THE
VISITANT
BOOK ONE
OF THE ANASAZI MYSTERIES

KATHLEEN O'NEAL GEAR
W. MICHAEL GEAR

TOR®

A TOM DOHERTY ASSOCIATES BOOK
NEW YORK

This is a work of fiction. All the characters and events portrayed in this book are either products of the author's imagination or are used fictitiously.

THE VISITANT

A Tor Book
Published by Tom Doherty Associates, LLC
175 Fifth Avenue
New York, NY 10010

www.tor.com

Tor® is a registered trademark of Tom Doherty Associates, LLC.

ISBN: 0-812-54033-6

First edition: July 1999
First international mass market edition: March 2000
First mass market edition: June 2000

Printed in the United States of America

0 9 8 7 6 5 4 3 2 1

PROLOGUE

Sun Cycle of the Great Horned Owl
The Buffalo Pawing Moon

A STRANGE QUIET *possesses the desert as twilight settles over the land.*

The sound of my sandals striking the long-abandoned road fills the night. Breathy. Urgent. Like the panting of a dying animal.

Tall and muscular, I can run all day. But I have been running for two days with almost no sleep. Exhaustion weights my limbs.

I trot to the edge of the sandstone rim and survey the canyon below. The color of the sheer cliffs has faded, changing from molten gold to a deep, dark crimson. A light dusting of snow frosts the ledges and coats the crumbling stone palaces that fill the valley.

My souls ache at the sight.

"The fools."

Once plastered with white clay and painted with the stunning images of the gods, the legendary towns now lay in ruins, their roofs collapsed, their glory as dead as their makers.

I prop my hands on my hips and grant myself a few moments of rest.

A ragged landscape spreads around me. Eroded drainages slice the uplands, meander down to the plains, and cut twisting canyons through the bottomlands. Here and there, wind-sculpted buttes rise into the sky like blunt fists.

"We share a purpose," I whisper. "We both wish to punch holes in the bellies of the gods."

The evil Spirit child, Wind Baby, toys with my long black hair, fluttering it before my eyes, trying to distract me from my duty.

I head east along the canyon rim.

Birds perch in the brush. They do not blink as I pass, but their eyes follow me, knowing instinctively that they dare not move until I am gone.

I reach the place overlooking the remains of Talon Town, and kneel.

A woman runs the road in the distance, her red cape blazing. She is alone. Long black hair sways around her slender body.

A whisper of wind climbs the canyon, and I hear her Singing—a beautiful, wrenching song.

I tip my face to the heavens, and Sing my own Power song, lending her my strength. The melody is the howl of a wolf on a blood trail; it echoes across the canyon, calling to the threads of Power that sleep in the drifting clouds and towering cliffs.

When the echo dies, I listen.

I wonder if Shadow is here. If, even now, she is hiding among the fallen stones, waiting for me.

I shiver.

Shadows live on light.

I am the Light. The source of her life.

She is the one who speaks with terror.

The woman on the road looks up, scanning the canyon. She shouts my name.

I feel it like a hot torrent flooding my bones.

"Blessed daughter, my daughter," I whisper.

Then. Behind me.

Steps.

She is nothingness, an empty place for the gods to fill. Writhing. Violent.

I breathe in the scent of the stone and night.

"Do not follow me," I order. "I do not wish you there."

Her laughter is wind through the brush.

I walk away.

I do not hear her.

But I am afraid.

"Two Hearts?" Ash Girl cried.

A tall woman, Ash Girl had seen twenty-two summers. As she hurried along the narrow trail, her red cape flapped like wings, and long black hair whipped around her oval face.

The sheer canyon wall rose two hundred hands high in front of her. Shadows filled the rocky crevices, and snow glistened on every lip of stone. Ash Girl broke into a run, pushing herself harder. Sister Moon hung above the jagged rim like a bright shining eye. Her gleam had chased away all but the strongest Evening People.

When Ash Girl reached the base of the cliff, she stopped. The brittle scents of dry winter grasses filled her heaving lungs. High above, a dead pine leaned over the rim. Its limbs had been blasted away by a lightning bolt, leaving only a rounded hump of trunk, and twisted roots that stretched over the cliff like spindly legs. She shivered and held the collar of her cape closed beneath her pointed chin.

The path led to the right, into a tumbled heap of boulders, and stunted juniper trees. Many of the boulders stood three times her height.

"Hello! Are you here?"

Her cry echoed from the canyon.

"Please? I must speak with you!"

She spun when she heard a whisper from the boulders,

low and muted, like the deep-throated groan of a waking Earth Spirit.

"Two Hearts?"

Ash Girl pulled up the long hem of her cape, and ran up the trail into the rocks. Juniper branches slapped at her shoulders as she sped by them, her feet crunching the frozen snow that lined the path. Moonlight sheathed the tops of the boulders, turning them a pale blue, but as she pushed deeper, the path at her feet grew darker, until the shadows devoured all light.

She blinked, letting her eyes adjust. The entry to the cavern could not be more than ten or fifteen body lengths away, but she could not see it. She nervously dried her palms on her turkey-feather cape.

"Hello?"

The boulders tilted over the trail ahead. Ancient paintings covered the rocks, but tonight she could see only the largest. Near the sharp tips of the boulders three white spirals shone. Zigzagging lines—like lightning bolts—radiated out from the spirals, warning all who approached that Power lived and breathed in this place.

Ash Girl could feel it, like sticky ant feet on her skin. She reached beneath her cape, and touched the sharp chert knife tied to her belt.

She had discovered the cavern by accident six moons ago. Thirsty and tired after a long day of harvesting the cornfields, she had come to sit in the shade of these boulders. Her nostrils had caught the gentle, caressing smell of water. She had followed the scent to a large pile of brush. When she'd removed it, shafts of sunlight had streamed into the cavern. She had returned frequently to sit by the pool in the rear of the cavern, and think about the many troubles her people faced.

She toyed with the smooth wooden handle of her knife, listening. Wind Baby whistled through the boulders, his voice shrill, desperate.

Ash Girl searched the darkness. She took two more steps.

Over one hundred sun cycles ago, the Straight Path Nation had fractured, and the different factions had fallen upon each other like ravening wolves. Three summers ago, a new faction had arisen. Calling themselves the Katsinas' People, they had proclaimed they were searching for the legendary white palaces of the First People. Ash Girl had listened raptly to their stories. The Blessed prophet, Poor Singer, had foretold that one day their people would return to the most holy place on earth, the First People's kiva—a magnificent subterranean ceremonial chamber—and restore it to its original glory. He had prophesied that when they had completed that task, a sacred doorway to the underworlds would open, and their people would be able to go to their Blessed ancestors, and ask them to bring the world back into harmony. The leader of the Katsinas' People, an old woman named Flame Carrier, claimed that her mother had known Poor Singer personally. Flame Carrier said that restoring the kiva would bring the wars to an end, and vanquish the evil Spirits that roamed the land.

Ash Girl had lost her mother in a raid four summers before. She ached for the prophecy to be true. She had shouted and ridiculed her husband, Browser, until he had agreed to join the Katsinas' People. He hadn't wished to. He would have been happy to live out his life in Green Mesa Village. Nevertheless, he had packed their few belongings, settled his newborn son into the little cedar cradle-board, and followed her to join the migration.

Since that time, things had been difficult between them. As the moons turned into sun cycles, and the prophecy failed to come true, Browser grew bitter and reclusive. He went on war walks that lasted three moons, and returned home with a sullen expression. He walked the cliffs at night, just to be free of her. The only thing

in life that seemed to bring him joy was their son, Grass
Moon.

Ash Girl believed Flame Carrier's teachings with all
her heart, but even she had wearied of the old woman's
promises. They had been traveling a long time. No one
knew which great kiva had been the original First
People's kiva. Two summers ago they'd rebuilt the magnificent kiva at Flowing Waters Town in the north, and
last summer they'd rebuilt one of the kivas in Straight
Path Canyon. They began work on another large kiva just
last moon, hauling out fallen roof timbers, cleaning up
the debris from collapsed walls. One of the village Elders
had dreamed the town was Talon Town. Ash Girl carried
away hundreds of baskets of crumbled plaster, shattered
mortar, exquisitely fitted pieces of sandstone, and de-
cayed wood. The entire time she prayed that old Wading
Bird's dream had been true, that they were indeed working on Talon Town, and the First People's cherished
kiva, and that their labors would bring the people peace.

Instead the warfare had intensified. Raiders visited the
canyon constantly, stealing women and children, killing
and burning. They brought evil with them. Many of the
Katsinas' People had Spirits feeding in their lungs.

"Including my son."

At this very instant, Browser would be washing Grass
Moon's hot face, and wondering where she was, why she
had left him. She had vowed she would not return to
Hillside Village until she'd found her Spirit Helper, and
that might take days. By then Browser would be wild
with fear, and angry enough to strike her.

Ash Girl braced a hand on the nearest boulder and
edged through the darkness until she smelled the mingled
fragrances of water and moss and saw the rounded outline of the cavern entry.

"Hello?" she called. "Are you here? Please, answer
me!"

The trail sloped downward. She placed her feet by memory, cautiously descending through the entry.

The floor flattened out, and Ash Girl turned around in a slow circle. How terribly black it was. Light might never have penetrated such a dark hole. She could not see the walls or ceiling, but she knew the cave spread around her like a dark womb, one hundred fifty hands across and fifty high. Water dripped steadily in the rear of the cave, splashing into the pool.

"Please?" she called again. "My son is sick. My people are sick. You *promised* you would help me. I need your help!"

When she still received no answer, she shouted, "You're my Spirit Helper! Where are you? I have done everything you've asked. I fasted for four days and nights. I ran all the way here. I need you more than I have ever needed you!"

The darkness closed in around her, pressing on her eyes and ear drums. The splashing water gave a lonely voice to the quiet.

"Two Hearts?" Ash Girl cried. "Please. What have I done? Why will you not speak with me?

He had come to her the first night she'd slept in this cavern. She'd thought she was dreaming when she heard those familiar steps, like long-dead echoes seeping from her memories, and saw him. He stood tall and thin in the crimson glow of the dying fire; the light sheathed his sacred mask, and struck terror into her heart. A katsina! The Blessed katsinas did not visit people like her. She had nothing, no power, no possessions. Yet, there he stood: part man, part wolf. One of the sky gods fallen to earth.

Since that time, she had seen him almost every night in her dreams, and twice at dawn, wandering along the canyon rim above her village. He frequently asked her odd questions. Questions about little girls and dark forest trails, and snakes with human eyes. Questions that had no meaning. When she'd told him this, his huge bottomless black eyes had flared as though lit by an inner fire. But he had only laughed.

"Two Hearts?" she shouted into the clinging darkness. "I think my son is dying. Please. I beg you. Hear me?"

A gust of wind penetrated the cave, and tousled Ash Girl's long hair. When it calmed, the silence deepened.

She sank to the floor.

"Why won't you come? Did you hear me? My son is dying! You told me you would help me! You are supposed to be my Spirit Helper. Where are you?"

The words boomed around the cavern.

Ash Girl stretched out on her side on the cool stone and fingered the bracelet that encircled her right wrist. Made from the blackest jet, it had been carved into the shape of a slithering snake. Browser had given it to her on their joining day. He'd been happy, smiling.

Ash Girl's throat went tight. She had not seen him smile at her in sun cycles. His love had slipped away, and now she was losing her only child. A soft cry escaped her lips. If she had been home, Browser would have knelt beside her and sternly ordered, "Stop this. If the people see you, their Spirits will turn to water. You must be strong for them."

She had tried.

But as her son wasted before her eyes, his cheeks growing gaunt, his eyes sinking into his skull, desperation had taken hold of Ash Girl's senses.

"I thought you would help," she choked out. "You told me you would. You promised!"

She buried her face in the soft feathers of her cape.

Images flitted across her souls. Disconnected. Haunting. Browser's worried eyes peered at her, and she thought she could hear him calling her name, his voice panicked, loud . . .

She jerked, and sat up, panting into the darkness.

The voice seeped from everywhere at once, the ceiling, walls, the floor.

"Why, my daughter?"

Ash Girl stopped breathing. "Two Hearts?" She twisted around to see him. "Where are you?"

She could make out the lighter gray of the rounded entry. A shadow blackened the right side. Fear and relief vied for control of her senses.

"Oh, Two Hearts, thank the gods. I was so afraid, I—"

"I asked you why?"

She stammered, feeling small and stupid, as she always did in his presence, "I—I do not understand your question."

"Why do you believe your son is dying?"

She spread her arms. "He can't breathe. Fever rages through his body. I have tried every Healing plant I know, but none has eased his suffering."

The shadow wavered like a man straightening to his full height. *"Blood comes from his lungs."*

It was a statement, not a question, but Ash Girl said, "Yes. Every time he coughs. He spits it up and gasps for air."

"But you are not ill?"

"No."

"What of the voices? Do you still hear them?"

Ash Girl's muscular legs trembled, but she rose to her feet. "No. And I—I do not care about them now! It is my son that wrenches my heart. Please, help him. He has seen only four summers. He is a good boy. Let him stay on this earth for a time longer." She reached out to the god. "He needs you. If you would only . . ."

She grabbed her head and staggered, suddenly dizzy.

Two Hearts' voice softened. *"Did you take the herbs I recommended?"*

"Yes, but . . . I am no better. The pain continues to

strike me at odd moments, and makes me sick to my stomach."

"The last time you lost your power to speak. What about this time?"

Ash Girl shuddered. Sometimes his voice sounded so much like her husband's, it stunned her. Did he do that on purpose? Did he know Browser and imitate his voice to frighten her? Two Hearts usually did it when he was loving her, and it acted like a lance in her heart.

She answered, "Just pain. And some weakness in my right hand. I—"

The shadow vanished.

Ash Girl's gaze darted over the empty entry. "Two Hearts?"

She lunged for the entry and raced out into the cold night air. After the utter blackness of the cave, the tumbled boulders resembled hunching giants. She searched the darkness.

"Two Hearts? Where are you?"

Juniper branches snagged at her cape as she hurried up the trail, tearing the red feathers loose, and scattering them in her wake.

A low cry, like a dying rabbit, pierced the quiet.

"Two Hearts?"

Somewhere in the distance a coyote yipped, then the whole pack broke into song. Their howls rose and fell with the wind.

Ash Girl gazed up at Sister Moon. As she climbed higher into the night sky, the cold air sparkled.

A whisper, barely audible, touched Ash Girl's ears: *"Come this way. This way."*

Ash Girl cried, "Where are you?" and trotted up the trail.

He stood in a pool of moonlight twenty body lengths from the cliff. His pointed ears and gray fur glimmered as though carved from ice.

He lifted one foot, then brought it down with a powerful thump. Then he lifted the other foot, but left it suspended in the air.

"Do you know Death's name, Ash Girl?"

She edged toward him. "Death has a name?"

"You used to know. Don't you remember?"

"No." She shook her head.

His foot came down violently, and he began Dancing, his arms swaying up and down. The fringes on his white buckskin shirt and pants licked out like tongues of silver flame.

"Hurry," he said, *"run past me. Before she sees you."*

Ash Girl looked around. "Who? Before who sees me?"

"Hurry! Don't you see her? There she is!" He tore the war club from his belt and pointed behind Ash Girl.

She whirled in terror. "What?" Only black shadows met her gaze, but in places the darkness seemed to ripple and sway. "I see nothing! What are you talking about?"

She started to turn back, and glimpsed the war club just before it slammed into her head, staggering her. She screamed. "No, please! Not now!"

Two Hearts waved the club, and the wooden muzzle of his mask dropped open. A fetid coppery odor gushed out, as though he'd been gnawing on a long-dead carcass.

Ash Girl cried, "I don't care where the voices live! Leave me alone!"

His mask lowered, and eerie, inhuman laughter split the night.

Ash Girl ran.

Two Hearts' feet pounded after her.

"Why are you doing this?" she cried, and glanced over her shoulder.

He Danced less than a body's length away, spinning and leaping, swinging the club over his head. *"Do you know Death's name?"*

"No! I already told you, I . . ."

Her foot tangled in a clump of dry grass, and she sprawled face-first across the ground. Before she could rise, he stood over her, his wolf's mask glowing. The fringes on his white sleeves trembled.

He whispered, *"Death stalks the desert, Ash Girl. She has been in the south, skimming creeks for moss, and chewing on rotting bones to survive. At this moment, she watches you, begging you to call her by name, so that she might spare you. She is hungry. Too hungry to control herself unless she knows you. Call out to her, Ash Girl. Call her by name. Tell her she knows you."*

Ash Girl shook her head. "But I do not know her name!"

He gripped his war club in both hands. *"Come closer, Ash Girl. Look at her reflection in my eyes, and you will remember."*

Ash Girl forced herself to look, but she saw only emptiness, and darkness.

"Two Hearts, please, I see nothing."

"Oh, gods." Sobs strained his voice. *"She relishes terror even more than living flesh!"*

His muzzle fell open again, and he began breathing on Ash Girl. His breath warmed her ankles and legs, then touched her hand and moved up her arm toward her face.

"What's happening?" she cried. Gods breathed upon the dead to bring them back to life. "Why are you breathing life into me? I'm not dead!"

A shudder went through him.

As though waking from a terrible nightmare, he slowly lifted his head. Moonlight gilded his fur. He knelt so still that his sharp teeth caught the light and held it like polished pyrite mirrors. He turned toward the ruins in the distance.

Ash Girl jerked around to look.

They had built their own village, Hillside Village, alongside the massive half-moon-shaped structure that they believed to be Talon Town. In comparison, the rectangular buildings of Hillside looked pathetically small and crude.

"*At the end,*" he whispered, "*witches filled the town. Did you know that? Talon Town became a hive of evil. The witches dug up the burials and robbed the corpses, taking any object that contained a shred of the First People's Power. They wove the Power around them like capes of stone and used it to destroy the First People. That's why they are gone. Their fire has gone out of our blood, because they were too stupid to realize—*"

"*Our* blood?" Ash Girl asked, surprised. "But you are a god, not a man."

He turned toward her.

Moonlight filled the eye sockets of his mask and illuminated the interior. He stared at her through intense black eyes, and she saw something familiar in their shape.

Ash Girl scanned the long lashes, the delicate brow visible through the right socket.

He must have known the instant she knew.

"*Yes. Go on. Scream, Ash Girl. Scream her name before it is too late.*"

She grabbed for her knife.

He caught her hand and, as they struggled against each other, he whispered, "*I've never forgotten the feel of you, my daughter.*"

1

WILLIAM "DUSTY" STEWART looked out over the desert-worn hood of his battered Bronco. A thin layer of dust had sifted over the older, rain-pocked dirt that had been partially cemented to the seared blue paint.

How like this elemental land to claim everything for its own—to mark it, infiltrate it, and become one with it.

Behind his Bronco, a convoy of vehicles threaded across the picturesque New Mexican terrain. A land of colored earth surrounded them, dotted with turquoise sagebrush, vibrant green rabbitbrush, and a pale scattering of chamisa.

Stewart rubbed his jawline with a callused right hand, feeling the stubble. He'd had trouble remembering to shave all of his life. This morning had been worse than usual. Today marked the beginning of a lifelong dream. Today he'd sink his first shovel into Chaco.

Six feet tall, blond and muscular, he wore faded Levi's, a pair of worn Nacono boots, and an oversize T-shirt emblazoned with a Mimbres lizard and the logo for the Casa Malpais site over in Springerville, Arizona. The desert had punished his fair complexion. His oval face with its straight nose and blunt chin had a weathered look. Eventually he would have to pay for those years of sun, wind, chill, and dust. Crow's-feet already etched the corners of his blue eyes. Not good for a man in his mid-thirties. He'd overheard women say he was too damned good-looking. A blond Adonis. Not that good looks had ever gotten him anywhere with women.

A familiar unease crept around just under his consciousness. *Don't even consider it. Open that door to the past, and you'll spend all day dwelling on it.*

Funny how something that happened long ago could stick with a man, screw up his whole life.

At the crest of a low ridge, Dusty glanced back through the dust boiling up behind the Bronco. The land could not be escaped, not here. Grains of sand infiltrated clothes, homes, and machinery. Its tan, gritty texture eventually came to permeate everything.

The vehicles that followed his were strung out across the sage-speckled desert like gleaming beads, a quarter mile apart, linked by fading plumes of dust. To follow any closer meant clogged air filters, jammed cassette players—critical equipment in a land of only two distant radio stations—or stuck doorlocks, or automatic windows. Any other mechanical thing that liked to function in a clean, lubricated environment existed at its own peril.

Automotive engineers in Flint, Dearborn, or wherever these trucks were designed, didn't quite understand what "off-road" really meant in the West. Over the years, and with the development of the "Sport Utility" class, something had been lost in the translation. Suburban mothers braving three inches of slush in Peoria as they carried four kids to basketball practice wasn't quite the same challenge as being buried up to the fenders in slimy brown Kayenta mud fifty miles from the nearest pavement.

As Dusty's Bronco rocked and jolted along the rutted dirt road, he glanced out the side window at the gnarly cactus and yellow-tufted rabbitbrush. Here and there the buff-colored sand had collected in small dunes—called sand shadows by the geomorphologists. In other places bare outcrops of sandstone concentrated the sun's heat, ironic reminders of the ancient ocean that had once covered New Mexico and Arizona tens of millions of years past.

In another time, a mere thousand years ago, this same desert stretch had grown Ponderosa pine, juniper, and lots of grass. But that was before the Anasazi had come with their stone axes, before the frenzied building of the "Great Houses," when over two hundred and fifty thousand trees had been cut for construction alone, not to mention the wood needed to light the giant pueblos, fire the exquisite pottery, cook their meals, and heat their homes. That was before the Anasazi population had burgeoned, and they had planted every arable hectare in corn, beans, and squash.

By the end of the eleventh century these eroded ridges had been denuded. Violent monsoon rains had washed away the topsoil, exposed the slick rock, and carved deep arroyos into the flood plains. Each centimeter had lowered the critical water tables. After the exhausted soil finally dried out, most of the people left.

Dusty crossed the cattle guard that separated Chaco Culture National Monument from the surrounding Navajo lands, and sighed as his all-terrain tires hummed on the irregular pavement. He waved at the stone-and-wood Park Service entry sign, its white letters looking so crisp on the brown background.

To his right lay Pueblo Alto, the nexus of the fabulous Anasazi road system that radiated out to the north, east, west, and south. The ruined pueblo stood hunched and broken against the western horizon. Incongruously, the cell phone chimed. Dusty rounded the curve that led into Mockingbird Canyon, blew the thin coating of dust from the gray plastic, and punched the "Send" button. "Stewart here. It's your nickel."

"You're dating yourself, Stewart," Maggie Walking Hawk Taylor's familiar voice chided. "It's like a dollar a minute out here, when you can get any reception at all."

"I like dating myself." Stewart smiled, his left hand resting on the use-polished steering wheel. "It's cheaper, and I don't have to impress myself with a forty-dollar bottle of wine."

"No wonder no woman will have you for more than two months. You're also late. Where are you?"

He ignored the comment about women. He'd just avoided falling into that funk, and he'd be damned if he'd let Maggie edge him into the abyss. "Just dropping down into the canyon. We got held up in Albuquerque. Had a major disaster. The usual place, the one that carries Guinness, was out of stock. We had to convoy across half the city, including a stop at Page One Bookstore—"

"You had to go to the bookstore to find Guinness?"

"I wish. Anyway, I'll be at the Park Service headquarters building in five minutes."

"Great, but I'm out at the site. Like I said, you're late. Knowing how you play fast and loose with the rules, I thought maybe you'd decided to screw the paperwork and gone straight to the dig."

"I always obey the rules. Oh, and it's not a dig until we get a shovel into the ground. Technicalities, you know, Maggie?"

"If you weren't such a brilliant archaeologist, I'd nail you, Stewart." He heard the smile in her voice. "Anyway, I wanted to get out of the office. You know, away from the phone. I've got all of the paperwork here: excavation permit, a list of ten thousand park rules, the special camping permit, tons of safety requirements, and all the other bureaucratic horse pucky they pay me to enforce." A pause. "Oh, by the way, you're not packing that big pistol around, are you? No, firearms—"

"I left my pistol at home, Maggie," Dusty interrupted and used his heel to jam his Model 57 Smith & Wesson back under the seat out of sight. "See you there in about fifteen."

"I'll be waiting."

He punched the "End" button and dropped the phone onto his seat. During the conversation, he had followed the serpentine blacktop through sheer-walled Mockingbird Canyon and out into the flat bottom of Chaco Canyon. At the stop sign, the Park Service sign pointed the way to various ruins, the campground, and visitor center. To his left, up Chaco Wash, he could see Fajada Butte, home of the Sun Dagger astronomical site, place of legend, where Spider Woman descended to earth. All across the sere landscape he could feel the Power.

Chaco called to him, beyond the centuries, across the bridge of cultures, peoples, and worlds. Only the soul-dead left Chaco Canyon unaffected.

He took the right and glanced into the rearview mirror. Sylvia's Jeep, Michall's Durango, Steve Sander's ratty old Toyota Land Cruiser, and the University Suburban accelerated behind him.

At the end of summer most of the field crew returned home to prepare for next semester. The students he had left were true diehards, the stuff great archaeologists were made of. Even then, two of them would be gone in a few days. Michall Jefferson, a short woman with red hair, would be leaving for the University of Colorado, and Steve Sanders, a tall black man, for the University of Arizona.

Dusty drove west past the Visitor's Center, and gazed out at the weathered sandstone cliffs, and the rubble of thousand-year-old pueblos that hemmed the canyon.

Chetro Ketl, its massive columns like blunt teeth stood with its straight-walled back to the cliff. The second-story hanging balcony had allowed the Anasazi to enjoy the shade during the midday heat.

Then came Pueblo Bonito, the largest Anasazi ruin in

the world. In its heyday it had stood five stories tall, with over eight hundred rooms; the walls had been plastered in white clay. The place still ruled the canyon. He couldn't help but cast sidelong glances at the stunning walls. They threw crisp shadows over the empty, ruined rooms. Where once thousands of people had walked in the light of a hundred torches, now only ghosts slipped across the courtyards.

The loop road passed Pueblo del Arroyo, then Kin Kletso, and curved southward; there, just before the road crossed Chaco Wash, a brown steel-pole barrier had been opened, the little wooden sign beside it proclaiming AU-THORIZED PERSONNEL ONLY.

Dusty slowed and turned off the pavement. After passing Casa Chiquita, the road narrowed to an overgrown two track. Behind him, his caravan followed like a weaving mamba line, each vehicle swaying over the ruts. Sunlight reflected from chrome and glass. Greasewood made squealing sounds as it scratched the sides of his Bronco.

A single puke-green Park Service truck had been parked off to one side. No more than thirty meters beyond it, a woman stood on what looked like a rocky outcrop, the stones studded with brush. Another two hundred meters beyond her, the sheer sandstone canyon wall rose against the pale blue New Mexico sky.

Maggie Walking Hawk Taylor turned, hands propped on her hips. She stood five feet six inches tall. Her round face betrayed her Indian ancestry. The faint breeze teased unruly strands of her short black hair around her dark eyes, and broad cheekbones. She wore a Park Service uniform and tan boots on her feet. The belted brown pants hugged a trim waist. She cocked her head and smiled.

Dusty nudged his Bronco past her pickup and into a flagged area that would be the field crew's parking lot. He set the brake and turned off the ignition. Then he fiddled through the clutter of notebooks on the passenger seat and retrieved an aluminum clipboard that held a fieldwork authorization and a site map.

Dusty opened the door and walked over to where Maggie waited on the pile of cracked rock. Her large brown eyes reflected amusement and excitement. During the excavation she would be the "Authorized Officer," meaning the Park Service person in charge, since the government didn't speak real English.

"Good to see you again, Maggie." Dusty extended his hand, and she shook it.

He looked out over the rubble. In the background he could hear the slamming of truck doors and the chatter of the field crew as they began unloading the vehicles.

"You ready for this?" Maggie asked, looking out at the section of desert. Six yellow stakes, each made of freshly sawed lath and topped with blaze-orange flagging tape, created a long rectangle in the greasewood. The stakes marked the future location of a weather monitoring site for NOAA. A tower would stand on a huge concrete slab, and solar powered antennae would beam satellite information back and forth. In all, over three thousand square meters of desert would be disturbed during construction.

"I've been waiting all of my life for the chance to dig here." He opened the metal clipboard and produced his excavation permit with a flourish. "Here you go. All signed, sealed, delivered, and official." Then he added wryly. "Just what a good, rule-bound boy like me would do."

She took the paper, scanned it quickly, and said, "You and Dr. Robertson are listed as Co-principal Investigators. Sylvia Rhone will be the Crew Chief. Is Sylvia here?"

As if on command, Sylvia appeared, trooping through the sagebrush with a transit and tripod slung over her shoulder. Beneath a ball cap that proclaimed: "Member,

Chinle Yacht Club," her shoulder-length brown hair had been tied into a pony tail. A sleeveless red T-shirt exposed muscular, tanned arms, and she wore her faded-blue Levi's tucked into scuffed hiking boots.

"Hey there, Magpie," Sylvia called "Maggie" by her real name: Magpie Walking Hawk Taylor. "Long time no see. How's life as a tourist herder?"

"Hi, Sylvia. Same old thing. The tourists still want the thirty miles of road between here and the highway paved. People keep picking up bits of pottery and stuffing them into their pockets. A couple of the rock art panels on the canyon wall were vandalized last week. We've had to restrict more of the park to protect what's left."

"People suck." Sylvia settled the tripod's pointed feet onto the dirt. "Imagine how they'd trash it if that thirty-mile stretch was paved." She looked around, her green eyes narrowing as if sighting a rifle. "It's better like this. A private and peaceful jewel." She paused. "Uh, we got a datum here anyplace?"

"Datum?" Maggie asked.

"The reference point we use to lay out the excavation grid," Dusty told her. "Come on, let's go see."

As he walked, he pulled out the survey map Dale had drawn months ago when he first came to inspect the construction site for archaeology. The site had been given the Smithsonian number 29SJ10003. Twenty-nine for the state of New Mexico, SJ for San Juan county, and ten thousand and three for the number of sites in the county.

The pile of rocks where they stood—actually a small collapsed Anasazi pueblo—was clearly labeled. Dusty glanced around, oriented himself to the west, and paced out from the edge of the tumbled rock for six long paces. "According to the map, X marks the spot. Look around."

"Got it," Maggie cried, pointing down. "29SJ10003."

Sylvia settled the heavy tripod over the aluminum cap.

"Mama, we're home." She immediately began extending the legs and leveling the instrument.

Leaving her to fiddle with the transit, Dusty walked out into the middle of the lath-marked rectangle. Maggie paced silently beside him.

Hot wind tugged at his blond hair, and whispered softly through the brush. In the distance, a red-tailed hawk shrieked. Shadows had lengthened on the canyon wall. If he just loosened the bonds of reality, he could step back, hear that hawk's call eight hundred years ago, and feel this same hot breeze.

A clatter erupted as Michall Jefferson dropped a bundle of wooden stakes by the transit and asked Sylvia if she needed help.

"Hey, you still here?" Maggie asked from Dusty's left elbow.

"Huh?" He glanced at her, this world coming into focus again.

Maggie studied him through serious brown eyes. "I've seen eyes like that before. You were looking back, weren't you?"

"You bet."

"Grandma Slumber used to get that look. My aunts still do. But they're of the people, White Eyes."

"Of the people," Dusty mused. He bent down, clutching a handful of the silty sand. "I'm about to uncover artifacts that haven't been touched in over eight hundred years, Maggie. Trust me, when you do that, it makes a bridge. I can feel them. We both touch the same bit of stone, see the colors, feel the flaking on the sharp edge."

"You're different, then."

"Different?"

"Yeah, most archaeologists I know just see the science. That and the damned statistical proofs."

"Yeah, well," he said, and let the sand trickle through his fingers. "There are two kinds of archaeologists, the kind who dig for theories, and the kind who dig for people. Each site is a special miracle that lets me touch those people. If only for a tiny sliver of time. I've wanted to touch the Chaco Anasazi all of my life, Maggie."

Maggie's eyes had grown larger, seeming to swell in her round brown face. "Just be careful, Dusty. The old ones will be watching you." She paused. "Will they find you worthy?"

He tilted his blond head. "I doubt it. I can't imagine why they'd be different from everybody else."

Maggie smiled. "I have to get back. See you later."

She turned, and walked away. The hot wind teased her straight black hair, and the brush scratched hollowly at her cotton pants.

Dusty closed his eyes, straining, hearing the faint whisper of the breeze through the succulent leaves of the greasewood. Every time he walked out onto a site for the first time, the quickening came to his blood. Each site had its own unique personality, and guarded its secrets. A site became an obsession, a challenging seductress who lured him, tried to mislead and obscure as she was coaxed to reveal her most intimate details. And like a woman, it needed to be coddled and caressed before it would finally yield to his advances.

Am I worthy? The question rolled around his mind like an off-balance wheel.

Seeking to escape the wreckage of his youth, he'd driven himself to become the best in his field. But he never really felt good enough. Sometimes he could sit in an excavation unit and feel as if he were having a lengthy conversation with people who'd died ten thousand years ago, and other times his greatest efforts failed to open even a pinprick view of the past.

"Hey, boss man?" Sylvia called. "We're ready over here."

Dusty straightened. "On my way."

2

VOICES WHISPERED.

Browser wearily leaned his shoulder against the pine-pole door frame and pulled the deerhide curtain aside. As he moved, shoulder-length black hair swung around his face, accentuating the tight lines near his dark brown eyes. Twenty-eight summers had passed since his birthing, but this morning he felt as old as the weathered cliff behind Hillside Village. It had taken an act of will to remove his soiled clothing and slip the clean knee-length leather shirt over his head. Lines of jet beads decorated the shirt's collar and hem; he'd belted the tan shirt at the waist with a red sash, then hung a war club and belt pouch from the sash.

The whispers stopped.

People approached.

I am here to bury my son. Browser forced himself to stand straight. The day had dawned clear, cold, and bright, the sun low on the southern horizon. Browser watched his breath rise and dissipate—like dreams that had been held too close to the heart.

One by one, the six Elderly Keepers of the Sacred Directions ducked past him, through the low T-shaped doorway, and into the room. He could hear them as they surrounded his boy's body, and old Flame Carrier began the death chant. The other members of the burial party remained outside, their expressions taut as they watched him.

Several of the women carried infants on cradle boards. They had tied their babies' heads to the boards to flatten the rear of the skull and broaden the cheekbones, making them more attractive. The babies gurgled and waved tiny fists.

His two best warriors, Catkin and Whiproot, stood to his right near the base of the towering cliff. They had just returned from four days of surveying the canyon rim, making certain no enemy warriors lurked there. They looked tired, their faces drawn. Both wore white ritual capes, the feathers dotted with chunks of polished stone.

Tall and lanky, Catkin was a beautiful woman. And a brave fighter. During a raid, eight moons ago, the Fire Dogs had wounded and captured her. There had been too many of them to risk his warriors in a direct attack, so Browser had sneaked in after dark, alone, killed the two Fire Dogs raping her, and carried her out on his back. Since that time she'd looked at him differently, her eyes softer, filled with a longing he could not allow himself to fulfill.

For both their sakes.

Whiproot held a ceramic pot in his two strong brown hands. From the top tendrils of smoke rose and wavered in the heat cast off by the coals taken from the eternal fire. Over the last couple of years, Browser had come to rely on Whiproot the way a roof did a support post. A head shorter than Catkin, the man had a thick, muscular body. A series of terrible scars received in battle ran across his nose and cheeks. Though disfiguring, he wore them with a warrior's pride. Proof of his courage.

Catkin carried a small ladder, a delicate thing made of branches, the rungs tied crossways with neat square knots. At the end of the burial ceremony, they would lay the ladder in the grave, so that his son's afterlife soul could climb out and be on its way to the Land of the Dead.

He returned his gaze to Catkin, and she gave him a reassuring nod, as if willing him strength across the narrow space that separated them. He closed his eyes. Every time he fought with Ash Girl, he ended up in Catkin's chamber. She might have been the whirlpool, and he the water. He could tell her anything, and she always offered solid advice. In truth, she was his best friend.

The sickly sweet scent of death drifted through the door, affecting him like a blow to the stomach. Browser pulled deep breaths of clean cold air into his lungs as he gazed across the desert.

Father Sun had not yet crested the cliff behind Hillside Village, but his light flooded the canyon, glistening from the buff-colored sandstone and burnishing the underbellies of the drifting Cloud People. It had snowed less than a half moon ago. White frosted the ledges of the north-facing cliff, and a patchwork dotted the ground. Most of the snow had melted into the sand, then refrozen, turning it as hard as stone.

Browser reluctantly reached for the door curtain, and let it drop behind him as he ducked into the room. The crimson gleam cast by the bowl of glowing coals sheathed the faces of the six Elders. His son's wasted body lay on a worn mat in the middle of the floor.

The old men stood on the east and west sides of the room. The old women stood in the north, to his left, and the south, to his right. Old Man Down Below and Old Woman Up Above crouched in the rear of the house, ahead of him, facing each other, softly chanting the Death Song: *"A plume we are bringing, A plume we are giving . . ."*

Each of the Elders carried a folded blanket and wore a finely tanned buffalohide cape, painted with the red images of wolf, coyote, eagle, and raven, the special Spirit Helpers of the Katsinas' People. Alternating feathers and seed beads knotted the ends of the long fringes on their capes.

Browser said, "Please. Begin."

Old Man East nodded, and gazed at the naked body lying on the willow twig mat. Tears blurred Old Woman North's eyes. She made a soft sound of mourning, and Old Man West bit his lip.

Browser could not physically force himself to look down. His gaze roamed the small room. Three body lengths square, dried sunflowers, corn, and beans hung from the pole rafters. Orange squashes lined the bases of the walls. Baskets and pots sat stacked in the far corner to the right of Old Woman Up Above. In the opposite corner, near Old Man Down Below, Browser's bow, quiver of arrows, and stone hatchet rested beside a pile of rolled hide bedding. The big corrugated pot beside the hides contained shelled beans, and the small black-and-white pot next to it held beads, thread, turkey bone awls, dyed porcupine quills, bone punches for making holes in leather, and other sewing tools—all necessities of Ash Girl's life.

Without thinking, he glared at the four gods she had painted on the walls. In the wavering reddish gleam they seemed to be Dancing, their masks swaying to the beat of a drum he could not hear. The Ant katsina dominated the south wall, Bear on the north, and Buffalo Danced on the east wall. He knew without turning, that the Badger katsina peered down at him from the west wall behind his shoulders.

Ash Girl had painted the gods with painstaking care, but they had failed her. As always.

Anger and guilt stirred his heart. Browser reached for the only reliable protection in the world, the heavy war club tied to his belt.

"Death is not an enemy, War Chief," Old Man East murmured. His ordinary name was Springbank. He had a long hooked nose and wrinkled lips that sunk in over toothless gums. Sparse white hair clung to his freckled scalp.

"Not your enemy, perhaps. But I have been fighting her all my life, Elder."

"Fighting, yes. But winning? Life Dances, War Chief. It chases and sleeps. Summer and winter, rain and drought, planting and harvesting, war and peace, everything travels in gigantic circles, engaged in an eternal process of becoming something else. We are all raw dough in the hands of the gods."

"I, of all people, know that, Elder." Browser clutched his war club more tightly. He had gone on his first war walk before he'd seen fourteen summers. He knew the gods for what they truly were, fickle, and vengeful.

Unlike his wife, Browser had never trusted them.

Springbank squeezed Browser's shoulder. "Your son is free of the sickness. Let us help him on his way to the Land of the Dead."

Browser forced himself to look down.

He had washed his son and prepared him as the Elders had instructed. The boy's naked body looked as thin as a reed. His ribs had stuck out, the knees like knobs. His cheeks and eyes sunk into the skull. The lips had pulled back, each tooth outlined in the disease's dried lung blood.

The ache in Browser's chest threatened to double him over. He spread his feet to brace himself.

Everyone had lost someone in the wars, but now they had the sickness to contend with as well. Rumors said that the evil Spirits that caused the sickness had first come from the Fire Dogs who lived in the south. He believed it. Nothing of any good had ever come from the Fire Dogs.

The Katsinas' People called them Fire Dogs because the raiders believed they had originally come to earth in the form of wolves made from gouts of Father Sun's fire. Browser believed it. Wild and brutal, they did not think like humans.

Old Woman North, Matron Flame Carrier, set her folded blanket aside and drew a small pack from beneath her cape. She had seen seventy-four summers. Gray hair straggled around her wrinkled face, but her small narrow eyes gleamed. Over the long summers, her eyebrows had vanished, leaving a few kinky gray hairs as reminders. She was sensible and friendly, though she had a stern voice. As she knelt beside Grass Moon, the lines in her forehead deepened. "Help me lift him," she said.

Springbank handed his blanket to Old Woman South and slipped his hands beneath Grass Moon's right knee and shoulder. Flame Carrier took the boy's left side. When they lifted the child, Old Woman South carefully spread the blankets they'd brought over the willow twig mat and smoothed them flat with her gnarled hands.

Springbank and Flame Carrier lowered Grass Moon to the soft bed of white blankets.

The boy's mouth opened in a silent cry, and Browser could barely stand it.

He clamped his jaw so tightly, his head shook.

Flame Carrier tenderly stroked Grass Moon's hollow cheek. She said, "Bring the objects of the breath-heart."

"Yes, Matron," Old Woman South responded.

Each person had two souls, a soul that stayed with the body forever, and a breath-heart soul that kept the lungs moving, and the heart beating. At death, the breath-heart soul seeped out, but it hovered around the body, not certain where to go until the Keepers prepared the way to the Land of the Dead.

Old Woman South, one of the *Kokwimu,* a sacred Man-Woman of great power, knelt and brought her own pack from beneath her painted buffalohide cape. *Kokwimu* had male bodies but female souls. This allowed them to see and do things that ordinary men and women could not. Younger than the other Keepers, she had coiled her long gray-streaked black braids over her ears and fastened them with rabbitbone pins. Graceful brows curved above her slanting eyes. Her triangular face and sharply pointed nose shone wetly with tears. Her ordinary name was Cloudblower. She was known for telling long stories filled with moral teachings that people only sometimes understood.

Cloudblower laid out two small yellow bags, a magnificent white shirt covered with red beads, and new moccasins. They shone with a reddish hue in the diffused light.

Browser had taken Grass Moon's old clothing and tied it into a bundle that now rested to the boy's right. At the end of the Death Ritual, Old Man East would take the coals from the eternal fire, kindle a blaze, and burn them, making certain to destroy all of the Evil Spirits that had sickened Grass Moon.

Browser bowed his head.

His son had drowned in his own blood, and his mother had not even been there to comfort him. For eight hands of time before he'd died, Grass Moon had choked out, "Mother . . . mother . . . mother . . ."

Browser had rocked him back and forth, whispering, *She's coming. She'll be here soon.*

A thread of rage wound through his grief. She had been gone for two days, without a word. He clenched his fists, vowing not to think of her. Not now.

Cloudblower opened one of the yellow bags and poured white cornmeal into Flame Carrier's cupped hands then filled her own. They rubbed Grass Moon's body with the meal, purifying it for the long journey to the afterworld.

When they finished, Flame Carrier slipped the beautiful burial shirt over Grass Moon's head. Cloudblower opened the other yellow bag and poured jewelry onto the blanket at the boy's side—jet ear loops, carved shell necklaces, and two cast copper bells. Very gently Cloudblower pulled the new moccasins onto Grass Moon's feet. She slipped the ear loops through the holes in his ears and tied the two copper bells to the laces on his moccasins. Finally she draped the necklaces over his head and centered them on his chest.

Cloudblower sat back with her eyes closed. Tears beaded her lashes.

Flame Carrier lifted a hand. "It will take the boy's Spirit four days to reach the Land of the Dead. He will be distraught and confused. No one must speak his name, or dream of him, lest they call his ghost back from its journey to the underworld."

She untied a blue bag from her belt. Blue was the color of the north and signified the Land of the Dead. She bent over Grass Moon and began pouring out a line of blue cornmeal as she slowly backed toward the door. The other Keepers of the Sacred Directions Sang softly, their brittle voices like sand against wood:

> In a sacred manner, we send a voice.
> We send a voice.
> The path of Father Sun is our strength,
> The path of Sister Moon is our robe.
> A praise we are making.
> A praise we are sending.
> In a sacred manner, we send a voice.

Browser lifted the door curtain. Flame Carrier exited, pouring her cornmeal trail through the burial party and across the cold village plaza. A whirlwind of snow careened along the south wall of Hillside Village, bobbing and twisting.

Springbank said, "The sacred trail will lead your son

to the Great North Road. From there he will be able to find his way to the Land of the Dead."

It would also lure his hungry ghost away from the village before it could grab onto any of the living and take them with him.

Wading Bird shuffled for the door, and the other Elders followed, ducking out into the icy morning wind.

Catkin stepped forward with the burial ladder. Made of juniper branches, it looked feeble and small. But it would be enough to carry his little son.

"Come," Browser said. "He is ready."

For such a tall woman, she moved with remarkable grace. Her white cape swayed around her strong body. Beneath the cape, she wore a knee-length blue warshirt. She had painted a black coyote on the front. Whiproot followed her, his face made all the more sober by the ribbed white scars.

Catkin placed the ladder beside Grass Moon's white blankets and murmured, "Whiproot, help me lift him onto the ladder."

Whiproot set his pot of coals aside and gripped the edges of the burial blankets. They lifted Grass Moon as if moving a mortally injured man. Whiproot set the pot of coals by Grass Moon's side and took one end of the ladder, while Catkin took the other.

Browser exchanged a soft look with Catkin as they passed and bent to pick up the tied bundle of Grass Moon's clothing. He clutched it to his breast and stepped out into the cold.

Mourners lined both sides of the cornmeal trail, weeping, and tearing at their clothing. Many had cut their hair short in grief—as he would when the ritual ended. Several people coughed, suffering the same illness that had taken Grass Moon. They had a haunted look, a thin grayness to their pallor. Their eyes had grown cavernous in their heads.

Catkin and Whiproot filed slowly past them, allowing each person to touch the boy or lay gifts on his chest.

The lavender shadows coated Grass Moon's face like liquid amethyst.

Browser stood numbly.

Grass Moon's bubbly laugh rose in his memory, and he saw the boy's shining face smiling up at him, his arms reaching out, wanting to be held . . .

Browser's chest seemed to expand, filling with black tingling emptiness.

You can do this. Just walk. See this through.

He forced himself to place one foot in front of the other.

Propped Pillar, a massive slab of sandstone that had broken away from the canyon wall, stood to his right, leaning threateningly over the ruins of what they prayed was Talon Town. The top of the pillar glowed golden.

Browser followed the burial ladder out onto the path that curved around the massive eastern wall of the town. Painted katsinas danced across the cracked white plaster. Three times the height of a man, the gods wore fearsome masks. Once, long ago, they must have stirred awe. Now, they looked pitiful. Chunks of the paintings had flaked off with the plaster, adding to the pile of debris at the base of the wall. Several of the gods were missing eyes, arms, or legs. Only the last painting remained disturbingly intact. The Badger katsina stood tall and black, his eyes glistening with life. Four terraces of blue thunder clouds adorned his chest, and white streaks of falling rain striped his kirtle. He carried a fire ball in his right hand.

The Badger katsina had been repainted recently. Not by his village or any of the other small villages in Straight Path Canyon, but by someone. The red fire ball looked molten.

As Browser passed, a whisper, like wind through sage,

pricked his ears. The katsina seemed to lean toward Browser, trying to get his attention.

Browser shot him a hard look in return. Unlike his wife, he had never longed to speak with the gods. He did not understand them, nor did he wish to.

Catkin and Whiproot rounded the southeastern corner of Talon Town and headed west along the road. Six body-lengths wide, the roadbed sparkled with crushed pot sherds.

The straight east-west wall of Talon Town faced south. Huge patches of plaster had fallen off, revealing the extraordinary sandstone masonry beneath. Pieces of stone no bigger than his hand had been rubbed together until they fitted so tightly an obsidian knife blade could not be forced between them. To his left, two mounds rose. Long and square, they'd been built atop trash heaps. Ash, bits of animal bones, broken pots, and the refuse from stone tool-making, constantly eroded out of the mounds. After heavy rains, the trash washed down across the road, and had to be raked aside.

A line of mourners followed Browser beyond the western wall of Talon Town and across long abandoned fields grown tall in sage and greasewood. Ahead of them, the six Keepers marched in single file toward the burial site. The hole had already been hacked into the frozen ground at the base of the cliff.

It won't be long now, Browser promised himself. *You can finish this without giving in to grief. Your son would want you to be strong for others.* He knotted his hands at his sides.

A large fire burned twenty paces from the pit, sending coils of blue-gray smoke into the brightening sky. The Sunwatcher, Hophorn, sat unmoving beside it, her back braced against the cliff, her head bowed. How still she was. So lost in contemplation. She wore a red-feathered cape around her shoulders.

She did not even raise her head as they approached, and Browser's heart constricted. She had loved Grass Moon as much as he had. During the time Grass Moon had been ill, Hophorn had checked on the boy as often as she could, given her other duties, helping Ash Girl to wash and care for Browser's son, going for any supplies Ash Girl needed. But she had been away when his child died, Healing at Starburst Village at the eastern end of the canyon. The boy's death must have shredded her souls.

Browser marched forward with his heart thudding. The long leather fringes on the sleeves and hem of his tan shirt flapped in the cold breeze, creating an irregular cadence.

In what seemed like another lifetime, he had loved Hophorn. He had seen fifteen summers, and she was not yet a woman. Browser's people had found her wandering the forests alone, bruised and battered. She had escaped from the Fire Dogs, that much she remembered, but she couldn't recall her family or clan. In six moons, they had become best friends. Her frailty and innocence had drawn him like a starving man to food. That was the summer before his grandmother forced him to marry Ash Girl. Blessed gods, how he wished Hophorn had agreed to marry him. He'd asked her to, but she was not a woman. She could not say yes, nor could he approach her adopted mother about courting her. Browser's grandmother had arranged his marriage to Ash Girl instead. His grandmother told him that Ash Girl needed a strong man to care for her, that her father had run off when she'd been a child, and that she'd never gotten over the loss. Ash Girl had begged her grandmother to wed her to Browser.

Deeply religious, Hophorn had entered the priesthood, and vowed not to marry until one of the katsinas soared down from the skyworld and gave her permission.

As Browser gazed at her, the ache in his heart expanded. On occasion, over the lonely sun cycles, they had been lovers. Holding her affected him like a cool Healing salve on a fresh wound.

Hophorn had left Green Mesa Village to join the Katsinas' People the same day Browser had. She'd followed on his heels every step of the way, smiling gently at him, soothing his misgivings in her soft musical voice, promising that everything would be all right.

But nothing had been right since he'd left Green Mesa Village. He and Ash Girl had started fighting and never stopped. His wife's zeal to find a Spirit Helper and restore the First People's kiva interfered with everything he—

A woman screamed.

Browser whirled.

Near the burial pit, Flame Carrier reached frantically for Cloudblower's arm. The other Keepers rushed forward to peer into the pit. Old Woman Up Above fell to her knees, wailing.

Browser ran.

As he passed Catkin and Whiproot, he ordered, "Put my son down! Follow me!"

Chaos erupted among the mourners. People grabbed children, and shouted questions. A din of coughing exploded. Babies shrieked as people hurried after Browser. The elderly hobbled in pursuit as quickly as their ancient legs would carry them.

Browser shouted, "Flame Carrier? What's wrong? What do you see?"

Springbank turned, his mouth round in shock. He stammered, "Q-Quickly," and waved a hand.

Cloudblower helped Flame Carrier to sit down, then knelt over the pit. She put a hand to her lips as if to quiet a cry that pressed at the back of her throat.

Browser halted at Cloudblower's side.

At first, he did not understand what he saw.

The man seemed to be resting on his stomach with his arms and legs thrown out at his sides, as though he'd been hurled face-first into the yawning grave. He wore an exquisite white buckskin shirt and pants. From the lengths of his pant legs, he must have been very tall. At his feet lay the sacred mask of the Wolf katsina. The gray fur shimmered.

A heavy sandstone slab covered the man's head.

Browser went stiff. People placed stones over the heads of witches to keep their breath-heart souls locked in the earth forever. Was this man a witch? Was that why he'd been killed?

Mourners crowded around the pit, shoving to get a better view. When they saw the horror, screams split the morning, and a shoving contest began. Like a herd of frightened buffalo, the villagers practically ran over each other trying to get back to Hillside Village before any of the witch's evil Spirit Helpers could fasten onto them.

Browser gazed at the handful of people who had stayed behind: the Elders and a few others.

Catkin knelt beside him. The shiny blue and red chunks of stone on her white feathered cape gleamed like bits of morning sky. "Who is it? Can you tell?"

"No."

Catkin shifted, her movements uneasy as she studied the grave. "Something's wrong," she said, and pointed to the places where the hands and feet should be.

Then it struck Browser. The victim had neither. The ends of the pant legs and the sleeves appeared to be empty.

"Mutilation?" Catkin turned hard eyes on Browser. "Someone should remove the slab so that we may name the victim."

"Remove the slab from a witch?" Peavine shouted. Thirty summers old, she had a square, pocked face with a bulbous nose. She'd coiled her hair on top of her head and fastened it with a wooden comb. "Are you mad? You will release his soul, and it will fly about trying to destroy us!"

Catkin wet her lips, and seemed to be nerving herself. "We must know who it is." She started to climb down into the pit.

Cloudblower gripped her arm. "No. I'll do it. You returned just last night from a war walk. You have not been ritually cleansed. I smoked myself in pinyon pine smoke this morning. If there is evil, it will not be able to enter my body."

Browser said, "Go with care."

Cloudblower sat down on the edge of the pit, then gingerly lowered herself to the floor. Shallow, the pit sank only six hands into the earth. She stood straddling the body for several instants. Finally, she bent forward, slipped her fingers beneath the rock, and shoved it aside.

The victim's face had been crushed. Bloody pulp filled the caved-in skull. It looked as if once the murderer got started he couldn't stop. The man's hair had been hacked short, as though in mourning. Browser frowned.

Catkin said, "We'll never be able to name him. He has no eyes, or nose—"

Browser interrupted, "Can you turn him over, Cloudblower? Perhaps he painted clan symbols on the front of his shirt."

Cloudblower grabbed the right arm and tugged. The rigid body flopped onto its back. As Cloudblower lowered the arm, the long sleeve pulled back, and a small, delicate hand adorned with a snake bracelet fell out.

Stunned silence came over the assembly.

A painful stinging sensation flooded Browser's veins. "No. No, it . . ."

The words died in his throat. He jumped into the pit and took the stiff fingers, examining the bracelet.

"Oh," Cloudblower whispered, and stumbled against the pit wall. "Blessed gods."

People surged forward, hissing.

Flame Carrier cried, "Is it . . . ?"

Cloudblower said, "Yes. I think so."

Flame Carrier shook her gray head. "Why would someone kill her and throw her into her own son's burial pit? It makes no sense!"

Catkin said, "It did to the killer." She rose to her feet, looming over Browser.

Browser rubbed his thumb over the back of Ash Girl's death-cold hand, feeling nothing. No pain, no horror, only a numb sensation. His heart slowed, but each time it beat, it felt like a concussion in his chest.

People shouted questions and a deep-throated rumble of coughing filled the morning.

Browser looked up and, for the first time, noticed their brightly colored clothing and jewelry. They had worn their finest to honor his son. Terrible grief and pity for him filled their eyes. He stared at each person, his soul moving slowly, methodically, trying to recall their names. When he came to the end of the line, a sudden stab of naked terror went through him.

"Blessed gods, where's Hophorn?"

3

CATKIN FOLLOWED THE trail of red macaw feathers she had noticed at the burial site. Wind Baby had blown the feathers about, but they appeared to lead from the burial pit to where the Sunwatcher sat with her head bowed.

As Father Sun climbed higher into the sky, the sand gleamed like powdered amber. The fresh scents of thawing earth and wet grass carried in the cool air.

She moved forward with her war club in her fist, her dark eyes searching the boulders, and brush.

Shadows mottled the face of the cliff to her left, turning the eroded sandstone into a patchwork of gray and gold. The larger crevices could hide a man.

With witchcraft lingering on the wind, Catkin would take no chances.

Wreaths of sparks spiraled up from the Sunwatcher's fire, which meant that someone had recently thrown wood onto it. Less than a quarter hand of time ago.

Catkin stopped five paces away. The Sunwatcher did not move. Her long braid fell over her left shoulder, looking startlingly black against the red cape.

Catkin gripped her club more tightly. She called, "Hophorn?"

A flock of pinyon jays flew over the cliff, their blue-gray wings flashing in the sunlight.

Catkin glanced at them. Witches often changed themselves into animals to elude capture, but these birds did not circle or appear unduly interested in the commotion below. They soared and dove in the sunlight, as if offering prayers to Father Sun.

Catkin took another step. No tracks ringed the fire pit, but she walked wide around it, careful not to disturb anything. When she reached the Sunwatcher's side, she crouched. Ashes sheathed Hophorn's hair and cape, and four lines led away from the body, pointing in the sacred directions. Two ash-coated eagle feathers stuck out from beneath her sandals.

Catkin's eyes slitted.

Shamans dipped ashes from fire pits and scattered them to the four directions for physical purification. What could this mean?

She reached for Hophorn's chin, and tipped her pretty face up. Blood matted her hair to the left side of her skull. A trickle of crimson ran down Hophorn's neck onto her red-feathered cape.

Feet pounded behind Catkin.

Browser's voice had turned frantic. He yelled, "Is she alive?"

"I don't know yet. A moment."

He ran to Hophorn's side and grabbed her hand to test her pulse. The fringes on the hem of his tan knee-length shirt flipped in the wind. "Gods, she's alive," he exhaled the words, and clutched Hophorn's hand to his chest. "Thank the gods."

Chaos broke out as people left the burial pit to rush in their direction. The rustling of clothing and hissing of questions assailed the quiet.

The crowd massed ten paces from the fire pit, whispering, wringing their hands. When Catkin glanced at them, she saw a wall of frightened eyes.

Browser gently tipped Hophorn's head, and studied her slack expression, her half-open eyes. "Her pupils are two different sizes."

"I know." Catkin tied her war club to her belt, and reached beneath Hophorn's cape to touch her chest. "She's cold. She must be in shock."

Browser tenderly stroked Hophorn's hair, and whispered, "I'm here, Hophorn. Don't be afraid. You're safe. Everything is going to be all right."

Cloudblower shoved through the crowd. Graying black hair straggled around her cheeks. She indicated the path Catkin had taken. "If I walk here, may I come?"

"Yes, but take care."

Cloudblower nodded. When she reached Catkin, she fell to her knees and gently took hold of the Sunwatcher's head. "Blessed Ancestors." She ran her fingers over the indentation in the skull. "Evil Spirits must be flying in from everywhere to feed on her brain. The brain will be swelling with them. If we do not relieve that pressure, she may die."

Cloudblower lurched to her feet, and yelled, "Whiproot, help me carry her. We must get her to my chamber immediately!"

Whiproot ran the path Cloudblower had taken. Gusts of wind ruffled his white-feathered cape and chin-length black hair. He had only seen eighteen summers, but each showed on his face. His scars twitched as he neared Hophorn, and Catkin saw the tears that welled in his eyes.

"What—"

"Take her feet. I will take her shoulders."

Whiproot did as the *Kokwimu* instructed. They lifted the Sunwatcher and started for the crumbling town where Cloudblower lived. Most of the crowd went with them, leaving less than a handful of onlookers. They milled about, speaking ominously to each other, gazing back and forth between Catkin and Browser, and the burial pit where Flame Carrier and Springbank still stood.

Browser rose. His wife and son were dead. His lover had been injured and might die, too. The very ground seemed to quake beneath his feet. "Did you see any sign of the attacker?"

Catkin shook her head. "Nothing except the red feathers. The sand is frozen solid. None of us are making tracks. Even with fifty people out here, we've barely scuffed the ground."

Browser walked to the fire and stopped suddenly. His eyes widened, as he caught sight of something on the ground.

"Catkin?" he said. "Come over here."

"What is it?"

Browser picked up the object and turned it in his hand. "A turquoise wolf."

For a moment she was too stunned to say anything, then she blurted, *"What!"* She ran forward and grabbed for the precious talisman.

During the Age of Emergence, there had been two kinds of "people": First People and Made People. The First People were related to those who had bravely climbed through the four underworlds; led by a blue-black wolf, they had emerged into this world of light. Originally, all First People had lived in Straight Path Canyon, near the sacred tunnel from which they had emerged. Legends said the First People had built their kiva around that hole. The four clans of the Straight Path nation were, on the other hand, Made People. The Creator had fashioned them from "animals" to provide company for the First People. The Buffalo Clan, Bear Clan, Ant Clan, and Catkin's own clan, the Coyote Clan, had originally been the animals their names implied. The Creator had breathed upon them, and they had turned into humans. But the First People had considered them inferior because they had once been animals, whereas the First People had always been human.

Catkin closed her fingers around the turquoise wolf. All of the First People were dead. Their legendary palaces lay in ruins. Their precious knowledge had turned to dust.

Except for stories. Glorious, unbelievable stories.

Because the First People had climbed through the underworlds, it was said that they possessed a secret knowledge of those worlds that the Made People did not. They had sold that knowledge for a price. From generation to generation, they whispered about the trip through the underworlds, the traps laid by the monsters who haunted the roads, and the landmarks that guided souls along the right path. And sometimes, for special, chosen seekers, they provided a turquoise wolf Spirit Helper to guide them on their way.

Catkin opened her palm and stared at it. The workmanship was magnificent. The wolf had her muzzle up, howling. Catkin said, "Do you think—"

"It can't be anything else," Browser answered. "That kind of work takes a master. A person who has spent all of his life carving and grinding turquoise. No one today can work turquoise like that."

He held out his hand, and Catkin reluctantly dropped the wolf into his palm.

Catkin's fingers tingled, as if the wolf had left a trace of Power on her skin. "Blessed Spirits," she whispered. "Do you know what someone would do to possess that wolf? The First People and their secret knowledge of the underworlds might be gone, but who needs it when they have a personal Spirit Helper to lead the way?"

Browser held the wolf out to the sunlight, and watched the light shimmer off the polished turquoise. "The killer must have dropped it."

"The killer?" She shook her head. "Why? It is more likely that it was dropped long ago by one of the First People who lived here."

Browser reached down and lifted a red feather. "It was laying on top of this, Catkin." Wind Baby tugged the feather out of his hand, and it pirouetted through the air, rising higher and higher until she lost sight of it.

Catkin scrutinized the spot where the feather had rested. The faint outline of something pressed into the sand. She said, "What's this?" and drew the odd arcing shape in the air above the impression.

Browser's eyes widened. He leaned forward. "Perhaps part of a heel mark? The sand around the fire pit has thawed. It is the only place we might find such a print."

She frowned. "If it is a heel print, he was a *big* man." She put her hand down, and the impression stretched from her wrist to the tip of her little finger. "A big, heavy man."

Browser nodded. "Yes."

"Big enough to fit into the clothing your wife was dressed in?"

They both turned when Flame Carrier and Springbank left the burial pit, taking the onlookers back to Talon Town with them.

Catkin stared at Browser's hand where he held the wolf. "If anyone today possessed such a wolf, he would be famous. I have never heard of such a person."

"Nor have I," he said through a long exhalation. Browser massaged his forehead as though a headache pounded behind his eyes. "Which means either the murderer found it recently, or the First People are not gone."

Catkin shifted. "But no one has seen one of the First People for more than fifty sun cycles, Browser."

Browser tucked the wolf into his belt pouch, and stood. "Maybe. Maybe we see them everyday, and do not know it, because they do not claim the privilege."

"So they may be hiding among us?"

"Perhaps."

Instinctively, her gaze shot upward, searching the sky for the pinyon jays she'd seen earlier. Perhaps that's how they'd done it. The last surviving First People had turned themselves into witches and moved unnoticed through the Made People.

"Catkin?" Browser said. "Tell no one about the turquoise wolf. When the time comes, I will speak of it. Do you understand? If anyone knew of this discovery, there would be a war over who should possess it. I do not wish—"

"Of course, I understand."

Browser scanned the boulders and crevices in the cliff. "Catkin, after we have buried my son, and wife . . ." His voice broke. He took a few instants to collect himself. His mouth worked, opening and closing. More softly, he said, "After that, I wish you to complete a task for me."

Catkin folded her arms to keep her hands under control. She longed to touch him, to ease his hurt, but that would just make things worse. She said, "Of course. What is it?"

He turned to her, and his eyes sparkled with tears. "We do not know why someone would wish to kill my wife, but we must assume that it was not an accident. The Ceremony of the Longnight begins in seven days. If we have not discovered who did this before then, we may all be in grave danger. Major ceremonials make excellent hunting grounds. With all the commotion, the Dances, the masks people wear, a killer could walk through the gathering unhindered, picking his targets one by one."

"Why do you think the killer is a man?"

"If my wife had been dragged, we would see the evidence of it. There would be bits of scraped-off skin on the rocks or hair tangled in the brush. He must have carried her. After we have searched the canyon, we will know more. For now, just call it a feeling."

"What makes you think he wishes to kill again?"

"His souls are twisted." Browser reached down and retrieved another red feather from near the crackling fire.

"Did you realize that the red cape Hophorn was wearing belonged to my wife?"

Catkin started. "Are you certain?"

"I recognized the yucca ties on the front. My wife wove them for many people, but she used a mixture of rabbitbrush and ground lichen to dye her ties a distinctive shade of yellow. She breathed part of her souls into her own ties." He nodded. "It was hers. That is why the trail of feathers led from the burial pit to Hophorn. The killer removed it from my wife's body, and placed it around Hophorn's shoulders."

Catkin's gaze roamed the cliff while she thought about that. Father Sun had chased away most of the shadows, leaving the weathered sandstone bright and golden. "Why would a killer take the time to remove a cape and walk sixty paces to—"

"Why would he take the time to undress his victim and then redress her in a man's clothing?"

Catkin could think of no answer.

Browser massaged his forehead again. "I don't know either, but I know someone who might."

"Who?"

"I want you to find old Stone Ghost, Catkin. Bring him here."

Catkin's jaw dropped. When she'd been a little girl, her mother had told her stories about the terrible crimes the old madman had solved and several he'd committed. No one dared speak his name too loudly, lest he hear and chase them on his flying rawhide shield.

She said, "I—I thought he was dead."

"No, I don't think so, though I haven't seen him in twenty summers."

"You know him?"

"He used to have a house down near Smoking Mirror Butte. I will give you directions—"

"You were there? You *visited* him?"

Gently, he said, "No, but he is my grandmother's brother."

Catkin had never heard the old lunatic spoken of with anything other than loathing and fear. Browser's reverent tone captivated her.

She stared into Browser's eyes. "Is he mad?"

He shrugged. "Everyone says so. But I never saw it. He . . ."

Browser stopped and seemed to be struggling for what to say next. Then he closed his eyes a long moment. As if in apology he placed a hand on Catkin's shoulder, and got to his feet.

"Later," he said. "We will speak more later. I must go and see about Hophorn, and consult with Matron Flame Carrier. Will you"—his hands started shaking—"could you guard my son while I am gone?"

"Of course."

"And let no one disturb this place. I want to search for a sign more carefully when I can." He looked toward his son's burial ladder, and a tortured expression creased his face.

Catkin rose to her feet. "Go. I will take care of this."

Browser lightly touched her hair, and walked away like a man about to face his own death, his chin up, shoulders squared.

4

Two DUST DEVILS—the *chindi* of the Navajo—danced in the flats to the west of the site. Dusty watched them as he planted a foot squarely in the soft back-dirt pile and supported the wooden-framed screen with his thigh. Digging, like anything else, had its moments. This wasn't one. The temperature had topped out at one hundred and four just after noon. Dust-caked perspiration had dried to a white stain on his T-shirt.

The sounds of the site surrounded him. The hollow metallic song of a trowel being scraped across hard sand, the clang of the flat shovel as it encountered a random rock tumbled from one of the pueblo walls. A symphony of *shish-shishing* came from the screens as they separated the tan sandy loam from bits of pottery, flakes, and the occasional stone tool. The idle chatter of the field crew had dropped to a bare mumble as the heat pressed the last vestiges of energy out of their dirty bodies.

That, more than anything else, gave Dusty a definite understanding of how the heat was affecting his people. Even the word games, the final resort of field archaeologists in the middle of a dig, had dribbled to the essentials of communications—and most revolved around motel rooms in Gallup, iced drinks, cold showers, and air conditioners.

Dusty ran his callused fingers through the pebbles, bits of root, and insect shells in the screen. He came up with a big, fat zero. Not a single artifact. He artfully lowered the back of the screen, and flipped the junk onto the back-dirt pile.

Bending down, he reached for his half-empty thermos —the iced tea had turned tepid hours ago—and nodded to Bruce Thompson, who tossed another shovelful of dirt into the screen.

"Hey, Dusty!" Michall shouted. "There's a truck coming! Swing lo, sweet chariot, coming for to carry me to Santa Fe and cold beer, I hope!"

"Dream on," Sylvia countered. "It's probably some Park Service control freak coming to ensure our tents are in the right order before he goes to measure the depth of the contents in the Sanolet."

"Shows what she knows," Bruce muttered as he pitched another shovelful onto the screen. "No bureaucrat measures smelly stuff. They order the seasonal temporaries to do it."

Dusty straightened and looked. The truck bobbed and lurched down the dirt track, trailing a thin yellow plume of dust. "Okay, Dr. Thompson, the pit is yours. Don't exceed a ten-centimeter level, and don't pocket any golden idols while I'm a co-principal investigator."

"Right, chief." Thompson gave him a crooked grin. The kid was still working on his B.A., couldn't tell ten centimeters from ten feet unless his eyeball was stapled to the tape measure, and probably wouldn't have recognized a golden idol unless it stood up and announced the fact. Fortunately, so far "Four north, Eight east," the two-by-two meter square that Thompson was digging, had been a "sterile" pit, meaning it had produced no artifacts.

Dusty walked along the line of stakes that made up the site grid. The datum line ran north-south, the baseline, east-west. Any artifact located would be mapped in according to its Cartesian coordinates, the distance from those two lines. When the site had been excavated, it would look something like a waffle: big empty squares separated by narrow walls of dirt.

Dusty ran a grimy forearm over his sweaty brow. The dirt on his arms streaked his forehead. As he walked out to the road, he slapped dust from his Levi's and brushed at the sweat stains on his T-shirt.

The approaching truck clattered and growled, its diesel idling along. The vehicle, a big Dodge extended cab pickup, sparkled, rich metallic red paint gleaming as it pushed through the gnarly greasewood.

It looked new, which meant it didn't belong to a dirt archaeologist. They generally made do with older, ragged out four-by-fours that left greasy puddles wherever they parked. The Dodge's hot metallic red also excluded Park Service personnel.

The big truck rolled to a stop, the chrome wheels catching the sunlight. Dust boiled up from the huge knobby all-terrain tires. The dark, tinted windows obscured any hint as to who the occupant might be.

Dusty stepped around as the door opened, and he could almost imagine the cool air-conditioned air puffing out and dissipating in the heat.

For as flashy as the truck might be, the old man who clambered stiffly out stood in stark contrast. He wore a battered, thirties-style fedora over a mat of steel-gray hair. His bushy eyebrows puffed out from his brow, and the thick mustache might have been tightly packed bristles. Seventy-plus years of sun and wind had turned his age-lined face into something resembling leather. About average in height, he hadn't gone either to a pot belly or bones, as the elderly were wont to do. In fact, the term elderly just didn't apply—especially not if you gazed into those sharp brown eyes. He'd stuffed his brown pants into the tops of old hiking boots, and wore a blue plaid western-cut shirt, the snap-down kind with fake pearl buttons.

Dale Emerson Robertson, the grand old man of south-western archaeology, stroked his gray mustache as he looked Dusty up and down. Robertson had lived as a giant among peers, as a boy working with Neil Judd, A. V. Kidder, and Harold and Mary Colton. He had carved out his own niche along with Lister, Haury, and John McGregor. Unlike so many of his colleagues, Dale had jumped into the "New Archaeology" of the sixties, and made the most of "Cultural Resources Management" in the seventies and eighties. For the nineties, he had taken to remote sensing, the electron microscope, and other advances in technology.

"William! Good to see you." Dale glanced sidelong toward the site. "All's well, I hope?"

"Hello, Dale." Dusty rubbed the hot hood, feeling the fresh wax. The dust had settled on it in mottled patterns. "What's this? A new truck?"

"The scout was getting a little old. Have you tried to find parts for an International recently? It's easier to find Folsom points in England." He glanced at the archaeologists working in the sun, their lower halves hidden by the brush. "Find anything interesting?"

"Not yet, but we've named the site. '10K3,' for ten thousand and three. We recovered some potsherds. Nothing diagnostic. We'll get a better handle on it in the lab. Meanwhile, I've got master scientist Thompson digging his second sterile pit. I can't believe a kid with a four-point-oh grade point average can be such a klutz when it comes to fieldwork. He's crumbled the pit wall twice. His idea of level makes the Himalayas look flat. In all my years of digging, I've never seen anyone who couldn't get the hang of a line level, but young Thompson is baffled by it."

Dale grinned. "So, the site's that dry, eh?"

Dusty grinned back. "It's only the second day. It's there, I feel it."

"You and your gut. Not exactly science."

"My gut proved right in New York two years ago. I demonstrated that the achrondoplastic dwarf was Iroquoian, didn't I? And really miffed that Seneca witch—"

"I wish you wouldn't refer to Dr. Cole that way. She's a rather special lady."

"Of course, she is. She was just born fifty years too late for the Nazi party."

Dusty and Maureen Cole had reacted like vinegar and baking soda. As the excavation near Buffalo, New York, progressed, his intense dislike of her had transformed into out-and-out contempt.

As though reading his mind, Dale exhaled wearily. "I always thought you'd outgrow this irrational fear of women, that you'd find someone who would cause you to reevaluate your opinions. Not every woman is your mother, you know—"

"What my mother did to my father has nothing to do with the fact that Maureen Cole is a viper."

Dale pursed his lips. "Only Freudians—and rodents—fear snakes. Are you a rat or a mouse?"

Dusty stamped on a low greasewood bush. The brittle stems snapped satisfyingly under his boot. His father had killed himself over the worthless woman he'd married. Dusty hadn't gotten over it. He *couldn't* get over it, but he hated to have anyone point out that failing. "If I didn't love you so much, I'd break your neck."

"Well," Dale said and shoved his fedora back on his head. "We archaeologists are a murderous lot of misfits. I suppose I should have turned you over to an accountant to raise. You would have been better off."

"It so happens that you were an excellent father," Dusty said. "You took me to every major archaeological site in the world. Every time you went off to a conference, you dragged me along. I grew up using a trowel during the day and listening to the best archaeologists in the world argue at night. Any sane kid would give his left arm to have a childhood like that."

"Maybe, but it stunted your social development. Archaeology doesn't exactly draw people with a 'normal' psychological composition. We drink too much. Infidelity and short-term relationships are the norm. Minor academic squabbles become blood feuds that last decades, and few of us ever demonstrate any kind of long-term responsibility." Dale's bushy gray brows lowered. "Do you realize that when you weren't living in a tent in the middle of the desert, you were stuck on a reservation?"

"I do. I learned Hopi, Navajo, some Zuni, and even a bit of Arapaho. How many white kids are initiated to a kiva when they turn thirteen?"

"That's the point." Dale sighed. "You never had a chance to be a normal child."

"Thank God."

"Yo! Massa!" Steve Sanders called out. He stood up, dust caking his ebony face. "Y'all wanna come see this?"

From the corner of his mouth, Dusty said, "I wish he wouldn't do that." To Steve, he called, "If it's another utilitarian potsherd, you can toss it with the rest."

"No, suh, Massa," Steve said. "I got bones."

Dusty glanced at Dale. "If he's right, you arrived just in time for the first excitement. Come on."

As they walked, Dale said, "Steve just made my point. The man received his master's degree summa cum laude, has an IQ of one hundred and seventy-six, and is leaving next week to pursue his Ph.D. at the University of Arizona. But he thinks it's funny to talk like Uncle Remus. I tell you, William, that's not normal."

Work stopped across the site. People gathered over Steve's excavation unit. Dusty elbowed his way through the dirt-caked bodies to peer over the pit wall. Steve was on hands and knees, sweat beading his neck. With the trowel, he dexterously pulled dirt back from the bones.

"What have you got?" Dusty asked.

Dale put a hand on Dusty's back for stability and moved up alongside him.

Steve looked up thoughtfully. "I cut the scapula first." He pointed to the shoulder blade; it had a white nick where the shovel had shaved the acromian process. "I put it back in place, and started troweling around it, figuring I'd pedestal it. That's when I uncovered this." He used the point of the trowel to indicate a row of bony protrusions sticking up from the pit floor. "Looks like the vertebral column to me, Massa boss."

"And the rock?" Dale asked, pointing to a flat slab of sandstone that canted at a slight angle where the head should be.

Steve glanced up, "Hey, hi, Dr. Robertson. Welcome to Feature One."

"He arrived just in time for the jive talk," Dusty said disapprovingly.

Steve grinned. "Being the smartest, best, and *only* African American on this project, I have decided not to report myself to the NAACP."

"Politically incorrect wretch," Sylvia said. She brushed her shoulder-length brown hair back from where the wind teased it. A sparkle animated her bright green eyes. "Are you going to pull the dirt back from that rock or wait until we all die of sunstroke?"

Steve moved with a careful grace, his trowel carving the sandy soil back from the rock.

"Whoa," Dale called. "Watch it. That's a discoloration."

"Whoops," Steve said. He followed around the lighter dirt with his trowel. "You're right. Looks like this was dug out, and filled back up. Want to take bets that the discoloration runs around the body?"

"A burial?" Sylvia said. "Why the rock on his head?"

"First things first," Dusty said in measured tones. "Somebody hand Stevie Wonder here a Ziploc. I want a soil sample."

Dusty watched as Steve troweled fresh dirt into the plastic bag, measured in the location, and pulled his line level out to take a depth from the pit datum stake. Then he handed it up for Sylvia to label.

Dusty glanced at Dale. "Are you thinking what I'm thinking?"

Dale shrugged. "Steve, trowel down around the cervical area, see if you can follow the spine up to the back of the skull. If you have to coyote under the rock for the moment, it's all right."

Sylvia frowned. "What are you thinking, boss?"

Dusty just shook his head, waiting.

Steve carefully positioned himself so that he wouldn't crush the fragile bone, and scraped the dirt away from the neck area, chiseling under the rock. "All right, race fans, I've got cervical vertebrae here, and . . . yes, I can feel the skull." Steve glanced up. "Okay, the guy's definitely got a rock on his head. What's it mean?"

Dale gave Dusty a warning look, followed by a slight shake of the head.

Taking the cue, Dusty said, "Well, in the Anasazi days, the cemetery commission didn't make you set the headstones in concrete. You'll have to take it up with the local 10K3 undertaker. In the meantime, make sure you've got everything mapped in, photographed, and recorded. You are not to remove a single bone. Got that? We're in NAGPRA land now. This unit has just been removed from the rule of science and placed under the rule of law."

His crew nodded. NAGPRA, the Native American Graves Protection and Repatriation Act, required archaeologists to stop digging and wait for further instructions from the federal agency. They could excavate other units, just not one with a burial in it.

"You'll have to call Maggie," Dale said as he stepped back from the pit.

"As soon as I can get to the Visitor's Center," Dusty said. "I told you, Dale. I've just got a feeling about this site."

"I hope your *feeling* doesn't have to do with that rock."

Dusty looked down at the rock and narrowed an eye. Maggie's words haunted him. He could feel the old ones watching from across time, their souls fluttering just at the edge of his.

"Me, too," he answered, genuinely worried.

5

CATKIN STOOD BESIDE Grass Moon's burial ladder. Everyone else had gone.

Father Sun hung like a fiery red ball over Talon Town. The cracked white plaster gleamed a bloody hue. Voices rose from the plaza. People must have gathered outside of Cloudblower's chamber.

Catkin knelt and propped her war club across her knees. She whispered to the dead boy, "Don't worry, little one. I will make certain you reach the Land of the Dead. No one will desecrate your body."

Two hundred paces to her left, Browser's dead wife lay at the base of the towering canyon wall. Toppled boulders jutted up around the grave. When Wind Baby gusted, a fine mist of snow whirled up and bobbed along the cliff face.

If a body were not properly cared for, cleansed, and rubbed with cornmeal, the confused soul would not know where to go or what to do. It would become a wicked, desperate ghost, wandering the land, crying. The only fate worse belonged to witches. A stone kept their souls locked in a space barely big enough for the body, where they squirmed in the darkness forever.

Who could have hated Ash Girl enough to have killed her and treated her like a witch? Or perhaps she had been a witch and had gotten what she deserved.

Catkin glanced around.

As always when fear taunted her, her thoughts turned

to her dead husband, Wind Born. He smiled at her from the room in her soul where she kept all precious things hidden.

She had been a warrior for two summers before he became a man. As a boy, he had looked up to her. Every time she returned from a raid, she found him waiting at the edge of the village, his eyes searching, eager for a glimpse of her. At first, she had trotted by him with the other warriors, her chin high. Later, she had made a point of stopping to speak with him, to satisfy his insatiable curiosity about her life and the battles she had fought.

Wind Born had once asked her, *"You are tall and strong, of course, but aren't the men stronger than you? How can you fight them?"*

She remembered smiling at the thin, frail-looking boy, and saying, "Each blow of my club, each arrow I shoot, must hit its mark exactly. Men can afford to be careless, to strike three or four times, or to shoot several arrows. They know that even if their wounded victim reaches them, they will probably be able to fight him off. I do not know that. So. I do not miss. Ever."

Wind Born had gazed up at her with worship in his wide eyes and then trotted at her heels as she'd made her way into the village.

It had been a full sun cycle before he'd become a man. In the moons that followed, he had courted her, often shoving his way through throngs of warriors to sit quietly at her side, gently touching her hand, and listening to the war talk. Dimly, gradually, Catkin had realized that his soft voice, and the way he tilted his head when he smiled, were very dear to her.

They had joined during the Falling River Moon when the aspens turned golden and the last mountain wild-flowers blossomed. Wind Born had seen fourteen summers. He'd been ill since boyhood, but the Evil Spirits had finally nested in his lungs that summer. Catkin had

spent their joining night holding him while he gasped for
air.

She had lost him two summers ago, ten summers after
they'd joined.

Catkin touched the malachite pendant she wore. When
Wind Born could no longer walk, he'd lain in their chamber and carved. The malachite teardrop gleamed like
green fire. Part of his soul lived in the pendant. She could
feel him, loving her, smiling at her in that boyish way
that always wrung her heart. He'd promised her that the
pendant would protect her from all evil.

Catkin thought about Stone Ghost.

No one had ever dared call him evil, but Catkin wondered. One of the many stories her mother had told her
described Stone Ghost as a young man. He had supposedly lived in a brightly lit cave in the northern mountains.
The light had come from the skulls that encrusted the
walls, hundreds of them, filled with a fire that never died.
Whenever anyone approached his cave, they heard
snakes hissing and coyotes and owls making hideous
noises.

It sounded like witchery to Catkin.

She suspected, however, that whether or not a person
was accused of witchcraft depended on how much Power
people thought he had. No one wanted to incriminate a
witch who could point a finger and turn them into a pile
of mouse droppings.

Singing rose in Talon Town. It sounded like the entire
village had joined to pray.

Catkin bowed her head.

Poor Browser.

Catkin knew some of what he must be feeling. The
tingling emptiness. The fear that withered the souls.

After Wind Born's death, she'd been lost and lonely.
Her grandmother had tried to marry Catkin to anyone and
everyone who might be interested. Last sun cycle, she

had tired of arguing and run away to join the Katsinas' People.

She'd hoped to find a quiet place to heal, and think. A place where no one knew her.

Only three moons after joining the migration, she'd been captured by the Fire Dogs. A despicable people, the Fire Dogs raided constantly, killing, stealing food, burning entire villages, then taking the survivors as slaves and driving them southward to dig and haul stones for their filthy towns.

Browser had risked his own life to free Catkin. He'd carried her out of the Fire Dog camp on his back, hidden with her, tended her wounds, and held her at night to keep her warm.

Now she had two holes in her heart.

One for a man she had lost. The other for a man that, until a hand of time ago, she had thought she would never have.

Hope vied with guilt inside her.

What would they do now?

Her gaze lifted to Talon Town. Soon he would come to her, longing to talk, to pour out his fears and agony. She would listen. She would soothe him. And he would say good night and leave.

He allowed little else. A touch on the shoulder. A private smile or exchange of glances.

Catkin gripped her war club when movement caught her eye.

Whiproot trotted around the corner of Talon Town, his white-feathered cape flapping, his young face stern. His chin-length black hair swayed as he ran. She studied the grisly scars that crisscrossed his face. She'd killed the Fire Dog who had done that to him, but not soon enough. Every day for the rest of his life, Whiproot would be reminded of that man and his knife.

For three moons after the battle people whispered that

Whiproot's wife, Silk Moth, could not bear to look at him. He had, briefly, moved into a chamber in Talon Town. The Elders had urged Silk Moth to go on a vision quest to ask guidance from the Spirit World. She had, reluctantly, and returned happy and smiling, saying she had gained a powerful Spirit Helper. Whiproot had moved home again, and they seemed to be doing well.

"What is it, Whiproot?"

"Forgive me, Catkin. I know that the War Chief asked you to guard his son, but Matron Flame Carrier has duties for us."

"What does she wish?" Catkin saw the shining new war club tied to his belt. Beautiful. Strange that she hadn't noticed it before. Had he taken it on the war walk?

"She says the boy's"—he looked down at Grass Moon, and his voice softened—"the boy's burial pit has been desecrated. She wishes you to dig a new one while I keep watch from the south wall of Talon Town. If you keep me in sight, I will be able to see both the boy and you from there. Do not fear. If you yell, I will be there."

Catkin nodded. "Very well. I will need to get a digging stick."

"The slaves stacked several between the big trash mounds. After you have finished the new grave, come and fetch me. Flame Carrier also wishes us to lift the War Chief's wife from the defiled pit and carry her back to the village where the War Chief can care for her. She does not believe his wife was a witch."

Catkin gave him a curious look, wondering how Flame Carrier could be so certain. "Why just us? Where is everyone else?"

"While Elder Cloudblower is opening the Sun-watcher's skull, they will be Singing. Praying for peace, and safety. Honestly, they are very afraid."

"How is Hophorn?"

Agony lined his face. He twisted his war club in his

hands. "She does not look well, Catkin. More than that, I cannot say."

The Singing stopped. They both focused on the town in silence.

Catkin tucked her war club into her belt. "Well, I had better begin the new grave. The sand is frozen. It will take some time."

"And I had better get to my guard position."

They walked back together.

When they reached the wide, shining road that ran in front of Talon Town, Whiproot trotted for the ladder. He climbed to the roof of the low one-story line of rooms that created the south wall, scanned the plaza inside the town, then looked out across the canyon. Finally he walked to the southwestern corner, and crouched down, overlooking Grass Moon's burial ladder.

Catkin climbed into the space between the two enormous mounds that bordered the road. Snow covered the tools. She kicked them to knock it lose, and selected a good fire-hardened chokecherry digging stick.

As she walked back out into the sunlight, the Singing started again.

The melody rose into the cold air like sad wings.

Maggie Walking Hawk Taylor squinted as the headlights of her Park Service truck lit the narrow greasewood trail. For a moment, the brush seemed alive, reaching out to her with spindly arms, then it recoiled as the truck rolled by. Out here, the Ancient Ones were not dead. They peered through the veil of time with little effort, examining the curious ways of modern people.

The first time she had felt them was eight years ago. Fresh out of the university, she'd come to Chaco Canyon as a Park Service summer temporary. She'd walked down to the great kiva at Casa Rinconada and heard flute music. The park closed at sunset. Tourists were prohibited in the ruins after dark. With her ticket book in hand, she'd sneaked silently into the giant subterranean ceremonial chamber, ready to write a citation.

She had flicked the big black maglight on and seen no one. The place stood empty, the stones bathed in the moonlight.

She had taken a deep breath, turned the flashlight off, and leaned against the cool stone, head back, to look up at the moon. She would have sworn she'd heard flute music. Like something Carlos Nakai would play.

Her soul responded to the chanting before her ears did. Distant, but oh, so close. The harmonic voices rose and fell as if to the metronome of her heart. At the edges of her hearing, the flute lilted.

A tape player? Something left by a tourist? She had slowly walked around the great kiva.

In the peaceful moonlight, her grandmother's words had come back to her: *"Only when your soul is still will you hear the Singing."*

Something electric kindled deep down in her soul. Just beyond the senses she could *feel* them around her. Ecstasy claimed her, carried her up, as if she were part of the moonlight and the ancient voices that whispered from the time-worn rock.

How long she stood, caught in that rapture, she did not know.

But that night had changed her life. For the first time she'd felt whole.

Maggie guided the truck through a series of dips and thought about her life.

She'd grown up hard. Her mother died in car wreck when Maggie was eight, killed when she passed out at the wheel after drinking too much whiskey in a Taos bar.

Her grandmother, Slumber Walking Hawk, and her two aunts, Hail and Sage, had used subtle but effective pressure to raise Maggie traditionally. At the same time, she'd had the radio, television, basketball shoes, and computer game arcades. They had irresistibly drawn her toward the White world, and the University with its challenges and excitements. She'd earned her Bachelor of Arts degree in History, specializing in Native American history.

She'd met her husband at school. Richard had been tall and dark, with a keen mind and a playful way about him. They'd loved each other for two years, then Maggie had noticed him pulling away, slowly at first. He'd made up excuses to go into town. Later he'd stayed away all night. They'd divorced three years ago, after she discovered he had several other women on the side. She still missed him. She also still longed to kick his ass.

The lights of her passing truck sparkled on eyes that bounded away. Deer? Or ghosts? Grandmother Slumber would have told Maggie that the other world had been stirred up by something.

Maggie smiled. Her "Western" rational side no longer fought with her "Traditional" side. Depending upon the situation, she could play in either court. Her heart and head worked in unison, each knowing when to give way to the other.

She bounced through a shallow wash and followed the two tracks through a sinuous turn. In her headlights, the reflectors on the archaeologist's trucks gleamed like little red flames. Then she saw the flicker of the campfire illuminating the greasewood.

Maggie pulled up behind Dusty's Bronco and turned off the ignition. She sat for a moment, allowing the stillness of the night to settle into her weary bones. The day had been long and complicated. A little boy from New Jersey had defied the warning signs and tried to climb the cliff behind Chetro Ketl. He'd gotten scared halfway up the Jackson stairway. Park personnel had been forced to rappel down from above to pluck the boy off the cliff.

Maggie's job had been to calm down the obnoxious parents, who kept shouting they were going to sue and have the entire monument shut down as unsafe.

She turned off her lights and stepped out of her truck. Dusty stood at the edge of the parking area, his back to the campfire, a bottle in his hand.

"Is that you, Maggie?"

"It's me." She smiled in the darkness. "Sorry I'm late. I had quite a day."

"Yeah, I heard. Dale was at the Visitor's Center when they pulled the boy off the cliff. New Jersey, huh? Is the suit filed yet?"

She chuckled. "I don't know. What is it about people? A thousand signs in the canyon saying don't climb on anything, and they still climb, then figure it's your fault. You'd think that common sense would tell somebody that if they let their kid scramble up a sheer cliff, he might get into trouble."

From around the fire, Sylvia said, "It's another sign that civilization is doomed. Humans are too stupid to survive."

"You might have something there," Maggie called back, then paused, and looked at Dusty. They'd been friends for five years. She usually knew what he was thinking, but not tonight. "Dale said you *really* need a monitor."

Dusty seemed suddenly reluctant. "We found another one today."

She heard the wary tone in his voice, and said, "You didn't do anything disrespectful, did you?"

"Who do you think I am?" He paused. "I want to talk to you about this alone, okay? Away from the fire."

"If it's a pass, forget it."

"I don't make passes."

"Right. Your reputation for being a real hot dog with women is all made up, huh?"

Dusty said, "You've known me for five years, and you still believe the things I say about myself?"

He led her away, toward his blue Bronco.

"Why can't we talk in front of the crew?"

He leaned against the rear of his Bronco, and firelight glimmered in his blond hair. In a low voice, he said, "From the delicate nature of the bones, body number one looks like a woman. Body number two, another woman. Body three, a woman. Body four, same thing."

"These were matrilineal people. Men went out to war and to trade. They worked in the fields, and hunted. They didn't come back as often. What's the problem?"

"Each woman has a fractured skull. They were beaten to death."

Maggie sat down on the bumper. "Really? Go on."

"You're not shocked?"

"Of course, but I'm not one of these people who takes it for gospel that the ancient ones were peaceful farmers. That 'Red Saint' thing is for romantics. What else?"

Dusty twisted his beer bottle in his hands. "The first victim had a rock dropped on her head." Dusty waited in silence.

Maggie stared. Then she blinked and straightened. "You're sure? The rock didn't roll down off the cliff and accidentally wind up there? You're positive it was intentional?"

"We're not sure of anything. We located the burials and stopped. We're waiting for that monitor. I just want you to know what the monitor *might* be getting into."

"Since when would an archaeologist care what an Indian monitor was exposed to?"

"Since the archaeologist was me," he said firmly. "I don't want to be responsible for bankrupting somebody's family to pay for a cleansing."

Maggie's heart constricted. She whispered, "You really think this is witchcraft?"

Even saying it aloud made her quake. She glanced around at the shapes that fluttered in the firelit darkness.

"It's a possibility. That's why I wanted to talk to you alone. For now, I don't want this to go any further than you and me. I'm not interested in having this turn into a circus."

She studied him. "I thought archaeologists loved circuses. You know, publicity, your picture in the paper, chairing a symposium at the next Society for American Archaeology meeting, et cetera, et cetera. Since when does a White archaeologist turn down a chance for fame?"

Dusty frowned at his beer. He peeled more of the label off the bottle and seemed to be thinking about what to say next. "Maggie, I don't talk about this, so I'm only going to say it once and trust that you won't repeat it. I was thirteen when I was initiated into a kiva. My life was wreckage. Dale had just taken me under his wing. I was headed for trouble, and Dale was friends with this old Hopi. They thought I should undergo this ceremony. I was an angry, hurt kid, drowning in hate and guilt. Really screwed up. My mother was gone. My dad was . . ." His voice softened. "He was dead. I thought I was tough. But when I went down the ladder into that kiva, my world changed. Let's just say I don't need any fame. I need balance and harmony in my life. Turning this into a circus wouldn't accomplish that."

A long silence stretched between them as she studied his firelit face. He raised the bottle and took a drink. She caught the earthy odor of dark beer.

Maggie said, "You know, there's more to you than meets the eye. I'm going to have to rethink my opinions of the renegade, Dusty Stewart."

Dusty gave her a closed-mouth smile. "I'd wait if I were you. I'm sure in another week I'll do something to prove your first opinion right."

Maggie smiled, rose, and took his arm. "Come on," she said as she led him away from the Bronco, and back toward camp. "You can buy me a can of Coke. I'll sit around, enjoy the fire, tell Sylvia how stupid tourists can be, and give this thing some thought. I'll find you the right monitor."

"You'd better do it fast," he said. "We're running out of time to complete this excavation. NOAA wants to lay a concrete pad in three months. We're already behind schedule."

"Dig faster."

"I'd like to, but every time we sink a shovel we hit another body."

Deadly sober, she whispered, "Do me a favor?"

He turned. "What?"

"Don't touch that rock until I can get someone in here who knows what to do."

Dusty looked at her from the corner of his eye. "Don't worry. I have no desire to see a witch's soul running around loose in my camp."

6

BROWSER SAT WITH his back braced against the door frame of Cloudblower's chamber. From here, he could look out to the west, across the ruined plaza of Talon Town. What a place it must have been when the Straight Path nation had been whole. Even now, Power radiated from the stones, the burned poles, and crumbled roofs. Five stories. How had they managed it? He marveled at the First People's perfectly fitted stone work. The elegance of their architecture. In comparison, the chunky, irregular design of Hillside Village seemed childlike.

To his left, above the toppled fifth floor, Propped Pillar leaned menacingly as if it might fall at any moment and crush the last of Talon Town's dreams.

Browser looked into the chamber, and his heart throbbed. Hophorn lay on a pile of soft hides in the middle of the floor. A red-and-blue striped blanket covered her tall willowy body. He longed to go to her, to touch her just to let her know he was near.

Hovering over the warming bowl, the *Kokwimu,* Cloudblower, prepared her tools for the delicate operation. Beside her, the slave girl, Redcrop, chewed her lip, her anxious brown gaze darting between Hophorn and the *Kokwimu.*

Redcrop had seen fourteen summers, almost all of them as a slave. Flame Carrier's son had captured Redcrop and her mother when Redcrop had been a little over a summer old. They had worked her mother to death, but Flame Carrier had taken a liking to the quick-witted girl. She treated Redcrop more like a granddaughter than a slave. Even now, the girl wore a finely painted yellow cotton dress with olivella shells decorating the collar. Most slaves wore plain coarse garments.

Cloudblower pulled Hophorn's long black hair up over her head, then used a sharp obsidian blade to scribe a semicircular line around the wound. The light glinted from the stone, blood welling along the slit scalp. The *Kokwimu*'s skilled fingers changed their grip on the sliver of stone and slipped it between the skull and skin as she pulled back on Hophorn's hair, curling back a hand-size piece of scalp. The depression could be seen in the blood-streaked curve of bone.

Browser could not take his eyes from her. Images of her beautiful naked body flitted across his souls, her long legs, the feel of her moving against him. Her eyes had always shone with a strange luminescence when they'd loved each other.

The jet pendant Hophorn had worn since last summer glittered. The spiral serpent coiled inside a broken eggshell. It had a single red coral eye. Ash Girl had given it to Hophorn. She'd found it while crawling around exploring the abandoned chambers in Talon Town. Hophorn considered it a stunning gift. She constantly commented on its beauty and extraordinary workmanship. Browser did not see it. When Browser gazed upon the serpent, a chill went through him. The serpent always seemed to be watching him, its gaze malignant, evil.

Cloudblower said, "Redcrop? Hand me that obsidian drill. I need to enlarge the holes in the circlet of skull I'm going to remove."

"Yes, Elder," the young slave girl responded.

Browser watched. It grew harder every moment to teeter around the edges of the chasm that had eaten a hole in his soul. Some part of him longed to fall in, to lose himself in that inner well of darkness. Perhaps then the guilt would end.

Ash Girl's face fluttered across the warp and weft of his souls, appearing exactly as it had the last time they'd spoken. He had known only that she was upset with him, perhaps tired of caring for Grass Moon, and needing Browser's help. He had excused himself from the war discussions—which, for the sake of their people, he should not have done—and gone to care for their son. Now, he wished he'd tried talking with Ash Girl, perhaps if he'd—

"I must find my Power herbs," Cloudblower said. "Just sit quietly, Redcrop."

Wrinkles cut the skin around Cloudblower's eyes and across her forehead. Her long graying black hair hung wetly over her cheeks, accentuating the triangular shape of her face. She searched several of the black-and-white pots that lined the rear wall. A pot slipped from her blood-slick fingers and fell. It struck a woven mat and rolled around in a circle before she could grab it, and right it.

Cloudblower poured a small amount of herbs from the pot into a bowl and reached for another pot. "There," she said, "that should be enough."

Redcrop shifted, and the red gleam sheathed her oval face and large black eyes.

Cloudblower turned back with the small bowl in her hands. She poured water from a gourd into the bowl, and used her bloody finger to mix the herbs. The distinctive scents of sage leaves and ground juniper bark filtered through the chamber.

Cloudblower set the bowl beside Hophorn and stretched her weary back muscles.

"May I pour you a cup of sunflower tea, Elder?" Redcrop asked and reached for the pot that hung on the tripod over the bowl of coals.

"I'll drink when we are finished here."

"Yes, Elder," the girl said.

Browser's gaze drifted over the magnificent paintings on the walls. Life-size, the katsinas wore brilliant feathered masks and carried dance sticks in their hands. The Buffalo katsina danced on the south wall in front of Browser. He had one foot up and his arms out at his sides, marching to a sacred Song that Browser could not hear. His long curving horns and black beard looked strangely iridescent against the white wall.

Only Cloudblower and Hophorn had enough courage to take up permanent residence in Talon Town. Many people believed the place cursed. Others said witches flew in and out every night, unseen, unheard, except by the lost souls who roamed the abandoned rooms.

Hophorn had moved here because of Browser. So they could be alone, beyond the direct gazes of Hillside villagers.

Cloudblower's ground-floor chamber nestled in the southeastern corner of the plaza. From the doorway, Browser could look due west across the plaza to the narrow line of rooms that bisected the massive semicircular town. The great kiva they'd begun restoring sat in the middle of the line of rooms. Though mostly subterranean, the upper quarter of the structure rose above the ground. The fresh white plaster shone in the noon sun.

Flame Carrier had ordered everyone home to Hillside Village, except Redcrop, himself, and Whiproot. He could see Whiproot crouching on the roof of the long south-facing wall. Dressed in his white ritual cape, he resembled a huge snowy owl. Above Whiproot, dark clouds drifted northward, silent as the shadows of the masked gods.

The only way in or out of the town was by ladder over

the southern wall where Whiproot perched. Browser himself had pulled up the ladder, and stowed it on the roof. He could see it laying to Whiproot's right.

"I'm ready," Cloudblower called, and Browser looked back into the red-hued chamber.

As Redcrop held Hophorn's head steady, Cloudblower slid two long chert flakes beneath the circlet of skull she had drilled and gently lifted it, separating the circlet from the rest of the skull, but she left it attached to the thin membrane that encased the brain. Almost immediately, the membrane puffed out like a fawn bladder balloon. The fluid inside looked faintly yellowish.

Cloudblower sighed, and sat back. "That should release some of the Evil Spirits feeding in her brain," she said. "When the swelling goes down, we will pull the flap of scalp back and sew it in place again. Then we'll plaster it with the Healing herbs."

"How long will that take?" Redcrop asked.

"That is up to the gods, girl. But pray it is not too long."

Redcrop's eyes widened. "What will happen if it takes too long?"

"The flap of scalp will die and Hophorn will have a spot of bare skull for the rest of her life." She gestured to the soot-blackened pot hanging from the tripod. "You may pour me that cup of tea now."

Redcrop picked up a gourd cup and dipped it into the pot. The liquid steamed as she handed it to Cloudblower.

The old woman blew on the cup, and her soft brown gaze centered on Browser. She gave him a sympathetic look. "War Chief, would you like a cup of tea?"

"Yes, Elder. Thank you." He sat up straighter.

Redcrop dipped another gourd cup into the pot, and Browser took it.

As he sipped, the fragrance of sunflowers rose. His round face reflected in the pale green liquid. Dirt streaked his flat nose, and dust glittered in his thick brows and shoulder-length hair. His eyes resembled those of a dead animal: wide and glassy. A ravening wolf lived in his body, silently slinking through him, eating him alive.

"You have killed many warriors, have you not?" Cloudblower softly asked.

"What?" Browser asked in confusion.

Cloudblower turned to Redcrop. "Please, go and tell Matron Flame Carrier that we have opened the skull, that Hophorn is alive, and she may proceed with the burial of Browser's son whenever she wishes."

Browser's son. His insides shriveled. After the burial, he would spend all night cleaning his wife, bathing her body in pine needle tea, washing her hair, trying not to see her crushed face . . .

"Yes, Elder." Redcrop rose. She stepped over Browser's extended legs, and trotted across the plaza. He heard her call, "Warrior Whiproot, please lower the ladder!"

Browser studied Cloudblower. "Why did you ask me about the people I've killed?"

Cloudblower slid backward, away from Hophorn, and braced her back against the wall. She drew up her knees and propped her elbows on them. For a time she did not speak, then she smiled gently at him, and said, "I knew a man once. His name was Sunrunner. A small, feeble man. He—"

Browser lifted a hand. "Please, Elder. Another time."

As though she hadn't heard him, Cloudblower continued, "On first glance, there was nothing impressive about him. He was short and skinny—"

"I have no interest in hearing a story, Elder. I—"

"We had both been captured and taken as slaves by the Fire Dogs. They took us to live in the south. It was not a pleasant life. But when Sunrunner was close, none of us felt the hunger, or blows, or saw the death all around us. It was nothing he said or did. I am telling you the truth. He was an ordinary man. In fact, he was a man who did not hope."

"And why was that?" Browser sighed, resigned to his fate.

Cloudblower swirled the liquid in her cup. "I had hope. Everyone around me hoped. We spent every moment locked in our souls thinking of home and family, of good food, and being able to sleep in warm hides. We didn't wish to be slaves."

"Of course not," Browser said. "No one does."

A sad smile touched her lips. "Sunrunner did not mind, because he did not hope. Why would he? He found joy in the smallest of things. The singing voice of another slave. Someone's talent for mending holes in leather. I would see him coming, walking through the heat and misery of the stone quarries, and I would long to shout, 'Why are you smiling? Don't you see what's happening around you?' But I never said those words because Sunrunner's eyes seemed to be focused entirely upon our agonies, but they did not wither his souls, as they did ours. Still, he was no hero. He was quite ordinary. He did not console, or preach, or take great suffering upon himself."

"Then what made him special?"

Cloudblower smiled. "He was not afraid."

Browser lifted his brows. "Forgive me, Elder, but as a warrior, I consider that heroic."

"Yes, I suppose so. But if you had known him, you would not have thought so. Truly. On one of the few occasions when he spoke to me, he said, 'Cloudblower, there are men who die because others kill them, and there are men who die because they are afraid to live. They carefully cut a hole in their hearts and invite death to come and nest there.' Which are you?"

She tilted her head.

Browser gazed at her, until he realized the question was meant for him, not part of the story. Or perhaps it served two purposes.

He said, "You think I'm cutting a hole in my heart?"

"I think you are very adept with a knife, War Chief, and not the one you carry on your hip."

Browser sloshed the remains in his tea cup. "I can't seem to help myself, Elder. I have been thinking, and there are many things I wish I had done. Things I should have done. If only—"

"Guilt is an excuse, Browser. Let it go. Accept what you did, learn from it, and get on with living."

Browser stared into his tea. "Your words sound right to my ears, Elder, but my heart isn't listening."

Cloudblower tucked a loose strand of graying black hair behind her ear. "Then your heart is foolish, War Chief."

Some of the weight lifted from Browser's shoulders. His gaze rested on Hophorn, and desperation ate at him. He leaned into the chamber to stroke the blanket over her feet. "I'm here, Hophorn," he whispered. "Right here."

Cloudblower looked away, as though to give him privacy.

Browser straightened and took another sip of his tea. The flowery taste warmed his throat and belly. "What happened to Sunrunner?"

"Oh," she said, "a woman came to me one day and told me Sunrunner was dead. I never knew how. Probably he did something to annoy the guards."

"I'm sorry."

Cloudblower's eyes shone. "Don't be. Sunrunner was a living prayer. I haven't forgotten the words."

Browser's eyes drifted over her triangular face and sharply pointed nose. He never knew quite what to think of her. The fact that she possessed a male body created

a natural bond of friendship between them, but her female soul, gestures, and tones of voice, often left him
puzzling what to say. In truth she was wholly "other":
Neither male nor female, but some grand blending of
both. He had seen her fight and been stunned by her skill
with bow and club. But her reputation as a Healer
spanned half the world. She had saved far more lives than
she had taken.

Browser could not say the same. He finished his tea,
and set the cup aside. "How is Hophorn?"

Cloudblower leaned forward to put a hand on the red-
and-blue blanket over Hophorn's chest. "The injury was
not as bad as I feared. In some people with head wounds,
when I remove the circlet of skull, the membrane swells
to the size of a fist. Hophorn's was less than one-third
that size."

After several moments of feeling the Sunwatcher's
breathing and heartbeat, Cloudblower leaned closer and
whispered, "Hophorn your breathing has slowed. You
seem to be resting easier. I know your breath-heart soul
is flying, and it feels wonderful, but please don't fly too
far. Remember the time you helped me open old Saw-
tooth's skull? He enjoyed flying so much that he flew
straight to the Land of the Dead. I do not wish that to
happen to you. I love you too much. I want you here
with me for a few more sun cycles."

Cloudblower picked up her cup and went to refill it
from the pot over the coals. From somewhere outside
childish laughter rang out.

Browser said, "Aren't you late for the morning races?"

"The children will have to do without me today."

Every day at about this time, Cloudblower went out to
run races with the children. She never won, of course,
but she cheered a good deal. Grass . . . his . . . his son had
cherished racing with Cloudblower because she insisted
upon running at least one race where no one won. The

children had to strive to come across the finish line at exactly the same time. If they did, Cloudblower would lavish praise upon them, saying, "See, isn't it more fun when all of us win together?"

His son had glowed with pride when he'd come across the line next to Dull Knife, the biggest, fastest boy in the village. Browser recalled one morning—

"Browser?"

He leaned out into the plaza and saw Catkin climbing down the ladder. Browser rose to his feet.

When Catkin hit the ground, she trotted toward him with her white-feathered cape flapping about her broad shoulders. Her beautiful oval face looked as if it had been carved from some pale stone.

Flame Carrier must have sent her to fetch me to the burial. He felt sick.

He turned back to Cloudblower. "Thank you for your story, Elder. It helped."

She nodded. "I'm glad."

Catkin stopped two hands in front of Browser, her dark eyes wide, nostrils flaring with swift breaths, and Browser knew she had not come for the burial.

He hissed, "What is it?"

"War Chief, I do not know how to say this, except to say it. Your wife . . . her body is gone."

He stared at her, uncomprehending. "What do you mean? Where is she?"

Browser lunged into the bright sunlight that flooded the enormous plaza, and met Catkin's eyes. She looked as if she feared he might crumble to pieces at her feet.

Catkin said, "Matron Flame Carrier asked me to dig a new grave for your son, then I was supposed to bring your wife's body back to the village. I found the pit empty, except for this." She opened her cape, and gingerly, as if touching a snake, pulled out a small bundle

of white cloth. She unfolded the cloth and revealed an
owl feather.

Cloudblower gasped, and Browser whirled to see her
standing in the doorway with her hands clasped over her
mouth.

Witches often turned themselves into owls and flew
about spying on people.

Browser shouldered past Catkin and ran for the ladder.
Who would take his wife's body? It made no sense!

As he climbed, he heard the commotion outside.
Shouts and cries of shock. Flame Carrier's voice carried
over the din: *"Stop this! We know nothing yet!"*

Whiproot offered Browser a hand and helped him step
off the ladder onto the roof, saying, "Take care, War
Chief. People are wild with fear. They do not know what
they are saying."

"What are they saying?"

Whiproot closed his mouth as if he wished he'd never
opened it. A swallow went down his throat. He answered,
"Some of the young women suggested that perhaps your
wife was a witch, and someone found out and"—at the
expression on Browser's face, Whiproot continued more
softly—"and that's why she was buried with the stone
over her head. Peavine . . ." Whiproot hesitated when
Catkin stepped off onto the roof and joined the circle.

Browser ordered, "Tell me."

"Well, Peavine—she's such a gossip. She said that
someone may have stolen the body because they feared
you would bury your wife without the stone, and her
spirit would wander the village murdering people."

Browser pulled the ladder up and flipped it over the
opposite side of the wall. He descended the rungs two at
a time and ran through the milling crowd. They hissed
and pointed as he passed, but no one dared say such
words to him.

At the edge of the crowd, he saw Flame Carrier and

Peavine. Peavine stood rigid, her black eyes blazing. Thirty, she had an ugly square face and gray-streaked black hair. She lifted her chin defiantly as Browser passed, and shouted, "She was a witch! I knew it all along!"

Flame Carrier cried, "Hush!" and reached out to Browser. "War Chief? Wait!"

He ran harder, his long legs stretching out, cutting the time to the burial pit. He raced by his son's burial ladder without stopping, but the well of darkness in his souls inched outward, devouring his chest.

The buff-colored canyon wall reflected the sunlight with a blinding intensity. Ravens soared over the pit, cawing, and *thocking* at each other. They tilted their heads to watch Browser. He slowed to a walk ten paces short of the pit, and began checking the sand for sign.

Catkin ran up behind him, breathing hard, and said, "I already looked. There's nothing."

"What about leading away from the grave?"

"Nothing. It is as if she was lifted from the pit by eagles and carried off." Catkin glanced uncomfortably at the circling ravens.

Browser shouted, "These are the acts of a *madman!* Why would someone do this?"

His eyes scanned every nook, every root protruding from the soil.

He could hear people coming up the trail, their voices low and forbidding. One man kept yelling, *"But where is the body? What happened to it?"*

Peavine responded, "Thank the gods it is gone! Would you have her wicked soul sucking the breath of life from your child tonight?"

Flame Carrier cried, *"Enough!"*

Browser swallowed the bitterness that rose into his throat. He closed his eyes, and stood, just breathing. Golden sparks danced behind his eyelids.

Finally, he said, "Catkin, there is a trail that parallels the Great South road. My grandmother told me that Stone Ghost's house was built into the side of Smoking Mirror Butte. Please. Get your weapons, and pack, and hurry."

She nodded. "Yes, War Chief."

"HERE'S ANOTHER ONE!" Sylvia Rhone shouted. Dusty left his dental pick lying in the eye socket of a long dead woman and straightened. He stood in unit 6N 4W, a two-by-two meter excavation unit he had laboriously dug until his shovel chipped the forward point of a hip bone. Immediately resorting to a trowel, he'd followed out the rest of the woman's skeleton.

Dusty called, "You're joking?"

Sylvia crossed her heart. "I swear." She had a curious expression on her lean face, half excitement, half fear. She'd tucked her brown hair up beneath a broad-brimmed straw hat. Dirt streaked her sweaty cheeks.

Before Dusty could climb out of his unit, he saw Dale trotting across the site, his battered fedora pulled down to shield his face from the fierce glare of the summer sun. He might be seventy-two years old, but he could keep up with the kids. Maybe not when it came to shoveling out a kiva, but he made sure the records were being kept, along with the pit logs, artifact bags, and other minutia of an expanding dig. The hot air left his thick gray hair dry and dust-coated. He wore jeans and a faded red cowboy shirt.

Dusty carefully braced his hands on the pit wall and lifted himself out. Drenched blond hair framed his tanned face and glued itself to his cheeks. Every part of him spilled sand: his green T-shirt, khaki shorts, and hiking boots. Grains even trickled from behind his left ear. He brushed at them as he headed toward Dale.

Chaco Canyon at this time of year could be brutal. Either the sun roasted you, or the thunderstorms filled your excavation units until they resembled small square lakes.

He passed eight other excavation units, dug in a line between his and Sylvia's pits.

Michall, occupied with cleaning up around what appeared to be a twelve-year-old girl, didn't even seem to notice when Dusty passed.

Steve Sanders, however, stood up and wiped sweat from his rich black skin. He'd been patiently brushing sand from a black-and-white pot rim. "Another woman?" Steve asked.

"I'll let you know," Dusty said.

Plastic bags filled with artifacts—mostly lithic debitage, the chips left over from stone tool making—and a large number of Mesa Verde black-on-white potsherds—nestled on the edge of Steve's pit. The sherds probably dated the site to the Big House Period, from A.D. 1250 to 1300, when migrants from the Mesa Verde region of southern Colorado had reoccupied the canyon, but Dusty didn't consider that definitive yet. A great deal about this site left him puzzled.

He veered wide around the bags and stepped carefully over taut strings until he reached Sylvia's unit. Dusty knelt beside Dale. Fifty centimeters below, Sylvia bent over a partly exposed human skull. The frontal bone, and the superior borders of the orbits, the eye sockets, were visible in the sand.

Dale shoved his fedora back on his head. "Good God, that makes eight so far."

"Another female," Dusty added. "At least that's my guess from the brow ridge and the bossing of the frontal bone. The others have ranged in age from ten to forty-five. I wager this one will, too."

Dale's thick gray brows lowered. "Where is that Indian monitor we asked for?"

"I talked to Maggie yesterday. She promises the monitor is coming. Probably after our next break."

Dale frowned at the skull. "Well, she'd better hurry. Do you want to lay bets on the condition of this one?"

Dusty brushed sweaty blond hair from his forehead. "No, I think I'd lose."

Dusty eased over the side of the pit, careful not to disturb any of the artifacts Sylvia had pedestaled, meaning she had cleaned away the dirt, but left them in place on a short pedestal of sand while she continued digging. Dusty said, "Sylvia, hand me your trowel."

She delivered it with a flourish. "All yours, boss man."

He crouched to the left of the skull and began removing thin layers of sand—definitely a woman's delicate brow ridge, not that he knew much about this physical anthropology stuff, but that's what it looked like to him. Elevated concepts of human anatomy, and evolution, didn't much interest him.

He reached for one of the brushes near Sylvia's feet and gently swept the dirt away.

When the first fractures appeared, Dale whispered, "They're all alike. What on earth happened here?"

Dusty kept brushing, revealing the dents in the smooth outer table of the woman's cranium. "Battered just like the others."

Dale studied the skull, then glanced at the few artifacts in the unit, and said, "It's time we called in a physical anthropologist."

"I agree, Dale, but I don't want some lab rat that can't stand dirt under his fingernails."

"No, we need someone accustomed to the rigors of field work. I know just the person."

Dusty's brush halted in midair. He felt his facial muscles tighten as they tried to pull his mouth into a rictus.

"Tell me you're not thinking what I think you are."

Dale rubbed his shirt sleeve over his gray mustache. "I am. She's the best."

Dusty threw the trowel to Sylvia, and scrambled out of the pit. "Over my dead body!"

Every time he thought about Dr. Maureen Cole, his stomach churned.

Dale pulled his fedora down and walked away.

Dusty ran after him, calling, "Wait a minute. Let's discuss this!"

"Maureen Cole is one of the finest physical anthropologists in the world. If we can get her, we'll be lucky."

Dale checked his watch and stepped up his pace, heading for Dusty's Bronco; it sat parked near the five tents that formed a neat circle around a central fire pit.

"Are you really going to do this to me, Dale?" Dusty pleaded. "No matter how I prostate myself before you—"

"That's *prostrate,* you illiterate."

Dusty thought about it. "Whatever. Listen Dale, I genuinely despise that woman. I do not—"

Dale finished, "—want to work with any woman who knows more than you do. Yes, I know."

Dale opened the door to the Bronco and tossed his hat inside. As he wiped sweaty gray hair from his forehead, he added, "This is not open for negotiation, William."

Dale got into the Bronco and pulled out Dusty's cellular phone.

Dusty propped his dirty hands on the roof of the Bronco. "You're a sadist, my friend. And very likely an accomplice to murder. Don't you realize I'll have to kill her just to preserve my masculinity?"

As he punched in the number, Dale said, "After this discussion, I'd say you're already too late."

When her phone rang, Maureen Cole closed the latest issue of the *American Journal of Physical Anthropology* and placed it on the table beside her wicker chair.

She wavered on whether or not to answer it. She had one more week at home before she had to return to Hamilton to prepare for classes and wanted to savor it. She reached for her cold glass of mint iced tea. She picked the mint fresh from her garden every morning, and it gave the brew a naturally sweet, cool flavor.

The phone continued to ring.

She turned away. What a beautiful day. Hot, but not too hot. She wore faded blue jeans and a red T-shirt. Sunlight glistened through the trees and dappled the floor of the porch that encircled three sides of her small house in Niagara-on-the-Lake. A cool breeze tousled long black hair around her shoulders.

Maureen drew her bare feet up onto the chair cushion and heaved a sigh. She'd turned thirty-seven last Tuesday. Lines had just started to crease the skin around her eyes and mouth. Her aquiline features, the straight nose, dark eyes, and full lips, came from her mother, a full-blooded Seneca. She had passed away just six months ago. Maureen swirled her tea and listened to the cubes clink. God, how she missed her.

The phone stopped ringing.

Maureen sighed and took a long look at Lake Ontario. The water turned a magnificent shade of blue this time of year. Autumn had already touched a few of the trees, dotting the shoreline with clumps of yellow and orange.

She took no joy in the fact that classes would start soon. Three years ago, when her husband, John, was alive, they'd spent every night discussing grand ideas about the future of the human species and sharing interesting questions their students had asked; it had made teaching fun. Since John's death, she'd found joy only in the physical anthropology lab, talking to dead people. She'd discovered that they carried on far more interesting discussions than most living people. She—

The phone rang again.

After ten rings, Maureen grudgingly got to her feet and started for the screen door.

The oak floorboards felt cool against her bare feet as she walked across the living room to the phone on the table in the bay window. A notepad and pencil rested on the seat of the chair.

She picked the phone up, and said, "Hello."

"Good afternoon, Dr. Cole, I understand classes start soon, are you anxious to get back to training the next generation of great physical anthropologists?"

Maureen smiled. "Dale Emerson Robertson, you old coyote. Are you in town?"

"No, I'm sitting in a Ford Bronco in northern New Mexico. It's ungodly hot, too, one hundred six degrees."

"Let's see, that's about forty degrees to those of us who live in the enlightened world. I've been telling you for a decade that you ought to move to Canada. It's a lot cooler here in civilization."

Dale chuckled. *"Maybe in my old age."*

Robertson was one of the truly great anthropologists of the twentieth century. He'd led expeditions into the jungles of the Yucatan to find lost Mayan cities, dug in Egypt, explored Thule archaeology in the frozen tundra of the Arctic, and pioneered the field of underwater archaeology. If he lived long enough, she expected him to be the first archaeologist on the moon. He was particularly legendary for his work in the southwestern United States.

"What's up, Dale? Or is this a social call?"

"No, business, I'm afraid. Stewart and I are working on a project that's turning up some burials, and I was wondering—"

At the mention of Stewart's name, her eyes narrowed to slits. She said, "Good-bye, Dale."

And hung up.

She'd tramped halfway back to the screen door when the phone rang again.

She lifted a brow. This time she didn't wait for Dale's customary greeting. She walked back, picked up the phone, and said, "You can tell the 'Madman of New Mexico' that I wouldn't work with him again for all the well-preserved mummies in South America."

Dale paused. In a stern professorial tone, he said, *"This is a very important project, Maureen. I'm sure you can both put your personal feelings aside for—"*

"What do you mean 'both?' What did that glorified pothunter say about me?"

"Let me tell you about the site, Maureen. It's far more interesting."

She clenched her jaw. Two years ago she'd had the misfortune to work with Stewart on an Iroquoian excavation in New York state. Never again. The man was not a scientist.

Maureen said, "I'm listening, Dale. Go on."

He did.

After a minute, her heart rate increased. She said, "Really? Mass graves among the Anasazi? That is fascinating."

"It gets better. They're all women."

"All?" she blurted.

"Women and children, yes. But that's not the only anomaly, Maureen. I really need your expertise."

"Dale, I—"

"This will only take a couple of weeks. You can find a graduate student to teach your introductory classes, and give your master's degree students special research projects while you're away. I'm sure one of your colleagues would be willing to cover any other—"

"Dale," she said, and propped her foot in the seat of the chair. "I really *hate* that guy."

A pause.

She could hear someone else's voice in the background.

Then Dale covered the receiver, and she heard muffled voices. It sounded like a spirited debate, but she couldn't make out any of the words.

Dale returned, *"Sorry, Maureen. We have a Kokwimu on the site who can be very annoying."*

"A what?"

"Never mind. As I was saying, I understand the fifth Earl of Carnarvon was no piece of cake, either, but it didn't stop Howard Carter from working with him so that he could dig King Tut's tomb."

Duly chastened, she sighed, "It's that important, eh?"

"More important than I can tell you over the phone. You have to see the site to believe it. The number of healed cranial depression fractures—"

"What do mean 'healed'? These women were struck in the head repeatedly, and lived?"

"No, the last blow killed them."

"Well, right, but I mean before that."

"Before that they had half their brains knocked out."

The longer Maureen listened, the more powerfully her blood rushed. "You're sure it's not just some odd form of cranial deformation?"

"I know cranial deformation, Maureen. The Anasazi tied their children's heads to cradle boards to flatten the skull. They didn't abuse them. These women show dramatic abuse."

She looked out the bay window at the *v* of geese flapping over the crystal blue lake. "So what are we talking about? Spousal abuse? Ritual warfare, where people hit each other in the head to demonstrate courage? Or maybe polygyny, where cowives beat each other?"

"If I knew the answer to that, do you think I'd be on the phone to you?"

Maureen paused, thinking. "Don't I remember something about mass graves of women somewhere down there? It was a paper I heard at the American Association of Physical Anthropologists meetings a while back. Women sprawled in graves—"

"The La Plata Valley stuff. Yes."

"Is that what you have there, Dale?" She could see the images in her mind: Skeletons of battered women thrown face-first into holes and covered with trash.

She could almost hear Dale smile. *"Come and see for yourself. There's an 'E' ticket waiting for you at the United terminal in Toronto."*

"Dale, I have obligations here. Classes start—"

"I'll let Dusty do the analysis, then. It's high time he learned something about paleopathology." He hung up.

Maureen stared down at the receiver.

Outside, birds chirped, and a gust of wind tinkled the chimes on her porch.

She settled the receiver into the cradle and gritted her teeth.

"I'm not going to do this, Dale. I refuse to subject myself to Stewart."

The last time, in New York, they'd spent the entire month at each other's throats. Stewart knew nothing about science, and she couldn't fathom his peculiar brand of cultural "hunches." Stewart could look at a site, study the artifacts, and stratigraphy—the soil layers—and arrive at an immediate intuitive understanding of what had been going on a thousand years ago. Despite the fact that he was generally correct in his guesses, it smacked of the worst kind of pseudoscience to Maureen. In her opinion, either anthropology was a hard science, with experiments anyone could replicate, or it was irrelevant.

As she stared out the French window, she could see the grapevines draping her fence, the clusters of immature grapes green in the late summer light. The image faded to that of earth-yellowed bone, rounded skulls, and gaping orbits.

Women. Battered. Why so many? And what had that hesitation been in Dale's voice? She'd known him for a long time. Something about this site worried him. What?

Maureen drifted around the house like a dandelion seed on a current of air and somehow ended up in her bedroom.

"I'll let Dusty do the analysis," she mimicked Dale's throaty voice, as she pulled her suitcase from the back of the closet, and tossed it on the bed. "You should have just put a gun to my head, Dale. The result would have been the same."

8

BROWSER DRAPED HIS door curtain over its peg. Cold wind blew into his chamber, rustling the dried sunflowers, corn, and beans that hung from the rafters.

He had buried his son less than half a hand of time ago. His wife had been murdered, her skull crushed and left to be discovered, then her body had been stolen.

This isn't real. It can't be real.

Browser touched his son's corn-husk dolls, the tiny bow and quiver of arrows he'd made for the boy. When his gaze landed on the carved wooden dog that rested near the baskets, his eyes blurred. He walked over and picked up the toy.

"Oh, my son."

According to tradition, for four days after the boy's death, Browser should not dream of him or speak his son's name aloud. Grass Moon was on his way to the Land of the Dead, and no one had the right to pull him back to this world of misery and pain. But Browser longed to say his son's name, to hear it again.

He paced the three body lengths of the chamber, turned, and paced back. In the diffused light, the brightly painted faces of the katsinas looked dull. The Badger katsina stood straight ahead of him, on the west wall. The god wore a black mask with turquoise eye slits and an eagle feather headdress. Sharp teeth gleamed in his long muzzle. He carried a spear in one hand and a bow in the other. Was it imagination, or did the god seem to be watching Browser with mild curiosity?

"Hophorn prayed to you every night. She offered you cornmeal and rare shells. Where were you when she needed you? Could you do nothing to save her?"

Anger swelled his heart, and he swayed on his feet. He'd barely slept in two days.

Two days? Has it only been that long since my wife came to me in the plaza?

He clutched the toy, and his gaze drifted over the chamber.

How could everything look the same when his life had been destroyed? Different-sized baskets and a stack of pots sat in the far corner to his right. His weapons lay next to his rolled hides in the far corner to his left; beside them stood the big corrugated pot of shelled beans. But an empty spot marked the place where his son's bedding had rested along the rear wall, and only a circular impression in the dirt reminded him of his wife's black-and-white sewing pot.

Browser stared at it.

After they'd discovered his wife's body missing, the entire village had combed the canyon, searching for tracks, drag marks, bits of clothing, or hair. They'd found nothing.

Out of respect, he had buried his wife's sewing pot, sending it to the Land of the Dead for her. Then he'd burned her clothing to kill any evil Spirits that might have nested in them.

Browser turned the toy in his hands, over and over, studying the angles of the running legs, the tilt of the dog's muzzle.

An eerie feeling of wrongness tormented him. It went deeper than the loss of his family. He felt as though a hideous monster stood right before his eyes, and he could not see it.

He had never before experienced this kind of fear. It had no object, nothing he could lash out at, or fight. The terror just squirmed in his belly, as though growing, readying itself to spring to life.

Browser knelt and touched a finger to the impressions left by the burial ladder.

"Where are you now, my son?"

Once a soul passed the traps, monsters, and snares set on the road to the underworld, it saw two trails: one leading to the left, and one to the right. The Sun Trail on the left was broad and sprinkled with corn pollen. Good people took that trail to the Land of the Dead.

People who had caused great pain and grief in their lives, however, saw smoke rising down the right trail, the Trail of Sorrows, and were drawn to it. Along the way, some turned into dung beetles. The worst people had to walk the trail carrying a heavy basket of grinding stones on their back. They could only take one step a sun cycle.

At the end of the Trail of Sorrows, Spider Woman waited with her sacred pinyon pine fire blazing. Some souls were purged in the smoke and allowed to return and take the Sun Trail. Others were cast into her fire and burned to ashes. The gods trod upon those ashes forever.

Browser knew which trail his son would take, but he couldn't say about his wife.

He used a finger to trace the outline of the burial ladder. The dirt felt cool and gritty.

When anger with the gods did not consume him, anger with his wife did.

She'd run away when her son had needed her most. If she'd been home, where she belonged, she would be alive today.

He squeezed his eyes closed.

With the guilt, came the shaking.

He tucked the toy into his shirt pocket and glanced at the doorway, praying no one would see.

A war chief who showed weakness, weakened everyone around him.

He needed to talk with someone, to pour out his fears and culpability, but Hophorn was incapable of speaking with anyone, and Catkin would not return for at least another day. The storm might delay her for two or even three . . .

Steps crunched the snow.

Browser clenched his fists. When the trembling came upon him like this, he couldn't stop it. "I am here," he called. "Come."

The young slave girl, Redcrop, leaned into his doorway. Snow coated her long hair, and frosted the shoulders of her elkhide cape.

"Forgive me, War Chief," she said. "Matron Flame Carrier sent me to fetch you. She wishes to speak with you."

Browser took a deep breath and said, "Thank you," as he ducked through the doorway.

Redcrop ran in the direction of Flame Carrier's chamber, and Browser followed.

Four ladders stood against the long south-facing wall of Hillside Village. Out of necessity his chamber had a doorway on the ground floor, but the seventy-two other chambers were more secure, reachable only by ladder. Smoke curled from the roof entries, and coiled up the cliff face into the snowy heavens.

Redcrop took the second ladder. Browser climbed up behind her.

Redcrop knelt over the roof entry and announced, "Matron, I have brought the War Chief."

"Fine, girl," a scratchy old voice answered. "You may go to Cloudblower now. Find out how the Sunwatcher is."

"Yes, Matron."

Redcrop rose, bowed hastily to Browser, and trotted for the ladder again.

Browser knelt over the circular entry and called, "May I come, Matron?"

"Yes, War Chief."

Browser descended. Flame Carrier stood below him, leaning on her walking stick in front of the warming bowl. She'd coiled her gray hair into a bun and wore a tan blanket over her hunched shoulders. Her large chamber stretched three-by-four body lengths across. The Sun katsina stood tall on the white wall behind Flame Carrier, his red-and-yellow mask covered with glistening stars, his eagle headdress painted in such extraordinary detail that the feathers looked real. Pots and baskets lined every wall, and two piles of bedding hides lay rolled to Browser's left.

A pile of sticks lay to the left of the warming bowl, and a teapot hung on a tripod to the right.

Flame Carrier did not look at Browser as he stepped to the floor, but said, "Sit, War Chief," and gestured to the mat on the opposite side of the warming bowl.

Browser knelt. "What did you wish to see me about, Matron?"

Flame Carrier prodded the wood pile with her walking stick, and the kinky hairs that made up her eyebrows knitted. She heaved a breath, and said, "Did you do this thing?"

"Do this . . ." The question struck Browser like a blunt beam in the stomach. He stared wide-eyed at her. "Matron. *No!*"

Flame Carrier slowly turned to face him. Her rich brown eyes shone. "I waited to call for you because I wished to speak with others first." She pointed at him with her stick. "Do you know how many of our people believe you killed your wife?"

Browser sank to the floor. "No."

"*Too* many. Thundercloud's chamber is next to yours. He says he has often heard you screaming at your wife, threatening her. Wading Bird reminded me that only last moon your wife went for days refusing to speak to anyone, and her left eye was black. Did you strike her?"

Browser felt as though his heart were melting and flowing down his back bone. "No."

Flame Carrier's wrinkled lips tightened. "Peavine told me—"

"Peavine?" he said in a strained voice. "She hated my wife. She hates me."

"That may be, War Chief, but she came here this afternoon to tell me the number of times you have visited Catkin's chamber in the middle of the night. Peavine says she did not blame you because she believes your wife was a witch, and Peavine assumed you did not wish to be a part of the hideous ceremonials she performed in your chamber."

"In our chamber?" He shook his head vehemently. "I know nothing of these things, Matron. No. No, I do not believe *any* of this!"

"Do you deny going to Catkin—"

"We are not lovers, Matron! Catkin is my deputy. We often have things to discuss, war plans to lay, plots to sift out. And . . ." He opened his hands. "And, more than that, she is my friend. Have you never had a man who was simply your friend, Matron?"

Flame Carrier's stern expression softened. "What do you say to Wading Bird's suggestion that you beat your wife, blacked her eye?"

"She would not speak with me either during that time! I asked her over and over what had happened. On the fifth day, she finally answered. But she said only that her Spirit Helper was healing her."

"Healing what?"

He spread his arms. "I do not know."

Flame Carrier lowered her voice, and whispered, *"Witchcraft?"*

"Matron, I have never seen any evidence that my wife was a witch. I will admit that my duties often take me away from home, but I think I would know if my wife were involved in such wickedness."

Flame Carrier's small eyes narrowed. "For the moment, let us assume that you did not kill your wife. Who did?"

Browser tucked his hands beneath his armpits to hide their trembling. "I do not know, Matron."

"You must have some suspicion."

He shook his head. "No. None. It could be anyone."

Flame Carrier adjusted the tan blanket over her shoulders. "Who hated your wife?"

"Peavine. More than that, I cannot say."

But in the deepest corners of his souls, oddly different voices hissed: *Peavine, Whiproot, Catkin.*

Browser glared at the glowing coals. Catkin had never spoken a word against his wife. Why would his souls name her? As snow filtered down through the roof entry, the coals spat and steamed. He suddenly found it hard to breathe.

Flame Carrier's wrinkled face fell into contemplative lines. "You are lying to me, War Chief. Why? Do you have something to hide?"

"No, Matron," he quickly defended. "It is just that if I speak poorly of people in my own village, it might appear that I am accusing them. I do not believe someone here did this terrible thing. The murderer must have been an outsider."

Flame Carrier grunted, "Indeed? You just said it could have been anyone."

She used her walking stick to brace herself while she eased down to the deerhide opposite Browser, and tucked her blanket around her feet. The warming bowl nestled between them, the coals glowing redly.

"What about Catkin?" Flame Carrier said in a calm voice.

"Matron? What do you mean?"

Flame Carrier tossed another stick into the warming bowl, and sat quietly, watching the flames lick around the wood.

Finally, she asked, "Where is Catkin?"

Browser's stomach muscles clenched. He'd been dreading this. He leaned forward and peered directly into Flame Carrier's narrow eyes. "I sent her to the south, Matron. To Smoking Mirror Butte."

"Without my approval?"

A swallow went down Browser's throat. "Matron, I have heard you speak of Stone Ghost before and your words were never kind."

"Of course not. He's an old fool. His souls flit around like bats."

Browser opened his hands in a pleading gesture. "But he has discovered the truth of many crimes, Matron. Do you recall the terrible murders at Faithful Hawk Village twenty summers ago?"

Flame Carrier's brows lowered, but she might as well have lifted a bow and aimed it at Browser. His mouth went dry.

"I do recall," she said. "But you would have seen barely eight summers. How do you know of it?"

Browser laced his hands in his lap. "My grandmother was one of those killed. I was there the day our warriors hauled her mutilated body into the plaza."

The scent of wet pine needles filled him, and he could feel the rain on his face and hear the thunder rumbling in the distance. The warriors had been splotched with her blood, their faces sprinkled with raindrops. The cries of Browser's mother rang in his ears.

Four old women had been brutally murdered that summer. None of them related. All suffering from the coughing sickness. The murderer had slit their throats and cut gaping holes in their bodies.

"Stone Ghost came to our village because my mother asked him to."

The old man had wandered the village like an imbecile, breaking into people's chambers in the middle of the night, brushing at walls and clothing, claiming the murderer had left a trace of red corpse powder on the dead bodies, but it could only be seen at night.

The villagers had roared with laughter.

Until another midnight corpse powder raid. Stone Ghost had leaped into a chamber and started howling. He'd acted like a foaming-mouth dog, urinated on blankets, baskets, and even a warrior's sacred Power bundle. He'd smashed pots against the walls. And "accidentally" discovered the blood-encrusted knife the murderer had used on his victims. Naturally, the man screamed his innocence and tried to kill Stone Ghost, but by that time half the village stood peering down through his roof entry with their weapons shining in the moonlight.

"What makes you think he will come?" Flame Carrier asked, and coughed into her hand.

"He may not, Matron. And if he does, with the snow, it will take him another two or three days."

Flame Carrier gave Browser a look that would have wilted a stout cottonwood. "Since you have already done this thing, it will do little good to counsel you on the errors of your judgment, War Chief. You were grieving, and your souls were not quite connected to your body. I will excuse you, this time, and have a chamber prepared in case the old fool arrives. But in the future you will remember that *I* am the clan Matron, and I bring all such decisions to the vote of our people. We are not—"

Feet pounded the roof.

They both looked up.

Redcrop called, "Matron? Matron! Cloudblower sent me for you. The Sunwatcher is awake!" The girl leaned down over the roof hole, her face bright red. Wet black hair stuck to her cheeks. "Cloudblower said for you to come quickly. The Sunwatcher has not spoken yet, but her eyes are open."

Browser got to his feet, eager to leave. After Flame Carrier's accusations, he *had* to find out what Hophorn had seen the day his wife was murdered.

The Matron waved a bony hand. "Go along, War Chief. I will come as soon as I am able."

"Thank you, Matron."

Browser climbed the ladder and ran across the roof. He took the rungs three at a time and hit the ground running. He passed the pitiful katsinas painted on the eastern wall of Talon Town and turned right onto the road. Hundreds of feet had trampled the snow, turning it filthy and treacherous. Mud oozed up around Browser's sandals.

Slaves, and two guards, walked the road, carrying wood and pots of water. They nodded to him as he passed.

Browser had not taken any slaves since he'd joined the Katsinas' People. Flame Carrier said it cost too much to feed them, clothe them, and care for them. But many of the older members of the Katsinas' People had slaves that had been with them since childhood, cherished slaves who required little or no guarding.

Whiproot stood on top of the one-story line of rooms that formed the long southern wall. Chin-length black hair fluttered around his buffalohide hood. He called, "Good morning, War Chief! Let me lower the ladder."

Browser grabbed the foot of the ladder as Whiproot let it down and braced it on the muddy ground.

He took the rungs two at a time, jumped off onto the

roof, and said, "Who else knows that Hophorn is awake?"

Whiproot's scarred face tightened. "Redcrop was supposed to tell you, and our Matron, first, but I'm sure by now she—"

Browser pointed a stern finger. "Let no one enter this town without my order or the Matron's order. Do you understand?"

"Yes, War Chief. I understand."

Despite his youth—eighteen summers—Whiproot obeyed quickly and never questioned an order. That made him one of Browser's most trusted warriors. He clapped Whiproot on the shoulder and reached for the ladder. "Help me pull this up."

Whiproot took the other side of the ladder.

Together they pulled it up and lowered it into the enormous plaza. Ahead of Browser, on the curving northern wall of the town, the faded thirty-hand-tall figures of the *Yamuhakto*, the Great Warriors of East and West, stood. They carried lightning bolts in their hands, aimed down at the plaza and anyone who would dare to defile this holy ground. Browser bowed to them, then stepped onto the ladder and clambered down.

When his feet hit the ground, he trotted toward Cloudblower's chamber. Snow had begun to accumulate and blow about the plaza. Drifts piled against the walls.

As he neared the chamber, Cloudblower softly called, "Enter, War Chief."

Browser ducked through the low doorway and into the crimson glow cast by the warming bowl. After the icy cold of his own chamber, the heat made him shiver.

"How is she?" he asked.

Cloudblower sat cross-legged near Hophorn's head, washing her face with a cloth. A bowl of melting snow sat to Cloudblower's left. The *Kokwimu* looked very tired. The lines around her slanting eyes cut deeply into her flesh, and her long gray-streaked black hair hung about her triangular face in damp strands. Soot smudged the bridge of her sharply pointed nose and mottled her long blue dress. "Better, War Chief."

Hophorn lay on her back to the left of the warming bowl, a red-and-blue-striped blanket pulled up to her chin. Long black hair haloed her swollen face. Her dark eyes kept drifting, apparently unable to fix on anything. When she saw Browser's face, her right hand lifted slightly off the blanket, as though trying to greet him, but fell before she could complete the gesture.

Browser rushed to take her hand. "My heart soars to see you awake, Hophorn. Everyone in the village has made themselves sick worrying about you. Now, perhaps, we can get some rest."

A faint smile tugged at the corners of her mouth, and Browser felt her trying to squeeze his hand. She had no more strength than an infant. Fear and love for her swelled inside him. He clutched her hand to his heart.

Cloudblower said, "She is having trouble speaking, but I'm sure it will pass."

"She feels hot."

Cloudblower rinsed her cloth in the melting snow, and mopped Hophorn's forehead. Hophorn leaned into the cloth, as though the coolness eased her suffering.

"Yes, she is fevered, but that is to be expected. Now that she is awake, I'll begin giving her willow bark tea. That should bring the fever down and ease her pain."

The left side of Hophorn's skull, around the injury, had been freshly washed. Cotton stitches outlined the rough oval of wet scalp that Cloudblower had pulled back to open the skull. The flesh remained red and puffy, crusted with dried blood.

Browser smiled down at Hophorn. "You may not feel well," he said, "but you look much better. There is color in your cheeks, and your eyes are bright. I wager you will be up in time for the Celebration of the Longnight."

A confused expression creased Hophorn's face. She tipped her head to look at Cloudblower.

Cloudblower said, "The celebration is in six days, Hophorn. But do not worry yourself. If you are not able to conduct the ceremonial, I will. I have acted as your assistant often enough to know what to do. It will not be as grand as the ceremonials you lead, but it will do for this cycle."

Hophorn smiled weakly, and her eyelids fluttered closed, then open, and finally closed again. Her head lolled to the side.

Browser looked up, frightened by her sudden loss of consciousness. "Is she all right?"

"Yes, just sleeping. I told her I was sending for you and Flame Carrier. I think she forced herself to stay awake until you came."

Browser gently placed her limp hand on the blanket and rose to his feet. "Cloudblower, may I speak with you outside?"

Cloudblower frowned, but followed him into the falling snow.

Each of the five stories that composed Talon Town had been stepped back, giving it a stairlike appearance. Snow sheathed the collapsed roof timbers and mounded the crumbling walls, softening the appearance of the ruins.

Browser led Cloudblower a short distance away from her chamber, and whispered, "Tell me straightly. How is she?"

Cloudblower's slanting eyes tightened. "She is very ill, Browser. Evil Spirits are still feeding in her brain. For some reason when they nest in injuries on the left side of the head they often eat away a person's ability to speak."

"Are you saying she may never speak again."

Cloudblower folded her arms across her blue dress and

shivered in the cold wind. "I am saying that it is possible."

Gods. All his prayers, and now this. "I can't lose her, too, Cloudblower. For the sake of the gods—"

"I will do everything I can to save her, Browser. But you realize, don't you, that if she cannot speak, we may never know what she saw that morning. *Who* she saw."

The muscles in his shoulders contracted and bulged through his leather shirt. "Has she said anything? Anything at all? A word? A phrase?"

"Browser, she just awakened, and even if she does speak again, she may not remember. Head blows—"

"Yes, yes," he said, "I know. I, too, have seen them many times."

An insane killer might be wandering the canyon, and he had no way to identify him. *If only old Stone Ghost were here! Perhaps he would see something that I cannot. I am upset, grieving and frightened. What if my pain has blinded me to—*

"Cutting another hole in your heart, War Chief?" Cloudblower asked in a concerned voice.

Browser gazed into her soft eyes, and said, "Forgive me. I have been praying that Hophorn would awaken and tell me who did this terrible thing. That way, I could kill the man, and it would end. Now . . ." He gestured to the collapsed rooftops and the snowy canyon rim beyond. "He could be watching us this instant."

"Hophorn may yet tell you who did this thing. We must wait."

Browser laughed, a soft desperate sound. "That is all I do these days. Wait, and hope."

Cloudblower placed a hand on his shoulder. "You are tired. How long has it been since you've slept?"

He honestly could not recall. Every time he tried to close his eyes, images of his son's sightless eyes, or the stone on his wife's mutilated head, flitted across his souls, and he sat bolt upright in his hides, gasping for air.

Cloudblower said, "Come back to my chamber. You can lay beside Hophorn and I will keep watch over both of you while you sleep. The memories will not be as strong here."

"I do not think—"

"Just try," Cloudblower said. "Besides, having you close will make Hophorn feel safer. I cannot say for certain, but I think she still fears for her life."

Browser jerked his head up. "Why?"

Cloudblower folded her arms, and snow silently coated them. "I thought she might wake yesterday. Her eyelids began fluttering in the manner of a waking person. Then, throughout the night, she tried to wake up, but each time she came close to opening her eyes, she moaned, and went limp. It was the way she did it, Browser. It made me think that if she'd been awake, the moan would have been a scream."

"I will post a guard in front of your chamber."

"You should return with me yourself. We will all feel better."

"I cannot." He shook his head. "I have duties." After a short hesitation, he added. "Flame Carrier accused me of killing my wife. Do you think I did it?"

Her mouth gaped. "Blessed gods, of course not."

Browser watched the snow fall. "Apparently many of our people here have gone to speak with her. They think I beat my wife . . . wished her dead."

"That's foolish," Cloudblower said, and glanced around, as if afraid their conversation might be overhead. "Did you tell her you were nursing your sick son the entire time your wife was away? More than a dozen people came to visit you; they will tell her that."

Browser clenched up inside, his heart like a fanged beast, ripping at his chest. He said, "It won't matter."

Whiproot pulled up the ladder, and slipped it over the other side of the south wall. Browser could hear Flame Carrier's stern old voice speaking to someone on the other side.

Browser stood quietly for a long moment, then he murmured, "I must go. Thank you, again, Cloudblower."

"When your duties allow, come back, War Chief."

"If they allow," he said, and walked away through the swirling snow.

9

THE BOEING 757 shuddered and dropped onto the runway, waking Maureen from a sound sleep. "Ladies and gentlemen," the flight attendant called over the speakers, "We would like to be the first to welcome you to Albuquerque. The temperature here is a balmy one hundred seven degrees, and the time is exactly three-oh-seven in the afternoon. Thank you for flying with us today. We hope you had a pleasant flight and that you enjoy your stay in Albuquerque, or wherever your final destination takes you. We know you have a choice of air carriers and want to thank you for flying United. Please stay seated with your seat belts fastened until the captain turns off the seat belt sign. It will just be a few more minutes."

Maureen yawned. Dressed in blue jeans, a white T-shirt, and denim jacket, she was just barely warm. She always froze on plane flights. She'd stowed her carry-on bag and purse beneath the seat in front of her. She propped a hiking boot on her bag, and looked out the window. Her long black braid fell over her left shoulder. What desolate country. The desert stretched in every direction, except one. To her left, a mountain rose into a brilliant blue sky. Already, she missed the lush green environment of Ontario.

Despite the insistent warnings of the crew, before the plane stopped rolling, people lurched out of their seats, flung open the overhead compartments, and dragged baggage out. It took less than five heartbeats for them to pack the aisles.

Maureen stayed in her seat, watching the suited businessmen stare at the ceiling, or their watches, or their polished shoes—anywhere except at the little old lady they'd pushed out of the aisle to make sure they were first off the plane.

People filed by toward the exit.

When the plane emptied, Maureen stood up, pulled her bag from beneath her seat, and made her way past the nodding flight attendants, the captain, and copilot, and two people in dark blue clothing, whom she assumed to be maintenance.

She walked up the jetway and out into the bustling airport crowd. She saw so many smiling faces and people hugging each other that she almost missed the one scowler.

Maureen stopped dead. She looked around, didn't see Dale, and took a fortifying breath. She headed for the scowler. He hadn't changed. Still a blond god. Tall, with a killer tan and reflective sunglasses, he wore tan Wrangler jeans, and a dark green T-shirt.

She stopped in front of him and said, "Dusty Stewart. I'd recognize you anywhere. You have a very distinctive expression. Digestive problems? Have you tried prune juice?"

"It's a joy to see you, too, Dr. Cole. How was your flight?"

"Fine."

"Do you have any other baggage?"

"Yes. One suitcase."

He pulled keys from his pocket, shook them, and peered at her over the rims of his sunglasses. In an accusing voice, he said, "You don't want me to carry your bag, do you?"

"Not on a bet."

"Fine. Right this way, then." He jangled his keys as he walked.

Maureen studied him from the corner of her eye. He had his teeth clenched.

"So," she said, trying to be pleasant. "Where's Dale?"

"He claims he had an unexpected family emergency."

"Nothing serious, I hope?"

Stewart gave her a bland look. "Don't be ridiculous. You don't believe that hooey, do you?"

"You think he's throwing us together, hoping we'll arrive at some mutual 'understanding' before we get out of the airport?"

"You know Dale. Always a rabid optimist."

Stewart pointed to the sign that said BAGGAGE CLAIM and turned right. He walked like a man on a mission, his pace swift, purposeful.

Maureen readjusted her shoulder strap and lengthened her stride to keep up. Her long black braid slapped her back.

They passed shops filled with turquoise and silver jewelry, real Navajo rugs, imitation Navajo rugs, kachina dolls, bows and arrows, really ugly pottery in putrid pastels, cactus candy, and some great "My Life Is in Ruins," T-shirts covered with petroglyph symbols.

They skirted the security station, and Stewart headed for the escalator. Maureen stepped on behind him. So, Dale had thought she would ride out to the site with this guy? Wrong! She considered her options as they waited for her bag to appear on the carousel. Maureen glanced at the big gleaming signs behind her.

"Look, Stewart, there's no reason for you to squire me around like some visiting dignitary. I'll probably have to be running in and out of town a lot. You know, to the university library, things like that. It would be better all around if I just rented a vehicle for a couple of days until I can bring this to a conclusion."

His lips twitched, failing to hide his wan amusement. "Run in and out of town? Bring this to a conclusion in a couple of days? You are a city girl, aren't you?"

"Ever hear of hard science, Stewart? That's where it's down, not out in the middle of nowhere. We need little things like electricity."

He turned on his heel. Over his shoulder, he asked, "Avis counter, right?"

"Right."

"Better get a four-by-four. You know, for your zipping back and forth to town."

Grabbing her bag, Maureen trundled across the baggage area to the red-and-white AVIS sign. When she finally made it through the line to the counter a bright-eyed, pudgy woman with gray hair greeted her. Her name badge proclaimed: MARTY. She had a wide genial smile on her wrinkled face.

"I'd like to rent a four-wheel drive for a couple of days."

"Do you have a reservation?"

"Well, no, this is a last-minute development."

"I'm terribly sorry, but all of our vehicles, four-wheel drive or otherwise, are reserved. We have two conventions in town, as well as the big festival up in Santa Fe. We're booked solid until next Friday."

Maureen discovered the same at Hertz, National, and Alamo.

"Want to try Rent-A-Wreck?" Stewart asked.

She gripped her suitcase and leaned forward. "How far is the site from a paved road?"

"Around thirty-five miles."

"And this is the rainy season?"

"The *monsoon* season."

"Ah."

The women passing by glanced casually at Stewart, then their eyes shot back to look him over more carefully,

and smiles curled their lips. Tall, with sun-bleached
blond hair and muscular shoulders, they probably just
assumed he had a soul.

Women were such poor judges of these things.

Though Maureen had to admit he was a very handsome man. Stunning, in fact.

"Look," Stewart said, "the crew's coming off their four
day. I don't have time to fool around. I have to get out
there."

"What's a four day?"

"We work 'ten fours.' Ten days on, four days off.
When you're out in the middle of nowhere, it makes
more sense. Two days isn't enough to get home and relax
before you've got to drive back to the site. With four
days, it's like a little minivacation. How about I take you
to the site and you and Dale can figure out transportation
later."

Maureen's stomach churned. "It looks like I've exhausted my other choices. All right, Stewart."

"This way."

He marched to the door below the PARKING sign, and
held it open for her.

"Thank you," she said, surprised by the courtesy.

"Think nothing of it. Westerners hold doors open for
everything. Horses, dogs, women."

She gave him an askance look, but just as she'd pre-
pared a comeback, the heat hit her like a sledgehammer.
She staggered as sweat popped out across her forehead.
"Good God," she said. "How can you work in this?"

"We try not to work in the heat of the day. Which
means we get up very early, and go to bed very late."

She studied the long rows of parked cars and trucks.
"Which one is yours?"

He pointed. "That blue Bronco over there across the
parking lot."

"Across the parking lot" translated into as far from the

front doors of the airport as a person could park.

Hitching up her suitcase, buffalohide purse, and backpack, she leaned into the effort. "How long will it take us to get to the site?"

"Providing it hasn't rained, about three hours."

"Well, I'm starved. I had a feast of pretzels for lunch. Where can we eat?"

Dusty glowered. "I'm driving straight to the site. Either you ride, or you don't."

Maureen stared at his reflective sunglasses. "I'll bet you wear those things so people can't see how blue your eyes are, don't you?" She added, "Look, let's make this easy. Drop me at a hotel. Draw me a map and I'll steal a car and meet you at the site tomorrow."

He crossed his arms over his chest. "You'll never find it without me."

"My, goodness." Maureen's eyes narrowed. "Have you thought about seeking professional help for these delusions of grandeur?"

She fought the urge to pant, both from the effort of carrying her luggage and the heat. Sweat had begun to dampen her armpits and the collar of her T-shirt. The effect was like walking through an oven.

"Forget it. I like my delusions."

"And I like to have my stomach full. Where's the food?"

"There's a town called Crownpoint a few miles up the road. You can grab something lavish there."

She glanced at him suspiciously. "Are you lying to me?"

"No."

But he looked oddly stoic. She hesitated, then said, "Oh, all right. There's no sense in fighting this. Tell me about the site. It sounds rather spectacular."

The sensation of the hot dry air on her face made her certain her skin would eventually crack like old leather.

She gave in and panted, sucking the hot air into her lungs.

"This site is fascinating. We call it 10K3. I've never seen anything like it. For years we've been arguing about whether or not there was warfare in the southwest. I think this is pretty persuasive evidence."

"Really? Why?"

Stewart walked nonchalantly, as if the heat had no affect on him whatsoever. "Puebloan stories, for one thing. They talk about warfare. History for another. We know that when the native peoples fought, they'd go in, kill the warriors—who were usually male, although not always—then they'd steal the women and children and turn them into slaves. I—"

"So you believe the cranial depression fractures are the result of slavery?"

"That's what it looks like to me." He gestured with a tanned hand. "Slaves are often beaten to get more work out of them, or keep them in line. I think these women were worked hard, beaten frequently, and when their owners had no more use for them, they hit them in the head and threw them in a pit."

Maureen watched the other cars driving by in the opposite direction, and considered the idea. "What does the stratigraphy indicate? Were all of these women killed at the same time? Have you processed any C-14 dates yet?"

"No. Our Indian monitor is supposed to arrive this afternoon. In the U.S., we can't process samples at a burial site without approval from a duly appointed tribal representative." He lifted his blond brows. "And this monitor is interesting, to say the least. Her name is Hail Walking Hawk. Her own people call her 'Ghost Talker.' Anyway, you'll meet her tonight. That's one of the reasons I can't wait around to find you a set of wheels. As to the stratigraphy, that's another intriguing thing about this site. It looks like the bodies were interred one by one, but within a short time frame. One body was thrown in"—he turned to peer at her over the rims of his glasses again, and his blue eyes glinted—"a thin layer of dirt was shoveled over her, and another body was thrown in, and so on. This may be a slave burial ground."

"Artifacts?"

"A few, mostly trash. Broken bits of pottery, lithic debitage, and a lot of stone slabs."

Maureen frowned. "Stone slabs?"

"Um-hum," he turned to face her. "Over the heads of several of the victims."

Maureen huffed her way to the back of his faded blue Bronco, and dropped her suitcase to the cement. "What does that mean?"

"Well, in this part of the world, that's how people handle witches. They place a stone over the head to keep the evil person's soul locked in the earth forever."

"Why would you do that to a slave?"

He shrugged. "Maybe they thought the slaves were witches, and that's why they killed them. Maybe—"

"Maybe it's a witches' burial ground."

"Possibly, but several of the victims don't have stones over their heads."

Stewart jangled his keys, found one, and inserted it into the tailgate. A motor whined tiredly as the window slid down. Actually, grated and squeaked its way down. She saw coolers, a couple of wooden-framed screens, shovels, what looked like olive-drab military ammunition boxes, two red gas cans, pin flags in assorted bundles of color, and the ugly end of a "handy man" jack. With one hand, Dusty picked up her suitcase and tossed it effortlessly onto the thin space between the roof and a mound of accumulated junk.

"Hey! That's my equipment! My calipers, microscope, and my—"

"Relax," he said. "If they survived the apes in baggage

handling, they'll survive anything I can do to them."

As Maureen headed for the passenger door, she muttered, "Yeah, right." *It takes an ape to know an ape.*

As Stewart unlocked her door, Maureen glanced into the Bronco. It had a beige interior, she thought; the layer of dust made it impossible to tell for sure. The backseat burgeoned with bags labeled "soil sample, unit 2N2E, level 4," or "Mesa Verde black-and-white potsherd, unit 4S4W, level 7." Eight cases of beer—good stuff, Guinness stout—two more ice chests, and four bags of what looked like potato chips.

Maureen studied the stack of beer flats. "How many people are on your field crew?"

"Full time? Two. Me and Sylvia. The rest just went back to school."

Her brows lifted. "You must not get into town much."

"Sure we do. Every ten days. As a matter of fact, that's where Sylvia is today. Shopping for next week's supplies."

Probably another truckload of beer. "Who is Sylvia?"

"Sylvia Rhone. She's finishing her B.A. at the University of New Mexico. A few other students show up when they can. Dale comes out on weekends. He spends most of his time at home in his lab cataloging and processing the artifacts and samples we've recovered. Why did you ask?" He gave her a cold smile. "Afraid to be alone with me?"

"No. With your beer."

His smile froze. His fingers tightened on the door handle. "Don't tell me. You're the leader of a new prohibition movement in Canada, right?"

Maureen propped her hands on her hips. "Prohibition has too many cultural stereotypes. We call it *Teetotalism.*"

Stewart stared.

Maureen smiled. After her husband's death, she'd

started drinking to help her sleep, then to ease the pain and loneliness, then to forget how much she hated herself for drinking. The phrase, "drowning in the bottle," had a personal meaning for her. She could proudly say she hadn't had a drink in two and a half years, but the longing had never gone away. Especially not for the creamy richness of Guinness stout.

"Figures," Stewart said. "I get stuck with a cross between Mary Baker Eddy, and Atilla the Hun."

"Best drop the Baker Eddy part," Maureen informed him. "I'm Catholic."

"Oh. How about, 'Mary the Hun?'" He opened the Bronco door, and dust boiled out.

Maureen coughed, and waved it away.

Out of curiosity, she bent forward and rubbed her finger across the dash.

"What are you doing?" Stewart asked.

"Just checking. I was afraid the interior might be white and the scorching sun had blinded me."

"White is a color for physical anthropologists who spend their lives in laboratories, Dr. Cole. No self-respecting archaeologist would own anything white."

Maureen wondered about his underwear, but decided not to ask. Stewart was the kind of guy who'd feel compelled to show her, and she'd experienced enough nausea on the rocky flight in.

Despite her effort at self-control, her lip curled as she stuffed her pack into a space in the backseat. She kicked empty bottles out of the way to make room for her feet, and ground her teeth as she placed her beautiful Bison Legacy buffalohide purse on the filthy floor. As she settled into the seat, she could feel the dust sneaking into her clean clothing, infiltrating around her collar, and the waist of her pants. It took three tries to slam the door.

"The hinges are a little sprung," Stewart explained.

"I noticed." She smacked the dust off her palms.

Stewart stuck the key into the ignition and the Bronco roared to life. He watched the gauges closely. A slight frown lined his forehead.

"Something the matter?"

"The oil pressure gauge." He knotted a fist and hammered the top of the dash.

Maureen jumped as dust billowed up in a mushroom cloud.

"There, see," Stewart said happily. "Oil pressure. The gauge is working after all. It gets a little jammed up on occasion."

He backed out of the parking space and drove down to pay the parking fee. The heat was boring into her, each pore screaming. Not even trips to the sweat lodge had prepared her for this.

As Stewart received his change, she turned the knob on the air conditioner and placed a hand on the dust-encrusted vents.

"Doesn't work," Stewart said, eyes on the traffic as he wheeled out of the airport drive and onto busy Gibson Boulevard. He turned west at the light, reached behind him with one hand for a battered straw hat, and flipped it onto his head. "I haven't had time to take it to a mechanic. The system needs recharging, and a packrat ate the wiring that runs the fan."

"I should have guessed," Maureen whispered.

"You'll have to make do with 'two-seventy' air until sunset."

"Two-seventy?"

He grinned. With the mirrored sunglasses, gnarly straw hat, muscular arms, and worn T-shirt, he looked like a rednecked rapist from a Peckinpah movie. "Yeah, two windows open at seventy miles an hour."

Maureen rolled her eyes, reached for the crank and started to roll the window down. She made a half a turn before the handle came off in her hand.

"Oh," Dusty called over the roar of the truck, "I forgot. You have to use your other hand to keep the crank on. That little screw fell out last year."

"Gee. Thanks for the warning." She managed to crank the window down, then leaned back, and let the hot wind blow over her. Relief, of sorts. Her gaze scanned the plastic molding for the seat belt. "So, Stewart, where's the seat belt?"

"Oh, that's a story in itself." He frowned at the traffic as he took the exit onto Interstate 25. "I got stuck in an arroyo south of Ganado. I finally found an old Navajo who'd pull me out. Problem was, I didn't have a tow strap."

"You used the seat belt for a tow strap?"

"It was that or walk twenty miles to the nearest phone."

Maureen gripped her seat as Stewart accelerated into traffic, weaving to miss the potholes. "Good Lord, I'm going to die."

"We all do, Dr. Cole. Wouldn't be much call for people in our professions if we didn't."

He didn't swerve fast enough, and the Bronco bounced through a hole. The window crank fell off and clattered to the floor. Stewart saw it out of the corner of his eye. "You might want to pick that up and shove it back onto the splines really hard. It can be a mess when you have to fish around for it in the dark on this floor."

Maureen bent over, staring down between her knees for the crank. Among the detritus, she noticed Guinness bottles, Arizona iced teas, squashed plastic orange juice bottles, two screwdrivers, a pair of pliers, several empty sardine tins, the interiors lined with crusted brown deposits, a piece of fossilized toast, and no crank.

Must have bounced under the seat. Maureen grimaced at the idea of reaching into that no-man's-land. In Stewart's Bronco, it might be reaching into a whole different universe inhabited by woman-eating mold monsters, or black widow spiders.

As she groped, her fingers slipped along a smooth handle. Not the window crank, but she pulled it out anyway. She let out a sharp cry, and dropped the pistol as if she'd just grabbed a snake. It thumped heavily onto the floorboards, and lay there among the empty bottles, malignant, deadly.

"Stewart," she yelled, "why is there a pistol in your Bronco?"

He watched her through those enigmatic mirror glasses, mouth expressionless. "You don't have guns in Canada, Dr. Cole?"

She gripped the fabric over her heart, and concentrated on breathing normally. "Is that *thing* loaded?"

"Well, it wouldn't be much good if it wasn't. But please don't pull the trigger inside the truck. Discharging a pistol inside a dusty vehicle makes a hell of a mess. Once I took a shot at a coyote through the passenger window. You know, just like so." Left hand on the wheel, he extended his right arm until his index finger pointed past her nose. "When I touched off that forty-one mag, it blew everything—dust, field notes, a can of Copenhagen, everything—right off the dash."

Maureen shoved his hand away, and stared out the open window as they took the exit onto west I-40.

"Good God, I'm in hillbilly Hell."

Dale, I'll get you for this. I promise.

THE DESERT SPREAD around Catkin like a vast white blanket, rumpled here and there with low hills. She had run all night, eating only snow to quench her thirst, and her stomach kept reminding her that she carried deer jerky in her pack.

But she could not stop to eat or rest.

The fear she had seen in Browser's eyes drove her onward. If the storm continued, it would take her two days to get home, and she did not know what he would do in the interim. He had no one else to talk to, no other friend. War chiefs dared not reveal their frailties to ordinary people for fear of losing their confidence, which meant they led lonely lives, able to speak only with their spouses late at night.

Browser had not even had that luxury.

Catkin focused on the butte that rose from the desert like a square tower, and pushed herself harder. Smoking Mirror Butte stood perhaps one thousand hands tall. Clouds encircled the top, creeping and curling over the tan sandstone.

On late nights, her mother used to whisper about the traps and invisible snares that lined the path to Stone Ghost's house. The closer you ran, the more there were, and when a person neared Stone Ghost's house, growls and screeches rose from the monsters he kept leashed to rocks.

Catkin didn't believe the stories, of course. Only a fool

would believe such things. But it wouldn't be wise to discount them. She had learned the hard way that caution was the foundation of courage.

And survival.

She leaped a snow-covered bush, and continued on in her determined dogtrot. With each breath from her laboring lungs, a white cloud formed, hung for a moment. Then she ran through it. Her legs felt like boiled grass stems. The trail slithered around bluffs and hills like a gigantic white snake, heading toward Smoking Mirror Butte.

From the depths of her memory, her mother's soft voice murmured: *"Old Stone Ghost gives wicked, unholy feasts. They commence at sunset, and sometimes last until well after dawn. He holds them in dark caves, or canyons, away from the prying eyes of normal people, and Stone Ghost's Spirit Helper, a gigantic white rattlesnake, always comes. Before revelers are allowed to enter the celebration, they must kiss the snake's tail, and allow it to embrace them."*

Catkin shivered. She had suffered nightmares for a full moon after she'd first heard that tale. She still recalled the evil glint in the snake's eyes, and the cold, clammy feel as its body wrapped around her throat. She . . .

She saw a house.

Catkin stopped dead in her tracks, breathing hard. The fragrances of damp leather and brush filled her nostrils.

Long ago, a huge square of stone had cracked away from the butte, and fallen. The owner had built his house into the remaining gap. The butte itself made up the south and east walls. The other two walls were fashioned of irregularly shaped stones, mortared together, and covered with tan mud, most of which had flaked off. Catkin squinted at the roof. It slanted to the west, toward the hide-covered doorway, and had holes the size of small dogs. She couldn't tell which happened faster, smoke trying to get out of the holes, or snow trying to get in.

Hands propped on her hips, she gulped the cool air in an effort to regain her breath as she walked slowly forward.

Polite people did not shout in front of someone's house. They waited, milling about, until the occupants noticed they had visitors.

As snowflakes collided with the sparks rising through the roof holes, a hissing filled the air.

An eerie sensation crept along Catkin's arms. Without moving a muscle, her gaze searched the snow-covered ground and brush. In a snowstorm, a white Spirit snake would be virtually invisible.

Blood flushed her cheeks.

Catkin kicked the rabbitbrush in front of her, and leaped back, pulling her war club from her belt.

When nothing rattled, she lowered the club, and exhaled hard, feeling like an imbecile.

Her gaze went uneasily to the enormous boulders that piled around the base of the butte. The juniper trees rooted among them cast ominous shadows on the snow. An entire army could hide in that rocky forest. Why would a Spirit snake bother laying around in the middle of a trail?

Catkin scanned the snowy crevices, and proceeded toward the house on the balls of her feet, her club at the ready.

When she stood no more than five paces from the house, she caught movement, and whirled around.

"Look out!" a old white-haired man shouted, and charged forward with a digging stick lifted over his head. He wore a brown-and-white turkey-feather cape, and had three black spirals tattooed on his chin.

"Quickly!" he shouted, "before it leaps upon you! Kill it!" He started slamming his digging stick into the snow.

Catkin jumped to his side, and expertly wielded her

club, smashing the snow, and the chunk of sandstone beneath it, to bits.

Finally, the old man staggered back, and panted, "Excellent work."

Catkin studied the powdered stone that scattered the snow. She prodded it cautiously with the tip of her war club. "What was it?"

The old man tucked his digging stick under his arm and grinned. Half Catkin's height, wispy white hair clung to his scalp, and his features seemed slightly too large for the lean frame of his face, his beaked nose too long, his mouth too wide. The digging stick he carried had been carved into the shape of a snake, and painted white.

"It was a rock," he answered.

"What?" Catkin said, annoyed. "I just crushed a lifeless rock?"

"My dear girl, what makes you think it was dead? It might be dead now. But!" He lifted a finger and shook it. "This could be fortuitous. Did you know that the entire history of Our Mother Earth can be read in grains of sand? Of course, you have to smash a lot of rocks, and make sure you scoop up every grain, then they must be rearranged just as the layers were in the rock, but somewhere here I have a drawing of the Age of Monsters . . ."

"Elder," Catkin said, as the old man begin patting himself down.

He halted with one hand in his belt pouch, and the other stuck through the front of his cape. "They don't like being smashed, you know."

"I suppose that's a sign of intelligence."

"Oh, they're very intelligent." He gazed up at her with wide, gentle, and curiously luminous eyes. "I once knew a rock who could recite every bird call known to humans. Can you do that?"

Catkin's mouth opened; but, what did one say? She could see the falling snow reflected in the dark wells of his shining eyes. "Who are you, Elder? What are you doing out here in the storm?"

He used his digging stick to point. "I was planting a prayer," he said, "over there by the corner of the butte. I was hoping Coyote Above would find it the next time he trots by."

He paused, taking in the butte, and his dilapidated house, then his gaze came back to her. "Wait! Are you the Coyote Clan girl? Why, you must be!"

He rushed forward, walked right underneath her war club as if it were invisible, and seized Catkin's hand, squeezing it with genuine delight. "You're late, but I'm glad you've come."

"Late?" Catkin jerked her hand away. "What do you mean late?"

"I expected you last night, but with the storm—"

"How did you know I was coming?" A creeping sense of dread tingled along her arms. She gripped her club more tightly.

"Well, that's a long story. You must be starved. Please, come inside and let me give you food and drink while we discuss it." He gripped Catkin's hand and dragged her toward his house.

"Wait." Catkin tugged him backward so hard he almost toppled.

The old man's bushy white brows arched. "Yes, child?"

"Elder, I am Catkin, of Hillside village. I come at the request of my war chief to find Stone Ghost. Are you Stone Ghost?"

The little man's black eyes went wide. "Why, of course, child. I'm sorry. I thought you knew that. Is there anything else you must know before you can allow yourself to rest?"

He seemed genuinely concerned about her. Catkin shook her head. "No."

"Good. You're shivering. You'll feel better after a cup of warm tea, and some prairie dog soup."

Stone Ghost hobbled to his door, ducked beneath the leather hanging, and Catkin heard him mutter, then pots clattered.

She gripped her war club. Clearly his souls flitted about like moths around a flame, but he didn't seem dangerous. Though anyone who would pounce on a rock couldn't be trusted. She cautiously headed for his door.

As she ducked beneath the curtain and into the cold blue shadows, she smelled the mingled fragrances of flower petals, and meat boiled with dried cactus fruits. Small and square, the house stretched barely two body-lengths across. A mound of snow had sifted down through the holes in the roof and drifted along the western wall near the door. She stepped over it, and stood awkwardly. After the brilliance of the snow, the house looked unnaturally black. To her right, along the southern wall, she saw six plain pots. To her left, three crudely woven baskets leaned against each other.

Stone Ghost sat on a mangy looking hide on the far side of the pit in front of her, humming to himself as he added twigs to the glowing coals. He had removed his tattered turkey-feather cape, and draped it over a pile of rolled blankets behind him.

As Catkin unslung her bow and quiver, she examined him. Ribs stuck out under his faded brown shirt, and she could see every bone in his skull, as though only a thin film of skin tied his head to his neck.

"Sit down, child." Stone Ghost indicated the willow twig mat on the opposite side of the fire. "Once I have this fire blazing, we can talk."

"Yes, Elder." Catkin eased one knee down on the mat; her right hand still gripped her war club.

A teapot was sunken into the ashes near the hearth-stones, and beside it, another pot hung from a tripod.

Spirals of steam rose from both pots. Ceramic cups and spoons sat neatly stacked at the base of the tripod. Despite the extravagant ventilation and the drifted snow by the door, the house felt warm.

Catkin said, "Elder, how did you know I was Coyote clan?"

Stone Ghost grinned, and bent down to gently blow on the coals. Ash puffed, and spun. Finally, the twigs caught, and fire crackled to life. Sparks shot upward toward the soot-coated ceiling. As he added larger branches, he said, "There," and sat back with his gnarled hands extended to the warmth of the flames. Orange light flickered over his white hair and wrinkled face. "I knew because Coyote loped through here last night around moonset. He told me you were coming, he also told me the Blue God is hunting."

Catkin tilted her head. He could have known her clan just by studying the symbols on her war shirt, or club, though she didn't entirely dismiss the notion that he'd spoken with Coyote. Catkin said, "The Blue God? That is an old belief. I recall hearing stories about her when I was a child."

Stone Ghost's lips parted, revealing toothless gums. "Do you no longer believe in her?"

"Well, no one I know believes in her. We are the Katsinas' People. We follow different gods."

Stone Ghost shook his head as if greatly distressed. "Well, that's unfortunate."

"Why is that?"

"Because it makes you easier to hunt. You are like rabbits unaware that a cougar hides in the brush." He shuffled through the cups at the base of the tripod. "Would you like a cup of tea?"

"Yes, Elder, please."

Stone Ghost selected a plain red cup, chipped around the rim, and dipped it into the teapot. He handed the cup to Catkin, and the sweetness of silktassel petals rose.

Catkin sipped it. "This is delicious. Thank you."

Stone Ghost drew up his knees and propped his elbows on them. "So," he said. "Tell me who the Blue God is hunting?"

Trying not to sound disrespectful, Catkin replied, "I know nothing of the Blue God, Elder. I am here because yesterday morning we found our war chief's wife sprawled in her own son's freshly dug burial pit. A stone slab covered her crushed skull."

Stone Ghost's luminous eyes flared. "Tragic," he said softly. "Your war chief lost his son and his wife in a matter of days. How is he?"

"I cannot say, Elder. I left immediately after we discovered his wife's body."

She could feel his eyes upon her, suddenly alert, probing, as if he'd heard something in her voice that she did not realize was there.

A branch broke in the fire, and the burst of light threaded the walls with bright gold.

For the first time, Catkin saw the fabric bags that hung from pegs at the junction of walls and roof. They appeared to hold large gourds.

Stone Ghost dipped a cup into the soup pot on the tripod, and tucked a horn spoon into it. As he handed it around the fire, he said, "Here. You will need your strength to fight the Blue God. I've tangled with her before, and she's very tricky. She almost took my head off once. I was walking along the rim of Orphan Butte—"

"The Blue God does not frighten me, Elder," Catkin said. She took the cup, and set it on one of the hearthstones, while she finished her tea.

Stone Ghost leaned forward, and hissed, *"She should."*

They stared at each other for several heartbeats.

Catkin calmly responded, "Elder, with all the warring these days, dead gods are the least of my concerns."

"Incorrect, child. The Blue God is your only concern. She is death itself. Don't you recall any of the stories your mother told you?"

"Just pieces of stories."

"Curious." Stone Ghost regarded Catkin with unwavering black eyes. "I'm surprised you're still alive."

Peeved, Catkin snapped, "Elder, I did not come here to discuss dead gods! My war chief, Browser, sent me to ask you if you will come to Hillside Village and help us find his wife's murderer. Will you?"

The firelight flashed on Stone Ghost's beaked nose as he sharply looked up, his cup halted midway to his mouth. "Why me?"

"Because he trusts you."

"I can't imagine why."

"Well, I suppose it's because you are relatives."

A blank expression creased Stone Ghost's ancient face. "Really? Which relative?"

"You do not recall Browser?" Catkin asked. She found it inconceivable. Browser's presence affected people like a Spirit plant in the veins. No one who had ever met him could forget him. "Browser is your sister's grandson."

"Which sister?"

"I do not know, Elder! I expected you to know."

She picked up her soup cup, and dipped her spoon. Seasoned with yucca fruit and chokecherries, the broth tasted rich, and tart. Prairie dogs were fat, the meat greasy—exactly the sort of thing her hungry body craved after such a long run. Around a mouthful, she added, "You may not recall him, but Browser remembers you quite well."

Stone Ghost almost dropped his tea cup. After he'd steadied it, he said, "The last time someone told me that, it was at the point of a spear." He glanced up at Catkin. "What else did he say?"

"There was not much time to speak about you. But I

did ask him if you were mad." She paused, gauging his reaction to this. His expression remained blank. Catkin continued, "Some people say you are, as I suppose you know, but Browser said he'd never seen it."

Stone Ghost chuckled. "I wonder which of my sisters produced such a dimwit? Probably Bee Sage. She never had the sense the gods gave a moth." He scratched his wrinkled cheek. "Of course, all my sisters are dead now, but that doesn't mean Browser, or the Blue God, for that matter . . ."

He stopped, and Catkin lowered her spoon to her cup. "Doesn't mean Browser what?"

Stone Ghost jerked around to look at her. "What about Browser?"

"The fact that your sisters are dead doesn't mean Browser what?"

"Well"—he picked up a branch and briskly prodded the fire. Flames roared and leaped—"I suppose it doesn't mean a lot of things. Why did you ask?"

"Why did *I* ask!" Catkin yelled. "I asked because you said . . . !" At his intent look, she sighed, and clamped her jaw.

Stone Ghost's stick hovered over the flames. "What did I say? Oh, wait! I was telling you about the Blue God. I'm getting so forgetful! I meant to ask if you knew that the Blue God is a huge bloody-headed woman? She meets the breath-heart soul as it climbs up the burial ladder out of the grave, and leads it to the shores of a deep black lake where the lights of the dead shimmer like a thousand torches. A soul has to dive into the lake, and swim down to find the Land of the Dead."

"Elder," Catkin growled in exasperation, "we weren't speaking of the Blue God, we were discussing the murder of Browser's wife." Catkin carefully enunciated: "He-wishes-to-know-if-you-will-come-to-Hillside-Village-and-help-us-find-the-madman-who-did-it."

Stone Ghost looked at her as if she'd just sprouted antlers. He said, "What makes you think he's mad?"

"He murdered an innocent woman. He must be."

"My dear child," Stone Ghost sighed, "there are only two forms of nourishment in life: love and death. All else is slow starvation."

Catkin understood the love part. Love sustained every moment of her life, but how could death provide nourishment? She ran a finger around the rim of her cup. Unless he meant hunting? Of course people killed to eat, but what did that have to do with murder? She repeated, "No one sane would murder an innocent woman, Elder. It is unthinkable."

"What makes you think she was innocent?"

Catkin lowered her cup to her lap. It had never occurred to her that Ash Girl might have been guilty of something. The only crime Catkin had seen the woman commit was against her husband. She'd treated Browser like a mangy camp dog, kicking him in the belly whenever she could. Browser had wandered the cliffs at night just to get away from her. When he'd needed a friend, he'd come to Catkin. Ash Girl was no one's friend.

"Ah," Stone Ghost whispered, and made a delicate gesture, as if pushing at a tuft of mist. "I see."

"What do you see?"

Stone Ghost stared straight at her, but did not seem to see Catkin at all. His eyes had an empty faraway look. "You must understand. For a murderer life is bondage, and murder is emancipation. To find the murderer, you must discover what binds him."

"Why would murder free someone? Even when I kill an enemy who deserves it, I feel hollow, and chained by guilt."

He blinked, and his gaze returned from wherever it had been to pin Catkin. "Why didn't you like Browser's wife?"

Catkin stiffened. "I-I did not dislike her. Not really. She was not a kind person, but—"

"She was not kind to you?"

"She was not kind to anyone, Elder, especially her husband. She shouted at him constantly, and was always wringing her hands, and making demands he couldn't—"

"And her son? Was she unkind to him?"

"Not that I ever witnessed, but I would not doubt—"

"And the others in the village? Did she slap old people, or children? Did she throw rocks at birds? What about ugly puppies? Did she kick them?"

Disarmed by the barrage of questions, Catkin just sat there.

"So," he said. "She was only unkind to her husband. That you are aware of. What had he done to her? Did he beat her? Berate her in public?"

"He did nothing to her! He tried to please her in every way he could! Less than a moon ago, she went for days without speaking to him, or anyone in the village! And, once, after she'd harassed him all day long, I found him around midnight wandering the cliffs, weeping as though his heart had been torn from his body. He was crying out to someone I'd never heard of, then the next day, he— he came to me—"

"What name did he cry out?"

Catkin shook her head, wondering what possible point this discussion could have. Stone Ghost wouldn't know the person anyway. "I don't recall. Shadow something, I think. But it doesn't matter. I had never heard the name before. I'm sure you wouldn't recognize it either." Blood pulsed very loudly in her ears, she could barely think. She looked across the fire, and found the old man staring at her with obsidian sharp eyes.

"Why are you looking at me like that?"

"Oh," he said, and shoved his empty cup around with his finger. His white hair glimmered as though sprinkled with gold dust. "I was just wondering if she knew you loved her husband?"

Catkin could not answer.

In a kindly old voice, Stone Ghost asked, "Does he know?"

"Does he know what?"

"Oh, well, of course he does. Silly of me to ask. That's why he comes to you. How do you think that made his wife feel? That he came to you for comfort? Do you think she resented you? Hated you?"

"Gods, Elder! She—she used to fall asleep when he touched her! He would start to love her, and she would go limp in his arms. He would look down and find her sound asleep! What kind of a wife is that?" Catkin waved a hand. "I wouldn't have cared how she felt. He needed me."

"What?" Stone Ghost shouted at the top of his lungs, and spun around.

Catkin leaped to her feet, bouncing on her toes, her war club poised. "What's wrong?"

The old man peered wide-eyed at one of the fabric bags hanging near the roof. To the bag, he said, "How do you know that?"

"Who are you talking to?" Catkin's skin had started to crawl. She searched the house for anything that might be white, or slithery.

Stone Ghost turned back and gazed at Catkin like a surprised stork. "What? . . . Oh! Crooked Nose says you saw her. Did you?"

"Who's Crooked Nose?"

Stone Ghost rose, went to the wall, and carefully lifted the red bag from its peg. He carried it back to the fire like a precious child. After he'd reseated himself, he began untying the laces.

"What is that?" Catkin asked, on the verge of bolting.

Stone Ghost's bushy white brows lowered. "An old

enemy. Of course, he's a friend now. Death has a way of smoothing even the most vile insults."

Catkin watched as he drew out a skull. Her gaze flitted across the other bags on the walls, counting sixteen. She'd thought they contained gourds!

"This is Crooked Nose." Stone Ghost ran his hand over the skull as if petting a favorite dog.

"Are all of those bags filled with skulls?"

"Hmm?" Stone Ghost frowned up at the bags as if he'd never seen them before. "Why, I haven't the slightest idea. Why don't you bring some down and we'll open them and look? They've been hanging up there for, oh, perhaps thirty sun cycles." He grinned like a mad dog. "I was a fine warrior back then."

"Elder—"

"Shh!" Stone Ghost pressed his ear to the mouth of the grinning skull. "Really?" he murmured, and looked at Catkin. "Crooked Nose says you saw the Blue God."

"I don't even believe in the Blue God."

Stone Ghost squinted one eye so that he could peer deeply into the skull's left eye socket. Firelight gilded the flattened rear of the head. "Um, yes, that's possible. She may not have realized what she was seeing." Then, "I suppose."

Stone Ghost cradled the skull against his bony chest and said, "Where were you the night of the murder?"

Catkin lowered her club. She had been out running the canyon rim with three other warriors, searching for raiders. "How do you know it happened at night?"

"Very well, where were you the day it happened?"

"I do not even know *when* it happened! I heard Matron Flame Carrier say the War Chief's wife had been gone for two days, but that is all I know. I was away on a war walk."

"Where did you walk?"

Exasperated, she waved her club. "Around the rim of

Straight Path Canyon. Over the past sun cycle, several women and little girls have gone missing from the smaller villages. We know it must be raiders. Probably Fire Dogs. We—"

"Which villages?"

"Well. Many. Whitetail village, Badgerpaw, Frosted Meadow. And others."

"Browser sent you on this war walk?"

"Yes, but I don't see—"

"How many warriors accompanied you?"

She gripped her war club as though to strangle the life from it. Catkin forced her voice to be low and controlled. "Elder, I did not kill Browser's wife. Is that what you are asking? Three warriors accompanied me on the war walk: Whiproot, Jackrabbit, and He-Who-Flies. They will tell you I was with them every moment of those four days. Well, except He-Who-Flies. I dispatched him a day early to run home and tell the War Chief all was well, and we were coming home."

Stone Ghost stretched out on the deerhide, and rested the skull in front of him. "Thank you," he said softly, and petted the skull.

Catkin glared at the empty eye sockets. "Are you thanking me, or Crooked Nose?"

"You, dear girl. You have told me many things in the past finger of time. Things I suspect you've never told anyone."

She shifted her weight to her opposite foot. What? That she'd disliked Ash Girl? That she loved Browser?

"What have I told you?"

"More than you know, child. Details you do not even realize you are aware of."

As she gazed down into his luminous eyes, Catkin felt physically exhausted.

The fire crackled and spat, but no sound penetrated from the outside except occasional moans of wind whipping around the butte. She wondered how the old man could stand the isolation.

She sank back to the floor and propped her club over her knees. It hadn't occurred to her until now that for almost a sun cycle Browser had lived within a day's run of his great-uncle, and never once come to see him. She wondered about that, about what it said about the old man. And, perhaps, about Browser.

"I should tell you, too," Catkin said. "When we found his wife's body, we also found our Sunwatcher injured. Hophorn had been tending the burial fire, and was apparently struck in the head by whoever threw Browser's wife into the burial pit."

"Is she alive?"

"I cannot say, Elder. Our Healer, Cloudblower, removed a circlet of skull from Hophorn's head to release some of the evil Spirits feeding in her brain, but Hophorn had not yet awakened when I left."

Stone Ghost lightly touched the firelit skull on the hide in front of him. "Risky, opening the skull."

"Yes, but Cloudblower has done it several times, though in the past Hophorn has been there to help her. This time Cloudblower had to make do with a slave girl's aid."

"Cloudblower," Stone Ghost said. The wrinkles in his face rearranged themselves into reverent lines. "I have heard of her. She is one of the *kokwimu,* is she not?"

"Yes, Elder. A very powerful one."

He nodded and went silent.

When he said no more, she asked, "Elder, there is one other thing you must know."

"Yes?"

"Browser's wife? Her body disappeared."

He sat up. "What do you mean? How?"

Catkin tied her club to her belt again. "No one knows. While Cloudblower opened Hophorn's skull, the rest of the village went home to think and pray. Our Matron, Flame Carrier, decreed that the burial pit of Browser's son had been defiled, and ordered me to dig a new one. I went out to do that, and found the body gone."

"Tracks?"

"Elder, the sand was frozen. I could make out nothing unusual. There was a strange mark near the fire pit, where the sand had thawed. It might have been part of a footprint. I cannot say."

He hesitated, and smoothed his hand over the skull. "How many people live in Hillside Village?"

"Fifty. Ten of those are slaves. Fifteen are children. We have only seven full-time warriors, Elder."

Stone Ghost whispered, "Interesting."

Catkin, watching his knotted fingers where they rested on the shining skull, saw them tremble, and she frowned.

She said, "Why do you think that's interesting?"

"Well, you are a warrior, and a fine one, I imagine. You would have searched for anything out of the ordinary. The fact that you didn't find it can mean only one thing."

"Witchery?" she whispered, and her spine prickled. She kept her voice low. "That's what we all feared. I found an owl feather in the grave."

She turned to look over her shoulder through the doorway. Snow fell in huge white flakes, coating the ground, and adding to the mound inside the doorway. She had the haunting sensation that someone stood just outside, listening. Witches had great Power. They could change themselves into animals by jumping through a hoop of twisted yucca fibers, and lope around in the darkness spying on people. They robbed graves to gather corpse flesh, which they dried, and ground into a fine shiny powder. When the breath-heart soul left the body, it took everything good with it. Only evil and depravity remained. Corpse powder concentrated that wickedness. If a witch sprinkled it on a path someone routinely walked, or mixed it with their food, the person could go mad, or even die.

"We are safe," Stone Ghost assured her. "Go on. What were you about to say?"

"We all feared a witch had flown in, struck Hophorn, and stolen the body, but we found no real evidence. Just the stone over the head and the owl feather."

Stone Ghost said, "The murderer may have left both of those, hoping you would be so frightened you would just cover the body up and leave."

"Possibly," she agreed. "But if a witch did not fly in, and we found nothing unusual around the site . . ." As the truth dawned, her jaw slackened.

The old man tilted his head. "It surprises me that you are surprised."

"No. No, Elder!" She shook her head vehemently. "No one in Hillside Village could do the bizarre things I saw yesterday!"

Stone Ghost turned slightly, and his hooked nose shone orange. "What bizarre things?"

Catkin threw up her hands. "Crazy things. The acts of a madman! Or a witch. The murderer killed Browser's wife, then stripped and dressed her in a man's clothing. He smashed Hophorn's skull, then he took the red cape Browser's wife had been wearing and draped it around Hophorn's shoulders."

Catkin could see thoughts racing in the old man's keen black eyes, and her own begin to dart about, eliminating the elderly, the small children, the sick, and those who had been gone.

"Elder," she said. "We need your help. Will you help us?"

He hesitated. "Will you help me, Catkin?"

She hesitated, unnerved by the request. "What is it you need?"

"I will come to Hillside Village," he said, and held up a hand to stop her from interrupting to thank him. "But I do not wish to go with you. I want you to run home alone. Tell your Matron that I will be along soon."

Catkin nodded. "How soon, Elder?"

A gust of wind swirled through the house and lifted the white hair from Stone Ghost's shoulders. The firelight glinted in the black depths of his eyes.

"Soon enough, Catkin. After people know I am coming, I wish you to watch what they do. That is all. Watch carefully *and remember.* When I arrive, I will want you to tell me in great detail."

"Very well, Elder. Is there anything else?"

Stone Ghost shook his head. "No, Catkin. That will be enough."

"Thank you, Elder. I will post a guard to watch the roads and try to meet you before you enter the village." She started to turn away.

"I don't think he'll let you," the old man said in a voice so low that Catkin, startled, couldn't be sure she'd heard it.

She looked back, and found Stone Ghost whispering into the ear of the skull, his lips twitching like a wolf's when it bares its teeth. She asked, "Did you say something to me, Elder?"

Stone Ghost's eyes reflected the flickering firelight. "The murderer is a man of great patience, Catkin. He watches and listens before he moves. By now, he knows where you went. He knows the trails you will be running. He probably knows you are tired and not thinking well. Go with *great* care."

It had not occurred to her that the murderer might have followed her here. That he might be waiting for her along the trail. *Stalking her.*

Catkin reached for her bow and quiver and backed toward the door. As she stepped over the mound of snow, she said, "I will, Elder. You, also," and she ducked out into the storm.

Low clouds tumbled over each other as they scudded northward.

She felt for the thong around her neck and pulled out the malachite pendant Wind Born had carved for her. It shone a deep dark green. Exhaustion trembled her limbs. By noon she would have to sleep.

As she forced her legs into a weary trot, she clutched the pendant, and scrutinized every place a killer might hide.

I DON'T SEE ANYONE, Aunt Hail."
Maggie Walking Hawk Taylor guided her great-aunt away from her old black Dodge pickup and into the archaeological field camp. To her left, five canvas tents stood in a circle around a fire pit. Tools, ice chests, and lanterns scattered the area in front of the tent flaps. Over at the site she could see conical piles of back dirt from the excavation.

"Where do you think they went?" Hail Walking Hawk asked in a frail voice. Her blue dress shone in the late afternoon sunlight.

"They have four day breaks, but they're supposed to be back today. I told them we were coming. Maybe something delayed them."

Maggie scanned the excavation units directly in front of her. Screens, for sifting the dirt, lay beside three of the rectangular holes. The other holes had been covered with black plastic. Rocks, shovels, and picks weighted down the edges of the plastic.

Maggie wiped damp strands of short black hair from her forehead and sighed. Ordinarily she'd be here dressed in her green ranger's uniform, driving a National Park Service truck, but she'd taken a few days off work to pick up her Aunt, and drive her out here. She felt oddly out of place in her white T-shirt, tan shorts, and black tennis shoes.

She looked around. "Well, there's a stack of folded

lawn chairs over there beside the fire pit. Let's go sit down."

As they started walking, Hail held tight to Maggie's arm, breathing hard. Soft pained sounds escaped her lips.

Maggie frowned. Her great-aunt claimed to be in excellent health, but she bit her lip as she shuffled along, her eyes squinted, as though against pain.

At the age of eighty, her aunt had a face like a James Bama painting, rusty and wrinkled, wise in a way beyond the comprehension of most whites. Age-spotted skin hung off her arms and throat. Arthritis had crippled her hands, leaving them clawlike, but she still worked around the pueblo, cooking bread and fashioning corn-husk dolls for the children.

"Just a little farther, Aunt Hail," Maggie said, "then you can rest."

"I'm all right, girl." Hail smiled and affectionately squeezed Maggie's arm.

They walked into the shade of the tents, and the temperature dropped ten degrees.

"Hey now, that's better," Maggie said. "Why don't you wait here, Aunt Hail? I'll unfold chairs for us."

"Sure, I'll listen to the quiet."

Maggie walked away. As she set the chairs up, she maintained her vigil on her aunt.

Maybe bringing her out here wasn't such a good idea. When her aunt first heard the details of the site, she had insisted, demanded, in fact, that she be the one to monitor the archaeologists. She had waved off protests of conflict of interest, the factional politics in the pueblo, and every other objection.

Hail looked around through white-filmed eyes. Maggie had explained to her once that doctors these days could remove cataracts quickly and painlessly, but Hail had chuckled. *"I see better with them,"* she'd replied, and Maggie had dropped the subject. The Walking Hawk sisters had a variety of names. Her grandmother had been called, She Who Haunts the Dead. Aunt Hail was known as Ghost Talker, and Great-Aunt Sage was Empty Eyes, for the way she looked when she was seeing into other worlds. What her aunts thought important to see were often things that Maggie, and most people, didn't even know existed.

Maggie unfolded the last chair, walked back, and took her great aunt's arm. "It's three steps to the chair, Aunt Hail."

Hail smiled, and counted aloud, "One. Two. Three. Am I there?"

"Yes. Hold on." Maggie pulled the chair around behind her, and said, "All right. You can sit now."

Hail lowered a skeletal hand to the chair arm, gripped it, and grunted as she eased onto the woven seat. "I'm down," she informed, and pointed to the other chair. "Your turn."

As Maggie dragged the chair closer, she said, "I wish you wouldn't do this, Aunt Hail. Working as a monitor is hard enough, but sleeping on site will be even worse."

Monitoring the excavation of a burial site required not just physical strength, but at this time of year it meant coping with extreme temperatures and unpredictable weather. A thunderstorm could roll in and turn the road into an impassable river. If her grandmother suffered a medical emergency during one of those storms, they'd have to airlift her out and pray they could reach Gallup in time.

And then the repercussions would land on Maggie like the proverbial ton of bricks. As the "Authorized Officer," the federal government's representative, she could get into a great deal of trouble for appointing her aunt to this position.

Hail chuckled and her head tottered on the slender stem of her neck. "You just don't want to set up my tent."

"You know that's not true. I don't mind setting up your tent. I'd just feel better if you let me come get you every night. I'll bring you back in the morning."

"I need to be here," she said. "The ghosts have been calling me."

Maggie reached over and brushed away the lock of gray hair that had tangled with Hail's stubby eyelashes. Her aunt had been hungry most of her life, including these days. Though Maggie made sure she had plenty of food, Aunt Hail gave away almost everything she had: *"Hunger is like a worm; it crawls into the bones, sleeps there until you feel safe, then wakes up and starts gnawing just to remind you. A child shouldn't have to feel that way."*

Maggie patted Aunt Hail's hand. "Grandma told me once that most ghosts couldn't talk to her. She said that she didn't understand their language, and the ghosts didn't understand hers."

Maggie's grandmother, Slumber Walking Hawk, had been one of the greatest Seers in the history of their people. She'd died in this canyon three years ago. Every time Maggie walked into one of the magnificent Anasazi ruins, she thought of Grandmother Slumber lying dead with that ancient turquoise knife clutched in her hand.

Hail affectionately clasped Maggie's hand. "Do you miss her?"

"Oh, yes. I think about her every day."

Hail's bushy gray brows drew together. "Me, too. She haunted the dead much better than me, Magpie. There were things I wanted to learn from her, and I never had the chance."

"What things, Aunt Hail?"

Hail stared southward, across the canyon. Heat blurred the tan cliff, turning it into an ethereal shimmering wall. "Your grandmother could walk in ghost worlds. I always wanted to know how she did that."

Maggie slipped an arm around her aunt's shoulders, and hugged her. "Did you ask her? I'm sure she would have told you."

"I asked."

"What did she say?"

"Oh, Slumber said she saw a kind of fuzzy picture frame around the ghosts, and that if she lifted her foot over the bottom of the frame, she could step into the picture."

"You don't see the frame?"

Hail's head wobbled. "Wouldn't matter. Every time I see a ghost, my toes dig right into the ground and plant themselves." She smiled. "I couldn't take a step if I wanted to."

"Maybe you should stop trying. Going into ghost worlds sounds dangerous to me. What if you couldn't get back?"

"I'd just make new friends."

Maggie laughed. "You've always been better at that than me."

After a short pause, Hail asked, "Don't you like these White Eye diggers?"

"One of them, the lady arriving today, is Indian, Aunt. Her name is Dr. Maureen Cole."

"I know." Hail's white-filmed eyes turned in Maggie's direction, but she gestured to the excavation units in front of them. "She's been coming out here. Every night."

Maggie considered that. Maureen Cole had never been to New Mexico, and her aunt had never been to this site, but none of that mattered. This was one of those instances when her Western skepticism gave way to traditional truth. Souls wandered, especially at night when a person slept. As a girl, Maggie, and the other children, had hunted for soul tracks in the sand around the pueblo. She'd never found any, but she still believed.

"What is Dr. Cole looking for out here, Aunt?"

Hail waved a transparent old hand. "A young woman. I don't know who she is."

Maggie turned when she heard the sound of a truck coming up the dirt road. Two dust plumes billowed into the sky.

Maggie got to her feet. "Somebody's coming."

"Hmm?" Hail said, and turned. "Did you hear something?"

"Yes, a truck. It's probably Dusty Stewart and Dr. Cole. Dusty said they'd be in around five. He's late. It's almost seven o'clock." Maggie peered between two of the tents, and saw the blue Bronco bouncing up the rutted road. "I'll go—"

"Bring back some of those cold drinks when you come." Hail said.

"I will, Aunt." Maggie bent to kiss Hail on the cheek. "I won't be long."

Hail waited until Maggie was gone, then bent forward, and gasped air into her lungs. The pain deep within her left breast had grown fiery.

It took several breaths before it eased enough for her to sink back in her chair.

A month ago she'd talked one of the reservation social workers, Carolyn, into taking her to a doctor in Albuquerque, fearing it might be her heart. The doctor had run a bunch of tests, told her she had a strong heart for a woman her age, then he'd run more tests. A week later, he'd called the social worker.

Hail sighed. Her sister had died from the same thing, and before that, her mother. The doctor said sometimes cancers ran in families. Hail hadn't told Magpie yet. Her great-niece would insist that Hail return to town with her, and she didn't want to do that. Being out in the desert soothed her. But it wasn't just that, she needed to be away for a while to think about things.

The doctor hadn't come right out and said that he thought treatment was a waste of time, but Carolyn's voice had made it sound that way: *"He says the cancer is pretty far along, and he wants to run more tests before he recommends radiation or chemotherapy."*

Hail gazed down at the fire pit. The shadows of the tents stretched across camp like long dark fingers, and the tangy scent of old campfires filled the air. She could make out the roughly circular shape of the pit. What looked like coals lay at the bottom. They might be rocks, though. She didn't see nearly as well up close. A pile of sticks rested a few paces away. They were clearer. These diggers must be smart. Out here you didn't put your wood pile close to your fire, or the whole desert could end up in flames.

"Hello, Dusty," Maggie said.

Hail swiveled around in her chair to look at the blond man who stepped out of the truck.

"Hi, Maggie," he called. "I'm sorry we're late. Dr. Cole had to stop in Crownpoint to pick up some food."

"No problem," Magpie said and smiled at the tall Indian woman who stepped out of the passenger side. "We've only been here for fifteen minutes."

"Yes," Dr. Cole said. "We stopped at a *lavish* little convenience store. I ate the shrink wrap with the sandwich and didn't notice any difference."

The woman walked forward and extended her hand to Magpie, saying, "I'm Maureen Cole. What is your name?" She had deep black hair, and wore blue jeans and a white shirt. More than that, Hail couldn't tell.

"Maggie Walking Hawk Taylor, Dr. Cole. How was your trip?"

"The flight was fine. The rest was : . . interesting. Please, my friends call me Maureen."

"I was just going to grab some cold drinks out of my ice chest, Maureen. Can I get you something?"

"If you have an unsweetened iced tea in there, I'll throw myself at your feet. I couldn't find any in Crownpoint."

"I do. How about for you, Dusty?"

He brushed dirt from his pants. "Nothing, Maggie. I filled up both of my ice chests in town."

Hail smoothed the wrinkles in her blue dress, and tucked a wayward lock of gray behind her ear.

Magpie called, "Aunt Hail, do you want a Coke or an iced tea?"

"Iced tea," she answered. "That ginseng stuff in the pretty bottle. I think it's made down in Arizona somewhere."

"Canada, actually," Maureen replied. "I like it, too."

Hail smiled. She could hear Magpie rustling around in the back of her truck. Bottles clinked against ice cubes. Those coolers were really something. She could only wish that they'd had such good ones when she was younger. Back then, the only cool drink came from a "desert bag," one of the canvas kind that evaporated to cool itself.

Memories of family, friends, and long-past times drifted through her mind. Almost all of those people were dead now. As she would soon be.

Hail folded her hands in her lap. The thought of dying didn't bother her much unless she was outside in the sunshine and around her family. She'd lived a good long life, fifty-five years of it with a man who'd shared her souls. She'd loved five children, twelve grandchildren, and six great-grandchildren, as well as an assortment of nieces and nephews. There wasn't much more to life that she could see.

Magpie led the two people into the tent circle, set the drinks she carried on the ground, and said, "Aunt Hail, this is Dusty Stewart and Dr. Maureen Cole. Dusty and Maureen, this is my great-aunt, Hail Walking Hawk."

Stewart removed his sunglasses, and knelt in front of Hail, putting himself in a lower position. "Thank you for coming, Elder." He extended his hand, and Hail shook it, and smiled.

The Indian woman stepped forward and extended her hand, too. "I'm pleased to meet you, Mrs. Walking Hawk."

Hail took her brown hand, and smoothed her knotted fingers over it. It felt cool, damp from sweat. She said, "What tribe are you?"

"My mother was Seneca," Maureen Cole said.

"And your father?"

"Oh, he was a mongrel. A little English, some French, and a lot of Irish."

"What do your people call you?"

Maureen smiled as though it pleased her to be asked. "Washais. It's a knife we use for carving sacred masks. Kind of a drawknife—"

"Figures," Stewart muttered under his breath. "I'm surprised they didn't call you 'Knife-in-the-Back.' "

Washais glowered.

Hail tried the name on her tongue, "Wah-sha-ees. Your mother must have thought you had a lot of Power to give you a name like that. Sacred knives are powerful things."

Washais smiled again, and Hail saw a faint blue glow behind her.

"And the man?" Hail said, and pointed. "Who is he?"

Washais turned, looked at the green tents, and the desert, and asked, "What man?"

Hail drew her hand back to her lap, and fingered her blue dress. Some people reacted funny when she told them about the Spirits that walked along with them. Softly, she said, "He's behind you. He has light brown hair, and green eyes. He . . ."

Washais's face slackened. She stared at Hail as though a monster had just leaped from her mouth. The blue glow wavered around her, as if touching Washais to reassure her.

Dusty Stewart shot glances back and forth between Hail and Washais, then smiled broadly, grabbed Washais's limp hand, and shook it hard, saying, "I should have warned you, Dr. Cole. This is definitely not Kansas. I do hope you brought your ruby slippers."

Washais jerked her hand away. "Next time, Stewart, you'll draw back a bloody stump."

Magpie stepped between them, edging Stewart aside, obviously concerned about Washais. "Why don't you sit down, Maureen. You look a little pale."

"No, I—I think I'll walk around, thank you. It'll be dark soon. I'd like to take a look at the site. Would you excuse me?"

"Sure," Magpie said.

Hail watched as the tall Seneca woman walked out to the square holes the diggers had made. She rubbed her arms as if they tingled.

Stewart leaned toward Magpie, and whispered, "See if your Aunt Hail can keep that up. Cole will be gone in no time."

Magpie answered, "It's my fault. I just assumed, since she's Indian—"

"She's Catholic."

Magpie's mouth fell open, and her dark eyes blazed. "Many Indians are Catholic! All of the marriages at Acoma are performed in the Catholic church. We take Power where we find it, be it in a rainbow or a cross."

Dusty glanced away self-consciously. "I know that. Sorry. What I meant is that I think her brand of Catholicism is a little less open-minded than yours."

Magpie lifted her brows. "No rainbows?"

"I doubt it."

Hail gripped her chair arms and tried to shove to her feet. Her first attempt failed; she fell right back to the seat, but her second attempt worked. She rose and shuffled a few paces away.

Magpie and Dusty both ran to grip Hail's elbows, supporting her.

Hail smiled, and said, "Magpie, where's that walking stick you made me?"

"Oh, it's in the truck. Hold on, Aunt Hail. I'll get it."

Magpie exchanged a look with Dusty, transferring the responsibility for Hail's welfare from her to him, and trotted away.

Dusty gripped Hail's elbow more tightly. He asked, "Elder, who did you see near the good doctor?"

Hail patted his tanned hand. "A man who loves her. Very much. Too bad, though."

"Why is that?"

"Oh, these things are hard. His soul ought to be in the Land of the Dead by now."

Dusty shoved sweat-soaked blond hair from his forehead and appeared to be on the verge of saying something unkind as if wondering how anyone could have loved Washais.

Hail said, "When he died, he left a hole in her soul." She glanced at Dusty, blinking against her filmy vision to read his response. "You might think about that. And the hole in your own soul."

"What hole?"

"The one your mother tore out of you."

Dusty didn't say anything, but he tilted his head as though to avoid her gaze.

Hail smiled. "You two are a lot the same. Maybe that's why you rub on each other like sandstone."

"The rubbing part is right. I'll have to take your word for the rest, Elder."

Dusty looked out across the square holes to where Washais knelt, frowning down at something in the bottom of the pit. She had lifted the black plastic from the hole and weighted it down with a rock. The corner flapped and rattled in the breeze.

"I found it," Magpie called, and trotted up with the fine oak walking stick in her hand.

Magpie had cut the branch, sanded it until it felt like silk, then attached a rubber foot to the point, and laid a piece of elk antler sideways on the top. A beautiful thing, Hail loved it.

"Thank you, child." Hail took the stick and politely said, "I'll be fine by myself now. You two go on. I'll be right behind you."

Magpie nodded to Dusty, and they both walked in front of Hail, but less than a pace away. Just in case they had to whirl around fast and grab her, she guessed.

Hail propped her stick, and studied the uneven ground. She made three steps and stopped to breathe, then took another two and rested. That miserable cancer throbbed in her chest, burning and aching. Every time she stopped Magpie turned.

"I'm still up," Hail called.

"But you're not moving," Magpie said.

"Yes, I am." Hail took three more steps, and leaned on her walking stick. "I'm just moving like Tortoise, slow and smart."

Stewart put his sunglasses back on and said, "I'm going to go see what Dr. Cole has found. Just yell if you need me."

Magpie nodded. "Thanks, Dusty. I will."

He went to kneel on the opposite side of the pit from Washais.

Hail could see him pretty well from where she stood, well enough to see his tanned forehead furrow. He propped a clenched fist on his knee and seemed to be waiting for Washais to say something.

Hail took three more steps, then two, gasped a few

times, and made four good steps before she had to stop. She could almost see into the pit.

Magpie stood beside her. She murmured, "Are you sure I can't help you, Aunt Hail?"

"I have to learn to make do for myself. You're going to be gone soon, child." She studied the fuzzy ground, put her stick down, and made her way to the edge of the long rectangular pit. She could see the bones. They resembled winter-bleached branches, but she couldn't make them out very well. A big flat stone rested to the side of the skull.

Dusty said, "So?"

Washais stared down for several moments. "Dramatic example of *hyperostosis frontalis interna*. She must have—"

"What the hell is that?" Dusty demanded, as if angry.

"It's a scientific term that real anthropologists use, Stewart. I assume the rock is what cracked her skull wide open?"

"That was our guess," Stewart said.

Washais stood up, and propped slim brown hands on her hips. "I won't need to guess. When we remove the cranium, I can match the impact fracture to the stone. Scientists do that sort of thing. Please continue. You were saying?"

He gave her a cold smile. "I was saying it looks like the stone was thrown in on top of her. Now why don't you explain this hypershit to me."

Washais pointed to where the skull bones were crushed like an egg shell. "Do you see the thickening of the frontal bone of the skull? It's called the *squamous* portion."

"I do."

"Despite the fact that the outside of the skull looks smooth, if you crane your neck, you will see that beneath that thickened area is a series of bumpy bone growths."

Stewart braced a hand on the ground and climbed over

the edge. He eased to the floor and crouched near the skull. "Hmm," he grunted. "What does it mean?"

"It means the dead woman had an impressive endocrine imbalance." Washais appeared to be thinking. "But usually cases like this are found in older, postmenopausal women. On the other hand," she added, as if speaking to herself, "pregnant women often develop *osteophytes,* bone growths, on the *squamous* portion of the frontal bone, but they're generally flat, and disappear after pregnancy." She slapped her hands on her blue jeans. "I need to take a closer look at that skull, Stewart. Why has it only been partially excavated?"

"Because, my dear doctor," Stewart informed her in an authoritative tone, "in these United States, we have something called the Native American Graves Protection and Repatriation Act, and the American Indian Religious Freedom Act, which require us to consult with native peoples before we excavate burial grounds."

"Well, if you expect a scientific evaluation of what caused this woman's death, I need to see her up close. I brought a few tools with me, a microscope, calipers, some other things. How soon can I start work?"

Dusty climbed out of the pit. "Elder Walking Hawk, what do you think?"

Hail shuffled over to stand beside Washais. Her long black braid fell down the back of her white T-shirt. "Washais, tell me what you see? My eyes aren't so good anymore." She affectionately took hold of Washais's arm.

Washais returned the affection, squeezing Hail's knotted fingers. "I don't see too much either. But this woman was fairly young, in her early twenties. Her arms and legs are sprawled out, as if she were hurled face-first into the pit. I suspect that Stewart is correct that someone crushed her head with that stone and with as much force as he could muster. It takes a lot to crack a skull, especially one resting on sand. I also think—"

They all turned when a dust-streaked Jeep Cherokee jounced down the two track followed by a side-slipping cloud of dust that edged out into the greasewood to slowly fade into nothingness. After parking beside Dusty's Bronco, a skinny young woman with a lean face and shoulder-length brown hair jumped out.

Magpie lifted a hand and waved. "Hello, Sylvia!"

"Hi, Magpie!"

Magpie turned back to Washais. "It might have been frozen sand," Magpie said, "if this happened in the winter."

"Yes," Washais agreed. "Possibly. I'll be able to tell from the nasal sinus."

"Really?" Dusty asked with exaggerated politeness. *"How?"*

"By the pollen, Stewart." She brushed her hands off.

"I've never heard of that before."

"I'm not surprised. You're an archaeologist. Correct me if I'm wrong, but isn't 'pulling a burial' the technical term you people use? Do you have any idea of the amount of information you destroy when you 'pull' a human being out of the ground?"

"Can you really do that, Maureen?" Magpie asked. "Tell what time of year she died?"

"I can tell you the time of year. I can tell you if that rock really smashed her skull. I can probably even tell you her blood type."

Stewart's blond brows lowered. "Yeah, right, you've got all the answers. I don't believe this . . ."

The words faded. Hail blinked her cloudy eyes, and turned away, listening. But not to the living. Somewhere close by a child wailed. Crying and coughing, as if he couldn't get enough air.

Hail propped her walking stick, and walked eastward through the dry grass, and lengthening shadows, until the crying stopped. Hail tapped the ground, and the boy coughed again.

She whispered. "Don't cry. I'm here."

From behind her, Magpie called, "What is it, Aunt Hail? What did you find?"

"One of the Haze People."

Steps patted the ground as the three young people surrounded her.

She looked up at Dusty Stewart's reflective sunglasses. "Tomorrow, while Washais is looking at that woman over there, I want you to dig here." She pointed with her walking stick.

Dusty frowned, and tilted his head as if vying with his own better judgment. "Elder, I don't think I can. This is outside of the impact area."

"Dig here," she repeated. "You tell him, Magpie. This boy is sad."

"What boy?" Washais asked, confused.

"Aunt," Magpie said in that tone that told Hail she didn't understand something. "The archaeologists can only dig where the ground is going to be disturbed by the weather station. This part of the site won't be bothered."

"This isn't about sites," Hail said. "This is about this sad boy."

"Aunt," Magpie said, "the Park Service has rules about where we can dig and where we can't."

"Then maybe you better get your boss down here and tell him this boy needs our help."

Dusty ran his hand through his blond hair and said, "If you want me to dig there, Elder, then I will. Can you tell me more about this boy?"

Hail shook her head, turned, and shuffled back for the camp, her steps wobbly. The pain had grown unbearable, clawing at her like a wildcat. Her ribs and backbone throbbed.

Magpie ran to hold Hail's arm, supporting her. "Aunt Hail, are you all right?"

"Yes," she panted. "I just—" her voice cracked. She took a moment to steady it, then finished, "I just need to sit down and drink something."

The boy started wailing as she walked away, and the sound pierced Hail's soul, mingling with the pain in her breast. She hadn't expected that, the pitiful cries of a lonely little boy. Something was wrong here. Something that had gone wrong a long time ago.

Are you sure you're the one who can fix it, old woman?

A chill breath blew from between the worlds, icing her souls.

Hail hurried for camp.

Dusty sat in front of the fire with a warm Guinness in his hand and pondered his problem. He was working within a National Monument, administered by the National Park Service. You didn't feed the bears or pet the buffalo in Yellowstone. You didn't pick up rocks for your collection in Zion or pluck the flowers from the Grand Canyon. And, if you were an archaeologist working on a government contract, you didn't so much as stick a pin flag in the ground outside of the designated impact area.

He glanced to his left at Maggie. She had a can of Coke in her hand and a bewildered look on her face. He could read her expression like an open book: half of her was frantic to stay within the rules, while the other half was just as desperate to follow her aunt's instructions.

That was why he was going to shoot-in that grid tomorrow morning, and dig the pit.

What the hell. The contracting officer is in Washington, D.C. I'll just claim I made a slight mistake. I was a few degrees off when I laid out the site boundaries. What can he do once the pit's been dug?

He can jerk your Antiquities Permit, you fool.

Every archaeologist who worked on federally administered lands had to be permitted. No permit. No work. Well, he'd worry about that later.

Maureen sat across the fire from him, her long legs crossed, quietly sipping coffee. A thoughtful expression creased her oval face. The black braid over her left shoulder fell to her waist. He hadn't noticed before, but a few strands of silver had entered her hair; they glimmered in the firelight. She had enormous black eyes and full lips. If he didn't know her, he'd think she was one of the most beautiful women he'd ever seen. Unfortunately, he did know her.

A cool wind swirled around the camp, fanning the flames. Whirlwinds of sparks coiled into the dark starstrewn sky. Dusty watched them rise, and tried to picture Cole in a laboratory. How could anyone choose to spend her life under fluorescent lights, breathing recycled air? He lived for this, working all day with the scent of dirt in his nostrils, cooking meals over open fires, sitting around at night talking with people who shared his passion for understanding the past.

His parents had started him down this road. Ruth, his mother, had come to the southwest to study the Keres at Acoma. She'd met Samuel Stewart there, an archaeology graduate student under Dale Robertson's guidance at the University of Arizona.

Dusty had been born fifteen miles shy of Tuba City, on the shoulder of US 160, when Ruth hadn't quite made it to the tiny clinic for the delivery. Dusty had been five years old when his mother left for the Pacific Islands. By his sixth birthday, Dusty's life had collapsed and he was living in Dale Robertson's apartment, sleeping on the couch. By the time he turned ten, Dusty had seen every major archaeological site in the western United States, grown up on them, in fact. He'd lived with the Navajo,

Hopi, Zuni, Apache, and Arapaho. He even spoke a smattering of their languages.

It had been a long, hard road to this campfire, and the
decision to excavate a unit outside of the authorized impact area. But he'd always been a maverick.

Maggie shifted and drew his attention. Her white shirt,
tan shorts, and black tennis shoes bore a thick coating of
dirt.

Dusty glanced behind her at the red nylon tent Maggie
had set up for her great-aunt. Something was wrong. He
felt it in his gut. Hail Walking Hawk had barely made it
back to camp. She'd collapsed into a chair, and started
rocking back and forth, murmuring softly to herself. He
did not know the Keres language—a curious language
isolate, not related to anything else in the world—but he
knew from the tone that the words expressed fear. Was
she ill? Maggie had been unusually silent.

Dusty sipped his stout and worked at peeling off the
black-and-gold label. He had known Maggie for five
years. As a National Park Service ranger, she routinely
endured a lot of stress, but he'd never seen her like this.
She hunched forward in her chair with her elbows
propped on her knees, staring into the fire as though she
could see the future there, and it wrenched her heart. Her
round face, short black hair, and tight eyes had an orange
tint. If Dusty were a guessing man, he'd say she'd just
seen a ghost, and didn't know what to do about it. Given
her family history, that possibility was real.

Sylvia, who sat to Dusty's right, popped the top on
another Coors Light. She wore a faded pair of Levi's,
and a sky-blue T-shirt that proclaimed: BUFFALO! THE
MEAT OF THE FUTURE! She had a lean face, with a
pointed nose, and freckles. Her green eyes maintained a
perpetual squint—like every archaeologist who worked
for hours on end in blinding sunlight.

Sylvia took several swallows from her can and said,

"Anybody heard from Dale? Did we ever find out what kind of family emergency he's having?"

Dusty replied, "I called his number from my cell phone on the way in. He left me a message on his machine. It said: 'Give Maureen my finest regards. I'll see you on Friday night.' "

"Oh, all right," Sylvia said with a grin. She shook brown hair away from her eyes. "It's Tuesday. We have three days of freedom."

"Freedom?" Dusty said. "I'm going to work your buns off. I'm assigning you to Dr. Cole. You're going to finish digging unit 8N 4E by yourself, while I open Elder Walking Hawk's unit."

Sylvia looked across the fire at Maureen and lifted her beer. "Here's to women ruling the world. We'll have fun."

A faint smile tugged at the corners of Maureen's lips. "Well, maybe. But you should know that your commander in chief has nicknamed me 'Mary the Hun.' "

Sylvia lowered her beer. "Wow. Sounds like the heroine of a porno flick."

Dusty took a long drink of his Guinness and let out a satisfied sigh. As he added another piece of greasewood to the fire, he said, "Dr. Cole provoked me."

"I did no such thing," Maureen defended.

"You did so."

"How?"

Greasewood burned fast and hot. Sparks filled the space between him and Maureen. Dusty leaned forward to see her better through the haze. "I said you were a cross between Mary Baker Eddy and Attila the Hun. You said I'd better delete the 'Baker Eddy' part because you were Catholic. So—" He made a sweeping gesture— "Mary the Hun."

Sylvia finished her beer, crushed the Coors Light can

in one hand, and dropped it with a flourish. "You could have called her 'Mary Attila.' "

"It didn't have the same ring."

"Yeah, guess not," Sylvia replied. "Nobody remembers who Attila was, but everybody knows what a 'Hun' is."

"Right," Dusty said. " 'Hon,' as in honey, eh, Sylvia?"

Sylvia made a face, and responded, "No, stupid. Hun as in 'anal retentive.' "

Maureen's perfectly etched brows drew down over her straight nose. "I beg your pardon?"

"You know?" Sylvia insisted. "Haven't you ever heard that phrase?"

"What phrase?"

"You know, like, 'she's an anal retentive Hun.' "

Maureen's mouth pursed with distaste. "I'm sure I have *not* heard that phrase."

Dusty tore off another piece of his label, and said, "It isn't her fault, Sylvia. Canadians have no sense of humor." He put a finger under his nose and tipped it up, demonstrating "uppity," then flared his nostrils for effect.

Maureen stared at him with a quizzical expression, then said, "You've either discovered astronomy, which is unlikely given your abhorrence of science, or the amount you've 'retented' is even getting to you."

Dusty lowered his hand. A comeback did not immediately spring to mind, which meant she'd certainly earned points.

"Oh, hey." Sylvia nodded in admiration. "Can I borrow that? I've always wanted to know a genteel way of telling people they were full of shit."

"Be my guest." Maureen reached for the coffeepot, which sat on one of the hearthstones, tested the handle, and filled her cup. Steam rose in a firelit veil. She added, "Besides, I'll probably never have the opportunity to use it again. Physical anthropologists aren't nearly as obsessed with excrement as archaeologists."

Sylvia's green eyes widened. "Yeah, but you have to admit, some feces are *fascinating*. I heard they found a coprolite in Colorado that was three feet long, and had a whole packrat skull in it. Can you imagine that? Dang. That wasn't just any old floater. I—"

"Sylvia," Dusty interrupted, seeing Maureen's expression turn sour, "hand me another stout. It's in the ice chest behind you."

"Oh, sure." Sylvia turned, opened the lid, and rummaged through what sounded like an ocean of melting ice. When she pulled out the Guinness, water poured from her hand. The puckered label hung sideways.

Dusty reached for it, found the church key in his pocket, and flipped the cap off. Rich creamy foam boiled up. He clamped his mouth over the top so he wouldn't lose any. It tasted heavenly. After several swallows, he eased back, studied the bottle, then smiled and wiped his mouth on his green T-shirt sleeve. "Now, that's beer."

"Yuck," Sylvia replied, and turned to Maureen. "Have you ever tasted that vile stuff? It's just like the scum from a burned peat bog."

Maureen took a sip of coffee, and sighed, "Oh, yes. I've tasted it. Magnificent stuff." She closed her eyes as if tasting it again and a look of utter joy came over her.

Dusty's bottle halted in front of his lips. "You liar. You told me you were the founder of the Teetotalism Movement in Canada."

She opened her eyes, and they caught the firelight, reflecting it like huge black mirrors. "That's now. Not then."

"When was then?"

"*Then.*"

The tone told Dusty the discussion had ended. He rotated his bottle in his hands, and calmly peeled off the bottom of the label. Perhaps, he'd misjudged her. Anyone who truly appreciated Guinness had to be all right in her heart. Of course, it didn't make up for her personality.

Sylvia leaned her head back and gazed at the glistening night sky. "God, look at all those stars. You think there's life on any of them?"

Dusty glanced sideways at her, then examined the infinite well of star-spotted indigo. "Well, let me see, the average star burns at about five jillion degrees. That would mean it could only support a vaporous life form. Or maybe—"

"You mean," Sylvia interrupted, "something that floats around aimlessly? With no mind? No purpose?"

"Well. Yeah."

"Wow," she said in true awe. "The stars could be filled with government employees."

Dusty peeled off the rest of his label and tossed it into fire; it sizzled and spat, before shriveling up.

Sylvia suddenly sat up straight, and looked at Maggie. "Oh, hey, Magpie, I didn't mean to include you in that crack. You know, Park Service people are different."

Maggie started, as if hearing her name for the first time. "What?" She focused her eyes. "Did you call me?"

Sylvia said, "Yeah, but forget it. If you didn't hear it, you can't get mad at me."

Maggie gazed around the fire. "I'm sorry. I'm not very good company tonight, am I?"

Dusty frowned down at his bottle. Puebloan peoples cherished privacy. A person who inadvertently violated that privacy might never get the opportunity to make amends. He wanted to ask about her aunt's health, but he couldn't do it straight out. Not right away. Instead, he began, "This afternoon your aunt said something I didn't quite understand. Right after you asked her what she'd found?"

Maggie exhaled. "Yes. She said she'd found one of the Haze People."

"The boy she was talking about is one of the Haze People?"

"That's what Aunt Hail says."

Maureen set her empty coffee cup on the ground beside her chair, and said, "Who are they? The Haze People?"

"I didn't really understand what she meant." Maggie shook her head, and short black hair fluttered over her broad cheeks.

Maureen pressed, "But your aunt meant that there's another burial there, correct?"

Maggie's shoulders hunched. "That's the part I didn't understand. You see, Haze People are people who were never born."

"The unborn?" Sylvia said. "Oh, man. That's not like the 'undead,' is it?"

Dusty said, "*Sylvia,*" and lowered his brows reprovingly.

Maggie frowned down at her Coke can. The red lettering had deepened to black in the fire's glow. "I don't know for sure. I need to ask Aunt Hail about it tomorrow."

Dusty turned. "I thought you were leaving tomorrow."

"No," Maggie whispered. "If it's all right with you, I think I'll call in and take two weeks of annual leave. I'm afraid that—that my aunt might need me."

"We'll be happy to have you out here," Dusty said, then tipped his head toward Maggie's tent where Hail Walking Hawk slept. "Is she . . . all right?"

"She tells me she is."

Fear edged Maggie's voice. Dusty saw the way her hands fumbled with the Coke can.

He hesitated, then softly said, "If you need me, just ask. For anything. You understand?"

Maggie jerked a nod. "Yes. Thanks."

Maureen studied Maggie intently. "Maggie, tell me

more about the Haze People? Are they human? Earth Spirits? Sky people?"

Maggie opened her mouth, about to make the effort to answer, then apparently thought better of it. "I'm really tired," she said. "Please excuse me. I think I'll hit the sack." She got to her feet.

Maureen leaned back in her chair. "Good night, Maggie."

"Good night everyone."

Sylvia said, "See you tomorrow, Magpie."

Maggie slipped her Coke can into the cardboard box marked TRASH, that set outside of her tent, then tiptoed through the red flap, and lowered it. Dusty heard her take off her boots, and unzip her sleeping bag, then her aunt murmured something soft and affectionate, and Maggie said, "I love you, too."

Dusty took another drink of stout. Maggie's grandmother had died just down the road at Pueblo Bonito a few years ago. She must be thinking about that. He'd heard the eerie story from the president of the local hiking club, Kyle Laroque, who'd been there when it happened. Kyle said he'd been talking with Maggie when the notes of an ancient flute had eddied around the ruins, then he'd heard a man's deep beautiful voice whisper, *"You may stay if you wish. You do not have to come today. I just thought you might wish to."* Kyle and Maggie had found her grandmother on the other side of the gigantic crumbling pueblo, dead, holding half of a broken turquoise knife in her hand. Slumber Walking Hawk had been dying of cancer. Maggie believed the voice Kyle had heard belonged to one of the *Shiwana,* the spirits of the dead who became cloud beings.

Tomorrow, he would tell Maggie that he'd be happy to shut down the excavation until she could find another monitor for the project. The good doctor would probably be livid, but he didn't care.

Sylvia yawned, and stretched her arms. "I assume we're still rising with the ducks?"

"That's right," Dusty said. "Five A.M. sharp. If you're not up, I'll kick you out of your bag."

Sylvia grinned at Maureen. "He's not kidding. One time, about a year ago, I'd imbibed a wee too much wine the night before, and didn't get up when dawn cracked. So Dusty simulated another dawn by setting off a shotgun over the top of my tent."

Maureen's jaw dropped. "You *what?*"

Dusty smiled. "Tell her what happened after that, Sylvia."

"Well, after I got my hearing back and threw up on him—"

"*After* that."

"Oh, you want the litany." Sylvia clasped her hands as though in Sunday School. "I learned a valuable lesson that day. Now I never drink too much when I know we have work to do the next day." She rose, said, "G'night y'all," and headed for her tent.

"Sleep well, Sylvia," Maureen said, and suppressed a smile. When Sylvia had zipped the front of her tent closed, Maureen added, "What a character."

Dusty nodded. A strange sober tone entered his voice. "Sylvia and I have a lot in common. Sometimes I think she knows me better than I know myself. That fact isn't particularly soothing, but she often keeps me from making a complete fool of myself. That's why I keep her around. And if she sticks with it, she'll be one of the great archaeologists of the next century. She has natural talent, but don't tell her I said that. She—"

"*I heard that.*"

Dusty looked over his shoulder at Sylvia's tent. "What ears. I need a bigger shotgun."

Maureen laughed in genuine delight.

Dusty smiled and toyed with his empty bottle. "You

know, I may have misjudged you. You're not as bad as I thought."

Maureen wiped her eyes, and her laughter turned into a closed-mouth chuckle. "Well," she said, and leaned forward, fixing him with dazzling black eyes. "That's because I haven't had a chance to tell you that your idea of a slave burial ground is sheer, unadulterated nonsense."

Dusty stared at her. Her braid had fallen from her lap, and almost brushed the ground by her foot. Every hair shimmered.

"I knew 'Mary the Hun' was only a breath away," he observed. "Okay. Tell me why?"

She rose to her feet. "After you've finished excavating, I'll *show* you."

She walked for her tent.

Dusty muttered, "Women," flopped back in his chair and searched the ground for a Coors Light can to crush.

12

WATER SKIMMER, MATRON of the Badgerpaw clan, sat on a soft red blanket in the village plaza. To her right, the canyon wall gleamed in the bright morning sunlight. As the stone warmed, a dusty scent filled the cold air.

Her clanspeople stood around, muttering behind their hands, pointing at the strange old man who balanced on his head in front of Water Skimmer. He looked like a stink bug with his rear thrust into the air. His mangy brown-and-white turkey feather cape covered his face. Actually, his entire head.

Water Skimmer adjusted the black blanket over her shoulders and leaned sideways to whisper to her husband, "What is he doing?"

Birdtail lifted his hands, and shrugged. Wind Baby teased the three hairs left on top of his bald head. "He hasn't said a word since he started this."

"What did he say when he first entered the plaza?" She had been inside her chamber, sewing porcupine quills onto a finely tanned buckskin shirt.

"He said he wished to speak with you. Then he turned himself into a dung beetle."

At the age of sixty-two summers, Water Skimmer had seen many curious things and had learned to watch and wait. The meaning of this eluded her, but perhaps it would become clear.

She tucked loose strands of chin-length white hair behind her ears and lifted her wrinkled chin.

The old man's rump wiggled, then he shoved his cape aside to look at her. His wrinkled face glowed bright red. "Ah," he said. "You must be Water Skimmer.".

"I am. Who are you?"

The old man collapsed to the ground, his cape in a mass of feathers over his left shoulder. He pulled it straight, and said, "I am the Blue God."

Water Skimmer smirked. "No, you aren't. I've seen her close up. Last sun cycle the Fire Dogs attacked and ran a lance through my chest. I know the Blue God personally, and you are not even related to her."

The old man's face fell. "But I know the names of all your dead relatives."

"So do I. That doesn't make me the Blue God."

"Do you believe in her?"

Water Skimmer eyed the old man, wondering at his purpose. "I am ancient enough to remember the days when everyone believed in her."

He cocked his white head like a demented stork. His narrow face, long beaked nose, and wide mouth added to the impression. In a low solemn voice, he said, "Then you are a wise woman, indeed. Did you see her when she came here hunting your niece, young Cactus Wren?"

Water Skimmer leaned back on her blanket.

Eight moons ago, her twelve-summers-old niece had vanished without a trace. No one had seen raiders. No one had even seen Cactus Wren leave the village. It was as though she had been lifted straight up into the air by a whirlwind.

In a hard-edged voice, she replied, "No. Did you?"

The old man shook his head. "I regret that I did not. Was the girl ill?"

Brilliantly painted capes flashed as villagers closed in around them, hissing and nodding their heads.

Water Skimmer said, "How did you know she was ill?"

"I didn't until now. What was wrong with her?"

She debated on whether or not to tell him, but could see no harm in it. "The child had gone on her first vision quest three moons before. She had received a very powerful Spirit Helper. We were excited, and hopeful. But every time he came to speak with her, she suffered headaches. The last time the headaches were so terrible we called for help from the Blessed *Kokwimu* at Hillside village. She—"

"Cloudblower," the old man said the name reverently. "Did she come?"

"She always comes. Whenever anyone needs her, she rushes to help. She brought her assistant, Hophorn, and they felt around on my niece's head, and gave her many herbs to drink. The girl felt better, and they left. Cactus Wren disappeared that night."

"Did you search for her?"

"Of course we did. We found nothing." She extended a hand to the murmuring crowd. "Many here believe that my niece was abducted. That a witch flew in on a rawhide shield, scooped her up, and carried her away to eat her."

The old man asked, "And you, Water Skimmer, what do you believe?"

She glanced around at her clanspeople. All eyes had fixed upon her, awaiting her answer. In the blue sky over their heads, stringy Cloud People sailed northward.

"I believe she is gone," she answered. "And we must now think of ourselves."

The old man got to his feet, and hobbled toward Water Skimmer with his black eyes shining. When he stood less than three hands away, he asked, "Tell me, when you hear about a witch being tortured to death for his crimes, do you see through the eyes of the witch or the people in the crowd?"

"The witch," she answered without thinking. In her souls she also suffocated with every child who had the coughing sickness and every mother who labored in childbirth. "Whose eyes do you see through?"

The old man's wrinkled lips pulled into a smile. "One of the onlookers, of course."

"Hmm." She tapped a finger against her knee. "Now tell me why you asked such a question."

He brushed at an invisible speck on his feathered cape. "I am confident, Matron, that I have power over my own deeds. I know I will never be before those torturers. You, however, are not so sure. You fear yourself. You fear what others think of you. Most of all, you fear what you are capable of that no one else realizes."

The villagers burst into laughter. They knew how confident and courageous she could be. They had seen her pull herself from a sickbed, grab her bow, and rush out to fight invaders. They had seen her stand up and curse the most powerful gods in the sky. They knew she feared nothing.

As the villagers drifted away, slapping each other on the backs and shaking their heads at the old man's foolishness, Water Skimmer looked at him more carefully.

"I think you are Trickster Coyote in disguise," she said. "What are you trying to get from me that I don't wish to give up?"

The old man smiled. "What you really wish to ask me is why we see differently. Let me tell you a secret, Matron. You are afraid because you have always felt isolated and lonely. Different from others. That is why you are a strong, powerful woman. You had to gain a position where you did not have to feel that way as often. I suspect you would do anything to keep from feeling that way again. I, on the other hand, am afraid of evil. It is my greatest fear, and always has been. That is why I see through the eyes of an onlooker."

Water Skimmer's mouth quirked. "So. We can all rest at night knowing you will never be a leader. Is that what you came here to find out?"

His eyes widened, and he blinked owlishly at her. "Why, yes, Matron. It is."

Irritated, she said, "Then why did you ask about Cactus Wren?"

"Because I thought she was a witch, just like the young woman at Whitetail, but I wasn't sure until we spoke. Thank you for your help, Matron."

Before she could tell him what an outrageous accusation that was, he turned and left.

Water Skimmer watched him hobble across the plaza, humming loudly to himself, his ratty turkey feather cape flapping around his scrawny legs. He took the road to Frosted Meadow village.

Water Skimmer turned to Birdtail. "Did you understand any of that?"

Birdtail squinted, scratched his wrinkled throat, and said, "Not a word, my wife."

MAUREEN WOKE TO the sound of singing. The elderly voice lilted softly.

She blinked her eyes open and looked at the pale blue light that filled the canvas tent. Even without knowing Hail Walking Hawk's language, she could tell the song greeted Father Sun. The melody had the same pleasant rhythm as Iroquois morning songs. Maureen lay quietly in her sleeping bag, listening.

Cool wind played with the tent flap, blew it out, then gently ruffled the edges. The scent of last night's fire and the sweet earthiness of the desert rode the breeze.

A curious sensation filtered through Maureen, as though her body knew this peaceful ritual from eons ago and found the familiarity comforting.

She checked her watch: four forty-five.

She sat up, brushed and braided her long hair, and pulled on the same jeans she'd been wearing yesterday. She added on a clean red T-shirt and hiking boots. As she unzipped the front of her tent, the singing briefly stopped then started again.

Maureen crawled out into the fragrant wind and looked up. An infinity of slate blue sky arched over her head, the west strewn with a glittering of fading stars. Thousands of them. Awe expanded her breast. Skies like this didn't exist in the northeast. There was too much moisture in the air and too many trees in the way. It seemed appropriate that her first glimpse of this sky was on her knees.

Despite the cool breeze, she could feel the day beginning to warm. Heat oozed from the very pores of the earth. By noon, she suspected it would be over thirty-five degrees centigrade again. Unbelievably hot for someone who had spent her life romping through the lush forests of Ontario.

She saw Hail Walking Hawk. The old woman wore a white sweater over a long yellow dress. She had her cane tucked under her right arm. Wisps of gray hair blew around her ancient face as she bent over and tied a feather to a bush. She had already tied half a dozen to a nearby bush, and the feathers twirled and bobbed in the morning breeze.

Maureen didn't know this ritual, but it fascinated her. The act of tying feathers and watching them blow seemed beautiful.

She walked wide around the fire pit and toward Mrs. Walking Hawk.

When the elderly woman heard her coming, she turned slightly and smiled. "Good morning, Washais."

"Good morning, Mrs. Walking Hawk. It looks like we're up before anyone else."

Her toothless mouth spread wider. "That's because you and me aren't as lazy as some other people." She hobbled toward Maureen, pulled two strings of feathers from her palm, and extended them.

Maureen took the feathers, and looked them over. She thought they might be mourning dove feathers. They had a blue-gray sheen. "Tell me what to do."

Hail Walking Hawk put gnarled old fingers on Maureen's arm and guided her to a nearby bush. She pointed. "Tie yours to this one. Each feather is a prayer. When Father Sun rises, he will see our prayers and smile."

Maureen knelt and tied the first feather to the bush. "What are we praying for?"

Mrs. Walking Hawk gazed out toward the eastern horizon. A lavender halo marked the place where the sun would rise. "Oh, many things. Health, and happiness for living people." She touched a finger to the last feather in Maureen's hand. "That one is for the Haze child in the ground over there."

Maureen tied the feather to the bush where it lifted into the air and danced on the wind.

As the sky brightened, the dark canyon walls began to gleam a rich golden-hued blue. She wouldn't have believed the color if she weren't staring at it.

"This is magical country," Maureen said.

Hail shrugged. "The gods live here, Washais. That's all."

"That is enough, Elder Walking Hawk," she said. "I didn't expect to find God here."

Hail craned her neck to look up at Maureen. Her white-filmed eyes caught the morning light and flashed. "You knew the gods were here," she said and tied her last prayer to the rabbitbrush.

In a way, of course, Maureen had known. God inhabited every tree in the woods. God lived in the eyes of the deer, and raccoons. Of course God must also live here in this vast treeless expanse of desert. She had always just associated God with living things, not sand and sky.

Hail Walking Hawk chuckled suddenly. "What makes you think the sky isn't alive?"

Maureen turned. "How did you know I—"

"Washais, your face tells everyone your thoughts. You were looking up at Brother Sky as though gazing at a corpse. There was no love in your eyes, just an appreciation of his beauty."

Maureen smiled in relief. "Elder, would you tell me more about the Haze child? Maggie told me a little last night, but I didn't really understand. What are Haze People?"

Hail Walking Hawk took her cane from beneath her arm, and leaned on it. "They are Spirits who walk in haze because they were never born. They never got to come out and see Father Sun with their own eyes, so they can only dream of him. They live in their haze dream. Kind of a sparkling haze," she said and tipped her deeply wrinkled face, as if seeing it herself.

"Are Haze People evil?"

"Oh, no, child. Not usually. Though some of them get very frustrated." She pointed to her own cataract-covered eyes. "I do, too, when I can't see things I want to. Mostly Haze People are sad."

"So they're sad Earth Spirits?"

Hail lifted her hands to the brightening bowl of the heavens. "Some of them live in the sky, hoping to be born. Others are stuck down here like that boy child over there. He wanted to be born, too, but he never was. I think his mother did some bad thing."

Maureen looked over at the place where Mrs. Walking Hawk had tapped the ground yesterday. "You mean"— she paused, not knowing the cultural taboos she might be violating—"you mean his mother aborted him?"

Most preliterate cultures knew the proper plants to induce abortion: milkweed and mugwort, star grass, and the dried roots of the cotton plant, among many other uterine irritants. But they were only used during times of extreme stress, natural disasters like droughts, floods, hurricanes. When the survival of the tribe was at issue, it was preferable to kill the unborn than to watch cherished loved ones die.

Hail Walking Hawk studied the fading stars before answering, "Maybe. That boy was really little. He hadn't learned to talk, so he can't tell me." She propped her cane and started for the camp a few halting steps at a time.

Stewart had risen. He crouched near the fire pit, adding sticks to the small blaze he had going. Maggie emerged from behind the tents and pulled up a chair. She wore khaki shorts, a dark blue shirt, and black tennis shoes. Sylvia hadn't appeared yet.

Maureen gently took hold of Hail Walking Hawk's left arm, and the old woman smiled.

As they walked, Maureen said, "Have your people always been here? In the desert, I mean?"

Mrs. Walking Hawk stopped. "In the beginning we lived in the belly of the earth with our mother, Iatiku. When the proper time came, birds, animals, and insects helped my people climb through four underworlds—the white, red, blue, and yellow worlds—to get to this fifth world of sunlight. We came out up north, near Mesa Verde, Colorado. That's mountains. Pine forests."

Mrs. Walking Hawk started walking again. She eased down through a dip in the sand and climbed the other side, leaning on Maureen one instant and her cane the next.

Maureen cocked her head. "Interesting. Your people believe the mother of human beings came from beneath the earth. My people believe she came from the sky. But if your people came up from the underworlds in Colorado, how did you get here, to New Mexico?"

Mrs. Walking Hawk halted to catch her breath. After a few inhalations, she said, "The place of emergence was too sacred for humans. We came here, to this canyon, and built the great White House." She turned back the way they'd come and gestured to the rapidly brightening east. "These diggers, they call it Pueblo Bonito. Now it's just red stone, but it used to be covered with white clay. We lived at White House with the gods for a long time. Then my people got to arguing with the *Shiwana*, the rain-bringers, and they left us. Without rain our crops wouldn't grow. We got hungry and started fighting with each other. We had to leave, to move on."

"Where did you go?"

She used her cane to poke at a clump of grass, as though testing to see what it was. "Some of us went north, back to Mesa Verde. Some south. My clan, the Antelope Clan, moved south to the sky city, Acoma."

Hail Walking Hawk started for camp again, and Maureen heard Dusty say, "Listen, Maggie, I've been thinking about what we discussed last night. If you want, I can shut down the excavation for a couple of weeks. That will give you time to—"

In a frail voice, Hail Walking Hawk called, "That Haze child can't wait a couple of weeks. He's crying. He needs to be free."

Maggie looked at her great-aunt and lowered her eyes to the ground. As sunrise neared, it cast a purplish glow over the camp. Maggie's round face and short black hair had a pale lilac sheen. "We should do what she wants," Maggie said to Dusty.

He nodded. He wore dark green shorts and a brown T-shirt that reflected the firelight. The battered straw cowboy hat sat on his head at a jaunty angle. "Just remember that the offer is open."

Maggie said, "Thanks."

Maureen guided Mrs. Walking Hawk to the chair beside Maggie and steadied it while she lowered herself to the seat. Hail said, "Thanks from me, too."

Dusty smiled, but Maureen could see the worry in his blue eyes. He said, "Any time, Elder." His sun-bleached hair glowed starkly white as he turned around to the boxes and ice chests piled behind his chair. He rummaged through them, pulled out a white plastic water jug, soot-coated coffeepot, and, finally, a bag of New Mexico pinyon coffee.

"Good morning, Aunt," Maggie said and leaned sideways to kiss her aunt's cheek.

"Good morning, Magpie." Hail tenderly touched Maggie's arm. "Me and Washais have already sent our prayers up. We can rest."

Maggie said, "I'll send mine after breakfast. That way I can offer part of my meal to Iatiku."

Dusty dumped half the bag of pinyon coffee into the pot's basket, shoved the lid on, and set the pot at the edge of the flames. "I don't pray until I've had at least three cups of coffee to brace myself."

Maureen said, "I suspect God needs a stiff scotch before you pray."

She walked behind the tents to the fiberglass Sanolet, and stepped inside. The thing reminded her of rock concerts in a different age. God, how long had it been? But John had been with her then, his wry smile and the sparkle in his eyes just for her. This time, when she stepped out the door, unlike those long years ago, she would be alone in an alien land.

She let the door bang behind her, crossed to the fire, grabbed a chair, and carried it out of the smoke. Unfortunately that meant setting it down to Stewart's right. He gave her a wary sideways glance.

"Am I too close?" Maureen asked.

"You'd be too close in Ontario, Doctor."

Maureen sat down. Orange firelight mixed with the shades of dawn and fluttered over the tents and people's faces. "Maybe you'd better consider a new continent, Stewart. I've heard Libya is looking for people of your caliber."

"Oh, they'd like an American caliber, all right. But more likely a .223 coming out of an M16A1."

Maureen lifted a brow. "I forgot. This is America. I'll bet you have one of those for home defense, don't you, Stewart?"

"No"—he glanced at his watch, turned around in his chair, and shouted—*"I prefer my shotgun!"*

"What!" Sylvia's tent wobbled as though a bear had just run through it. *"I'm up!"*

Dusty turned back to Maureen and showed her a perfect set of white teeth. "Thanks for the gun talk, Doctor. It gets lonely being the only man out here."

Sylvia stuck her head out of her tent. Shoulder-length brown tangles framed her freckled face. She sniffed the air and gazed at the sky.

"What are you doing?" Dusty asked.

"The testosterone is like a bug-bomb out here. I was just checking to see if the crows were falling out of the sky."

Dusty smiled. "It's good of you to join us, Sylvia."

"Hey, no problem." She crawled out of her tent wearing green camo shorts, a tan T-shirt, and hiking boots. "How's the coffee?"

"Not quite, but soon." Dusty bent over the glass top on the battered coffeepot. "It's foaming. Another two minutes ought to do it."

Maureen watched the soot-blackened pot for a moment, and said, "Somehow, I just don't think this is going to be Tim Horton's."

"What?" Dusty asked.

"The finest coffee in all the world is made at Tim Horton's. They serve it in these wonderful big white cups. And their chocolate-dipped donuts are enough to make angels swoon." She closed her eyes. "God, I'm a million light years from civilization."

"Thank God," Stewart said. "No blaring horns, or smelly air, or crime, or traffic jams, or frantic lines. Just peace, tranquillity, and fresh air. But if you're desperate for donuts, I think we've got some. Probably as good as Tim Horton's. Whatever that is. Picked 'em up back at

the convenience store in Crownpoint. They're the powdered sugar kind with—"

"Stewart, that is heresy."

Sylvia pulled up a chair between Maureen and Maggie,
and took a comb from her back pocket. As she ran it
through her tangles, she said, "Outside of vituperosity,
what's for breakfast?"

"Vituperosity?" Dusty asked. "Is that a word?"

"It is now."

"Well, you have a choice," Dusty told her. "You can
have eggs, bacon, and dark rye bread, or any combination
of the above."

"Cool. Ethnic food." Sylvia finished her hair and
tucked her comb into her back pocket again, then she
turned to Maureen. "I've been telling Dusty for two years
that burritos three times a day makes your pit partner go
away. He wouldn't listen until one time—"

"Sylvia," Dusty interrupted, "why don't you find the
cups. The coffee's done."

"Oh, sure." She got up and went to search through the
wooden footlocker near her tent.

Hail Walking Hawk laughed silently and shook her
gray head. Maggie had a hand on her great-aunt's arm,
smiling.

Maggie whispered to Maureen, "Be glad Dusty
stopped her. I've heard the conclusion before."

Dusty echoed the sentiment with an exaggerated nod.
He picked up a stick, and dragged the coffeepot out of
the fire onto a hearthstone. Thick brown foam bubbled
over the spout. "And if she ever starts the story about the
strippers in Cortez, Colorado," he said to Maggie, "I expect you to save me."

Maggie leaned forward in surprise. "What strippers in
Cortez?"

"Oh, hey," Sylvia said as she walked back, fingers
looped in the handles so the cups hung in a cluster. "You

haven't heard that story? It's really nauseating. Dusty took the field crew to this place called the 'Slit and Run' for dinner. I thought it looked kind of dark, you know. Then we got inside, and there were these two women onstage who must have weighed four hundred pounds each. Man, I got to tell you. The place didn't even serve food. My gag reflex started early and went into overdrive when Dusty got up to dance with Muffet—"

"Muffet?" Maureen narrowed her eyes at Stewart. "You danced with Muffet?"

"I—"

"Not for very long," Sylvia answered for him. "Muffet did one those twirly things and her size-fifty triple C's knocked Dusty off the stage and onto a table filled with empty Coors bottles. We got him to the hospital as soon as we could, but we spent half the night waiting for him to be sewed up. I mean, wow. No wonder they called it the 'Slit and Run.' That's what happened to us."

Maureen looked at Stewart. He was staring at Sylvia as if he longed to strangle her.

Maureen tapped him on the shoulder to get his attention, and in a fair imitation of Sean Connery, said, *"You call this archaeology?"*

LITTLE BOW SAT at the edge of Frosted Meadow Village's plaza. Across from him, his relatives gathered in front of the clay-washed face of the village, a two-story rectangular building that served as both living chambers and storage rooms. Children squirmed in their grandparents' laps, whispering questions. Warriors in knee-length blue war shirts encircled the plaza. Occasionally one man would lean sideways to whisper to another, but their expressions spoke more of curiosity, than apprehension.

They had assembled to watch the madman who pranced in the firelight.

Beyond the ring of warriors, at the very edge of the firelight, Little Bow's brother, Singing Mantis, stood tall and muscular, his backbone rigid as he observed the proceedings. He wore buckskin pants and a finely tanned white leather coat with long fringes on the sleeves. The fringes shimmered in the firelight. Singing Mantis was a renowned Trader. He ran the roads all the way to the great ocean in the west, where he obtained rare seashells, which he traded to the northern wild peoples for exquisitely colored cherts, and buffalo horn spoons. Grief strained his young features, making him look more like forty, than eighteen summers. He had lost both his wife and son in the past quarter moon. They had died of the wasting disease while he'd been away. He had yet to forgive himself.

Little Bow looked beyond the bizarre show in the plaza, and watched the mist that crept along the dark rim of Straight Path canyon. Thin starlit streamers twisted and billowed, blowing about like enormous spider webs. Evening People glittered across the night sky. He folded his arms, and his braid tumbled over the front of his gray-and-white rabbitfur cape. He had a chiseled face, his cheekbones sharp, his chin squared bluntly.

"Please, my husband," his wife, Marsh Hawk, asked in her weak voice. "Sit down."

She knelt on a deerhide at his feet. Shoulder-length black hair fell over her buffalo fur collar. She had a beautiful round face with a petal-shaped mouth and soft brown eyes. That is, until the wasting disease had consumed so much of her. Now her face had a sunken look, and despite her pregnancy, her bones stuck out. Her energy had ebbed away and a dullness had begun to creep into her eyes. When she coughed now, she brought up blood as often as phlegm.

As he exhaled, Little Bow's breath shimmered. Returning his attention to the ragged old man who spun around in the firelight, he said, "I don't like this."

"Wait . . ." Marsh Hawk began, and started coughing. The fit shook her entire body.

Little Bow leaned over and put a hand on her shoulder. "Do you need a cup of tea?"

Marsh Hawk shook her head.

Three moons ago they had lost their last child, a son, to the coughing sickness. Many people in the village suffered from it. A few whispered that the evil flew about on a witch's wings. In the past sun cycle, two of their children had died of the disease, and young Tadpole, their eldest, had disappeared without a trace. It was almost too much to bear.

Little Bow tenderly touched his wife's hair. "Are you warm enough? Shall I fetch you a blanket?"

"I'm fine, my husband." She gave him a frail smile, and touched her swollen belly. The baby had been growing for about five moons. "I just wish your daughter would stop kicking me in the lungs."

A shout rang out, and they both lifted their gazes to the old man who danced, or more correctly, stumbled around the fire. He looked like an outcast. Large patches of feathers were missing from his ragged cape, and his sparse white hair stood out at odd angles.

Little Bow whispered, "Do you think that is truly Stone Ghost?"

Marsh Hawk shrugged. "He says he is."

"But Stone Ghost is supposed to be a Powerful shaman. This old man looks like a derelict."

"Shh," the village Matron, Corn Mother, hissed. She sat to Little Bow's left with a blue-and-white blanket over her bony shoulders. Sixty-seven summers old, she had a skeletal face and jutting lower jaw. Thick gray hair matted her head. "I've also heard him called a witch," she said. "We do not wish to anger him."

Little Bow's gaze shot back to the old man. A witch? He had never heard that. Powerful shamans could be frightening, but they worked for the benefit of their people. Witches, on the other hand, thought only of themselves. Hatred and wickedness drove them to do inhuman things. They might extract their enemy's heart with a spindle and put it inside their own chests so they could live twice as long. Sometimes they stole the eyes of animals and left them in odd places to watch people. Little Bow's aunt had once found a bobcat's eye staring up at her from her tea cup.

Little Bow knelt beside his wife. "I thought the old man wished to speak with us about Tadpole's disappearance?"

"Yes, he does, but he said he had Dance to appease the Earth Spirits first."

"He calls *that* Dancing?" Little Bow grunted.

Short and as thin as a corn stalk, the white-haired old man kept whirling and stumbling, laughing, then whirling around again. His deeply wrinkled face glowed orange in the firelight.

"Have you ever heard that?" Little Bow murmured in Marsh Hawk's ear. "That Stone Ghost was a witch?"

"No, but—"

Stone Ghost suddenly stopped in midwhirl, and stared at Little Bow, as if he'd heard the whisper. The old man's bushy white brows lowered.

Little Bow went as still as a mouse under an eagle's shadow. His heart slammed his ribs. "Blessed Ancestors," he croaked to Marsh Hawk. "You don't think he . . ."

Stone Ghost turned away.

Little Bow grabbed the cape over his heart and let out the breath he'd unwittingly been holding. "Gods, for a moment, I thought he might have heard—"

"That is why you must keep your voice down!" Corn Mother hissed. "Witches have ears like a cougar's."

Stone Ghost dropped to the ground on his hands and knees and sniffed the sand like a dog.

Little Bow exchanged uneasy glances with Marsh Hawk and Corn Mother.

The old man was crawling around the firepit, smelling the hearthstones, and using his long hooked nose to poke at the cooking pots. When he stuck his nose to the hot teapot at the edge of the fire, he yipped and leaped sideways. His nostrils flared. He slowly crept forward again and lowered his head to the sand beside the teapot. The watching villagers had gone as still as rabbits, a new anxiety in their eyes.

Little Bow said to Marsh Hawk, "Gods. He's as dimwitted as a clubbed grouse. You don't think he's going to attend the Ceremony of the Longnight at Hillside village, do you? I may not go."

"You will go," Corn Mother ordered. "I have already sent word to Flame Carrier that we will attend."

"But, Matron! What if this old man is a witch? I do not wish to—"

"Shh!"

From inside his cape, Stone Ghost pulled a wooden bowl, and began scraping up sand.

Corn Mother studied this act for several moments then said, "Little Bow, why don't you go over, and ask him what he found?"

"Me?" he said, surprised. "You want me to go talk to a witch? I don't think that's a good idea. I'm not—"

"Don't speak so loudly!" Corn Mother said. "He could whistle and turn all of us into dung beetles!"

Little Bow closed his mouth.

Stone Ghost got to his feet and hobbled toward them with his bowl. Dark brown age spots showed through his wispy white hair and dotted his hooked nose.

The old man stopped in front of Little Bow and looked up through radiant eyes. "I found this footprint over there by the fire. I think it belonged to your daughter."

Little Bow peered into the sand-filled bowl. "I don't see a footprint."

Corn Mother looked, squinted, and pulled back.

Marsh Hawk looked, too. She lifted her brows and said to Stone Ghost, "How do you know it belonged to Tadpole?"

"Because the girl walked alone." Stone Ghost looked back and forth between Little Bow and Corn Mother. Then he turned to Marsh Hawk. "Your daughter did not have many friends, did she?"

Marsh Hawk nervously wet her lips. "No, Elder."

"It wasn't her fault," Stone Ghost said in a sad voice. "She didn't have the same strength as the other children. She couldn't play as they did, because of her headaches."

Little Bow's mouth gaped. His daughter had suffered

terrible headaches, and backaches. "How did you—"

"Her footprints." Stone Ghost shook the bowl of sand. "She stumbled a lot, like a duck that's been hit in the head with a rock."

"She *had* been hit in the head!" Corn Mother said. The white stripes in her blue-and-white blanket shimmered with an amber gleam as she leaned forward. "Tadpole claimed her Spirit Helper had done it to teach her lessons."

Stone Ghost peered at Corn Mother like a lizard seeing a shining fly. He edged over and sat down cross-legged in front of her. Corn Mother looked as if she might bolt.

Firelight gilded the left side of the old man's wrinkled face. "You didn't think it was her Spirit Helper."

Corn Mother shook her head. "Well, no, I—I thought it was one of the other children, but Tadpole would never name her assailant."

"Who was her Spirit Helper? Did she say?"

Corn Mother's gaze darted here and there across the sky, anything to avoid meeting the old man's intense stare. "It has been a long time, but I believe she said Wolf was her Helper? Is that not correct?" She turned to Little Bow.

He nodded, swallowing hard, his mouth suddenly dry. "Yes. Wolf. He visited her for six Blessed moons before she disappeared, told her wonderful stories of great heroes, and brought her strange gifts."

"Gifts?" Stone Ghost asked.

Marsh Hawk said, "Yes, Elder. Wolf brought Tadpole many gifts: turquoise bead anklets, exquisitely carved shell bracelets, pendants made from magnificent stones that we had never seen before. Tadpole said that Wolf had brought the gifts from the belly of the world."

Stone Ghost studied the elders seated before the clay-washed village and the dogs that lay beside them. He surveyed the ladders sticking out of the rooftop entries.

"And how many times a moon did this visitant come?"

Little Bow said, "Two or three times a moon, Elder."

Stone Ghost didn't say anything for a time.

Little Bow asked, "What are you thinking, Elder?"

Stone Ghost lifted his chin toward the village. "Show me where your chamber is, Little Bow?"

Little Bow pointed to the far western end of Frosted Meadow, to the little square window under a line of roof poles. "There, Elder. In the corner on the first floor."

"You enter from the roof, yes?"

"Yes, Elder. . . . Well, adults do. We have another window that you cannot see from here. It faces west. Our children often go in and out that way, though we discourage it, of course."

The wrinkles drew tight around Stone Ghost's mouth. As if speaking to himself, he whispered, "That's how he lures them out."

Marsh Hawk twisted her hands in her lap. She got on her knees. "Elder, may I speak? Another woman went missing from Starburst Village a few days ago. I heard they found her mutilated body in the village plaza, but before they could properly care for her, she vanished. I'm frightened."

Stone Ghost nodded. "Speak."

"Sometimes our daughter would wander home very late at night and crawl in through that window. Her head would be bloody. It terrified me. I begged her to tell me who was doing that to her, but she would only mutter, and weep, and claim that her Spirit Helper was punishing her. We called in Healers from as far away as half a moon's run, but none of them could cure her. The headaches finally got so bad, we asked the *Kokwimu* from Hillside village to open her skull to release the evil Spirits."

"Cloudblower." The old man bowed his white head, and his hooked nose glimmered with a fine coating of dust. "She is a great Healer. Did her treatment help?"

Little Bow saw his wife's eyes blur, and gently put a hand on her arm. When Marsh Hawk didn't answer, he said, "It seemed to, Elder. But shortly after Tadpole recovered, she disappeared."

"Indeed?" Stone Ghost said. "How did it happen?"

"Tadpole went out to collect kindling for the fire one night and never returned. We hunted everywhere for her but found nothing."

Stone Ghost poked at the sand in his bowl, and frowned as though he could see images shimmering there. "Did she vanish during the winter?"

Corn Mother blurted, "Yes!" and she gazed curiously at the sand. "It snowed the night she disappeared. You saw that in the bowl?"

Stone Ghost's eyes flared. "Why, yes. Did you think I made it up?"

"N-no."

Stone Ghost turned back to Little Bow. "You found no tracks?"

"We found nothing," Little Bow said. The same anxious futility he'd felt that night returned to gnaw at his belly. Long after the village had ceased searching for his daughter, he and Marsh Hawk had climbed the cliffs, calling her name, searching the rocks for threads, or tracks, or any sign that she might have passed that way. They'd found only sand and stone.

"When the headaches began," Stone Ghost asked, "did you check her to see where she had been struck? What part of the head?"

Marsh Hawk answered, "The right side, Elder. Always on the right side. I did not understand it. If she were being tormented by another child, surely he would strike her wherever he could. And the blows grew more fierce over time. At first she complained of mild headaches, then she stayed in bed for three days, and finally she began coming home bloody-headed and vomiting."

Stone Ghost stared unblinking at Marsh Hawk, but thoughts churned behind his luminous eyes. "The right side," he said in a low voice. "Of course."

"Why?" Little Bow asked.

Wind Baby gusted through the village, and the old man leaned over to watch the grains in the bowl blow about. Tiny curls of sand whipped across the surface. "How long ago did your daughter disappear?"

"Nine moons, Elder."

Stone Ghost watched the sand, but he had a look in his eyes that eluded Little Bow—not fear, not anguish, more like a man suddenly confronted with a horror too bizarre, too abominable to believe.

Little Bow said, "What is it, Elder? What do you see?"

The old man's bushy brows drew together. He hesitated, his mouth open.

Then, in a mink-soft voice, he said, "The strange agonizing grief that turns a human being into a monster."

Maureen squinted in the scorching sunlight that fell across the canyon. The distant cliffs wavered like heat-spawned illusions. Though she'd dressed in tan shorts, a white T-shirt, and hiking boots, the extreme heat made it almost impossible to breathe. She pulled her white canvas hat low over her dark eyes, and shifted to sit cross-legged on the edge of the excavation unit. Three feet below, Sylvia worked, carefully brushing away the centuries of sand that had accumulated over the young woman's bones. They'd begun work at six-thirty, rested between the hours of noon and two, and been working for two hours since then. It stunned Maureen that at four P.M. the heat could still be this suffocating.

Thirty paces away, outside the perimeter of lath stakes, Stewart excavated the site where Mrs. Walking Hawk claimed the Haze child rested. Maggie and her aunt sat in lawn chairs a few feet from the edge of the pit, watching. Both wore straw cowboy hats. Maggie kept patting her aunt's arm affectionately. They spoke in voices too low for Maureen to hear, but she could see Mrs. Walking Hawk smiling.

Maureen shifted uneasily. From the instant she had met Hail Walking Hawk, she'd sensed something amiss, as though the kindly old woman had reached inside her and scattered the pieces of Maureen's carefully ordered world. The man that Mrs. Walking Hawk claimed to have seen standing behind Maureen fit John's description. And that was a problem. Her own gut feelings lent weight to the vision. She often felt John nearby, talking just below her ability to hear, touching her with hands she could almost feel. Sometimes, when she missed him desperately, she sat down, closed her eyes, and tried with all her strength to summon him, to see him standing before her with that loving smile on his face—and she almost could. Perhaps that's what Mrs. Walking Hawk had seen. A longing so intense it had form.

"What are you thinking?" Sylvia asked. "You have a weird look on your face."

"I was thinking that people who would work in this kind of heat have to have rocks in their heads, eh?"

Sylvia grinned. She'd tucked her brown hair beneath her broad-brimmed straw hat, but sweaty locks glued themselves to her freckled forehead. Dirt streaked her face and ringed her green eyes. Her brown shorts, hiking boots, and the pale green long-sleeved cotton shirt and tank top bore a thick coating of dust. In a poor German accent, she replied, "Ve archaeologists must get used to all climates, Doctor, from ze Sahara to ze arctic." She turned to the notebook that lay to her right and jotted down a few notes. "You ought to give yourself a few days to get used to this. Why don't you go rest in the shade of the tents? I'll yell when I've bagged the skull."

"I'd rather fry. Two minutes in the shade and 'Cool Hand Luke' over there would never let me live it down. He'd start calling me a 'lab rat' to my face."

"There are a lot worse things you could call him back. If you need suggestions, let me know." Sylvia ran her shirt sleeve over her sweating chin.

Grasshoppers leaped at her movements, buzzing as they flew away, then rattling through the dry grasses. As the sun descended in the western sky, the slanting rays of light turned the sand into a sparkling golden blanket.

"Tell me the truth, Sylvia. Did Stewart really dance with Muffet."

Sylvia stood up and stretched her back muscles. "Not even I could make up something that gross. And the worst part came afterward. Dusty was, like, devastated. He wouldn't date for weeks. He kept telling women that he'd taken divine vows, which they naturally translated as VD."

"Sounds more like he didn't have any *v* at all."

"Yeah, I told him he should have claimed he was venereally challenged. Women take pity on men like that. You know? War wounds?"

Maureen swiped at a fly that dive-bombed her nose, missed, and said, "I don't know. I suspect the women might have reacted to Stewart's wounds like those killer bees in Texas. Did you read about that? The males were sterilized by a blast of radiation then released into the wild."

"No. What happened to them?"

"The females bred once, and died." .

Sylvia brushed sweaty brown hair from her freckled cheeks. "Wow. That really gives the name 'killer bee' a new twist."

"I'll say."

"Fortunately dancing with Muffet is about as close as Dusty gets to women, so I guess it's irrelevant."

"He really has problems, eh?" Maureen frowned at him where he stood in the pit across the site. His tanned face had an unearthly sheen. "Hard to believe. He has the looks of a blond god."

"Yeah. And the nightmares of Frankenstein."

Maureen looked down into Sylvia's green eyes. She seemed to be appraising Maureen, gauging her reaction. "He has nightmares?"

Sylvia nodded. "Every time he starts getting close to a woman he has really scary ones about being locked in darkness. He wakes up and can't breathe." She took a deep breath of the hot air. "I don't know all of it, but I think it goes back to his mother."

Wind blasted the site, flapped the green tents, and threatened to tug off Maureen's white canvas hat. She grabbed it just before it went and held onto the brim until the gust passed by and continued on down the canyon.

Sylvia wiped her trowel off on her brown shorts and knelt again. "So. Let's talk about you. Are you a lab rat? Is that what you really do?"

A puff of cloud passed overhead and the cool shadow briefly touched Maureen's face. It felt heavenly, soothing. Maureen breathed in the coolness, then the shadow drifted westward, and the heat beat down upon her again. She sighed and gazed at Sylvia.

"Pretty much. I enjoy that a good deal more than the classroom."

"God, where do you get the strength? I could never work in a lab day in and day out." Sylvia blew dust from the smashed cranium of the dead woman. It puffed around her face and settled on the brim of her straw hat. "I have to be outside or my soul grows snake eyes. I start looking at human beings like I'm the queen mother on LV426."

Maureen tried to place the reference. "Is that the planet in *Aliens*?"

Sylvia nodded. "Yeah. Remember that scene in the nursery where the queen hisses, and drops her jaw? That's just how I feel after a few days of being locked in a building with other people."

"You are definitely not a big city girl. Were you born in New Mexico?"

Sylvia squinted against the blazing sun. "I don't really know. I spent the first eight years of my life in foster homes in Idaho, being traded around, shoved from one pair of 'loving' arms to another."

The way she'd said "loving" shriveled Maureen's heart. "Sounds like a tough way to grow up."

"I didn't know any different. Not at first. I thought all kids traded parents four times a year. Then I turned six, and started school. That was rough. I'd make friends, then the angels at Social Services would move me to a new family halfway across Boise. I—"

"Were your foster parents that bad? I didn't think the state moved a child unless it had a reason to."

Sylvia's mouth quirked. She twisted her trowel in her dusty hands. "Well. Some of them were bad. I remember this one old man. God, I hated him. He used to come into my room late at night. I think I was about four at the time. I swear all I remember is the feel of his mouth over mine, sucking the air out of my lungs, and his rank smell—like gin mixed with stinking saltwater. The social worker told me the other foster kids in the house claimed it had gone on for months, but it's like my mind just blocked it out."

Maureen stayed silent. Sylvia's matter-of-fact voice was as haunting as the picture it painted of a lonely, frightened little girl, trying to figure out what was happening to her, why the people supposedly taking care of her were, instead, hurting her—a child so traumatized by the pain that her mind simply severed the neural pathways to the memories.

No wonder she and Stewart were friends. They'd both lived through difficult childhoods. Perhaps that's what he'd meant when he'd said, *"Sometimes I think she knows me better than I know myself . . ."* Sharing that kind of past must create a bond that outsiders couldn't really understand.

In a soft voice, Maureen said, "I've heard that the mind does that to protect people."

"I guess," Sylvia said. "Too bad it doesn't work better. I still wake up on occasion swinging my fists." She gave Maureen a sheepish smile. "By the way, don't ever walk into my tent unannounced."

"You want me to use a shotgun to get your attention first?"

"That'll work." Sylvia tipped her straw hat back on her head. "One time Dusty decided he'd play a joke on me. This was before he knew about the problems I'd had as a kid. He reached into my tent, grabbed the bottom of my sleeping bag, and started to drag me out. Ha, ha. What fun, you know? Thank God he has a distinctive scream. Woke me up before I had a chance to finish the job the Coors bottles started. I was just about to smash his nonexistent *v* to smithereens with my baseball bat."

"You sleep with a baseball bat?"

"Yeah." She used a paintbrush to whisk dirt away from the occipital bone that made up the base of the skull. "I'm not the sort of person who should own a pistol."

Maureen just stared.

"I still don't know how you got to New Mexico, Sylvia."

"When I turned eight, I was adopted by these great people in Idaho Falls. We moved to Albuquerque when I was ten."

"You've been in New Mexico since then?"

"Except for a few trips to nearby states. I'm pretty happy here. The archaeology is fabulous. The Mexican food is out of this world. That's all I need in life. Give me lots of sunshine, some broken rocks, a bushel of jalapeños, and I'm yours. What about you? Have you always been into anthropology?"

"My family did it to me. We used to travel to archaeological and historical sites for summer vacations. I guess I never got over that sense of wonder."

"Yeah, but that's field stuff. How did you wind up buried in a laboratory?"

A little defensive, she said, "The lab is where the real science begins, Sylvia."

"But it's cold and sterile. Where's the thrill of discovery?"

Maureen chuckled. "It's there every moment, Sylvia."

She thought about the bones that lay arranged on her lab table. Many tribes in North America believed that humans possessed two or even three souls, and that one of those souls stayed with the body forever. In a strange way, she believed it. When she first touched a bone it always seemed as though a long-dead person reached back to her across an infinite gulf of time, grateful for the sudden companionship.

"I don't know how to explain it," Maureen said, "but working on human remains is different from a potsherd or a stone tool. Bones *talk* to you."

Sylvia blew dirt from the hole in the dead woman's skull and answered, "I've heard something like that before."

"Really? Where?"

"Dusty invited a Hopi woman into one of our classes last year. She was a museum curator, and lectured about the museum's treatment of kachina masks. Talk about spook city. She said that each mask had a soul, and that she had to feed them blue corn, and rub them with sunflower oil to keep them happy, or they'd get pissed and wipe out the museum."

"She was serious?"

"Dead serious." Sylvia wiped her dirty palms on her shorts. "One of the other students in the class was Cheyenne. She added that her people believed that medicine bundles had souls, and she thought it was cruel to keep them locked in a museum, because they'd be lonely."

Sylvia stood, slapped the sand from her pants, and reached for the olive-drab ammunition box on the lip of the pit. She withdrew a thirty-five millimeter camera and a scaled "north arrow." She placed the arrow parallel with the pit wall, focused on the exposed burial, and snapped two quick shots before replacing the camera and the arrow. As she wrote the shots down in the photo log, she said, "So, like, do you believe stuff like that?"

"I'm a scientist. If I can't prove it I can't believe it." But that wasn't quite true. Maureen thought about her bones. They always seemed to be comforted by the warmth of her touch. "What did the Hopi woman say about the lonely Cheyenne medicine bundles?"

"She said, 'Why would they be lonely? They have each other.' " Sylvia gave Maureen an askance look and added, "I had bad dreams about talking artifacts for weeks. If you think the babbling toilets on TV are grotesque, you should see a coprolite chatting with a kachina mask. 'Hey, Wolf Kachina, check out this next tourist. What a babe, huh?' "

Sylvia brushed dirt away from the super orbital torus, the brow ridge, and Maureen frowned at the cranial depression fractures that scarred the bone. All had healed, except for the section smashed by the stone that had landed on her head. None of the fractures appeared to be the cause of death, though Maureen wouldn't know for sure until she had the skull in her hands.

Her gaze lifted to Dusty. As he bent over in the shallow pit, his T-shirt conformed to the muscles in his broad shoulders. Before she knew it, Maureen found herself studying the lines of his tall body, and the way the sunlight glistened from the sweat on his tanned legs.

"Enchanted by something, Washais?" Sylvia said in a knowing voice.

Maureen gave her a bland look. "How are you coming with that skull?"

"Give me another fifteen minutes, and it's yours. I still have to—"

Maggie Walking Hawk blurted, *"Where?"*

Maureen shielded her eyes.

Hail Walking Hawk pointed at something in Stewart's excavation unit. Excited murmurs broke out.

"When you're finished with the skull, Sylvia, give me a call. I'm going to go see what Stewart found."

"You got it." Sylvia waved "good-bye" with her trowel.

As Maureen walked, her eyes drifted over the canyon. Thick streaks of black minerals flowed down the buff-colored canyon walls, giving them a mottled, melted appearance. Two large ravens floated on the searing air currents above the rim, cawing and clucking.

As Maureen approached, Mrs. Walking Hawk glanced up. Gray hair blew around her wrinkled face, tangling with her eyelashes. She said, "Hello, Washais. We found that lost boy. No wonder I could hear him so good. He wasn't buried very deep."

"Really?" Maureen stopped at the edge of the pit, and gazed down. Stewart's green T-shirt clung to his back in sweat-drenched folds, and sun-bleached blond hair matted his temples under his rumpled cowboy hat. A thin coating of tan dust sparkled on his reflective sunglasses.

In the bottom of the pit, the tiny bones of a fetus rested in the abdominal cavity of a young woman. A stone rested over the woman's head, but Maureen could see the bones from the shoulders down. The excavation unit couldn't have been more than thirty centimeters deep.

Maureen knelt, gauging the size of the delicate bone

structure with a practiced eye. "The fetus was about three months," she said.

Stewart didn't answer. His attention rested on an artifact between the woman's third and fourth ribs. Maureen said, "Isn't it odd that this burial is so shallow?"

Stewart blew dust from the artifact, and reached for a brush. As he worked, he said, "It's not odd if you look at the stratigraphy of the other burials, doctor. This site looks fairly flat now, but when the burials were interred the site sloped to the south at a five-degree angle. Centuries of wind and rain redeposited the soil, filling in the low spots. None of these burials were dug very deep."

"Another argument for winter interment?"

Stewart used his tape measure and line level to record the provenience, then repeated the photo ritual Maureen had just seen Sylvia perform. As he opened his clipboard and painstakingly drew the artifact in on the excavation form map, complete with the measurements and depth, he said, "It certainly is, Doctor."

He set his clipboard aside, reached for a dental pick, and gently levered the artifact from between the ribs. A low admiring whistle came from his lips. "This is beautiful."

"What is it?" Maureen asked.

Stewart handed it up to her. "It's a jet pendant."

Maureen carefully rubbed away the dirt that clung to the red coral eye, and gaped at the exquisite workmanship. "Gorgeous."

Maggie walked around the pit, and said, "May I see it?"

"Of course." Maureen gave it to her, and Maggie took it back to her aunt.

Mrs. Walking Hawk felt the pendant with her knobby old fingers. "Tell me what it looks like, Magpie?"

Maggie said, "It's a shiny black stone, Aunt. It's been carved into the shape of a coiled serpent lying in the center of a cracked eggshell." Maggie tipped the pendant, and the coral eye flashed in the sun. "The snake has one red eye. It—"

Hail Walking Hawk gasped, threw the pendant to the ground, and began frantically wiping her hands on her yellow dress. "Get it away!"

"Why?" Maggie shouted. "What is it, Aunt? What's wrong?"

"*Basilisk!*" she hissed.

"What? I've never—"

"Go get me some eggs, Magpie! From the ice chest. Do it right now!"

Maggie ran.

Stewart's forehead furrowed. He studied Mrs. Walking Hawk for several moments, then said, *"El basilisco?"*

Hail Walking Hawk nodded. *"Si. El basilisco es como los brujos, duerme con los ojos abiertos."*

Stewart leaned against the pit wall. Without being asked, he translated, "The Basilisk is like the witches, for he sleeps with his eyes open."

Maureen said, "What's a basilisk?"

Stewart removed his sunglasses, and looked up at her with bright blue eyes. "A mythical creature. In South America it's a snake born from an egg laid by a cock. But in the southwestern U.S., any bird can give birth to a basilisk, and it's usually described as a shapeless, hideous creature, not a snake, but more closely resembling a malformed chick."

Maureen studied the agony on Mrs. Walking Hawk's wrinkled face. Her lips trembled. Maureen said, "Why is that terrifying?"

"It isn't. Unless you're afraid of monsters. If the monster sees you before you see it, you die. Lots of southwestern tribes believe that only witches can look into a basilisk's eye and live." From the corner of his mouth, he added, "Which is, incidentally, what you just did."

"I did?"

He nodded. "Uh-huh. A number of people die every year from doing the same thing. People suspected of witchcraft are forced to look at a pendant like that, and if their toes don't curl up on the spot, they're obviously witches and are put to death."

"Dead if you do, and dead if you don't?"

"Right."

Maureen turned when Maggie ran up with the bottom half of her T-shirt filled with eggs. Sweat coated her round face, and matted short black hair to her cheeks. "I brought six, Aunt Hail. Is that enough?"

Hail Walking Hawk said, "First, we have to get rid of the snake . . ." She used the toe of her shoe to push the pendant toward Stewart. "Put it back in the ground, Dusty. Cover it up. Hurry."

Stewart used his trowel to pick up the pendant, and it seemed to take an act of will for him bury it in the corner of the excavation unit, but he did it. Maureen suspected he would have looked the same if he'd just been forced to swallow cyanide.

Hail Walking Hawk waved a frail old hand. "Magpie, give everybody here an egg, then start rubbing yourself down. The pure white shell draws the evil of the monster out of the body."

Maureen took the egg Maggie offered, and watched Mrs. Walking Hawk. The old woman rubbed the egg over her face, then her arms, and finally, she lifted her yellow hem and started rubbing her sticklike legs. Maureen felt foolish, but she did the same, as did Stewart. When they'd all finished, Maggie collected the eggs, and said, "What should I do now, Aunt?"

"Go bash the eggs on rocks. Make sure they all break. That destroys the evil."

Maggie walked away and began dropping the eggs

onto a flat piece of sandstone. The yolks splattered the ground.

Hail Walking Hawk held her gnarled hands up to the sere blue sky, and began singing. The song had a soft haunting quality.

The commotion must have been too much for Sylvia. She crawled out of her excavation unit, and walked across the site with a curious expression on her lean dirt-streaked face. Her pale green shirt billowed in the breeze. "What's going on?"

Stewart put a finger to his lips, and waved her over. When Sylvia knelt beside him on the edge of the pit, Stewart whispered, "I found a witch's pendant. We've all been contaminated by the evil."

"Cool," Sylvia said, examining the bones of the woman and unborn child in the pit. "Where is it?"

"I buried it."

Sylvia's green eyes flared. "Why?"

"It was either that, or slit Mary the Hun's throat. She's the one who looked the monster straight in the eye, and refused to drop dead."

"Wow," Sylvia said, and squinted at Maureen. "Can I try next?"

Stewart put his reflective sunglasses back on and paused thoughtfully, watching Hail Walking Hawk. Under his breath, he answered, "Not unless you want bean burritos for breakfast the rest of the week."

The setting sun shot golden rays across the sky, and lit the mountains to the east. The snow-capped peaks shimmered with a rosy fire. At midday, Catkin had rolled her cape and tied it over her pack, running in her knee-length blue war shirt. But she could already feel the chill of night eating at her arms. Soon, she would have to stop and put her cape on again.

The day had been warm for the Buffalo Pawing Moon.

Most of the snow had melted. Mud puddles filled the trail, and sparkled like silver eyes across the desert.

Catkin had barely eaten in three days. She felt weak and light-headed. Thank the gods that old Stone Ghost had forced her to share his prairie dog soup. That was the only real meal she'd had. Otherwise she had contented herself by chewing on jerky strips as she ran, dipping handfuls of water from the puddles when she grew thirsty.

Stone Ghost. She shook her head. *What an odd old man.*

His daft demeanor one instant, and lance-sharp questions the next, made it seem like two people inhabited his body: one perfectly rational, the other utterly mad. His lunatic appearance, however, did have advantages. The old man could pry loose a person's most deeply held secrets before he realized what had happened.

What would he find when he questioned Matron Flame Carrier or the obnoxious Peavine?

Catkin leaped a large puddle and sprinted on down the trail. She could see the rim of Straight Path canyon in the distance, shining like a winding strip of pure gold. To her left, Father Sun sank through a frothy layer of Cloud People. If she could keep up this pace, she might make it home before full darkness veiled the land.

Catkin pulled her war club from her belt and carried it in front of her.

The trail curved around a drainage channel, and, for a time, headed west toward the sunset. Catkin watched the last molten sliver of Father Sun's face vanish below the horizon. The Cloud People gleamed in iridescent shades of crimson, orange, and the palest of yellows.

Over the past three days, she had considered every possible person in Hillside village who might be the murderer, but she just could not believe any of them capable of such a heinous deed. Granted, she had known the villagers for less than a sun cycle, but none of them showed signs of madness or of harboring a hatred deep enough to make sense of what had happened. Not even the loathsome Peavine would do such a thing.

Oh, Peavine had hated Ash Girl. Everyone knew that. Her rage began the day Ash Girl ran into the village proclaiming she had received a Spirit Helper. Peavine had refused to believe it. She had spent half her life seeking a Helper and never received one. Peavine accused Ash Girl of lying, of claiming she had received a Spirit Helper to get attention. Then Peavine started a rumor that Ash Girl had turned to witchery to advance herself. Several people sided with Peavine. Others did not.

But whatever side they took, few people liked Peavine. Catkin often wanted to whack her in the head to stem the maliciousness that poured from the woman's mouth, but Peavine would never think of killing someone and then redressing the corpse in a man's clothing. More important, Peavine, and everyone else, loved Hophorn. She wouldn't have hurt her.

Near the canyon rim, a line of wind-smoothed boulders stood. They looked like gigantic eggs that had melted together and frozen. The pale blue gleam of twilight turned them a rich shade of lavender. At the base of the boulders a natural cistern always held clean water this time of sun cycle. Catkin had drunk out of enough muddy hoofprints during the last two days. She longed for a drink that she didn't have to strain through her teeth.

As she neared the boulders, she heard a sound. Soft and muted.

She stopped.

The sound stopped.

Catkin clutched war club, remembering what Stone Ghost had said about the murderer. She quietly circled around to the right.

Moccasins scritched on gravel as the man eased around the boulders.

"Browser!"

He did not smile or greet her. He tucked his war club back into his belt and straightened his dark brown war shirt. His round face, thick black brows, and flat nose bore a sheen of tan dust. Cut in mourning, his hair hung around his ears in jagged layers.

"War Chief, what are you doing here? You are a hand of time from Hillside village."

"Things are much worse than when you left, Catkin. I feared that someone might lay a trap for you and old Stone Ghost. I have been coming up here every night. Just in case."

"Worse? What's happened?"

Browser looked around. "Where is Stone Ghost? Did he refuse to come?"

"He's coming, Browser. In a few days. He wanted to come alone. I cannot say why." She studied the deep lines that incised his forehead, and the weariness in the eyes. "Tell me what has happened?"

"Matron Flame Carrier called me to her chamber and asked where you were. I told her, of course. The next thing I knew, everyone in the village was racing about, carrying the news that Stone Ghost was coming to Hillside."

"She told people? Why would she do that?"

"Partly to shame me for dispatching you without her approval. And, I think, because she wished to warn people."

"But by alerting people, she has given the murderer time to escape."

"Or," he said pointedly, "to kill Stone Ghost."

"Blessed gods." Catkin heaved a tired breath, and walked by Browser to the sandstone cistern at the base of the boulders. Clear water sparkled in the catchment.

She dropped to her knees and drank until relief flooded through her like a cool tide, then she wiped her mouth, and looked at Browser. "He said something like that to me."

"What?" Browser came over and knelt in front of her, his brown eyes concerned. "What did he say?"

"Just before I left, I told him I would keep watch on the trails so that I could meet him and escort him into the village, and he said, *'I don't think the murderer will let you.'* I wasn't actually sure he was speaking to me, but now I wonder. Perhaps he knew this would happen."

Browser's cold expression thawed. "Perhaps."

Catkin dropped her head into her hands for a moment and enjoyed the sensation of being off her feet. Her legs tingled. When she looked up again, she found Browser staring at her.

"Forgive me, Catkin, for meeting you this way. I have not been sleeping well"—he shook his head—"but that is no excuse. I am grateful for your help. I know it was not easy for you to go to Stone Ghost. Not after the stories people tell about him. You were very brave to do this thing. I will not forget."

He looked away. Spider Woman's Butte thrust up like a square tower in the middle of the canyon. He seemed to be studying it. "That crazy old Trader, Mossmouth, came through yesterday, Catkin. He said that a woman is missing from Starburst Village. She disappeared four days ago."

Starburst sat at the western end of the canyon. Small, and very poor, barely twenty people lived there. Fire Dogs had raided them last autumn, taking all of the corn, bean, and squash the villagers had stored for the winter. Every day they scrounged for food.

"Did the raiders kill anyone?"

Browser shook his head. "No."

"What did they steal?"

"Nothing."

Their gazes held, hers curious, his desperate.

"I don't understand."

He clenched his jaw, and his teeth moved beneath the brown skin. "The Trader came through to deliver a message, Catkin. One of minor importance, but it caused me to think and wonder—"

"A message for whom?"

He got to his feet, and paced back and forth, his hands up as though in surrender. "I do not even wish to think about it. I—"

"But you are thinking about it, so tell me."

Browser slowly lowered his hands. "Cloudblower."

"Yes? And?"

"Mossmouth stopped to tell Cloudblower that the little girl she had Healed in Starburst Village was much better."

Catkin's eyes narrowed when she caught his meaning. "Browser, Cloudblower and Hophorn go on a Healing trip to the smaller villages every half moon. There is nothing strange about that."

"I know. It just seems odd that the woman disappeared the same day they were there."

"Coincidence. Cloudblower and Hophorn are not killers." Catkin watched him struggling with himself, desperate to find the person who had murdered his wife. "Leave it, Browser. You are looking in the wrong place."

"Probably," he granted, and kicked at a loose stone. "The Trader also said that he'd heard Stone Ghost was visiting Whitetail Village."

"Whitetail?" She scowled. "What was he doing there?"

"Whitetail is on the way here. That is another reason I came tonight. I was certain he would be with you."

Catkin tugged at a clump of mud on her sleeve. Perhaps the old man had friends in Whitetail Village. He had told her he would be along "soon enough," not as soon as possible. He had the right to stop anywhere he wished.

Catkin said, "How is Hophorn?"

"She has moved back into her own chamber, but she has not regained the power to speak."

Catkin jerked as though she'd been struck in the belly. "She has lost her power to speak?"

Browser closed his eyes a moment. Catkin knew that they had been lovers in their youth. He must be hurting for her.

"Forgive me. I forgot you did not know. Cloudblower says people often lose the ability to speak when they are struck on the left side of the head. She also says Hophorn may relearn to speak, or that her ability might return in a flash."

"Blessed Spirits," Catkin murmured. Hophorn loved nothing better than talking, and laughing with people. This must be like a knife in her heart. Catkin suddenly felt too tired to move. "How is Hophorn taking it?"

"Better than I would be. She called me to her chamber three times yesterday to try and tell me something. She grunted, and gestured, and fought to make words, but she couldn't, Catkin. I asked her a hundred questions about who had attacked her, but all she could do was moan and wave her arms. It tears my souls to see her like this."

Hophorn and Cloudblower were the two most beloved people in Hillside. Villagers must be frightened and angry.

"Why her, Browser? I do not understand any of this."

"I think she just happened to be there when the killer came, and he—"

Catkin's head snapped up. "You think he was surprised to see her there?"

"Yes. He must have been. I mean—"

"Then the murderer was an outsider."

Browser frowned. "Why?"

"Because, Browser. Everyone in Hillside Village knew Hophorn would be keeping the burial fire. The Sunwatcher always does. If the killer did not—"

He stared hard into her eyes. "Perhaps he was a Fire Dog after all."

"Or one the northern Tower Builders. They worship animal gods, and know nothing of our ways."

In elation, Browser gripped her hands. Then, just as quickly, his smile vanished. "No, Catkin. An outsider would have killed Hophorn, not just wounded her."

"But, didn't he try to?"

Browser released her hands, and got to his feet. "I don't think so. Cloudblower said that the injury was not that bad. She opened the skull anyway, to release some of the evil Spirits, but she told me yesterday that she thinks Hophorn would have lived without her efforts." Browser gave Catkin a sidelong look. "I think the murderer wanted Hophorn to suffer."

A slow fire built in Catkin's veins, part hatred, part fear. She rose on shaking legs and looked at her soaked moccasins and mud-spattered blue war shirt. She had been dreaming of her first meal at home, eager for the warmth of a fire and a hot bowl of cornmeal mush flavored with pine nuts and dried beeweed leaves.

She said, "How are you, Browser? Are you well?"

Browser's thick black brows pulled together over his flat nose. He let out a breath. "No. Gods, no." He shook his head. "I can't think. I can't sleep. I can't even concentrate on important things people tell me. By the time they've finished, I've forgotten why they came to speak with me at all. I—I feel like a kicked dog, Catkin. I just want to run away."

Catkin put a hand on his broad shoulder. "Come. Let's go home and talk."

CATKIN LAY ON her side, wrapped in a thick buffalo hide. The crimson gleam of the warming bowl fluttered over the ring of blue diamonds she had painted on the white walls near the ceiling. She watched it absently.

She and Browser had returned home to an eerily quiet village. No fires had burned in the plaza. No dogs had barked to greet them. The sounds of playing children had vanished. Flame Carrier had sent for Catkin immediately, had questioned her about Stone Ghost, and had told Catkin that most of the villagers had retreated to their chambers, afraid to come out until the murderer had been caught.

Catkin had walked to Hophorn's chamber to check on her health and found Jackrabbit standing guard. The Sunwatcher had been sound asleep inside, her face twitching. Next, she'd tried to visit Cloudblower, but the Healer's chamber had been empty.

Catkin sighed.

Usually at this time of night, laughter and the crying of infants rang out from nearby chambers. Tonight, only the sound of coughing competed with the wind. A powerful gust shook the ladder that led through the round entry hole in her roof.

Catkin snuggled into the furry warmth of her hide and closed her eyes. Red wings of light danced across the insides of her lids. She wondered what Wind Born would say to her tonight. What advice he would give her. About the insanity in the village, the murders. About Browser.

A sad smile touched her lips. The first instant her heart began to yearn for Browser, Catkin had seen Wind Born peek from her soul, frowning gently in disapproval. Wind Born would think Browser brash and headstrong——a buffalo bull who rampaged about, growled, and waved his horns for no reason. Browser could be, of course, though he usually tried to think before he acted.

Perhaps that's why he had snared her heart. Browser had not thought before he'd rescued her from the Fire Dog camp. No thoughtful war chief would have abandoned his fleeing war party and risked his own life to save one person. In similar situations, Catkin had seen Browser leave men behind.

She still did not know why he had come for her.

She took a deep breath of the warm smoky air, and sleep taunted at the edges of her souls, tugging at her like the arms of a lover.

She yawned and rolled to her back. Starlight streamed into her chamber. The room sparkled. She watched the elusive wisps of smoke that fluttered through the chamber, licking at the ceiling poles. Each wisp that escaped through the roof hole flashed in the starlight before it vanished.

Just as sleep began to overcome her, she heard a faint voice call, "*Catkin? Are you awake?*"

She braced herself on her elbows and blinked the sleep away, then she dragged herself to a sitting position. "Come, War Chief."

Browser climbed down the ladder into her chamber. His flat nose and jaggedly shorn black hair gleamed with a reddish hue. He wore a plain buckskin cape over a long red war shirt and black leggings. He stood awkwardly.

Catkin rubbed her tired eyes. "Are you well, War Chief?"

"I came to apologize." His arms flapped against his sides in frustration. "When I met you on the trail, I acted poorly. I knew you would be exhausted and hungry. I should have at least offered you the jerky I carried in my belt pouch. I just—I was not thinking, Catkin. I do not seem to think at all these days. Forgive me."

"Do not fret about it. I was fine. I am still fine."

Browser ran a hand through his black hair, and his gaze searched her chamber, as if eager to look at anything but Catkin.

"War Chief," she said. "Please. Sit down." She gestured to the mat on the opposite side of the warming bowl.

"Yes, all right. If you're sure I'm not disturbing you."

"Sit."

Browser sank to the floor, and tossed another twig onto her warming bowl. Flames danced around the fresh tinder. "I don't know what's the matter with me, Catkin. I feel like I am falling to pieces inside. I no longer know who or—or even what I am. I—"

"Browser," Catkin said and leaned back against the wall with her buffalo hide around her shoulders. Long black hair streamed down the front. "You just lost your wife and your son. Did you expect to feel whole? Of course you are wobbling."

His buckskin cape draped his tall body in firelit folds, accenting the breadth of his muscular shoulders. When he lifted his gaze, Catkin could see anguish in every line of his handsome face.

"What is it, War Chief?"

He shook his head, and gestured to the teapot that hung on the tripod to the right of the warming bowl. Cups, bowls, and horn spoons nested beneath it. "May I?"

"Of course. It's yucca petal tea. It should still be warm."

Browser dipped a gourd cup full and sipped. Steam swirled around his face. "Did you eat?"

"Yes. Are you hungry?"

"No, I ate with He-Who-Flies and Jackrabbit. There wasn't much conversation. All of our warriors are exhausted, Catkin. I've had Whiproot and He-Who-Flies standing guard with me at night, then Skink, Jackrabbit, and Water Snake stand guard during the day. Worse, people are frightened, so they often go to visit warriors during their sleep time, to ask them questions, to share theories with them. No one is sleeping well."

"You least of all."

He stared unblinking at her and pain welled in his dark eyes. His voice came out low. "Catkin, have you ever had the sense that you really knew what was happening, yet you didn't know at all? As though your souls had suddenly stopped speaking with each other?"

Wind gusted through the roof entry, and the warming bowl spat and crackled. Catkin pulled the worn softness of her buffalo hide more tightly around her.

"I think I know what you mean. Why? What do you sense is happening?"

His thick brows drew together, and he turned his gourd cup in his hands, as though not certain he wished to answer. Finally, he extended his right hand, the palm open. Firelight flickered through the hair on his arm. "Sometimes I feel the answer right there, in my grasp, but I can't close my fingers around it. The only thing I know for certain is that everything is tied to my wife. She is the center of this whirlwind, Catkin." He tightened his hand to a fist, and shook it. "I *know* it."

As though suddenly needing room, he set his cup on the floor, got to his feet, and paced across her small chamber. When he passed through the stream of starlight, his face glowed a silvery blue.

Catkin smoothed her fingers over the warm buffalo fur,

thinking about things Stone Ghost had asked her. "Browser?"

He stopped and looked at her. "Yes?"

"Did you ever . . ." She hesitated. It was none of her concern, and he might tell her that flatly, but she had to ask. "Did you ever beat your wife?"

His mouth opened in disbelief. "Why would you think that, Catkin?"

"I don't, but, Stone Ghost asked me if you had ever beaten her, or berated her in public, and I—"

"What purpose did the question serve? Why did he ask?"

She gestured lamely. "He told me something I didn't understand. He said that for a murderer 'life is bondage, and murder is freedom,' and that if we wished to find the murderer we must discover what binds him. Then he . . . he asked me why I didn't like your wife."

"What did you say?" he asked mildly.

"I said that she was not a kind person, Browser."

"Go on."

"Stone Ghost asked who she was unkind to, and I said you." She stared into the dark wells of his eyes. "That's when he asked me if she'd had a reason to be unkind to you, if you beat her or berated her in public."

Browser knelt in front of the warming bowl again and picked up his gourd cup. As he frowned down into the pale green liquid, he said, "I never hit her, Catkin. I give you my oath. There were times when we argued outside, in the plaza, or down near the drainage, and there were people nearby. I may have embarrassed her in front of others, but not because I wished to hurt her. I just lost my wits for a moment."

"All of us can say the same, Browser."

He sloshed the tea in his cup, and gazed at her from beneath his lashes. "I never understood her, Catkin. When she was angry, she changed, became someone I did not know. Her eyes would suddenly burn, and her voice grew husky, and menacing. She would shout into my face, and wave her fists. I know it probably sounds cowardly, I am so much bigger than she was, but I always felt threatened." He tipped his chin up, and grimaced at the smoke crawling across the ceiling. "Many times, I admit, I wished to strike her. But I never did, Catkin." His eyes tightened. "I swear."

Wind Baby whipped around Hillside Village, battering the chamber ladders. A sustained clatter rose. People, awakened from sleep, started coughing. Infants wailed.

Catkin lowered her hands to her lap, and frowned at them. His every movement, every word, revealed the agony that ravaged his heart.

"Browser, has it occurred to you that you may think your wife is the center of this whirlwind, because her death is the center of your personal whirlwind?"

"It's not her death," he said, and clenched his fists. "If it was only grief, I could manage it. But it's much more, Catkin. Guilt is eating my souls alive." He opened his hands and spread them. "I tell you truly, the gods will punish me for what I have done. I—"

"What have you done?" She had heard this same pleading tone in his voice a hundred times. He was a grand one for accusing himself of things he had not done, things he'd had no control over. "Tell me."

Browser's thick black brows drew together. He peered at the red coals in the warming bowl for a time. "Why didn't I go after her, Catkin? Why? When my wife came to me in the plaza the night we were organizing the war party, I knew she was frantic. I could see it on her face. If I had gone after her, she wouldn't be dead. She went out alone and got into some kind of trouble she could not get out of. If I'd been there, to protect her—"

"As I understand it, then, you are not sorry she's dead, just that you shirked your duties as her husband."

Browser stared at Catkin nakedly, his hurt reflected in his shining eyes. "I did not say that."

Catkin clamped her jaws. *It is not you the gods will punish, but your worthless wife.*

They would punish her for her incessant whining and the way she bullied Browser into doing things he did not wish to. For her storms of temper, and the way her voice could turn cutting and deep and send shivers up people's backs. For shaming Browser in front of his friends. But she could not say any of those words. Not when Browser looked so tormented.

Catkin extended her long legs across the white plastered floor. "Forgive me. What did you mean?"

He shifted his weight.

"I keep seeing her smashed face, and feeling the cold stiffness of her hand. The images stick to my eyes like boiled pine pitch." He unconsciously wiped his hands on his cape. "I am sorry she's dead, but I—I cannot find it in me to forgive her. She ran away when our son was dying, Catkin. How can I forgive that?"

"I'm not sure I could forgive that either, Browser. Tell me, would you have her back? If she were alive, and walked into your chamber tonight, what would you do?"

He shook his head. "I do not know, Catkin. I—"

"I think you do know."

His lips pressed into a tight line. "We would fight. That is as far ahead as I can see."

"Tell me what you would have done differently the night she disappeared? Would you have left your dying son alone, and run off to chase your wife?"

"No."

"Perhaps you could have asked someone else to hold your son, to comfort him during the last few hours of his life, while you chased after her?"

He shook his head vehemently. "Never."

"You could have sent one of your warriors after your

wife. Of course, everyone would have known you were using him to spy on her. Everyone would have snickered behind your back, but—"

"I wouldn't have *cared* about that! My wife—"

"On the other hand, she didn't have to run away, did she? She was a free woman. She could have stayed with your son. With you. She chose to go out that night, and it turned out to be a bad choice. But you could not have known. Could you?"

Browser lifted a hand and massaged his forehead. "That sounds very mixed up."

Catkin folded her arms. "You have asked yourself these same questions. I know you have. Why does it disturb you to hear the truth?"

Browser sank to her floor cross-legged, and dropped his head in his hands. "I tell you, she's the center of all this, Catkin. I do not know how, or why, but *she* is the heart of this insanity."

Catkin slid forward, picked up a gourd cup, and dipped it full of yucca petal tea. She took a long drink and said, "I believe you. When you figure out how to unravel the tangle, tell me. I will help you in any way I can. But right now, my friend, I'm fatigued. I need to rest."

Browser gazed at Catkin with an odd expression on his face. "Sometimes you are very blunt."

"I am always blunt. That's why you come here. You know everything I'm going to say long before I say it, but you let me tell you anyway. Browser, you are an honorable man. That is why you cannot say things you know to be true, and that is also why I do it for you."

He threw another twig into the bowl, and a flurry of sparks winked and drifted lazily toward the roof hole.

"I fear you are the only person left who thinks I am honorable. Over the past few days, almost everyone in the village has turned their backs on me. Some have even dared to ask me directly if I killed my wife." He smoothed out a fold of leather in his buckskin cape. "It's my fault. All of it."

"Why?"

Wind gusted down the roof entry and fanned the warming bowl. The coals flared, and the red gleam flickered in his hair and eyes.

"If I had been kinder to my wife, treated her better, people would not now suspect me of hurting her."

"Blessed Ancestors, Browser," Catkin said. "You *would* have been kinder to her if she had given you one instant of kindness herself. Love requires watchfulness and nourishment or it withers. You stopped watching long ago. And she stopped nourishing. The soul of your joining has been dead for sun cycles. The only thing she ever gave you that brought you joy was your son."

At the mention of Grass Moon, he bowed his head, but she could see the torment on his face. He had loved that little boy more than his own life.

Gently, Catkin said, "Browser, you must stop this. You are shredding your heart over something you could not have changed. Surely, you know that."

A weary smile bent his lips. "I thank you for caring enough to speak straightly with me. I'm going to go now. I know you are exhausted. I probably shouldn't have come at all, but I—"

"Before you go," she said, "there is something I wish to ask you."

He looked at her, nodded. "Ask."

"For almost a sun cycle you have lived within a day's run of your great-uncle. Why have you never gone to see him?"

Browser waved a hand. "I barely know him. I suppose I feared he wouldn't remember me."

Catkin's dark eyes narrowed. "Did it never occur to you that he might be lonely? Or need help? He lives by himself in the middle of the desert."

"No," Browser said, and propped his hands on his hips. "It never occurred to me. Holy people seem to need privacy more than ordinary people. I have always assumed my great-uncle lived alone, because he wished to be left alone."

Catkin finished her tea and placed the cup beneath the tripod. "Have a pleasant evening, War Chief."

"And you also, my friend."

He climbed up the ladder and out into the starlit night. Catkin could hear his steps patting across the rooftop.

She sucked in a breath of the smoky, cedar-scented air and watched the crimson light flutter over her walls. The blue diamonds that ringed the ceiling shone a deep dark purple.

The tone in Browser's voice when he spoke about his dead wife had pricked her nerves. His gut feelings usually turned out to be correct. If she were the heart of this insanity, he might be the only one who would know.

But what had his wife ever done to cause such a calamity?

Perhaps it had begun long ago, before Catkin joined the Katsinas' People.

Catkin curled onto her side and drew her furry buffalo-hide up to her chin.

That would merit some thought.

As he walked across the site, evening light streamed across the canyon, lavender and glowing. Dusty glared up at the hazy sky. They had passed into the first week of September; the weather patterns had to break sometime, didn't they? Looking around at the sere land, he could imagine how the Anasazi must have felt as the drought deepened.

He stopped in camp and poured a glass of water from the jug that sat on the Bronco's shaded north side. He drank half and poured the rest over his head, savoring the feeling as it ran down his sweaty face, neck, and into his dust-streaked brown shirt.

Opening the Bronco's door, he leaned in, opened the center compartment, and pulled out the cell phone. He checked the battery charge and signal. Not too bad today: he had four bars of power.

He pressed in the numbers and hit "Send."

While it rang, he turned, looking back toward the excavation. He could see Sylvia perched on a back-dirt pile, head bent as she recorded the locations of each bone Maureen lifted from the pit floor.

After seven rings, Dale's gruff voice greeted, "Robertson. Go ahead."

"Hey, Dale, it's Dusty."

"Good to hear from you. I tried calling earlier."

"The phone's been out. No signal. I—"

"I'm about to leave here. Is there anything I need to bring?"

"That's why I called. We need burial boxes. We're up to ten skeletons now, counting the little guy."

"Little guy?"

Dusty shoved wet blond hair behind his ears. "I guess you might as well know now as later, we're outside the impact area. I've got a woman with a fetus—"

"How *far* outside the impact area?"

"About five meters."

Silence.

"Listen, Dale, Hail Walking Hawk, our Keres monitor, told me there was a body there. She insisted that I dig the unit, so I did."

Dusty winced at the curse words.

"You know, don't you," Dale continued, "that we are now in violation of our Antiquities Permit, our fieldwork authorization, the project scope of work, and with the proper incentives, the government could prosecute us for violations of the 1906 Antiquities Act, the Archaeological Resources Protection Act, and a host of other rules and regulations."

"Yeah, but . . ."

"Yeah, *but?* William, I allow you a great deal of free rein, but this is—"

"Necessary," Dusty finished. "The Indian monitor demanded we dig the unit. You can use that to rock them back on their heels at the next Pecos Conference. Not only that, Maggie agreed. That means that if anything comes of this, we were acting in compliance with NAGPRA, the American Indian Religious Freedom Act, and the authorized officer was on our side."

A pause. "We need something in writing, William. I don't want the Department of the Interior nailing my butt to one of their bureaucratic walls. A dead archaeologist is the sort of thing they'd consider decorative."

Dusty smiled. "I'll talk to Maggie about an authorization letter."

"Please do." Displeasure dripped from his voice.

"Remember the burial boxes, okay? About fifteen. You know, the ones you pirated from University of Arizona when the NAGPRA people cleaned out their comparative collections. Oh, and we need another ten rolls of film, another stack of forms, ten more boxes of Ziplocs, and that box of empty soil sample sacks that's back behind the floatation equipment."

"Done." Dale said, "How is Maureen adapting to the site?"

Dusty stepped onto the running board, boosting himself high enough that he could see over the Bronco's blue top to the excavation. Maureen had coiled her long braid on top of her head. Her sweat-soaked T-shirt clung to her body like a second skin, accenting her full breasts and narrow waist. Dusty sighed. If he had to dislike a woman, why couldn't she be ugly?

"The good doctor is on her hands and knees, Dale. She

wanted to remove the burials herself. She didn't like the way that Sylvia and I were doing it. She says that archaeologists do better work with backhoes than we do with trowels. But she's spent half the day on a single skull. It's like she's never had to deal with a timetable in her life." He made a face and uttered the worst slight he knew. "She's definitely an *academician*."

"Besides spending your time digging units outside of the impact area, and Maureen's attention to detail, how is progress otherwise?"

Dusty stepped down to the ground, and braced a hand on the open door. "Behind schedule. I don't suppose you could find us some more field crew? I'll take any warm bodies you can scrounge."

"William, we have to be out of there by the first of November. That's the scheduled date for completion of the fieldwork." Dale's voice had taken on that no-nonsense tone that Dusty had come to hate over the years.

"No one expected a dozen burials, Dale. The preservation is extraordinary. Dr. Cole thinks she can even get a handle on stomach contents from the phytoliths."

"Well, do what you have to but we need to move more dirt, William."

"Right. See you when you get here. And don't forget the drinks. We're down to warm water in the coolers, and the Guinness is thinning out."

"A tragedy of Biblical proportions. I'll be there this afternoon."

Dusty pushed the "End" button and slipped the phone back into the Bronco's central compartment. As he leaned over the hood, he thought about the woman he'd exposed and the fetus cradled in the curve of her hips. He'd buried the basilisk in the corner of the pit, but it still gnawed at him. It hadn't felt evil to him, but it did have an odd "presence." Every time he got near it, he found himself straining to listen, as if for a voice that might or might not be there.

He stared at the pit. "I know you're calling me," he whispered. "I just don't know what you want."

WIND BABY RACED through the scrubby weeds and whimpered across the fallow cornfields. Wraiths of dust traced his path.

Browser walked across the roof of Hillside Village toward the ladder that led to the ground below. The juniper rungs had iced with the coming of night. He placed his sandals carefully. As he climbed down, he scanned the darkness. Boulders cluttered the base of the canyon wall to his left. Lingering patches of starlit snow veined the rocky crevices.

Preparations for the Celebration of the Longnight had begun that morning. The scents of blue corn cakes, simmering beans, and roasted pine nuts wafted from the roof entries. In two days, people would begin trickling in from the smaller villages, expecting to hear the news, to feast, and to Sing and Dance. Each person would be in a constant state of prayer, sending their sacred energy to Father Sun. After the long sun cycle, Father Sun was often too weak to start the journey back to the north by himself. His people had to help him. They did this willingly, with all their hearts.

Browser stepped to the ground and walked toward the towering ruin of Talon Town. Wispy clouds blew in from the west. They raced through the darkness as though fleeing some hidden sky monster. Browser had passed most of the day stalking back and forth from Hillside Village to Talon Town, avoiding his own chamber, because he could not bear the sadness that came over him when he was there. Few people spoke to him these days. They passed by, their glances wary, troubled. The entire world seemed to be waiting to see what he would do next.

Thank the gods for Catkin. Though her callous manner often upset him, she had an uncanny ability to ferret out his deepest fears, and lay them before him like a collection of cups and bowls. They lost their power when he could see them clearly. Without her, he suspected he might go mad.

Browser rounded the southeastern corner of Talon Town, examined the frost-coated road that ran south from Talon Town's entry, cut across Straight Path wash, and headed for the far canyon wall. Stone Ghost should come up that road. Browser held his cape closed at the throat and gazed at it longingly. The road resembled a broad glittering swath of crushed seashells.

Why *hadn't* he gone to visit the old man?

The question disturbed him, mostly because he'd never even considered going to see Stone Ghost. If his grandmother had lived, perhaps he would have felt differently. She insisted on family and clan unity and worked very hard to properly arrange marriages to assure that unity. With her death, however, the clan had disintegrated. Browser's father had been killed in a battle when he'd seen four summers. His mother was barely twenty-two when she became clan Matron. She did not have the power or the personal strength to convince people to do what was best for them. Green Mesa clan had fragmented almost immediately. The in-fighting went from vociferous arguments to outright warfare. People separated into seven different villages. Each established their own rules and traditions and called their relatives "outcasts." Browser's village had been renamed "Green Mesa."

Browser had never heard Stone Ghost labeled an outcast, but after the old man solved his sister's murder, he left and never returned. No one in Green Mesa Village spoke of him, though the number of rumors that circulated outside the clan grew every year. By the time Browser had seen fourteen summers, he'd feared Stone Ghost as much as everyone else.

Still, he *should* have gone to see his great-uncle. His grandmother would have been greatly saddened by Browser's failure to care for her aging brother.

Burdened by his thoughts, he followed the curving wall around to the front of Talon Town. That sense of old Power, of darkness and blood, seemed to hang on the chill wind, as if pain had soaked into the very stones of the old ruin.

Whiproot stood guard on the roof at the southwestern corner of Talon Town. His chin-length black hair whipped in the wind as he lifted a hand to Browser.

Browser called, "I'm coming up, my friend."

Whiproot trotted along the roof, picked up the ladder, and lowered it over the side.

Browser climbed slowly, trying to avoid the worst ice.

No matter how much work the Katsinas' People did, cleaning and repairing, the smell of ancient destruction seeped from these rooms. The mixed odors of moldering plaster and smoke-blackened timbers offended his nose. Now the wind, moaning around blackened timbers and broken stone, mocked the wailing voices of the past, as though releasing them to the night.

He stepped off onto the roof. "How is everything?"

"Fine. Nothing unusual." In the starlight, Whiproot's heavily scarred face reminded Browser of a tangle of thin white ropes. "Cloudblower left and has not returned. Jackrabbit is still guarding the Sunwatcher's door. The night has been quiet."

Browser surveyed Talon Town. Frost covered every stone in the toppled walls and painted the five stories with glittering white. He turned his attention to Cloudblower's chamber. It sat in the southeastern corner, straight ahead of him, but he couldn't see it very well. Piles of debris surrounded the collapsed kiva that sank into the ground in front of Cloudblower's chamber. As he gazed along the line of rooms that faced west, he saw Hophorn's chamber. It nestled in the middle of a three-room block about ten body lengths to the left of Cloud-blower's chamber. The plaster had flaked off, leaving the front of the room-block mottled, a splotchy mixture of white plaster and red stone masonry. Behind her chamber, four stories rose, each stepped-back, giving the ru-ined town a stairlike appearance.

He said, "Where did Cloudblower go? I was hoping to speak with her."

"Peavine's daughter, Yucca Blossom, the one with the coughing sickness, has a bad headache and fever. Cloud-blower went to see if she could help." The red-and-white blanket Whiproot wore rippled in the wind. He pulled it more tightly about his muscular shoulders.

Jackrabbit stood in front of Hophorn's chamber, watching them. Fifteen summers old, the youth had a guileless face, with wide brown eyes, and a pug nose. He held his shoulder-length black hair in place with a red headband. Browser waved at him. Jackrabbit lifted a hand in return.

"Has Jackrabbit been there since midday?" Browser asked, worried.

"I told him to go have supper two hands of time ago. I watched Hophorn's chamber while he was away."

"Why hasn't He-Who-Flies come to take his place?"

"Oh," Whiproot said in surprise. "I forgot to tell you. While you were away, He-Who-Flies developed a stom-ach ailment. He's been vomiting since early afternoon. Redcrop came to tell me. Jackrabbit said he did not mind standing guard for the night. It is his honor to guard Hophorn."

Billowing Cloud People crowded the western horizon, tumbling and shining, pushing toward Browser. He said, "Very well, but by midnight he will be growing weary. Call out to him now and then, just to make sure he is awake."

"I will, War Chief."

They stood quietly for a time, then Whiproot asked, "How is Catkin? Jackrabbit said she came in earlier, but I was asleep when she arrived."

"She is well. Just very tired."

Browser gazed southward, across the two mounds, to the shadowy canyon wall in the distance. In the brilliant light of the Evening People, he could make out every boulder and drainage. Dozens of small villages glittered along the length of the canyon floor. Their fires dotted the dark cliff face like strewn amber beads.

"Did Catkin say when we should expect Stone Ghost?" Whiproot unconsciously toyed with the war club on his belt.

"Soon. That is all we know."

Whiproot chewed on his lower lip. "Have you heard the news?"

"What news?"

"The Trader, Old Pigeontail, came through this afternoon."

"Indeed? What did he want?"

"He Traded for a few bags of corn and squash seeds." Whiproot hesitated. "He also said that Stone Ghost visited Frosted Meadow Village yesterday."

Browser's stomach muscles bunched. What was the old man doing? Selling his powers for handsome jewelry when the people of Hillside Village might be in danger?

"Why? Did Old Pigeontail say?"

"Oh, yes. It was a strange tale, War Chief. He said that Stone Ghost spent the evening collecting ghost footprints in a bowl."

"In a bowl?"

Whiproot nodded. "So he claimed. Apparently everyone else just saw sand in the bowl, but Old Pigeontail said that when Stone Ghost shook the sand, pictures formed."

"What kinds of pictures?"

"Pictures of a dead girl. Her parents and the clan Matron were apparently amazed by what he saw. Then, just before he left, Stone Ghost planted a prayer in the sand, and gave the bowl of footprints to the clan Matron."

Browser thought about that. "Frosted Meadow is less than a day's walk away. Why isn't he here already?"

Whiproot gestured lamely. "I cannot say, War Chief. He is very old, perhaps he has the joint stiffening disease, and cannot—"

A loud grunt split the darkness, followed by the sounds of a struggle. Jackrabbit cried, *"Help!"*

Browser and Whiproot spun around in time to see a katsina, a masked god, slam his war club into Jackrabbit's head.

"Blessed Ancestors!" Browser shouted. "Hurry! Get the ladder!"

Whiproot grabbed the ladder, pulled it up, and flipped it over the wall into the enormous plaza below.

Jackrabbit screamed and rolled, trying to crawl away. The katsina ran through a gaping hole in the wall near Hophorn's chamber and vanished.

Browser took the rungs down three at a time and hit the ground running. Whiproot's feet pounded behind him. When they neared the gasping Jackrabbit, Browser ordered, "Whiproot! See to Jackrabbit. If he is well enough, send him for help, but do not leave the Sunwatcher's door! Do you understand? Do not leave her alone!"

"I understand, War Chief!"

Browser sprinted for the gaping hole the *katsina* had disappeared into.

As he stepped inside, darkness enveloped him. He had been here once last summer. The walls formed a confused maze of interconnected chambers and kivas, like a rabbit's warren. Rubble cluttered the floors, and charred roof beams dangled from the ceilings. Finding his way would be . . .

Soft laughter filtered through the darkness, somewhere up ahead.

Taunting, daring him to walk deeper into the maze.

Browser drew his war club. He kept his gaze focused on the middle of the wall where the doorway stood, and placed his feet like a hunting cat. Despite his care, grit whispered beneath the tanned leather of his winter moccasins.

As he neared the wall, a lighter patch of gray defined the doorway. Browser stopped and listened.

He heard nothing and stepped through.

Starlight shot beams through a ragged hole in the ceiling. Dust glimmered in the silver shaft kicked up by a man's passing.

Browser gripped his war club and edged forward. He passed through two more rooms and entered a well of cold blackness. He crouched, blinking against the darkness, his war club raised. In the blackness, he could discern no doorway.

The silence ate at his nerves. Silence was a hawk's shadow just before it dropped on its prey. A wolf's eyes the instant before it leaped. It started as a mere lack of noise, then crept into a man's bones, and grew to a deafening roar that shook him apart.

Something moved ahead of him and to his right. The barest of sounds, like corn silk dropped on the floor.

Sweat trickled down Browser's jaw.

Had Jackrabbit gone for help? Even if he'd had to run

all the way to Hillside Village, it should take no more
than five hundred heartbeats for armed warriors to stream
to the rescue. How many times had his heart beat? One
hundred? Two?

*Wait. Someone will come. Then you can comb these
ruins until you find . . . what?*

The sight had stunned his senses. He could not be certain, but he thought the katsina had been wearing the
same clothing as his dead wife. The gloriously carved
wolf mask looked different, however, the colors bright,
as if freshly painted.

A god? Or a man?

Browser's lungs started to suck at the cold air, threatening to give away his position. He had to move to relieve the tension.

He took a step.

And a step sounded behind *him.*

Blind terror gripped Browser. He clasped his war club
in both hands, and turned to gaze back through the last
doorway.

A black silhouette stood in the shaft of silver light.

Browser lifted his club with shaking hands.

"War Chief?"

Browser did not answer. It could be a trick.

The man stepped closer, and Browser saw the oddly
shaped spikes on his war club glitter.

He called, "Jackrabbit?"

"Yes, War Chief! Are you well?"

Browser swallowed the lump that had grown in his
throat and turned back toward the far corner where he'd
heard the sounds earlier. They had stopped. He could not
recall how the chambers connected here. Was there a
passageway that led outside?

Browser backed out of the room, and said, "I lost him,
Jackrabbit. He could be anywhere in this crumbling hive
of rooms. How are you?"

Jackrabbit touched his head. "I feel sick. Whiproot told me to run for help, but just as I made it to the ladder, young Goathead called out from the road on the other side. He'd heard my cries. I told him to run for help, and I returned to aid you."

"I appreciate that. I—"

An agonized wail, like a cry ripped from a man's throat, carried to them.

Jackrabbit jerked around, and Browser gripped his arm with talonlike fingers. "Don't move."

"But what if Whiproot—"

"We can't rush out into the starlight. The killer might be waiting on the roof with his bow ready."

"But we can't just wait here like cowards!"

"*Jackrabbit!*" shrilled a voice that could have come from the deepest darkest underworld. It echoed through the ruins. "*Jackrabbit! Helllp meee!*"

Jackrabbit blurted, "Who is that? I don't recognize the voice!"

Browser edged to the next doorway, and stopped to examine it before he entered.

"*Oh, gods, helllp!*" The scream was inhuman.

Browser clutched his club with painful force and ran heedlessly through the next two rooms.

Another prolonged shriek cut the night.

He halted at the katsina's hole and peered out into the starlit plaza. Jackrabbit trotted up behind him.

"What do you see?" Jackrabbit panted.

Browser searched the piles of fallen stones, and heaps of windblown dirt. Nothing moved. But a sharp tang rode the wind.

Torn intestines. Blood.

"Stay here," he said to Jackrabbit. "I'll call if it's safe."

"But War Chief—"

"Just do as I say! Help will be here soon. Wait!"

Jackrabbit sank back against the wall. "Yes, War Chief."

Browser lurched through the hole and ran with all his might, his legs pumping, for the closest pile of rubble. He dove behind it and crawled on his belly until he felt safe enough to peer over the top. He didn't see Whiproot.

A cacophony of voices rang outside the walls, and Browser heard Catkin shouting, *"Hurry! Get the ladder up!"*

Browser's souls withered. He and Whiproot had left the only ladder on the inside of the town. Catkin had been forced to send someone back to Hillside to fetch another before they could get over the wall.

A long ragged scream erupted, followed by suffocating sobs.

Browser recognized that voice. He leaped to his feet and charged across the plaza, shouting, "Hophorn? Hophorn, I'm coming!"

As he ran, he caught a glimpse of Catkin as she raced down the ladder. People gathered on the roof, waiting their turns to climb down. Frightened shouts and cries filled the night.

Browser shouted, "Someone bring a torch!"

Catkin met him in front of Hophorn's door, and they both stopped dead in their tracks. She had risen directly from her robes. A wealth of long black hair cascaded over her knee-length blue shirt. She gripped a bow in her hands.

Pools of black blood filled the hollows in the hard-packed ground. The stench of death nearly overpowered them.

Browser called, "Hophorn? It's Browser."

She mewed pitifully.

"Hophorn? Where's Whiproot?"

Sobs.

Oh, gods. He reached for the leather door curtain, and

Catkin jerked him backward with such force Browser almost lost his footing.

Catkin glared at Browser and called, "Hophorn? Are you alone in there?"

A long pause.

Hophorn weakly answered, "Nnnooo. B-Browser?".

Those were the first words she'd spoken since her head injury, and they affected Browser like a Spirit plant in his veins. His heart raced.

Catkin and Browser took up positions on either side of the doorway. Three other warriors lined up in a semicircle around them, their bows nocked and aimed at the door. Jackrabbit stood among them, his feet braced, breathing like a hunted animal.

"I have the torch!" Cloudblower called.

Browser watched her climb down the ladder into the plaza with a blazing juniper bark torch. She wore a turkey-feather cape and white leggings. Long gray-streaked black braids framed her triangular face. The torch bounced as she ran.

Cloudblower handed the torch to Browser and backed away.

He nodded to Catkin.

As he jerked the door curtain back, they lunged inside at the same time, Browser holding the torch and his war club, Catkin with her bow swinging around for a target.

The instant light filled the room Browser saw blood; it splashed the ceiling and trickled down the walls. He couldn't move without stepping in it. The stench almost gagged him.

Orange torchlight fluttered over Whiproot's body. He lay on his back, his mouth covered with blood, his eyes open and staring sightlessly at the ceiling poles. His war club lay to one side. The right arm was rigidly extended; the left arm was tucked beneath his back, as if he'd twisted as he fell. His war shirt had been pulled up, the blood-soaked material wadded, as if by a fist.

Words caught in Browser's throat. A slit had been cut into Whiproot's exposed belly, and two sections of severed intestine protruded from the bloody wound.

Hophorn huddled like a terrified child in the corner to his left. A black-and-white blanket covered her body; she held it against her trembling mouth. A fine spray of blood speckled her face and long black hair.

Browser ran to her.

She gazed up at him with huge eyes.

"It's Browser," he said softly. "Are you all right? Did he hurt you?"

Her shoulders heaved, and it took Browser a few moments to realize she was being wracked by silent sobs. Her mouth opened, but no sounds came out. Pink rivulets rolled down her cheeks—tears mixed with blood—and dripped onto the blanket she clutched in her hands. He took her in his arms, and rocked her gently. "You are all right, Hophorn. He's gone."

She shook her head violently.

Catkin knelt beside Whiproot and placed her fingers against the big artery in his neck. Disbelief, followed by anger, tightened her eyes. She tipped him onto his side to check his back. "I'm sorry I wasn't here to help you, my friend," she murmured and gently lowered him.

Browser tenderly stroked Hophorn's hair. "Can you tell me what happened, Hophorn? Who did this?"

She whined: the cry a dying rabbit makes when it stares up into the eyes of a weasel smeared with its blood.

Catkin said, "I can tell you what happened," and got to her feet.

Browser looked up.

Catkin pointed to the sandal prints that had tracked through the blood. They looked like the work of dancers circling each other in some depraved ritual.

Catkin indicated the overturned pots along the north

wall, the scattered coals from the broken warming bowl. "Whiproot was wounded outside," she said, "that's what the splotches of blood are out there. Then he was forced to back into Hophorn's chamber." She pointed to the prints on the floor, "after that the killer ordered him to kneel down. These oval spots are knee prints. But Whiproot did not go without a fight. See these tracks? Whiproot was trying to shield Hophorn, to cut the killer off from reaching her. He must have leaped for the killer and knocked him backward into the pots over there. During the struggle, they crushed the warming bowl and scattered the coals."

Browser pointed to the blood on Whiproot's head. "Is that what killed him?"

"I cannot say. Probably. I'm sure it dazed him. He has two knife wounds on his arms and one on his neck. Maybe he was stabbed in the belly before the killer yanked his intestines out."

She bent over a shriveled length of bloody tissue that lay at the base of the wall. "This is gut, Browser. After he cut it out of Whiproot, he must have swung it around like a rope." She swallowed hard.

"Blessed gods," Browser whispered, cringing at the stippled clots of blood.

Catkin turned to Hophorn, a frantic glitter in her eyes. "Who did this, Hophorn? Did you see his face?"

"Easy," Browser said. "She's terrified."

Hophorn tried to answer, but it came out a suffocating series of pants.

Browser tightened his grip on the torch to stem the sudden trembling in his hand. "He was wearing a mask. A wolf mask. She would not have seen his face anyway."

Catkin jerked around and their gazes locked.

"The same mask—"

"I—I don't know. It looked freshly painted. Even in

the darkness, I could see black, red, and white bands—"

"War Chief?" Cloudblower called from outside. "May I come? Is Hophorn hurt? Are you hurt?"

Hophorn stuttered, "Nnn-no," and shivered as if freezing to death. She shoved out of Browser's arms and backed into the corner as far as she could.

"She is not wounded," Browser said. "But she is not well. Come."

Cloudblower stepped into the torchlit chamber, and Hophorn let out a blood-chilling scream.

Browser whirled, shocked.

"Hallowed gods," Cloudblower said, and shoved by him to get to Hophorn. "She has lost her senses!"

Hophorn flung off her blanket and scrambled madly for the door on her hands and knees, babbling, "B-B-Browssser! She. Knows. She . . . *knnnows!*"

Browser went rigid.

"Don't!" Cloudblower yelled and fell to the floor. She grabbed Hophorn, gathered her in her arms like a baby, and rocked Hophorn back and forth while she whispered into her ear. Hophorn's teeth chattered so loudly Browser could not hear Cloudblower's words.

He stared at Hophorn dry-mouthed, uncertain of what to do.

Catkin tipped her head toward the door, and Browser followed her outside. A mumbling crowd of about twenty people had coalesced in the starlight, and more climbed down the ladder as fast as they could. Browser could hear Flame Carrier shouting orders outside the town.

Catkin led Browser a short distance away, then demanded, *"What happened?"*

FLAME CARRIER'S BREATH puffed whitely as she climbed the ladder. Young Redcrop waited on the roof above, her oval face and large dark eyes shining in the light of the Evening People. She wore a red-and-black-striped turkey-feather cape that matched Flame Carrier's. Just seeing the girl made Flame Carrier feel better. Redcrop had left her chamber shortly after supper and had not returned. Flame Carrier had been concerned. A murderer was stalking the canyon, and the girl was out, by herself, taking unnecessary chances.

Frightened voices rose from inside the ruins of Talon Town.

Flame Carrier tried to hurry. When she reached the ladder's top rung, a gust of wind threatened to hurl her to the ground. Redcrop caught Flame Carrier's hand in a strong grip and helped her off the ladder and onto the roof.

"Thank you, child," she said, and patted Redcrop's hand. "Where is the War Chief?"

Redcrop turned and long black hair whipped over her face. "To the left, Elder. Near the First People's kiva." She pointed.

Most of the village milled in the broad plaza, their low voices hissing like a den of newborn serpents. As each person saw her standing on the roof, they elbowed the person next to them, and a hush fell.

Flame Carrier searched the huge crumbling town.

"What happened, child? Has anyone seen fit to tell you?"

Redcrop nodded. "Whiproot is dead."

"That much I've heard. Does his wife know?"

"No, Elder. Not yet. Wading Bird just went to fetch her."

Flame Carrier's chest felt like it was being squeezed by a huge rawhide band. She braced her feet to keep her shaking knees from buckling. "How did this begin?"

Redcrop gestured toward the knot of warriors outside of Hophorn's chamber. "Jackrabbit told me he was standing guard in front of the Sunwatcher's chamber when someone leaped upon him from the roof above. The tall man wore a sacred katsina mask. A wolf mask. Whiproot and Browser stood here, where we now stand. They heard the commotion, and climbed down as quickly as they could, but by the time they reached Jackrabbit, his attacker had fled into the dark passageways of the town."

"Did they catch him?"

"No, Matron. Browser and Jackrabbit went after the man, but they did not find him. Whiproot stood guard alone in front of the Sunwatcher's chamber. I don't know exactly what happened after that, except that he was killed."

"Is the Sunwatcher safe?" she asked anxiously. Hophorn had always been one of her favorites, a cherished friend and loyal supporter. The thought of losing her wrenched Flame Carrier's souls.

"Cloudblower took the Sunwatcher to her chamber. Hophorn looked terrified, but she seemed unharmed."

Flame Carrier heaved a sigh of relief. "Well, help me get onto this other ladder, child. I must speak with the War Chief."

"Yes, Elder."

Redcrop took Flame Carrier's left elbow, and steadied her while she maneuvered her sandaled feet onto the top rung. She descended slowly. Peavine waited at the foot of the ladder, her black eyes slitted against the wind that whirled through the plaza. A white blanket waffled over her shoulders; her short, black-streaked gray hair fluttered around her homely face.

As Flame Carrier neared the bottom rung, Peavine gripped Flame Carrier's right arm, and helped her to the ground.

"Thank you, Pea—"

Peavine hissed, "This is witchery, Matron."

Flame Carrier disentangled herself from Peavine and said, "Why do you say that?"

"The murderer was wearing the same white deerhide clothing that the War Chief's wife had on when you found her in the burial pit."

"Who told you that?"

"Jackrabbit." Peavine straightened, as if proud she'd discovered this appalling fact.

Flame Carrier's kinky gray brows drew down over her bulbous nose. "What sort of madman would do such a thing? What is he trying to prove?"

Peavine shook windblown hair away from her square face. "I think the clothes and mask are witched, Matron. They *give* him his Power."

"Blessed Spirits, Peavine!" Flame Carrier glanced around to see what might have been overheard. "Do not say such things aloud! You will have our people jumping at their own breathing!"

Peavine's black eyes tightened. "Perhaps we should be, Matron. Look what happens when we lower our guards." She extended a hand toward Hophorn's chamber, where Jackrabbit stood with a torch in his hand. The waves of wind blown light flashed on the blood that pooled outside the chamber.

Flame Carrier started across the plaza, and Peavine matched her stride.

"You should also know, Matron, that Hophorn spoke.

For the first time since her injury! It happened just before the War Chief entered her chamber."

Flame Carrier stopped, and turned. "What did she say?"

"No one told me, but she has not spoken since. I asked Cloudblower myself."

"I thank you for telling me. Now, go, Peavine. I wish to speak with the War Chief."

"Yes, Matron."

Peavine scowled at Browser and Catkin where they stood very close together in front of the doorway that led to the newly restored kiva, then she stalked across the plaza.

Flame Carrier watched her feet as she walked, careful not to step in any holes. Without her walking stick, her balance often failed her.

Catkin caught sight of Flame Carrier and ran to help her. "Let me help you, Matron," she said as she extended a hand.

Tall, and lanky for a woman, Catkin had a beautiful oval face. Her long hair, recently unbraided, streamed around her like rippled black silk.

"Gladly," Flame Carrier said and closed her clawlike fingers around Catkin's forearm. "It seems you did not get much rest. I assure you that all was quiet while you were away. We . . ."

Flame Carrier's voice faltered. She gazed at Catkin from the corner of her eye. Catkin had returned very late in the evening the night the War Chief's wife died. She had also been the one to "discover" the body missing the next day. And then, tonight, she had supposedly been asleep in her chamber.

"What were you saying, Matron?" Catkin asked, as she guided Flame Carrier toward Browser.

"Nothing. Just mumbling to myself."

Flame Carrier's blood rushed. Catkin loved Browser.

Everyone knew it. Had she so wished his wife dead that she could have killed her and now sought to eliminate anyone who might suspect? Passion often twisted a person's souls.

Especially a woman's.

Most women were mothers at heart. The gods had made them that way, whether they liked it not, whether they actually became mothers or not. Women often saw the man they loved as a child. When that man happened to be married to a unkind woman, they tended to see him as an abused child—one in need of salvation—and that vision formed the rationale for terrifying acts. Getting the child away from the abuse became an obsession. Flame Carrier had seen it. She had known a woman named Maypop, who had dreamed her married lover's hurts every night, hurts much worse than he had ever experienced, but once her heart became inflamed with those images, they could not be erased by reality. They had flayed her souls with unimaginable pain. To save her lover, Maypop had murdered his wife. Two days later, her lover had set fire to the kindling beneath Maypop's feet, and watched her scream until the blaze consumed her.

Flame Carrier glanced at Catkin again. Wondering.

Browser strode out to meet Flame Carrier. His buckskin cape, and shorn hair whipped in the wind. His thick black brows had knitted over his flat nose, forming a solid line across his forehead. "Have you been informed, Matron?"

"I've heard several things, but I wish to hear the tale from you, War Chief. I understand that you were standing with Whiproot at the guard position when Jackrabbit was attacked. Is this true?"

"Yes, Matron." He turned and pointed to the ragged hole in the toppled wall near Hophorn's chamber. "The katsina fled through there. I followed. Later, when he was able, Jackrabbit joined me. We lost the katsina in the dark passageways."

Flame Carrier pulled up the hood on her cape, shielding her face from the brunt of Wind Baby's chill breath. "And Whiproot? What happened to him?"

Grief and regret strained Browser's round face. "I ordered him to guard the Sunwatcher's chamber. I thought it would be safer than chasing down the katsina." He exhaled hard. "I was wrong, Matron. I do not know the way of it, but Whiproot was young and as strong as a buffalo. The killer must have surprised him."

Flame Carrier looked at Catkin. "What tale do the tracks tell?"

"We think the katsina leaped on Whiproot from the roof above Hophorn's chamber and struck him in the head. They struggled—"

"The blow must have dazed Whiproot, Elder," Browser said. "That is the only way the killer could have stabbed him twice."

"He was stabbed?" Flame Carrier asked. "No one told me that."

"Yes, Matron. The man who killed him also cut open his belly, cut out some intestine, and twirled it around." He grimaced, as if forcing himself to speak the rest. "The blood and contents spattered the room. He ended by throwing the empty length of gut against the wall."

Flame Carrier stared blindly at the ground. She had brought her people here to rebuild the ancient ceremonial chamber in the hopes that they could stop the violence, and restore harmony to the unbalanced world. She *believed* the prophecies! How could this be happening?

Flame Carrier clenched her knobby fingers and shook her fist at Browser. "Find out who is doing this, War Chief!"

"I am trying, Matron. Stone Ghost should be here very soon. I expect him tomorrow."

Flame Carrier struggled to control the futility that shook her limbs. "In the meantime, *do* something to protect our people!"

"Yes, Matron," he said, and bowed. "I will, I—I will."

Flame Carrier started to say something else, but a buzz of voices rose around her. She turned and saw Silk Moth scrambling down the ladder into the plaza. Seventeen summers, with short black hair, and a broad catlike face, she wore a gray rabbithide cape. When her feet touched the ground, she ran for Hophorn's chamber.

Jackrabbit blocked her way, speaking softly to her, clearly trying to prepare her for what she would see inside.

Silk Moth cried, "Get out of my way! Where is my husband?" Her voice rose to a shrill wail. *"Whiproot? Whiproot, where are you?"*

Jackrabbit said, "Please, Silk Moth, don't just run in. Let me tell you—"

"I want my husband!" she screamed and slammed a fist into Jackrabbit's shoulder. "Let me by! *Whiproot?"*

Silk Moth tried to shove by Jackrabbit, but he held her sternly by the shoulders, saying, "He is dead, Silk Moth. I'm sorry. He was attacked by someone—"

Silk Moth shrieked, "No!" then tore loose from Jackrabbit's grip and lunged into Hophorn's chamber.

For a single stunned instant the silence held.

Then an insane cry split the night.

Jackrabbit rushed into Hophorn's chamber and came out carrying Silk Moth draped limply over his arms, unconscious.

"Oh, gods," Flame Carrier said in a tortured voice. "The sight must have—"

"Yes." Browser's face tensed. "I told you, there is blood everywhere, Matron. The ceiling, walls . . ."

Flame Carrier's old heart cramped, skipped a beat, then stuttered to life again. She grabbed Catkin's arm for support. "War Chief, find someone to carry Whiproot back . . . No. No, don't." Ordinarily the dead were taken home to be prepared by their families for the journey to the Land of the Dead, but she doubted Silk Moth could stand it. "Have Whiproot placed on one of the foot drums in the newly restored kiva. I will see to him myself. Tomorrow."

"Yes, Matron."

Over the long sun cycles, Flame Carrier had cared for many of the dead, including her husband and seven children. All of them had died from the coughing sickness. She had washed their bodies, rubbed them with cornmeal to purify their flesh, then prepared their burial ladders and the clothing they needed for the journey. She would do the same for Whiproot.

Flame Carrier scanned the plaza. She found Redcrop standing at the base of the ladder, helping people down. "I will ask Redcrop to clean Hophorn's chamber. Terrible chore to give a girl, but someone must do it."

Catkin said, "I will help her, Matron."

Flame Carrier gratefully touched Catkin's wrist. "Redcrop will appreciate that. Thank you."

She looked at Browser. The lines around his eyes cut deeply into his skin. He appeared to be waiting for a reprimand. Flame Carrier said, "I'm going back to my chamber to rest. Wake me if you need to."

"Yes, Matron."

Flame Carrier nodded to Catkin, and hobbled toward the ladder. When Redcrop saw her coming, she ran to Flame Carrier's side and took her elbow.

Flame Carrier affectionately said, "I do not know what I would do without you, child. You are my only true friend."

Redcrop beamed up at her, her eyes filled with love. "And you are mine." She squeezed Flame Carrier's arm. "Did you see that Jackrabbit carried Silk Moth home?"

"No, I didn't, but I'm glad of it. She has endured enough for tonight."

Redcrop maneuvered Flame Carrier around a heap of cracked plaster, and toward the ladder. "Silk Moth will not be able to prepare her husband will she?"

"No. She will not. I will do it."

"I will help you."

Flame Carrier looked at the wide-eyed girl. "I have another job for you. One that is more difficult."

"Yes?" Redcrop looked up.

"Someone must clean Hophorn's chamber. It will not be pleasant. From what I have heard—"

"I can do it, grandmother. I'll start after I take you home."

"I can go by myself, child, but thank you."

"Are you certain?"

"Yes." Flame Carrier stood at the base of the ladder, and gently stroked Redcrop's cheek with the back of her hand. "When I get back, I'll place your blankets by the coals. They will stay warm until your return."

Redcrop smiled. "Thank you, grandmother. I will see you soon."

"Very good, girl."

Flame Carrier took hold of the ladder, and lifted her feet onto the rungs. As she climbed, she heard the fear in people's voices. It rang across the plaza like the lingering notes of an echo. By dawn, the terror would have reached gigantic proportions. It would grip them all by the throats. No one would be able to breathe without pain.

Flame Carrier stepped off the ladder onto the roof and looked out across the canyon. Frost glimmered and twinkled in the starlight, outlining every ledge and sheathing the fallen boulders and juniper trees. Straight Path Wash cut a jagged swath of darkness through the shining white blanket.

She turned back to Talon Town. The enormous semicircular structure gleamed, hiding the dark, twisting passageways within. A killer who understood the maze could hide there forever.

Flame Carrier's stomach knotted as she stepped onto the ladder that led down to the road. Her sandals slipped repeatedly on ice, but she held tight with her hands and managed to make it to the ground without incident.

Several people moved in the shadows cast by the mounds. Flame Carrier saw Wading Bird huddled with his family. His bald head glowed. His gnarled hands clenched at his sides.

"Is there more we can do tonight?" he asked as Flame Carrier neared. The lump in his long nose shone in the silver light.

"No." She lifted her voice so that everyone could hear her. "Go home! We are all safer in our chambers than standing out here in the open. The murderer is still loose! He may be watching us right now."

Frightened murmuring erupted, and people began to disperse, slowly heading back toward Hillside Village.

To Wading Bird, Flame Carrier whispered, "The murderer wore the mask of the Wolf Katsina."

He stared, his eyes jerking wide. "Like the mask—"

"Possibly."

"Hallowed Ancestors."

Flame Carrier touched Wading Bird's shoulder as she passed and continued up the road.

Her legs ached in cold weather, especially her ankles. Every step hurt. By the time she reached the ladder that leaned against the side of Hillside Village, she was favoring her right leg. Flame Carrier panted as she climbed to the roof.

The rich sweet scent of baking squash rose. She savored the smell as she walked, passing three roof entries before she came to her own. Darkness filled the chamber.

Without her there to add an occasional twig, the warming bowl had dimmed.

Flame Carrier grasped the top of the ladder, and stood just for a moment, squinting down, before she stepped onto the first rung. A sudden chill shivered her backbone.

She could imagine how Whiproot must have felt, being hit by something heavy, knocked to the ground, slammed in the head before he could rise . . . then stabbed as he tried to get to his feet. And poor Hophorn, forced to hear the cries, the shuffling feet, to see the men stumble into her chamber in a fight to the death.

What had she seen? What had she *said*? Flame Carrier had forgotten to ask Browser. Well, there would be time enough tomorrow.

A curious scent met her nose as she descended into the darkness. Sage smoke. But her coals came from juniper wood.

The blackness exploded into light as someone tossed a twig onto her coals, momentarily blinding Flame Carrier.

"Who's there?" she called, and squinted.

Below her, in the corner to her left, a dark figure coalesced from the shimmering darkness.

Flame Carrier's legs went weak. She clung to the ladder as if it were a life raft in a raging river.

A brittle old voice said, "He is here, you know. Close by, watching us. You must stop walking alone, Matron."

18

DUSTY LEANED BACK in his lawn chair and tipped his chin to the breeze that buffeted the tents. Early that morning, they'd pulled the green rain flies from the tents and attached them to posts to create four ramadas around the central fire pit. It felt much cooler beneath them. Blond hair fluttered around his deeply tanned face. His tie-dyed black-and-white shirt, and Army green shorts, clung to his body like wet snakeskin. The noon temperature sat at an ungodly 108 degrees Fahrenheit. He'd just called an end to work and told the crew to take their two-hour midday break. People had immediately headed for the shade.

Hail Walking Hawk napped in her red tent.

Maureen and Maggie sat to Dusty's left, hunched over a fold-out table that Maggie had brought them from the Park Service headquarters. The wood-veneer top was strewn with the bones of two females. One appeared to be an adolescent girl—Maureen said she was probably eleven or twelve—and the other was the woman Sylvia had excavated, about twenty-two years of age. A magnifying glass, microscope, calipers for measuring the width and breadth of skeletal materials, and a bottle of Lipton's unsweetened iced tea sat in front of Maureen. She'd braided her long hair and clipped it up in back, but damp black wisps fringed her forehead. At dawn, she'd appeared wearing a white T-shirt and tan shorts. Now, her shirt matched her shorts.

Maggie quietly watched Maureen pick up the magnifying glass and study the length of a femur, the large leg bone. As Maggie leaned forward, short black hair framed her round face, accenting her rich brown eyes. She wore Levi's cutoffs, black tennis shoes with white socks, and a cream-colored T-shirt.

Dusty gazed across the fire pit, between two tents, and down the length of the canyon to the west. The cliffs wavered like golden phantoms. Not a single cloud adorned the pale blue sky, which meant there was no relief in sight. Without an afternoon thundershower, the heat would remain high well into the evening.

Sylvia rummaged around in the ice chest to Dusty's right. "God. This heat is almost too much even for me."

Locks of soaked brown hair straggled from beneath the brim of her straw hat and glued themselves to her freckled cheeks. She looked like a skinny drowned rat. Her soaked khaki shorts, and brown tank top, had a spiderweb of muddy folds where her perspiration had mixed with the tan dirt. She dragged two cans of Coke from the chest, and grabbed a plastic bag of snacks. As she handed one of the Cokes to Dusty, she said, "I feel like the Wicked Witch of the West: *I'm melting, melting.*"

"Let's not talk about witches, hmm?"

He glanced at the open tailgate of his Bronco. He'd carefully packed the *basilisco* out of sight, buried beneath neatly labeled brown paper sacks, soil specimen bags, and Ziplocs. Maggie and Mrs. Walking Hawk, of course, did not know he'd mapped and collected it—as he would have any other artifact.

Dusty popped the top and took a long drink of the cold sweet liquid. It went down like the nectar of the gods. "We'll see how the temperature is later this afternoon. If it hasn't dropped to below one hundred by three, we might just take the rest of the day off."

"Hallelujah," Sylvia said.

"Don't hallelujah yet If we take the afternoon off, we'll go over to the headquarters, take showers, and refill the water jugs. After that, I want field notes updated and an inventory done on the collections to make sure the artifact bags match the field specimen log."

"Ugh," Sylvia said, and walked over to the ramada in front of her tent. She dropped into her lawn chair and set her bag on the ground. For several seconds, she held the cold Coke can to her forehead, then rubbed it over her sweaty neck, before finally opening it, and swallowing half the can in four gulps. "If I pass out, just leave me until dark."

"Well, if you feel it coming on, throw me the rest of your Coke. We're running low."

Sylvia clutched the can to her chest. "Dale is supposed to bring supplies tonight. Do you think we ought to call and tell him to bring two more cases of Coke and another six cases of beer?"

Maureen looked up, shook her head in disgust, and went back to rearranging her bones.

Dusty said, "Might not be a bad idea."

Sylvia tipped her can up, and finished her soda, then reached for the snacks. She dragged out her favorite meal: a package of flour tortillas, a bag of those awful little cheese-flavored fishes, and two strips of teriyaki jerky. She laid out a tortilla, filled it with cheezy fishes, rolled it up, and took a bite. In between crunches, she ripped off hunks of jerky and chewed.

Dusty made a face. "I can feel the rigor mortis settling into your blood vessels."

Around a crunchy mouthful, Sylvia said, "Don't you ever look at those 'food group' charts they plaster on the college dormitory walls? A perfectly balanced diet is white, yellow, and brown."

"You're supposed to *read* the posters, Sylvia, not scan the colors as you pass. Those white, yellow, and brown things are cheese, bread, and meat. Not polysorbate substitutes."

Sylvia took another bite. "You should talk. Your favorite meal is sour-cream-and-onion potato chips, washed down with brown bog scum."

"At least I get my vegetables."

A broad smile spread across Sylvia's face. She said, "God bless America."

Maureen scowled at the two of them. "Nero fiddling."

"Fiddling with what?" Sylvia asked with genuine interest. "Wasn't he like a king or something?"

Maureen went mute. She lifted a brow, and something akin to puzzled dismay crossed her face. "The American school system is certainly going to bring about the Second Coming. I'm sure God wants your history to end as much as everybody else does."

Dusty reached for the paper bag of snacks by Sylvia's chair, and pulled out a big package of jalapeño crackers. "Hey," he said. "I didn't know you'd bought these."

"Yeah, I thought we needed more fiber in our diets."

"I love these." Dusty opened the bag and ate one of the green jalapeño-shaped crackers. "Umm-umm." He pulled out another one, and held it up for Maureen to see. "What sort of god could destroy a people with this kind of cultural legacy?"

Maureen studied the cracker through slitted eyes. "The sort who realizes Canadians should inherit the earth."

Sylvia tore off another hunk of jerky. "You and cockroaches. You'd better start stocking up on Raid."

Dusty lowered an eyebrow. "If Canada's so great, how come Quebec wants to succeed? Not enough Tim Horton's?"

"I believe you mean *secede,* you moron. As in secession, to leave a political body." Maureen gave him a disgusted look.

"Yeah, well, if you ask me, those guys in Quebec just

want to join the United States so they can unthaw."

"Unthaw?" Maureen lifted a pair of stainless steel calipers. "How does one 'unthaw?' Either you thaw, or you freeze. Or is this another example of the way Americans are exterminating the English language?"

Dusty dug out a handful of the spicy crackers and shoved them into his mouth. He washed them down with the last of his Coke, stood, and went to sift through the ice chest. Around the collection of half-melted cubes and bottles, soggy pieces of labels swam. He grabbed a naked bottle of what looked like root beer, and went to sit down again. As he unscrewed the lid, he gestured to the skeletal remains. "So, tell me how those bones disprove my war and slavery theory?"

"I need to see the other skulls, first, Stewart. The ones that are partially exposed, and currently covered with black plastic, as well as the ones that are still under rocks."

He had been going very slowly with the Haze child burial, making sure that every curiously shaped pebble was documented, just in case it turned out to be an artifact under the microscope. "Tomorrow," he said. "I'll have the Haze child, and his mother, pulled. Sylvia can finish burial number three, too, I think."

"Yeah, boss," Sylvia said with a nod.

Maureen held up the chunk of bone she'd been studying, and turned it over in her hands. "I can already tell you, though, that this was a very sick group of people."

Sylvia took a big bite of white and yellow, and slurred, "How do you know?"

Maureen placed two malformed pieces of bone together. "You may not recognize them, but you're looking at the eleventh and twelfth thoracic vertebrae. They've been eaten away by infection. For it to have so severely eroded the anterior bodies of these vertebrae, this poor girl must have had a huge paravertebral abscess. I'll bet the abscess cavity contained ten cubic centimeters of pus, enough to . . . What's the matter?"

Maureen squinted at Sylvia who had an enormous half-chewed mass of food in her cheeks. She looked like a wide-eyed, but well-fed, chipmunk.

Dusty leaned forward. "Okay, so she was filled up with pus. What caused it?"

"For a twelfth thoracic lesion? Rampant tuberculosis. This girl must have been in constant pain. Her back muscles would not have relaxed in any position. She would have suffered incapacitating spasms, and probably had difficulty standing, let alone walking. I'd even wager she had to support her upper body with her arms while sitting, or the pain of the collapsed vertebrae would have been unbearable. Just the pressure of the gigantic pus sack on the nerves—"

Sylvia made a disgusting deep-throated sound.

Dusty said, "I thought tuberculosis was a lung disease?"

"Pulmonary tuberculosis is. What we're seeing here is a case of advanced extrapulmonary tuberculosis, the type that affects the body outside of the lungs. Extrapulmonary tuberculosis infects the joints, eyes, lymph nodes, kidneys, intestines, even the larynx, and skin. When the tuberculosis bacteria enters the brain, it causes meningitis, meaning it attacks the meninges—the three membranes that cover the brain. As the membranes swell, the pressure inside the skull changes, producing violent headaches, often accompanied by vomiting and disorientation. When I was in Iran several years ago, I dissected the brain of a tubercular victim with so many abscesses, it literally oozed in my hands."

Maureen propped her elbows on the card table and extended her fingers, as if Dusty could see them dripping.

Sylvia choked down her lunch and flopped back in her

chair with a sour expression her freckled face. "God," she said. "No more yellow in my diet."

"Who's going to finish all your Coors?" Maggie asked.

"Not me. I don't drink anything that smells like a fire hydrant. I'd rather die," Dusty vowed and unscrewed the lid on his root beer.

Sylvia said, "I can't wait to see what Maureen finds when she dissects you. Or worse, doesn't find."

Dusty's blond brows lowered. "Don't you dare bring up Cortez again."

Sylvia grinned, but Maggie and Maureen gazed at him as if they hadn't the slightest idea what he was referring to.

When Maureen's right brow arched, Dusty rushed to say, "Let's get back to the bones. All right, tell me how this tuberculosis bacteria works? It's passed through sneezing and coughing, right?"

Maureen nodded. "Primarily, yes, though it can also be passed by contact with items touched by an infected person or even by drinking unpasteurized milk from a cow with tuberculosis."

"How long is a person contagious?"

"An untreated person can be contagious, off and on, for his entire life. I've seen cases of long-latent tuberculosis suddenly flare up, particularly in older people, and cause epidemics in third world countries."

Dusty crossed his legs and propped his root beer on his knee, wondering how the Anasazi would have interpreted the disease. He remembered hearing an elderly Zuni woman talk about an illness that had carried away a number of her people during the 1940s: *Their blood turned to water, and came out their mouths mixed with white spots. Some of them took a long time to die. We could do nothing for them. Witches caused it. They buried bad medicine bundles around the village. Whenever*

*anybody stepped on one of these bundles, they got the
sickness and died."*

Maureen said, "The tubercular lesions aren't the only
interesting thing about these bones though." She picked
up the battered skull of the young woman. Dusty could
count at least three cranial depression fractures, dents, on
the right side of her head. "Did southwestern peoples
practice cannibalism?"

Dusty glanced up sharply. The issue was hotly debated
in the southwest. "Tim White, Christy Turner, and I say
'yes,' but there are a lot of people who want to slit our
throats for that. Why do you ask?"

Maureen picked up her magnifying glass and studied
the top of the skull. "There are unusual cut marks on this
skull, and several of the long bones."

Sylvia wiped her hands on her dirty shorts, and
reached for the bag of jalapeño crackers. "Are you sure
they aren't marks left by animal teeth? Mice? Wolves?"

"I'm sure. These are long, straight cuts. Rodents make
parallel marks from the incisors that look like gouges
under the microscope. The canines and carnasials . . . uh,
wolf fangs, leave irregular shallow grooves. These cuts
look like deep *v*'s, as though someone carved through the
muscles, to the bone, and sliced the meat off in long
strips. Only sharpened stone tools make this kind of in-
cision."

Sylvia peered seriously at the skull. "Like butchering
something?"

"Yes."

"Or . . ." Dusty left the word hanging for affect. He
consciously didn't glance toward his truck, and *el basilisco*. "It could be witchcraft."

Sylvia, mimicking his exact tone of voice, countered,
"Or . . . it could be an upset daddy using stone cutlery to
carve his point into mommy's head."

Maggie met Dusty's gaze. She didn't say anything for

a few seconds, then began, "I remember a strange story I heard when I was little. Witches from Tesuque pueblo went to Nambe. They spent a few days there, making evil dolls that would cause people to cough. They stuffed chili seeds, dirt, and rags into the dolls and placed them around the village. Then they turned themselves into cats and dogs and escaped up the arroyo that runs through Nambe."

"What happened to the witches?" Sylvia asked.

The lines around Maggie's eyes tightened. "They were caught and tortured until they vowed they would stop their witchery, but I think they all died from the torture."

Dusty nodded. "I remember that story. By 1910 the leaders of Nambe had executed so many witches the village population had dropped by half."

"The way I heard it, it was a real reign of terror," Maggie agreed.

Maureen turned the skull in her hands. "I don't understand. Why would you think these long cuts might be witchcraft?"

Dusty leaned forward, his eyes on the skull. "Corpse powder."

Sylvia suddenly whispered, "God! Of course!"

A look of revulsion tensed Maggie's face. She pushed her chair away from the table.

"Corpse powder?" Maureen frowned. "What is that?"

Dusty took a long drink of root beer and wiped his mouth on his shirt sleeve. "Don't you read Tony Hillerman? You know, Jim Chee and Leaphorn?"

At Maureen's blank look, Sylvia said, "Wow, the only anthropologist in the world who's illiterate."

"Right," Maureen agreed dryly, "so, enlighten the benighted heathen from the north, okay?"

Dusty took a moment to bask in her scowl. "Some southwestern tribes believe that at death the good soul leaves for the afterlife, and all that is left in the body is evil. Witches harvest this evil by stealing corpses and reducing the flesh and bones to a fine powder, which they sprinkle on their enemies. Supposedly corpse powder can drive a person crazy or even kill him."

Maureen's hand crept up to clasp the silver crucifix at her throat. She casually rotated the clasp around to the back of her neck, as though the action had nothing to do with the discussion, but when she dropped her hand to the table again, she drummed her fingers uneasily.

Maggie stared at Maureen. "Maybe I should wake my aunt. She might be able to tell us more. She—"

"No," Dusty said gently. "Let her sleep. I think this heat has been harder on her than anyone. We can ask her later tonight."

Maggie nodded. "Yes, you're right. She didn't sleep well last night, either. She woke me in the middle of the night to ask me if I heard the ghosts walking around the tents."

Dusty straightened when he saw Maureen's face suddenly go pale.

"What?" Dusty asked.

Maureen looked up. "Hmm?"

"Don't 'hmm' me. What's wrong?"

A gust of wind shuddered the tents. Maureen turned away until it passed. When she turned back, her eyes had narrowed as if against some hidden strain. "Oh, nothing, really. It's just that I had the strangest dream last night."

"What dream?"

"Well, it—it was odd." She put the skull down, and folded her arms tightly across her chest. "It began with the sound of a baby crying. Then frantic steps ran past my tent. Soft steps, like sandals in sand, and a man and woman shouted at each other. I couldn't understand their language, but I knew they were upset and frightened. I thought it had to do with the child." She looked at Maggie. "Isn't that strange, that your Aunt would hear steps in the night and that I would dream . . ."

Maggie's brown eyes fixed on Maureen. "Aunt Hail told me you were a Soul Flyer."

"*Me?*" Maureen smiled in genuine amusement, and pointed at herself. "Sorry, Maggie, this time you've got the wrong person."

Maggie tilted her head as though debating whether or not to say something else. It piqued Dusty's curiosity.

"Is that all your aunt said?" he asked.

Maggie ran her fingers around the base of the adolescent girl's skull. She answered, "Yes," but the way she said it meant "no."

Dusty finished his root beer and placed the bottle in the trash box behind him. It clacked against a wealth of tin cans. He gave Maureen a suspicious glance.

She said, "I'm no Soul Flyer, Stewart."

Dusty smiled. "Me thinks the good doctor protesteth too much."

"What is that supposed to mean?"

Maggie touched Maureen's hand lightly. The silence stretched between them before Maggie murmured, "I'm sorry. I shouldn't have said anything. Especially not in front of others."

"You're not telling me you believe in ghosts?" Maureen accused her.

Maggie lifted a shoulder. "Sometimes, Doctor. Sometimes."

Dusty said, "Well, she may not, but I do."

"*You,* I would expect it of," Maureen replied. "You're full of nonsense, but Maggie has a scientific mind."

"*If* I'm full of 'nonsense,'" Dusty replied, "it's because I've seen a lot of strange things out here, Doctor. I don't discount any explanation. Unlike you, I don't think science answers all questions."

Maureen picked up the woman's battered skull again

and turned it slowly in her hands. The gaping hole, where the sandstone slab had crushed the back, caught the light. "Maybe not, Stewart, but it's still the best way of 'knowing' that we have."

Dusty laced his fingers in his lap. His gaze drifted from Sylvia's wide green eyes to Maureen's stoic authoritative expression and finally landed on Maggie's politely bowed head.

"It's one way of knowing, Doctor. It is not the only way."

Maureen bent forward, as though truly interested in what he'd said. "My goodness, we have a philosopher in camp. I didn't realize you were skilled in epistemology, Stewart."

"He's not a philosopher," Maggie started to defend him, "he's just sensitive to other cultural—"

"I am so a philosopher," Dusty cried indignantly. "I can instantly tell the difference between the teachings of Jean-Paul Sartre and Yoda."

Sylvia's brows lifted in admiration. "Wow. I'm pretty good with Batman and Spock, but Yoda is way beyond me."

Another gust of roasting wind battered the camp, rattling the ramadas, and sending Sylvia's empty Coke can tumbling for the hinterlands. She leaped up and ran through the greasewood after it.

When she returned she dropped the can into the trash box behind Dusty's chair and trudged for the ice chest with the beer. As she dug around through the meltwater, she said, "It's definitely time for Coors. Anybody else want one?"

19

A SCREAM SPLIT the darkness, echoed from the canyon wall, and dwindled into choking sobs.

Browser looked up at the thousands of Evening People glittering across the night sky. A pale blue glow haloed the eastern horizon. Off and on throughout the night Silk Moth had shrieked her husband's name. Peavine, and several other women in the village, had been taking turns, sitting with Silk Moth, trying to comfort her, but it had done little good.

Browser gazed down at his meal. He crouched on the roof of Talon Town eating corncakes and a hot bowl of soup that Redcrop had made for him. The soup, a mixture of squash, roasted pumpkin seeds, and dried yucca petals tasted sweet and flowery. He dipped his corncake into the steaming bowl, scooped up a large chunk of squash, and ate it while his gaze drifted.

He'd posted five guards on Talon Town, including himself. To his left, in the plaza below him, Jackrabbit and He-Who-Flies whispered outside of Cloudblower's chamber. On the toppled fifth story, near the cliff behind Browser, Skink and Water Snake stood, silently surveying the distant canyon.

Browser took a bite of his corncake and chewed slowly. The cold night air carried smells of cedar smoke, damp earth, and the lingering taint of blood and torn intestines.

After the villagers had returned to their chambers,

Browser and Catkin had carried Whiproot's body into the newly restored kiva and placed it on one of the long footdrums. They'd stood in silence, neither saying a word, but both thinking the same thought: Whiproot should have died in battle fighting his enemies, not taken by surprise at home. How could it have happened?

Many things made no sense. At first, Browser had assumed the murderer had attacked Jackrabbit and run to draw everyone away from Hophorn's chamber so that he could kill her—but he was no longer certain of that. The murderer must have seen Browser and Whiproot standing together on the roof before he attacked Jackrabbit. Why had he chosen that moment? If he had waited another finger of time, Browser would have been gone, leaving only two foes to battle.

Browser dipped his corncake again. As he chewed, he frowned out at the dark canyon. It was almost as if the murderer had waited for Browser's arrival. Had *known* Browser would come, and wished him to be there when he murdered Whiproot.

Browser's belly knotted. He stared down at his soup. Earlier in the evening, an unthinkable possibility had flashed across his souls. For just an instant, he had feared that the murderer might be using Hophorn against him— dangling her safety in front of his nose like a piece of meat before a starving coyote, luring Browser in, then murdering people while he stood helplessly by.

Browser picked up his horn spoon and stirred his soup. The pumpkin seeds swirled around the yucca petals.

He looked out at the dark zigzagging slash of Straight Path Wash, wondering if the murderer used it to approach the town? Or to escape when he had finished his foul deeds? At first light, he would search for tracks in the frost. If he found none, he would crawl through Talon Town on his hands and knees by himself.

Browser swiveled around and studied the giant half-moon-shaped structure. He saw Skink and Water Snake standing tall, silhouetted against the canyon wall. The roof of each crumbling, stepped-back story, glittered. Collapsed timbers thrust up through the fallen stones like huge spears aimed at the sky gods. Predawn light streamed through gaping holes in the walls.

Many of the holes could not be seen from his current position. The largest, most dangerous openings, gashed the towering rear wall of the town, near the cliff face. A man with a hook tied to the end of a rope might be able to climb in and out of those holes at will, especially given the fallen rocks and deteriorated plaster piled at the bottom.

Browser tipped his soup bowl up and swallowed the last of the sweet broth. As he set it down, he noticed Redcrop trotting up the road to his left. Her long hair fluttered with her stride. She had been up most of the night cleaning, cooking, and running errands for Flame Carrier. The poor girl must be as exhausted as Browser.

She stopped beneath him, and called, "War Chief? The Matron wishes you to come to the Hillside plaza."

"Tell her I'm coming."

"Yes, War Chief." The girl sprinted back toward the village.

Browser slung his bow and quiver over his shoulder and walked along the roof until he stood over Cloudblower's chamber. At the edge of the roof, he called, "He-Who-Flies?"

The muscular warrior stepped out of the shadows and looked up. He stood twelve hands tall, and had a chest like a grizzly bear. His round flat face gleamed in the predawn glow. "Yes, War Chief?"

Jackrabbit leaned against the wall outside of Cloudblower's chamber. His eyes glinted in the starlight.

Browser said, "The Matron has summoned me. I wish you to take my guard position. I will try to return soon."

"Very well, War Chief." He-Who-Flies reached for the ladder that lay on the ground near Jackrabbit, propped it against the south wall, and started to climb up.

Browser walked to the ladder he'd stowed at his guard position and lowered it over the side to the road below. By the time he set foot on the frozen ground, He-Who-Flies stood tall and straight above him, his bow and quiver over his right shoulder.

Browser removed his war club from his belt and clutched it in his right hand as he headed for Hillside Village.

As he rounded the southeastern corner of Talon Town, he saw two people standing before the small blaze in the fire pit, both small and hunched, wearing long capes. One of them leaned on a walking stick. At the edge of the orange gleam, four guards stood.

Ten paces from the fire, a little old man turned suddenly and called, "My dear grand-nephew!" and hobbled toward Browser in a swirl of feathered cape. He had wispy white hair, a hooked nose, and thick gray brows.

"Uncle Stone Ghost?"

The old man passed between the guards as if they didn't exist and gripped Browser's free hand. He held it to his heart and smiled. "You cannot imagine how happy it made me to know that you had moved here, barely a day's run from my house. Remind me. Which nephew are you?"

"I am not surprised you don't recall. The last time I saw you, I had barely seen eight summers. You came to Faithful Hawk Village after Grandmother Painted Turtle was murdered."

"Painted Turtle! Of course. She was always my favorite sister." A look of old grief touched his expression. In a softer voice he said, "Then you must be Prairie Flower's son."

"Yes, Uncle."

Stone Ghost started to return to the fire, stopped, and gazed back at Browser with kind brown eyes. He gripped Browser's hand tightly. "I was sorry to hear about your wife and son. Are you well, my nephew?"

"Well enough, Uncle." Browser gestured to the fire. "The Matron is waiting. I think we should—"

"Perhaps later we can speak of this together. I would like to know more about your wife."

Browser nodded. "Of course." He took a breath, and steeled himself. How strange that in the midst of his pain and guilt, a flame of anger still burned. She was dead. Why couldn't he let it go?

Stone Ghost affectionately clutched Browser's hand as they walked to the fire. In the wavering gleam, the old man's wrinkles looked like rain-carved crevices. Several strands of tawdry pottery-disk necklaces glinted around his throat. Among the poorer villages a dropped pot became jewelry. They smoothed the pot fragments into round disks, strung them, and wore them. Was his uncle this destitute? From the corner of his eye, Browser scrutinized Stone Ghost's clothing. Patches of feathers were missing from his cape, and his moccasins had holes in the toes.

Browser slipped his war club through his belt and put his hand over the old man's. Before Stone Ghost left, Browser would make certain he had a warm cape, moccasins, and whatever else he needed.

Flame Carrier tapped her walking stick. "Come. Let us get started."

Her gray hair and bulbous nose shone amber as she lowered herself to one of the rocks that encircled the fire.

Browser guided Stone Ghost to the rock beside Flame Carrier and helped him to sit down. Browser took the rock beside his uncle. A teapot hung on a tripod at the edge of the fire. Cups nested beneath it.

Flame Carrier said, "Stone Ghost arrived last night

during the insanity. He could hear the commotion from the road and decided to go to my chamber to wait for me." She scowled at Stone Ghost. "After I shoved my liver back down my throat, we spent most of the night talking. I have told him everything I know about the murders. He wishes to question you now, before dawn brings dozens of onlookers."

"I understand," Browser said and turned to Stone Ghost. "What is it you wish to know about the murderer, Uncle?"

Firelight flashed in Stone Ghost's eyes when he jerked. His bushy brows drew down over his hooked nose. "Do you know something about the murderer, my Nephew?"

"Well. Yes. I mean, I saw him last night."

Stone Ghost leaned closer, and his white hair caught the firelight. "What did you see?"

Browser shifted. "A tall man, slender. Though it was hard to tell. He wore—"

"How tall?"

Browser shrugged. "Eleven hands, perhaps twelve. I only saw him for a moment, when he was struggling with Jackrabbit, but Jackrabbit is about eleven hands. The murderer seemed taller to me."

Stone Ghost turned to the teapot and said, "May I, Matron?"

Flame Carrier nodded. "That is why I had Redcrop make it."

"I'm grateful." Stone Ghost picked up a cup, dipped it full, and handed it to Browser. Then he filled one for himself. The fragrance of sunflower petals rose.

Browser added, "But the man was wearing a large mask, Uncle. It would have made him at least two or three hands taller."

As Stone Ghost sipped, a veil of steam wavered around his wrinkled face. "What else?"

Browser rested his cup on his knee. "The killer struck

Jackrabbit with a war club and fled through a gap in the wall near Hophorn's chamber. Whiproot and I immediately climbed down and ran to Jackrabbit. I ordered Whiproot to guard the Sunwatcher's chamber and told him that if Jackrabbit recovered, he should send him for help."

"Then you followed the killer, yes?"

"I tried to, Uncle. I didn't make it very far."

Flame Carrier watched them through keen old eyes, her elderly face stern.

Wind fluttered the wisps of white hair clinging to Stone Ghost's spotted scalp. His eyes narrowed. "Inside the town, what did you see?"

"Very little." Browser frowned down at his tea. The firelight dyed the rising steam the deep gold of squash blossoms. "I entered the gap in the wall and proceeded cautiously, listening every step of the way. I heard laughter ahead of me, then I thought I heard something just before Jackrabbit came up behind me, but it might have been a rodent. The crumbling town is filled with them."

"How much time passed between the moment you entered the gap and Jackrabbit appeared?"

"Oh," Browser said through a long exhalation, "four hundred heartbeats, at most five."

Stone Ghost frowned and shifted to peer at Flame Carrier. Firelight flowed across her still face. They appeared to be exchanging thoughts. Flame Carrier tilted her head, and her kinky gray brows twitched.

Stone Ghost turned back Browser. "In those five hundred heartbeats," he said, "did you hear anything from outside?"

Browser's hand arrested in midmotion lifting his tea cup. His gaze darted over the clay-washed face of Hillside Village, noted the coils of smoke rising through the rooftop entries and the way the firelight played on the cliff. "I do not recall hearing anything, Uncle."

"Did you not think that strange? Jackrabbit had just been attacked. Surely he would have been questioning Whiproot, or Whiproot questioning him."

A hollow sensation expanded Browser's chest. He watched the light of the flames sheath his uncle's ancient face and twinkle in his curiously gentle eyes. "What are you saying?"

Stone Ghost smiled. "Tell me, do you think the walls of the town are so thick they eliminate sound?"

"No, because later Jackrabbit and I both heard a voice screaming. It called—"

"It? You did not recognize the voice?"

"No, Uncle, but that is of little import. I have been in battles where my own best friend cried my name and I did not recognize his voice. Panic twists the souls, makes voices come out in ways they never have before."

"True," Stone Ghost said. He smoothed his thumb down the side of his cup. "When you first entered the Sunwatcher's chamber, what did you see?"

The images flashed across Browser's souls, and he closed his eyes a long moment. "Whiproot lay on his back. His mouth was covered with blood, and his war shirt was pulled up. His belly had been sliced open. Blood streaked the walls and ceiling and pooled on the floor. Hophorn was huddling in the corner, trembling. Blood and stuff from the intestines speckled her face and the blanket around her. Clearly two men had fought. Their sandal prints had tracked through the blood. The way the tracks circled each other, it appeared that Whiproot was trying to protect Hophorn, to keep the murderer from reaching her." Browser shook his head. "As best we could determine, the murderer leaped on Whiproot from the roof and struck him in the head. The blow dazed Whiproot enough that his attacker could stab him. From the cuts, Whiproot tried to defend himself. Then the murderer forced Whiproot to back into Hophorn's chamber and kneel down. But Whiproot must have seen his chance and leaped for the man, knocking him backward. They had overturned the pots on the north wall and stumbled through the warming bowl. Coals and broken potsherds scattered the floor. Instants later, I ran from the passageway where I had chased the katsina and out into the plaza."

"Tell me about the passageways?"

"Well, I—I know almost nothing, Uncle. None of us have spent much time inside. The town is falling apart. Every day we hear crashes and thuds as new sections of walls collapse. No one willingly enters that decaying hive. It is very dangerous."

Flame Carrier added, "When we first arrived, ten moons ago, a twelve-summers-old girl was killed running through the passageways. Browser's wife was with her. She said a roof collapsed on top of the girl. I have forbidden children to enter the town, except with an adult."

Browser could see thoughts churning behind Stone Ghost's eyes. Suspicion glinted.

"We found her body beneath a pile of rubble and fallen timbers, Uncle. It must have been an accident."

"Where did you find her?"

Browser turned, and pointed to the northeastern side of Talon Town, near Propped Pillar. "There. In a fourth-story chamber."

Stone Ghost gazed at it, then swirled his tea in his clay cup. For a time, only the moan of wind stirred the silence. Stone Ghost pulled the worn softness of his feathered cape up around his throat and sipped from his cup.

"Did you know," he said, "that the last Matron of Talon Town was as mad as a foaming-mouth skunk?"

Browser blinked, wondering what that had to do with the murderer. "No."

"Oh, yes, it was a calamity for the First People. The Blessed Night Sun ran away with her lover, the War

Chief Ironwood, and the next woman in line was completely daft. Let me see. I think her name was Featherstone. Yes. I believe that's right. As a child, Featherstone had been captured and taken slave by the Fire Dogs. They had beaten her in the head until her souls hung by the thinnest of webs, sometimes in her body, frequently not. She—"

"Uncle," Browser said reprovingly, "what does this have to do with the murderer?"

Stone Ghost looked at Browser with unwavering concentration. "Why, everything, my nephew."

"Why should it concern us that more than one hundred sun cycles ago, Featherstone was struck in the head?"

"Because she was," Stone Ghost responded. "I heard that tale from my own grandmother, the Blessed Orenda. You don't think she lied to me, do you?"

"No, Uncle. I just don't see how the story is related—"

"Oh, all things are related to all other things, my nephew. Whether we like it or not. Yes?"

Browser glanced at Matron Flame Carrier, saw her mouth turned down. He replied, "I wouldn't know, Uncle."

Stone Ghost cocked his head like a curious bird. He pointed to a chunk of sandstone twenty hands away. "Do you see that rock? If we went back far enough, I guarantee you we would discover that it hit someone in the head." He paused to examine Browser's expression. "Humans are like that. We bash each other all the time and for the most trivial of reasons." He lifted a finger. "But, if you make a careful study of bashed heads, you learn a lot about rocks and the people who throw them. Do you see what I mean?"

Flame Carrier gruffly folded her arms beneath her turkey feather cape, and gave Browser a disgruntled look. "I told you his souls flitted around like bats."

Stone Ghost swerved to stare at her. "Well, I should

think that fact would comfort you, considering that I am here to study people whose souls flit around like bats."

"What?" Browser asked in confusion.

Stone Ghost swung back. "Oh, come, my Nephew. Your wife had no friends, did she? People feared and distrusted her. Many accused her of witchcraft and whispered that she sent her souls 'flitting' about at night to harm others. She suffered violent headaches and on occasion went for days without speaking—"

"How do you know that?" Browser leaped to his feet in sudden fright. The old man's reputation for Power, and possibly even sorcery, dropped on Browser's chest like a landslide. His hand instinctively lowered to his war club. "You never knew my wife!"

Stone Ghost gazed at Browser through strange, glowing eyes. "No, but I know a great deal about her, Nephew. Because I know her Spirit Helper."

Silk Moth let out a wrenching cry, and the world seemed to go still. They all turned to look behind them, toward her chamber at the western end of Hillside Village. Her cries dropped to a series of suffocating gasps.

Browser gripped his club to halt the quaking of his hand. "Is Wolf your Spirit Helper, as well?"

"Mine? No." Stone Ghost shook his white head. "This katsina is a very selective god. It takes him moons of careful observation and much thought before he chooses those he will visit. He makes certain they are outcasts in their villages, and either sick themselves, or with desperately ill family members. He claims he can cure the coughing sickness if only the woman, or girl, will release her souls to him." Stone Ghost rose to his feet and took a step toward Browser. "She tries, of course, very hard. She doesn't wish to die, or to see precious family members die. But she fails. Always. The punishments inflicted by The Visitant for this failure are severe."

Browser's nerves had started to hum. "How do you

know these things? Did Catkin tell you about my wife?"

"Catkin is very loyal to you, my nephew. I have a different source of information. The families of the dead in Whitetail Village, Badgerpaw, and Frosted Meadow Village."

"What would they know about my . . . wife . . ." Browser's voice faded.

"Each of those villages had lost members over the past sun cycle. Women. Girls. Everyone assumed raiders had stolen them."

Browser stared unblinking at Stone Ghost. "Are you telling me that all of these females were murdered? By the same man?"

"That appears to be the case, Nephew."

Flame Carrier's small brown eyes flared. "Are you certain of this?"

Stone Ghost smiled. "The first rule of investigation, Matron, is that if you are certain, you've probably got it wrong."

Stone Ghost hobbled back toward his rock but before he seated himself he said, "Tell me one last thing. During the turmoil in Talon Town last night, where was the Blessed Cloudblower? Is her chamber not there? In the town?"

"Her chamber is there, yes, but she was not," Browser said. "We have many people ill with the coughing sickness. Cloudblower was in Hillside, Healing."

Stone Ghost nodded mildly. "Yes, I'm sure she was." He sat on the rock and sighed, "It will be dawn in another hand of time. When we have enough light, Nephew, I would like you to show me the passageway where you chased the katsina."

"I will gladly show you, Uncle, but I wish to examine Straight Path Wash first. Before the frost melts."

"Ah." Stone Ghost nodded. "Yes, of course. For tracks. I will wait in the First People's kiva. I must examine Whiproot anyway. I am in no rush."

"Well, I am," Flame Carrier replied. She rose and propped herself on her walking stick. Gray hair fell around her wrinkled face. "The Ceremony of the Longnight begins day after tomorrow. I don't like the idea that a murderer might be moving among us, choosing his next victim." She stabbed her walking stick at Stone Ghost. *"Find him."*

"Oh, that won't be necessary," Stone Ghost said with a smile. He finished his tea and poured the dregs on the hearthstones where the droplets sizzled and popped. "I assure you, he will find me. They always do."

CATKIN WOKE AT the sound of sandals on the roof. She rolled onto her back and squinted against the morning light that pooled on the western wall.

"Catkin?" Redcrop's young voiced called. "Are you awake?"

Catkin sat up in her buffalo hide. Her breath formed a white cloud in the cold air. Through her roof entry, she could see the girl's pretty oval face and large black eyes. She wore a yellow-and-red painted deerhide cape. Behind her, the dawn sky shone glistening and golden. "What is it, Redcrop?"

"Matron Flame Carrier requests that you meet with her in the First People's kiva. Stone Ghost arrived last night. The clan Elders—"

"What?" She threw back her hide, and lurched to her feet, sleepily looking around for her cape, comb, and a number of other things she knew she needed, but could not think of right now. "Why was I not informed?"

"The Matron knew you were exhausted. She did not wish to wake you. The clan Elders and the War Chief are already in the kiva. They were about to begin but Stone Ghost insisted that I come and fetch you first."

"Please tell the Elders that I will be there shortly."

"Yes, Catkin."

Redcrop's face disappeared, and Catkin heard her steps retreating across the roof.

Disoriented and groggy, Catkin stumbled toward the

big red pot that stood in the northeastern corner of her
chamber. She opened the lid and surveyed the array of
folded war shirts, cotton socks, hair pins, shell bracelets,
combs, and pendants. The icy wind last night had knotted
her hair. She pulled out a comb, and tugged it through
the tangled mass, and winced as she ripped out strands.

She had been up half the night reliving the events,
hearing the disturbance, leaping out of bed, and running
to Talon Town only to discover no ladder there. Panicked
by the cries coming from inside, she had dispatched He-
Who-Flies for a ladder, and tried to climb the south wall
of the town, to no avail. Then, after He-Who-Flies delivered the ladder, and she had made it inside, the sight of
Whiproot, the look on Hophorn's face when Cloudblower
had entered the chamber . . . How could anyone sleep?

Catkin pinned up her long hair and fastened it with
two plain wooden hair combs. As she slipped off her tan
sleeping shirt, she examined the folded clothing in the
pot, and selected a knee-length red shirt with white lines
zigzagging around the collar and hem. She slipped it over
her head, and reached for her buckskin leggings, then
stepped into her sandals. She grabbed her cape and
climbed the ladder into the morning cold.

Around twenty men and women stood in a whispering
ring around the plaza fire pit below, their backs stiff,
expressions taut. A group of unnaturally quiet children
squatted a short distance away, playing a dice game.
Their young eyes kept darting about, as if anxiously waiting to see what would happen next. A half-dozen dogs
slept on the warm sand near the fire, their ears pricking
when someone got loud.

Catkin climbed down the ladder and headed for Talon
Town. As she passed the fire pit Peavine yelled, "Wait!"
and shouldered through the crowd. Black-streaked gray
hair straggled around her ugly square face, and deep lines
cut her forehead, making her appear much older than her

thirty summers. Her doeskin cape flapped as she hurried toward Catkin. "I have been talking with the others. We wish to know if the stories are true."

Irritated, Catkin said, "Peavine, I have been summoned by the Matron. I do not have luxury of discussing—"

"Is it true that Stone Ghost has spent the past several days visiting the other villages in the canyon where young women have gone missing?"

Catkin spread her arms. "I have also heard that, but I do not know for certain. I have not spoken with him since I left his house days ago."

Peavine whispered, "Is it true that he is related to the War Chief?"

Catkin hesitated. Peavine would know soon enough, but Catkin did not wish to be the one to stoke rumors. "You will have to ask the War Chief, Peavine."

Peavine's black eyes glittered with suspicion. "How can we expect fairness from the War Chief's great-uncle? Surely Stone Ghost will not question his nephew."

Catkin glared. "Peavine, when Whiproot was killed last night, Browser was with Jackrabbit. He could not possibly be the murderer."

"That is not what I heard," Peavine said and cocked her head, peering at Catkin through one eye. "Jackrabbit told me that the War Chief ordered him to stay inside the dark passageways while he went out into the plaza alone. She lowered her voice. "Who is to say what happened in the time the two men were separated." Peavine shrugged. "Perhaps Hophorn knows, but she has told no one."

Catkin took a threatening step toward Peavine, and hissed, "If Jackrabbit told you that much, then he also told you the War Chief was standing with Whiproot on the roof when Jackrabbit was first attacked." She jammed a finger into Peavine's chest. "If you are going to tell the story, tell the *whole* story."

Catkin stalked away.

Behind her, Peavine called, "The whole story? How about this? The War Chief bribed someone to attack Jackrabbit to create a diversion, so that he could kill Whiproot!"

Catkin clenched her fists to quell her anger and walked straight to the road that ran in front of Talon Town's south wall. The crushed potsherds on the road shimmered and winked in the morning light. Jackrabbit stood guard on the roof ahead of her. When he saw her coming he lowered the ladder over the side.

"Thank you, my friend," she called.

"It is good to see you, Catkin."

As Catkin climbed, she studied his face. He looked every bit a frightened fifteen-summers-old youth. He nervously brushed his shoulder-length black hair behind his ears and bit his lip, watching her.

Catkin stepped off the ladder onto the roof and said, "How long have you been here?"

"Here? Not long. Two hands of time. I spent most of the night guarding Cloudblower's chamber."

Catkin peered down at the kiva that formed a large circle in the middle of the plaza below. Smoke rose through the hole in the roof, scenting the air with the rich fragrance of cedar. If Jackrabbit had stood guard most of yesterday, then all night long, he must be growing muddleheaded, perhaps even feeling ill.

Catkin pulled up the ladder and lowered it into the plaza. She stepped onto the top rung and said, "How are you, Jackrabbit?"

He gestured awkwardly. "Tired. I—I keep hearing Whiproot's screams."

They stared at each other in shared pain. Whiproot had been a good friend to both of them.

"And your head?" She pointed to the place he'd been struck last night.

He touched it and winced. "The blow glanced off my

skull. I have a headache, but it is bearable. Cloudblower made me drink several cups of willow root tea. They lessened the pain."

Catkin said, "Good," but gazed at him worriedly. Jackrabbit should be home wrapped in thick hides and fast asleep. Yesterday, they'd had seven full-time warriors. Now one was dead. Browser had clearly made the judgment that after Catkin's long run, she needed the sleep more than Jackrabbit. She wasn't certain he'd made the right choice. Injured, fatigued men tended to say things they did not mean.

"Jackrabbit, Peavine stopped me near the plaza fire. Did you . . ." She hesitated, then finished, "Did you say anything to her that might have led her to believe the War Chief murdered Whiproot?"

Jackrabbit's mouth fell open in shock. "No! Catkin, I would never do that! Last night, she asked me what had happened, and I told her. I do not know how she could have misunderstood—"

Catkin waved it away. "Forgive me for asking. Peavine deliberately misunderstands when it suits her purposes. You are tired, and have enough to concern you. When I am finished in the kiva, I will take your place here."

Jackrabbit nodded his gratitude. "Thank you. I—I could use sleep."

Catkin clasped him on the shoulder. "I won't be long."

She climbed down and walked across the plaza. Ahead of her the thirty-hand-tall figures of the Great Warriors of East and West peered down. The rich reds, blues, and yellows of their terrifying masks gleamed with an unearthly brilliance in the morning sun. The lightning bolts in their upraised fists seemed to blaze. An eerie gloom hovered in the plaza, like the stench of carrion on a hot day. Catkin's shoulder muscles bunched as she walked.

Long before she reached the doorway that led into the altar room outside of the kiva she heard soft voices.

Catkin ducked low to enter through the T-shaped doorway and stared up at the katsinas painted on the walls. Their gaudy, inhuman masks were hateful, fierce. They had their fangs bared and bows drawn, aimed at the person who had just stepped through the entry. At this moment, her. To her right stood a long rectangular stone altar, freshly plastered in white and painted with the images of mountain lion, coyote, rattlesnake, a rainbow, the sun, moon, and morning and evening stars. To her left, a narrow recessed stairway led down into the subterranean ceremonial chamber. Firelight gilded the steps.

Flame Carrier called, "Catkin? Is that you?"

"Yes, Matron."

Catkin climbed down. Torches burned on either side of the stairs, casting a haunting yellow light over the magnificent circular chamber. They would initiate this chamber tomorrow during the Ceremony of the Longnight and spend the rest of the evening praying that their efforts would open a tunnel to the underworlds, as the Blessed Poor Singer had prophesied.

One hundred hands away, at the opposite end of the kiva, Stone Ghost and Browser tended the ritual fire. Stone Ghost added sticks, while Browser blew on the coals to help them catch. The richness of cedar infused the chilly air.

Four square pillars, painted red, supported the pole roof. In the middle of the pillars that ran north and south, two long rectangular foot-drums stood. During ceremonials, musicians sat on the edge of the drums, and tapped the leather surface with their feet. Whiproot's body lay to her left on the eastern foot-drum, covered with the blanket Catkin had thrown over him last night. Gray-and-black geometric designs banded the top and bottom of the white blanket. Dried blood splotched the center.

Catkin lowered her eyes. *My friend. Gone.*

Somewhere in this room Whiproot's ghost stood and

watched, wishing they would proceed with his burial so that he could be on his way to the afterlife.

Soon, I promise you.

Three levels of benches encircled the chamber. The lowest bench had been painted yellow, the next red, and the highest bench shone blue. Above the blue bench, thirty-six glorious katsina masks stared at Catkin through hollow eye sockets. Crypts, filled with offerings, sank into the white walls just beneath the masks. Catkin's gaze took in the bowls of corn pollen, buffalo horn spoons, elaborately carved shell pendants, dance sticks, and beautifully painted gourd rattles. The Katsinas' People possessed little, but they had given their best to these gods.

The four Elders sat in a line on the yellow bench to her left. Catkin bowed to them.

Wading Bird sat closest to Catkin, his bald head shining in the firelight, his gnarled fists propped on his knees. His fringed brown cotton shirt and pants looked freshly washed. Despite his age, he had lost none of his keen sensibilities. He had not taken his eyes from Stone Ghost.

Springbank sat beside Wading Bird in a red-feathered cape. He had his wrinkled lips sucked in over toothless gums. Sparse white hair matted his freckled scalp. After sixty-five summers, Springbank did not see very well. He had to squint to focus his eyes. He seemed to be scrutinizing Whiproot's body.

Cloudblower nodded to Catkin. Catkin nodded back. The sacred Man-Woman had plaited her gray-streaked black hair into two long braids and left them to drape the front of her white doehide dress. Her triangular face with slanting eyes and sharply pointed nose appeared frozen as though she held onto her emotions with an iron fist.

Flame Carrier sat to Cloudblower's left. Her brown-and-white feathered cape shimmered in the firelight. She had fastened her gray hair over her ears with shell combs. The style did not enhance her appearance. Her bulbous nose resembled a dark brown egg tucked into a wrinkled nest.

"I came as you ordered, Matron," Catkin said.

Flame Carrier gestured at Stone Ghost and Browser. "As soon as we have a reliable fire, we will begin."

Stone Ghost grunted as he rose to his feet and grinned at Catkin. "It's good to see you again, child! I passed you on the road the day you left. You were sleeping, and I didn't wish to wake you. My heart soars to see you alive."

Browser stood and his thick black brows drew together. His round face and black hair gleamed in the flickering firelight. "Were you in danger?"

"No, War Chief."

By noon that day Catkin had been too haggard to run another step. She had curled into a snow shadow on the lee side of a large boulder and fallen into a dead sleep. She had awakened late in the afternoon, made a watery soup of boiled snow, deer jerky, and cornmeal, then had run until the darkness and falling snow halted her for the night. Had Stone Ghost bulled ahead through the darkness and storm?

"Your dedication surprises me, Elder," she said. "If you hadn't made several stops, you might have beaten me back and shamed me before my people."

Stone Ghost's cheap pottery-disk necklaces clicked as he hobbled forward, a warm smile on his ancient face. Soot streaked the front of his threadbare green shirt. "And terrified your war chief, I fear."

Browser wiped his hands on his buckskin cape. A thin layer of ash coated his flat nose and bushy eyebrows. He smiled at Catkin. "Yes. I would have imagined my finest warrior dead."

Stone Ghost gave Catkin a sympathetic look, apparently sensing how Browser's soft tone must have affected her. "Now that you are present, we may begin. I wish you to assist me."

She stepped forward. "What is it you require, Elder?"

Stone Ghost took her hand and dragged her toward the foot drum where Whiproot rested. "I wish you to be a witness, child. Just watch and remember."

"Of course," she said, but wondered why he needed her when there were five other witnesses in the kiva.

Catkin glanced at Browser, and Browser walked to stand behind her, looking over her shoulder. He moved in a bone-weary manner. Dark circles swelled beneath his eyes, and his breathing had fallen into the deep tortured rhythms of exhaustion.

Catkin whispered, "You need rest, War Chief."

He shook his head.

Did he still have trouble walking into his own chamber? The memories of his beautiful dead son must haunt his sleep. What did he dream of his wife? Did he dream of her at all?

"When we are finished here, I am going to relieve Jackrabbit. I will be standing guard," she said softly. "Rest in my chamber."

He bowed his head as if thankful she understood. "I will. Thank you."

Stone Ghost gently pulled the blanket from Whiproot's corpse and said, "Please come forward, Elders. There are several things I wish to show you."

The Elders whispered among themselves, then Flame Carrier rose and the others fell into line behind her. They filed over and formed a half-circle around Browser, Stone Ghost, and Catkin. Browser backed away allowing the Elders a closer view and leaned against the red northeastern pillar. Springbank took his place at Whiproot's feet, his old eyes squinted.

Firelight fluttered over the katsina masks on the wall lighting carved beaks and bared teeth, feathered head-dresses and fur-shrouded faces. Catkin had the uncanny feeling that they, too, watched, and with an unnatural interest.

"First," Stone Ghost said and tugged on Whiproot's rigid arm, "I wish you to notice the stiffness of the body. Stiffness usually develops within two hands of time after death, and disappears within twelve hands of time." He turned to Catkin. "How long has it been since this warrior's murder?"

Catkin hesitated, silently calculating the interval. "At least twelve hands, Elder. Perhaps thirteen."

Stone Ghost nodded. "Heavily muscled people, especially those who die fighting, often remain stiff longer than normal. On the other hand, very slight individuals who die in their sleep may never develop much stiffness. Heat and cold affect this pattern somewhat. So." He looked at Browser. "Forgive me for asking, Nephew, but I must. Was your wife stiff when you found her?"

Browser's shoulder muscles bulged through his cape. In a tortured voice he said, "Yes, Uncle."

"How long had she been missing?"

"Two days."

Murmurs broke out. Stone Ghost lifted a hand to silence them. "Then your wife was not killed the first night she was gone. She had probably been dead less than twelve hands of time when Flame Carrier found her in your son's burial pit."

Catkin folded her arms, listening, not certain why this was important.

Stone Ghost smoothed wispy white hair from his wrinkled face and tucked it behind his ears, then held his hands out to Browser. "Did you notice cuts or bruises on her hands, Nephew?"

Browser shifted against the red pillar. "No. Why?"

Stone Ghost's hands flashed, cutting the air, as if warding off blows. "When a person fights for his life, he gets injured in the process. For example"—He lifted Whip-root's left hand. One of the fingers had been nearly sev-ered. It hung down over the gashed, bloody palm—"I assume that this warrior was right-handed, and holding a weapon in it because he used his left hand to fend off his attacker's knife. That is also why we have cuts on the outside of his forearm."

Catkin's breathing went shallow. She whispered, "He was right-handed."

Browser said nothing, and Catkin could tell from his haunted expression that his thoughts had riveted on Ash Girl, probably asking the same questions as everyone else in the chamber: Why hadn't Ash Girl defended herself? Had her murderer taken her from behind? Perhaps she'd known the murderer and let him get close enough to kill her before she realized what was happening?

Stone Ghost hobbled to Whiproot's head. "Next I wish you to examine the bruises beneath the blood around this warrior's mouth."

"Bruises?" Browser said, astonished. He shoved away from the pillar. "I did not see those last night."

"It was dark, War Chief," Catkin said. "Even when we carried him in here, Jackrabbit stood at the foot of the stairs with the torch. The dim light probably hid many things from our view."

Stone Ghost's brows lowered. "Nephew? Did you not tell me that you thought this warrior had been dazed by a blow to the head, then stabbed, and forced to back into the Sunwatcher's chamber, where he fought to protect her?"

Browser nodded. "Yes."

With great care Stone Ghost tipped Whiproot onto his side and pulled blood-stiff black hair away from the rear of his head, revealing the gashed scalp and split skull. Catkin could see the brain inside.

The Elders gasped, and Flame Carrier reached for

Cloudblower's arm for support. She whispered, "Blessed gods."

Stone Ghost looked at the Elders one by one. "Which of you imagines that Whiproot could have fought off an attacker after such a blow? This wound was not administered with a war club, but a stone hatchet."

The Elders pushed each other to get closer. Flame Carrier looked at Browser. She did not utter a word but her eyes accused him of missing the obvious.

Browser said, "He was struck after he was stabbed."

"Long after, Nephew." Stone Ghost let the clump of hair drop. "I suspect he was not quite dead, and the murderer wished to hurry him along. More interesting, though, are the bruises around his mouth. We will know more after he has been washed and prepared, but if you look closely, they appear to be fingerprints."

Catkin could feel the blood draining from her head, leaving her floating on a tide of shock. Her souls pictured the night, imagined it all happening . . .

Her eyes met Browser's like a clash of war clubs.

She said, "Someone was holding him—"

Browser finished, "—while someone else stabbed him."

Cloudblower let out a small cry and backed away. Her white dress and the silver strands in her braids gleamed yellowish in the fire's glow.

Stone Ghost watched Cloudblower like a coyote at a mouse hole.

"Oh, gods," Cloudblower murmured. Her triangular face flushed and tears sparkled in her slanting eyes. "I—I thought I could stop—" her mouth hung open as if afraid to finish. Then she said, "She tried to t-tell me."

Flame Carrier shouted, "Who did?"

Cloudblower looked straight into Browser's haunted eyes, then ran from the chamber. Her sandals clacked on the stairs and across the altar room above.

Flame Carrier swung around to Browser. "War Chief, what did she mean?"

"I do not know, Matron! This is the first I have heard of it!"

"Then go after her, and find out!"

Browser bowed obediently and hurried for the stairs.

While Flame Carrier, Springbank, and Wading Bird shouted questions at each other, Stone Ghost took Catkin by the hand and led her away from the Elders. He stopped in the fluttering torch light at the foot of the stairs. His brows arched, silently questioning her.

Catkin whispered, "I'm not certain. Hophorn. I think. It must have been . . ."

"Cloudblower, wait!"

Browser's buckskin cape flapped around his long legs as he ran across the sunlit plaza after her.

Cloudblower ducked beneath her painted leather door curtain and disappeared. The curtain swung.

Jackrabbit, who stood guard on the roof above, gave Browser a puzzled look and nervously glanced around as if fearing some other disaster might befall him.

Browser called, "All is well, Jackrabbit, but stay vigilant."

"Yes, War Chief!" Jackrabbit clutched his war club in both hands.

High on the fifth story near the cliff face, Browser saw Skink and Water Snake put their heads together and talk in low voices. Sunlight burned across the towering sandstone wall behind them and lit the shoulders of their hide capes. Browser could feel the tension rising.

He trotted for Cloudblower's door and stood outside shifting from one foot to the other.

"Come, War Chief," Cloudblower whispered.

Browser ducked under the door curtain into the dim chamber. Larger than most, this chamber stretched three body lengths by five. The warming bowl in the middle of the floor threw a dull reddish gleam over the katsina masks hanging from the white walls. Furred muzzles with sharp teeth shone. Dark hollow eyes peered at him.

Cloudblower's white dress flashed in the shadowed rear of the chamber, but he couldn't make out her face yet. A pile of bedding hides and baskets lined the western wall to Browser's right. To his left black-and-white pots, filled with blue corn, red-and-white speckled beans, and pumpkin seeds, sat in a clump. As Browser's eyes adjusted, he saw Cloudblower cradling Hophorn in her arms. She had her lips pressed against Hophorn's hair. Hophorn wore a long brown dress and badgerhide leggings. The patch of hair where Cloudblower had opened her skull had gone white, as though the roots had been starved and died.

"B-Browsser," Hophorn stammered and reached out to him.

Browser hurried around the warming bowl and crouched beside Hophorn. She sat on a thick pile of buffalo and elk hides. Hophorn looked gaunt. Her broad cheekbones stuck out sharply, making her small nose and full lips seem larger. Long curling lashes fringed her enormous eyes, but fear walked in those black depths.

Browser took Hophorn's hand and held it gently. "Are you well, Hophorn?"

Hophorn tried to nod, but it came out a jittery side-to-side movement. "H-helllp. Me."

Browser glanced at Cloudblower, and the Healer squeezed her eyes closed and shook her head. Browser did not know whether Cloudblower was signaling him not to ask or telling him she didn't understand the plea either.

Browser forced himself to smile, hoping it would reassure Hophorn. "I will help you in any way I can, Hophorn. You know this. You have only to ask."

Hophorn gazed up at him with her whole wounded heart in her glistening eyes. She struggled to say, "C-commming. Ssstop. Them."

"Who is coming?"

"T-Two. The . . . two."

Browser clutched her hand more tightly. Every muscle in his body prickled. Insistently he said, "Who are they, Hophorn? I must know."

"T-Two." Her strength seemed to fail her. She sank back into Cloudblower's arms, trembling. "C-Coming." Tears traced silver lines down her cheeks.

Browser looked imploringly at Cloudblower. "What does she mean?"

Cloudblower bowed her head and her long gray and black braids mingled with Hophorn's jet black hair. "She keeps repeating the same words about 'the two' coming. I didn't understand until Stone Ghost was explaining the bruises on Whiproot's mouth."

Browser laid Hophorn's hand on her chest and said, "It makes no sense. How could she know the murderers are coming?"

Cloudblower said, "I'm not certain she knows what she's saying. She may mean she *fears* they are coming, Browser, not that she knows they are coming. The past five days have been horrifying for her. She—"

"For all of us, Cloudblower." Browser slumped to the floor and ran a hand through his smoke-scented hair. "Gods, I am more confused now than when my wife was first killed. What did you think of the things Stone Ghost said about her death? The stiffness of her body? The fact that she did not defend herself? I—"

Hophorn leaned her head against Cloudblower's shoulder, but her gaze remained on Browser, her eyes huge, unblinking, as if anxious for him to say or do something.

"War Chief, your uncle was asking questions, not stating facts. There are many explanations for the things he noted."

He frowned at Cloudblower. "What? Tell me?"

"Perhaps your wife ran for a day, or—or she may have been sitting praying for a day before he found her. She was strong, Browser, but she was also alone and tired. She would have been easy prey." In a strained voice, Cloudblower added, "Especially if there really were two of them."

Browser dropped his head in his hands and massaged his temples. "Yes. One could have distracted her while the other clubbed her from behind. She would not have had the opportunity to struggle against them. Gods, I wish . . ."

Browser looked up when Hophorn shifted.

She pushed away from Cloudblower, shivered, and her trembling arms flopped against her sides, as if they'd gone numb. The horror melted from her expression. Hophorn crawled to her bedding to his right and stretched across a rumpled pile of red blankets like a cat in warm sunlight. Before she closed her eyes a strange ghostly smile came to her face. Then she seemed to be asleep, immediately. Her entire body went limp. Her face slackened.

Browser could not take his eyes from her.

Cloudblower whispered, "Since the injury, she . . . I can't explain it. Often, she seems to simply leave her body. I will be speaking with her and her eyes go blank. She stares into the distance as though her souls have fled. And, perhaps, that is what's happened. I have sat with her for hands of time, watching. Were it not for the rise and fall of her chest I would think her dead, Browser."

Cloudblower gripped her white doehide skirt and stared at her hands. Her gray-streaked black braids dangled around her triangular face. "I'm afraid for her, Browser."

Browser got to his feet and stood looking down at Hophorn's beautiful face. Her long hair streamed across the blankets, creating a shining black halo. She seemed almost too peaceful, her tall, lithe body like a magnificent sculpture.

Outside sandals scraped the frozen dirt and he could hear Catkin speaking softly to Stone Ghost.

Browser murmured, "I am afraid for all of us, Healer."

He reached for the door curtain and drew it aside.

BROWSER LOOKED OUT at Catkin and Stone
Ghost. The ruined wall behind them resembled a
patchwork of red stone and crumbling plaster. Only the
First People's kiva, to Browser's left, gleamed with fresh
plaster and paint. Strings of red spirals ran around the
circumference at the top and bottom of the white ceremonial chamber.

Catkin stood tall, her broad shoulders squared, her face
unreadable.

Stone Ghost gave Browser a grandfatherly smile and
gestured to the door curtain. "Will the Healer allow us
to enter, Nephew?"

Cloudblower called, "Yes. Please, come."

Browser stepped aside, and Stone Ghost hobbled by
him into the sage-scented dimness. His white hair
gleamed reddish as he passed the warming bowl and went
to sit down on a deerhide to Cloudblower's right. The
light shone on his long hooked nose and thick white
brows. His green shirt showed through the holes in his
mangy turkey-feather cape.

Browser continued to hold the curtain aside, but Catkin
did not enter. He cocked his head, silently asking why,
and she took a step backward, as if she feared to enter
the Healer's chamber.

Catkin said, "I promised to relieve Jackrabbit, War
Chief. If you need me, that is where I will be."

Browser examined her stiff expression, and an uneasy

sensation curdled his stomach. "Very well. I will find you when we are done, and tell you what passed here."

Catkin said, "Until then," and strode toward the pole ladder to the roof.

Browser let the curtain drop. Cloudblower sat with her head bowed, as if unwilling to meet Stone Ghost's keen old eyes. The fringes across the breast of her white dress trembled.

Stone Ghost waited, his knotted hands in his lap.

Browser said, "Thank you for what you revealed in the kiva, Uncle. I am grateful for your help."

Stone Ghost smiled, and stuck a finger through one of the holes in his cape, as if he'd never seen it before. "And you, Healer, what did you think of my words?"

"You did not come here to ask me that, Elder," she said softly.

"No," Stone Ghost answered. "I came to ask you what it was you could not stop and what Hophorn tried to tell you."

Cloudblower studied her fists. They shone with a crimson gleam. "The day we—we found the War Chief's wife"—she gestured to Browser—"I opened Hophorn's skull to release the evil Spirits feeding in her head wound. Hophorn could not speak at first, but she kept making sounds, frantically trying to tell me something. She would draw two lines on the floor, and repeat words over and over, as if it were urgent that I understand, but I did not, Elder."

Stone Ghost leaned closer to Cloudblower, his eyes shining. "What did you think she was saying? You must have tried to guess."

Cloudblower lifted her hands. "I thought, for a time, the words were *bat* and *fight,* or perhaps *black* and *white.* Something like that." Cloudblower closed her eyes again, and took a breath. "Later, I thought she said, 'the bright one,' which made me think that her earlier words might

have been *black* and *bright,* but how can I know, Elder?"
A pleading expression creased Cloudblower's triangular
face. "Hophorn has been too ill to explain, and I—"

"That is true," Browser defended. Cloudblower looked
as if she teetered on the edge of a precipice. To give her
time to collect herself, he said, "I myself have questioned
Hophorn on what she saw the day my wife was killed.
The first word she spoke clearly was last night, when
she—she called my name."

It had not occurred to him until this instant that it may
have taken an overwhelming act of will for Hophorn to
find his name inside her, that desperation had torn it from
her injured souls.

Stone Ghost's gaze lifted to Hophorn. A lifeless expression slackened her face.

Browser said, "Uncle, when I first entered this chamber, Hophorn told me that 'the two' were coming. She
begged me to stop them. To help her."

"The two?" Stone Ghost asked.

Cloudblower shook her head, as if denying what
Browser had just said.

Stone Ghost said, "You disagree?"

"No, I—I mean, yes, she did say that, but I think she
meant she *fears* they are coming, Elder. It was the tone
in her voice; it was not one of knowledge, but terror."

"Perhaps," Browser granted, "but we—"

Hophorn moved. She drew up one knee, and resettled
herself on her side, facing them. Her brown dress fell in
sculpted folds around her, and her black-and-white
badgerhide leggings looked startling against the red blankets. Her eyes opened and fixed on Browser.

Quietly, Browser asked, "Hophorn? Are you awake?"

Her eyes had gone glassy.

Browser returned his gaze to Stone Ghost. "We cannot
afford to ignore the possibility that one of the murderers

spoke to her last night, Uncle. Spoke to her and told her he would be back."

"You are right, Nephew. Murderers often make threats. Take whatever precautions you must."

Browser nodded. "Later in the day, when people from the distant villages begin arriving for the Ceremony of the Longnight, I will go to Flame Carrier and ask that she speak with the clan matrons. Perhaps they will assign several of their warriors to help guard the village during the ritual. Surely 'the two' will not risk challenging—"

"Surely they will, Nephew. Do you know the faces of every villager who will be here? No? I doubt that they know the faces of every person in Hillside Village either. There will be many strangers present. Two more will be of little consequence." Stone Ghost touched Browser's shoulder. "Though, you are right, of course. More guards mean more eyes. But do not suppose that more eyes will stop them. They won't."

"I don't understand?" Browser frowned at the old man. "I would not risk killing someone if I thought I might be captured by her relatives."

"No," Stone Ghost answered. "You would not. But you are sane, Nephew."

Stone Ghost grunted to his feet and hobbled across the room, halting five hands from Hophorn. As he knelt, his tattered turkey feather cape spread across the floor. "Blessed Sunwatcher?" he called respectfully. "May I speak with you?"

Hophorn's full lips parted, but her eyes remained on Browser.

"Can you hear me, Sunwatcher?" Stone Ghost waved a hand in front of her open eyes.

Cloudblower's face tensed. She whispered, "It's another of her blanking-out spells, Elder. They come upon her swiftly and often take hands of time to pass. She—"

"I know. She is not well," Stone Ghost sighed, and got to his feet. "I will try again later, when she is rested."

As though some part of her had taken his words as an order, Hophorn's eyes closed, and her head lolled sideways on the red blankets. She appeared to be sound asleep.

Stone Ghost stood silently for several moments, studying her. "Nephew, I wish to walk with the Healer. Alone. Do not consider it a reflection upon you, rather—"

"Do not apologize, Uncle." Browser rose to his feet. "I promised to speak with Catkin. I ask only that you remain in the plaza, in my sight. I do not wish to worry that someone is sneaking up on the two of you."

Stone Ghost turned to Cloudblower. "Healer? Will you grant me a finger of your time?"

"Yes, of course," Cloudblower said but sounded reluctant. She reached for her painted deerhide cape and swung it around her shoulders. "I will meet you outside. I need to cover Hophorn. In a few moments, she will start growing cold."

"Of course." Stone Ghost ducked beneath the door curtain. Browser followed him out into the cool morning air. He could hear Cloudblower whispering to Hophorn, and knew from the few words he caught that she was reassuring Hophorn, telling her not to worry, that she would return soon.

He-Who-Flies straightened to his full height, over twelve hands, and a breath expanded his massive chest. He scrutinized Stone Ghost with slitted eyes. His round, flat face showed the strain of a long night. Lines cut deeply around his mouth and across his forehead. "War Chief?" he said to Browser. "A word with you?"

Browser nodded, and stepped closer. "Yes?"

He-Who-Flies kept his deep voice low. "What did you find this morning? At the wash? Were there tracks?"

Browser shook his head. "No."

He-Who-Flies grimaced. "I heard what Hophorn said about 'the two' coming. Does that mean you think there are two people working together?"

"It appears so. There are other things, as well, which bolster her words. Whiproot has bruises on his mouth, as though a hand—"

"Clamped his mouth shut while someone else killed him!"

Browser nodded.

He-Who-Flies glanced around. "If the murderers are human, how are they getting in? And out after they commit their crimes?"

Browser searched the enormous crumbling town that surrounded them and the stone and dirt that piled against the walls. "This town is like an ancient rabbit warren, He-Who-Flies. If men are brave enough to risk being crushed by collapsing walls, there are dozens of entries and exits."

"But humans would leave tracks, War Chief. We would see some sign of their passing!"

Browser frowned. After Whiproot's murder and Silk Moth's screams last night, no one felt safe. Less than a hand of time ago, he'd heard Peavine tell Redcrop that perhaps Ash Girl's wicked soul had gotten loose and was tormenting the people who'd spoken ill of her during her life. He had not wished to mention that if that were true Peavine would have been the first to die.

"There are tracks, He-Who-Flies, inside the passageway where the katsina fled last night."

"The tracks of two people?"

"No. One. But it tells us we are looking for men, not gods."

"Not gods," He-Who-Flies agreed, "but maybe witches who can transform themselves into gods. Very powerful witches who kill with a word."

Browser replied, "These people prefer real weapons.

They struck Hophorn with a club and killed Whiproot with a stone hatchet."

"A hatchet?" He-Who-Flies asked quietly. "I had not heard that."

"I did not know myself until a short time ago."

To his right, high in the rear of the town, Skink and Water Snake watched from the rubble of the toppled fifth story. They clutched war clubs in their hands. On the roof to Browser's left, Catkin stood with her back to him, surveying the canyon beyond. Wind Baby had torn strands of raven hair loose from her combs and fluttered them over her back like the sinuous arms of a dancer. The sight had an odd affect on him, comforting.

Cloudblower pushed her door curtain aside and stepped out. Her graceful brows lowered, accentuating the bladelike sharpness of her nose. She appeared unhappy. "I am here, Elder," she announced and spread her feet as if preparing for a fight.

Stone Ghost slipped his arm through hers and said, "I am not as steady as I once was, Healer. You'll help me, won't you?"

"Yes, Elder. Tell me where you wish to go."

The lines at the corners of Stone Ghost's eyes crinkled as he smiled and pointed. "Let us walk toward the hole in the wall where the killer fled last night. We will talk along the way."

Cloudblower glanced uncomfortably at Browser and He-Who-Flies, then led the old man toward the hole in the crumbling wall.

Browser said, "I will speak with you more later, He-Who-Flies. I promised to inform Catkin of what passed here. Stay vigilant."

"I will, War Chief." He-Who-Flies returned to his guard position outside Cloudblower's door. His eyes scanned the plaza and the cliff that loomed behind Skink and Water Snake.

As Browser climbed the pole rungs of the ladder, he felt exposed, vulnerable. His backbone seemed to turn to ice. The cold sensation spread through him. By the time he'd reached the roof where Catkin stood, he felt as if his insides had frozen solid. Catkin seemed to know. Apprehension strained her beautiful oval face.

"What is it? What's happened?"

"Let us talk away from anyone's hearing." He lifted a hand toward the southwestern corner of the roof.

They walked in silence. Finches flitted through the ruins, chirping and fluttering their wings, hopping from stone to stone. In the distance, the western sky sparkled as though carefully polished.

Browser stopped at the edge of the roof and gazed at the sunlit canyon wall. The pile of fresh earth where they'd buried his son shone darker than the rest of the desert. The boy would be in the Land of the Dead now. Responsibility for his care had shifted from Browser's shoulders to that of the Blessed Ancestors. He prayed that they would care as much for his son as he had.

He forced his eyes away. The grave where they'd found his wife remained a gaping hole. No one had wished to fill it. Nearby, the windswept fire pit Hophorn had stoked lay cold and dead. Large chunks of black charcoal filled the center.

"Hophorn said that 'two' are coming." Browser watched Catkin's face go pale.

"Did she say when?"

He shook his head. "No, but I have known her since we were children, Catkin. The look in her eyes told me she meant *soon*."

A swallow went down Catkin's throat. The morning breeze fluttered her hair around her face. Her eyes lifted to the towering canyon wall. Snow filled the shadowed crevices, and wispy Cloud People sailed through the blue above the tan sandstone.

"What are you looking for?" Browser asked.

Catkin tipped her chin to the rim. "For the place where they must stand."

"Who?"

"Hasn't it occurred to you? The perfect place to watch from is up there. Men could sit on the rim, unnoticed, all day. They could study people's habits, when they rise, when they go for water, how often, and at what times of day they walk alone. It would take little effort. They could bide their time until they saw their chance."

Browser felt as if he'd been bludgeoned. "Blessed gods," he whispered. "We have to post guards on the rim. Why didn't you tell me this before? When did you first—"

"The day we found your wife," she said. "That was when I . . ." She paused. A strand of black hair blew across her turned-up nose and tangled with her long eyelashes, but she did not seem to notice. "Browser, how well can a person hear from up there?"

A light-headed euphoria filled him. "The canyon wall seems to magnify sound. I have stood on the rim many times and heard every word spoken by people in Hillside Village. You think they—"

"Listen," she finished. "Yes."

The slanting light touched the dark circles beneath her eyes and flashed from her juniper hair combs. She shifted to examine the road that ran in front of Talon Town, and Browser gripped her hand to make her look back at him. He was conscious of the warmth of her skin and the frail bones beneath her long fingers.

"Catkin, why didn't you wish to enter Cloudblower's chamber?"

The longer he held her hand, the more swiftly her pulse pounded.

As though choosing her words with care, she whispered, "There is something . . ." A shiver went through her.

"What?"

"I do not know, War Chief!" she hissed angrily. "There is something in her chamber. I have never seen it, but whenever I go near her chamber, I *feel* it, like a serpent slithering through my veins!"

Browser stood rigid. "Is it a—a Spirit, or a thing? Perhaps a witch's charm? We must tell Cloudblower. She may not even know it's there."

In the long silence that followed, Browser saw Redcrop and another slave, an old man named Hawkfoot, walk down to the drainage with water jars swinging in their hands. The shell bells on their sandals clicked. As Father Sun rose higher into the sky, the shadows scuttled back, clinging against the cliffs like dark frightened children.

Catkin whispered, "Cloudblower knows it's there."

"How can you be so certain?"

She disentangled her arm from his grip and walked away into the slanting rays of sunlight that fell through the clouds. She held her head down, as if disinclined to continue their discussion.

Browser matched her stride. "Do you think Cloudblower is involved in these murders?"

"Do you?" she said, and a half-hearted smile touched her lips. "I doubt that either of us do."

He took her hand again, forcing her to stop. "Explain."

Catkin gazed down into the plaza. Two hundred hands away, Cloudblower stood beside Stone Ghost. "Haven't you ever noticed? Whenever I must go to her chamber, she never invites me in. She always comes out to meet me, as if she knows that *I* know."

"Know what?"

"That she is hiding something. That she has a terrible secret. Something she wishes no one to know."

"Are you accusing her of—"

"Nothing! I would never accuse Cloudblower of harming anyone, War Chief! I love her. She is a good and kind woman. She works very hard to Heal the sick and injured. She loves children and tirelessly cares for the old people. How could I accuse Cloudblower of anything wicked?"

Browser searched her tormented expression. He was not sure if she'd meant that last statement to be taken seriously or if it had been a cry of frustration, meaning no one would believe her if she did.

He reluctantly released her fingers, and propped his hands on his hips. "You are not being wholly truthful, Catkin. I know you. Why aren't you sharing your thoughts with me?"

Her eyes evaded his.

Browser fumbled with the polished handle of his war club. Over the sun cycles the wood had absorbed the oils from his hands, the blood of his victims. The club felt solid beneath his fingers: the only thing in the world that did.

He glanced up at Catkin. Loneliness always drove him to her, and he'd never felt more lonely in his life than he did at this instant.

"Please, my friend," Browser said softly. "There are many good reasons for not trusting me, and I know them all. I am often foolish. But"—he looked up and she held his gaze—"you must know that you are the only person in the world I trust completely. I know you keep my confidences locked in your heart, and you must know that I do the same for you."

"Yes. I do."

He spread his arms wide. "Then trust me now. I am worried that there are many things you have kept from me, and I need to hear them. Do you understand? I should have posted guards on the rim the day we found my wife. I was confused and grieving." He tightened his fists and frowned at the rim above Skink and Water Snake. A flock of pinyon jays floated on the air currents, flapping and diving. "I am still grieving. I need you to help me, Catkin."

She looked vulnerable. Her hair combs winked as she turned to look southward, across the canyon. The sparse grasses gleamed like a mottled golden blanket.

Browser moved to stand close beside her, his face no more than two hands away. He could smell the delicate fragrance that clung to her hair, and see the sweat that beaded the elegant line of her jaw. "Please. Help me."

Catkin closed her eyes. "The night I—I found you . . . on the cliff? Last summer?"

"Yes?" he said, but shame filled him. He'd fought half the night with Ash Girl. His son had been huddled in his blankets with his head covered, coughing and whimpering. When Browser had lifted his fist to strike Ash Girl, he'd suddenly stopped, realizing what he was about to do. He'd run from their chamber like a madman. Catkin had found him on the rim, bent double, sobbing like a five-summers-old child.

"What about that night, Catkin?"

She wet her lips. "What name were you calling?"

Browser frowned in confusion. "What do you mean?"

"You were calling a name. *Shadow* something. I heard you, as I climbed the stairs cut into the cliff."

"I called out to no one, Catkin."

She looked at him as though angry that he would lie to her at a moment like this.

"I swear I called to no one. Why do you think I'm lying?"

"It was your voice, Browser. I would know your voice anywhere. Unless . . ." Her anger vanished in an instant, replaced by naked fear.

"What is it?"

She whispered, "Did you know that Cloudblower was there?"

"You mean . . . on the rim?"

"Yes. When I helped you to your feet I heard her whispering."

His bushy brows drew together, not sure he understood why that bothered Catkin. Cloudblower had probably heard his fight with Ash Girl, and had been worried about him. "And?"

"She was not alone, Browser. At first I thought she was speaking with He-Who-Flies. The man had a deep voice."

"Go on."

Catkin's eyes scanned the ruins behind them and the roads in front of them. In the distance, several people walked toward Talon Town.

"Browser, just before we left, I saw eyes flash in the darkness. The man and I stared straight at each other. His eyes blazed, as though I had stumbled upon a private ritual, and he hated me for it. Or perhaps he hated me for being with you, I don't know. I—"

"It was dark, Catkin. If you could not see Cloudblower—"

"I am not finished," she cut him off.

Browser closed his mouth. "Forgive me."

"I have heard that man's voice at least one other time."

"When?"

Catkin shivered. "Last night. The voice that cried 'Help me!' That wasn't Whiproot, Browser. *It was him.*"

Stone Ghost released Cloudblower's arm and peered through the jagged hole in the wall. Fallen pieces of red sandstone scattered the floor. A musty scent suffused the darkness. He could make out the sandal tracks of at least three people in the soft windblown dirt.

"Have you ever been in here?" Stone Ghost asked.

Cloudblower's face tensed. "Yes, Elder. Last Moon of Blazing Sun. I came looking for a cool place to sleep."

"The interior chambers stay cool in the summer heat?"

Cloudblower nodded.

Stone Ghost patted the stones in the crumbling wall, and sighed, "My grandmother told me that. She said that winter or summer the temperature varied little in the innermost chambers."

Cloudblower cocked her head, and her long graying black braids fell over the front of her painted deerhide cape. "That is true, Elder. Though few people know it. Did your grandmother live here?"

"No, but she grew up with the Blessed Poor Singer, and he told her many tales of this place."

In a soft, reverent voice, Cloudblower said, "Your grandmother knew the Blessed prophet? I would have given anything to have seen him just once in my life. What was your grandmother's name?"

"I'm sure you've never heard of her. She came from a great people who live far to the east. They are mountain builders. They carry dirt in baskets for hundreds of sun cycles until they've piled up small mountains, then they place their houses on top of them. Her own people called her Orenda, though later in her life she came to be known as The Blessed Mother, because no one was allowed to hurt a child in her presence. She would not even allow a parent to utter a harsh word or give a misbehaving child an unkind look. She spent much of her life loving and protecting children." A fond smile warmed his wrinkled face. "I think she missed her people, though. She often spoke of their magnificent artwork, the brilliant fabrics they wove, the extraordinary stoneworkers who labored for the Sunborn."

"The Sunborn?"

"Her people."

"Curious," Cloudblower murmured. "Why would people do that? Build mountains?"

Stone Ghost stepped inside the dark chamber, and blinked until his eyes adjusted. Refuse clotted the floor. A large packrat nest of juniper needles, grass, feathers, and bits of fur filled the corner to his right. Ahead of him, he could just make out a dark T-shaped doorway.

"My grandmother's people believe that Father Sun and Mother Earth were torn apart at the moment of creation and that by building mountains they help Mother Earth to touch fingertips with Father Sun."

"They believe that the earth is their mother?" Cloudblower said disdainfully. "Not their grandmother?"

"Yes. That's right."

Cloudblower folded her arms. "That is foolishness. Our Grandmother Earth gave birth to first woman, then she gave birth to the Great Warriors of East and West who helped the people to climb through the underworlds. The twins ridded the surface world of monsters, in order that we might walk unhindered through the light, and—"

"Yes, that is what we believe. The Mountain Builders would think our stories just as foolish as you do theirs, Healer."

Stone Ghost backed out into the wan winter sunlight and smiled. Cloudblower did not return the gesture. Her expression was that of a man accused of something he had not done.

Stone Ghost sat down on the pile of fallen stones beside the hole in the wall and propped his hands on his knees. A chill breeze blew around the plaza, kicking up plumes of dust. Cloudblower remained standing. Stone Ghost examined the red and yellow images of the gods that danced around the hem of her cape. The Wolf katsina led the procession, followed by the Sun katsina, and Badger.

Stone Ghost hooked a thumb at the wall behind him. "My nephew and I are going to search these ruins this morning. What do you think we will find?"

"I can't say, Elder."

Stone Ghost braced his hands on his knees and gazed up into her troubled face. "On my way here, I visited several villages."

Cloudblower's teeth ground beneath the thin veneer of her cheeks. "Yes, I know."

"I discovered some interesting and terrible things. In the past sun cycle, each of those villages has lost a woman or a girl. Many of the victims were dragged through the villages and left in the plaza for all to see. Then their bodies were stolen. Just like my nephew's wife. Most of the relatives of those women believe raiders are responsible."

Cloudblower did not respond.

Stone Ghost studied the hard set of her lips, as if she were straining against words that longed to be spoken. "The people in Whitetail Village, Badgerpaw Village, and Frosted Meadow Village, told me sad tales of lonely, sick little girls. They also told me that you had been very good to them. They said you ran to their village when they called, and stayed up all night nursing the sick. They told me you left only when you believed the girl was out of danger."

"I do what I can."

Stone Ghost smoothed the brown-and-white turkey feathers over his knees. "Yes, but these girls had many problems, didn't they?"

"I tended their head wounds and their coughs, Elder. I did not notice if something else was wrong with them."

Stone Ghost waited for her to continue. When she didn't, he said, "Shortly after you left, they vanished."

Cloudblower looked up, as if surprised. "What?"

"You knew they were missing."

"Yes, of course, but . . ."

Stone Ghost scanned her face. "But not when it happened?"

Cloudblower didn't seem to be breathing. Her head trembled.

"Many of them disappeared within hands of time after you left, Healer."

Cloudblower violently shook her head as if to deny it, then, suddenly, the certainty seemed to drain away. She went still. Her eyes darted about, searching for something or perhaps gathering and fitting disparate pieces together.

Stone Ghost gave her more time to think. His gaze drifted over Talon Town, trying to see it as it must have been one hundred sun cycles earlier, filled with playing children, women grinding corn, and traders displaying their wares.

"What did you mean in the kiva, Healer, when you said 'I thought I could stop . . . ?' Stop what?"

"Nothing. I—I meant nothing."

Stone Ghost's eyes narrowed. "You live here, in Talon Town, but you were away last night when your friend was killed. Yes?"

"I was tending Peavine's young daughter, Yucca Blossom. She was ill. I boiled willow bark tea for her pain and Sang to her. She needed me. There were warriors here protecting Hophorn. I thought it was safe to leave." She twisted her hands as if punishing herself for making the wrong decision.

"When did you first learn that something had happened in Talon Town?"

"I heard young Stonehead yelling for help. By the time I reached the town, Catkin and several other warriors had already arrived and were trying to find a ladder to climb over the wall. The screams coming from inside were . . . were hideous, Elder. I knew a torch would be needed. I ran back to Hillside for one, and when I returned people were frantically pouring over the wall into the town."

"Did you see anyone outside the walls? Perhaps running away?"

"Elder," she said in exasperation, "people were running in all directions."

"Ah." Stone Ghost nodded. "Of course."

The Healer's expression had turned frantic, as if she teetered on the verge of desperate actions.

Clouds billowed over the plaza, pushing westward like a gleaming white army. He pointed. "Did you know that the Thunderbirds build nests of lightning bolts in the Cloud People?"

Cloudblower squinted.

He continued, "It's truly amazing. They weave the lightning bolts into blazing baskets, then tuck them into the soft hearts of the Cloud People. When the hatchlings are born, they shake the baskets apart with their thunder. Lightning bolts fly and the hatchlings soar free."

Cloudblower watched the sky for a few moments, then lowered her gaze to the ground.

"I fear," Stone Ghost said, "that the Cloud People may be rushing to join us for the Celebration of the Longnight. I hope they do not bring snow with them."

Cloudblower frowned.

"You were captured by the Fire Dogs, weren't you? Many summers ago?"

She flinched. "Why do you ask?"

Stone Ghost rubbed his hands together. The morning air had chilled them. "I have heard they do terrible things to slaves."

Cloudblower stared at him.

"Were you beaten?"

She whispered, "Often."

"Raped?"

She didn't answer.

"You must have a special sympathy for others who have suffered the same fate."

Cloudblower's shoulder muscles swelled through her cape, as if suspecting and fearing his meaning.

Stone Ghost nodded to himself. Her reaction told him a great deal.

She said, "Would that be bad?"

"Not at all. But it might lead you to hide things that you would not otherwise." He smiled. "Do you see what I mean?"

Cloudblower's cheeks flushed. "No, I do not."

"Well, it is a curious coincidence, perhaps, but I often find that murderers have suffered much pain in their lives. Many of them were beaten senseless by their parents or other close relatives. A few endured true horrors, things that sane people could not even imagine. Torture, mutilation. I will not describe the heinous acts for you, because I do not wish those images to live in your dreams as they do in mine. I mention them only because I wish you to understand that I, too, have sympathy for those who have been tormented."

Cloudblower's expression softened. She stood rigidly for a long while, then eased down onto the dirt pile beside Stone Ghost.

The wind changed. The sweet woody scent of roasting pine nuts blew over them. Stone Ghost inhaled deeply. For the next two days, women would be cooking, cleaning, decorating the villages, and preparing costumes for the ceremony. He had lived alone for so long, he hadn't realized how much he'd missed this.

Gently, Stone Ghost said, "Is there something you wish to tell me, Healer?"

She lifted her gaze to the bright colorful paintings of the Great Warriors on the wall to the right. Their terrifying masks glowed in the sunlight.

"Elder," she murmured. "I ask that you listen to me

for a time. I do not know if I will ever be able to say these things again."

"I'm listening, Healer."

Cloudblower's words came softly: "You speak about suffering and its results. The Katsinas' People are all wounded souls, Elder. Each suffers in a different way, but that is why he or she is here. We were all desperately seeking a way out of our agony and found it in the teachings of Matron Flame Carrier." She clenched her hands tightly. "I came because I could not bear to live as an ordinary person should. After serving the Fire Dogs, the needs of my souls were different, greater, much more demanding. I craved the companionship of others who understood what it was to be hurt. For many sun cycles I lived as an outcast in my own heart." She lifted a hand to the big warrior who stood guarding her chamber. "He-Who-Flies came because his wife and children had been massacred. He lost everything. When he first joined us, he moved through our society like a man walking in his sleep. He spoke little. He asked for nothing. Except hope, Elder. Hope that the wars would end, that the dead would rise from their graves and walk the earth again. The Katsinas' People give hope, Elder. That is what we do."

Reverently, he said, "I know that, Healer."

Cloudblower paused. "Jackrabbit, the young warrior who stood on the roof this morning? He does not even know where he came from. He woke one morning at the bottom of a cliff, his head bloody and bruised. He could recall nothing. He may have slipped and fallen, or been attacked in a battle and left for dead. He wandered for days before he chanced upon Matron Flame Carrier at Flowing Waters Town two summers ago. She took him in and cared for him. He never left."

Stone Ghost said, "And Catkin? Why is she here?"

Cloudblower fumbled with her hands, lacing and un-lacing them in her lap. "I know little of her, Elder. I have heard it said that her husband died, and her clan tried to force her to marry a man she despised. But I cannot tell you if that is true. Catkin is a quiet one. She speaks little of herself. At least to me. She may reveal more to Browser. You might wish to ask him."

They exchanged a glance. Stone Ghost nodded and wondered how many others here knew that Catkin loved his nephew. It might make a difference.

"What of my nephew's wife? What did you know of her? The things I have heard disturbed me."

The painted hem of Cloudblower's cape waffled in the wind. She seemed to be watching it while she contemplated what to say.

"Elder, she—she often did unkind things to people. Shouting, lashing out with her fists for no reason. For over a sun cycle I feared that her souls had left her body. She seemed to be hovering like Hawk over a precipice of madness."

"Madness?" Stone Ghost asked. "You are the first to suggest that. Why?"

Cloudblower's voice dropped to a whisper. "At night, when she slept, she had terrifying experiences in the Land of the Dead, Elder. Near dawn, two moons ago, she shrieked like a madwoman, and ran to me in terror, claiming she'd heard strange, inhuman voices coming from Browser's mouth while he slept."

"What did you say?"

"I questioned her, Elder, on what had actually happened. I believed, then and now, that she was deep asleep when she heard the sounds. I think something, or someone, in the Land of the Dead was tormenting her, making the voice enough like her husband's that she would think the eerie sounds came from him."

"Why would one of the ancestors do such a thing, Healer?"

Cloudblower shrugged. "The dead are mysterious

beings, Elder. I have never been able to fathom their ways."

"Did you perform a Healing for Ash Girl?"

Cloudblower shook her head. "I tried. She wouldn't allow it. She said that her Spirit Helper cared for her and that was enough."

Stone Ghost moved his sandal across the frozen earth. It left white streaks. Why hadn't Browser forced his wife to undergo a Healing? The mad could not make such decisions themselves. They needed others to do it for them.

"And Hophorn?" he asked. "What is her story?"

"Oh, that is easy, Elder." A loving smile came to Cloudblower's face. "She followed Browser. She had taken care of him since they'd been children, soothing his hurts, easing his fears. When Browser and his family joined the Katsinas' People, and left Green Mesa Village, she could not stay behind. She loved him too much. Not as a lover, you understand, but as a cherished friend."

"I do understand," Stone Ghost answered. "I had a friend like that once. When the Tower Builders killed her, my souls tore loose from my body. For over a moon, I could not walk, or even feed myself. My body would not move."

Cloudblower gazed at him, concerned. "I have heard that grief can paralyze the souls."

Stone Ghost tipped his wrinkled face to the sunlight, and let it warm him. "It can, Healer. That is why I fear for Hophorn. These 'blanking-out' spells, are a sort of paralysis of the soul. I must find out what she has seen, and why she cannot bear to face it."

"What do you mean? Face it?"

"I think that is why she blanks out. She sends her souls flying to escape."

As though surprised by the suggestion, Cloudblower said, "She is ill, Elder. Her head injury—"

"Why does it disturb you that she might wish to escape? Is she escaping you, Healer?"

Cloudblower's face slackened.

Five women climbed onto the roof where Catkin and Browser stood. They carried baskets, pottery jars, and decorations—strips of colorful fabric, ears of corn, strings of bright feathers, and other things Stone Ghost could not make out from where he sat.

As they climbed down into the plaza, Cloudblower bowed her head. Stiffly, she said, "I must get back, Elder. Hophorn cannot care for herself, and she is terrified that the murderers are going to return to kill her. As well, I have preparations to make for Whiproot's burial and the Longnight ceremony. Hophorn usually leads the ritual. Because of her illness that duty has fallen to me."

Stone Ghost nodded. "I thank you for speaking with me, Healer."

Cloudblower rose and her painted cape flapped around her as she walked toward her chamber.

Stone Ghost watched until she had ducked beneath her door curtain, then he stretched in the sunlight.

The women set their pots and baskets down on the long wall outside the First People's kiva and began removing things from inside. One of the women, around thirty summers old with an ugly pocked face and short black-streaked gray hair, watched Stone Ghost from the corner of her eye.

He walked toward them, smiling, and the ugly woman quickly turned away. Harsh voices came from within the kiva. Flame Carrier's panicked tone was accompanied by two scratchy male voices.

"Cancel the ritual!" Flame Carrier cried. *"Have you lost your wits! Hundreds of people are coming. Many have been walking for days. By nightfall their camps will surround Hillside Village. We can't greet them by telling*

*them we've decided not to hold the Ceremony of the
Longnight!"*

Wading Bird's brittle voice rose above Flame Carrier's, *"Isn't it worse to allow them to stay when murderers may be stalking their loved ones!"*

Stone Ghost hobbled past and climbed the ladder to the roof.

When he reached the top, he stood for a time, enjoying the majesty of the canyon. A large flock of ravens cawed as they flapped eastward toward Father Sun, their black wings flashing. Across Straight Path Wash, he could make out a line of people coming up the road. They had packs on their backs. Several children trailed in the rear, surrounded by dogs. He cocked his head and heard barks and laughter.

Stone Ghost walked east along the roof toward Browser and Catkin. His nephew looked as if he'd taken a blow to the stomach. As he turned, his round face and short black hair shone in the morning's gleam. A new fear had been born in his dark eyes.

Stone Ghost called. "It is time that we had a long talk, Nephew."

Browser's thick black brows drew down over his flat nose. His weary movements appeared sluggish. He said something soft to Catkin, then clasped her shoulder, and came to meet Stone Ghost.

"Yes, Uncle. What is it you wish to know?" His plain buckskin cape was mottled with the soot of many campfires.

"First, I would like you to take me to the place where you found your wife's body, then we must search this town, Nephew."

Browser seemed visibly shaken by the request. He swallowed. "I do not have much time, Uncle, truly.

Guests are beginning to arrive for the ceremony. I must sleep before the festivities—"

"I understand, Nephew," Stone Ghost said and took Browser by the arm. As he led him toward the ladder to the road below, he added, "I will not take long."

Browser could barely feel his sandals striking the sand. He did not know what to think of Catkin's words. He believed that she had heard Cloudblower speaking with a man, but, as one of the village elders, Cloudblower often entertained passing Traders, clan matrons, or even hunters running the roads. She also had many friends, mostly people grateful for Healings she'd performed.

But nothing explained the man's presence in Talon Town last night, or his ghastly pretense of being Whiproot.

Could Catkin be correct?

Cloudblower knew the murderers?

"You are marching like a condemned man, Nephew," Stone Ghost said. The breeze fluttered his wispy white hair, revealing the large freckles on his scalp. His thick brows knitted over his hooked nose. "Why is that?"

Browser did not wish to discuss this with anyone until he'd had more time to think about it. He replied, "I have not walked this path since my son's burial, Uncle."

"I regret the need to make you relive that day, Nephew. But it's necessary."

The cliff loomed ahead of them, the rim blazing golden against the blue sky. Browser searched every possible lump or shadow that might be a man. An eagle perched on a scraggly juniper that had rooted in one of the crevices. The big bird's head moved, watching them as they approached. But he saw nothing that looked threatening.

At the base of the cliff, his son's burial, marked by a pile of recently dug earth, stood twenty paces to the left of the empty pit where they'd found his wife. Twenty paces to the right, the long-dead ritual fire pit sank into the ground. He still could see Hophorn sitting with her head down, dressed in Ash Girl's red-feathered cape.

"Five days ago," Stone Ghost said, "the Keepers of the Sacred Directions came out here, then you led the procession of mourners, yes?"

"Yes, Uncle. I was lost in my grief, trying just to make it to the end of the ritual. I was watching my feet when I heard Flame Carrier scream." Browser pointed. "You can see the open pit. That is where we found my wife. When I looked up, Flame Carrier grabbed Cloudblower's arm and stumbled backward. Old Woman Up Above wailed like a homeless ghost. I ordered Catkin and Whip . . . another warrior"—he could not say that name again until Whiproot was well on his way to the Land of the Dead—"to put my son's burial ladder down and follow me. We ran to the pit as quickly as we could."

Stone Ghost walked with his arms folded beneath his brown-and-white turkey-feather cape. His hands showed through the holes. "What did you see when you arrived at the burial pit?"

"At first I didn't know what I was seeing, Uncle. I thought it was a man, a tall man. My wife lay on her stomach with her arms and legs sprawled, as if she'd been thrown into the pit. A stone slab covered her head. She wore a white buckskin shirt and pants. Near her feet, the mask of the Wolf katsina rested. When the mourners crowded around the pit and saw the stone, screams broke out. People begin pushing and shoving. Most ran."

"Wise people. What happened next?"

"Catkin realized that something was wrong. She pointed to the places where hands and feet should be.

The sleeves and pant legs appeared empty. We feared it might be mutilation. Catkin wished to climb down into the pit to remove the slab, but Cloudblower wouldn't allow it. Catkin had just returned from a walk and had not yet been ritually cleansed in pinyon pine smoke. So Cloudblower climbed into the pit and shoved the stone aside."

Browser's exhausted heart throbbed with the memory. He propped his hand on his war club. "Bloody pulp filled her crushed skull. My wife's long hair had been cut short, as if in mourning. I do not know why a murderer would do such a thing. It makes no sense."

"But thorough work," Stone Ghost murmured. His disconcerting eyes flared a little wider. "How could you tell it was your wife, Nephew?"

In his souls, Browser could see her small, delicate hand, and feel the stiffness. "She was wearing the snake bracelet I gave her at our Joining, Uncle."

Browser stopped in front of the burial pit, and Stone Ghost moved up beside him. He gripped Browser's arm for support. As the old man leaned over, his tawdry pottery disk necklaces swung. Owl feathers scattered the bottom of the grave.

Browser sucked in a sharp breath.

"The feathers aren't witchery, Nephew." Stone Ghost pointed to the cliff. "Owls perch in the crevices at night. I saw their eyes shining early this morning."

Browser squinted at the white splotches of droppings that streaked the wall. His uncle was probably right. Still, the feathers worried him.

"You have had a few days to consider what you saw, Nephew. Why do you think the murderer would dress her in white, cut her hair, and place a stone over her head?"

Browser's gaze returned to the rim. As the day warmed, the scent of damp stone rose. Had the murderers been watching that day? Peering over the edge of the cliff, smiling at the happenings below?

"He didn't want her breath-heart soul to escape, that's why he used the stone. And"—he kicked at a small chunk of sandstone—"perhaps he believed her to be a witch. Many people in the village whispered that she was, but I never saw it, Uncle. A man would know if his wife were a witch, wouldn't he?"

Stone Ghost lightly touched Browser's hand. "I think so, Nephew."

Browser's gaze strayed to his son's burial. From the depths of his souls, he saw Grass Moon smile and heard his son calling, *"Father? Father, come and play with me?"* The pain in his chest made it hard to breathe.

"Where was Hophorn sitting, Nephew?" Stone Ghost asked.

He pointed. "Over there. She had her back against the cliff. Catkin noticed the trail of red feathers that led from the burial pit to Hophorn. Apparently, the murderer had taken the red cape my wife had been wearing, carried it over, and draped it around Hophorn's shoulders. Hophorn was also sheathed in ashes, Uncle, and four lines led away from her in the sacred directions. As if the murderer had purified her."

"More likely, Nephew, he was absolving himself of the act of attacking her." Stone Ghost frowned at the fire pit. "What else, Nephew?"

"Two ash-coated eagle feathers stuck out from beneath her sandals."

"Two? Not four? He didn't leave one for each direction?"

"Two, Uncle."

Stone Ghost nodded. "And then your wife's body disappeared, yes?"

"Yes, Uncle."

Stone Ghost said, "Where was Cloudblower when the body vanished?"

Browser grimaced. "She is not the murderer, Uncle. You must trust me about this. I know her. She was in Talon Town, opening Hophorn's skull when it happened."

"Was anyone with her?"

"Yes," he answered. After Catkin's words, how could he still defend Cloudblower? His own emotions churned. "Redcrop was aiding Cloudblower in the Healing."

Stone Ghost scratched his wrinkled cheek. "The entire time?"

Browser thought about that. "I don't know. Whip— one of my warriors was standing guard over Talon Town that morning."

"And now that warrior is dead."

Browser's belly knotted. "Are you saying he was killed because he knew Cloudblower had left? That he saw her take my wife's body?"

Stone Ghost gave him a lopsided smile. "Why, no, Nephew. You're the one who said that. Were you trying to tell me something?"

Browser frowned, then shook his head. "No."

A brown-and-white feather tore loose from Stone Ghost's cape and flipped away, somersaulting through the air. Stone Ghost smiled and gestured to it. "Was the wind blowing the morning you discovered your wife's body?"

Browser struggled to recall. "Yes. I think so. Just a breeze, but it made the morning seem colder."

"Yet Catkin could follow a trail of feathers, Nephew? Did that not strike you as odd? Surely all such feathers would have blown away less than one-quarter finger of time after being dropped."

As the cliff absorbed the morning sunlight, it warmed

and gave off a faintly sweet scent, like a mixture of dust and cactus flowers.

Browser looked down into his uncle's strangely glowing eyes. "Blessed gods. Are you suggesting—"

"No, I'm telling you. The red feathers must have been dropped only moments before the burial party arrived. That's also why you found only two eagle feathers. Wind Baby pulled them loose."

The cawing of the ravens suddenly turned loud, raucous, as if in warning. Browser listened to them with blood pounding in his ears. "Which means the murderer was here. Close by. Probably watching."

Stone Ghost took Browser's arm and guided him toward the ritual fire pit where Hophorn had been attacked. "They always watch, Nephew. If they can. That's their triumph. Why create a pageant if you can't see the audience's reaction?"

They walked into the shade cast by the cliff; Stone Ghost released Browser's arm and carefully walked around the dead fire. Charcoal chunks thrust up through a layer of ice.

"Catkin told me that you found a strange mark near the fire pit where the sand had thawed. She thought it might have been part of a footprint. Is it still here?"

Browser knelt and tapped his finger to the ground. "This is the mark, Uncle."

Stone Ghost examined the arc in the soil. "Did you think this was a heel print, Nephew?"

"I thought it might be. If so, it was made by a big, heavy man."

"Indeed." Stone Ghost got down on his hands and knees, and scrutinized the shape with great care. "Was the fire blazing when you arrived? Or burning low, and steady?"

"Blazing, Uncle. I remember because I thought Hophorn must have heard us coming and added wood."

Stone Ghost grunted to his feet. "Did you find anything else?"

Browser hesitated, then reached beneath his cape, to the pouch he wore around his waist. He drew out the turquoise wolf and held it before Stone Ghost on his open palm. "This, Uncle."

Stone Ghost's wrinkled lips parted, as if in awe. "I haven't seen one of those in sixty sun cycles. Where did you find it?"

"There. It was resting on top of a red feather."

Rather than reaching for the precious object, Stone Ghost frowned at the place Browser pointed. "Where was Hophorn sitting?"

"In the rear, Uncle."

Stone Ghost skirted the pit and sat down in the same place Hophorn had been sitting, as if trying to imagine what she had seen that morning. His gaze moved from the empty burial pit, to the place where the wolf and feather had rested beside the heel print.

"Have you shown that wolf to anyone, Nephew?"

"Catkin knows, Uncle. She was here when I found it. But I've told no one else. I'm sure she hasn't either."

As he rose to his feet, Stone Ghost said, "That, my Nephew, is why you are both still alive."

Browser searched the rim again, and scanned the piles of rock behind Talon Town. "Why?"

"Because he was watching," Stone Ghost said calmly. "He knows that one of you has it."

"But if—if he knows—why doesn't he just kill us and search us?"

Stone Ghost grinned. "He can't risk killing you before he questions you, Nephew. Only a person with the wits of a blood-sucking fly would carry a legendary Power object in his belt pouch."

Browser looked down. The Turquoise Wolf had a curious, unnatural glint in her eyes, as if preparing to leap from his palm and run away like the wind. Browser tucked it back into his belt pouch. "I will hide it as soon as we return to Hillside Village, Uncle."

Stone Ghost affectionately slipped his arm through Browser's, and headed him back toward Talon Town. They followed an ancient, overgrown trail that slithered through a garden of toppled boulders.

Stone Ghost stopped in the shadow of the town's towering western wall and released Browser's arm. A curving line of cracked plaster and fallen stones heaped against the base of the wall. His voice went low. "I think these boulders shelter us from view, Nephew. So. Quickly, tell me what Catkin said that upset you."

MAGPIE, COULD YOU hold this?"

"Of course, Aunt."

Hail Walking Hawk handed her cane to Magpie, and dug around in the pocket of her yellow dress for the two pieces of bread she had saved from their supper of venison chili and biscuits. The pieces of fluffy white bread looked almost silver in the twilight as she withdrew them. She lifted the morsels to the pale blue evening sky, and Sang softly. The brightest Evening People had awakened, and sparkled on the eastern horizon.

Hail said, "This is for our mother, Iatiku," and bent over to place the bread on the flat slab of sandstone. Her yellow dress billowed around her legs. "And this is for you, Utsiti, creator of the universe." She placed the other piece of bread beside the first. They seemed to gleam against the tan stone.

Hail straightened. The temperature had just begun to drop, and her whole body heaved a sigh of relief. She had spent most of the day in her tent, watching the shadows of the bugs who walked on the red nylon. The pain and the ghosts kept crying out to her, trying to force her to sit up and take notice of them. As the evening cooled, she felt a little better.

"There," she said, "that should do it." She reached for her cane and propped it on the ground. The tip sank into the soft sand.

Magpie took Hail's left elbow and smiled. "Do you

realize, Aunt, that if everyone made offerings to the gods each night, all the wars would go away, and no one would ever be hungry again." Perspiration soaked the armpits of her white T-shirt.

Hail grinned. "Especially Iatiku and Utsiti. They'd be as fat as those wrestlers in Japan. What are they called?"

"Sumo wrestlers, Aunt."

"Sumo," Hail tried the name on her tongue. It tasted sticky, like the rice they served in those Chinese restaurants in Albuquerque.

Hail sighed and studied the cliffs that surrounded them. The darkness had turned the tan rock a grayish purple. Owls perched in the crevices, their eyes flashing as they searched the canyon bottom, waiting their chance to dive down and snatch up a juicy mouse or an unsuspecting kangaroo rat.

Hail turned toward the Haze child. He'd been gurgling for the past hour, like a baby blowing bubbles to occupy himself. A black piece of plastic covered the pit. Hail could feel his hope. He knew people had found him, and he could not understand why no one had taken care of him yet. He had been trapped here for a long time.

Not much longer, she promised. *As soon as these diggers get you out of the ground, I'll take care of you. Don't be afraid.*

Hail's filmy old eyes moved to the top of the pit where the stone rested over the witch's head. She had been a tall woman. Dusty had dug around her long limbs, revealing how her arms sprawled. Washais said it looked like the woman had been hurled into the grave.

Hail glanced at the other pits. All of these women and children had been thrown away like old rags—but from the marks Washais pointed out on the long bones, the muscles had been stripped from them before burial.

That frightened Hail.

When she had been a little girl, she'd heard the Pueblo

elders whispering about two *maleficiadores,* enchanters, who dug children from their graves, and cooked their flesh in a large pot in the moonlit graveyard. People could smell the foul odor for miles. Some witches ate only the organs of powerful shamans, to gain their powers. Other witches jerked the flesh of their victims and fed it to their enemies as a way to hide their crimes.

Hail glanced at the square holes.

Many of these women had stones over their heads, but she could sense they weren't witches. Someone had just treated them that way. Nevertheless, evil did live here. They had awakened it with their digging. She could still feel the *basilisco*'s malignant presence. Even after centuries of lying in the ground, the corruption was strong. Hail could taste it at the back of her throat, cloying, like the odor of rotten meat.

Dusty would have to get these bones out of the ground soon, so they could all leave, or the corruption would make them sick.

"Aunt," Magpie said, and gently touched Hail's white hair. "I've been having scary dreams."

Hail swiveled her head. Sweat glued Magpie's short black hair to her cheeks, and made her rich brown eyes appear deep and dark. Spirit Helpers often came to people in dreams, delivering messages to help the tribe. "What dreams?"

Magpie tipped her head, as if reluctant to say. "I see terrible things. You and Grandma are talking in the Land of the Dead, and I—"

"Is she letting me get a word in edgewise?" Hail asked seriously. "She could talk a dead rabbit away from a starving coyote."

Magpie smiled, but she gave Hail that look that told her she knew Hail had cleverly sidestepped the part about being in the Land of the Dead.

Hail tucked her cane under her arm and clasped her

knobby fingers over Magpie's. At the feel of her smooth skin, love swelled Hail's chest, easing some of the pain. "Help me back to my bottle of iced tea," she said. "We'll talk on the way."

Magpie supported Hail while she searched for steady footing in the sand, then they veered around a thick greasewood bush, and headed east, toward the firelight that haloed the tents and outlined the blocky shape of Dr. Robertson's square camp trailer. He'd towed it in that afternoon behind his shiny red truck.

Dusty sat next to Sylvia before the leaping flames in the fire pit. Washais and Dr. Robertson stood over a table scattered with bones to Hail's right. She could see them in the white sphere of light cast by a Coleman lantern. Frowns incised their foreheads.

Hail and Magpie's red tent nestled between the two groups; the rain fly that had been set up as a ramada out front waffled in the night wind.

"Please tell me the truth, Aunt," Magpie said hesitantly, fearfully.

Hail smiled up into her niece's dark eyes. "Oh, it's nothing so bad. Not for me, anyway. Death and I have been companions for many years, walking side-by-side, just like old friends."

Magpie's steps faltered. She looked down at Hail with pained eyes.

"Don't mourn me, child. I'm happier than I've ever been. I cherish every moment, every color. When you smile at me, my heart soars like that owl up there." She lifted her cane and pointed to the big bird wheeling silently in the slate sky above them. His body shone blackly as he passed in front of the brilliant crescent moon.

Tears glistened in Magpie's eyes. "Oh, Aunt."

"Listen," Hail said, "I'm going to need you to help me. I don't want anybody else to know about this, and the pain gets really bad sometimes. I have trouble breathing. When it comes upon me, you may have to get me back to the tent before I fall down flat."

Magpie jerked a nod. "Please let me take you home?"

"I need to be here." She gestured at the excavation. "These diggers, they don't know what's slinking around out here. Something old, something evil. I still have things to do. The time's not right yet, but when it comes, I have to be ready."

Magpie tenderly touched Hail's white hair and bit her lip. "Oh, Aunt, I can't stand to see you in pain."

Hail glanced her way. "I have a bag full of pain killers in the tent, child. I just haven't been taking them. I get wobbly, and I can't think straight when I do."

Magpie kept silent for a time. "What if your doctor needs to run a test? Don't you need to be close—"

"He can't do anything more, Magpie."

Magpie squeezed her eyes closed, and a tear rolled down her cheek. "Is he sure?"

"Yes, child. It's just my time. Like it will be yours someday. I want to live my last days out in the open, watching sunrises and sunsets, not in a white smelly hospital."

Magpie's jaw quivered. She seemed to be nerving herself to ask the question. "Is it . . ."

"Cancer, yes. Just like your grandmother."

Magpie clutched her arm so tightly it hurt.

Hail petted her fingers. "Now I know how packrat feels in Eagle's talons."

Maggie loosened her grip. "Breast cancer?"

"Yes, girl. Which means you have more to worry about than me dying. That doctor in Albuquerque said sometimes this sort of cancer runs in families. *You* have to go get checked. Soon."

Magpie's voice came out low. "How long, Aunt? Did the doctor tell you?"

. "A few months. Long enough for me to drive you crazy telling you how much I love you. Now, help me back to my chair by the fire. I want to finish my iced tea, and I don't want you looking like somebody in the family just died, because I'm still here. You see me, don't you?" Hail waved her cane.

"I see you," Magpie smiled, but it looked like it hurt.

Hail gripped Magpie's arm, and took one agonizing step at a time. Why did breast cancer make her hurt all over? It didn't make sense. Her chest, naturally, burned as if on fire, but her knees and elbows felt like an ice pick had been wedged between the bones. Her sister, Slumber, had never complained about these kinds of pains, but now that she thought of it, Slumber had never complained about anything. Her sister had stayed on her feet and busy to the end.

And so will I. But, unlike Slumber, she had one last battle to wage. And this one, she couldn't afford to lose.

The wind changed, blowing smoke in her direction. The fragrance of the fire pleased Hail. Dr. Robertson had hauled in four bundles of ponderosa pine logs, and the faintly sweet tang saturated the night.

Hail said, "Are you going to be all right?"

Magpie wiped her eyes on her white shirt sleeve. "I'll be fine now. Thank you for telling me straight out."

"I should have done it sooner. I was just being selfish. I wanted to see your eyes shining for me, and I was afraid the truth would dim them."

"It won't. I promise." Magpie suddenly turned and hugged Hail.

Hail stroked her niece's short black hair. "I love you, child. You're the reason I'm still here. You've taken good care of me these past few years."

Magpie couldn't speak. She swallowed and patted Hail's hand.

They walked in companionable silence, smiling gently at each other.

Dusty caught sight of Hail and Maggie as they appeared from the darkness. He stopped peeling the label from his Guinness bottle and studied them. Both wore curious expressions, almost desperately loving, as though each feared the other might disappear at any moment. He smiled at Maggie. She smiled back, and led her aunt to the lawn chair beside Sylvia. After the elderly woman eased down, Maggie pulled her chair up so close that the aluminum arms touched.

Maggie reached down for the almost empty bottle of iced tea laying in the sand, unscrewed the lid, and handed it to her aunt. "Would you like another bottle, Aunt? This one is almost gone."

Hail shook her gray head. "I'd just have to get up twice in the night, and the ghosts might get me."

Sylvia's green eyes widened. She had clipped her brown hair up in back, and the style made her face look as lean as a weasel's. She wore a tan tank top, Levi's shorts, and hiking boots. "Did you hear them again last night, Mrs. Walking Hawk?"

"I hear them every night. They're a noisy bunch."

"What did they say?"

"They were shouting at each other and shoving back and forth. I could hear their feet scraping the ground."

Sylvia glanced at Dusty, then whispered, "I wonder what they're fighting about?"

Hail said, "I don't know, but he's really mad. Last night his voice screeched, then her voice went soft, like she was afraid of him, begging him not to hurt her."

"He? I thought we just had women here." Sylvia's eyes scanned the darkness.

"I heard a man," Hail replied, with a distant look in her eyes. "I think he's the cause of all this. He's really bad. He touched the basilisk. I could feel him in the stone."

"Can you hear the ghosts now, Aunt?" Maggie asked.

Hail cocked her ear to the wind. White hair danced around her wrinkled face as she listened. "No. Even that Haze baby is quiet."

Sylvia sank back into her chair. "Good. I don't want to accidentally get in their way, you know? Getting whacked by a ghost isn't my idea of sacrificing for science."

"Whacked?" Maggie asked. "Ghosts whack you?"

"You betcha." Sylvia nodded. Her freckles looked larger in the firelight. "My mother used to tell me bedtime stories about ghosts when I was growing up. They were always whacking people by throwing chairs and making chandeliers fall on them. I remember one story that scared the bejeesus out of me. The ghost broke an icicle off the roof of the house, then slipped into a young woman's bedroom, and plunged it into her heart, but the woman didn't die right away. She ran around screaming until she stumbled through a window and a piece of broken glass lopped her head off."

Dusty reached for the top log in the woodpile to his left and tossed it into the fire pit. Ash puffed, and whirled upward into the night sky. As flames licked around the wood, sparks crackled and shot in all directions. "Your mother told you stories like that at bedtime? And you didn't run screaming?"

"Are you kidding?" Sylvia answered. "I loved those stories. After one of her tales, I'd pull the blankets over my head and fall fast asleep."

"You must have been suffering from oxygen deprivation. No normal child would sleep after a story like that."

Sylvia took a sip of her Pepsi. "I didn't have oxygen problems until she started telling us vampire stories. I slept with a sheet wrapped around my throat until I was eighteen."

"And discovered baseball bats," Dusty supplied.

"Right."

"I'm surprised you didn't choke—"

"*No, Dale,*" Maureen said sharply, "that's *not* what I mean."

Dusty looked over at them. Maureen and Dale stood behind the table in front of Maureen's tent. Two lines of skulls, and carefully laid out long bones, covered the fake wood veneer top. Dale had come in about sunset, the trailer full of groceries, drinks, and ice. He'd spent his years in tents. These days, he always arrived at an excavation with the old Holliday Rambler trailer in tow.

"Look here, Dale. See these fractures?" Maureen said. "They're all on the right side of the skull." The white lantern light profiled her oval face, and flashed in her dark eyes. Her long black braid draped the front of her light green shirt. The silver strands glittered. "These skulls come from burials on the easternmost side of the site. There's a pattern here. As you can see, each fracture is in a different place, as if he started at the linea temporalis, and worked his way back."

"The site as excavated," Dale pointed out. Deep wrinkles etched his elderly face. He wore a faded pair of jeans, and a red-and-black-checked shirt with pearl buttons. His dusty fedora—the kind Bogart always wore in the movies—sat on his head. About the same height as Maureen, his thick gray hair and mustache contrasted sharply with her dark complexion. "There may be more burials we haven't found yet. And, besides, you can't prove it's a pattern."

"Oh, yes, I can. The statistical probability of finding this order of fractures—"

"A *probability,* Maureen. Nothing more." Dale propped his hands on his hips.

Maureen frowned at the top row of skulls. All of them had been carefully placed in Ziploc bags to avoid contamination.

"True," Maureen said, "but based upon what I've seen so far, I can also hypothesize a cause. I wouldn't do it in print. Yet. But I'd tell you, Dale."

Dusty balanced his Guinness bottle on one knee. "I don't get this. If someone's killing slaves, they whack them wherever it's convenient."

Maureen looked up. "If you'll grace us with your presence, Stewart, I'll show you why that's hogwash."

Dusty rose and walked wide around the fire. When he stood opposite Maureen and Dale, he could see that Maureen had left the front of her tent open. Inside lay folded clothing, a microscope set up on a stack of books, and a carefully rolled sleeping bag. He unwrapped a finger from the warm beer bottle. "I'd zip my tent if I were you. This time of night, scorpions, spiders, sidewinders, anything could crawl into your bed. I'm not sure what effect they'd have on you, but I'm sure they'd think you were seriously infringing on their personal space."

"That's interesting, Stewart," Maureen said, as she stepped over and zipped her doorway closed. "You can't imagine how a human being might feel sleeping with a poisonous creature, but you know exactly how poisonous insects and reptiles feel sleeping with human beings. That sums up your character, doesn't it?"

Sylvia snickered, and when Dusty glared at her, she pretended to be choking on Pepsi. She coughed and slapped herself on the back. "Nasty. The carbonation I mean."

Dusty braced a hand on the corner of the table and nonchalantly gestured to the skulls with his bottle. "You were saying about the fractures, Doctor?"

Maureen walked back to the table. "I've arranged these skulls in order of the burials, moving east to west across the site. Notice that the first two skulls show cranial depression fractures on both sides and in two different planes."

"I see that," Dusty said. "So?"

"*So*, the killer didn't know what he was doing. The blows were random. But look at these." Maureen tapped the bags that held the fourth and fifth skulls. "These women were only struck on the right side of the skull, and these three"—She touched skulls in the bottom row—"were only struck on the left side of the head."

Dusty's blue eyes narrowed. "Your point?"

Maureen gazed at him as if he must be stupid. "It's right in front of your face, Stewart. Don't you see it?"

He studied the skulls more closely. The numerous dents, and radiating fractures, shone oddly yellowish in the firelight. "I see battered skulls. Is there something more here?"

Maureen exhaled hard. "After the first two women, the blows are calculated, strategic." She hesitated, as if waiting for him to supply the rest. When Dusty just stared at her, Maureen said, "The killer was systematically testing brain function, Stewart."

Dale's bushy gray brows went up. The pearl buttons on his shirt flashed as he turned. "You mean the murderer wanted to see what would happen if he struck the head in different places?"

"Of course, he did. Look at—"

"Nonsense," Dusty objected. "You're presuming these burials were deliberately laid out from east to west. We have no way of determining their order. This skull with fractures on both sides may have been the last one buried, not the first. It's more likely that the guy just had the chance to bash both of these women's heads before they could run."

"I'll grant you that's possible," Maureen said, "but I don't think so."

Dusty threw up his hands. "Good God, is this what physical anthropologists call science? I'd be hounded out of the archaeological profession if I openly spouted such baseless garbage."

Sylvia cupped a hand to her mouth, and called, "Let's not forget those who have tried!"

"And failed!" Dusty called. "Jealousy is rampant in this profession, Sylvia. When you're at the top you have to expect a few coup attempts."

In a curt voice, Maureen said, "Dale, I know I've already given you a list of the tests I want performed on these remains, but I want you to add another one."

"All right, Maureen. What?"

"I want a pollen analysis done of the nasal cavities. There's some desiccated tissue in a few of these skulls. If we—"

"We have a limited budget, Doctor," Dusty replied.

"I want to know what time of year they died, Stewart. If specimen number one has chimaja pollen in her nostrils, and specimen number two has sage pollen, we will know one died in the spring, and one in the autumn. Get it?"

He blinked. "Ah. You mean because that's when chimaja and sage bloom. Sure. I get it. Why is that important?"

"It's important because it might help us to determine the order in which they were interred. Is this coming into focus for you?"

"Oh, yes," he said with exaggerated interest. "Absolutely, your worshipfulness. It's just that the picture I see is a lot different from the one you see." He folded his arms, and braced his beer bottle on his left elbow. "You're hypothesizing a prehistoric serial murderer loose among the Anasazi, and I'm saying these women were all tortured by their slave masters and thrown into pits when they were no longer useful. I see it fine. You're the one who's myopic."

Maureen lifted her hands as if in surrender. "If you're going to stick with this slave hypothesis, we should have the bone collagen tested for stable-carbon and nitrogen isotopes."

"What in the name of God is that?"

Dale shoved his fedora back on his head. "Carbon and nitrogen isotope ratios," he explained, "can tell us what types of plants and animals the people were—or were not—eating."

"Be serious, Dale," Dusty said. "I can think of a dozen alternate hypotheses as to why one woman's diet would be different from another's. Especially if the doctor is right and they really were buried in sequence. Food shifts occur during different times of year."

Maureen braced her hands on the table and leaned toward him. "If there's testable collagen in these bones, Stewart, I'll be able to tell you whether these women were eating watery corn gruel or a lavish diet of deer, turkey, and rabbit. You don't think masters would feed their slaves the good stuff, do you?"

Wind gusted through camp, tousling Dusty's blond hair. He shifted his weight to his opposite foot. "No." He narrowed an eye. "You really can tell that?"

"Maybe. We'll see." She straightened up.

Dale watched them with shining eyes.

Maureen lowered her voice. "I also think I know where to find evidence to support my serial murderer hypothesis."

"Yeah? Where?" Dusty asked.

Maureen pointed to the site. "If I'm right, there's another burial between the Haze child and the woman in unit N4W6." Firelight flickered over her face as she turned to peer at Dusty. "And she has a depression fracture just posterior to the left coronal suture, right over Broca's Area of the brain."

"The what?"

Maureen lifted a slender finger and tapped the side of Dusty's temple, just ahead of his ear. "There, Stewart."

"Hmm," Dale said. He thoughtfully stroked his mustache. "It would be interesting to test your hypothesis. That area is, however, outside the impact area. Maggie?" he called. "What do you think?"

She massaged her forehead. "I don't know. Let me think about it. One pit dug outside of the impact area on the instructions of the Indian monitor is annoying but understandable. Digging another just to prove a hypothesis is going to rankle the Department of Interior bigwigs. The DOI motto is: 'Research is a waste of taxpayer dollars. We do land management, not science.' "

"But the pit I want dug is closer to the impact area than the Haze child unit that Stewart dug," Maureen said. "Why can't we just excavate the gap between?"

Sylvia called, "I agree! Let's dig it. I think Maureen's right. This is the work of a serial murderer."

Dusty turned toward Sylvia. A crushed Pepsi can lay at her feet. She had a Coors Light balanced on her chair arm. Brown hair straggled around her face. "Yeah? Why?"

"Well, think about it. A few blows to the head is pretty amateurish torture. I mean, the Apaches used to build fires in people's stomachs."

Dusty's mouth quirked. "Did you have a point?"

"Well, yeah, boss man. I mean, look at the black slave cemeteries in the South. Some of those people were beat up really bad, and over a long period. Last year, I read about two burials, a man and a woman, who were laid side-by-side behind slave cabins in Mississippi. During their lives, they'd both had their arms broken; their legs broken, several ribs broken. The woman's neck had even

been broken once. Now, *that's* slave torture. What tor-
turer would just hit his slaves in the head?"

Dusty walked back, and sank into his chair before the
fire. "If you want to talk about torture, nobody can hold
a candle to the good doctor's people, the Iroquois." Dusty
aimed his bottle at her. "They made torture an art. It
lasted for days. I remember one entry in the *Jesuit Relations* that described the capture of a British trader. They
hacked the guy apart a piece at a time. In the middle of
the torture, they stuck his hands in the fire, to cook the
flesh, then called the special children forward to chew
the meat off the bones. As a reward for good behavior,
you understand. Can you imagine watching smiling children eat you alive?"

Sylvia looked fascinated. She gripped her Coors in
both hands, and said, "What I can really imagine is all
the other kids in the longhouse." In a whining voice, she
said, "Oh, Dad, *he's* got one, *I* want one."

The fire suddenly spluttered and sparks popped. A
haze of smoke rose into the night sky.

Dusty grimaced. "You are a sick woman."

"No," Maureen corrected. "She just doesn't know
much about the Iroquois." She gave it the French pro-
nunciation: Irokwah. "They were matrilineal, Sylvia. The
kids would have said, 'Oh, *Mom*, he's got one, I want
one.' "

Sylvia's green eyes widened. "Hey, thanks for telling
me. That's the kind of mistake that could get me killed
in the wrong circles."

Dale loudly said, "Getting back to the burials, Maureen. Tell me about the irregularities I see in the squamous portion of this frontal bone. Osteophytes?"

Dusty knew the skull Dale meant. It was the burial
Maureen had commented on when she'd first arrived. The
crushed skull had come out of the ground in three pieces.
After they'd bagged them, Maureen had spent hours

looking at them through a magnifying glass. The entire inner table of the skull undulated with white lumps.

Maureen said, "This a classic case of *hyperostosis frontalis interna.*"

Dusty translated, "Which means she had one hell of an endocrine imbalance."

Dale gave Dusty a penetrating look. "Maureen must have told you that. You'd never think of it yourself." He turned to Maureen. "What are the clinical considerations in such cases?"

Dusty made a face, and took a swig of his beer.

Maureen said, "*Hyperostosis frontalis interna* is observed almost exclusively in women, primarily postmenopausal women. Several studies have documented it. One of the best known was carried out on women who had died and were being autopsied. In that case, forty percent showed thickening of the skull, and these same bony growths. Another study was done in a home for the aged. Sixty-two percent of the women there suffered from HFI, but none of the men."

Dale seemed to be weighing this information. His bushy gray brows twitched. "What happens to the women involved? This sounds like a painful condition."

"Not always," Maureen answered. "Sometimes the victims suffer insomnia, urinary difficulties, disturbances of equilibrium, that sort of thing, but nothing severe. On the other hand, some are in agony. They have raging headaches, fainting spells, even convulsions. One researcher discovered a dramatic frequency of HFI in women who were insane."

Sylvia's chair squeaked, and Dusty glanced at her. Her eyes had gone huge. She was listening to the discussion literally on the edge of her seat.

"So these bony growths," Dale said, "must extend themselves into the brain."

"They certainly put pressure on specific areas. The

larger they are, the more brain tissue they squeeze."

Dale touched the pieces of skull in the clear plastic bag. "Dusty? Didn't you say you thought this woman's skull had been split by a rock?"

"Maureen matched the fractures to the stone," he said without looking at her. "That's exactly what happened. The rock was thrown into the pit on top of her head, cracking her skull, but—"

"Wow! Hold on! This is coming together!" Sylvia shouted. "Maybe she was crazy, and her people thought she was a witch. Did you ever read that great book by Marc Simmons on *Witchcraft in the Southwest*? In the past four hundred years, lots of crazy women have been accused of being witches. After they were captured, their own people would torture them to get a confession and force them to undo their evil, then they were killed, and in some pretty gruesome ways."

Hail Walking Hawk lifted a frail old hand, and the camp went silent.

Gray hair blew around her ancient face as she propped her elbows on the arms of her chair. "Many years ago, my grandmother told me about two witches who lived over at Zuni pueblo. They could change themselves into animals by jumping through yucca hoops, and once they turned a man into a woman. Everybody said they were crazy, but people were too scared of them to try and kill them. My grandmother said that the oldest witch ran around at night in the body of coyote, howling in pain, because her head always felt like it was going to explode." Hail Walking Hawk looked at Maureen. "Do you think those women might have had these growths in their heads, Washais? Is that why they were crazy, and became witches?"

Maureen's midnight eyes resembled deep dark holes in her firelit oval face. "It's possible. I can't say for certain without examining their skulls, but I wouldn't be surprised."

Dusty asked, "But you said earlier that HFI was found primarily in postmenopausal women. The skull on the table is from a woman in her early twenties. What's the overall occurrence in the general population?"

"About five percent of all adult women suffer from it," Maureen said, "but only ten percent of those are under thirty."

Sylvia flopped back in her chair. "Thank God. I still have a few years before I go crazy."

"Don't be hasty," Dusty said. "What if you're in the ten percent of the five percent?"

Sylvia turned her Coors can in her hands. "I wonder if HFI is related to the incidence of depression among women? I mean, wow, these things grow in your head, and you start thinking crazy thoughts. Who wouldn't be depressed?"

"That's an interesting hypothesis, Sylvia," Dale said. "I think you should do a paper on it next year. In the meantime"—he stretched, and yawned—"it's been a long day for me. I'm going to bed. Good night all."

" 'Night, Dale."

He lifted a hand, and walked behind the tents into the darkness, headed in the direction of the Sanolet.

Hail Walking Hawk said, "I'm going to sleep, too. Give me a hand, Magpie," and reached out to her niece.

Maggie helped the old woman out of her chair and tenderly slipped an arm around her shoulders. "Good night everybody. We'll see you in the morning."

"Good night," Sylvia said and lifted her Coors can in a salute. "Don't let the ghosts get you."

Maggie chuckled. "I won't. You either, White Eyes."

Sylvia grinned.

As Maggie and her aunt slowly made their way to the red tent, which nestled between Dusty's tent and

Maureen's, Sylvia finished her Coors, crushed the can in one hand, and tossed it into the trash box behind Dusty. It landed with a soft metallic clank.

"Heavy discussion," Sylvia said. "Ghosts, torture, murder, insanity. I'm going to rub my bat with garlic before I go to sleep." She got to her feet, and stretched.

Dusty said, "Good night, Sylvia."

"Good night, boss." She headed for her tent.

Dusty used the toe of his hiking boot to rock the pot at the edge of the coals. "There's still coffee in the pot. Are you interested, Dr. Cole?"

Maureen ran a hand through her hair. "I guess." She sat down across the fire and reached for the cup she'd used at dinner. "We need to dig that pit, Stewart."

"I've got to hand it to you, a serial murderer?" He shook his head. "An Anasazi crime site? They'll be laughing from the Pecos Conference to the SAAs."

"What's the Pecos Conference?" she asked as she poured coffee into her cup.

"The oldest conference on Southwest Archaeology. A. V. Kidder started it back in nineteen twenty-four. It happens every year. People go and talk about their research. The SAAs, I assume you've heard of."

"The Society for American Archaeology." She nodded. "I am going to dig that pit, Stewart."

He sat back. "*You* don't know how to dig, Doctor. If anybody digs that pit, it's going to be me, and I can't scuff the surface without Maggie's approval. Get it?"

She sipped her coffee. "The only thing I get is that the American government is run by antiscience fundamentalists bent on destroying any research that threatens their—"

"Their what?" he demanded, trying to keep his voice low. "Their respect for other traditions? I thought Canadians were all for the 'Cultural Mosaic'? Or did you miss that lecture in Canadian History one-oh-one?"

"The concept of the Cultural Mosaic is based on understanding other cultures, Stewart. We don't take their religious beliefs, turn them into laws, and shove them down the throats of nonbelievers."

He glared at her. "No wonder you're alone. Who in the hell would have you?"

For a moment, she just stared at him as though sideswiped by the comment. Then her lips quivered, she tossed her coffee into the fire, and walked out into the darkness.

Dusty bowed his head, and squeezed his eyes closed. "God, I'm an idiot. I've always been an idiot. I will always be an idiot." He opened his eyes, and stared unblinking into the fire. He had to find her. He couldn't let her leave thinking he . . .

"Maureen? Wait!"

24

I WISH TO lead the way, Uncle. You understand? If we trap the killer in there, it will be up to me to kill or disable him. I don't want you to get in the way."

Stone Ghost stood leaning into the hole in the wall, surveying the dark interior. His thin white hair fluttered around his head. "I have no objections, Nephew."

Browser poured hot bear grease from a small pot onto the tightly wrapped top of the cedar bark torch, then dipped it into the warming bowl that rested on the ground. Smoky flames curled around the wrapping.

"There is no way that we can travel silently or secretly through these dark warrens, Uncle. The light of the torch, the grating of our sandals on the crumbled floors, will provide plenty of warning to anyone inside. Let us proceed slowly."

Stone Ghost stepped out of the room and gestured for Browser to enter. "I'll be following right behind you, Nephew."

Browser led with the torch, sticking it in to light the square room. The white plaster had cracked away from the intricately laid stone walls, and crusted the floor. Charred roof beams dangled from the ceiling. Stone Ghost stared closely at the finely fitted rocks, many no larger than the palm of his hand.

"People hide the most curious things. Imagine, this fine stonework, and they covered it with plaster." He canted an eye toward Browser. "Just like people, wouldn't you say?"

"He went this way." Browser walked across the room, and ducked through the low doorway into the next chamber.

Sunlight slanted through the gaping hole over Browser's head. He could see a mound of fallen stone resting on the lip of the hole. The beams sagged beneath its weight. "Careful, here, Uncle. A good breath of wind will cause this ceiling to come crashing down.

Stone Ghost entered, gazed up at the hole, and silently followed Browser through two more rooms.

Browser stepped into the next room and the rounded wall of a small clan kiva curved to his right. He hadn't seen that last night.

Stone Ghost whispered, "Is this as far as you went the other night?"

"Yes, Elder." Browser held his torch high, illuminating the litter on the floor. A layer of fine dust and ash covered burned beams, half-rotten wood, old plaster, and torn matting. Footprints had churned up the dust.

Browser identified his own prints, and Jackrabbit's. The third set mystified him. The man had been wearing yucca sandals. Browser knelt and measured the prints against his hand.

Stone Ghost whispered, "My feet are bigger than his."

Browser rose, and narrowed his eyes. "His tracks lead around the curve of the kiva."

Browser walked forward cautiously, searching every pile of rubbish.

"Through there," Stone Ghost pointed to a corner doorway, partially obscured by the sagging roof poles. "I would say, Nephew, that's how he managed to lose you the night your warrior was killed. There, behind the fallen timbers, see it?"

Browser walked forward, following the curving wall,

until he saw the ladder stuffed into the corner. Above it, a small hole let sunlight into the chamber.

"It appears," Browser murmured, "that the killer climbed back up on the roof, then dropped on Whi—my warrior."

Stone Ghost came up behind Browser and frowned at the doorway. "Let's make sure, Nephew."

Browser nodded, handed the torch to Stone Ghost, and set the ladder into the hole. "Be ready for anything, Uncle," he whispered, and took the torch back.

Browser climbed slowly, listening for sounds from above. He heard nothing. He climbed out into a small rectangular room. The curiously rich and earthy smell confused him for a moment. The floor beneath his feet felt soft. He helped Stone Ghost up and frowned.

"What is this spongy brown layer we're standing on? My moccasins are sinking into it."

Something fluttered on the ceiling, and Browser whirled to look up. No more than an arm's length away, the roof seemed to be moving, undulating in the heat of the torch.

Browser flinched. "Bats."

He hated bats. Creatures of the night, they associated with owls and shared the same skies with witches.

"I don't think they like your torch," Stone Ghost whispered. "It's the middle of the winter. They want to be asleep. Bats are a great deal smarter than people. If you sleep all winter, you don't have to go out in the cold, or store food, and gather wood. Let's leave them in peace."

Browser lowered his torch and picked his way across the droppings into the next room. The entire ceiling had collapsed, covering the floor with crossed beams, stones, and powdered plaster. His haste to get away from the bats almost killed him.

"Oh, dear gods!" he shouted, and stumbled back as the floor beneath his feet gave way, and crashed down.

Stone Ghost grabbed Browser's cape and tugged him backward through the doorway.

Dust rose in a smothering veil.

"Thank you, Elder." Browser gasped for a breath and fought to still his pounding heart.

"That was close, Nephew." Stone Ghost poked his head past Browser's shoulder and peered down into the darkness. "Lift your torch. Let's see what's down there."

Nerving himself, Browser stepped back into the doorway and raised the torch. The fallen floor lay in a heap in the center of the room, but beautiful black-and-white pottery lined the walls, dust-streaked and stained with packrat urine. In one corner lay a desiccated coyote, in another, a bobcat, apparently animals that had fallen in and couldn't find a way out.

"Where do we go from here, Uncle?" Browser asked.

Stone Ghost pointed. "The killer went that way. If you will notice, the dust and packrat pellets have been kicked off around the edge of the wall to the right. The dirt has also been polished by someone's sandals."

"What kind of fool would edge his way around this rickety floor?"

Stone Ghost smiled. "The kind who has done it many times, Nephew." Stone Ghost edged out onto the path, hugging the wall.

"Uncle, wait! What makes you think a man made that trail? It might have been a coyote or a bobcat."

"Come, Nephew," Stone Ghost whispered. "If this is the killer's trail, it will support our weight."

"I don't like this, Uncle. It's not safe!" But Browser held his torch low and felt his way around the gaping hole, following in Stone Ghost's footsteps. "If I go crashing down—!"

"You won't, Nephew," Stone Ghost called from where he waited in the T-shape doorway on the opposite wall.

"Look around you. The spiders tell us this is the trail of the killer."

Browser finished the perilous journey without falling into the abyss and even more miraculously, without setting himself afire. He slipped into the doorway beside Stone Ghost.

Stone Ghost stuck his head into the next room and sniffed loudly.

Browser gripped his uncle's bony shoulder. "This time, I'm going first, Uncle."

Browser stepped by him into the next chamber. Two ladders led into the chamber above. There was no other way out. Browser lowered his torch to the floor around the ladders.

Ceramic beads from a broken necklace scattered the dust, along with smashed pottery, and pieces of a basket. The plaster on the wall to his right had cracked off, leaving only the head and shoulders of the Badger katsina. The masked god stared at Browser through glittering blue eyes. The artist must have mixed ground turquoise with his paint.

Bracing a hand on the ladder, Browser lifted the torch.

Stone Ghost sniffed again. "Wait, Nephew. Notice the air?"

Browser sniffed. "What about it?"

"It's still. No wind." He pointed to the thick spiderwebs that filled the corners of the room. "Raise your torch high. No wind penetrates this chamber, but look at the webs. How many have you wiped from your face so far?"

Browser lifted the torch. "None, Elder."

"See, the spiders tell us that someone, at least as tall as we are, walked here before us."

Browser's eyes widened. "I understand."

He tested the strength of the ladder, and climbed up into the next chamber. There were two doorways, one on either side of the room. An intact web hung from the lintel in front of Browser. The web on the door behind him, however, was gone.

He reached down to help Stone Ghost off the ladder.

The old man licked his lips, and sighed. "Which door, War Chief?"

"This one, Uncle." Browser led the way.

As he stepped into the small, dark chamber, the light of his torch gleamed over corncobs, a splintered war club, and shreds of dusty cloth.

A path had been kicked through the clutter into the next room. Browser followed it. When he ducked into the next room, he stopped suddenly. "Uncle, come and see this."

The sound of Stone Ghost's steps crunching on broken pottery seemed loud in the stillness.

Browser walked forward. The man's skeleton lay hunched in the far corner, propped against the wall, and covered with a crumbling stack of mats. Mice had gnawed the extended leg bones, but a single patch of hair clung to the rear of the skull.

Browser lowered his torch and pulled back the mats to examine the man. A broken arrow shaft, partially packrat gnawed, lodged in his ribs like a malignant sliver.

Stone Ghost bent over Browser. "He's been here for a long time."

Browser let the mats down and straightened. "Do you think he was one of the First People?"

"Perhaps. But if so, someone in the past one hundred sun cycles stole his turquoise wolf pendant. All of the First People had one." Stone Ghost gestured to the next doorway. "Have you looked in there yet, Nephew?"

"No, Uncle."

Browser walked to the entry, and thrust his torch inside.

Behind him, he heard Stone Ghost whisper to the dead

man, "No, I'm sorry. I haven't seen the Blessed Stern-light."

Browser's grip tightened on the torch handle. "Uncle, isn't Sternlight the priest who first brought word of the Katsinas? Back in the days before the Blessed Poor Singer became a prophet?"

"Yes, that's right," Stone Ghost answered, and casually stepped by Browser into the next chamber. "He was captured and killed by the Fire Dogs."

Browser's skin prickled as he followed the old man through the chamber toward the ladder that stood in the hole in the floor. The air had a musty, heavy feeling.

Stone Ghost gripped the poles of the ladder and started to step onto the rungs.

"Uncle, please don't do that," Browser said and trotted forward.

His breathing had gone hoarse, as if he'd been running for days. Despite the cool air, perspiration soaked his war shirt.

"Very well, Nephew," Stone Ghost said and stood aside.

"Thank you." Browser climbed down two rungs and extended his torch into the chamber. In the corner to his right, a shining mass of what looked like wet rope lay. The opposite corner was filled with over a dozen standing poles, as if someone had brought them in to shore up the roof, but hadn't used them yet.

Browser climbed down, and waited.

Stone Ghost panted as he descended, and his legs were shaking.

Browser gripped his arm and supported him to the floor.

Stone Ghost smiled and turned.

He froze.

Browser spun around, searching the room for some threat he'd missed.

"Easy, Nephew," Stone Ghost whispered. "It's the middle of the winter. I think if we stay away from them, they won't bother us."

"What?" Browser held out his torch.

"I wouldn't do that, if I were you. They are dormant now, but like all of their kind, heat brings them to life."

"Blessed Katsinas!" Browser leapt back with his heart in his throat. "I didn't see them!"

His torch sparkled from a hundred eyes. Their triangular heads rested on gleaming scales. The diamond patterns on their backs resembled mottled weavings.

"I don't think the rattlesnakes arrived here the same way that we did, Nephew." Stone Ghost looked around. "There must be another entrance."

The old man picked his way through the crumbling matting that scattered the floor, and headed into the blackness to the left.

Somewhere above them, a rodent scurried across plaster, its claws clicking.

"Ah," Stone Ghost barely whispered. "Here, we have it."

Browser followed. Only the faint hissing of the burning grease, and the sputter of the flames could be heard.

Stone Ghost walked behind the upright poles, and vanished. Browser ran after him.

As he stepped into the chamber, a cold shaft of light shot across the room to illuminate a spiral painted on the far wall.

"It's a solstice room," Stone Ghost said as he walked toward a large oblong bundle in the middle of the floor. It was wrapped in yellow cloth, and two small pots sat on either side of it. Each pot had a flat piece of sandstone waxed to the rim to seal the pot. "Since we are nearing that day, the spiral behind you is illuminated. At any other time of the year, however, this room will be in shadow."

The old man bent down next to the bundle and frowned.

"What is that, Uncle?" Browser examined the room behind them, then turned back.

"You wouldn't have to ask if you were closer. The smell of rotting flesh is very distinctive, even wrapped in thick fabric."

Browser leaned against the door frame, where he could watch their back trail. "Human, or animal?"

"I don't know yet."

Stone Ghost began unwrapping the yellow fabric.

He had to tug the last layer loose from the blood-caked skull. The bones of the nose, cheeks, forehead, and jaw had been crushed. The hair was cut short in mourning.

Browser suddenly felt lightheaded. Blood pounded in his ears as he stepped forward. "Uncle . . ."

Stone Ghost ripped the cloth away to expose the ribs, the empty gut, and hips. The bones had been stripped. The thigh bones were welded stiffly to the pelvis by dried ligament and tendon. Even the thin strips of muscle between the ribs had been cut out.

"Curious." Stone Ghost reached down, and slipped off the anklet that adorned her foot. Made of carved jet beads threaded on a braided yucca string, it was beautiful. He slid it onto his own wrist, and reached for the bracelet.

"Blessed Katsinas," Browser whispered.

He ran forward and bent over the corpse. The familiar jet bracelet, carved into the shape of a serpent, caught the weak solstice light.

"Uncle, this . . . this is my wife."

Browser's knees went weak.

"What happened to her? Uncle? Why is her—her flesh gone!"

But as he said it, he knew.

Browser sank to the floor and gasped for breath. "Oh, gods, dear gods."

The dawn horizon glowed with an eerie luminescence that only a desert could spawn. Maureen tipped her head back, enchanted by the sight, wondering at the diffuse pastel aurora. The lilting calls of coyotes rang from the canyon walls.

All night long, she had walked down the dirt road, alternately cursing Stewart, and teetering around the edges of the abyss left by John's death.

Around midnight, she had ended up in the huge ruins of the giant pueblo where she now sat on a low sandstone wall, shivering, hunched over for warmth. How could a place roast you during the day, and freeze you at night?

Whether she looked inside herself or out at the greasewood, chamisa, and sagebrush, the view was the same: Dry, empty, and lonely.

The first plaintive songs of the morning birds filled the air. Bats fluttered around the dark face of the cliff to her left. She watched them in an odd haze of memory, seeing John's body sprawled on the kitchen floor, his wide eyes staring sightlessly into hers, feeling his hand, all the strength and warmth gone. The stench of burning spaghetti sauce mixed poignantly with the fragrances of the desert and dawn. She'd come home late from a faculty meeting. The shock of finding him still numbed her.

Maureen rubbed her arms.

She wanted to go home. This wasn't her place. None of her ancestors had ever trod this sere landscape. Her place was faraway. Cool, with slow, dark rivers, and billowing white clouds. The spirits of her ancestors, Seneca and white, moved in the Ontario shadows, not here.

She surveyed the ruins. Tumbled, ghostly walls—the wreckage of ancient dreams—thrust up around her. To her right, the gaping circle of a kiva yawned. A wooden marker bearing a white "10" indicated that she had stopped at some tourist point-of-interest. She rose from the stone wall and stared into the giant subterranean ceremonial chamber. Eyes seemed to peer back at her from the shadowed depths. For the briefest of moments, she could have sworn she heard singing, then the booming of a jet high overhead drowned it out.

She rubbed her eyes. "You're tired. Hurting. You've been up all night wandering around with ghosts. No wonder you're hearing things."

After John's death, she'd worked herself pitilessly, never missing a class. Weekends had been the worst. She'd rushed to her car after her last class, driven down Queen Elizabeth Way to her favorite liquor store in Niagara-on-the-Lake, then gone to their lonely home, locked herself in, and drunk herself into oblivion. Beyond feeling. Beyond any . . .

The sound of gravel crunching under a boot made her turn.

He stood silhouetted against the dawn, tall, his blond hair shining. A stab of fear went through her in that instant before she placed the rumpled straw cowboy hat.

"Get away from me, Stewart."

He thrust his thumbs into his jeans' pockets, as if cowed. "I'm truly sorry, Maureen."

"You certainly are."

He winced, shifted uneasily, and looked at the sunrise. The iridescent sky glittered with bands of indigo and orange. "I've been tracking you all night. It's given me a lot of time to think."

"You? Think? Did it give you a headache?" She crossed her arms, not wanting to shiver against the cold. Not in front of him.

His face was in profile, but she saw his brow line. "Tracking you wasn't so bad at first. In the moonlight, I could follow your tracks down the dust to the road. After that, I had to search every room in Kin Kletso and Pueblo del Arroyo. You wouldn't believe the size of the rattlesnake I stepped on. I guess he lives in the Mesa Verdean addition over at Arroyo."

She looked at the ruins to the south. "Mesa Verdean addition?"

He nodded. "Anasazi migrants. They reinhabited the canyon around A.D. twelve-fifty." He pointed behind her. "They also rebuilt the great kiva behind you. Roofed it, plastered it, painted it. We think it was a messianic movement, maybe the start of the kachina religion."

She took a deep breath. "What's the name of this place?"

The massive stone walls had solidified in the growing light. "This is Pueblo Bonito. Up until about eighteen-thirty, it was the largest building in North America. As best we can guess, it stood five stories tall and had over eight hundred rooms. When it gets a little lighter, I'll take you around. The masonry will stun you."

She could see the regret in his eyes. He really was trying hard to apologize.

"You're an enigma to me, Stewart. I can't figure you out."

To her surprise, he said, "That's all right, I'm an enigma to myself. I have this black place inside me. I don't like to admit it, but it's there. Sometimes, it opens up, and I say outrageous things like I did last night. Then I spend the rest of my life kicking myself for it."

"For the sake of efficiency, I hope your knees are double-jointed."

He peered down into the shadowed depths of the kiva. After a long silence, he added, "A lot of Power was concentrated down there. You can still feel it. Some good, some bad. The old gods still dance, echoing the beginning times and the journey up from the underworlds." He paused. "That black place inside me, it's my own kiva, I guess. I keep the past locked up in there."

As though uncomfortable, he bowed his head. "I'm going to dig that unit you want me to."

Maureen frowned, trying to figure his angle. "Why?"

He vented a deep sigh. "If we don't, we'll never know which of us is right. Is it a slaves' burial ground, or a murderer's hiding place?"

She gave him an askance look. "Can we dig the unit? Will Maggie authorize it?"

"Well," he said and scanned the brightening sky. "It's about three miles back to the site and asking her that exact question. Which means we ought to get started." He held out a hand. "If you're ready."

"Do you need to rest?" Little Bow asked Marsh Hawk.

She stood bent over, her beautiful round face twisted in agony. Marsh Hawk's cough had grown worse. She could barely take ten steps before another fit doubled her over.

Marsh Hawk shook her head. "No, I am well enough, husband, and it—it isn't much farther. When we get there I will have all night to rest." The curly brown hair on her buffalo cape looked black in the twilight.

Since noon, they had been falling farther and farther behind, straggling at the rear of the Frosted Meadow procession. His brother, Singing Mantis, walked just ahead of them, his bow in his hand, anxiously studying the canyon bottom.

Little Bow stroked Marsh Hawk's shoulder-length black hair. "Very well, but I am planning to rest on the other side of the wash."

She smiled. "All right, husband. I will do as you say."

As Sister Moon rose higher into the sky, her silver gleam flooded the canyon shimmering in the twisted junipers and outlining every dark crevice in the sandstone walls. Shadows draped the rocky rim like a string of polished black beads.

Ahead of them, Talon Town gleamed. The fifth story had collapsed into a heap of jutting timbers and fallen stones. Most of the plaster had cracked off and scattered the ground around the enormous half-moon-shaped structure like a dirty white apron, but torches burned everywhere, and he could smell the scent of cedar fires and frying bread. To the right of the town, Hillside Village sat against the cliff, white and rectangular. A large fire burned in the plaza.

Many small camps scattered the flats, and he could see groups of people standing in the wavering firelight.

"Hallowed Ancestors," he murmured. "I would not have believed it if I hadn't seen it with my own eyes. Talon Town looks alive."

His great-grandmother, the Blessed Horned Bird, had told him many tales of the rise and fall of the grandest town in the Straight Path nation. On cold winter nights, she'd held Little Bow close and whispered of the wicked First People and their evil courtship of the lost ghosts who roamed the canyon.

She had often spoken about the Blessed Cornsilk. Her father had been a great warrior, one of the Made People and her mother had been the highest Matron in the land. Horned Bird had vowed that if Cornsilk had only taken her rightful place as Matron of Talon Town when Night Sun left, the Straight Path nation would still be strong: "The Blessed Cornsilk would have built alliances, not waged wars. She would have extended the trade routes so her people would have had food in the dark times. Cornsilk would have sniffed out the plots and stopped the First People before they started hiring assassins to take each other's lives."

Then, immediately after telling this story about the great and Blessed Cornsilk, Horned Bird would speak in low tones about the death of the last of the First People, and the celebration that lasted for a full sun cycle.

Marsh Hawk started down the road into the steep, jagged ravine, and Little Bow followed. Gravel grated beneath his sandals.

"You don't think that crazy old man will be here, do you?"

Over her shoulder Marsh Hawk called, "Everyone else is coming. I don't see why Stone Ghost wouldn't."

Little Bow leaped the trickle of water flowing in the bottom of the wash and started up the opposite side of the drainage. Marsh Hawk weaved in front of him and started coughing, the sound raw and wet.

He trotted to her side and wrapped an arm around her shoulders, holding her up while she trembled and gasped. The effort coaxed tears from her eyes. Marsh Hawk leaned against him until the fit passed, then she gulped air and wiped her face with her hand.

"I'm sorry, husband. I know I'm the reason we have fallen so far behind."

She rested her chin on his shoulder, and Little Bow hugged her. Her swollen belly pressed comfortingly against him. He patted her back. "In a finger of time, we will catch up."

He held her as they climbed up out of the wash and onto the sandy flats. Moonlight sheathed the desert, casting odd shadows. Mixed with the flickering amber glow cast by Talon Town and the fires of the smaller camps, the shadows seemed to crawl toward them in a rush, then scamper away as if frightened by their human scents.

"I want you to sit down and rest, my wife. You are ill and with child. A few moments will harm no one."

Marsh Hawk sank to the ground and heaved a tired breath. "Just a few moments, Little Bow, then we'll be on our way."

"Rest as long as you need to. We are in sight of the town. This night will be filled with nothing but reminiscences and feasting anyway. Tomorrow, the holy work begins."

As he knelt by her side, an uneasy sensation crept through Little Bow. He squinted for a long moment at the darkness, wondering what had happened to everyone else. They must have descended into a dip, or perhaps the firelight had blinded him. A large boulder tipped precariously over the bank to his left. Little Bow reached for his club. The boulder cast an oddly shaped shadow. His souls could conjure the shape of a tall man's shoulder, and a leg almost hidden by the rock. He stared at it.

"Look, husband. The rest of the village is almost there," Marsh Hawk said and tipped her chin toward the fire blazing in front of Hillside village.

The first in a straggling line of people walked into the crowd, and voices rose. Matron Corn Mother strode directly toward a woman wearing a red-feathered cape, and they embraced.

"That must be Flame Carrier."

"Yes," Marsh Hawk said. "The new Matron of Talon Town."

Little Bow smiled at the irony. Flame Carrier was one of the Made People, a member of the Ant Clan, masons, architects, and artists. The First People's ghosts locked inside Talon Town must be shrieking at the insult.

He dragged his gaze away. Inside Talon Town, he could just see the upper torsos of the Great Warriors. The eye sockets in their fierce masks gleamed with a curious fire, as if anxiously gazing beyond the people, and the camps, to the desert where Marsh Hawk and Little Bow knelt. Little Bow had the discomforting feeling that they saw something he did not.

He put a hand on Marsh Hawk's shoulder. "If you are rested, wife, we should go."

She looked up. "I thought you told me to take as long as I wished, husband?"

"I did, but . . ." he paused, his senses suddenly on alert. An owl hooted in the darkness, and he caught sight of a dark body sailing over their heads. "I think we should leave."

Marsh Hawk shoved to her feet and scanned the moon-lit desert. Barely audible, she murmured, "Why? What do you—"

He cut the air with a fist. *"Walk."*

She did.

Little Bow drew his war club, and held it at his side. He followed on his wife's heels, protecting her back.

"Shh," someone hissed from behind them.

In one fluid movement, Little Bow shoved Marsh Hawk to the ground, and whirled around with his club up. "Who's there?"

A shadow detached itself from the boulder, and hoarsely whispered, *"Run away before it's too late!"*

Little Bow took a step toward the man. "Who are you?"

"Great evil lurks in these ruins, Little Bow. Did they not tell you?" He sucked in a desperate breath, as though he'd been running for a hand of time to get here. The shadow seemed to turn around, as if fearfully gazing over his shoulder. *"If you do not leave, you will have to do battle with the Wolf Witch, the most powerful witch in the world. Leave. Now!"*

Little Bow's mouth dropped open, but no words came.

The shadow hissed, *"Ask them about the ashes. Ask them, Little Bow."*

"What ashes? What are you talking about?"

The man seemed to dissipate into the air. The shadow vanished.

"Wa-wait!" Little Bow called. "Who are you? I don't understand!"

Marsh Hawk cautiously sat up, her eyes wide with fear. Pale sand caked the front of her buffalo cape. Neither of them spoke for three or four hundred heartbeats, then Marsh Hawk whispered, "Hurry. Let's go."

Little Bow wavered. If he'd been on a war walk, he would have run the man down, and demanded an explanation at the point of a deerbone stiletto, but he couldn't leave his pregnant wife alone in the darkness.

Little Bow reached down and helped Marsh Hawk to her feet. She was shaking, her gaze on the place where the man had vanished.

"Stay to my right," Little Bow instructed. "Walk quickly, but do not run. I must watch and listen. If you get too far ahead of me, I cannot protect you."

Marsh Hawk nodded.

They started for Hillside village.

He heard nothing. No steps. No breathing. No leggings catching on brush.

But the owl's shadow wheeled over the ground, as if circling them.

Little Bow dared not look, but his heart fluttered. What if the man were a witch? Witches were canny. They could change themselves into whirlwinds, and career around villages unnoticed, or leap through magical hoops of twisted yucca fibers, and turn themselves into animals.

They were especially fond of night birds.

It took all of his strength, but he kept his gaze on the surrounding brush, searching for a human foe. Ordinary flesh and blood could be killed. He did not know about enchanted witches.

When they came to within fifty paces of the crowd in Hillside village, Little Bow turned to Marsh Hawk and shouted, *"Run!"*

She gripped handfuls of her long skirt and ran hard, her hair flying out behind her.

Only when she had entered the crowd, did Little Bow grant himself the luxury of flight. He whirled and his muscular legs drove into the ground. He blasted into the crowd, and shouldered through the sea of people, following his wife.

Marsh Hawk saw him behind her, and stopped. Little

Bow waved her ahead. "Go on!" he called. "Tell Corn Mother."

Marsh Hawk headed for her.

Corn Mother halted her conversation with Flame Carrier. Her wise old eyes fixed on Marsh Hawk.

Marsh Hawk knelt before Corn Mother, and breathlessly said, "Matron, forgive me, but we must speak with you."

"What is it, child?" Corn Mother clasped the hood of her blue-and-white-striped cape at the throat. Thick gray hair stuck out around her hood, and her skeletal face, with its jutting lower jaw, appeared unnaturally pale in the fire's sheen.

Flame Carrier, who sat beside her, frowned. She had small narrow eyes, and a bulbous nose. A few kinky gray hairs made up her eyebrows. She sat on a deerhide, dressed in a beautiful red macaw-feather cape.

It took Little Bow a while to work his way through the two hundred or more people in the plaza. Some sat in small groups, others stood, talking and laughing.

"Forgive us, Elders," he said as he bowed to the matrons, "but this is urgent."

Corn Mother searched his face, then Marsh Hawk's, and said, "Tell me."

"A man stopped us at the wash, Matron. Well, I—I think it was a man," Marsh Hawk corrected herself. "It seemed to be a man."

Flame Carrier's expression turned grave. She quietly asked, "What man?"

"We could not see him, Matron," Marsh Hawk answered, "but he called to us from the shadows."

"Yes?" Corn Mother asked. "What did he say?"

"He said that great evil lurked in these ruins, Matron, and told us if we stayed here we would have to do battle with the Wolf Witch, the most powerful witch in the world."

"He said something else, Matron," Little Bow added. "He told us to ask about the ashes."

"Then vanished into the night."

Corn Mother mouthed the words: *the Wolf Witch.*

Flame Carrier gripped her arm. "Do you know what that means?"

The people closest to them went silent, and their gazes riveted on the matrons. A din of whispering broke out.

Corn Mother said, "Stories. I remember stories from when I was a child."

The crowd rearranged itself, creeping forward, forming a ring around the two old women.

Another coughing fit struck Marsh Hawk. She tried to cover the sound with both hands. The fit affected her like a seizure, her whole body tensed, and quaked.

Little Bow slid over, put his arm around Marsh Hawk's back, and drew her against him.

Matron Corn Mother waited until the fit had eased then began slowly, as if the words took effort. "It began about one hundred sun cycles ago. They knew they were in trouble. They began sealing exterior windows and doorways—actually walling them up with stone and mortar. Talon Town was originally open in the front, allowing people to come and go as they wished. Did you know that?"

"No, Elder," Little Bow answered.

"Yes, when they first grew scared, they built that string of rooms on the south side, but they left two gates. Then they closed off the gate to the eastern half of the plaza, and narrowed the western gate to the width of an ordinary doorway. Finally, that gate, too, was walled off. They even closed the small vents that allowed air to circulate through the town. The only way in or out was over the walls by ladder."

"It must have been difficult for the elderly and the sick," Marsh Hawk said.

"That was the least of their concerns. The First People who lived in Talon Town were being murdered one by one. Their bodies were thrown into shallow graves. Stones were dropped over their heads to keep their wicked souls locked in the ground forever. When the town was abandoned, the bones of those people became priceless. To witches." She laced her hands in her lap, and gazed into the faces of her listeners. "About—oh, let me see—it must be fifteen summers now—the most powerful witch in the land moved into Talon Town. He was called the Wolf Witch, but his real name was Two Hearts."

"Two Hearts?" Flame Carrier said.

"Yes. Blessed gods, he was evil. Common witches gather putrefying corpse flesh to make their corpse powder, but legends say that Two Hearts made his from the bones of stranded ghosts. By grinding the bones, and carrying the powder with him, he could force a ghost to do anything—even kill entire villages of people. He—"

From the rear of the crowd a man shouted, *"His corpse powder was always lethal because he made it from the bones of First People!"*

Villagers began shuffling back, shoving each other to get out of the way. In the narrow alley that formed, Stone Ghost appeared, wearing the same ratty turkey-feather cape he'd worn days ago at Frosted Meadow village.

Little Bow gaped.

The old man was covered head to toe with gray ash. He hobbled forward, and extended his cupped hands, as if silently asking people to look at what he carried. "Even a single grain of Two Hearts' corpse powder could kill. Several people in nearby villages had this powder sprinkled in their hair, and died writhing like clubbed dogs." More loudly, he added, "And it was rumored that Two Hearts stashed entire pots of corpse powder in the burials of people he truly hated. To drive their souls mad for eternity!"

A roar went through the gathering.

Little Bow shuddered. He could imagine no more terrible curse. Even in death the witch's enemies could not escape his evil.

As Stone Ghost came closer, Little Bow craned his neck, trying to see what the old man held.

Stone Ghost grinned, stopping often to allow puzzled people to look into his hands. His sparse white hair stuck out as though he stood on a high mountain during a lightning storm. The dark age spots on his scalp showed through the thick layer of ash.

"What's he been doing?" Little Bow whispered to Marsh Hawk. "Sleeping in the trash mound?"

As Stone Ghost came closer, he spied Corn Mother and a look of genuine excitement brightened his face. "My dear Corn Mother!" he called. "How good to see you again. I hope you buried that footprint as I instructed." He shouldered between Little Bow, and Marsh Hawk, dumped his rocks at Corn Mother's side. Then he reached out, seized her hand. "We wouldn't want to have it running around trampling people's souls."

"I buried it properly." Corn Mother jerked her hand away. "What happened to you? You look like someone shoved you face-first into an old fire pit!"

"Well, that's almost right," he said, and flopped down on the hide beside Corn Mother. As he brushed at his filthy cape, a choking veil of ash rose.

Corn Mother waved at it. "Where did you find so much ash?"

"Hmm?" Stone Ghost said, and his eyes narrowed, as if he'd no idea what she meant. "What? Oh! It's remarkable what a man must do to dig out the truth. You see, I thought it was very odd that there was no woodpile beside the ritual fire. Wouldn't you think that odd? The

Sunwatcher knew the burial would last for another hand of time, and she would be responsible for burning the boy's clothing, and then smoking the burial participants in pinyon smoke to cleanse them. Why wasn't there a woodpile?"

Corn Mother turned to Flame Carrier. "What's he talking about?"

Flame Carrier's face turned a mottled crimson. "I knew there was something strange that day, but the woodpile . . . gods, I should have noticed."

Stone Ghost scooped up the rocks he'd dropped, gathering them into a pile before him. As he began to arrange them, he said, "After I thought about the missing woodpile, another thought occurred to me. You know how, on a freezing night, snow falls into a fire, melts, puts out flames, then freezes over the ash bed?"

"Of course. What of it?" Corn Mother squinted.

Flame Carrier released her blue-and-white hood, and bent forward to point at the white rocks. "What are those?"

"That," he said, and shook a finger, "is the question, Matron."

Stone Ghost lifted a rock, turned it on end, and tried to fit it to another rock, as if reassembling a shattered pot.

Little Bow gestured to the rocks. "Where did you find them?"

"Beneath the ice in the ash bed. That's why the mysterious messenger tonight told you to ask about the ashes. It took half the day, but I finally sifted them out."

The hair at the nape of Little Bow's neck tingled. "How did he know you would be looking through an ash bed?"

"He watched me until well after sunset. He knows what this is, of course."

"What?"

"I said *he* knows, Little Bow, I don't."

Little Bow gave Marsh Hawk an askance look. The rocks had broken jaggedly, along the tiny white lines that veined the stones. Such fractures appeared when you threw a chert cobble into a very hot fire and it exploded.

"You think this was once whole?" he asked. "Like a hammerstone?"

"I think it was whole, yes. Here." He shoved several rocks toward Little Bow. "Help me piece it together."

Little Bow squatted. The white chert cobble had probably been pulled from a creek bed, but what it had been used for, he could not tell. "Who is the man who spoke to us, Elder?"

"How would I know?"

"Well, if you saw him watching you, you must know—"

"I never saw him."

Little Bow's mouth quirked. He debated asking the old fool how he could possibly have known he was being spied upon if he never saw the spy, then decided against it. He suspected Stone Ghost would just spout something equally ridiculous.

The evening's merriment had faded to an eerie anxiety. Only the people on the farthest edges of the plaza continued to talk and laugh. At least one hundred people ringed them, listening.

"Tell me, Little Bow, the man who stopped you tonight, was he tall?"

"Yes, Elder."

"Slender? Or a heavy, broad-chested man?"

"We could not see him very well, Elder. He clung to the shadows. But I would say heavy."

Moonlit clouds massed over the towering sandstone wall behind Hillside Village, blotting out the Evening People. Thunderbirds slept in the clouds, their deep voices rumbling.

"Elder, is it possible that the man who spoke to us is the Wolf Witch?"

Stone Ghost fitted six pieces together, and the object began to take shape. It resembled an elongated egg, a little more pointed on one end than the other. "I cannot answer that. If so, he has seen the passing of at least fifty-five sun cycles."

Marsh Hawk said, "This man was much younger, Elder. He—"

Corn Mother interrupted, "Witches can prolong their lives by removing their relatives' hearts with a spindle, and putting the hearts into their own chests."

"Yes, that's true," Stone Ghost said, "but it is difficult for me to believe that Two Hearts is alive. I have not heard anyone speak of him in at least fifteen summers. Witches are vain. They take pride in their despicable acts. If Two Hearts is alive and working evil, he would make certain people knew."

Little Bow picked up a rock, and fitted it in place. "Hmm," he said, "this piece is grooved. Do you see this?"

Stone Ghost's eyes flared. He pulled Little Bow's hand close to examine the groove. "Where does it go? Can you tell?"

Little Bow turned it over, tipped the rock up, and placed it in the middle. It wasn't connected to any other pieces, but that's where it went. The smooth outer edge of the stone fitted the curving line of the "egg."

"Elder," Little Bow said, then paused while he thought about Talon Town and Two Hearts. "Why did the First People seal up every window and door? Were they afraid of witches? Fire Dogs?"

Stone Ghost looked up, and their gazes held. "Neither, warrior. Humans can fight witches. Humans can fight Fire Dogs. What they often cannot fight are the shadows that whisper to them from their own souls. That's what they were afraid of. As we all should be."

Little Bow tilted his head, wondering what that meant. Shadows whispering from the souls? Lofty sounding nonsense. He fitted another rock into place.

As he drew back his hand, he paused. "Elder," he said, and studied the emerging shape. "This is the head of a war club."

Stone Ghost froze with a rock halfway to the blanket. White hair fluttered around his face and tangled with his stubby eyelashes. He did not bother to brush it aside. His dark pained eyes lifted to Flame Carrier.

"Matron, would you send for my nephew?"

THE SHARPENED EDGE of the shovel caught on roots as Dusty lifted and tossed the dirt into Maureen's screen. She threw her weight into rocking the mesh-bottom box. Dirt cascaded through onto the back-dirt pile.

All in all, it hadn't been too traumatic. Maggie had reluctantly agreed. Dale had crossed his arms and firmly forbade them to make further excavations outside the designated impact area. His bulldog jaw had been set, his wiry gray hair poking out from under his fedora.

Dusty had immediately set up the transit, and while Maureen held the rod, shot in the elevation for the control corner. He wanted to get it down before anybody had time to reconsider. After they'd measured out the two-by-two unit, he'd started digging.

Sylvia knelt in her unit ten paces away, continuing the slow process of skeletal removal. Maggie and Hail sat under the ramada, sipping tea, talking softly.

Dusty took a minute to pull the line level tight and extended his tape measure to check the depth of his pit floor while Maureen sifted through the root mat, gravels, and small stones in the screen.

"This is hard work." Maureen sighed, flipped the junk out of the screen, and wiped her forehead on her white T-shirt sleeve. "I'm going to have great arm muscles when I get back to Ontario."

"And every other kind of muscle," Dusty said, as he

jotted notes on his clipboard. "There are no out-of-shape, pudgy women archaeologists. Unless they're *academicians,*" he said the word like a five-syllable curse.

Maureen leaned on the screen. "Did your mother excavate or just do cultural fieldwork?"

Dusty hesitated, his pen hovering over his clipboard. Without looking up, he said, "If I talk about my mother, I don't want any flippant comebacks from you, all right?"

"Sure."

Dusty took a deep breath. "She never sank a trowel. She never washed a potsherd. Her kind of fieldwork was walking around a village, taking notes about what people were wearing or eating. If she ever got dirty, she went into town and took a shower, so she'd look 'pretty' the next day. The Zuni used to make jokes about her behind her back. They called her 'The-Woman-with-No-Eyes,' because she never looked at them, just her papers."

Maureen toyed with a root that had lodged in the hardware cloth of the screen. "She must have had a knack for languages though, if she could understand what they're were saying."

"She did." He left it at that.

Maureen worked the root out of the screen and tossed it onto the dirt pile. "How did you end up with Dale?"

Dusty finished making his notes, closed his clipboard, and set it aside. "There wasn't anybody else. After Dad . . ."

"When did he die?"

He met her gaze. "Actually, that's the wrong word. He didn't just die. He killed himself."

To his surprise, her voice softened. "Were you the one who found him?"

He shook his head. "No. A nurse in the hospital did."

Maureen rubbed her fingers along the wooden rim of the screen. "I found John. He'd been making dinner. He was in the kitchen. I came home late."

She had said the words matter-of-factly, but he heard the buried pain.

"My father electrocuted himself. The nurse said that he didn't give any sign. Just took off his slippers, jumped up on the sink, and by the time the orderly got the door open, Dad had unscrewed the lightbulb, and stuck his finger into the socket. He had his bare foot on the metal faucet."

Dusty sank his shovel again, and Maureen extended the screen to catch the dirt. She sifted it back and forth, before reaching down and lifting something. "Potsherd," she said, and flipped it to him.

Bracing the shovel handle on his hip, Dusty rubbed it clean with his thumb, and studied the decoration. "Mesa Verde Black-on-white. I'd say we're coming down on our cultural layer. You're going to have to go over and fill out an artifact bag for this level."

"On my way." She let the screen down, and walked for the green ammo box where Dusty kept supplies.

He studied the ground, looking for the soil discoloration that indicated the old ground surface. Root casts— the places where brush had grown, died, rotted, and been refilled with dirt trickling down from above—spotted the soil.

Maureen pulled a Ziploc sandwich bag from the dig kit. She used a Sharpie pen to mark it with the unit provenience, and level depth.

Dusty frowned at her. She was a striking woman. Her face aquiline, her eyes the deep black of velvet.

He smiled grimly at himself. He'd known a lot of striking women. They tended to gravitate to him. They usually hung around for about two weeks, just enough time to peel back his good looks and see what lay beneath.

"Did he . . ." Maureen proceeded slowly, as if moving through a mine field. "Was it a terminal illness? Is that why your father was in the hospital?"

Dusty used his shovel to scoop up loose sand and tossed it into the screen. "It wasn't that kind of hospital."

She set the artifact bag down and gripped the handles of the screen. The muscles of her slender forearms tightened. "I'm sorry to hear that."

"It was a long time ago." He knelt down to retrieve his notebook, blew the sand off the page, and jotted his level notes. He made a quick description of the soil, the root casts, and the single potsherd. Setting the notebook aside, he glanced up at her, and an odd prickling sensation went through him. The veil that generally covered her eyes had vanished. She was gazing at him somberly.

"I don't think I'll ever be able to look back at John lying on the floor, and say, 'It was a long time ago.' "

"Yes, you will. Pain goes away, Doctor. Eventually. That or it tears you apart."

He focused on the pit floor, trying to gauge where he'd most likely come down on the burial. If the soil horizons continued to slope, he ought to hit it just to the left. He made his first shovel scrape, then a second. They worked in silence, him shoveling to the *shish-shishing* of her screening.

He had almost dug another ten-centimeter level when he noticed the discoloration, a subtle distinction of color and texture. He stopped. "Curtain time."

She set the screen aside and knelt on the lip of the unit. "What did you find?"

Dusty indicated the changing soil horizons with a finger. "This," Dusty told her, "is the darker stain from the organic content of the old site surface. That's from the ash, organic trash, and stuff left over from the occupational phase of the pueblo. This," he indicated a lighter soil that curved in an irregular arc, "is intrusive. Younger silt and sand washed in."

"The grave?" She looked at him with sudden anticipation.

"Apparently."

She started to get down into the pit. "Let's get her uncovered."

Dusty held up a hand. "How about you stand back and let me map this in first? You know, do a little *real* science along the way."

Maureen sank down on the edge of the pit with a disappointed expression. "Just don't take too long, Stewart."

Dusty measured in the soil discoloration, took notes, and began troweling, pulling out the intrusive soil until he encountered jumbled dark soil, several chunks of stone from the toppled pueblo wall, and three sherds of pottery.

"What is all this?" Maureen asked.

"Trash. He shoveled it on top of the grave to cover her up." Dusty took a soil sample, and bagged it. "Do you see the ragged edge of the grave?" He pointed to the irregular pattern. "Normally we'd see long scars left by the digging sticks as they levered the soil loose. This is choppy, as if the digging was difficult because the ground was frozen."

"Pollen in the nasal sinus will tell us, but I'll bet you're right."

He worked quickly but diligently, troweling for a time, then mapping in the broken sandstone rocks, potsherds, and stone flakes. When he finally stood up to stretch his back muscles, Dusty studied the outline of the soil discoloration, the grave, and tried to imagine how the skeleton might be laid out below. If this burial followed the pattern set by the others, her body should be laid out with the head to the north.

For a reason unknown to him, Dusty suddenly said, "My father was committed for his own safety."

Maureen's eyes tightened. She frowned at the ground. "By your mother?"

"She was long gone by then."

"Your grandparents?" she asked gently.

"They weren't on speaking terms with Dad. He was supposed to become a lawyer, or doctor, or something productive. I don't know the history of it. Just bad blood between them."

"Then who?"

"Dale did." He rolled the trowel in his fingers. "I think it's one of the toughest things he's ever done. God knows, because of it, I've hung like an albatross around Dale's neck for years."

"What happened to your mother?"

"She teaches at Harvard, manages a big collection of Australian Aboriginal and Maori artifacts at the Peabody. That's where she made her name for herself."

Maureen sat back, stunned. "You mean, Ruth Ann Sullivan is *your* mother?"

Dusty knelt and started troweling dirt again. "You know her?"

"Everyone knows her. Her books are classics. After Margaret Mead died, Ruth Ann Sullivan filled her place, writing about culture for the popular audience." She frowned at the top of Dusty's blond head. "You really hate her, don't you?"

"If I gave her any thought, I probably would. But I don't. In fact I—"

Bone grated beneath his trowel. Dusty's blue eyes narrowed. He slowly pulled back the darker earth, exposing the rear of a skull.

"My God," Maureen whispered. "There she is."

Dusty stood, smacked sand from his hands and pants, and said, "I need to get the camera. Would you like to *gently* excavate around the skull while I do that?"

"Would I!" She jumped into the pit and grabbed for his trowel.

Dusty got out and walked over to the ammo box. By the time he'd removed the camera, placed the North arrow and scale, and snapped a couple of shots, Maureen had excavated around the side of the skull. He'd just started walking back to the ammo box to put the camera back when Maureen called, "Dusty?"

It was the first time she'd ever called him by his first name.

She stood up in the pit and looked at him. Her breathing was coming fast, and her voice had a higher pitch than normal. "You'd better take a look at this."

Dusty hurried back and knelt, looking down at the skull. "What did you find?"

Maureen used her trowel to point to the dent in the woman's skull. Fractures radiated out from the temple on the left side. Just where she'd predicted. "Language skills, Stewart. He was trying to find the source of language in the human brain."

He got into the pit with her. "Amazing," he said in awe.

Beside the skull, Maureen had exposed a small patch of what looked like ground stone. "Can I have my trowel back?"

"Why?"

"This looks like a metate, but it doesn't seem to be very big. It may be a fragment of a broken metate."

He took the trowel and cleaned the dirt away until he could see the metate fragment had been inverted, its smooth grinding surface carefully stuck to the top of a pot with what looked like beeswax.

"This is curious," Dusty said and wiped his forehead with the back of his hand. "The person who did this was taking special precautions to preserve whatever's inside this pot."

"Can we open it?"

Dusty's trowel hovered over the pot. "I don't know if that's wise. This is an unusual burial artifact. First, we'd better . . ."

He heard Hail Walking Hawk's cane tapping the

ground and Maggie's soft voice: "We can see it once they get it out of the ground, Aunt."

"I want to see it now, child," Hail answered.

Dusty shielded his eyes against the sunlight and looked up at the old woman. Gray hair framed her wrinkled face.

"Did you find that woman, Washais?"

Maureen said, "I think so, Mrs. Walking Hawk. We also found a pot that's covered with a grinding stone. The stone is held in place by wax. Do you know what it might be?" Maureen pointed to it.

Hail squinted her ancient eyes, as if trying to see the pot, but not quite able to. "Might be food for the after-life."

Dusty asked, "Is it all right if we take it out and open it?"

Hail didn't answer for a time. Wind blew her hair around her face. "Do you think it will tell us something about the murderer, Washais?"

"It might. We won't know until we open it."

Hail's head tottered in a nod. "Open it up, then, and let me know what you find."

Maureen slid behind the cramped table in Dale's camper and carefully placed her microscope and dissecting kit on the Formica top. A Coleman lantern sat in the middle of the table, hissing softly. As she reached into her travel bag for slides and stain, she looked around. A tiny gas stove and cupboards filled the space to her left. To her right, a small window reflected the lantern's silver gleam. The booth had once been upholstered in reddish brown fabric, but years of dust, spilled coffee, and sweaty archaeologists had turned it gray. The battered old trailer possessed the faint metallic smell of mice.

Dale opened the camper door, and the hinges complained as he stepped inside, followed by Dusty. Dale cradled a black-on-white ceramic pot in his hands, the heavy sandstone cap still in place. The trailer rocked as they came to stand over the table.

"We just lifted it out of the grave. Ready?" Dale asked.

"Ready." Maureen turned on the battery-driven light of her portable microscope.

Dale settled the round-bottomed pot on a fabric donut, a device used to support either human skulls or fragile pottery.

"I have plenty of bags." Stewart reached into his back pocket and produced a roll of translucent Ziplocs.

"Good." Maureen opened her dissecting kit and removed a scalpel, then she studied the dark brown wax. "The wax apparently once covered the entire top, as though the person who sealed it melted the wax and poured it over the metate cap." Brown splotches mottled the cap, filling the depressions in the stone. "My God, there are dermatoglyphics in this wax. I'm going to try and pry the wax around the edges loose so we don't destroy them."

"What?" Stewart raised a blond eyebrow.

"Fingerprints," Dale said. "If Maureen is correct that these women were murdered, the prints probably belong to the killer."

"Well," Maureen said, "in that case, the murderer was a woman."

The camper went silent. The hot wind outside seemed suddenly loud, shrieking and whimpering as it rocked the camper.

Maureen frowned at their stunned faces. "What's the matter?"

"A woman?" Dusty whispered in awe.

"I can't say that for certain yet, of course, but look at the palm width demonstrated by these fingerprints." She pointed. "It's small. The size a woman, or a child, would make. Maybe a small man, but I doubt it."

Maureen took her scalpel, and carefully pried on the

sandstone cap. It didn't budge. "This stuff is like concrete."

"It's had eight hundred years to harden." Dusty said. "Here, let me help." He reached out, grasped the sandstone cap, and wrenched it free with a twist.

Maureen barely caught the pot before it spilled. "Good Lord, Stewart! Who do you think you are, Indiana Jones in the tombs of Venice? Too bad you didn't have a stick of dynamite and jackhammer, eh? Maybe some rare thousand-year-old fabric to make a torch so you could melt it off?"

Dale gave Dusty a reproving look, then picked up the sandstone cap, and held it to the lantern light. "Open a Ziploc for me, William. We can probably obtain good pollen, phytolith, and maybe even some macrobotanical samples from the protected surface within the wax ring."

Stewart opened a gallon Ziploc, allowed Dale to slip the cap inside, then promptly "zipped" the bag closed.

Maureen tipped the pot to the light, and frowned at the contents. At first glance, the stuff looked like shredded jerky. A thin gray layer of mold gave it a silvery look.

Dale peered at it, and shook his head. "I thought it might be food or precious gifts for the afterlife. Apparently not."

Dusty took a Sharpie pen from his green T-shirt pocket and labeled the bag containing the stone cap. "It still might be food. Shoshonean tribes in the Great Basin and Plains dried squirrels and rabbits and then ground them up on metates. Sort of a flaked meat. The prehistoric precursor to hamburger."

"Give me a minute and I'll settle this discussion." Maureen used forceps to lift a thin brown strand from the pot, then pulled scissors from her dissecting kit, and clipped off a tiny sample. She dropped the rest of the strand back into the pot and fixed the sample to a slide. "Let's see what we have here."

She started at ten power and grunted.

Dale said, "What?"

"Muscle tissue," she replied.

The memory of striations on some of the earlier burials caused her forehead to line.

"What are you thinking?" Stewart asked.

"Hold on." She rummaged through her kit, located a test tube, a small vial of clear liquid labeled "Human Juice," and a length of string wrapped around what looked like a heavy cigar tube.

"What's that?" Stewart asked.

"This is my traveling physical anthropologist's down-and-dirty field lab. Dale, I need a *clean* porcelain surface. Have you got a saucer? A plate?"

"I do." He unsnapped the latches on one of the cabinets. Reaching in, he pulled out a plastic bag of china saucers. "I bag them straight out of the dishwasher because I don't like the taste of mouse droppings. Will this do?"

"Fine," she said. She turned the saucer over and set it on the table in front of her. From her kit, she took a rag and two more small plastic bottles. "Bleach," she explained, and dripped two drops inside the ring on the bottom of the saucer. "Stewart, I see a roll of paper towels hanging from the bottom of the cabinet behind you. Unroll three squares, and give me the forth. Tear it off by holding it at the corners, and don't let it touch anything as you hand it to me."

Steward obeyed, frowning as he handed her the fourth towel. "I want you to explain this to me."

Maureen took the towel by the edges and curled it into a cone so that the unhandled portion of the towel made the point. "All right, the center of the saucer is glazed, and, for the most part, protected from scratches. There might be a fingerprint, so I'll use the bleach, and spread it around with the clean paper towel. Bleach denatures protein." As she spoke, she used the towel to swab the interior surface. "We'll leave that to set for a moment. Stewart, hand me another towel. Same procedure."

He carefully ripped another clean towel from the roll and handed it over.

Maureen used the towel to wipe the saucer bottom clean. "Now,"—she dribbled a little liquid from the second plastic bottle—"we'll apply distilled water and ask for yet another paper towel."

"You must have stock in a paper mill," Stewart said and gave her another towel.

"No," Maureen said, "I'm doing my best to minimize contamination."

She scrubbed the surface with the latest paper towel. "I'm trying to remove any of the remaining bleach." She squinted at the gleaming surface. "That's as good as we'll get out here." With the forceps she lifted the bit of tissue from the microscope slide and dropped it into the center of the plate. "Now comes the fun part." She carefully cleaned the scalpel handle and used the metal butt to mash the bit of tissue flat. For long minutes, she rocked the rounded end back and forth, flattening the bit of tissue. Finally, she picked up the test tube, unstoppered it, and used a needle from her dissecting kit to flick bits of pulverized tissue onto the scalpel blade, then she dropped them into the test tube.

"All right, we have a sample in the test tube." She lifted the little vial marked, "Human Juice." "This stuff is an antihuman antigen. It reacts with human tissue. I carry it around because it often comes in handy in the field."

She carefully measured out two drops, and set it aside. She added distilled water, stoppered the test tube, and dropped it in the weighted cigar-shaped holder. "Science

time, archaeologist," she said to Stewart as she handed
him the tube. "You're a big muscular man. I want you
to go outside, let out the string to its full length and spin
the tube around your head for the next five minutes while
Dale and I make ourselves a cup of coffee."

Stewart lifted his brows, hefted the weighted holder,
and asked, "Why don't you do this?"

"Because I've done it before. You haven't."

"Right," he nodded. The camper door squeaked as he
stepped outside. Wind slammed the door closed.

Dale gave her a smile and lit a match. When he turned
on the gas burner, blue flames burst to life.

Maureen leaned back, and smiled. "God, this is fun,
Dale. I haven't enjoyed myself this much in years."

Dale's gray mustache quirked. "You and Dusty seem
to have come to an agreement of sorts."

"Of sorts." She tilted her head, and watched Dale pour
water into the coffeepot. "He's a curious character. One
minute he seems like a perfectly rational adult, and the
next minute he displays the emotional development of a
twelve-year-old. What's the thing between him and Ruth
Ann?"

Dale dumped coffee into the old fire-blackened pot,
pushed the lid down, and glanced at her from the corner
of his eye. "Did he tell you about that?"

"Not much. Just that his father committed suicide in
an asylum."

Dale set the pot on the flames and turned around. He
folded his arms and leaned against the counter. "That's
more than he's told anyone in years, I think."

"Why did she leave?" Maureen lowered her voice,
glancing cautiously at the door.

"Another man. His name was Carter Hawsworth. He
was out here studying social structure at Zuni Pueblo.
Ruth offered to show him around. Professional courtesy,
you know. Sam was working in Blanding, Utah, at the

time. When he got back a week later, Ruth had a one-way ticket to Cambridge. She waved it at him when he walked through the door."

"That quick?"

Dale nodded, reached into his pocket for his pipe, then went through the careful ritual of filling the bowl, tamping it down and lighting it with a match. After puffing it alight, he looked at her from the midst of a hazy blue cloud. "Sam worshiped that woman. Her betrayal destroyed him."

"If their marriage could be broken that easily, what ever got them together in the first place?"

"Oh, who can say? I think Sam was new and exciting to her. They came from the same roots, old money, East Coast high society. She was young, out on her own for the first time, and here was this handsome young archaeologist living a romantic life in field camps. She was pregnant before they were married and, from her perspective, trapped, because Sam wasn't going back East to a university. He'd virtually come to blows with his parents when he turned down a teaching job at Harvard and left for what they called 'The Wild West.' Sam was a field man, one of the best. His soul would have died in a university."

Maureen laced her fingers on the table. "How old was Dusty when this happened?"

"He'd just turned six. For most of those years, Ruth had endured. She never showed him the kind of love that a child needs to survive. I remember one night in December"—he gestured emphatically with his pipe stem—"I came over to show Sam a curious artifact I'd found and couldn't identify. Dusty was four. He'd done something, I never knew what, but Ruth had locked the boy in the basement. It was pitch black down there and icy cold. He'd been there since early morning. I could hear him screaming her name, telling her he was sorry, begging her to let him out." Dale blew out a stream of smoke. "I couldn't stand it, Maureen. I had to leave."

Her heart clutched up. "Why didn't Sam do something?"

"He was a good man, Maureen, but he wasn't a strong man. I think he knew, even then, that he was going to lose Ruth, and was trying so hard to keep her that he let her do things to his son that no sane man would have." He paused and frowned at his pipe. "After she left, Sam disintegrated before my eyes. He attempted suicide three times the first month. He couldn't take care of himself, let alone a six-year-old boy."

"Was Dusty there?" She shot a glance at the door and lowered her voice. "When he tried to kill himself?"

"Every time."

"My God." Maureen bowed her head. "That's why you committed him and took Dusty?"

He nodded. "Somebody had to. I called Sam's parents, and they didn't want him. I tried to find Ruth's parents, but couldn't. I didn't know it at the time, but they'd both been killed in a car accident the same week that Hawsworth showed up at Zuni. I'm sure Ruth was dazed, hurting—"

"That's no excuse . . ."

Dusty opened the door and stepped in, followed by a filthy Sylvia. Her green T-shirt and khaki shorts were covered with dust. Half-moons of mud arched beneath her armpits. She'd pinned her brown hair up, but wet brown locks straggled around her freckled face.

Dusty panted slightly as he walked forward. "That's more of a shoulder workout than I'd have thought."

"Careful Dusty," Maureen warned. "Don't shake it up."

"Of course not, Doctor. I may have never acted as a centrifuge before, but I'm smart enough to understand the process."

Maureen lifted her brows in surprise. "What are you doing? Impersonating a scientist?"

He gave her a bland look. "Yeah. Right. I thought I'd give it a try. Were you convinced?"

"No way," Sylvia said as she slid into the booth across from Maureen. "You'd be better at impersonating a woman. It wouldn't take as much effort."

Dusty scowled at her as he handed the tube to Maureen, perfectly upright. "I'm going to buy you a nice batch of anthrax to go with your cheezy fishies, Sylvia."

Her green eyes widened. "Thanks, boss. After the Hez Bullah pays me for it, you can come visit me on my island."

"After you sell it to the Hez Bullah there won't be any islands, you dope."

Sylvia sighed, and sank back against the booth seat. "Wow. I figured there'd be something upwind of D.C."

"Yeah, well, trust me. Santa's headquarters at the North Pole isn't all it's cracked up to be. Ask Rushdie."

Maureen gave them a disgusted look, then unscrewed the cap, extracted the test tube, and held it up to the lantern light. "Well," she whispered.

"What is it?" Stewart squinted at the little red blob in the bottom of the test tube.

"A positive reaction," Maureen said. "The precipitation we've just completed tells us that this pot is full of powdered people."

"Uh-oh," Sylvia whispered.

Dusty gave Dale an uneasy glance. "Jesus. We're in trouble."

"That's an understatement," Dale said.

"I don't understand." Maureen propped the tube on the table. "In many cultures around the world, people macerate their dead and save the flesh. It's a variation of keeping your husband's ashes on the mantle. Among the Chocktaw, Chickasaw, Cherokee—"

"This is the southwest, Maureen," Dale said, and his gaze locked with Dusty's.

Dusty nodded and exhaled hard. "Well, at least we know something more about Maureen's serial murderer."

"What?" Maureen asked.

Dusty looked at her with bright blue eyes. "He was into a lot of things. He specialized in young women, did a little basic experimentation in neurophysiology with a war club. After he killed his victims, he stripped the flesh from their bones, and . . ." He let the word hang, and turned to Sylvia.

Sylvia finished, "And used it to make corpse powder."

"Right."

"Corpse powder?" Maureen said. "You think that's what this is?"

"No question about it," Dale replied. "And we've opened it up without taking any precautions. The evil is loose."

Dusty ran a hand through his blond hair. "Let me be the one to tell Maggie and Elder Walking Hawk. This will probably shut the excavation down for a few days while we undergo a cleansing, but—"

"A few days if we're lucky," Dale said. "Things like this can *end* an excavation."

No one seemed to hear the coffeepot as it began to perk.

SISTER MOON'S GLEAM penetrated the gathering
clouds and streaked the cliffs with soft dove-colored
light. Where it fell upon patches of ice, they shone like
glassy eyes.

Browser sat with his elbows propped on his knees,
throwing pebbles into Straight Path Wash. He had deliberately taken the guard position farthest from the village.
If the murderer wanted to find him alone, now was the
time.

He longed to see the man face-to-face, with his war
club in his hand.

And he could think out here. All the conversations, the
laughter, the running children, and the barking dogs had
frayed his nerves.

He drew his buckskin cape more tightly around him.
Seven warriors walked the torchlit tiers of Talon Town,
and another six perched on the roof of Hillside Village.
Most of them, he did not know. After Flame Carrier had
approved his plan, Browser had gone to the newly arrived
matrons from the other villages and explained that he
needed additional warriors to maintain the "harmony and
sanctity" of the celebration. Everyone knew that large
gatherings tended to provoke arguments. Two summers
ago in Flowing Waters Town, a man had been killed.
The matrons were happy to oblige. He had posted half
of the warriors, sixteen men and four women, in strategic
locations: on roofs, the mounds in front of Talon Town,

and three men on the rim. They would stand guard through the night. Tomorrow, while they slept, he would post the other sixteen warriors.

Wind Baby ruffled Browser's hair with icy fingers and whistled in his ear, as if taunting him, trying to get him to rise and return to the village.

Browser tossed another pebble into the wash. Moonlight gleamed from the stone as it fell, then he heard it splash into the water.

Dozens of campfires sparkled at the base of the northern canyon wall, running like twisted strands of beads from Kettle Town on his right and well past Talon Town on his left.

At least two hundred and twenty guests had already arrived, and Flame Carrier expected another forty before dawn. Many of the visitors had moved in with friends from Hillside Village. Others had settled into the cleaner rooms in Kettle Town. No one would brave Talon Town. They all knew the legends about the ghosts and witches who roamed the abandoned chambers at night.

Most people had made simple camps in the flats. They'd dug a fire pit, spread out their hides, and arranged their belongings around the camp's perimeter. Large water pots, painted with tadpoles and baby snakes, stood close to the fires. Beside them sat small-handled pots painted with the sacred images of the Corn Dancers; they contained white cornmeal for making the sacred breads they would share tomorrow night.

A prayer pole stood at each camp. Four perfect ears of yellow corn clothed in glittering beadwork topped the poles. Below them hung magnificent masks draped with necklaces of olivella shells, red coral beads, carved jet bears, and obsidian mountain sheep, as well as fans of mallard, macaw, downy eagle, pinyon jay, and crow feathers. At the base of the pole, a rawhide basket nestled on a willow twig mat. The basket held all colors of corn kernels, squash seeds, pine nuts, sunflower seeds, tobacco, and red-and-white beans. Each was a promise forgotten, but not abandoned. Tomorrow they would be presented to the gods. Gods remembered every vow a person had made to their clans or families and, if properly asked, would gently remind the penitent, so that his loved ones would not know he'd forgotten.

Browser picked up another pebble. He had promised to make Grass Moon a yellow dance stick for this celebration.

His son had seen two summers when Browser first told him the story of the journey through the dark underworlds. *"When humans finally stepped into Father Sun's blinding light, it hurt them, my son. Tears ran from their eyes, and each place a tear fell, yellow lilies, and sunflowers grew."*

From that instant, Grass Moon had loved yellow. Ash Girl had dyed all of the ties on their clothing yellow, because it pleased their son.

Browser picked up another pebble.

Ash Girl.

His rage had melted, but he could not describe the emotion that had replaced it. He felt numb, drained of everything human in his souls. After seeing her mutilated body, he could barely think. A part of him still loved Ash Girl, and the realization brought him pain. He also remembered the adoration in Grass Moon's eyes when he'd looked at his mother.

Browser clutched the pebble and whispered, "I needed her too much. That's what drove her away. And that's why she's dead."

The sicker Grass Moon became, the more demands Browser had made, and the more time Ash Girl spent searching for a Spirit Helper—as if desperate to ease both his, and their son's, hurts.

Why hadn't he seen that?

He'd interpreted her long absences as neglect. Proof that she really hadn't cared about them at all.

He hurled the pebble into the drainage.

Stone Ghost had said that Ash Girl's Spirit Helper was a very selective god, only choosing desperate women who were sick themselves or with sick families. He'd said that this "Visitant" promised to cure the illness if the woman would release her souls to him, and that when the woman failed, he killed her.

But now it appeared there were two murderers, not one.

A single madman, Browser could understand. But two? What purpose could they have? What goal would their brutality achieve?

Cloud People sailed in front of Sister Moon, and a well of darkness enveloped Browser. Movement caught his eye.

Across the drainage, a tall dark figure wavered against the firelight. It had no depth, like a cutout of black cloth.

He eased his club from his belt. The blood rushing in his veins turned hot. Sweat ran down his chest. As always before a battle, he felt lightheaded.

As the Cloud People passed, moonlight drenched the canyon again.

Very softly, a voice called, "Browser?"

"Gods, Catkin!" he said, and got to his feet. "Call out to me earlier next time! I was ready to bash in your skull!"

She halted on the opposite bank. "Call out? So the murderers can hear me?" She folded her arms.

He vented a tingling breath. "I thought you were resting?"

"Not anymore."

Browser stiffened at her tone. "Why not?"

"Come over here, and I'll tell you about it."

He trotted for the trail across the wash. As he ran down

the slope, and up the other side, some of his tension fled.

Catkin met him at the top of the trail. A black blanket covered her tall lanky body from throat to knees, and she wore black leather leggings, and sandals. Her long braid fell down her back. When Browser got close enough to see her oval face, with its turned-up nose, he noticed how quickly she was breathing.

"Hurry," he said. "Tell me."

"Your great-uncle found something interesting. Come and see."

Catkin turned and headed back for Hillside Village.

"Tell me! I want to know now."

"He wants to tell you."

They walked in silence to the edge of the crowd, then Catkin extended a hand. "Stone Ghost is sitting by the plaza fire with Flame Carrier and Corn Mother. Go. I will take your guard position until you return."

Browser pushed through the crowd, saying, "Forgive me . . . I'm sorry, I must reach the matrons . . . Pardon me, please."

He shouldered through the last throng of about thirty people who blocked his way and stepped out into the firelight.

Stone Ghost sat on a blanket with a pile of rocks between his scrawny legs. Ash coated his wrinkled face and mangy cape and even caked in the creases of his eyelids. The resulting black line gave him a bizarre appearance.

Flame Carrier looked grim. Wet gray hair framed her small narrow eyes, and bulbous nose, as if she'd been perspiring despite the cold. The beautiful red-feathered cape that Ash Girl had made for her glimmered in the wavering firelight.

Corn Mother, from Frosted Meadow Village, sat to the right, whispering with a young man. A woman sat next to him, her face pale and strained from the coughing sickness.

"Nephew?" Stone Ghost called. "Come. See what we've discovered."

Browser walked wide around the fire and squatted in front of the old man. People must have been waiting for Browser's arrival. The throng pressed closer, hissing and pointing, their eyes wide.

Browser frowned down at the rocks on the blanket.

It took several moments before he understood.

He reached out and touched the fragments. "That's the head of Whip—of a dead warrior's club, Uncle. The way it's cracked, you must have found it in a fire. Where?"

"Catkin said it was his too," Stone Ghost answered in a calm voice. "It had been cast into a blazing fire, a fire built up so high and hot, it would be certain to shatter chert. The murderer, or murderers, never thought anyone would sift through the bed of ashes to dig out the tiny pieces that remained."

Browser drew his hand back, and clenched it in his lap. "You found this . . ." His voice faded as his souls started to ache. "In the ritual fire pit? The one where Hophorn was sitting?"

Stone Ghost's dark gaze affected Browser like a lance in his heart. He seemed to sense that the news about Whiproot would wound Browser deeply.

Stone Ghost clasped Browser's wrist in a gesture of sympathy. "Matron Flame Carrier has set a pot of pine pitch on to boil. As soon as it is ready, we must glue these pieces back together. Will you help me?"

"Of course. Yes, Uncle."

"Good," he said, "then we will see if the shape matches."

"Matches? You mean the—the dent in Hophorn's skull?"

Stone Ghost shook his head sadly. "No, Nephew." He prodded the pieces of the rock, shoving them closer together. "I am more concerned about the strange mark by the fire pit. The one you thought might be a 'heel' print."

Confused, Browser said, "I don't understand."

"Don't you?" Stone Ghost asked gently, and his smile warmed as he cryptically added, "That's good."

"Let me fetch a torch, Uncle." Browser's voice sounded hollow, as though his insides had been kicked out. He could not take his eyes from the fractured head of the war club. "I will meet you at the southwestern corner of Talon Town."

Stone Ghost rose to his feet, and two more feathers fell out of his ash-coated cape and fluttered to the ground. His brown socks showed through the holes in his moccasins. "We will be there shortly, Nephew."

Browser bowed to the matrons and shouldered through the whispering crowd. People watched him with worried eyes.

He took the trail that curved around the eastern wall of Talon Town. Each time his sandals landed he felt as if another chunk of his souls had shaken loose and shattered to nothingness.

It couldn't be true. Not Whiproot. Not the man he'd warred beside, and relied upon, even entrusted with his life.

When Browser ran beneath the enormous images of the gods, he glanced up at Badger. The magnificent katsina's eyes gleamed. He seemed to watch Browser as he hurried around the corner of the town and onto the road. At dusk, he'd staked two juniper bark torches on either side of the ladder to the roof. He ran for the closest one and pulled it out of the ground.

Jackrabbit crouched on the edge of the roof, his wide brown eyes and pug nose glowing orange in the wavering gleam. He'd tucked his shoulder-length hair behind his ears. His doeskin cape flapped in the wind.

"War Chief?" he yelled. "Is all well?"

Jackrabbit turned when a long line of people filed around the corner and marched up the road toward Browser. Stone Ghost and Flame Carrier led the procession.

"What's happening?" Jackrabbit hissed. He wet his lips as if his mouth had suddenly gone dry.

Browser called, "Stone Ghost found the head of a war club in a fire pit. We—"

"Whose war club? Why was it in a fire pit?"

The procession, at least one hundred people, stopped, and began shoving on the road behind Browser, trying to peer around each other to hear what Browser was saying. As they moved, the brilliant reds, blues, and yellows of their clothing appeared to be a fluid rainbow.

"Everything is well, Jackrabbit. This is just another thing we must look into."

Jackrabbit gazed down at the crowd. He could tell from people's expressions that it was not "just another thing," but he said, "Yes, War Chief."

Stone Ghost hobbled by Browser with the glued chert cobble clutched in his right hand. It resembled an oddly shaped black-and-white egg. The pitch had not taken long to set in the cold, but the head of the club was not whole. Many small gaps remained. Stone Ghost had filled them with pitch as best he could, but one end of the cobble had a deep notch in it. The piece that fit there had probably exploded into a thousand tiny fragments in the blazing fire. Browser suspected they'd never find it.

Flame Carrier stopped beside Browser and pulled the torch from his hand. "I'll carry this. You lead the way, War Chief."

"Yes, Matron."

Browser pulled his club, and caught up with Stone Ghost in four long strides. "Uncle, allow me to go first. Just in case there is someone—"

"I would rather you walked at my side, Nephew. So that we may talk."

"The Matron asked me to lead—"

"Then do not get too far ahead of me."

"Yes, Uncle."

Browser stepped out in front. The whispers and rustles of clothing made it impossible to listen to the darkness. Browser prayed the murderers were not . . .

From behind him, Stone Ghost said, "They are, Nephew. Be certain of it. They're out here watching us right this instant."

His fingers tightened around his club. "How do you know? Do you see them?"

"No, but less than a hand of time ago, one of them spoke with stragglers coming in from Frosted Meadow Village."

Browser's steps faltered. He had to force his legs onward. "What did he say?"

"Nothing important. He spoke to them to let me know that he'd been watching me all day. But I knew that already. Of course, he didn't know I knew that."

Frustrated, Browser said, "Uncle, just tell me what he said!"

"Very well, Nephew, no need to growl. He told Little Bow and Marsh Hawk that they might have to do battle with the most powerful witch in the world, and urged them to ask about the ashes."

"The ashes?" Browser glanced at the old man over his shoulder. His uncle's wispy white hair bore a thick coating of gray. "The ashes in the ritual fire pit?"

"Of course, Nephew. He was just threatening me. Do not let it disturb you."

Flame Carrier walked up beside Stone Ghost, and said, "What are you two whispering about?"

"I was just telling my nephew—"

Flame Carrier said, "Well, hush! People are frightened.

They're like a covey of quail back there, ready to burst into flight at the sight of their own shadows!"

Browser said, "Yes, Matron," and led the way to the fire pit near the canyon wall.

People started to rush forward, coming in like a wave. Browser shouted, "Stay back! You'll destroy what we're looking for!"

Shouts and curses rang out as the crowd settled into an irregular semicircle. People shuffled and jostled for position but stayed about five paces away.

Stone Ghost knelt beside the curious mark in the soil, and Flame Carrier bent over him. Her red cape glittered in the torchlight.

"Bring the torch closer, Flame Carrier," Stone Ghost instructed as he held the mended chert cobble over the mark.

Flame Carrier lowered the torch.

Browser tried to watch the crowd and Stone Ghost, shifting his gaze back and forth.

Stone Ghost rotated the cobble onto its side and compared it to the mark, then grunted unpleasantly. He spun the cobble in his hands, tipped it on end, with the point aimed at the sky, and tried again.

"Ah," he said softly. "Nephew, I wish you to see this."

Browser knelt opposite Stone Ghost and watched as his Uncle lowered the heavy end of the cobble to the ground, and inserted it into the impression. "You try," Stone Ghost said and handed the cobble to Browser.

Browser took the cobble, bent down, and carefully placed it into the niche in the soil. The right side sank more deeply than the left, but it fit perfectly. Browser lifted the cobble and handed it to Flame Carrier. "Matron, do you wish to see?"

"I have seen all I care to, War Chief," she said. "Tell me what this proves? One of our warriors dropped his club here before your son's burial. That does not mean he used it to strike Hophorn. Or that he is the one who harmed your wife."

"No, Matron. But if not, why was the club thrown into the fire? Someone obviously did not wish for it to be found."

"Perhaps it was destroyed, War Chief. That does not prove that our warrior harmed people with it first."

Stone Ghost shoved up on wobbly legs. "Matron Flame Carrier is correct, Nephew. We have proven nothing. All we can say is that it looks as if the club struck the ground here, and then, at some point, all of the wood was thrown into the fire, along with the club. Now that we've determined that, let's return to the plaza and rejoin the festivities. I'm thirsty for more of Flame Carrier's excellent yucca blossom tea."

"But, Uncle—"

"*Come,*" Flame Carrier ordered and walked back up the trail.

The crowd turned and followed her, casting backward glances at Stone Ghost and Browser.

Stone Ghost slipped his arm through Browser's and fell in line at the rear of the assembly.

Stone Ghost whispered, "I wish you to consider something, Nephew."

"Yes, Uncle?"

"The voice Catkin heard that night on the rim, and the voice she heard in Talon Town last night . . ." He looked up at Browser, as if expecting him to finish the sentence.

Browser said, "Might have been—that warrior—after all."

Stone Ghost nodded. "I am not saying it is so. Only that you should think on it, and on the reasons that warrior might have had to murder someone."

"There were times when I thought he wished to murder his wife, Elder, but I never heard him wish anyone else ill."

Stone Ghost stepped around a rock in the trail. "The warrior had difficulties with his wife?"

"Moons ago, Uncle. You saw how badly his face was scarred. It happened in a battle last summer. When he returned home, his wife would not touch him. His heart was crushed. For three moons, he moved into one of the chambers in Talon Town. He did not stay long. Silk Moth asked him to come home in early autumn."

"I see."

Browser glanced down at the thin old man beside him. Stone Ghost had said the words slowly, deliberately, as though he really did see something Browser did not.

Browser said, "Uncle, that warrior returned from a war walk late the night before the burial. He helped carry my son's burial ladder to the grave. He was my friend. I cannot believe in my heart that he—"

"Hmm?" Stone Ghost said as though he'd just noticed Browser was speaking. He blinked owlishly. "Oh, well, of course not, Nephew. I don't believe he did it either."

Browser stopped, letting the procession move on ahead of them. They stood near the southwestern corner of Talon Town, just beyond the gleam of the torches.

"Why did we just take the cracked head of his war club out to the fire pit if not to prove that he—"

"Not he. His war club. Did he ever mention to you that it was missing?"

Browser sifted his memories. Had it been missing, Whiproot would have demanded that Hillside Village be searched, and the culprit punished severely. War clubs were not weapons, they were alive and part of a warrior's souls.

Browser said, "No."

"Then he loaned it, or gave it to someone, didn't he? Who? Why? A warrior and his club are usually inseparable. I doubt he would have given it to a passing stranger."

"You think the murderer was a friend of his?"

"Or a relative. Maybe someone powerful enough to demand he turn his club over. One of the elders in Hillside Village? Who would you give your club to, Nephew? And why?"

Stone Ghost started walking again.

As they rounded the corner and headed up the road, Browser said, "My wife, perhaps, if I thought she were in danger, and I knew I wasn't going to be there to . . ."

I was never there. Ever.

He let the sentence hang and grimaced.

Stone Ghost stared at him with unnerving concentration, "What?"

"Nothing, Uncle."

Browser lifted a hand to Jackrabbit, who stood on the roof, and said, "I must tell my warriors this news, Uncle, before they hear it from someone who does not know the facts."

"Of course, Nephew."

Stone Ghost started to walk away, then stopped and turned. "Catkin is standing guard in your position, is she not?"

"Yes, Uncle."

"When you go to relieve her, Nephew, take great care. The two of you, together in one place, and away from the village fires—"

"I understand, Uncle. I will. Sleep well."

Stone Ghost inclined his head, smiled, and walked up the road.

Browser looked at the two guards, one standing on each of the mounds to his right, then cautiously went to the ladder and climbed.

Jackrabbit extended a hand to help Browser from the ladder to the rooftop, and said, "I don't believe it! Our friend would never—"

"That's right, he wouldn't."

Jackrabbit stared openmouthed at Browser. "But I heard people talking as they passed. They said our friend—"

"His club, Jackrabbit, not him. Do you ever recall him loaning it, or giving it to anyone?"

At the very thought, Jackrabbit clutched his own club in both hands. "No, War Chief."

"Well, he must have. Start asking around among our people. *Quietly.*"

"Yes, War Chief."

Browser gazed out across the moonlit canyon to the place Catkin should be standing. Dark cloud shadows roamed the canyon bottom, flowing like water over the low hills.

"I must return to my guard position, Jackrabbit. Remain alert. He-Who-Flies will relieve you at dawn."

He jerked a nod. "Yes, War Chief."

CATKIN ROLLED ON to her back in her buffalo hides and gazed at the big fluffy flakes of snow tumbling through her roof entry and onto the coals in her warming bowl. A soft sizzling filled her chamber. A few Evening People gleamed through the gaps in the clouds, sparkling against the indigo blanket of night.

Catkin stretched. The rich scents of ritual cooking filled her nostrils. For the past two days women had cooked rabbits, band-tailed pigeons, deer, and a variety of corn flour breads. They'd roasted gourds, pine nuts, sunflower and pumpkin seeds, boiled enormous pots of beans, and made a delicious jam by boiling dried yucca fruits and chokecherries until they became a paste. All of those scents clung to the village. Her stomach growled.

Catkin sat up and tossed a few twigs into the bowl. The wood crackled and spat, and flames licked up around the tinder.

She rose in the soft yellow gleam and walked to the big red pot across the chamber. On this, the shortest day, and longest night of the sun cycle, she had sacred duties to perform.

As she pulled her tan sleep shirt over her head, she Sang:

> *My breath-heart is calling to you Father*
> *Sun,*
> *Hear me calling,*

> *I am coming,*
> *I am coming,*
> *Dark purple rises in the east,*
> *I am coming,*
> *Begging you to awaken, and light the*
>   *world,*
> *I am coming, Father Sun.*

She drew out her long blue war shirt, a white dance sash, her white feathered cape, polished slate mirror, and a small pot. Beautiful red, black, and white paintings of the katsinas covered the pot.

She hung her cape on the ladder that thrust up through the roof entry, then shrugged into her blue war shirt, and tied the white sash around her waist. As she slipped on two pairs of cotton socks and her sandals, she thought about Cloudblower. Catkin had never known anyone as kind or caring. Or secretive. She did not know what to expect today. They might simply climb the cliff, perform the sacred Turning-Back-the-Sun ritual, and return to Talon Town for the morning Dances. But Catkin had the uneasy feeling that, after all that had happened in the past few days, Cloudblower would feel obligated to speak with Catkin. And Catkin did not know what she would say.

She laced up her red leather leggings, then combed and braided her long hair.

As she lifted the lid on the small painted pot, the sweet perfumes of corn flour and ground evening primroses encircled her. Catkin dipped her fingers and rubbed the fine white powder over her face.

"In memory of White Shell Woman," she reverently whispered, "grandmother of Father Sun. We thank you for giving us light and warmth."

She studied herself in the polished slate mirror. The

powder shimmered a ghostly white, and her dark eyes looked huge.

Catkin tucked the pot and mirror back into her big red jar and stepped to her buffalohide bedding.

Her war club, as always, rested to the side within easy reach. She picked it up and tested its familiar weight. It felt comforting in her hand. She tied it to her dance sash and yawned.

As she walked to the ladder and swung her white-feathered cape around her shoulders, snow fell around her, landing on her hair and hands. Climbing the stairs cut into the cliff would be treacherous, especially in the darkness. They would have to go slowly.

Catkin started up the ladder, and stepped out onto the roof. Tendrils of blue smoke rose from the other roof entries of Hillside Village, and she could hear people talking softly, readying themselves for the sacred activities of the day.

Her sandals crunched snow as she walked across the rooftop. A few fires gleamed in the flats below. Her gaze landed on the place Browser stood guard. He would be tired and hungry, probably thinking about Whiproot's war club, speculating on how it had ended up in a roaring fire.

As she had all night.

She walked to the ladder, and took the slick rungs down one at a time. Scattered patches of starlight lit the canyon, gleaming from the freshly fallen snow.

When Catkin reached the ground, she turned and saw Cloudblower waiting for her near the plaza fire pit where a bed of red coals glowed. Cloudblower had her hands extended to the warmth. She wore her buffalohide cape, painted with the red images of wolf, coyote, eagle, and raven, the Blessed Spirit Helpers of the Katsinas' People. Feathers and seed beads knotted the ends of the long fringes on the bottom. Cloudblower had coiled her long gray-streaked black braid on top of her head and fastened it with carved deerbone pins. Her triangular face, slanting eyes, and sharply pointed nose looked somehow softer beneath the layer of sacred white powder.

She turned when Catkin neared, and said, "A Happy Longnight to you, Catkin. Are you ready?"

"I am ready, Elder."

Cloudblower nodded and led the way.

They walked in front of Hillside Village and out onto the dark trail that ran eastward along the base of the cliff. The massive bulk of Kettle Town, almost as large as Talon Town, loomed huge and black in the distance. Orange gleams lit a few of the chambers near the front of the town, and Catkin saw the dark shapes of people moving about on the rooftops. After they'd eaten, and sung their morning prayers, they would dress for the celebration, and make their ways to Talon Town. Only the Dancers would be allowed into the newly restored kiva. Spectators would sit in the plaza or on the roofs and wait for the Dancers to emerge from the subterranean ceremonial chamber.

They walked behind Kettle Town to the ladder that leaned against the rounded tower by the cliff. Cloudblower climbed up first, and waited for Catkin. When she stepped onto the tower's roof, Cloudblower took the next ladder. The cliff here was too steep for stone stairs. The ladder, coupled with handholds, took them to the slope in the cliff where the stairs had been cut a hundred sun cycles ago.

"Careful," Cloudblower said as she stepped off the ladder onto the stairs. "The steps are icy."

"I will be, Elder."

Catkin climbed slowly, actually it was more like crawling. She braced both hands on the top step, found a handhold, then slid her knees up, and reached for the next step.

Father Sun had just opened his eyes in the Land of the Dead. A deep blue gleam arched over the eastern horizon, lighting the tallest ridges and dying them an unearthly shade of purple. From this vantage, Catkin could see vast distances. Blunt buttes jutted up here and there across the eroded country. The early morning light threw their shadows across the uplands like arms stretched out in longing. Black slashes of drainages cut the hills and zigzagged into the bottomlands.

Cloudblower crawled onto the rim and extended a hand to Catkin.

Catkin grasped her fingers and allowed Cloudblower to pull her up. Golden spikes of grass grew in the rocky crevices. They swayed gently in the morning wind.

To the south, in front of her, the lands of the Fire Dogs rose in cool blue layers, the grass-covered flats giving way to pine-whiskered Thunder Peak. Billowing black clouds sailed over the canyon, trailing gray veils of snow beneath them. Turquoise Maiden formed a black hump on the eastern horizon, to her left. Westward, the fires of Starburst Town glittered like fallen stars.

Catkin inhaled the beauty and exhaled a prayer of thanks.

Cloudblower walked westward across the canyon rim, her head bowed, Singing softly.

Catkin followed. Father Sun would be very weak this morning, his strength exhausted from a sun cycle of rising to light the world. If he could not pull himself into the sky, he would stand still on the horizon, and Cloudblower would have to perform the sacred Turning-Back-the-Sun ritual. She would have to offer her own strength to Father Sun.

Two summers ago, in Flowing Waters Town, Catkin had played the flute for Hophorn while she'd performed the ritual. Hophorn had been fasting for sixteen days, drinking only dried squash blossom tea. Yet she had lain

on her side and wretched into the winter grasses for two
hands of time. By dawn, the vomiting had turned to dry
wrenching heaves. But her strength had been enough. Father Sun had risen and chased the cold and darkness from
the land.

Cloudblower walked around a shoulder-high pillar of
wind-carved sandstone, then turned, and looked eastward
across the point of the pillar. As she pulled out the four
small bags she wore as a necklace, snow coated the
shoulders of her buffalo cape. Melted flakes glistened like
tears in her hair.

Catkin folded her arms beneath her white-feathered
cape and waited.

Cloudblower opened the first sack, and her deep beautiful voice echoed across the canyon, *"In beauty we begin. In beauty we begin."*

She tipped the sack and poured white cornmeal to the
east. Wind Baby caught the meal and carried it out over
the rim in a fog. It shimmered among the snowflakes,
and fell.

Cloudblower turned and emptied the red cornmeal to
the south, the yellow to the west, and the blue cornmeal
to the north.

Then she lifted her meal-covered hands to the sky, and
finally, bent over to touch Our Grandmother Earth, as
she Sang: *"In beauty we finish. In beauty we finish."*

Catkin looked eastward. Usually, at this time in the
ritual Father Sun crested the horizon, but it appeared they
had some time.

Cloudblower said, "Forgive me. I am not as adept at
this as Hophorn. She always knows the exact moment to
empty the last sack."

"She has had more practice, Cloudblower. I don't think
Father Sun cares if our prayers are a little early."

Cloudblower smiled and walked to stand beside Catkin, gazing eastward. A translucent lavender halo marked

the place where Father Sun would first show his face. The Cloud People seemed to be waiting, hovering in the purpled light, with their bellies gleaming.

The longer they stood there, the more uncomfortable Cloudblower seemed to be. She finally walked a few steps away.

Catkin said, "Are you well, Cloudblower?"

Cloudblower's mouth tightened. She knelt and gently touched an ice-sheathed blade of grass that protruded through the thin layer of snow. "Beauty is such a frail thing, Catkin. I often wonder if humans understand how precious it is. Every time we love, or touch someone tenderly, or laugh in genuine delight, we should be deeply grateful. Each should be a prayer. I have always tried to live that way, but often, more of late"—Cloudblower gave Catkin a tremulous smile—"I fail."

"We all fail, Elder. It is allowed on occasion."

Cloudblower rose to her feet, and shook her head. "Not for me."

Wind Baby gusted across the rim, kicking up snow, and whirling it over the edge in a luminous haze.

"Why not, Elder?"

Cloudblower frowned at the eastern horizon. Father Sun had still not shown his face.

"I have made too many errors, done too many terrible things in my life, to be allowed to fail ever again."

Cloudblower took a step toward Catkin, and Catkin felt suddenly anxious. Sweat broke out beneath her arms, and trickled down her sides.

"I have only seen you do good things, Cloudblower. I think, perhaps, you demand too much of yourself."

Cloudblower tipped her head to the right, and stared at Catkin. The lines around her dark eyes deepened. "I can do many good things, when I—I live in my female soul. But often my male body takes over, Catkin, and you cannot imagine the things I long for. The things I do."

She took another step closer, and Catkin backed away toward the rim. Two hundred hands below, she could see Talon Town. The plaza fire blazed, and people had already begun to line the walls. Old people sat with blankets pulled over their heads, and parents clutched children in their laps. Even in the dim blue gleam, the bright colors and elaborate designs on their clothing made a gorgeous sight.

Catkin said, "What's wrong, Cloudblower?"

The sacred *Kokwimu* turned away, but not before Catkin saw the anguished expression on her face. "You see, it is because I understand the twists of male and female souls that I try so hard to help people."

"I can understand that."

Cloudblower turned back, and tears blurred her eyes. "No, Catkin, you can't. You see, not even I knew until a few moons ago, the—the violence—of the male soul." She held out a hand to Catkin. Her voice went low and shaky. "In that time, I have learned a terrifying truth."

"What truth?"

Cloudblower clenched her hand to a trembling fist. "Catkin, have you ever felt . . . I mean, has it ever occurred to you that there might be more than one person inside you? That perhaps, there is someone else who lives in your body without your permission?"

Catkin shrugged. "Often. When I am engaged in battle, I am a different person. I will catch myself about to slice a man's throat and wonder who it is inside me who can do this terrible thing. But if that other 'me' were to ask my permission to take over my body during a fight, I would give it without hesitation, Elder. 'She' is the one who keeps me alive."

Cloudblower kept silent, staring into Catkin's eyes. Finally, she whispered, "May I tell you a story?"

"Yes. Of course. I love your stories."

Cloudblower checked the horizon again and folded her arms tightly across her chest. The red paintings of wolf, coyote, eagle, and raven swayed. The birds appeared to be flying.

"I know a woman. When she was a child, she had a very wicked father. He hurt her, Catkin. She does not remember what I am about to tell you, but I swear it is true. When she'd seen two summers, he started lying with her, forcing things inside her. When she cried, he used to make her play a game he called 'beetle,' where he forced her to lie on her back, then push up with her arms and legs until she'd arched her back as far as she could. She had to stay that way for hands of time. When she couldn't, he beat her in the head with a fire-hardened digging stick. By the time she'd seen four summers, she fell asleep every time he came into their chamber. Just"— Cloudblower shook her head—"fell on the floor sound asleep. She would wake up bleeding, and imagine that some monster had harmed her while she slept. She envisioned hideous creatures with deep growling voices and sharp claws."

Horrors stirred in Catkin's souls. She could see a small, helpless little girl reaching out to a man who should have been protecting her, caring for her, and instead, he . . .

Cloudblower shuddered.

Catkin said, "Elder, if the girl cannot remember these things, how do you know about them?"

"There is a—a boy—a man. He comes by here often, to see the woman. He worries about her. We talk."

The man I heard you speaking with here on the rim? The man in the plaza the night Whiproot died?

"He lived in her village when she was little?"

Cloudblower nodded. "Yes."

"What else did he tell you?"

"Oh, many things," she exhaled the words. "He told me that the girl said something to the old women in the village, something they understood, even if the girl didn't. She was barely two at the time. All four of those old women were murdered, Catkin. They were horribly mutilated." She hesitated as if expecting Catkin to remember hearing about the event. It did strike a memory chord, but Catkin couldn't quite recall the context of the stories. She frowned, and Cloudblower continued, "In the girl's fifth winter, her mother finally discovered the truth, and her father ran away before he could be punished for incest."

"Did anyone ever tell her what he'd done to her?"

"Gods, no, Catkin. Do you think her mother wished for her daughter to be Outcast from the clan at the age of five summers? You know the incest laws. Everyone involved is tainted with the evil and has to be punished. It does not matter whose fault it was. The little girl would have died."

"Did you ever perform a Healing on the woman, Elder?"

Cloudblower squeezed her eyes closed. "I never had the chance. I . . ."

A tiny sliver of gold rose over the eastern horizon. Cloudblower walked back to stand behind the Sun Pillar. As she lifted her hands to frame the image tears traced silver lines down her cheeks.

"Father Sun rose in a different place," she said and let out a relieved breath. "He does not need our strength to journey across the sky today. We can return and join in the celebration."

Strands of graying-black hair worked loose from her braid and fluttered in the wind. She gave Catkin a pleading look. "Please do not mention these things, Catkin. I love this woman. I think it might harm her to hear my words repeated."

"I would never repeat anything you tell me, Elder."

Cloudblower steepled her fingers over her mouth. "Thank you, warrior. I had not planned on burdening you—"

"It is not a burden to ease someone else's hurt, Elder. It is a privilege."

Cloudblower touched her shoulder and softly said, "If we hurry, we can be back in time for the morning Dances."

LAVENDER THUNDERHEADS WALKED across the dusk sky on willowy iridescent legs of rain. Hail tipped her head back and inhaled the sweet scents of damp earth and dry grass. Thunderbirds rumbled in the distance, bringing the storm closer.

She groaned softly as she bent over and picked up a branch to prod her pinyon pine fire. A hand of time ago, Hail had boiled juniper needles in Magpie's big chili pot, poured equal amounts into five plastic bowls, and instructed each of them to take a ritual bath—which meant they had to dip a cloth in the water and wash every part of their skin and hair.

Behind her, in the red tent, Magpie, Sylvia, and Washais whispered. Dusty and Dr. Robertson had already been purified and returned to Dr. Robertson's trailer to dress.

Hail couldn't see the bottom of the fire too well, but the flames looked high enough. She used her stick to lift the pile of Dusty's and Dr. Robertson's clothes and dropped it onto the fire. Thick greasy smoke rose as the flames licked up around the edges and gradually worked their way to the center.

She leaned on the stick while she gazed out at the site.

Evil rode the air with silvered wings, flashing around, studying the camp and the people, waiting its chance to slip inside them and make a nest in their souls.

The Haze boy had been very quiet, as though afraid to breathe.

Hail had to purify everyone who'd been there when the pot was opened, then she had to figure out what to do with the pot itself.

When the fire had burned through the clothes, Hail threw another pine log onto the flames, and said, "All right, Magpie, you can come out."

The three women emerged carrying their plastic bowls, and bundles of clothes. Blankets covered their naked bodies, and the tang of juniper surrounded them. Washais had unbraided her hair, leaving it long and free. It fell over her pale blue blanket in a shining rippled wealth. Magpie and Sylvia stood in matching ivory blankets.

"All right," Hail said, "no one may ever use those bowls again. They've been tainted with the evil. Toss them into the fire." She tapped a heartstone with her stick.

The white plastic bowls landed in the flames and shriveled up into black knots. An ugly acrid smell rose.

"Sylvia," Hail said, "you first. Go stand over there, downwind from the fire."

"Gotcha." Sylvia walked to stand directly in front of Hail.

"Now you two"—Hail gestured to Washais and Magpie—"stand on either side of me."

Magpie stood on Hail's right and Washais on her left.

The coffeepot, filled with water, sat on the ground in front of Hail. She propped her branch and reached down for the battered black handle. "Okay, Sylvia, take off your blanket."

Sylvia tossed the ivory blanket aside and spread her arms. As skinny as a cottonwood twig, the white skin she kept covered looked corpsish against her deeply tanned face, lower arms, and legs.

"I'm ready, Mrs. Walking Hawk. Cleanse me."

Hail poured a little water from the coffeepot onto the coals, and a blue haze of smoke billowed up. "You and Washais help out, Magpie."

"Yes, Aunt. Follow me, Maureen." Magpie used the blanket around her shoulders like wings to fan the smoke across to Sylvia.

"I see," Washais said and fanned her blanket in rhythm with Magpie's.

Sylvia closed her eyes as the cleansing smoke blew over her. "I love this smell. Feels hot though."

Hail said, "You'll feel a lot hotter if that corpse powder gets inside you, and starts eating you alive. Turn around, Sylvia."

"Okay." Sylvia spun on one foot, military fashion.

Magpie said, "My God. That's the whitest butt I have ever seen in my life."

Sylvia grinned over her shoulder. "Blinding, ain't it?"

When the smoke dwindled, Hail poured a little more water on the fire, and Washais and Magpie blew it across to Sylvia.

Hail said, "Make sure it touches every part of you, Sylvia. Smoke is a cousin to the Thunderbirds who bring us rain and life. The Spirit of the smoke will drive away any evil that lived in that corpse powder."

"Cool," Sylvia said, and fluffed her shoulder-length brown hair out so the smoke would penetrate it.

"Good. You're done, Sylvia. Go put on clean clothes."

Sylvia picked up her blanket and walked for her tent. "See you soon."

Hail gestured. "Washais, your turn."

Washais took up Sylvia's position, except that she stood solemnly with her head bowed, as though saying a silent prayer.

Hail waited until Washais lifted her head, then she said, "Take off your blanket, child."

Washais pulled it away from her shoulders and

dropped it at her feet. A tall woman, Father Sun had roasted her in the past few days. Her chest had gotten it the worst, though. A scoop of reddish-brown curved down over the tops of her breasts.

Hail poured water on the fire again, and Magpie fanned the billowing smoke across.

Washaiṣ lifted her face to the sky, and started singing, a beautiful lilting song that soothed Hail. Magpie smiled broadly. Neither of them understood the strange words, but they both knew it was a blessing song, asking for-giveness, praying for good things for her people.

"Turn around, Washais," Hail instructed.

Washais turned, and spread her long arms and legs. When she finished the song, she feathered her hair in the smoke, and started speaking in a new language.

"*En archay ayne ha logos, kai ha logos ayne pros ton theon . . .*"

Hail looked at Magpie and they both shrugged. You didn't have to understand words to know when somebody was being reverent. It was the softness of the voice, the posture.

Hail poured more water on the fire, and Magpie fanned smoke over Washais.

When Washais went silent, Hail said, "You're done, Washais. You can put on clean clothes now."

"Thank you, Mrs. Walking Hawk." She picked up her blanket and headed for her tent.

Before she ducked through the flap, Hail asked, "What language was that last prayer, Washais? It was pretty. I don't think I've ever heard that before?"

"New Testament Greek. That's the opening of the Book of John." Washais smiled and entered her green tent.

Hail turned to Magpie and lifted a hand. "Give me your blanket, Magpie. I'll fan you."

"Thank you, Aunt, but I don't know why I have to be

purified. I was with you when they opened the pot."

Magpie handed over her blanket, and went to stand across the fire. Short black hair framed her round face. Even her arms, used to the sun, had tanned more deeply since they'd been here.

"I know, child," Hail said, "but I don't want to take any chances with you. When you talked to Dusty, you might have breathed in some of the powder on his clothes."

Magpie gave Hail a soft look, smiled, and closed her eyes. "All right, Aunt, I'm ready."

Hail poured water onto the fire, laid her stick down, and fanned the smoke over her great-niece.

Magpie gathered the smoke in her hands and rubbed it over her arms, and face, then the rest of her body. Next, she turned around and ran her hands through her short black hair.

"All right, child, you'll be fine now."

"Thank you, Aunt." Magpie picked up her blanket and headed for their red tent. "I'll be right back."

"Good. You and me need to figure out how to catch the evil that's running loose around us."

"I know, Aunt. I have some ideas about that."

From inside her tent, Washais called, "So do I!"

Sylvia ducked out of her tent dressed in faded blue cutoffs, a red tank top, and hiking boots. "Wow, I feel like a million dollars. I think it worked."

Hail smiled and used her stick to lift Magpie's contaminated clothing and dropped them into the flames.

Sylvia came to stand beside her. "Can I do that?"

"Yes." Hail handed her the stick. "But don't let the end of the stick touch you anywhere, and after you've burned all the clothes throw the stick in on top of the flames."

"No problemo," Sylvia said.

As Sylvia lifted Washais's old clothing into the fire,

Hail hobbled over to one of the lawn chairs and eased down. It felt good to sit. Sweat trickled down her neck and soaked the collar of the blue-flowered yellow dress. Magpie had insisted she take a pain pill about two hours ago, but Hail wasn't sure she felt better. The pain had lessened, but a groggy, off-balance, sensation had replaced it. For no reason at all, the world would just go out of focus, and Hail would stumble. She'd almost fallen into the fire when she'd been cleansing Dusty. If he hadn't snatched her sleeve and dragged her back, she'd have been scorched. She didn't like feeling this way.

Sylvia *tsked* to herself as she lifted her own clothes, a pair of shorts and a T-shirt, into the flames. "That was my favorite buffalo shirt. I guess I'll have to get back to Wyoming someday to find another one like it."

"You should get a real buffalo hide to make a shirt out of," Hail suggested. "It would keep you warm in the winter."

"I wonder where I'd get one? I've never seen them at Wal-Mart."

Hail chuckled. "I think you ought to call one of the buffalo ranches in New Mexico. Some of them sell hides. I had a cousin who . . ."

The door to the camp trailer squealed as Dusty and Dr. Robertson came down the steps. Dusty wore a yellow T-shirt, and pink shorts. They'd been white at one time, Hail thought, but he must have washed them with something red. His reflective sunglasses glinted as he walked. Dr. Robertson looked like a flag in his red-and-white-striped shirt, and blue jeans. They were talking in low tones as they approached the camp. Frowns incised their foreheads.

"Hey," Sylvia called. "I figured you two would be the first back into camp. What took you so long?"

A gust of wind whipped across the site, rattling the tents and trash box. Dr. Robertson pulled down his fedora to fend it off, and Dusty turned his head. Blond hair flipped around his face.

"We were discussing what to do with the pot of powdered people," Dusty said. "Before the cleansing, we put the cap back on and double-bagged it in Ziplocs, as Elder Walking Hawk instructed, but—"

"*But!*" Washais said as she ducked out of her tent. She'd replaited her hair and the braid hung down the front of her tan T-shirt to the waist of her jeans. "Now we have to get rid of it, right?"

"Right," Magpie said as she joined the group. She'd dressed in a white T-shirt and brown shorts. "The question is, how?"

"I'm not sure," Hail said in a frail voice and laced her arthritic fingers in her lap. "Maybe we should find another place, far away from here, and bury it again. That would keep wicked people from finding it and using it to hurt others."

As Dusty sifted through the ice chest, Dr. Robertson and Sylvia unfolded lawn chairs and sat down across the fire.

Washais pulled up a chair next to Hail. "Mrs. Walking Hawk, I have an idea that might sound strange to you, but I would like to take the pot back to Canada with me, for further study—"

"You're joking, right?" As Dusty turned, sunlight reflected from his glasses. He had a bottle of fruit juice in his hand. He twisted off the cap, and said, "Doesn't Canada have laws about the disposition of human remains?"

"Yes, of course. There will be a lot of red tape, but this is such a rare opportunity, I think—"

"We can't, Maureen," Magpie said. She dropped into a chair beside Sylvia, to Washais's left. "There are strong traditionalists here who will want to see the pot, and its contents, destroyed—or as my aunt suggests, at least put in a place where it can't hurt anyone."

"Well, we can't destroy it," Dusty said. "We'd be in violation of every historic preservation law on the books. Not only that, we'd be destroying federal property. So let's figure out something else to do."

"Give it to me," Washais said. "That's what else we can do. I'll take the evil far away."

Wind blew gray hair into Hail's eyes. She tucked it behind her ear and said, "We have to respect the Power there, Washais. People can die just from touching that pot."

Washais bowed her head and seemed to be marshaling her arguments. In a soft voice, she said, "I know this is difficult, but the contents of that pot might tell us how that woman lived, how she died, why this terrible thing happened to her. Isn't that important? Isn't it more respectful to learn from her? Elder Walking Hawk, I think she's just another, older Elder, one who can teach us new lessons."

Dusty said, "I don't agree."

"Why not?" Washais turned, and glared.

"If they were just slaves, like I thought in the beginning, I might have sided with you. But you've proven your point. These women were murdered, and at least part of this last one was turned into corpse powder. She's better off covered up. According to traditional beliefs—"

"Hold it," Washais said. "I don't understand this. Four years ago, I went to the rededication of an ossuary. We held our Feast of the Dead, and invited our ancestors to come visit us from the Village of the Souls. When it was all over, we each took little containers of earth from the burial pit, because we believe it contains bits of our ancestors. My container sits by my bedside table. That's *traditional,* isn't it?"

"Your tradition, not theirs," Dusty said, and took a sip from his juice bottle.

"What makes one traditional belief more important than another?" Washais's brows lowered.

Gently, Hail said, "Washais? I don't understand your ways, but I'm glad your ancestors hear you and help your people. This place is different, though. Our ancestors lived and died here. Their blood runs in our veins. We have different ways. That *stuff* you found today is dangerous." She blinked her white-filmed eyes at the clouds building in the sky. The scent of rain had grown strong. "It's bad enough that those NOAA people want to put a weather station here. With all the bad things that happened on this spot that weather station is never going to work right." She looked back at Washais. "I think we have to take that pot away, and cover it up. Maybe put a big rock on top so that the evil can never get loose again."

Dusty nodded. "I agree."

Dale pushed his fedora back on his head. "If that's what our Indian monitor wants, then that's what we'll do. Just tell us where to bury it, Maggie."

Magpie's brow furrowed. "I'll have to think about it."

"But, Dale," Washais said. Disbelief crept into her voice. "I *need* to do more work on this burial."

"I know it would be nice, Maureen, but it isn't going to happen. We're over the budget already, and I hate to keep bringing it up, but she's outside of the impact area."

Washais's gaze went from Magpie, to Dale, then rested on Dusty. She looked at him as if for support. He slowly shook his head.

"Not this time, Doctor," he said. "Sorry."

"I don't understand either of you." Her hot gaze went from Dale to Dusty. "You're telling me that you are willing to stop scientific inquiry based on religious fundamentalism? Do you realize the precedent this kind of decision sets? What happens if next week a group of Cherokee fundamentalists come out, say that the contents of that pot are the sacred remains of their ancestors, and claim it as a holy relic? Will you let them have it based solely upon religious mythology? What if a Navajo witch claims it because he wants its Power? Will you give it to him? How do you decide *which* religious beliefs are more valid than others?"

Dusty leaned forward. "I agree it's difficult, but—"

"Difficult? It's *insane*! And you're as nutty as your father if you let it happen!"

Dusty seemed to turn to stone. He stared at her through glittering blue eyes.

Washais rose to her feet, and stood quietly for a long moment. "I need to get away for a while, Stewart. To think about this. Would it be possible . . ."

Dusty fished in his pocket with his free hand. The keys rattled as he tossed them to Washais. "Drive carefully, obey the speed limit signs, and don't trust the gas gauge. Fill up at Crownpoint going and coming."

Washais nodded, said, "Thanks," and stiffly walked to her tent. She dragged out her purse, and headed for the Bronco.

As the engine roared to life, and she backed out, dust filled the air.

Hail watched the blue truck jounce down the dirt road for town. "I hope she's all right," she whispered in concern. "I didn't mean to hurt her."

"She'll be all right, Aunt," Magpie said, and came over to sit in Washais's chair. She took Hail's hand and stroked it. "Don't worry about her."

Dusty peered at Hail over the rims of his sunglasses; she could see a mixture of hurt and rage in his eyes. "She's fine, Elder," he said in a clipped voice. "She's just not accustomed to making decisions based upon real life cultural taboos. Physical anthropologists work with sterile facts. Life has just taught her a valuable lesson."

"Really?" Dale asked with mock interest. "What?"

"Sometimes science is irrelevant." Dusty adopted an authoritative posture, his broad shoulders squared, his chin up.

The first drops of rain started to fall, stippling the ground and hissing in the fire.

Dusty finished his juice, and threw the bottle into the trash box. It clattered through the other garbage. He stabbed a finger at Dale. "If we have trouble over this, I want you to remember that you're the one who invited her out here. I was against it from the start. A lab rat in a field camp! God forbid."

Sylvia examined Dusty through squinted eyes for several seconds, clearly on the verge of defending Washais, then as if she'd reconsidered, she smiled, and her gaze dropped to Dusty's pink shorts. "Tell me something, boss? Do those come with the panties built in?"

THE HOLLOW THUMPING of the foot drums in the First People's kiva echoed through the twilight, slow, steady, like a sleeping person's heartbeat.

As Browser and Cloudblower walked across Talon Town's crowded plaza, Cloudblower said, "Hophorn is afraid, Browser, but I think it will be good for her to watch the Dances. This is her favorite ritual of the sun cycle. If she does not attend, I think in a few moons, she will wish she had."

Cloudblower wore her painted buffalohide cape, red leggings, and moccasins covered with shell bells. They clicked pleasantly. She had coiled her long gray-black braid on top of her head. The style made her face appear starkly triangular.

Three lines of people encircled the plaza. Children sat in front, with the elderly behind them. Other adults stood against the wall. The bravest people perched on the flat roofs of Talon Town, wrapped in many-colored blankets. The village elders, along with Stone Ghost, sat on the roof of the great kiva. Each group of elders had their own colors and styles of ritual capes. The Hillside elders wore red-painted buffalohides; the Starburst Village people preferred yellow deerhides; the elders from Frosted Meadow adorned themselves with rabbitfur capes, covered with a thick layer of blue-gray pinyon jay feathers. The capes adopted by the Badgerpaw Village elders had an intricately woven layer of cotton lace

draped over the top of finely smoked leather. Stone
Ghost, of course, wore the same mangy brown-and-white
turkey-feather cape. His wispy white hair looked as if it
had been teased just for this occasion; it stuck out like a
frizzy halo.

In the northernmost corner of the plaza, beneath the enormous paintings of the Great Warriors of East and West, an
array of blankets had been spread. Haunches of roasted venison, whole cooked turkeys, and a variety of smaller game,
hung from racks above steaming pots of beans, plates of
breads, baked gourds, bowls of roasted pumpkin and sunflower seeds, large fabric bags filled with popped corn, and
several water jars. People were free to help themselves
throughout the celebration.

Peavine walked through the gathering, speaking to
people. She had an annoyed expression on her ugly face.
Her white doehide cape shone in the torchlight.

"You have spoken with Hophorn about this?" Browser
asked.

"This morning. She agreed to try. I don't know how
long she will be able to sit outside. The only place she
feels safe is in my chamber. But even if she sits for less
than a hand of time, it will help her, Browser."

Dusk fell over the canyon like a gray opalescent blanket, gleaming from the snow that had fallen at dawn. The
towering cliff behind Talon Town shone faintly blue.
Above the rim, the first Evening People sparkled.

The booming of the foot drums grew louder, and the
high wail of a flute joined in. The note hung like a hawk
in midair, before it lightly swooped down and fluttered.

Cloudblower stopped before her door curtain and
called, "Hophorn. We are here. Are you ready?"

A stammering voice responded, "Y-yes, I—I am."

Cloudblower drew back the curtain, and Browser saw
Hophorn sitting just inside the entry. She gazed at Cloudblower and Browser as if terrified by the sight of them.

She was trembling, her long black hair moving as if alive.

Softly, Cloudblower said, "Don't be afraid, Hophorn. I'm going to spread your hides right in front of the door in case you wish to go back inside. And Catkin will be standing guard on the roof above you."

"Yes, she will," Browser said.

Hophorn wet her lips, nodded, and reached for the black blanket that lay folded beside her. She drew it to her chest. She wore her usual Longnight ritual clothing, a scarlet macaw cape elaborately decorated with bone beads, and tiny red shale figurines carved into the shapes of frogs, birds, deer, and wolves. Her strange jet pendent, the serpent coiled inside the broken eggshell, hung down to the middle of her chest. "R-ready," she managed, and extended a trembling hand to Browser.

He helped Hophorn outside and held her up while Cloudblower ducked into the chamber to grab an armload of hides.

Cloudblower carefully spread the hides out next to the door curtain. "You'll be safe, here, Hophorn. I swear it. I—"

"Have you seen my daughter?" Peavine said as she strode up. Her pocked face had mottled with what appeared to be anger. "She was supposed to be here a half a hand of time ago."

"I haven't seen Yucca Blossom, Peavine," Cloudblower said. "But she is eleven. Several of the older girls gathered near the Hillside plaza fire to talk. Perhaps she is there."

"Well, she isn't supposed to be!"

"Do you wish me to send someone to fetch her?"

"No," Peavine replied irritably. "If she isn't here by the time the Dances begin, I'll fetch her myself. And she'll be sorry."

Peavine turned and stalked away.

Cloudblower exchanged a bewildered glance with Browser, then reached for Hophorn.

But Hophorn turned to search the roof, as if for Catkin.

Catkin lifted a hand and walked over. "It is good to see you, Sunwatcher. Are you well?"

Hophorn smiled, weaved on her feet, and sank to the hides as though her legs would no longer hold her.

Browser called, "The Sunwatcher will be sitting here for the Dances. You'll watch over her, won't you?"

"Of course, War Chief. And when Jackrabbit takes my place in another hand of time, I'll tell him to do the same."

An expression of relief slackened Hophorn's pretty face.

Cloudblower gently pulled the black blanket from Hophorn's hands. "Let me help you." She shook the blanket out, then draped it over Hophorn's head, and tied it in a knot in front. "There. You should stay warm now. I must go into the kiva to purify the Dancers, Hophorn, but I won't be away for long, and Browser will be close while I am gone."

Hophorn looked up at Cloudblower with huge eyes.

Cloudblower gently touched her cheek. "Browser? I know you are charged with maintaining harmony in the plaza, but if you are able—"

"I will stay as close to Hophorn as I can, Elder."

Cloudblower gave him a grateful look, backed away, and strode for the kiva.

Hophorn gripped a handful of Browser's buckskin pant leg and held tight.

He knelt beside her, and whispered, "You don't see them here, do you, Hophorn?"

She scanned the faces in the plaza, and on the rooftops, then she did it again, with great patience, before she shook her head.

"Good. I asked the village matrons to personally iden-tify each person before we allowed him or her into Talon Town. People will, however, be coming and going all night long." Browser pointed to the ladder that stood ten paces to Hophorn's left. "If you see *anyone* come down that ladder that you think might be—"

She gestured to the roof. "C-Catkin."

"Yes, good, Hophorn. Call out to Catkin, or to me if you see me. We will have those people face-down in the dirt before you can shout again."

Browser patted her hand where it gripped his pant leg. "I'm going to have trouble breaking up fights if I have to drag you with me."

Hophorn gazed at her hand, and slowly, a finger at a time, let go.

Browser said, "If you need me, I'll be close. Just call. Do you understand?"

The black blanket hid her face unless she was looking directly at him, but he saw her nod.

"Good. I'm going to go stand over there." He pointed to the door that led into the kiva's antechamber. "That's thirty paces away, Hophorn. I'll be there the entire time. I promise."

Hophorn gazed up at him with terrified eyes, but she nodded.

Browser smiled, and walked across the plaza to his ritual position beside the door. A total of two hundred and forty-three people had come for the ceremonial. Villagers from Starburst Town, the last to arrive, had trotted in just after dawn. Conversations and laughter filled the night.

Browser glanced back at Hophorn. Her eyes had not left him.

He waved.

Her expression didn't change. She watched him as if her life depended upon it.

Catkin stood tall on the roof right above Hophorn, her club resting on her right shoulder. Her long black braid draped the front of her white-feathered cape.

Their gazes met and held.

The lines around her eyes had tightened.

He braced his feet, and tried to get a full breath into his lungs.

The flute and drums inside the kiva went silent.

The crowd hushed.

Like a wave rolling toward shore, people turned as one, to watch the door beside Browser.

Cloudblower stepped out with a feathered prayer stick in one hand, and a red pot of sacred cornmeal in the other. As she walked she Sang in a deep melodic voice:

> *"I am planting the northern mountains.*
> *I am planting the western sea.*
> *I am planting the southern deserts.*
> *I am planting the eastern trees."*

She knelt in the middle of the plaza and planted the prayer stick in the snow. The downy eagle feathers on the top fluttered and swayed in the cold evening breeze.

As she rose, she tipped her pot and poured a line of blue cornmeal at the base of the prayer stick, then backed up toward Browser and the door to the subterranean ceremonial chamber. The Dancers would follow that line, symbolically retracing the path of the First People from their emergence from the underworlds to their arrival at Straight Path Canyon. They would Sing of the long journey in the brilliance of Father Sun's light.

Cloudblower halted on the other side of the door, and a haunting chorus crept from the kiva, soft howls, and yips, hawk shrieks, and the low roars of mountain lions.

Cloudblower lifted her meal-covered hands to the Evening People, and at that instant, a line of unearthly figures emerged from the firelit womb of the kiva.

They shuffled forward with their arms swinging and their sandals kicking up a haze of snow. Their Song was hushed, like the chirping of newborn birds. Their glorious masks, part animal, part astonishing god, bore sprinkles of raindrops, shining stars, and feathered halos. Ruffs of buffalo fur encircled their throats; and their bare chests, painted pure white, gleamed with black zigzagging lightning bolts. Their turkey-feather capes swayed as they trotted down the road of emergence, tossing their masked heads, and staring at the crowd through dark, empty eye sockets. They carried red-and-yellow dance sticks and gourd rattles.

When they reached the planted prayer stick, they broke into four lines and veered outward in the sacred directions, showing the different paths people had taken after they'd reached Straight Path Canyon.

Hophorn clutched the black blanket beneath her nose covering most of her face, but a reverent glow lit her eyes.

Browser smiled.

The Dancers shook their rattles, circled, and formed two concentric circles.

Each breath they released, each thump of their feet, called to Our Mother Earth, telling her that after this long night, Father Sun would hold her longer, love her more, and warmth would seep back into her bones.

The Dancers stopped circling and tilted their heads, as if listening.

The flute sounded again, the note so sweet and high it brought tears to Browser's eyes. He bowed his head.

Four women emerged from the kiva, their white doeskin dresses and boots shining as they trotted very close to the crowd—but hallowed, untouchable. Eagle feathers adorned their long black hair, twisting and bobbing in the breeze. The Deer Mothers circled the plaza four times, Dancing through the soft torchlight, their arms reaching for the sky, supernatural beings that had just emerged from the misty cloud of legend. Their hoarse breathy

voices resembled those of deer in the forest, calling warnings to each other.

The masked Dancers bleated or howled in terror. Some
ran for cover in the crowd. Others hunched down and
waited for the sacred Mothers to pass.

Spectators put their hands over their eyes and watched
through the weave of their fingers. No one could look
directly upon such Power and beauty.

Browser glanced back at Hophorn.

She was gone. The hides empty.

Panic went through him, then he saw the door curtain
to Cloudblower's chamber swinging.

Had she only been able to watch for a finger of time?

Browser looked up at the roof. Catkin knelt with her
back to him, speaking to someone below. Probably one
of the warriors standing guard on the mounds.

Several people perched on the roof near Catkin, watching the Dances, smiling.

Browser heaved a sigh and lowered his head again as
the Deer Mothers passed by.

---

*My white buckskin shirt and pants blend
with the snowy ground, but Shadow's
dress is the darkness.*
 *She paces behind me, her steps silent.
Her black eyes glittering. She is an
abyss in the night, invisible, dangerous.
A single flute wails.
It begins low, a shrike's whistle.
People line both sides of the Dancers'
path. Old people grin and clutch
squirming children to their chests. The
Dancers' moccasins shish as they
prance through the snow. The light of
creation lives in their hooves, claws,*

*furred muzzles, and polished wooden
beaks.*

*I rub my cold face, stunned by the
beauty.*

*As the Dancers sway and dip, they
watch me with the ancient eyes of long-
dead heroes, ancestors, the spirits of
clouds.*

*The flute grows shrill and breathy—
like a strangled scream.*

And I know it is time.

Shadow creeps up behind me.

I can feel her eagerness.

*On the fabric of my souls, I see her
smile. Death lives in the elegant curves
of her lips, the quivering of her
nostrils. She is magnificent.*

*Her fingers sink into the muscles of
my arm like blades.*

"Wait," I whisper.

*She is trembling, the longing so strong
it is a physical pain.*

*"Go to the pottery mounds," I say. "I
will bring her to you."*

She backs away.

*After several moments, I turn, but I
see only darkness and starlit snow.
Distant buttes are black blocks on the
horizon.*

*The scent of burning cedar rises from
the sacred fires, bathing my face.*

*I scan Talon Town and Hillside
Village.*

*I wonder if she sees me. If, even now,
she is shouldering past the onlookers,
hurrying to meet me. The face of death*

and the face of the beloved are often
indistinguishable.

I have experienced this myself when
Shadow becomes intoxicated with the
kill, and turns on me. The instant
before she attacks, there is a moment
when I would willingly throw myself
into her arms, and allow myself to be
consumed by the fires of her lust. I . . .

I see her.

Running away from the plaza fire in
Hillside Village.

She is so young. Achingly beautiful.

"Yes," I whisper. "Come to me. Have
I not told you that you must be bathed
in blood to be saved?"

Already I can feel it on my hands,
warm, sticky, the scent pungent.

I shiver.

As I rise, I gaze down at the dead
guard. The gaping hole in his chest
resembles a red-lipped mouth open in a
final scream.

He was standing on the edge like the
others, watching the Dances. The
firelight had blinded him.

I take no pride in such kills. They are
like slaughtering coyote pups in their
den. Easy.

I tiptoe along the rim.

The night is clear. By morning, we
will all be freezing, ready for the bowl
of life. The sacred meal. Hot. Steaming.
We will shudder as we eat.

I halt near the top of the cliff
stairway.

There is another. She follows the first,
though the girl does not know it.
Her mother?
I crouch like a cat.
Two of them.
One for each of us.

Shadow will be ruthless.

He stood on the sandstone rim one hundred hands above
Yucca Blossom, his white buckskin cape and pants glowing in the torchlight. She clung to the sandstone steps,
breathing hard. Gray feathers haloed his wolf mask, rising like silver rays behind the pointed ears. For a time,
he crouched so still and calm, the shells sewn around his
collar caught the night's gleam and shone like mirrors.

The world died around Yucca Blossom.

Her ears no longer heard the ritual chanting or flute
music that echoed across the canyon. Her eyes no longer
sought the Dancers in the plaza. The magnificent dresses,
turquoise and shell jewelry. The ornately decorated war
shirts which had flashed brilliantly moments ago, vanished as her world became the canyon rim.

Two Hearts lifted his right moccasin and extended a
hand to the Dancers in Talon Town.

Yucca Blossom glanced back and forth between them.

He mimicked the steps of the Dancers who snaked
around in Talon Town, shaking rattles, Singing in deep
resonant voices. Like the Serpent of the Heavens who
guarded the skyworld, his body glittered and swayed.

She reached for another handhold, and pulled herself
up. The stones were slick, icy with snow. But she hurried.

He stood like a dagger of silver flame. His long white
cape blazing.

The shell bells on her cape scraped against the rock,

and her white kirtle flashed around her blue leggings, as she scrambled up the cliff.

His breathing seemed loud, hoarse, his need for her unbearable.

Yucca Blossom climbed the last step and ran to him. Her two braids, woven with strips of red cloth, hung down to her waist.

He reached out, almost as if afraid, and stroked them.

She could barely hear his tight voice. *"Afraid?"* he asked.

"No. I want to be with you."

He nodded, but spread his white cloak and enfolded Yucca Blossom anyway, protecting her from the darkness and cold.

They stood close for several moments, and she smelled an odd scent, musty, metallic, like the dust that rises from fallen buildings.

He whispered, *"Do you know where the pottery mounds are?"*

"Yes. I have been there many times."

"Go. Wait for me. I will be along very soon."

Yucca Blossom obediently trotted away, heading north. She turned only once to look back.

At first she didn't see him, then the feathers on his mask quivered.

He lay stretched out on his belly in the snow just above the stairs.

As if waiting for someone.

31

CATKIN SAW THE seven warriors from Frosted
Meadow coming up the road, laughing and playfully
shoving each other. They wore red capes with the hoods
pulled up. Several weaved on their feet. Catkin had seen
them earlier, gobbling blue corn bread, and drinking co-
pious amounts of fermented juniper berry juice.

As they climbed the ladder to the roof, she walked
down to meet them.

The first man, built like a grizzly bear, stepped off,
smiling, and Catkin whispered, "The Deer Mothers have
arrived."

The big man turned and put fingers to his lips to hush
his companions.

The other warriors stifled their laughter and stumbled
off onto the roof, grinning. As a group, they went to stand
overlooking the Dancers. Wind buffeted their red capes
around their legs. Two of the warriors were women. As
their hoods flapped, Catkin saw their white face powder.
They'd applied it thickly, in honor of White Shell
Woman. One of the women looked familiar, tall and slender, but Catkin couldn't place where she'd seen her.

The big warrior elbowed one of his friends in the ribs
and laughed.

On the roof of the kiva to their left, Corn Mother,
Matron of Frosted Meadow Village, pointed a stern finger, and gave them all evil looks.

Cowed, the warriors shushed each other again and

climbed down into the plaza. They lined the wall in front of Cloudblower's chamber.

Catkin had seen Hophorn crawl into the chamber a finger of time ago, but she looked down anyway, making certain none of the warriors had staggered through the door curtain on top of her. They stood with their fingers over their eyes, whispering to each other, but they seemed to have calmed down.

Catkin checked the positions of the other six guards standing on the high crumbling walls of Talon Town, then returned to her own position at the southeastern corner.

Catkin folded her arms beneath her white-feathered cape and focused on the potsherds that paved the wide road below. In the torchlight, they glittered and twinkled.

The two guards on the mounds to her right, faced south, gazing out across the starlit canyon bottom. They wore the painted yellow capes of Starburst Village warriors.

Catkin expelled a breath and it frosted in the air before her. Her nerves, which had stretched tighter and tighter over the past quarter moon, hummed at the snapping point tonight. Something out there in the darkness watched her with feral eyes. She could feel that gaze upon her, unwavering, like a cat's as it stealthily closed in on prey.

A commotion broke out behind her, and Catkin saw the red-caped Frosted Meadow warriors climbing off the ladder onto the roof. They shoved and nudged each other, stumbled around, and choked back laughter. Two of the warriors supported another warrior between them, as if he'd passed out in the plaza. The incapacitated man's cape was much too long for him; it trailed the roof as they dragged him, grinning, toward the ladder down to the road.

Catkin called, "If you can't behave appropriately

during the sacred Dances, I suggest you return to the Hillside plaza fire."

As if eager to obey, the big "grizzly bear" warrior tiptoed toward the ladder, but he couldn't quite keep his balance. When he tilted too far in one direction, his friends shoved him back up and snickered.

Catkin's heart lurched into her throat when the big man almost toppled over the edge, but his friends snatched the hem of his cape and tugged him backward in a flurry of waving arms and cries.

Catkin scowled at them.

The big warrior sheepishly climbed down the ladder. The two warriors dragging the other went next. They jostled the unconscious man until he roused, then shoved him onto the ladder. He climbed down unsteadily. The others filed behind him, and they staggered in a weaving, colliding herd back toward Hillside Village.

Jackrabbit met them as they rounded the southeastern corner of the town, and hastily stepped back to let them pass. He wore a blue-and-green painted buffalohide cape, and his shoulder-length black hair shone as if freshly washed. He gazed up at Catkin and his pug nose crinkled. He said, "I saw them earlier. I didn't wish to be flattened."

"A prudent decision," she called.

Jackrabbit trotted to the ladder and climbed up. Just as he made it to the roof, the flute went silent, and the drums began, pounding out the heartbeat of Our Mother Earth, and introducing the Buffalo Dancers. They shuffled from the kiva with their curving black horns shining, shaking their shaggy heads. Long brown beards draped their red-painted chests. Buffalo brought the blessing winter snows that gave birth to spring grasses, and fed all creatures, small and large. They also possessed magical powers. They could live under lakes, and run to the skyworlds by leaping from one cloud to the next. They were cousins to the Thunderbirds. They both made deep rumbling roars, and both brought water from the sky. Healing teas were always drunk from a buffalo horn cup, if possible.

Cloudblower led the Dancers around the plaza on a sinuous path, uttering a deep-throated call, the rumble a buffalo makes when she's searching for another animal in the herd.

The people in the crowd "rumbled" back to Buffalo Above, saying "Here we are, mother. We're right here. Give us your blessings."

Jackrabbit walked to Catkin and whispered, "Are you going to stay for the Dances?"

She shook her head. "I've been here since dawn. I think I will return to my chamber and rest for a time. But I'll be back for the grand midnight Dance."

"Rest well. I will see you then."

Catkin started to walk away, then turned. "Jackrabbit, the Sunwatcher is in her chamber, but she may come back outside later. Please watch for her and let her know you are close."

He nodded, "I will. Is she still frightened?"

"Terrified. She came out for the first Dance, and saw the katsinas arrive, but went back into Cloudblower's chamber soon after."

"I will watch for her, Catkin. Don't fret."

She nodded and headed for the ladder.

Weary to the bone, her limbs felt like dead weights. She watched her feet as she walked toward the Hillside plaza fire. Six of the Frosted Meadow warriors clustered around the large jars of fermented juniper berry juice on the south side of the fire, dipping up cups, laughing too loudly.

The big bearlike warrior said, *"Is that what he told you when he borrowed your extra cape? He told me it was his sister, that he wanted us to help him play a joke on her. Some joke, she could barely walk!"*

His friends roared with laughter and stumbled around the fire.

Catkin passed them without a word. She was no longer on guard, and they were disturbing no one out here. Let them be happy.

As she neared the ladder that leaned against the side of Hillside Village, she stopped and frowned at the ground.

Though the snow had been churned up by hundreds of sandals and hide boots, these tracks were fresh. And made by bare feet.

Catkin knelt and studied the toe and heel prints. A woman probably. Maybe a youth. She'd been staggering.

Catkin's gazed followed the tracks back toward the fire. Another person, wearing hide boots, had stepped on several of the barefoot tracks.

Catkin rose and walked alongside the tracks, tracing them across the front of Hillside Village, and onto the dirt trail that led to Kettle Town. Several of the gaps in the town's tumbled walls gleamed redly. Perhaps the two warriors had decided to return to their chambers for the evening?

Movement caught her gaze. Her eyes lifted to the cliff stairs. Two people climbed up. The red hood of the person on top had fallen back, revealing long black hair. The windblown flames and torchlight made it impossible to see the people clearly, one instant they were there, the next gone, swallowed by the darkness.

Catkin cocked her head, wondering. It was probably nothing, warriors climbing to get a better view of the Dances from the rim, but barefoot?

Her boot struck something buried in the snow.

Catkin took a last look at the figures, and knelt. She dug around in the snow until she felt a leather strap. As she pulled it out, it swung in her hand.

A necklace with a jet pendant carved into the shape of

a serpent coiled inside a broken shell. The single coral eye glared at Catkin.

Her eyes jerked upward as her lungs started to heave. *She could barely walk* ... "Blessed gods. No. I—I can't believe ..."

The images of the Frosted Meadow warriors flashed. Dragging a man with a cape much too long. She felt sick, shaky.

Catkin slipped the necklace over her head, drew her war club, and ran for the round tower at the base of the stairs.

32

THE BUFFALO DANCERS trotted back for the kiva, breathing hard, their long beards shimmering with beads of sweat. Browser reverently lowered his gaze as they passed.

Cloudblower brought up the rear. She started to follow the other Dancers into the ceremonial chamber, but seemed to think better of it, and stopped beside Browser.

"How long did Hophorn watch?"

"Not long, Elder. Less than a finger of time."

Cloudblower sighed, "At least she saw the katsinas arrive. I'm grateful for that."

"I think she is, too, Elder. I'll look in on her as soon as I am able."

"Thank you, War Chief."

The next Dance would not start for half a hand of time.

The crowd rose and stretched, conversations broke out.

On the kiva roof above him, Browser heard the clan elders talking. Flame Carrier called, "War Chief? We are coming down."

"Yes, Matron."

Cloudblower clasped him on the shoulder, then ducked into the antechamber to attend to her kiva duties.

The elders walked from the kiva roof onto the roof of the long south-facing wall and toward the ladder. Their brilliant capes flashed. Flame Carrier chuckled at something Stone Ghost said.

Browser saw Jackrabbit crouching on the southeastern

corner of the town. He searched for Catkin. He had assumed that once Jackrabbit had taken her position she would remain for the Dances, though warriors who'd stood guard since dawn certainly had the right to rest for a few hands of time before the midnight Dances.

Browser strode to the ladder and waited for the elders to climb down. He extended a hand to those who needed help stepping off.

Flame Carrier, Wading Bird, and Springbank came first, followed by Stone Ghost. His uncle grinned up at him and walked around to stand behind Browser, waiting while Browser helped the others down.

Most of the elders headed straight for the blankets covered with food—except for one man from Starburst Town.

Dressed in a yellow-painted deerhide cape, he stood at the foot of the ladder, staring at Stone Ghost. About forty summers, he had thick gray hair that hung to his shoulders, and a pale oval face. His dark eyes blazed.

Browser turned to Stone Ghost. His uncle stood quietly watching the people in the plaza.

Browser looked back at the Starburst elder. "May I help you, Elder?"

The man stepped forward as if walking through a snake's den, his steps light, cautious. He grabbed Stone Ghost's wrist in a hard grip, and demanded to know, "Where did you get this?"

Stone Ghost blinked. "What?"

"This anklet you're wearing!" He wrenched Stone Ghost's arm, and hurled the old man to the ground. "Answer me!"

Browser leaped forward and shoved the Starburst elder away. "There is an explanation, Elder," he said. "Uncle?"

Stone Ghost frowned up in surprise, then as if sudden understanding washed over him, he removed the jet anklet and handed it to the man. "Did it belong to some-one you cared about?"

The Starburst elder studied the exquisitely carved jet beads, and swallowed repeatedly, clearly having trouble controlling his emotions. His gaze slowly lifted to Stone Ghost. "Answer me. *Where* did you get this?"

"From a corpse."

The elder squeezed his eyes closed in pain. "Oh, no, no."

Stone Ghost softly asked, "When did she disappear?"

The elder bowed his head. "Seven days ago. Our son had just died. She wanted to be alone, and she . . ."

An odd ringing filled Browser's ears. His fingers low-ered and tightened around his war club as if it could save him from the horror stirring in his heart. Disbelief vied with certainty. He felt as if he were floating, disconnected from the earth and sky, hovering in some terrible void between. Had his souls separated from his body? How could he stand here so calmly? Why wasn't he dashing across the plaza, shouting her name, running to find her?

The gray-haired elder held the anklet to his breast like a beloved child. "Where did you find her?"

"Here." Stone Ghost pointed to the southeastern corner of Talon Town. "She was in a room up there. The mur-derer had wrapped her in yellow cloth."

"That's what she—she was wearing. When she left. A yellow cape." Tears blurred his eyes. "I want you to take me to her. Now! I have to see her with my own eyes!"

Browser couldn't move. He could not even force his eyes to look down at his uncle. He stared unblinking at Cloudblower's door curtain. It swayed in the wind, as if someone had just entered or . . .

Stone Ghost took Browser's arm and tugged. "Nephew? Listen to me for a few moments. There are things we must discuss."

Browser flung off Stone Ghost's hand and ran.

The people in the plaza whirled to watch him. Conversations halted for an instant, then a din of whispers erupted.

Browser ducked into Cloudblower's chamber. The breeze fanned the coals in the warming bowl, and a reddish gleam fluttered over the interior. The masks on the walls watched him in mute silence. The bedding hides lay rolled and tucked in the corners. The chamber was empty.

"No!" Browser cried. He lunged through the doorway and dashed for the ladder to the roof.

Jackrabbit met him at the top, red-faced with fear. "What's wrong, War Chief!"

"Where is Hophorn? Where did she go?"

Jackrabbit shook his head in confusion. "I do not know, War Chief. I—"

Browser grabbed the youth by the shoulders and shook him hard. "You have been standing guard since Catkin left! You must have seen her!"

"I didn't! I swear! I haven't seen the Sunwatcher all night! I don't know where Peavine's daughter is either! War Chief, many people have been coming and going, crowding the roof. It is impossible to—"

"Peavine's daughter?" Browser said. "What are you talking about?"

Jackrabbit lifted his arms in a helpless gesture. "A hand of time ago, Peavine was terrorizing the village, searching people's chambers without their permission, screaming that her daughter was missing. Perhaps she is with Hophorn?"

Browser glared into Jackrabbit's worried young eyes. "Hallowed gods," he whispered and stepped back.

"War Chief, what is it?"

In a bizarrely quiet voice, he said, "Find Catkin. Tell her I have gone in search of Hophorn and, perhaps,

Yucca Blossom. Tell her to organize a search party and
follow me."

"Yes, War Chief." Jackrabbit bowed obediently and
ran for the ladder down.

Browser looked over the edge of the roof, down into
the plaza where Stone Ghost stood. The old man's wispy
white hair blew about his wrinkled face. Their gazes
locked.

Browser called, "I'm going after her."

"No, Nephew! *Wait!*"

The words died in Stone Ghost's throat as Browser
sprinted for the ladder and disappeared over the edge.
"Blessed Ancestors," he whispered, "give him the
strength to endure what he finds."

Voices rose across the plaza. Shouts rang out as people
huddled together, whispering, shaking their heads. Children, sensing danger, grabbed onto their mothers, and
peeked, wide-eyed, from behind the shelter of long colorful skirts. Flame Carrier examined the anklet that Rising Fawn held out. The other elders crowded around,
hissing questions.

Rising Fawn grabbed Stone Ghost's wrist and twisted
it. "I said *now*! I want to see my wife!"

Cloudblower stepped from the kiva's antechamber.
Her white face powder had been freshly applied and
glimmered with a ghostly radiance in the torchlight. She
frowned at the Rising Fawn. "I heard the commotion.
What's wrong?"

Stone Ghost replied, "Yucca Blossom and Hophorn are
both missing."

Cloudblower stared at him numbly, her mouth open,
as if she hadn't heard what he'd said. Then she ran for
her chamber, threw the curtain back, and ducked inside.
A sharp cry split the night.

The crowd surged across the plaza like a tidal wave
and massed outside her door.

Stone Ghost tugged against Rising Fawn's rock-hard grip. "I pledge that I will take you to your wife later, but at this moment, I must—"

"Healer?" Flame Carrier called to Cloudblower, "What's happening? Where is the War Chief? Why are you in there?"

Cloudblower ducked out of her chamber and shouldered through the sea of bodies, shouting, "Let me pass! Get out of my way! *I must speak with Stone Ghost!*"

She stopped in front of him with tears streaming down her face. "Elder, please. You must help me."

He disentangled his wrist from Rising Fawn's fingers. "I will help you. Tell me."

"Oh, Elder, no one knows. I'm sorry. I—I thought I could Heal her. I kept begging her to let me help, but she . . ." Sobs shook Cloudblower. "Elder, I tried so hard."

"I know you did, Cloudblower," he said gently, and took her by the arm. "Let us find a quiet place to speak."

"Not until I have more answers!" Rising Fawn shouted. He lunged for Stone Ghost's arm. "Who killed my wife? Was it you?"

"Please, I have no time for this now, I must—"

Rising Fawn grabbed Stone Ghost's cape and shook him until his head flopped on his shoulders like a rag doll's. Turkey feathers jerked loose and fluttered through the torchlight.

Flame Carrier yelled, "Water Snake? Skink? Hold that man!"

Catkin climbed the icy stairs with her war club in her fist. Light flooded the cliff. A man could be standing on the rim, watching her, and she would never see him.

She slid her knee over the next step, and pulled herself up. A strange musty scent clung to the trail, fear sweat, and urine.

As she neared the rim, blood rushed so loudly in her ears, she could barely hear the sounds of the people shouting in Talon Town below. She searched the darkness, trying to find form in it, an arm, a head, a flash of clothing.

She saw only blowing snow and flickering stars.

Catkin leaped from the last step onto the rim with her club in both hands, and spun around, panting, ready.

Wind Baby had blown large swaths of the rim clean, leaving an irregular black-and-white patchwork of pummeled snow, starlit rock, and a vast expanse of night sky.

Catkin stared into the darkness, forcing her eyes to adjust quickly. Familiar sandstone rises and distinctive lumps began to appear. Blades of grass thrust up through the snow-covered rock at her feet.

He-Who-Flies should be standing here. Where was he?

She held a hand up to block the glare from below and carefully searched the rim. At dusk, she'd seen three guards standing up here. Now, she saw none.

She stepped onto the beaten trail that led westward along the rim.

In the canyon below, the Dances had begun again. Drums beat, keeping time to sacred Songs. She could not look for fear of being night-blinded, but she knew that the twelve Antelope Dancers, led by Antelope Above, had just emerged from the kiva. Decorated alike, a white line would outline their chins, stretching from ear to ear. Their lower legs and arms would be painted white. Each would be wearing a fox skin over his back, a white kirtle, feathers in his hair, and beaded anklets. Antelope Above would carry a bowl of sacred water to be poured on the prayer stick, as the First People had done to bring trees to life.

The trail led down into a snow-filled depression, perhaps ten hands deep. An eerie sensation came over her. She stopped at the top, and glanced over her shoulder.

Nothing moved, but she felt as if a monster walked behind her, his steps matching hers, his breathing timed to hers. A chameleon of light and dark, his colors shifting as he silently pursued her.

She gripped her war club in both hands. To fight down the panic, she painstakingly identified each clump of brush and rounded boulder, each shadow in the snow . . .

Catkin's eyes narrowed.

An oblong splotch darkened the bottom of the depression.

Catkin edged toward it with her club up.

She heard shell bells rattling in the wind.

Her breathing went shallow. She took another step.

Below her, long hair fluttered, and softly spread across the snow.

Catkin ran down the incline.

A woman. She lay on her stomach, her face half-obscured by her hair. The shell bells decorated the collar of her white cape. Her open mouth and staring eyes formed three pitch-black holes in her white face powder.

Catkin gripped the woman's wrist, testing for a pulse. Wind whimpered through the depression, and a haze of snow momentarily blinded Catkin. She let the dead woman's wrist drop and gripped her club, concentrating on the sounds of the night. Voices rose from Talon Town. She could hear every word the Dancers Sang.

But she heard no feet crunching snow, no breathing, no clothing flapping in the wind.

Catkin grabbed the dead woman's sleeve, and rolled her to her back.

"Peavine."

A wet mat of hair darkened the left side of her head. Catkin could smell the blood. She pulled the white cape away from Peavine's feet. Bare. Toenails shone in the starlight.

"Was it you I tracked, Peavine?"

. Catkin touched the jet pendant she'd found in the snow, and searched her memory. She did not recall seeing Hophorn wearing this pendant earlier in the evening. Had Hophorn given it to Peavine? Or perhaps loaned it to her for the ceremonial? Hophorn would give away everything she owned if someone asked her.

Catkin studied the trail. Tiny tornadoes of snow bobbed and careened across the rim.

Catkin rose to her feet.

The lilt of a flute rode the wind, and she could hear the Antelope Dancers calling to the rain god, *"Hututu! Hututu!"* Rattles shook, and feet stamped the ground.

Catkin started up the opposite side of the depression. Just before the crest, she slipped and scrambled to get her footing.

Soft laughter . . .

Catkin spun.

He seemed to rise up out of the snow in the bottom of the depression. The wolf fur on his mask blew in the wind. He gazed at her through dark empty eye sockets.

"You are early," he whispered, and Catkin recognized that deep masculine voice. She'd heard him here on the rim last summer and in Talon Town two nights ago. *"I did not expect you until tomorrow."*

Heart thundering, she backed up. "Who are you?"

He laughed again, and tipped his chin, as if signaling someone behind Catkin. *"Yes, Shadow,"* he whispered, *"yours."*

"What—"

The blow took Catkin from behind, staggering her. She stumbled around, wildly swinging her club.

The next blow blasted through her skull with the force of a lightning bolt . . .

THE DANCES STOPPED.

Wind Baby thrust icy fingers through the holes in Stone Ghost's turkey-feather cape and poked at his ribs. Stone Ghost folded his arms to block the assault and leaned against the wall. They'd found an empty, roofless chamber in the rear of Talon Town. Three-by-three body lengths, a gaping hole marred the south wall, leading out into the plaza, and a thick layer of windblown dirt, old juniper needles, and the debris from the fallen roof covered the floor.

Cloudblower sat in the far corner, to Stone Ghost's left, her face in her hands, rocking back and forth. The red paintings of the katsinas on her buffalohide cape swayed.

"I did this," she whispered.

"No, Healer. You did everything you could to help her."

"Gods, how did this happen?"

Torchlight fluttered over the walls, filling the chamber like fiery wings. "Murderers are not born, Cloudblower. They are molded as children. It requires vicious, repeated, intolerable pain to chase away a child's souls and create a nest where a monster can be born inside them."

Cloudblower looked up through tormented eyes. "But she is a good, caring person, Elder. I thought she was just confused, heartsick."

"Confused?"

Cloudblower shook her fists. "Yes! Once, she came to me covered with blood, and told me she had done it while she was asleep. Then, a few months later, she insisted she hadn't done it at all. She claimed that her father had appeared out of nowhere, killed the girl, and forced her to drag the body away to a—a place she called the 'sanctuary.' I did not know what to believe! But I loved her, Elder. You must understand. I loved her, and I wanted to believe her."

"You didn't believe her father existed?"

Cloudblower ran a hand over her long graying-black braid. "No."

Stone Ghost pushed away from the wall, and paced the chamber. "She may genuinely believe she didn't kill anyone. The monster soul is very curious. In my experience, it comes at a time when frightened children give up hope, when they know they cannot endure the pain alone. It is as if their own souls fission, and give birth to someone stronger, a protector who can shield them from the pain."

Cloudblower exhaled and her breath drifted across the chamber in a white cloud. "But Elder, if that is so, why wouldn't she remember what happened to her? She did not. I swear to you! I could tell by the look in her eyes. She believed she was telling me the truth!"

People had gathered outside the chamber, whispering. Snow squealed beneath shuffling feet.

Stone Ghost kept his voice low. "Tormented children rarely recall what happened to them, Healer. Only the monsters remember. And hate. And wait."

Cloudblower shook her head. "But Elder, if she was hurt so much as a child, why would she hurt others? Surely she would realize—"

"She may. But I doubt that *he* does."

Cloudblower remained silent, listening.

Stone Ghost walked toward her. "I have seen it many times, Healer. When they are old enough to inflict pain,

the monster souls re-enact what happened to them, as if
by hurting others, they can exorcise the memories of their
own childish terror and weakness. I have often wondered,
if it isn't also an attempt to kill the terrified child who
still huddles inside them."

Cloudblower murmured. "What do you mean?"

"By driving the child's soul out of the body entirely,
the monster soul never again has to hear it crying or
begging for help. Monster souls often resent the children
they protected. After all, the monsters were the strong
ones. They took the pain, and survived, while the child's
soul huddled in terror with its back turned, unable even
to watch."

Cloudblower rocked back and forth, her expression
tormented. Tears had streaked the white powder on her
triangular face, revealing the brown skin beneath. "I do
not really understand this, Elder."

"Doesn't matter." Stone Ghost held up a hand. "The
question is, where would she go? Where would she feel
safe? We must find her, before she can kill again."

Cloudblower wiped the tears from her cheeks,
smearing the powder, and straightened. "She called
the place where she dragged the bodies the 'sanctuary.'
Perhaps—"

"Did she say where this sanctuary was?"

"No. No, she didn't, but she told me once that it was
on the road to the Land of the Dead."

"So. West, perhaps, where Father Sun slips into the
underworlds at night? Or she may have meant somewhere along the Great North Road, to the sacred lake
where the eyes of the dead sparkle."

"Perhaps." Cloudblower steepled her fingers over her
mouth for several moments, as if mustering courage. Finally she said, "Elder. There is something else I must tell
you."

Stone Ghost spread his feet. He was tired and

desperately worried about Browser and Catkin. Neither one of them understood what they would be facing. They would see the face of a loved one. Stone Ghost feared it might distract them until too late. "What is it, Healer?"

"It's about the club. The warrior who was killed two nights ago? He gave his club to Hophorn just before he left on his last war walk. They had"—she paused to swallow hard, as if it anguished her to reveal this secret—"last summer he was badly scarred in a battle, and his wife said she could not look at him. He moved into Talon Town for several moons. During that time, he and Hophorn became lovers. It ravaged her heart when he went back to Silk Moth, but they continued to care for each other. They became good friends. Hophorn told him, just before he left on the war walk, that she was frightened. He was worried about her. He gave her his club and made himself a new one. That is why—"

"Yes, I understand," Stone Ghost said, and nodded. "That explains many things. Thank you for telling me."

Stone Ghost walked to the gaping hole and gazed out at the plaza. A milling crowd of people waited for them. Flame Carrier stood in the front, her old eyes fixed on Stone Ghost.

"Elder?" Cloudblower called.

"Yes?" He turned.

She rose to her feet with her fists clenched at her sides. "Please? I know it will not be easy. Too many people have been hurt, but I beg you to bring her back alive. I can help her now. I'm sure of it. *Please.* Let me try?"

"I am willing, Healer," he answered, "but I am not so sure about the families of her victims."

Stone Ghost stepped into the plaza, and people rushed toward him.

Catkin woke, but did not move. A man whispered a short distance to her right.

It was his *voice.*

She lay on her back, her head throbbing sickeningly. Ropes bound her hands and feet. Wind Baby had quieted. Not even a breeze disturbed the morning.

Snowflakes landed softly on Catkin's hot face.

Father Sun must have risen, but only dim gray light penetrated the clouds.

Catkin inched her head toward the man's voice and froze, unable to look away.

Less than six hands distant, a body lay, the arms and legs sprawled. The flesh had been stripped from the bones. Only the head remained intact.

Hophorn's long black hair haloed her pretty face. Her lips had parted, and snow melted on her wide dead eyes, leaving them shiny as if brimming with tears.

The murderer knelt at Hophorn's feet, using a red chert knife to scrape her lower leg bone. Tall, his blood-spattered white cape swung around him as he moved. The gray fur of his mask gleamed with a silver hue. An exquisite mask, expertly carved, long leather ears pricked alertly on top of his head. The white muzzle sparkled with sharp teeth. A black line, the breath road, ran from his nostrils, over the top of his head, and—though she couldn't see it, she knew—down his back to the base of his spine. As he scraped flesh from the bone, he whispered to himself.

Catkin subtly tested her ropes.

He stopped whispering. And turned. An odd black gleam shone through his eye sockets.

"I thought you were awake."

He rose from his grisly task and walked to stand over her. The pungent scent of fresh blood wafted from his swaying cape. Softly, he said, "Cloudblower told you, didn't she? She told you about me?"

Catkin shook her head. "I—I don't know."

"Yesterday morning on the rim. I heard part of it. She told you what Ash Girl's father did to her when she was a child, didn't she?"

The discussion about the woman?

"She—she might have. She told me about a woman who'd been hurt."

"Hurt?" he snorted in derision. "He used to shove war clubs inside her when she two. Two!" He knelt and lowered his mask very close to Catkin's face, hissing, "Without me, he would have killed her."

Catkin choked back her nausea, and said, "Who are you?"

He sank down to the snow, his knees spread wide like an adolescent boy puffed up with himself. He toyed with the knife in his hands. "She was three. Maybe four when I came."

Catkin closed one eye, and the pain in her head dimmed a little. "What's your name?"

"Yellow Dove. I took care of her."

Catkin squinted. She'd never heard of him. He must not be from anywhere near Hillside Village. He seemed to be watching her intently, as if eager to talk.

Catkin forced a swallow down her dry throat. "What did her father do when you came?"

"He didn't even know I was there." With lightning quickness, he threw his knife and stuck it in the snow less a finger's width from Catkin's elbow. She flinched. He laughed, pulled the knife out, then he flipped it in his hands. His voice grew husky. "He'd taken her out into the forest, away from the village, because he didn't want people to hear her scream. When he started to hurt her, she fell asleep. Like always. That's when I came." He leaned forward, and Catkin could see a glimmer of black human eyes in the wolf's mask.

"Did you fight with him?"

"I made sure he couldn't hurt her anymore. I made her go away."

Catkin's vision blurred. The world spun around her in a haze of white, and gray. She closed her eyes. "Go where? Away from her village? Where did she go?"

Catkin eased onto her side, facing him, and opened her eyes.

He made a soft disgusted sound and got up. He started to walk away, then turned back. "He's the one who killed her, you know. She was going to have his baby and he knew it."

Nausea welled in Catkin's throat. She choked it back, and whispered, "Her father killed her?"

"Of course, he did. At the end, he kept asking her if she knew Death's name. But she'd never known. I knew. I could have told him. He used to threaten her with Shadow Woman as a child. He'd say, 'You'd better not tell your mother what we did today, or I'll tell Shadow Woman, and she'll chew your heart out of your body.' He'd repeat the name over and over, *Shadow Woman, Shadow Woman*, as if it meant something that Ash Girl should understand."

Catkin said, "Who was Shadow Woman?"

"She helped him to kill Ash Girl. They both killed her. They wanted to kill her baby, too, but I wouldn't let them." He lowered a hand to his belly as though a child rested inside.

"Ash Girl's baby? You mean—her son?"

"I don't know what it was. But she hadn't had her bleeding in three moons. She was pregnant with her father's child, believe me."

Catkin could feel herself on the verge of blacking out. A gray haze fluttered at the edges of her vision, and she was only hearing every few words he said. She had to keep him talking. The longer he talked the longer she lived. She laid her head in the snow. "How did her father kill her?"

"She thought he was a Spirit Helper. She begged him to make the voices in her head go away. The old fool told her he could do it. He said he knew where voices lived." He aimed the knife at the snowy ground. "He used these women and girls to find out. When he hit them in the head, and they lost their abilities to speak, he knew." He turned suddenly and spat into the snow. "The voices in her head. She meant *me!* She wanted him to kill me! Can you believe that? After all I'd done for her. I'm the one who took the beatings! I'm the one who had to look into his eyes when he groaned on top of her!"

He turned to peer at Catkin through the black holes in the mask. "Oh, he could kill voices, all right. It worked with Ash Girl. But not the way he'd expected. He's kept me tied up in a cave for the past seven days, trying to figure out who I am, and how to get his daughter back." His deep voice went high, pitiful. "He wanted to hurt her more! I couldn't let him. I remember the way it was. I wouldn't let him do it!"

Gods, help me. His souls are loose. He's completely mad.

The pain in her head blinded her for several heartbeats. When the world came back into focus, she saw strange snow-frosted shapes around her: *Frozen fingers reaching for the sky. Twisted faces.*

The women and girls . . .

She sucked deep breaths into her lungs.

The Wolf katsina rose and returned to loom over Hop-horn. "She knew," he said in a resentful voice. "She knew all about me. The War Chief used to whisper to her when they coupled. He thought his wife was talking in her sleep, using strange voices. He didn't know who I was, but he—"

"The War Chief?" Catkin said, barely audible. "Do you mean Browser?"

"Of course, I do. Oh. yes, he used to go to you for talk, but he went to her for what his wife wouldn't give him. And you were such a pathetic fool, you didn't know."

As Catkin's pulse rate increased, the pain seemed to jet through her veins. Browser and Hophorn? Lovers? In the past, yes, but . . .

The Wolf katsina grabbed Hophorn by the feet and dragged her to a shallow hole hacked into the ground. He threw her in face-first, then kicked at the snow until he found what he'd been searching for. He lifted a sandstone slab over his head, and hurled it down on top of Hophorn. The splitting skull made a dull, watery crack.

"Why did you do—do that?" Catkin demanded to know. "She was a g-good woman. She wasn't a witch!"

"I don't want her soul coming after me. She's going to think I did this. I didn't, but she'll think so."

"Why would she think you killed her?"

"She can't tell the difference between me and Ash Girl's father. He's tricky. He disguises himself. Not even Ash Girl knew it was her father when he first came to her here in Straight Path Canyon. Oh, he called her 'daughter' and acted like he loved her, but she didn't know who he was until just before he killed her."

He knelt and started to shove dirt over Hophorn.

Catkin said. "Wait. Please."

He stared at her for a disconcerting time, before whispering, "Why?"

Catkin used her bound hands to pull the pendant over her head. "She lost this at the bottom of the cliff staircase. Please, give it back to her. She would want it."

Catkin held it out. The jet pendant swung, flashing in the gray light.

He walked over, and ripped it from Catkin's hand, then

tipped his head to examine it through the eye sockets in his mask. "This is a Power object?"

"She thought it was. I don't know."

He slipped it over his own head, and stroked the pendant. "She won't need it. I might. He's coming back, you know."

"Who is?"

"Her father. He's coming back. I'll bet that girl is dead by now. Which means he'll be here any moment."

Sick fear washed through her. "Girl? Yucca Blossom? He killed her?"

The Wolf katsina seemed to take it as an accusation. He swung around and shouted, "Of course, he killed her! You didn't think I did it, did you? I didn't kill any of them! I may have stripped the flesh from the bodies, and sealed the pots, but I've never murdered anyone!"

"I—I didn't mean it as an ac-accusation," Catkin panted, and tested her ropes. "Forgive me."

He did not answer. He shoved dirt over Hophorn until he'd filled in the shallow grave, then he stood and brushed off his hands. "He's coming for you, you know?"

"Me?"

"He thinks you have his Turquoise Wolf."

"But I—I don't."

He laughed, a low hideous sound. "He has done so many evil things in his life, he knows he will never find his way to the Land of the Dead without it. He'll be drawn down the Trail of Sorrows, and Spider Woman will burn him up in her pinyon pine fire." He paused. "He dug in the ruins of Talon Town for ten sun cycles before he found that Wolf. He *wants* it."

"How did he lose it?"

"He didn't lose it. That woman"—he pointed to Hophorn—"tore it from around his throat when he jerked her club from her hand. She paid for it. He used her own club to strike her down, then tossed it into the fire and piled wood on top of it. The burial party was coming. He didn't have time to search for the Wolf."

Snow began to fall heavily, whirling around them in huge flakes. Catkin kept her eyes on the place he'd been, but he faded in and out of the storm.

"I am going to make sure he never finds that Wolf," he said softly.

Catkin caught movement, and saw his red knife flash as he walked toward her.

Browser lay on his belly next to the toppled house, less than ten body lengths from Catkin. He had been listening for a finger of time, and was shaking badly; he couldn't steady his aim. His arrow kept slipping free of the bow string. He fumbled to secure it again, and drew back, focusing on the man's chest.

How could this beast, this man-beast, know things about his wife that Browser had not? Could the things he'd said about Ash Girl and her father be true?

Why had no one in the Green Mesa villages ever spoken of his crimes? Had her mother kept the truth hidden so well that no one suspected?

The arrow shook loose from his bow again, and Browser rushed to get it back in place.

He'd thought when he left Talon Town that Ash Girl might be alive, perhaps being held captive. The hope had almost torn him apart. But this katsina had just said she was dead, that her father had killed her.

A new and desperate grief tightened his heart.

His bow wavered, and Browser clenched his teeth and hardened his muscles to keep it steady.

The Wolf katsina knelt beside Catkin. "If I kill you, then Browser, Two Hearts will never find the Wolf." His voice had the menacing hiss of a rattlesnake about to strike.

"No," Catkin said, and squared her shoulders. "Nor will you." She seemed to be fighting back nausea. She swallowed, and her head trembled. Blood clotted the rear of her skull, and hung in long frozen stringers from her braid, and the back of her white-feathered cape. "Don't you wish to find your way to the Land of the Dead?"

He hesitated. "Do you know where the Wolf is?"

"Of course. I can take you there. It's hidden in a safe place. We didn't want to carry it around with us."

The Katsina remained motionless, staring at her, wondering whether to believe her or not.

Browser held his breath. Aimed. Let fly.

The arrow sailed through the falling snow, striking the right side of the Katsina's chest.

The man gasped, dropped his knife, and lurched to his feet, shrieking, *"Who did this?"* He stumbled around in a circle, frantically grabbing at the blood-slick shaft. *"You can't kill me! Who will protect her if I die?"*

Browser nocked another arrow and ran.

When the Katsina saw him emerge from the thick blanket of snow, he let out a blood-chilling scream and turned to run.

Browser shot him in the back, and the man fell face-first into the snow. His legs kicked, as if he were trying to crawl away.

Browser knelt beside Catkin, pulled the red chert knife from the snow, and cut her bounds. "Are you all right?"

"Yes," she said hoarsely.

Browser gently touched her cheek, then rose to his feet, and ran for the Katsina. The man was still breathing, his back rising and falling. But both arrows had struck the lungs, he wouldn't breathe much longer.

Browser slung his bow, kicked the Katsina onto his back, and glared down into the dark eye sockets. *"Who are you?"* he shouted.

As he gripped the wolf fur and tore the mask from the

man's head, the world died around Browser.

He couldn't move, or speak. The mask dangled in his numb fingers.

Ash Girl lifted her hands and, like a small child, rubbed her eyes with her bloody fists, as though awakening from a long nap. When she saw Browser standing over her, she smiled, then her body convulsed. Blood gushed from her wounded lungs and poured down her chin.

"Oh. Gods . . ."

A hoarse scream tore from his throat.

Browser threw himself to the ground and pulled her to his chest, his muscular arms shaking. "Dear gods, what have I done? Ash Girl, Ash Girl"—he buried his face in her long hair—"I'm sorry. Gods, forgive me!"

Ash Girl's head trembled. She looked up at him through eyes drowsy with death. Her voice was that of a child, high and frightened, "R-Red Buck . . ." she called him by his boy's name. "Go. H-Hurry . . . coming. He . . . he's . . ."

Slowly, as if it took time for her muscles to realize what was happening, her head fell back, and she went limp in his arms. Browser watched the soul drain from her dark eyes.

"I don't understand," he choked out angrily. "What happened? Whose voice was that?"

He lowered her to the ground, and looked at the hot blood on his sleeves and hands. A hollow sense of terror expanded his chest.

"What have I done?" he shouted. "Catkin?"

She walked toward him unsteadily, her eyes squinted in pain. Blood-clotted hair framed her face.

Ash Girl's left hand jerked, and Browser grabbed for his war club, afraid that whatever it was that lived inside her was trying to rise, to get to him, or Catkin. The bloody hand rose into the air, and reached for Browser, the fingers spread wide, straining. Then the arm fell to the snow.

Browser's eyes went huge. He backed up. "What was that—that creature? *Who* was it? Catkin? Did you hear that voice?"

Catkin placed a hand on his broad shoulder and fought to keep her stomach from heaving.

"The only thing I know for certain, War Chief, is that I am alive because you killed it."

A chill went through Browser. He shivered and pulled away from her. Ash Girl stared up at him through still shining eyes. A serene expression slackened her bloody face.

I killed my wife. My wife!

His legs felt like granite as he turned.

He made it to Hophorn's grave before his knees gave way and he collapsed to the ground.

Browser curled on his side in the snow. Ash Girl had been in a hurry when she'd shoved dirt over Hophorn. She'd missed a few locks of Hophorn's long hair. They fringed the edges of the grave like delicate brushstrokes.

Browser's shoulders heaved. His body shook. But no tears came to wash away the sight.

As Catkin walked away from the burial, crimson light poured through the wispy clouds, turning the snow pink. One hundred hands away, Browser stood with his back to her, his hand braced on a large sandstone slab that leaned against the canyon wall. Twice his height, ten people could sit on the slab's flat surface.

Catkin made it as far as the small abandoned house and eased down onto the toppled western wall to watch him. The pain in her head grew unbearable if she opened her eyes all the way.

Eagles played over the cliff to her right. The female circled the male, shrieked, and tapped him with her wings. The male shrieked back. Snow striped the ledges of the cliff.

Browser was gazing upward, toward the eagles, but he did not seem to see them. He stood so still and quiet he did not even seem to be breathing.

Stone Ghost's search party had met them on the road back to Talon Town. He'd immediately sent a runner for the Hillside elders and insisted that Catkin and Browser accompany him back to the burial site to explain what had happened.

They'd waited for the elders for four hands of time.

A group of twenty guards had escorted the elders, including Jackrabbit and Skink, who now stood to Catkin's left, on the western end of the grave, murmuring, watching the elders.

Springbank, Wading Bird, and Cloudblower stood to the south. Flame Carrier and Stone Ghost stood on the north side of the grave. They wore white, the color of cleansing and renewal. Their elderly faces shone in the red light streaming across the canyon. Cloudblower sobbed silently. She had faithfully led the sacred Dances until dawn, then been called here for this ghastly duty. She looked exhausted. Black smudges marred the skin beneath her eyes.

Jackrabbit and Skink had worked for a full hand of time to scrape out the shallow hole where Ash Girl rested. No one had washed her body or dressed her in fine clothing. After hearing Catkin's story, they'd been afraid to touch her for fear that the evil would leech into them. Jackrabbit and Skink had used juniper poles to drag her to the grave, and roll her over the edge. She lay sprawled in the pit.

Browser had not watched.

He'd been standing with his back to the ceremony since it began. His short black hair blew in the wind. He still wore the buckskin cape soaked with Ash Girl's blood.

Catkin let her head fall forward and tried just to breathe. She hurt for Browser. She could not imagine how he must be feeling. The malignant soul he'd killed had not been Ash Girl, but it had lived in Ash Girl's body. He must be wondering why he'd never seen it before. Or, perhaps, wondering if he had. The fiery black eyes that glared at Catkin through the mask were born in nightmares. If Browser had seen them, he would remember.

Flame Carrier said, "Cloudblower, you have the soul sticks."

"Yes, Matron."

Cloudblower wiped her cheeks, removed a handful of feathered prayer sticks from her belt, and walked around the grave, sticking them into the ground at the cardinal directions. The sticks would form a defensive line against the evil, keeping it in the grave. The yellow goldfinch feathers bobbed and twirled in the breeze. Cloudblower returned to her position, and bowed her head.

"Jackrabbit? Skink? Bring the stone."

The two young warriors lifted the large sandstone slab and carried it to the head of the grave. They heaved it in unison, and it fell on Ash Girl's head.

Browser flinched, and Catkin saw him shaking. He braced his feet to steady himself.

Flame Carrier waved a frail old hand. "Fill the hole. Let us be done with this."

Jackrabbit and Skink shoved dirt over Ash Girl. Everyone else walked away.

There would be no sacred songs or speeches; no one would cut his hair in mourning or praise her life.

Catkin folded her arms and hugged herself. The stone, and the prayer sticks, would keep all of her souls locked in her bones forever, even the soul that had loved Browser and Grass Moon. Flame Carrier said they could take no chances the wicked soul might escape, and secret itself in another body. Everyone agreed, even Catkin. But it seemed wrong somehow. Shouldn't Ash Girl's soul be free to go to the Land of the Dead? Why did they have to condemn her as well as the wicked boy?

Catkin looked back at the grave. Jackrabbit and Skink stood to the side, whispering. The fresh mound of earth looked dark against the snow. The elders had gathered over Hophorn's grave to Sing her to the afterlife. Flame Carrier's gravelly old voice rang out above the others. She had loved Hophorn a great deal. Cloudblower knelt at the side of the grave, rocking back and forth, sobbing the Death Song.

Stone Ghost broke from the group and hobbled toward Catkin. His tattered turkey-feather cape caught the light.

The feathers that remained winked. It looked as if he hadn't combed his thin white hair in days. A spiky halo surrounded his wrinkled face.

He stopped beside Catkin, and studied the cliff. The fires of sunset turned the sandstone into a glittering wall of gold and white.

"Do you think he's out there watching us?" Catkin asked.

Stone Ghost's eyes narrowed. "I don't know. Maybe."

He sat down beside Catkin on the low rock wall and braced his hands on his knees. "It is curious that the witch, Two Hearts, disappeared less than a sun cycle before Ash Girl's birth. It's possible that he found a village where no one recognized him and took a wife."

Catkin's heart started to pound. "He must be cunning."

"Oh, he had a reputation for being exceedingly clever. He was being hunted at the time. I remember that very clearly. Several villages had joined together to search for him. The number of women he was killing had soared. First it was one or two a sun cycle, then it was two or three a moon, as if he couldn't get enough of the blood. It's possible that he cloaked himself in Green Mesa Village for a few summers." Stone Ghost bowed his head. "I do not even wish to think of it, but I may be partly responsible for this terrible act."

"What?" Catkin said. "How could that be?"

"Twenty summers ago, when my sister was killed in Green Mesa Village, I went a little mad. I began a desperate search for the killer." He blinked at the snowy ground. "I now fear that I may have accused the wrong man. Perhaps if I had searched longer and more carefully, I would have discovered Two Hearts and stopped him twenty sun cycles ago. Instead . . ." The lines around his mouth pulled tight.

"But the murders ended didn't they?"

"Yes. Still, I'm not certain the man I accused deserved to die."

Catkin scooped a handful of snow from the rock, and held it to the base of her head. It eased the hurt enough that she could get a full breath into her lungs. "It's so hard to believe, Elder."

"What is?"

"That Two Hearts cloaked himself among the Green Mesa clans and turned on his own child."

Stone Ghost smoothed his fingers over the stones in the low wall, petting them as if to ease some hurt. "His souls are sick, Catkin. He must be dying inside."

She glared. "You *pity* him?"

"Oh, yes, very much. People who commit horrible acts are deeply wounded, Catkin. Often, they endured intense pain as children, and they grew up struggling to hide their suffering. The child was helpless to stop the agony, so the adult craves control. Hurting others is a demonstration of the killer's power. Especially the power over his own suffering."

Catkin lowered her hand to the deerbone stiletto she had borrowed from Jackrabbit. "I would gladly end his misery for him, Elder, if I knew where he was."

Stone Ghost's bushy brows drew together over his hooked nose. "If Two Hearts really was her father, he's a tormented man, Catkin. After he left the Green Mesa Villages, he came to Talon Town, and apparently began a panicked search to save himself, digging up graves, searching room after room, until he found a Turquoise Wolf."

"You believe that story?"

Stone Ghost nodded. "It would not surprise me. Two Hearts is getting older. As the sun cycles pass, people think more and more about death. Two Hearts has good reason to worry. Spider Woman must be eagerly awaiting his arrival."

"I hope she's keeping her fire stoked up to a furious blaze."

Stone Ghost patted her knee, and gazed at Catkin with luminous eyes. "How are you feeling?"

"I waver between wanting to throw up and wanting to sleep."

"Well, it won't be long now. I asked Jackrabbit and Skink to cut poles for a ladder. They're going to carry you home. That way you can throw up, then fall asleep."

Catkin managed a smile that didn't hurt. "Thank you, Elder."

Stone Ghost glanced back at Hophorn's grave. "Flame Carrier says you will all be leaving here soon."

Catkin frowned. "Really? Where will we go?"

"I don't think she knows. The tunnel to the underworld did not open, as prophesied. She thinks you repaired the wrong kiva. She's going to keep searching."

Catkin blinked thoughtfully at the ground.

Stone Ghost said, "Will you go with her?"

She lifted a shoulder, and her gaze went to Browser. "I don't know, Elder."

A soft worried expression creased Stone Ghost's face. "What did he do when he found out it was his wife beneath that mask?"

"He fell to his knees and held her until she died. He kept telling her he was sorry."

The lines around Stone Ghost's eyes deepened. "He could not have acted differently, but he won't realize that for moons. You'll have to help him."

The love Catkin felt for Browser swelled painfully in her breast, and her head throbbed. She scooped another handful of snow and slowly ate it. "If he will let me, Elder, I'll help him in any way I can."

Catkin turned to squint at the rim, wondering. Jackrabbit told her that Water Snake was still out with a search party, combing the canyon for Yucca Blossom.

But it had been snowing off and on since she'd disappeared. There would be no tracks. There would, Catkin suspected, be no trace at all. The killer was shrewd, and he'd been at it a long time. She doubted he would make a mistake now that . . .

Stone Ghost clasped her hand tightly. "I must speak with my nephew."

Catkin nodded. "I think he's been waiting for you. Hoping someone can give him a logical explanation."

"In cases like this, we're dealing with the logic of dreams, Catkin. Nothing makes sense in an ordinary way." He got to his feet. "But I'll try."

The pink light of evening streamed through the clouds, and dappled the canyon around him as Stone Ghost plodded across the snow toward Browser.

Browser heard his uncle's steps crunching through the snow. He straightened, but didn't turn. Long ago, someone had carved a perfect spiral on the left side of the stone slab. It had four rings, one for each of the underworlds the people had traveled through to get here to this place of sunlight. The Sun katsina, and Wolf Katsina, stood above the spiral, guarding the pathway to the underworlds. A zigzagging lightning bolt shot across the rock beneath the spiral, warning of the dangers that would be faced by those who dared to walk that legendary trail.

Browser reached inside his cape and touched the lump sewn into the seam of his buckskin cape. The Turquoise Wolf felt warm. After Stone Ghost told him that only someone with the sense of a blood-sucking fly would carry such a Power object on him, Browser figured there was no safer place for it.

Stone Ghost stopped on Browser's left and softly said, "Are you well, my nephew?"

Browser looked down into the old man's luminous

eyes. The breeze fluttered white hair around his wrinkled face. "Do you . . ." Browser's voice came out hoarse, strained. "uncle, do you know what it was? Inside her. That—that boy?" Browser's shoulder muscles tensed and bulged through his cape. "The voice. The—the mannerisms. I can't believe that my . . ."

He couldn't say the rest. He couldn't even think about Ash Girl at the same time that he did that *thing*.

Stone Ghost folded his arms beneath his ratty cape and watched the eagles playing over the cliff for a several moments.

"Monster souls are rare, Nephew. I have met three in the past fifty sun cycles of solving murders. Each of those has had a profoundly different voice from the main soul. They are not easy to understand. They are often bizarre animalistic creatures that live in the deepest darkest corners of human beings. I remember one monster soul I met, oh, fifteen summers ago now. Her name was Silver Song. She lived inside a young man's body, but she was an old woman. She had come to live inside the boy one afternoon when his father had beaten him unconscious. The young boy had excellent vision, but the monstrous old woman couldn't see close up. She spoke in a high scratchy voice; the boy had a deep melodic voice. The boy could remember none of the terrifying murders committed by the old woman, but she reveled in every detail."

Browser looked down at the dried blood on his hands. He had washed them in the snow, but red still crusted his fingernails. In a barely audible voice, he asked, "Is it witchery, Uncle?"

Stone Ghost spread his arms. "Not in the way we usually think of witchcraft, Nephew. I don't think monster souls come about from curses, or Power amulets, not even wicked potions, but I have often wondered if monster souls are not lost ghosts."

Browser's spine tingled. "You mean the forsaken ghosts that roam the earth?"

"Yes. They are desperate souls. I imagine they would take any chance to live in a body again, to speak with people, to feel the warmth of blood surging through their veins. Most healthy people are strong enough to keep them out. But wounded children?" He shook his head wearily. "They are defenseless."

Browser clenched his hands into hard fists. "Uncle, the woman that my son loved could not possibly have known about the malevolent boy inside her. She would have killed it if she had known, even if she'd had to rip out her own heart to do it."

Stone Ghost said, "She knew, Nephew."

Browser searched his face. "How can you say—"

"From the things Catkin told me. Ash Girl begged her father to kill the voices inside her. She heard them. Probably often."

Browser shifted to brace his hand on the stone slab again. "I think, maybe, I heard him, too, Uncle."

Stone Ghost peered up at him. "The boy talked when Ash Girl was asleep, didn't he?"

Browser kicked a small stone that lay at the base of the slab. "Yes. I just thought it was . . . strange. I didn't understand—"

"I knew she had heard the boy at least once while she slept. She heard his voice, awoke lying beside you, and assumed it was you talking in your sleep. She ran to Cloudblower in terror. But it wasn't you, Browser. I'm fairly certain it was Yellow Dove she heard."

Browser's hand slowly fell to his side. "*Fairly* certain?"

"What I meant is that some people have more than one monster soul inside them. She may have heard Yellow Dove. But it might have been another soul that we know nothing about."

Browser mouthed the words, *another soul,* and closed his eyes, blocking out the world until he could get hold of his raging emotions. He longed to scream and slam his fists into something.

He breathed, "At least it's over. Thank the gods, it's over."

Stone Ghost didn't respond, and Browser opened his eyes to stare down into his uncle's serious face.

Stone Ghost paused for a long while, before saying, "I fear that none of the Katsinas' People understand what has happened. The tunnel to the underworlds of the human soul did open. It opened last night. It's been yawning black and bottomless before us all day."

Browser swallowed hard. "You mean . . . it isn't over?"

Stone Ghost held Browser's gaze.

"You still have his Turquoise Wolf, Nephew. He'll be back for it. *I promise you.*"

Dusty was thinking about his father when he heard the Bronco return. Over the years, he had come to know each sputter and metallic clink the Ford made.

He sighed and stretched out on the large sandstone slab that canted at an angle north of the site. It would hold five people stretched out side-by-side. He watched the last remnants of sunset burn across the sky. The cliff over his head glittered with a cinnamon hue. To his right, a spiral petroglyph etched the stone, along with two square-bodied kachina-like figures, and a zigzagging line.

Cool night air swirled around him, the desert coming alive after the long hot day. Field mice scampered through the dry grass around the boulder.

As nutty as your father . . .

The words were like stilettos in his heart.

In the beginning, it had been Dale who kept the lid on the nasty secret. Word was that Samuel had suffered a sudden "accident." Then, as the years passed, people simply assumed he'd died of a heart attack, or cirrhosis of the liver, or any of the other insidious things archaeologists fell prey to because of their rather peculiar lifestyles.

Finally, as in all things, Samuel Stewart simply faded away. Unlike a Lister, a Kidder, or a Fewkes, Samuel Stewart hadn't lived long enough to amass a large body of published works. His name still appeared in bibliographies of various theses and dissertations, and occasionally in an archaeological field report, but for the most part, he was forgotten.

Sometimes at the Pecos conference, or the Society for American Archaeology meetings, one of the old-timers would mention his father in a passing reference, but that was the extent of it.

He stared up at the sky. As the last light faded from the western horizon, an infinity of tiny lights frosted the heavens.

An owl hooted on the rim high above him, and the muted chirrings of the insects filled the greasewood. The day's heat still radiated from the rock, warming his tired muscles.

Though they'd covered her back up, the sightless eyes of the last skeleton stared at him, bridging the gulf of time, whispering to him. Mrs. Walking Hawk had Sung over each of the burials, and sprinkled them with cornmeal, but Dusty wondered: Had their souls been freed? Had they found their way to the trail of the dead, and that terrible fork where, according to some myths, they would be judged? Which way had each gone? To her long-lost family and friends? Or down that other torturous route where the evil were forced to atone for their deeds?

"May the kachinas guide you," he said into the night, hoping that their journeys, no matter what they deserved, might be easier.

He heard the soft sound of boots in sand, but stared up at the Big Dipper; it had just sparkled to life on a blanket of slate blue.

"Am I disturbing you?" she called.

"Yes."

She threaded her way through the greasewood, a darker blot in a landscape of shadowed rocks and brush. A plastic grocery sack hung from her left elbow. She wore a clean pale blue T-shirt, but dust coated her jeans and hiking boots.

"Sylvia said she thought you were over here."

"Did she? I'm going to make her catalog potsherds for the rest of her life."

Maureen stopped at the base of the boulder and looked up at him. He lay near the top, ten feet away. A frown lined her tanned forehead. He heard her exhale, then she said, "Mind if I come up?"

"Yes, but you'll come up anyway." Dusty leaned forward, braced his left arm on the rock, and extended his right. "So, here. Take my hand. There's a ledge at about your waist."

Her fingers were warm in his, her grip strong. Heaving, he pulled her up, and she climbed over the edge onto the flat stone.

"Welcome to my palace." He stretched out again, his hands behind his head.

Her Levi's scraped the rough stone as she sat down and drew the sack into her lap.

"I brought you a peace offering." She pulled a bottle of Guinness from the sack, along with an opener, flipped the cap off, and handed it to him.

He took it. "Thanks. Your offering is accepted with pleasure and appreciation."

"It was a real test of will."

"How so?"

"I was feeling miserable. About what I said to you. I always crave a drink when I'm unhappy."

"Being around a bunch of archaeologists with their lubricated elbows must be difficult."

"A battle every day. Some, like today, are worse. But I'm tough. I can stand it."

The glass clinked on the stone, as he set the bottle to one side and shifted to look at her. "You okay?"

Maureen reached into the plastic sack again and pulled out a bottle of sparkling water. She unscrewed the cap and took a long drink before answering, "I'm really sorry for the things I said. I still don't understand how religious fundamentalism can be allowed to stifle scientific inquiry, but I wish I'd expressed my views to you in private." She let out a breath, as if bolstering her courage. "I especially want to apologize for what I said about you and your father, I—"

"Apology accepted." He ran his fingers down the warm sides of the Guinness bottle. "I don't want to talk about it, okay?"

"Okay."

The silence stretched.

"This is a funny job, Maureen. I spend my time trying to serve three different masters with three mutually exclusive agendas. Archaeology demands science. The native peoples want to take care of their ancestors. The client, NOAA in this case, wants their project permitted as quickly and cheaply as possible."

She drew one knee up, and propped her bottle on it. "How do you keep them all happy?"

"I don't. I do the best I can for all three, but inevitably one or two of them will accuse me of favoritism, or shoddy work, or anything else to let me know they're displeased with the decisions I made." He lifted the Guinness and took a long drink of the rich dark beer. "The only thing I want you to know is that I *always* take care of the archaeology."

She nodded. "I believe that."

Dusty studied the elegant curve of her jaw, and the delicate lines around her mouth. "Incidentally, while you were away, Maggie decided to deny the NOAA permit. We can all pack up and go home tomorrow. We've already back-filled every excavation unit—"

"My God, what about the skulls! The bones!" she shouted, and started to rise.

Dusty grabbed her arm, and gently tugged until she sat back down. "They're still in your tent. Mrs. Walking Hawk said she wanted you to study them, and when you're finished, she wants them ceremonially reburied to make sure the souls are able to go to the Land of the Dead."

Maureen grabbed a handful of the blue shirt over her heart. "Thank God for small miracles."

"It *is* a miracle," Dusty said. "I want you to appreciate it. She didn't have to allow any further study."

Her dark eyes glimmered. "Dusty tell me something? Can a Christian fundamentalist, a deep believer in Creationism, come out here and shut down an excavation because you're uncovering ten-thousand-year-old burials? They believe the world is only six thousand years old. Your scientific discovery would be an affront to their religion, wouldn't it? Couldn't they shut down your excavation, just as Indian beliefs did today?"

He frowned at his bottle. "If we treated all religious beliefs equally, I guess so. Thank God we haven't had to face that one, yet."

"But you will someday. Don't you see that? If you give free reign to one variety of religious fundamentalism, albeit native fundamentalism—"

Dusty held up a hand. "Let it go, Doctor. Please? It's over. The decision's been made." His hand dropped to the rock. "And there's something else I want to talk to you about."

She sat for several seconds with her mouth open, as if wanting to press the issue, then finally sighed. "What is it?"

He toyed with his bottle. "I want you to know how much I've appreciated having you on site. You taught me things no one ever has. This burial site would still be a mystery if you hadn't come to New Mexico." He glanced up. "I guess what I really want to say is, thanks."

Maureen seemed taken aback. She pulled her gaze from his and squinted into the darkness. The shining path of the Milky Way splashed the sky, and bats flitted around the cliff face, diving and squeaking to each other.

"You taught me a lot, too, Dusty," Maureen said. "Thanks for taking the time."

He lifted a shoulder. "Digging is my life. I enjoyed showing you some of it. Dale says I'm driven to be perfect in the field because I'm a failure as a normal human being. A social misfit."

"Well," she said with a tilt of her head. "Physical anthropology is my life. When I'm not working, I'm home alone. In the summer, I sit on the porch and watch the lake. In the winter, I sit at the window and watch the lake."

He craned his neck to look at her. "What? No string of men knocking on your door? You're an intelligent, attractive woman. I thought men would be falling all over themselves to take you out to Tim Horton's."

She laughed, the sound musical. "Sorry, I have to buy my own each morning before I dodge the potholes in the QEW."

"QEW?"

"The highway that takes me to Hamilton. That's where my university is."

Soft strains of conversation rose from the camp. Sylvia

had just kindled the nightly fire. A wavering orange gleam sheathed the tents. Sylvia crouched in front of Hail's and Maggie's chairs, apparently blowing on the fire. Clouds of sparks periodically flooded into the night sky.

Dusty rubbed his fingers over the gritty surface of the rock. "Do you still miss him?"

"Who?"

"John."

As if he'd opened some private door, her voice turned guarded. "Why would you ask me that?"

"Isn't that why you stare out the window at the lake? You're living with John in your head? With what was. What might have been." He paused. "I used to do that after my father died. Except I was staring out at the desert."

She took another drink of sparkling water and wiped her mouth with the back of her hand. "For a while, I hated him for leaving me alone. As if by dying he'd betrayed me."

"I don't think he planned on having a heart attack that night, Maureen."

"Oh, I know. His death was just so unexpected. He was as healthy as a horse. Cooking supper one minute, dead the next. The doctors said it was a genetic defect, like that Russian figure skater, a flaw in the heart. Some odd form of arrhythmia." She lowered her head. "I miss him all the time."

Dusty saw the pain flash across her face, and wondered about John—about how much it must have hurt him to be torn away from a woman like this one. No wonder he had followed her halfway across the continent.

If somebody loved me as much as she loved him, I'd probably fight death, too.

In the distance, Dale's camper creaked, and he stepped

out and walked toward the blazing campfire. His gray hair had an amber gleam.

Maureen continued, "John's death left a big empty hole inside me, Stewart. I'm only half of a person. I spend a lot of time talking to my people about death."

"Your people? The Iroquois?"

She propped her elbows on her knees. "No. The dead I spend my days with are in the lab. I think physical anthropologists have a different perspective on the dead than most people. I'm not afraid of them. They're my friends. We talk a lot about John, about dying. About how easy it would be to let go, then I could find John, and be whole again."

Dusty sat up and stared hard into her sparkling ebony eyes. "If you ever get to the point where you're seriously contemplating 'letting go,' I'm a plane flight away. I'll send you a ticket. You can come down and spend a few days observing what suicide does to those who live through it." He thumped his chest with a finger.

She cocked her head, giving him that careful scrutiny he had come to appreciate. "Be careful, Stewart. That's the sort of thing a friend would say. Feeling dizzy? Slip of the tongue?"

"I've been feeling dizzy since I met you, Maureen. I thought it was the heat."

She laughed.

Dusty ran his fingers over the gritty surface of the rock. "Have you ever considered that maybe you need some time away? It can't be easy working and living in the same places where you built your life with John. Don't you see him everywhere?"

"Yes, I do." The lines around her eyes tightened. "I've considered taking a sabbatical. The university owes me one. For years I've covered everyone else's classes while they took time off for research, but I've never really had a reason to—"

"Well, you do now." He held a hand out to the site. In camp he saw Hail Walking Hawk rise from her chair and walk out toward the filled-in burials. "There are a lot of women down there who'd really like you to find out who they were, and why they died. You might say 'no' to me, but how can you say 'no' to them?"

Maureen used the bottom of her bottle to make small circles on the sandstone. A grating sound filled the night. "I'll think about it. That's all I can promise."

He propped himself up on one elbow, and inhaled the scent of the pinyon pine fire. The breeze had turned cool, soothing. It fluttered loose strands of hair around Maureen's face.

"That's enough, Maureen."

Hail took three steps and stopped to catch her breath. She could see the pile of dirt and fallen stone that marked the ancient pueblo to the east of the burials. The greasewood growing up through the middle shimmered pale blue in the evening light. She clenched the elk antler knob on her walking stick and fought the nausea that threatened to send her back to her sleeping bag. It had been a bad day. She'd been chewing pain pills like candy, but they'd barely dented the agony.

On the western horizon a single cloud hung, its charcoal center outlined with a brilliant pink halo. The night smelled sweetly of wood smoke and freshly turned earth. She forced her feet forward.

When she reached the pueblo she propped her walking stick and eased down onto the cornerstones. The rocks felt warm beneath her yellow-flowered white dress.

On the big rock to Hail's right Dusty and Washais talked, their voices rising and falling with the wind. They sounded happy.

Magpie still worked in front of their tent, packing things as Hail had ordered, but her eyes were fixed on

Hail. She lifted a bony hand to her niece to tell her she was all right, and Magpie waved back, but it was a tense gesture. Sweat matted Magpie's short black hair to her round face, making her dark eyes seem as large as a wounded doe's.

Hail smiled sadly. She knew what it was to watch a loved one fail before your eyes. You felt helpless and broken. But that was the way Utsiti had created the universe. People's times came and went. That was all.

Just like these poor women.

The freshly filled graves resembled dark freckles on the land. She'd sprinkled corn pollen on the Haze child, and sung his spirit to the Land of the Dead. As he'd climbed out of the grave and flown away, his joy had almost burst Hail's heart.

But . . .

She frowned.

The evil was growing, as though once loosed the witch's soul was pulling Power from the glistening stars and gusts of wind. She could feel him slipping around her on ghostly feet, watching and whispering in a language she did not understand. He'd been Powerful. Much more powerful than Hail, especially in her condition. His presence had left a stain on the very air she breathed, on the grains of sand, and the twinkling sky. What sort of creature had such Power? Only the Shiwanna, known as Kachinas by other tribes, could breathe their souls into the world and have them stay for a thousand years. Perhaps he had not been human at all. Maybe he—

"Aunt?"

Hail squinted her white-filmed eyes at Magpie. Her niece walked toward her with her arms folded over her chest. Her white T-shirt blazed against the background of dark cliffs.

"You just couldn't stay away, eh?"

Magpie tilted her head, embarrassed. "I came to tell

you that I've finished packing. We can leave whenever you want to." She sat down on the toppled wall beside Hail and gave her a worried look. "Are you ready?"

Hail pointed with a crooked finger. "Our red tent is still up."

"Sylvia said she would take it down tomorrow and keep it for me. I want to take you home, Aunt. Please?"

She'd watched Hail eat pain pills all day, even poured them out for her when Hail's hands shook too badly to open the bottle. With each pill Magpie's face had lost a little more color, her eyes had gone a little wider.

"I guess I'm ready. There's nothing more I can do here. The evil is too great for me."

"Too great for anyone, I imagine. That's why it's still here." Magpie took Hail's hand and held it tightly. Her skin felt cool. "Let's go, Aunt Hail."

Hail sucked in a deep breath of the fragrant night air and let it out slowly, savoring the feel of her lungs moving, and her heart beating.

"I'm ready, child."

Magpie helped Hail to her feet, and they walked back through the silver veil of starlight holding each other as if for the last time.

Just before they reached the campfire Hail heard a deep male voice. She stopped dead in her tracks, and her eyes lifted to the canyon rim. Ghostly laughter echoed, vicious, frightening. The hair at her nape stood on end.

"Aunt?" Magpie said in sudden terror. "What's wrong?"

Hail's eyes narrowed. Junipers swayed in the wind on the rim. "Nothing, child," she whispered. "He just knows he's won.

". . . Again."

EPILOGUE

A S NIGHT SETTLES *upon the land, the snow trail-*
ing beneath the clouds turns into a gray starlit veil.
I watch it blow across the canyon. Its movements are
sinuous, graceful.

The snowflakes cool my hot skin. The day has been
long and arduous. My hands are shaking. As the flakes
melt, and mix with the blood on my face, red tears roll
down my cheeks, and drop silently onto my white deer-
hide cape.

"Please!" *the girl calls from behind me.* "Don't hurt
me again!"

She breaks into sobs.

I inhale the fragrances of snow and damp stone.

From my essence and light, I have created six gods.
This girl is not one of them, but she will do until I find
the rest. I know where three of those gods sleep . . . in-
cluding the one lying beneath the fresh mound of earth
below. They put a stone on her head. I watched them do
it. Her souls are locked in the earth now. The wrenching
sounds of her little girl cries are gone, wiped clean from
my souls. She'll never be able to hurt me again.

I'm free. I have been forgiven.

For now.

"Two Hearts? I'm sorry for whatever I did! Please, I
beg you! Let me go!"

Shadow's footsteps on the bare sandstone are quick
and impatient. Breath hisses in and out of her nostrils.

At moments like this, just before the end, she has a pungent feral scent, like an animal in heat. It stokes the fire in my veins.

I hear her voice in the soft patting of snowflakes on the rim, whispering, "Now, now, now."

My hands shake more violently.

I turn, and my eyes fasten on the girl's young body staked out naked in the falling snow. Blood flows from a hundred small, carefully placed incisions. Shadow stanched each with a glowing stick, but the blisters ooze. She is so beautiful. Long black hair haloes her face.

"Two Hearts!"

"Yes, my daughter, I'm coming."

My steps are those of a wolf, graceful, silent. . . .

BIBLIOGRAPHY

Acatos, Sylvio. *Pueblos: Prehistoric Indian Cultures of the Southwest*. Translation of 1989 edition of *Die Pueblos*. New York: Facts on File, 1990.

Adams, E. Charles. *The Origin and Development of the Pueblo Katsina Cult*. Tucson: University of Arizona Press, 1991.

Adler, Michael A. *The Prehistoric Pueblo World* A.D. *1150–1350*. Tucson: University of Arizona Press, 1996.

Allen, Paula Gunn. *Spider Woman's Granddaughters*. New York: Ballantine Books, 1989.

Arnberger, Leslie P. *Flowers of the Southwest Mountains*. Tucson, Arizona: Southwest Parks and Monuments Association, 1982.

Aufderheide, Arthur C. *The Cambridge Encyclopedia of Human Paleopathology*. Cambridge: Cambridge University Press, 1998.

Baars, Donald L. *Navajo Country: A Geological and Natural History of the Four Corners Region*. Albuquerque: University of New Mexico Press, 1995.

Becket, Patrick H., ed. *Mogollon V*. Report of Fifth Mogollon Conference. Las Cruces, New Mexico: COAS Publishing and Research, 1991.

Boissiere, Robert. *The Return of Pahana: A Hopi Myth*. Santa Fe, New Mexico: Bear & Company Publishing, 1990.

Bowers, Janice Emily. *Shrubs and Trees of the Southwest*

Deserts. Tucson, Arizona: Southwest Parks and Monuments Association, 1993.

Brody, J. J. *The Anasazi*. New York: Rizzoli International Publications, 1990.

Brothwell, Don, and A. T. Sandison. *Diseases in Antiquity*. Springfield, Ill.: Charles C. Thomas Publisher, 1967.

Bunzel, Ruth L. *Zuni Katcinas*. Reprint of Forty-seventh Annual Report of the Bureau of American Ethnography, 1929–1930. Glorietta, New Mexico: Rio Grande Press, 1984.

Colton, Harold S. *Black Sand: Prehistory in Northern Arizona*. Albuquerque: University of New Mexico Press, 1960.

Cordell, Linda S. "Predicting Site Abandonment at Wetherill Mesa." *The Kiva* 40(3): 189–202, 1975.

———. *Prehistory of the Southwest*. New York: Academic Press, 1984.

———. *Ancient Pueblo Peoples*. Smithsonian Exploring the Ancient World Series. Montreal: St. Remy Press; and Washington, D.C.: Smithsonian Institution, 1994.

Cordell, Linda S., and George J. Gumerman, eds. *Dynamics of Southwest Prehistory*. Washington, D.C.: Smithsonian Institution Press, 1989.

Crown, Patricia, and W. James Judge, eds. *Chaco and Hohokam: Prehistoric Regional Systems in the American Southwest*. Santa Fe, New Mexico: School of American Research Press, 1991.

Cummings, Linda Scott. "Anasazi Subsistence Activity Areas Reflected in the Pollen Records." Paper presented to the Society for American Archaeology Meetings. New Orleans, 1986.

———. "Anasazi Diet: Variety in the Hoy House and Lion House Coprolite Record and Nutritional Analysis," in *Paleonutrition: The Diet and Health of*

Prehistoric Americans. Southern Illinois University at Carbondale, Occasional Paper No. 22, Sobolik, ed., 1994.

Dodge, Natt N. *Flowers of the Southwest Deserts.* Tucson, Arizona: Southwest Parks and Monument Association, 1985.

Dooling, D. M., and Paul Jordan-Smith, eds. *I Become Part of It: Sacred Dimensions in Native American Life.* San Francisco: A Parabola Book, Harper; New York: Harper Collins Publishers, 1989.

Douglas, John E. "Autonomy and Regional Systems in the Late Prehistoric Southern Southwest." *American Antiquity* 60:240–257, 1995.

Downum, Christian E. *Between Desert and River: Hohokam Settlement and Land Use in the Los Robles Community.* Anthropological Papers of the University of Arizona. Tucson: University of Arizona Press, 1993.

Dunmire, William W., and Gail Tierney. *Wild Plants of the Pueblo Province: Exploring Ancient and Enduring Uses.* Santa Fe: Museum of New Mexico Press, 1995.

Ellis, Florence Hawley. "Patterns of Aggression and the War Cult in Southwestern Pueblos." *Southwestern Journal of Anthropology* 7:177–201, 1951.

Elmore, Francis H. *Shrubs and Trees of the Southwest Uplands.* Tucson, Arizona: Southwest Parks and Monuments Association, 1976.

Ericson, Jonathan E., and Timothy G. Baugh, eds. *The American Southwest and Mesoamerica: Systems of Prehistoric Exchange.* New York: Plenum Press, 1991.

Fagan, Brian M. *Ancient North America.* New York: Thames and Hudson, 1991.

Farmer, Malcom F. "A Suggested Typology of Defensive

Systems of the Southwest." *Southwestern Journal of Archaeology* 13:249–266, 1957.

Fewkes, J. Walter, and J. J. Brody, eds. *The Mimbres: Art and Archaeology.* Albuquerque, New Mexico: Avanyu Publishing, 1989.

Fish, Suzanne, K., Paul Fish, and John H. Madsen, eds. *The Marana Community in the Hohokam World.* Anthropological Papers of the University of Arizona, No. 56. Tucson: University of Arizona Press, 1992.

Frank, Larry, and Francis H. Harlow. *Historic Pottery of the Pueblo Indians: 1600–1880.* West Chester, Pennsylvania: Schiffler Publishing, 1990.

Frazier, Kendrick. *People of Chaco: A Canyon and Its Culture.* New York: W.W. Norton & Co., 1986.

Gabriel, Kathryn. *Roads to Center Place: A Cultural Atlas of Chaco Canyon and the Anasazi.* Boulder, Colorado: Johnson Books, 1991.

Gumerman, George J., ed. *The Anasazi in a Changing Environment.* New York: School of American Research, Cambridge University Press, 1988.

————. *Exploring the Hohokam: Prehistoric Peoples of the American Southwest.* Albuquerque: Amerind Foundation; University of New Mexico Press, 1991.

————. *Themes in Southwest Prehistory.* Santa Fe, New Mexico: School of American Research Press, 1994.

Haas, Jonathan. "Warfare and the Evolution of Tribal Polities in the Prehistoric Southwest," in *The Anthropology of War*, Jonathan Haas, ed. Cambridge, U.K.: Cambridge University Press, 1990.

Haas, Jonathan, and Winifred Creamer. "A History of Pueblo Warfare." Paper Presented at the 60th Annual Meeting for the Society of American Archaeology. Minneapolis, 1995.

————. *Stress and Warfare Among the Kayenta Anasazi*

of the Thirteenth Century A.D. Chicago: Field Museum of Natural History, 1993.

Haury, Emil. *Mogollon Culture in the Forestdale Valley, East-Central Arizona.* Tucson: University of Arizona Press, 1985.

Hayes, Alden C., David M. Burgge, and W. James Judge. *Archaeoloical Surveys of Chaco Canyon, New Mexico.* Reprint of National Park Service Report. Albuquerque: University of New Mexico Press, 1981.

Hultkrantz, Ake. *Native Religions: The Power of Visions and Fertility.* New York: Harper & Row, 1987.

Jacobs, Sue-Ellen. "Continuity and Change in Gender Roles at San Juan Pueblo," in *Women and Power in Native North America.* Norman, Oklahoma: University of Oklahoma Press, 1995.

Jernigan, E. Wesley. *Jewelry of the Prehistoric Southwest.* Albuquerque: School of American Research; University of New Mexico Press, 1978.

Jett, Stephen C. "Pueblo Indian Migrations: An Evaluation of the Possible Physical and Cultural Determinants." *American Antiquity* 29:281–300, 1964.

Komarek, Susan. *Flora of the San Juans: A Field Guide to the Mountain Plants of Southwestern Colorado.* Durango, Colorado: Kivaki Press, 1994.

Lange, Frederick, Nancy Mahaney, Joe Ben Wheat, Mark L. Chenault, and John Carter. *Yellow Jacket: A Four Corners Anasazi Ceremonial Center.* Boulder, Colorado: Johnson Books, 1988.

LeBlanc, Steven A. *Prehistoric Warfare in the American Southwest.* University of Utah Press, Salt Lake City, 1999.

Lekson, Stephen H. *Mimbres Archaeology of the Upper Gila, New Mexico.* Anthropological papers of the University of Arizona, No. 53. Tucson: University of Arizona Press, 1990.

Lekson, Stephen, Thomas C. Windes, John R. Stein, and W. James Judge. "The Chaco Canyon Community" *Scientific American* 259(1): 100–109, 1988.

Lewis, Dorothy Otnow. *Guilty by Reason of Insanity. A*

Psychiatrist Explores the Minds of Killers. New York: The Ballantine Publishing Group, 1998.

Lipe, W. D., and Michelle Hegemon, eds. *The Architecture of Social Integration in Prehistoric Pueblos.* Occasional Papers of the Crow Canyon Archaeological Center No. 1. Cortez, Colorado: Crow Canyon Archaeological Center, 1989.

Lister, Florence C. *In the Shadow of the Rocks: Archaeology of the Chimney Rock District in Southern Colorado.* Niwot, Colorado: University Press of Colorado, 1993.

Lister, Robert H., and Florence C. Lister. *Chaco Canyon.* Albuquerque: University of New Mexico Press, 1981.

Lomatuway'ma, Michael, Lorena Lomatuway'ma, and Sidney Namingha, Jr. *Hopi Ruin Legends.* Edited by Ekkehart Malotki. Lincoln: Published for Northern Arizona University by University of Nebraska Press, 1993.

Malotki, Ekkehart. *Gullible Coyote: Una'ihu: A Bilingual Collection of Hopi Coyote Stories.* Tucson: University of Arizona Press, 1985.

Malotki, Ekkehart, and Michael Lomatuway'ma. *Maasaw: Profile of a Hopi God.* American Tribal Religions, Vol. XI; Lincoln: University of Nebraska Press, 1987.

Malville, J. McKimm, and Claudia Putman. *Prehistoric Astronomy in the Southwest.* Boulder, Colorado: Johnson Books, 1987.

Mann, Coramae Richey. *When Women Kill.* New York: State University of New York Press, 1996.

Martin, Debra L. "Lives Unlived: The Political Economy of Violence Against Anasazi Women." Paper presented to the Society for American Archaeology 60th Annual Meetings. Minneapolis, 1995.

Martin, Debra L., Alan H. Goodman, George Armelagos,

and Ann L. Magennis. *Black Mesa Anasazi Health: Reconstructing Life from Patterns of Death and Disease*. Occasional Paper No. 14. Carbondale, Illinois: Southern Illinois University, 1991.

Mayes, Vernon O., and Barbara Bayless Lacy. *Nanise: A Navajo Herbal*. Tsaile, Arizona: Navajo Community College Press, 1989.

McGuire, Randall H., and Michael Schiffer, eds. *Hohokam and Patayan: Prehistory of Southwestern Arizona*. New York: Academic Press, 1982.

McNitt, Frank. *Richard Wetherill Anasazi*. Albuquerque: University of New Mexico Press, 1996.

Minnis, Paul E., and Charles L. Redman, eds. *Perspectives on Southwestern Prehistory*. Boulder, Colorado: Westview Press, 1990.

Mullet, G. M. *Spider Woman Stories: Legends of the Hopi Indians*. Tucson, Arizona: University of Arizona Press, 1979.

Nabahan, Gary Paul. *Enduring Seeds: Native American Agriculture and Wild Plant Conservation*. San Francisco: North Point Press, 1989.

Noble, David Grant. *Ancient Ruins of the Southwest: An Archaeological Guide*. Flagstaff, Arizona: Northland Publishing, 1991.

Ortiz, Alfonzo, ed., *Handbook of North American Indians*. Washington, D.C.: Smithsonian Institution, 1983.

Palkovich, Ann M. *The Arroyo Hondo Skeletal and Mortuary Remains*. Arroyo Hondo Archaeological Series, Vol. 3. Santa Fe, New Mexico: School of American Research Press, 1980.

Parson, Elsie Clews. *Tewa Tales*, reprint of 1924 edition. Tucson: University of Arizona Press, 1994.

Pepper, George H. *Pueblo Bonito*, reprint of 1920 edition. Albuquerque: University of New Mexico Press, 1996.

Pike, Donald G., and David Muench. *Anasazi: Ancient People of the Rock*. New York: Crown Publishers, 1974.

Reid, J. Jefferson, and David E. Doyel, eds. *Emil Haury's Prehistory of the American Southwest*. Tucson: University of Arizona Press, 1992.

Riley, Carroll L. *Rio del Norte: People of the Upper Rio Grande from the Earliest Times to the Pueblo Revolt*. Salt Lake City, Utah: University of Utah Press, 1995.

Rocek, Thomas R. "Sedentarization and Agricultural Dependence: Perspectives from the Pithouse-to-Pueblo Transition in the American Southwest." *American Antiquity* 60:218–239, 1995.

Schaafsma, Polly. *Indian Rock Art of the Southwest*. Albuquerque: School of American Research; University of New Mexico Press, 1980.

Sebastian, Lynne. *The Chaco Anasazi: Sociopolitical Evolution in the Prehistoric Southwest*. Cambridge, U.K.: Cambridge University Press, 1992.

Simmons, Marc. *Witchcraft in the Southwest*. Bison Books, reprint of 1974 edition. Lincoln: University of Nebraska Press, 1980.

Slifer, Dennis, and James Duffield. *Kokopelli: Flute Player Images in Rock Art*. Santa Fe, New Mexico: Ancient City Press, 1994.

Smith, Watson, with Raymond H. Thompson, ed. *When Is a Kiva: And Other Questions About Southwestern Archaeology*. Tucson: University of Arizona Press, 1990.

Sobolik, Kristin D. *Paleonutrition: The Diet and Health of Prehistoric Americans*. Occasional Paper No. 22. Carbondale: Center for Archaeological Investigations, Southern Illinois University, 1994.

Sullivan, Alan P. "Pinyon Nuts and Other Wild Resources in Western Anasazi Subsistence Economies." *Research in Economic Anthropology* Supplement 6:195–239, 1992.

Tedlock, Barbara. *The Beautiful and the Dangerous: Encounters with the Zuni Indians.* New York: Viking Press, 1992.

Trombold, Charles D., ed. *Ancient Road Networks and Settlement Hierarchies in the New World.* Cambridge, U.K.: Cambridge University Press, 1991.

Turner, Christy G. and Jaqueline A. Turner. *Man Corn: Canabalism and Violence in the Prehistoric American Southwest.* Salt Lake City, Utah: University of Utah Press, 1999.

Tyler, Hamilton A. *Pueblo Gods and Myths.* Norman, Oklahoma: University of Oklahoma Press, 1964.

Underhill, Ruth. *Life in the Pueblos,* reprint of 1964 Bureau of Indian Affairs Report. Santa Fe, New Mexico: Ancient City Press, 1991.

Upham, Steadman, Kent G. Lightfoot, and Roberta A. Jewett, eds. *The Sociopolitical Structure of Prehistoric Southwestern Societies.* San Francisco: Westview Press, 1989.

Vivian, Gordon, and Tom W. Mathews. *Kin Kletso: A Pueblo III Community in Chaco Canyon, New Mexico,* Vol. 6. Globe, Arizona: Southwest Parks and Monuments Association, 1973.

Vivian, Gordon, and Paul Reiter. *The Great Kivas of Chaco Canyon and Their Relationships.* School of American Research Monograph no. 22, Santa Fe, New Mexico: 1965.

Vivian, R. Gwinn. *The Chacoan Prehistory of the San Juan Basin.* New York: Academic Press, 1990.

Waters, Frank. *Book of the Hopi.* New York: The Viking Press, 1963.

Wetterstrom, Wilma. *Food, Diet, and Population at Prehistoric Arroyo Hondo Pueblo, New Mexico.* Arroyo Hondo Archaeological Series, Vol. 6. Santa Fe, New Mexico: School of American Research Press, 1986.

White, Tim D. *Prehistoric Cannibalism at Mancos 5MTUMR-2346.* Princeton, New Jersey: Princeton University Press, 1992.

Williamson, Ray A. *Living the Sky: The Cosmos of the American Indian.* Norman, Oklahoma: University of Oklahoma Press, 1984.

Wills, W.H., and Robert D. Leonard, eds. *The Ancient Southwestern Community.* Albuquerque: University of New Mexico Press, 1994.

Woodbury, Richard B. "A Reconsideration of Pueblo Warfare in the Southwestern United States." *Actas del XXXIII Congreso Internacional de Americanistas*, II:124–133. San Jose, Costa Rica, 1959.

————. "Climatic Changes and Prehistoric Agriculture in the Southwestern United States." *New York Academy of Sciences Annals*, Vol. 95, Article 1. New York, 1961.

Wright, Barton. *Katchinas: The Barry Goldwater Collection at the Heard Museum.* Phoenix, Arizona: Heard Museum, 1975.

Don't miss

The Summoning God

the next exciting book in the series.
Available in hardcover July 2000

BROWSER REACHED FOR the ladder and almost missed the marks. Long dark streaks covered the roof. They might have been soot or mud, but they looked more like the claw marks made by bloody fingers.

He touched them, matching them with his own fingers, and suddenly pulled his hand away.

"Matron! I'm coming down."

He lowered the ladder through the entry and it hit the ground with a solid, ordinary thump.

The dark pit reeked of rot and corruption. It took an act of will to convince himself to put his feet on the rungs. Every instant he expected an arrow in his back. His gaze searched the village again, then he went down the rungs two at a time.

He stepped off onto the kiva floor and blinked at the darkness. Ash puffed beneath his feet, and the stench almost gagged him. If someone had wished to attack him, now was the time. He held his war club at the ready and fought to keep his breathing even.

When his eyes adjusted, he saw the fire hearth three paces in front of him and the woodpile stacked beside it. A faint crimson gleam lit the hearth's center. Browser went to the woodpile, pulled out a branch, and stirred the ashes until he found red coals. He broke his branch into pieces, placed them on the coals, and bent down to blow on the kindling.

The clawing again.

Desperate, erratic.

"Hello?" he called. "Is anyone in here?"

Something about the urgency of the clawing suggested human hands, someone trying to get to him.

Fighting his own sense of dread, Browser went back to blowing on the coals. A flame licked up. Then a branch popped in the fire, and sparks whirled toward the entry. Light flared.

Browser couldn't move.

The flickering images burned themselves into his soul.

The bodies had no heads.

The feral eyes of wood rats blazed as they scrambled from one bloody scrap of cloth to another. The rats must have gotten in through the kiva's ventilation shaft, a narrow opening in the wall designed to bring fresh air into the kiva.

Most of the bones had been stripped of flesh, then scattered, but a few still had tatters of clothing clinging to arms or legs. He saw an infant's head lying on the floor to his right. It looked as though it had been tossed. Was this a child he'd seen three days ago? One of the happy little boys playing in the plaza when he had arrived? He looked to be about four summers old.

Claws. Behind him.

Browser turned and stepped into a pool of blood. "Oh, dear gods."

Walker and Bole slumped against the curving rear wall. They were so recently dead the rats feared to approach them. The little animals would race forward, bite a piece of cloth, and scurry backwards, their feet scratching the floor for purchase.

"What happened?" Browser murmured.

The fools must have come down long before his signal. They must have disobeyed. . . .

Perhaps they'd been forced down.

"Right after Catkin and I left."

Walker's intestines had been pulled out onto the floor and his decapitated head stuffed into the gaping cavity. His wide eyes stared through the slit in his stomach, as though he'd been surprised by his killer.

Bole—he thought it was Bole—leaned against Walker. His face had been mutilated, but the obsidian-studded war club stuffed down his throat had belonged to Bole.

Browser locked his knees. He had seen a great deal of warfare and raiding. This was neither. Raiders killed in haste and stole food and trinkets to take home to their families. Warriors slaughtered their enemies and burned their villages. But this was calm, methodical butchery.

CHAPTER FIVE

AN AMISH SUMMER

OTHER BOOKS BY THE AUTHORS

SHELLEY SHEPARD GRAY

LONE STAR HERO LOVE STORIES
The Loyal Heart

An Uncommon Protector

Love Held Captive

CHICAGO WORLD'S FAIR MYSTERY SERIES
Secrets of Sloane House

Deception on Sable Hill

Whispers in the Reading Room

STORIES
The Courage to Love included in
An Amish Homecoming

AMY CLIPSTON

THE AMISH HOMESTEAD SERIES
A Place at Our Table

Room on the Porch Swing

A Seat by the Hearth

A Welcome at Our Door

THE AMISH HEIRLOOM SERIES
The Forgotten Recipe

The Courtship Basket

The Cherished Quilt

The Beloved Hope Chest

KELLY IRVIN

Sweeter than Honey included
in *An Amish Market*

One Sweet Kiss included in *An Amish Summer*

Snow Angels included in *An
Amish Christmas Love*

The Midwife's Dream included
in *An Amish Heirloom*

Mended Hearts included in *An Amish Reunion*

An Amish Summer

Four Stories

Shelley Shepard Gray, Amy Clipston,

Kathleen Fuller, and Kelly Irvin

ZONDERVAN

An Amish Summer

A Reunion in Pinecraft © 2017 by Shelley Shepard Gray

Summer Storms © 2017 by Amy Clipston

Lakeside Love © 2017 by Kathleen Fuller

One Sweet Kiss © 2017 by Kelly Irvin

This title is also available as an e-book.

Requests for information should be addressed to:
Zondervan, *3900 Sparks Dr. SE, Grand Rapids, Michigan 49546*

ISBN: 978-0-310-35442-0 (mass market)
ISBN 978-0-7180-7884-3 (trade paper)
ISBN 978-0-7180-7898-0 (e-book)

Library of Congress Cataloging-in-Publication Data

CIP data available upon request.

Printed in the United States of America

19 20 21 22 23 / QG / 20 19 18 17 16 15 14 13 12 11 10 9 8 7 6 5 4 3 2 1

CONTENTS

Glossary of Pennsylvania Dutch Words

*The German dialect spoken by the Amish is not a written language and varies depending on the location and origin of the settlement. These spellings are approximations. Most Amish children learn English after they start school. They also learn High German, which is used in their Sunday services.

ach—oh
aenti—aunt
appeditlich—delicious
bedauerlich—sad
bopli—baby
bruder—brother
bruders—brothers
bu—boy
buwe—boys
daadi—grandpa
daadihaus/dawdy haus—grandparents' house
daed—father
danki/danke—thank you
dat—dad
dochder—daughter

Englischer—English or non-Amish
fraa—wife
freind—friends
freinden—friends
froh—happy
gern gschehne—you're welcome
Gmay—church district, community
Gott—God
gut—good
haus—house
Ich liebe dich—I love you
jah—yes
kaffi—coffee
kapp—prayer covering, cap, woman's head covering
kind—child
kinner—children
lieb—love
liewe—love, a term of endearment
maedel—girl, young woman
mamm—mom
mammi—grandma
mann—husband
mei—my
mudder—mother
narrisch—crazy
nee—no
onkel—uncle
rumspringa—period of running around
schee—pretty
schweschder—sister
suh—son

schweschder—sister
sohn—son
Was iss letz?—What's wrong?
wunderbaar—wonderful
ya—yes

A Reunion in Pinecraft

Shelley Shepard Gray

This novella is dedicated to the wonderful group of ladies who joined me on my first "girlfriend getaway" in Pinecraft. It was an amazing weekend, and your kindness and enthusiasm always leaves me speechless. Bless you all!

Do not judge others, and you will not be judged. Do not condemn others, or it will all come back against you. Forgive others, and you will be forgiven.
LUKE 6:37 (NLT)

Things turn out the best for those who make the best of the way things turn out.
AMISH PROVERB

PROLOGUE

Dear Graham,

Thank you for replying to my letter. What a nice surprise! It was so thoughtful of you to send me those packets of lavender seeds. Since it's only January, I've planted them in a little pot in my room. And months from now, when they're filling our back patio with a lovely scent, I'll think of you.

> Sherilyn Kramer

Dear Sherilyn,

Thank you for your sweet note and get-well card. It cheered me up when I was suffering from the flu. I'm happy to tell you the flu has now left our house and none of us is too worse for wear. Only my sister-in-law, Katie Jo, was bedridden more than two days. But she is with child and my brother does dote on her, so that's a blessing in itself.

I hope this letter finds you still feeling well. Take heart. Winter is almost over! I'll write more soon.

> Graham Holland

Dear Graham,

I know I sent a long letter earlier this week, but guess what! I talked to my sister, Sharon, and she wants to go to Pinecraft too! She said she rarely gets a break from her job baking, so this will be a great opportunity for her. That makes four of us able to go, including our two friends. We're going to purchase our bus tickets tonight and will call tomorrow morning to get a room at the Orange Blossom Inn in Pinecraft.

Sherilyn

Dear Sherilyn,

Wow, your sister's name is Sharon. I bet that created quite a bit of confusion when you two were growing up!

Anyway, when I talked to Beverly Wagler at the inn, she said she hosts an afternoon tea around three o'clock every day. Let's plan on meeting then. I would come down to greet your bus since my friends and I will arrive in Pinecraft earlier than you will, but I've heard there's always quite a commotion and swarm of people there. I doubt we'd get more than a moment to talk.

I can't wait to continue our acquaintance in person. Just think, soon we won't have to wait days for replies to our questions. There's no telling the things we're going to find out about each other. Ha!

Graham

Dear Graham,

This is a quick letter I hope you'll receive before you leave. I wish you safe travels and lots of sunscreen. I'm for sure bringing a whole bottle for myself. Yes, I'll see you for afternoon refreshments at the inn. And just in case you've forgotten what I look like in the last six months (ha!), I'll be the girl with the red hair and freckles!

See you in person in Pinecraft. I honestly can't wait.

Sherilyn

CHAPTER 1

H uh," Sherry said, disappointment thick in her voice. "I thought Pinecraft would look different."

As Sharon Kramer followed her little sister out of the Pioneer Trails bus in the center of the small vacation community, she hid a smile.

She supposed, for someone as lovely and full of life as Sherilyn—or Sherry to pretty much everyone who knew her—Pinecraft, Florida, was somewhat of a letdown. From here, it wasn't all that picturesque or darling. It looked a bit weather-beaten and stuck in a time warp.

Then, too, they weren't near the beach or even Pinecraft Park. They were standing in the middle of a large, crowded parking lot next to a tiny post office. Another bus was parked nearby, idling listlessly, casting off noxious fumes and no small bit of heat. That extra blast certainly wasn't needed, given that the hot July sun was already beating down on them all.

"It sure is hot," Sherry continued. "Really hot."

It was so hot and humid Sharon could practically see steam rising from the pavement. But her main concern was that her sister sounded so disappointed, especially after all the exciting letter writing she'd been doing with her secret pen pal for six months. Sharon decided to try to console her a bit.

"Even the best vacation spots have parking lots. I bet the rest of Pinecraft is just as charming as everyone said it would be."

"Maybe. I don't know, though."

As Sharon scanned the great number of people who had come out to meet the bus, she added, "Oh, who cares? I know you don't. We both know you didn't come here to take in the sights."

Stretching her arms out in front of her, Sherry nodded with a sheepish smile. "You're right. I'm sorry. I think I'm just tired. And *neahfich*."

"*Nee* apologies needed. I feel nervous too. And it was a long trip. I didn't sleep more than a few hours of it."

"I'm exhausted too," Sharon's best friend, Vera, said as she tumbled out of the bus. Her arms were full of the two dozen items she'd claimed were necessities for the hour drive from their Amish community in Adams County to Cincinnati and the sixteen-hour bus ride from Cincinnati to the center of Sarasota, Florida. "I can't wait to get unpacked, organized, and take a nap."

"There's *nee* way I want to do any of that right now," Carla declared. She was the fourth and final member of their group. "I'm excited to see everything. And to get a peek at Sherry's mysterious pen pal." She turned to her best friend. "*Now* are you going to tell us his name . . . finally? All we know is that you met him at the wedding in January."

"Oh, all right," Sherry said. "His name is Graham Holland, and he's from Sugarcreek."

Vera frowned. "That name doesn't ring a bell."

"Maybe you'll remember him when you see him. We met a lot of people those couple of days in Shipshe."

"I remember meeting Graham, but I don't remember exactly what he looks like," Carla said. "Do you, Sharon?"

Sharon shrugged. "The name sounds kind of familiar, but there were over four hundred people there. I don't think I could match any of their names with faces. They've turned into a blur in my brain."

"It's *nee* wonder. Six months ago you were still getting over your breakup with John Marc," Sherry said. "You didn't pay much attention to anything."

"That is kind of true." Less than two months before that trip to Indiana, she and John Marc had called off their relationship. It had been obvious that, although they were both nice people, a future together wasn't meant to be. Sharon had supposed they were both disappointed about how things worked out in the end.

That belief evaporated when, just a week before leaving for Indiana, Sharon saw John Marc flirting with Viola, one of her good friends. Then, days later Sharon learned the two of them had been quietly flirting with each other behind her back even before Sharon and John Marc broke up. Neither had wanted to hurt her feelings, they claimed, so they hadn't said a word.

Which, honestly, made no sense at all. John Marc had still cheated.

She'd been so embarrassed—and angry too. She'd alternated between fuming and crying the whole journey to Indiana. Watching that happy couple recite their vows had felt excruciating. Though she had nothing but good wishes for them, witnessing their ceremony was a reminder that she was a long way from celebrating her own wedding day. She'd been so melancholy and hurt she'd barely talked to anyone.

The only person she remembered in any detail was a man with sandy-brown hair and blue eyes. He'd been so nice and kind, and a little flirty. Handsome too. And for a few minutes, he'd helped her forget her disappointment and hurt. Ever since then she'd wished she could remember his name. But she couldn't remember anyone's name from that day, and she'd never even mentioned the incident to Vera, let alone to Sherry.

Sherry, on the other hand, had been her usual self, making friends right and left. She'd come home with a list of people she wanted to correspond with, having boldly asked the host family for all their addresses. As the months passed, Sherry told Sharon about some of her pen pals, including the mysterious man she'd just identified as Graham Holland. But Sharon had never paid too much attention since they all seemed like strangers to her.

As they waited for the bus driver to open the luggage compartments under the bus, Sherry scanned the area nervously. "Do you think he's here? He said he wouldn't come on account of the crowds. And I told him in my last letter, assuming he got it, that I'd see him at the inn. But maybe he's here."

"If he said he was going to skip this zoo, I bet he did," Vera said in complete confidence. "There must be over a hundred people here, all milling around. I'd avoid it if I could."

Sharon said nothing, but she nodded at Vera, letting her know she privately agreed with her.

Sherry shook her head in exasperation. "You girls have *nee* sense of adventure. I shudder to think what's going to happen to you when I'm settled and you have *nee* one to organize adventures."

"We'll miss you prodding us. For sure," Sharon said, thinking she really did need to start being a bit more like her little sister.

It was all because of Sherry's strengths as a correspondent that this whole trip had gotten off the ground. She and her mysterious man had begun writing letters to each other, and soon they were writing every week. Five months later, the two of them set up this trip for July, with Sharon, Vera, and Carla joining Sherry. Two of his friends were accompanying him here, too, as well as some others from his circle. Now they also knew they all hailed from Sugarcreek.

Everyone had rented rooms at the large Orange Blossom Inn, and they were going to spend the next two weeks enjoying the beach and all the sights the area had to offer.

Of course, Sharon also knew her twenty-year-old sister was privately hoping her many months of letter writing to Graham Holland were going to blossom into a summer romance.

Although their parents had at first not wanted them

to go, in the end they encouraged it. They knew both their daughters needed this trip to Pinecraft, giving them some time away to figure out what to do next in their lives. Sharon was completely over John Marc's betrayal and was eager to meet new people. And though several men they knew had been attempting to call on Sherry, she wasn't interested in any man except the one she was writing letters to.

As the four of them walked to the side of the bus, where the driver and two burly men were unloading the luggage stored underneath it, Sherry was looking over her shoulder, scanning the thirty or so people standing closest to the new arrivals.

Suddenly Sherry gripped Sharon's arm and whirled them both around. "I think that's him! He must have decided he couldn't wait to say hello at the inn. Isn't that something?"

"Well, I think that means he's smitten," Sharon said, teasing her sister with a smile. She really was happy for Sherry. She had such a good heart, and it was so romantic to imagine that she and this Graham had fallen in love through a series of letters.

Still staring across the parking lot, Sherry gave a little squeak. "Oh my heavens . . . It looks like he's trying to find us." When she turned to Sharon, a dozen imagined insecurities flickered across her face. "Do I look okay?" She ran her hands over her apron.

"Of course. Even after our long bus trip, you look perfect." Sherry was animated—like she always was, especially when she was excited. Her dark-auburn hair was falling out of its pins. Her green eyes were sparkling.

And her slim, athletic build was showcased in her clothes. She looked like she was ready for anything.

"You look *wunderbaar*," Vera said with a wink. "I'm certain this Graham is going to be real excited to spend more time with you. Why wouldn't he want to?"

Sherry brushed her fingers down the skirt of her pale-yellow dress. "I hope you're right. I'm going to be so embarrassed if he's disappointed. You know how some memories are distorted. He might have remembered me being prettier."

"He won't be disappointed," Sharon said. "Please don't think such things. You are lovely, and more fun and vibrant than most girls we know. Just be yourself. You're a wonderful-*gut* person."

Looking marginally more optimistic after that little pep talk, Sherry turned to Carla. "Will you walk over there with me?"

"Try to stop me," Carla teased as she grabbed Sherry's hand and led her through the crowd.

As they snaked their way through—Carla's coral dress and Sherry's yellow one mixing with the vivid colors of the other Amish summer dresses—Sharon smiled. Carla and Sherry were best friends and set off each other in the best ways. Carla was boisterous yet looked like a timid, perfect doll. Sherry, on the other hand, looked like a modern-day Amish Anne of Green Gables, ready to experience all Pinecraft had to offer.

Sharon laughed. "What I would give for even a tenth of their exuberance."

"We're only five years older than our sisters," Vera said, "but they make me feel old as the hills."

"Hardly that."

"Well, older and stodgier. Look how cute and fresh they look too. I, on the other hand, feel like a wrinkled mess."

Pressing her hands on her hips, Sharon leaned to one side. "Me too. And I'm stiff and sore. Sleeping on a bus is not comfortable."

"Sharon, tell the truth," Vera said a minute later as she returned from retrieving her and Carla's suitcases from the bus. "Were we ever that impetuous?"

"I know I wasn't. Maybe you were?"

Vera laughed. "Maybe I was when Stefan and I first started seeing each other."

"If you were, he must have liked it. After all, you *are* an engaged woman now."

Vera stood a little straighter and smiled. "That I am. And you are a maid of honor."

Sharon smiled back. She didn't want to do or say anything to spoil Vera's happiness, but being only a maid of honor wasn't exactly what she'd been hoping for a year ago.

She helped Vera locate the rest of their bags, said good-bye and thank you to the bus driver, and then the two women put all their belongings in a neat grouping so no one would accidentally walk off with them.

The hot Florida sun felt as though it was toasting her skin, and she was already sweaty and in need of a shower and a change of clothes. She also needed a couple of hours' sleep in a real bed.

"Now that we have all our bags, let's go see if we can round up those girls and get to the inn," Vera said. "I need a nap."

Scanning the thinning crowds, Sharon smiled. "You read my mind."

"There they are. Boy, Sharon," Vera murmured, "I didn't remember those guys looking like that. Did you?"

Sharon turned her head and followed her friend's gaze. And then she felt like gulping.

Sherry and Carla were standing with two men. They were chatting with them like they were long-lost friends. Long-lost best friends.

And the man standing closest to Sherry was not only smiling at her, but appeared to be intently listening.

He was easily the most handsome man Sharon had ever seen.

Her stomach dropped. He was also *that* man! The only man she remembered meeting at the wedding.

"Vera, you remember them? Do you know their names? I talked to one of those guys for a while the morning after the wedding."

Vera adjusted her glasses. "Really? Which one?"

Sharon realized the meeting that had been blurry for months was slowly becoming clearer. "I think he was that man with the sandy-brown hair. The man standing closest to Sherry. Do you by any chance remember his name?"

"Sure I do, now that I've put the name and face together. I *did* meet him at the wedding. That's Graham Holland."

His name was Graham. For a few minutes he'd made her feel special, helped her forget how her dreams of marrying John Marc were over, how John Marc and Viola had hurt her. He was the man she'd thought about from time to time since, and had kicked herself over not remembering his name.

He was her sister's pen pal?

She was starting to feel sick.

It didn't matter to Graham that he'd flirted with both sisters. He simply made a choice between them, exchanging letters with Sherry, dismissing Sharon as if they'd never met.

What kind of man did such a thing? Worse, what kind of sister was she for feeling even the smallest bit jealous?

CHAPTER 2

Graham wasn't exactly sure why he'd decided to come greet the Pioneer Trails bus after all. Maybe it was because he was so eager to see Sherilyn. Maybe he was simply tired of his buddies, Matthew and Toby, asking questions. He'd been fairly secretive about his pen pal, never even agreeing to tell them what she looked like.

Or maybe it was because he was too nervous to be completely alone when he and Sherilyn were first reunited.

Whatever the reason, he was now thoroughly confused. Sherilyn looked nothing like he remembered. The Sherilyn he'd recalled had light-brown hair, green eyes, and lovely, high cheekbones. She had a reserved air about her, almost tentative. She made him feel as though she needed a friend, and that friend should be him.

But this Sherilyn was the girl he only now remembered talking to a few times at the wedding. She was redheaded, freckle-faced, rather petite, and bold—not his usual type at all. Definitely not the picture he'd had in my mind all this time, flattered that she'd obtained his address and initiated their letter writing.

How had his memory been so wrong?

Now, after exchanging a few minutes of awkward conversation—a smile plastered on his face, desperately trying to covering up his dismay when she'd said, "Hi, Graham! It's me, Sherilyn!" and listening to her regret that he hadn't received her last letter—he was wishing he had *anywhere* else to go. He needed a few minutes to wrap his mind around the fact that he'd been writing to this near stranger.

"Oh! Now that the crowd has started to thin out, I see our sisters," Sherilyn said to Graham as she moved a step closer to him. Almost as if they were a couple.

He scanned the area. "Where are they?"

"There. The woman with the rose-colored dress is my sister, Sharon, and the woman in the violet-colored dress and wearing glasses is Carla's sister, Vera. Vera is Sharon's best friend."

He scanned the area, then froze as he realized that, while he might not have remembered this woman beside him very well, he definitely remembered the woman in the rose-colored dress.

He almost sighed in relief. Maybe he wasn't going crazy after all.

"I see them too," Carla called out. Seconds later, she groaned. "Uh-oh. They're standing near all our suitcases and bags. Sherry, we better go help them."

Turning to Graham and his friend Toby, Sherilyn said, "Would you guys like to come over and say hello, or just wait to meet the girls when we get to the inn?"

"We'll go over so we can help you with the bags," Toby said. "There's *nee* way we're going to let you carry everything on your own."

"That's so sweet of you."

"That's because we are sweet," Toby teased.

Still staring at the woman in the rose-colored dress, Graham murmured, "*Jah*. We'll go help you." As they started to move through the remaining crowd, he swallowed hard. "Hey, uh, Sherilyn, I'm sorry, but what are their names again?"

"My sister is Sharon. Her friend is Vera."

"Your sister is Sharon and you're Sherilyn. Your names are mighty similar. And Carla just called you Sherry too."

"They are similar, and I remember you commenting on that in one of your letters. And Sherry is a nickname you can call me if you like. Sharon and I were named after our parents' two favorite sisters. Sharon is our father's oldest sister, and Sherilyn is our mother's oldest sister." She sighed, revealing she'd told this story more than once. "Both my parents wanted to honor their sisters. After they named Sharon, *Mamm* teased my father, saying since he got his way for the first baby, she was going to get her way for the second . . . if they had a girl."

Graham couldn't help but chuckle. "And they did."

Smiling back at him, Sherilyn nodded. "Indeed, they did. So that's how I got my name. To be honest, I don't think they considered how our similar names might sometimes be a problem, especially when *Mamm* got mad at us. She'd trip over both our names!"

"I can see how that could happen. Especially, say, if one didn't know either of you well."

Maybe it was because of the tone of his voice, but Sherilyn began to look a little confused. "Um, anyway, that's my sister and Vera. Vera is engaged."

"Is Sharon betrothed too?"

"Oh, *nee*." Looking at him curiously, she said, "Why do you ask?"

"*Nee* reason," he said quickly. "I'm, uh, just trying to get to know everyone a little bit better." He knew that made him sound like an idiot, but at the moment he didn't care. Especially because he now realized he'd been writing to the wrong sister.

How could that have happened? How could he have been so stupid? At the wedding, he hadn't even realized these two were sisters. They were such different ages too. At least four or five years separated them!

"Come on, I'll go introduce you."

"*Danke*." Following Sherry, Graham knew he had about ten seconds to get his composure and his tongue under control. He needed to not embarrass Sherilyn—Sherry—her sister, or himself.

He had a feeling it was going to be a bit difficult.

The fact of the matter was that Sharon Kramer was even prettier than he remembered. She was truly beautiful. And that pale-pink dress she was wearing set off her pale, porcelainlike skin. Her brown hair was neatly confined under her *kapp*, and as he got closer he noticed the color of her eyes leaned more toward hazel than the true green of her sister's.

But it was the way she carried herself that held his attention and made his pulse beat a little faster. When they met at the wedding, his first impression had been that she needed a protector. But perhaps he'd been mistaken. She looked icily composed and calm. Reflective.

"Whoa," Toby murmured, low enough that Sherry couldn't hear. "Ain't she something?"

Yes. Yes, she was. Torn between continued dismay about what was happening and being strangely possessive over this woman, Graham was feeling more and more awkward. And sweaty.

Then there they were, all standing together.

"Sharon, this is Graham Holland," Sherry said. "Graham, please meet my sister, Sharon."

He held out his hand and gently clasped Sharon's hand in his own. "We've met," he said, searching her face. "Do you remember?"

She smiled, though that warmth didn't spread to her eyes. "I do, now that you mention it. We talked at the good-bye breakfast the morning after the wedding."

Sherry raised her eyebrows, obviously surprised. "You never told me you knew Graham."

"I didn't." Looking a little apologetic, and not as calm, Sharon sputtered, "I mean, we met, but we didn't really talk. Much. We didn't really know each other. I mean, not like you and Graham obviously knew each other before we headed home. We only shared one brief conversation."

Sherry's expression cleared. "Oh." Turning to Graham, she said, "Isn't that something? We only had a couple of short conversations, and that was in groups. Yet it meant enough for you to write me back . . . and send me those lavender seeds."

He hoped she would never find out he sent those seeds because he thought she smelled like fresh, fragrant lavender.

Well, her sister had.

"That is something," he agreed, his mouth going dry.

After Graham managed to introduce Toby to Sharon and Vera, and after Vera—to Graham's further embarrassment—reminded him he had met her at the wedding, too, Toby reached for one of the suitcases. "Are you girls ready to leave this parking lot? It's time to go, I think."

Looking around in surprise, Graham realized most everyone else had left. He took hold of the nearest suitcase. "I'll take this one."

Sherilyn frowned. "That one's Sharon's."

As if it was burning hot, he quickly released the handle. "Is that a problem?"

Sharon shook her head. "Of course not. Sherry, I'll simply take yours."

Suddenly looking embarrassed, Sherilyn mumbled, "*Nee*, I'm being silly. I can take my own. Let's just go."

That was how they all ended up in the formation they did, each one carrying at least one bag or suitcase. Toby was walking next to Vera, Sherry was following—whispering to Carla by her side—and he and Sharon were taking up the rear.

Graham was so tongue-tied he had no earthly idea what to say, so he decided to just keep quiet.

Sharon must have felt the same way, because she seemed content to stroll at his side, glancing at the shop windows and various front yards they passed, never saying a word. After they'd walked two blocks without speaking, Graham gathered himself and cleared his throat. "So, Sharon, are you exhausted from the journey here?"

"I wouldn't say I'm exhausted, but I am certainly tired. I'm not quite the traveler my sister is, I'm afraid," she said in an apologetic tone. "I guess I'm more of a homebody."

"I am, too, though I suppose it's by circumstance instead of choice. Farmers are tied to the land."

She turned to him, fresh awareness shining bright in her eyes. "I had forgotten you said you farmed. Tell me about it."

"About what? Planting corn?" He smiled, giving her an out. After all, who really wanted to hear about a farmer's life?

"*Jah*, I want to hear about planting corn. And plowing fields and whatever else farmers do."

"You're serious?"

She shrugged. "I am. Tell me all about it, Graham. I really am interested."

He doubted that, but he figured conversation about plowing and ears of corn was better than anything else he could think of. So he started talking about crop rotation and rainfall and worms and mud.

Sharon gazed ahead as they walked, but whenever he glanced at her, he could tell she was listening as though he was telling her something of value.

And just like that, he knew. Sharon was exactly the woman he'd remembered. And she truly was more than just a pretty face. She was special.

But of course, now if he told everyone the truth it would only set off a real mess of emotions. No, it was better to keep his secret to himself and hope neither sister ever discovered his mistake.

But then, while he was keeping that secret, maybe he could find a way to extricate himself from Sherry's grip and get Sharon Kramer to give him the time of day.

That was all. *Just that.*

He sighed. This vacation—the one he'd been counting the days toward—suddenly felt like the worst idea ever.

CHAPTER 3

The reunion had been awkward, and she'd known exactly why.

Sharon couldn't think of a more accurate word to describe how she felt when Sherry introduced her to Graham. From the moment she'd met his gaze, she'd been flustered—though she was thankful that even Vera hadn't seemed to be able to tell. Even though she'd been sure she blushed like a girl far younger than twenty-five, she had done her best to pretend she wasn't shocked to see this was the man her sister had been writing to for six months.

And she had done her best to pretend to her sister and their friends that she could totally see the two of them together.

But she couldn't. She decided then and there that she'd never tell Vera anything more about this if she didn't have to, even if she was her best friend. It was too embarrassing.

It didn't mean she was right about Graham, however. She'd been wrong about men and relationships before, especially when it came to herself. And not just with John Marc, either. No, she seemed to make a habit of misjudging men's interests, imagining there was spark in places there wasn't.

Now here they all were in the living room of the inn, just a couple of hours after arriving and getting settled in their rooms. Sharon was beginning to wish she was anywhere else.

Not a great way to start a two-week vacation.

Holding a heart-shaped cookie liberally frosted with light-pink frosting, Sharon debated whether to simply set it down on a plate and hope no one noticed she hadn't eaten it, or to find a place to throw it away without anyone seeing her do it.

She couldn't eat a thing.

She was the only one, though. It seemed that every afternoon, Mrs. Beverly Wagler served tea, cake, and cookies to her guests. Today she had fresh-baked brownies too. From what everyone had been telling her, and from what she observed, half her neighborhood stopped by as well. The Sugarcreek crowd, who had already been there two days, told the new arrivals the gathering wasn't to be missed.

Realizing she was going to have to find a way to eat this treat so she wouldn't seem rude, Sharon continued to nibble. It was a perfect sugar cookie. Firm but not hard, sweet and tinged with the faint essence of both vanilla and lemon. This proprietor definitely had a way around the kitchen.

"I trust your room is all right?" the innkeeper asked as she came to stand beside Sharon.

"Oh, yes!"

Beverly visibly relaxed. "Thank you for understanding. I don't know how the reservations got so mixed up, but I've felt awful about it. I know it must be awkward with your sister and friends in the triple upstairs while you're in the single room down here, on your own."

"Please don't worry about it. I like being on the first floor. As you might have noticed already, I'm a little on the quiet side. If I was up in the attic room, I'd be up all night with three women who really like to talk. Now, at least, I can be assured I'll get some rest."

"I've had more than one group of girls here over the years. You may have a point. Plus, it's not as if I'll mind if you go up and down the stairs as often you like, at all hours of the night too."

Sharon liked that image of her sneaking back to her room after a long night of laughing in the attic room upstairs.

"Is the cookie okay?"

"Yes. I'm, uh, just not as hungry as I thought I was."

Beverly pointed to a trash can. "If you don't want it, you can throw it out, dear. I promise I won't be offended."

"Thank you. I don't want to do that, though. It's really good. I work in a bakery, so I know cookies like this are to be treasured."

Beverly's cheeks turned pink. "That's so sweet of you to say. If you work in a bakery, I'm guessing you like to bake too?"

"I do. Very much."

"Maybe we can sit down one day and discuss recipes."

"I'd like that a lot."

Beverly smiled at her again before walking to the next guest.

"Your sister mentioned you work as a baker," Graham said as he drew up beside her, a thick, chocolate-chunk brownie in his hand.

"Yep. I've worked there for eight years now, since I was seventeen. I started washing dishes in the kitchen, then began helping all the ladies with the baking. Now I'm one of the lead bakers. I really enjoy it."

"My aunt works in a bakery in Sugarcreek. She says it's hard work."

"It is. Hot and a lot of heavy lifting too. But I love creating something people can enjoy immediately."

"That must be nice. Nothing happens like that in farming."

"*Jah*, but you also help create something other people enjoy."

He chuckled. "I never thought of corn like that."

"You should."

"I will, then. Anyway, your job sounds interesting. In her letters, Sherilyn told me about her nursery school job. I have to say I don't know how she does it. Watching all those *kinner* sounds chaotic and crazy. She must have the patience of a saint."

"She is patient. Well, with *kinner*."

Graham's gaze settled on her again, this time almost a bit uncomfortably long.

Sharon might have been imagining things, but she was beginning to get the feeling he wanted to talk to her about something but was trying to figure out the best way to do it.

She decided to put him out of his misery. "Did you want to talk about something special?"

"What? *Nee.*" He looked away.

"Oh." She was disappointed. He was obviously lying. But then he looked at her again, this time a little sheepishly.

"Sharon, I'm sorry. Something has been on my mind, but *nee* matter how I try, I can't think of an un-awkward way to say it."

"Un-awkward, hmm? Well, now you have to tell me. You've got my curiosity piqued."

"All right. Do you . . . do you ever wonder why some things happen the way they do?"

"You're still being awfully vague there, Graham."

"I guess I can't help but wonder why it was Sherilyn and me who started writing to each other."

It was as if he'd read her mind. Her secret, most self-ish thoughts. And that stung. Both because he was asking and because there wasn't anything she could say without hurting her little sister's feelings. "Does it matter?" she asked lightly.

"*Nee.* I mean, I guess it doesn't. I was just thinking about how strange it is the way things worked out."

"I can only imagine you encouraged Sherry to keep writing to you. Didn't you?" She was sure she was red-faced by now, but she had to know.

He opened his mouth, looked around in frustration, then signaled her to come with him. She hesitantly fol-lowed him through the groups of people and out the front door. Luckily, the rest of their friends had been in deep conversation or sorting through travel brochures. They hadn't seemed to notice them leaving.

When they were standing on the wide covered porch, Sharon said, "This is nice out here."

He leaned against the railing. "I'm sorry I brought any of this up."

"You didn't. I asked what was on your mind, remember?"

He looked relieved. "This is true. Anyway, you were right. It doesn't really matter how things worked out. The Lord is in charge, after all."

She was all for believing in the Lord guiding her life, but she couldn't help but think Graham was making a bit of a stretch. "The Lord?"

"*Jah*. I mean, it could have so easily been maybe Carla and Matthew writing. Or if you'd met him, Toby and you." He swallowed. "Even you and me. But instead it was Sherry and me."

Now that she understood where he was coming from, Sharon relaxed. "I see what you mean now. But you have to know Sherry. She's a super letter writer. She writes to everyone. And, well, at the wedding, I wasn't myself. And I still wasn't myself for a while afterward. I wouldn't have written to anyone."

"Why not?"

"When we met, it was just two months after I broke up with my boyfriend. I was pretty upset about what I found out afterward. He and my friend had been flirting behind my back."

"Are you doing better now?"

"I think so. It took a while, but I realized even if John Marc hadn't cheated on me, we wouldn't have made a *gut* match. We're too different."

"I'm sorry he treated you so poorly."

"*Danke*. It was hard. I won't lie. Actually, it put me in a bit of a tailspin." She tried to smile to take the sting out of her words. "Now that we're here, I do remember meeting you and some others from Sugarcreek. Normally, I would have wanted to get to know you all better."

"But . . ."

"But because of what happened with my boyfriend and friend, I wasn't sure if I could trust you." Hearing her words, she winced. Not only because what she said was the raw truth, but because she no longer felt Graham had behaved so badly. After all, he made her feel special that day, and she'd needed that.

"I'm sorry. That sounds bad," Sharon said.

"It doesn't. It sounds like you're a cautious woman."

"I've become one. I especially don't trust men too much anymore. At least ones who don't tell the truth."

"I bet you don't," he said after a pause.

To her surprise, Graham now looked even more agitated. "Um, did I say something wrong?"

"Not at all." He'd said that quickly, but his voice had an edge to it.

He seemed to be avoiding her eyes. "Sure?"

"Of course." Taking off his hat, he ran a hand through his hair. "Well . . . I'm sorry, but the truth is, I am concerned about something. It ain't important, though. It's especially not anything you need to worry about."

Taking a stab at what he might be talking about, she

said, "If you have any questions about Sherry, feel free to ask them."

He blinked. And looked even more uncomfortable. *"Danke."*

"I'm happy to help. I bet it's a bit difficult for the two of you to learn to communicate face-to-face now. I think it's easier to be more open and honest in a letter, don't you? People can take all the time they need to find just the right words."

"I never really thought about that. You're right. Getting to spend so much time writing those letters felt like a gift. Now I'm doing my best to figure out how to have the same kind of conversations. It *is* difficult."

"Maybe you don't need to worry so much, Graham. I mean, you're doing just fine now."

He swallowed so hard she could see his Adam's apple move. "Honestly, I don't know if I am or not."

"I'm sure everything will work out like it's supposed to." For a second, she was tempted to rest her hand on his arm. To assure him everything was going to work out the way the Lord intended.

But that sounded condescending and would probably reveal that she cared a little bit more for him than she should. Ruthlessly, she pushed her discomfort away. "Just remember that my sister has a soft heart," she said quietly. "She might come off as a little brash, but that's because she wears her heart on her sleeve."

"I'm sure she does," he agreed as the front door opened and the focal point of their conversation popped out.

Sherry looked from Sharon to Graham curiously.

"Hey. I've been wandering around looking for each of you. I didn't think you'd be out here together."

Sharon felt guilty even though she knew she'd done nothing to feel bad about. "Graham and I were catching up. The living room was noisy. We were having a difficult time carrying on a conversation."

Sherry smiled at Sharon's hand, which still held three-quarters of a frosted sugar cookie. "At least you took a snack out here with ya."

"I guess so. I, um, had forgotten this was in my hand."

After looking at her quizzically, Sherry turned to Graham and said, "Would you like to go for a walk? I know it's awfully warm, but we could stay in the shade of the trees lining the street."

"Uh, sure. That sounds *gut*. Are you ready to go now?"

The joy that transformed Sherry's features was a sight to behold. "I am."

"Then I am too."

Sharon made sure she kept a happy, carefree smile on her face as the couple walked down the steps.

No matter what, neither of them could ever find out a big part of her wished she was the girl walking by Graham's side.

CHAPTER 4

This situation had to be one of the most awkward of his life.

Graham approached Sharon and then invited her to talk outside with the purpose of getting to know her better—and to admit he hadn't realized he'd been writing to Sherry and not her this whole time.

He'd been certain complete honesty was the right thing. After all, they were about to spend fourteen days together. That was far too long to maintain a lie. So, though he'd been nervous, he'd also been determined to tell her the truth. He would have tried to get her to understand . . . if Sherry hadn't joined them with such an excited, expectant look on her face.

How could he embarrass Sherry by revealing he hadn't meant to be writing to her all these months? That would be cruel. Besides, Sharon had obviously and firmly latched onto the role of the caring older sister, and there was probably no real way she would ever accept that he wanted to date her and not Sherry. There was never going to be a right time to confess his mix-up.

As he and Sherry walked along the street in front of the inn, Graham forced himself to concentrate on the girl beside him and respond to the comment she'd just made. "*Jah*. I mean, it does seem like a nice time to go for a walk."

"I'm relieved to hear you say that. I have a bad habit of being a bit too forward. I think it comes from organizing small *kinner*," she said, joking. "I start wanting to organize everybody around me."

"It's not too forward It's refreshing."

Sherry smiled. "Carla and Toby and I were making plans. We thought it would be fun to go to Siesta Key on Monday, the day after tomorrow. What do you think?"

There was no mistaking the look of excitement and longing she wore. "I think that sounds like fun. Do you think you girls will be up for a day at the beach so soon after your long trip? It's taken us two days just to catch up on our sleep."

"Carla and I thought we could sleep all day tomorrow. That's the plan, anyway."

"I'll be sure to be quiet if I'm anywhere near the attic," he teased.

Her eyes twinkled. "That will be appreciated. Anyway, we figure by Monday we'll be more than ready to see the ocean. I can't wait to see it."

"You have a point there. You should probably be going to the beach at every opportunity."

"So, um . . . do you want to join us?" Her question sounded awkward and tentative.

It shouldn't have sounded either way.

Fact was, he was definitely not opposed to going to the beach. His buddies had come to Florida for a vacation, not just for his suddenly drama-filled life. That said, he was also opposed to leading Sherry on. His letters had been bad enough, but now he really didn't want to make her think he regarded her as other than a younger sister.

Although . . . maybe he wasn't even sure about that? Her letters had meant something to him. He'd loved them. He'd looked forward to receiving them. Didn't that mean he owed it to Sherry to take the time to get to know her better? He decided to get some more information.

"Who else wants to go? Or is it just the three of you?"

"I haven't talked to Sharon about it yet, but I bet she'll go. And if she goes, then Vera will too."

Here was his answer. "If Vera and Sharon go, I'll go as well. You'll need more men with you."

Sherry looked taken aback for a second before nodding agreeably. "Yeah. Okay. That makes sense."

"What time do you want to leave?"

"Carla wants to be sure she gets some more sleep. Maybe around nine thirty? Is that time *gut* for you? It's late, but maybe not too late for vacation."

"It's a date then," he quipped, then wished he'd said just about anything else when he saw Sherry's look of pure happiness.

How in the world was he going to get himself out of this mess? And if and when he did, how was he ever going to get Sharon to give him the time of day?

He really was too old for this.

. . .

It was almost nine o'clock on the day of their trip to the beach, and Sharon was the first to arrive for breakfast.

Secretly pleased by this, she took another fortifying sip from her coffee cup and eagerly unwrapped her muffin.

The muffin had an orange marmalade glaze and swirls of cream cheese running through its center. Saying it was delicious was an understatement.

"Oh, good. I see you've already found the muffins," Beverly said when she entered the dining room. "I hope you're enjoying yours?"

"I think this is one of the best I've ever eaten. Do you share your recipes?"

"Of course. I'll write it out for you before you head back to Ohio."

"*Danke*. But I hate for you to go to any trouble. I'm happy to do the copying myself. I have a feeling I'll be asking you for several recipes. You really are gifted."

"That's very sweet of you to say." Pleasure lit her green eyes. "My husband, Eric, keeps telling me I should put together a cookbook for guests to purchase. I haven't wanted to tackle that project yet, but it might save me time in the long run."

"I bet it will. I can't imagine you aren't asked for recipes at least once a week."

"I am." Her cheeks flushed. "Now I just need to figure out how to get started on it."

"I could help you, if you'd like," Sharon offered. If she worked on the cookbook, she wouldn't have as much time to watch Graham court Sherry. It felt like a perfect solution.

"What? Of course you can't! You're on vacation."

"This would be a fun project for me." Sharon held up a hand. "But I don't want to overstep my bounds. If you don't want any help, I understand. It's just that I really love to bake and would enjoy helping you."

"I . . . well, thank you. I might take you up on that," she said, just as a handsome man in a wrinkled pair of shorts, a dark-blue T-shirt, and bare feet wandered in.

Right in front of Sharon, he pressed a kiss to Beverly's temple. "You sound like you're hatching a plan."

"I am. At least, I think I am." Turning to Sharon, Beverly said, "Sharon, please meet my husband, Eric. Eric, this is Sharon Kramer. She wants to help me work on that cookbook with my recipes while she's here."

Interest lit his eyes. "Really? That's terrific. I've been telling my wife I'll take care of getting everything typed, printed, and bound into books, but I can't do anything without those recipes. This is really kind of you."

"Not so much. Besides, if I help, I'll get to see all the recipes myself," she said, making a joke.

Beverly chuckled. "I like how you think. You just let me know when you want to get started, and we'll come up with a time."

"I will," Sharon promised as the room began to fill with her friends and other guests. "We're going to Siesta Key today, but while we're there, we're also going to make some tentative plans for the rest of our vacation. I'll touch base with you tonight."

"That sounds perfect." Smiling broadly, Beverly added, "I better go get more coffee going."

"I'll help bring out more platters of muffins and that hash brown casserole too," her husband said.

As they darted into the kitchen, the white door swinging in their wake, Sherry arrived at Sharon's side.

"Sorry we're late. I'm afraid we stayed up talking last night."

"I wasn't in any hurry. Actually, I was having a *gut* conversation with Beverly and Eric about cookbooks."

Sherry wrinkled her nose. "Only you would be talking about baking when we're heading to the beach."

"I know. I can't seem to help myself, though."

Sherry patted her on the arm. "You know I'm kidding! Now, I need coffee and something to eat."

Sharon took a seat as her sister, joining the other late arrivals at the sideboard, began filling her plate.

"Anyone sitting here?" Graham asked.

"Not yet," she said with a shy smile.

"Great." He set a glass plate piled high with fruit on the table. "I'll be right back."

When he returned with even more food, Sharon couldn't help but be impressed with the amount he planned to consume. "Do you eat like this every morning?"

"I wish, but *nee*. Usually I make myself a big bowl of oatmeal or cook a couple of eggs," he said after he paused for a moment to say a quick, silent prayer of thanks. "But I do eat a lot of food. That's what happens when you work in the fields all day long."

"I bet. You didn't say the other day. Have you harvested your corn yet?"

"*Nee*, it needs another three weeks, which is what made this the perfect time for me to get away. It's going to be a grueling few days when I get home."

"But you have a lot of help, don't you?"

"Sure. My two brothers, Robert and Caleb, plus my

father, an uncle, and a cousin. We also hire some temporary workers for two of the three days."

"I'm impressed."

He shrugged. "It's a pretty big farm. We plant over three acres of corn alone. A *gut* crop makes our year."

"*Jah*, I suppose it does." She sipped her coffee and smiled as he dug into his egg-and-sausage casserole with obvious gusto.

He paused in midbite. "Am I being rude?"

"Not at all. I've been here for a while."

"An early riser, hmm?"

"Not especially, but I guess I was today compared to everyone else," she said as Graham's friends Matthew and Toby joined them.

After the two men prayed and they all marveled at the array of breakfast food, Graham said, "Did I overhear you talking to Mrs. Wagler about working on a cookbook?"

She was embarrassed now. "You did. I know I'm on vacation, but I guess I can't help but lean toward all things food and baking."

"You shouldn't apologize for finding something that sparks your interest. It's kind of you to want to help her too."

"The project will do me *gut*. I am looking forward to going to the beach today, but I have *nee* desire to spend every day there."

Matthew held out an arm. "Me neither, Sharon. I'm so pale I'm going to have to slather on sunscreen every ten minutes."

She laughed. "I'm sure you're exaggerating, but I bet you can't be too careful."

"Matthew works third shift at the brickyard in Sugarcreek," Graham told her, explaining why his friend had no tan at all.

"So if you ever need someone to hang out with while everyone else is out in the sun, I'm your man," Matthew said with a grin.

"I'll keep that in mind."

"Now I, on the other hand, already have a *gut* base tan," Toby said, holding out a lightly tanned forearm.

"He works construction," Graham explained.

"That means if you ever need something built, I'm the guy to talk to," he said, winking at her.

His flirty comment was so fun, she giggled. "Careful, Toby, I may just take you up on that."

"I promise, you calling on me wouldn't be a hardship."

She giggled again, liking how lighthearted he was. As she picked up her cup, she glanced Graham's way and was startled to see he was frowning at Toby as though he'd just done something wrong.

Toby must have felt the tension, because he looked at Graham, raised his eyebrows, then smirked. "You got a problem, Graham?"

After a pause, Graham shook his head. *"Nee."*

"Gut."

As Matthew coughed, Graham's expression hardened. Luckily Vera stood up at one end of the table and diffused the burst of tension that had just risen.

Holding up a printed pamphlet, she said, "I've got

the schedule of the SCAT, the Sarasota County Area Transit system, and a bus for Siesta Key leaves in fifteen minutes. Can we make it?"

"I can," Sharon said. She stood up and walked to her girlfriend's side. She needed some distance between her and Graham before she began imagining there was something romantic between them.

That would be a huge mistake.

CHAPTER 5

Though the sun was shining and she was excited to be going to the beach, Sherry felt a little uneasy. She was beginning to feel as though something wasn't quite right between her and Graham. Oh, he'd been friendly. He'd also acted pleased to see her again when she arrived on Saturday. But something in his letters to her was missing now.

At first, she thought he was simply a little shy. Then she thought he was one of those rare people who communicated far better in letters than in person. Finally, she began to wonder if maybe his letters hadn't been all that warm or special after all. Maybe they'd simply been . . . letters. Friendly, to be sure, but not filled with hope for a future relationship as she'd imagined.

It was really too bad that she hadn't brought the letters with her. Then she could compare them to the man she was coming to know.

If she ever really got to know Graham, that is, since right now he seemed to be avoiding her.

As the SCAT bus made another stop, Sherry watched Graham and Sharon—and fretted. They were sitting together in front while she was sitting in the last row.

"If you sigh again, people around us are going to think you have some kind of lung ailment," Carla whispered. She was sitting next to Sherry, by the window. "What's wrong with you?"

"Nothing. I'm fine."

"Sherry, please, don't play this game. I know something is bugging you. Tell me. You know I won't give up until you tell me what has you so upset."

Knowing Carla wasn't joking—she would nag until Sherry finally told her what was on her mind—Sherry looked down the aisle. After making sure Toby, Matthew, and Vera weren't in hearing distance, she whispered, "I don't think Graham likes me anymore."

Carla's eyebrows rose. "What makes you say that?"

"A lot of things."

"Such as?"

"First of all, look who he's sitting next to. It's Sharon, not me."

Carla shrugged. "Don't go making a problem where there ain't one. You can see how crowded this bus is. We all had to take seats wherever we could find them."

Shaking her head impatiently, Sherry said, "It's more than that. Graham hardly looks at me. And when I mention something he wrote in one of his letters, he gets this weird expression on his face. It's strange. Almost like he's embarrassed that we wrote to each other for months."

"I'm sure he's not embarrassed. After all, if it hadn't been for you two writing to each other, none of us would be here now."

"Oh, I know that. But he's different, Carla." As she noticed Graham cocking his head, evidently to be sure he heard something Sharon said, frustration and jealousy churned in her stomach. "He's distancing himself. I know it."

"I haven't noticed him doing that."

"I have. And wouldn't I notice it more than you?"

"Not necessarily. We just got here," she said in her matter-of-fact way.

Continuing to stare at Graham and her sister, Sherry mumbled, "This is just terrible. I really . . . I *thought* I knew him." To her embarrassment, she heard her voice tremble. "I had such high hopes too."

Carla pursed her lips as the bus stopped again. Two English teenagers got off, and an older couple climbed aboard and took their seats. When the bus pulled forward, she said, "Sherry, I don't want to hurt your feelings, but I think you've put too much hope in those letters. *Jah*, you've been writing to each other for months. *Jah*, you probably also shared some things. But that doesn't mean you had a relationship. Be honest, now. You don't actually know Graham."

Sherry wanted to argue with her. She wished she could pull out one of those letters and prove to Carla that she hadn't been wrong to expect that she and Graham would be a couple when they reunited in Pinecraft.

But of course, she didn't have the letters with her. She wouldn't embarrass either of them by sharing their private correspondence anyway.

As the bus sped along the long causeway that led to Siesta Key, Sherry began to wonder if she had, in fact, put way too much emphasis on mere letters. Sure, they'd been lovely. The novelty of having a handsome pen pal was exciting too. But they weren't the same as having a real conversation with someone face-to-face—or, in Graham's case, avoiding that conversation.

Unable to help herself, she sighed again.

Carla groaned. "Sherry, you are driving me crazy."

"I'm sorry my pain is causing you to be uncomfortable."

"Your moping around is going to spoil a perfectly nice vacation," she said loud enough for the man sitting across the aisle to look at them in alarm.

"Hush, Carla."

"I'll hush if you promise to stop acting like this meeting in Pinecraft was supposed to result in a marriage proposal. Stop putting so much pressure on yourself and on Graham too. Why don't you just try to relax and enjoy our vacation? It's not going to be the end of the world if you and Graham don't get together. Or if you meet someone else you like better."

As the words sank in, Sherry was finally able to look away from Graham and Sharon. "Do you think that's possible?"

"Of course it is. We're only twenty! Let's just have fun. I mean, even if we go home with only tans and some *gut* memories, that's going to be more than enough."

"*Jah.* You're right." She felt self-conscious now that she was admitting to herself that she had actually dreamed about Graham and their practically running into each other's arms in the bus parking lot. She chuckled softly. "*Danke.* You gave me some perfect advice."

"You're not mad at me for bursting your bubble?"

"Not at all. You are exactly right. Here we are, under

the beautiful Florida sun, and I don't have to work for two weeks. I need to definitely start looking on the positive side of things."

"*Gut* job," Carla said as the bus pulled into the middle of a large parking lot next to the beach. "And just in time, too, because we've arrived."

"*Danke* again, Carla."

"*Nee* problem," she replied. "That's what friends are for."

"Indeed."

As everyone got to their feet, Sherry gazed out at the beautiful white sand and turquoise water that was so famous.

Now, this place, at least, wasn't destined for disappointment. She was fairly sure Siesta Key was going to surpass her greatest expectations.

CHAPTER 6

Graham's first impression of Siesta Key was that it was beautiful—right on the expansive Gulf of Mexico and no doubt one of the most stunning places on God's earth. The beach was wide and uncluttered and went on for miles. A person could walk for a solid hour without having to turn around. The fine sand looked almost pure white and felt like sugar slipping between his fingers and toes.

And the water! It was clear as glass, greenish-blue, and felt just two shades cooler than bath water. Boats and ships and other watercraft bobbed in the distance.

The only structures in sight were a snack shack and evenly spaced lifeguard shacks. All were built out of wood and painted primary colors. Their bright red, blue, and yellow forms dotted the landscape and made him smile. Feeling fanciful, Graham decided those buildings illustrated how absolutely picture-worthy and charming the small island was. Graham felt the builders had done a very fine job.

When they first arrived, Sherry, Carla, and Matthew had led the way. Even though none of them had been to the area before, they had definite ideas about where to set up camp. He, on the other hand, couldn't imagine any spot he wouldn't want to be.

He, Sharon, Vera, and Toby followed the trio and stood to one side while they debated. Graham was amused at how Sharon seemed more than happy to let her little sister take the lead. That was so different from the dynamics with his brothers at home. There was a definite pecking order there. His older brother, Robert, wanted to lead Graham and their younger brother, Caleb, all the time and no matter how old they got.

Once the perfect spot had been selected, Graham followed the rest of the group and laid his towel on the outskirts of their claim. He never liked to be confined and wanted to have room to spread out. Plus, he knew he would want to get up and walk around a lot, especially since it was so hot. He had no desire to disrupt everyone else's relaxation, stepping around them or getting sand in their food or drinks.

He couldn't help but notice Sharon picked the same sort of spot on the opposite side of their group. He wondered if she did that because she, too, wanted room to move around.

But now, from the way she seemed to be trying to look everywhere but at him, he suspected her reasoning had to do with creating distance she didn't have on the bus.

Their talk had been a little stilted, as though she wished she were sitting with someone else. That surprised him after their conversation on the porch Saturday night and this morning at breakfast. He thought she'd warmed up to him a bit.

Or maybe she, too, was aware of the strange connection that was happening between them? A connection she thought her sister wouldn't like? He hadn't been thrilled when Toby flirted with her earlier, but he didn't think she . . .

He didn't know what to think. And he didn't know what to do. He'd written to the wrong sister and hadn't even been brave enough to come right out and tell either of them. Instead, he was mooning over Sharon and avoiding Sherry.

He was fairly sure this wasn't going to end well, and it would be all his fault.

Just as he decided to let the Lord take care of his problems and exhaled, he saw Sherry pull off her dress to reveal a one-piece bathing suit.

Realizing his face was probably turning a deep red, he jumped to his feet.

"What are you doing?" Toby asked, brushing the sand he'd kicked up off his left arm.

"I'm going for a walk."

"Already? We just got here."

"Yeah, well, I like walking."

Turning away, he resolutely kept his gaze straight ahead as he raced away. He had no desire to encourage any further connection to Sherry, and he couldn't get away fast enough.

After a couple of minutes, Toby caught up to him.

"Something wrong?" Graham asked.

"Nah. All of a sudden I just decided I felt like walking too."

Graham doubted that. Toby worked construction in

Millersburg. The guy was active all day, every day. All he'd been talking about from the time they'd planned this trip was how great it would be to sit around and do nothing.

But if he knew anything about Toby, it was that he'd share what was on his mind when he felt the time was right. After they passed another lifeguard shack, Graham said, "The sand and surf feel great on bare feet. Ain't so?"

"*Jah.*"

Another couple of minutes of silence passed before Toby said, "Hey, Graham? I need to ask you something."

"Sure. What is it?"

After Toby looked at the waves for a couple of beats, he turned back to Graham. "Well, I need to know this. Which one of the Kramer sisters do you like?"

He was so caught off guard, Graham stopped and stared. He and Toby had been best friends from the time they were seven or eight years old. They'd discussed all kinds of things and had even gotten each other through their *rumspringa* when both of them had done some pretty foolish things.

But they'd never discussed women. At least, not like this. He'd never told Toby much about his correspondence with Sherry, or even Sherry herself. Good thing, since it turned out Sherry wasn't Sharon.

This made him uncomfortable, though he knew it was mainly because he didn't know how to confess what a mess he'd made with both women.

Feeling as though he needed to be walking to continue the conversation, he moved on. "Why are you asking?"

"Because you're making me pretty confused." Pulling up his sunglasses, revealing serious eyes, Toby added, "Maybe you could take a stab at clearing the air."

Ruthlessly, Graham picked up his pace. "I'm not dating either woman. You know that."

"I do know that."

"Then what's the problem?"

"Well, Sherry acts as though your letter writing has been a little more significant than you led me to believe. And when her bus arrived, she seemed like she could be expecting a relationship with you." He paused, then raised one eyebrow. "But on the other hand, it seems to me that you like Sharon as well. A lot. Do you?"

Did he? A lot? He didn't know.

And that was terrible. It was also embarrassing. No. Beyond embarrassing. The last thing he wanted was to be seen as a man who played with women's hearts.

In a poor effort to evade the question, he blurted, "For the last time, I ain't with either woman." Hopefully Toby would get the hint and drop the subject.

Unfortunately, he didn't. Sounding progressively irritated, Toby said, "You know why I'm asking. Don't act like you don't know."

Graham glanced at his best friend again, forcing himself to wrap his mind around the fact that Toby was feeling tentative about a girl. Most likely about Sharon.

The fact was, if Sharon was a woman who was much sought after, Toby was very likely her male counterpart. Blessed with dark-brown eyes, matching hair, and a perpetual tan, he stood out among many of the fair-skinned, fair-haired Amish men. Added to his list of attributes were his quiet, almost old-fashioned demeanor and his size. The man was easily two hundred and fifty pounds and over six feet tall. Yet because he worked construction, specializing in roofs and trusses, he had a grace to him that belied his size. Women all over Holmes County flirted with him. More than a few had let it be known they would love to be courted by him.

In addition, Graham didn't know one person who wasn't fond of the guy. Toby was loyal and friendly. He didn't deserve Graham's attitude.

"You're right," he said at last. "Sherry is the one I've been writing to, but—"

"Wait. Why don't you sound very glad about that?"

"Probably because I, uh, hadn't realized some things about her when we started corresponding."

Toby raised his eyebrows. "What did you discover?"

Graham wished he could blurt out his case of mistaken identity, but he was sure there was no way to admit such a thing without being unkind to both girls. "Um, first off, I hadn't realized how young she is."

"How old is she?"

"Twenty. I heard her tell someone she's twenty."

"Why is that a concern for you? Twenty ain't too young at all. She's more than old enough to be courting."

"That is true. But that doesn't mean I didn't think she was older. I thought she was twenty-two or twenty-three."

Toby scoffed. "You make that sound like a huge difference. It ain't."

Graham sighed. "You're right. It ain't."

"What else is the problem?"

Graham knew he needed to be more forthcoming. Looking off into the distance, he said, "Sherry's sister has been a surprise to me. I find Sharon easy to talk to. And, well, I don't think it's happenstance that she's here too. I'm wondering if maybe the Lord meant for me to meet Sharon through Sherry. So, um, that's why I've been talking to her as well."

Toby's expression turned chilly. "I find that excuse hard to believe."

Graham did as well. But that didn't mean he could back down. "You shouldn't find it hard to believe at all. After all, it's true. It's not an excuse."

"Graham, have you heard what you're saying to me?"

He had and he was embarrassed about it. But what was he supposed to do? Hating this situation he'd put himself in, he blurted again. "Toby, I haven't been trying to court two women at the same time. It's all just turned out that way."

"But you are. And if I'm noticing, everyone else is too."

"I feel certain everything will be resolved soon. Don't forget, it's only been a couple of days."

"I'm not forgetting that I've seen both women studying you with questions in their eyes. It ain't right."

Graham felt trapped. "You mean it ain't right for you. Don't you think you're sounding an awful lot like a moony teenage boy? I mean, who notices how much time other people spend together? Maybe the problem lies with you, Toby."

His best friend flinched. But instead of backing off, he raised his hands in frustration. "Comments like that are what I'm talking about. You never talk like this. Something with these women has hit a nerve." Before Graham could dispute that, he added, "Don't start lying again, either. I saw that look you sent my way at breakfast. There was something in your expression when you looked at Sharon and me. It sure wasn't that she meant nothing to you."

"I didn't—"

"Oh, *jah*, you did. You practically sent me a death glare when I offered to spend time with her."

Everything Toby was saying was right. But because he still wasn't sure what to do, Graham decided to stay on the offensive. "Instead of asking me twenty questions and chiding me for not being completely honest, why don't you share what's on your mind? Who are *you* after? Do you want to spend time with Sharon or Sherry?"

Toby laughed. "With Sharon, of course. Her sister is a firecracker. She'd wear me out in two minutes. Plus, those freckles and red hair? Not my type."

"Sherry is cute in her own way," he spit out automatically. Now, why did he feel the need to defend the girl he didn't want to date?

Seeing a fence signaling the boundary of a private resort, they turned around and headed back. Graham was surprised how far they'd walked. He couldn't see any of their group in the distance.

Not in any hurry to return, he slowed his pace. Toby matched it exactly, looking more than a little relieved as he wiped a sweat-soaked brow.

"So is that my answer, then? You like Sherry and you're all right if I spend time with Sharon?"

He cared. He cared a lot. But he didn't see how he was ever going to make his wants a reality. He was one of three brothers, but he'd heard sisters had an even stronger bond when it came to love and romance. Never would he want to hurt Sherry because he longed for her older sister.

It would be best to simply stay out of both women's lives.

Plus, Toby was a good man. He was hardworking and kind. And a little on the shy side, he'd be perfect for a quiet woman like Sharon. A kind person who would treat her well.

With all that in mind, was there really any doubt about what his answer should be? "If you want to spend time with Sharon, I think you should. I won't be mad, and I'll even support you in any way I can."

Toby exhaled. "Boy, you had me going there for a bit. *Danke*."

His buddy sounded so relieved, Graham almost smiled. "Sharon really means that much to you?"

"I don't know if she does or not. I do know she's intrigued me in a way few other women have."

"Ah."

"Graham, the reason I came to talk to you is that our friendship is what means so much. I don't want to step on any toes."

"You won't."

"*Gut*." Looking a far sight happier, Toby said, "I'm so glad everything is out in the open now. It's better that way, *jah*?"

"For sure and for certain." Well, it would if everything actually *was* out in the open. Realizing they were almost back to the rest of the group, Graham asked, "Is there anything else you want to discuss, Toby?"

"Of course not. We're at the beach to relax, not discuss every problem in our lives." Looking satisfied, he added, "I'm going to go buy myself a bottle of water and then sit on my towel for the rest of the morning and afternoon."

"Me, too, though I'll probably cool off in the water too. It's hot out here."

"Yeah, well, people say July is a hot month."

Toby and his gift for understatement. Graham grinned in spite of himself. "*Danke* for talking to me. And *gut* luck with Sharon." Realizing luck didn't have much to do with it, he said, "I mean, I hope you and Sharon will find yourselves to be happy together."

"*Danke.* I don't know if I'm what she's looking for, but I have to try, you know? Girls like her are few and far between," he said before veering over to the snack shack.

Unfortunately, Graham knew far too well what his buddy meant. Girls like Sharon were mighty special.

But friends like Toby were too.

CHAPTER 7

Although a lot of Amish girls wore bathing suits, Sharon wasn't quite ready for that. Oh, she'd bought one, of course. She and Sherry had gone into Millersburg and tried on swimsuits almost a month ago.

At first they'd been afraid of what their mother would say about making such a purchase. Sherry, being Sherry, hadn't wanted to tell *Mamm*. She said their mother would never need to know what they'd done. But Sharon hadn't felt okay with that. She'd hesitantly told their mother they intended to wear swimsuits at the beach in Siesta Key. Modest ones, of course.

To her surprise, *Mamm* had just laughed. "You act as if I've never been young, child. Wear one if you must. I'm sure it will be a great deal more comfortable than sitting on the beach in a dress."

They'd taken their mother's comments to heart and had quite a grand time picking out suits to try on.

Checking herself in the dressing room mirror had been a whole other story, however. She frowned when she stared at herself from every angle. Her skin had looked as pale as a newborn babe's, and her hips and thighs had seemed far bigger than the mannequins' in the store.

When Sherry knocked on her door and showed Sharon her choice, she mentioned the same concerns about herself. But they'd done it. They'd each bought a modest one-piece suit. Modest for the Englishers, that is.

But this morning even though she knew it covered her up sufficiently, Sharon felt her swimsuit was far too revealing. So she'd worn her lightest and baggiest dress over it, in case she chickened out. Then when Sherry revealed hers—practically the moment she'd sat down on her beach towel—Sharon had known she couldn't do it. Not yet.

Sharon knew her sister's look of triumph had been directed at her. Sherry was pleased she was pushing herself a bit and wanted Sharon to do the same. But although she was hot, Sharon was still too self-conscious.

Thankfully, her sleeves were loose enough that she'd been able to roll them a few inches above her elbows. When she'd sat down, she'd pulled the skirt of her dress up to reveal her knees. And now that was how she was sitting—modestly and mildly warm, with some of her dress's fabric sticking to the middle of her back. Soon after Sherry's big reveal, Carla and Vera had pulled off their dresses and were sunbathing in swimsuits too. Matthew was beside them, putting an awful lot of sunscreen on himself.

Sharon sighed and stretched out her legs, grateful Vera would never push her to do anything she didn't want to do. But boy, she wished she'd been braver! Now if she pulled off her dress it would look awkward. She was going to have to deal with her big reveal the next time they went to Siesta Key. And, she realized with a bit of embarrassment, she should also remember looks aren't that important. She mustn't be too prideful.

"You want a cold bottle of water?" Toby asked as he shook out his towel and sat down next to her.

He had shorts on, and his calves and knees were already starting to darken. Realizing how silly it was to stare at his legs, she diverted her eyes.

But what caught her eye next was the pleasant, kind way he was looking at her. Like he wanted to be her friend.

Forcing herself to examine the bottle he was holding out, she noticed it had droplets of condensation all over it. "*Danke*. Few things have ever looked so *gut*."

"Oh, I can think of a few," he said with a smile.

"Such as?"

"Why this beach, for one. The ocean for another."

He was absolutely right. She needed to stop worrying what everyone was thinking about her and simply enjoy herself. "I think I walked into that, didn't I? Here I am, sitting on one of the most beautiful beaches in the world, and I haven't even taken the time to properly give thanks for it."

"I'm sure the Lord knows you're pleased with His work, Sharon."

She smiled at him. "Indeed, I'm sure He does."

He unscrewed his bottle cap and promptly swallowed a good half of the bottle's contents. "Boy, was I thirsty."

She laughed. Toby was so open and vibrant! Almost like a puppy. She found him easy to be around and easy to talk to. "You and Graham went on a long walk."

"We went farther than I intended. I hadn't planned on walking with him that long."

Liking how he simply said whatever was on his mind, she added, "I thought maybe you were going to go for a swim, but instead it looked like you were racewalking."

"What you saw was correct." He grimaced. "We were race-walking. Practically running."

If they did it all the time, that meant he liked it, right? But he was acting as if he didn't care for it one bit. "Do you and Graham do that a lot?"

"Nee." After he finished the rest of his water, he put the cap back on the bottle and tossed it into a nearby canvas tote bag. "We had some things to talk about. Graham . . . well, Graham likes to walk and talk at a brisk pace. I reckon it has something to do with all those acres he walks when he inspects his corn."

"But not you?"

"Nee. I'm in construction. I spend most of my days running around whatever building I'm working on. I like to sit down when I can. I'm lazy that way."

Sharon firmly pushed down that little burst of appreciation whenever she heard Graham's name. He was her sister's beau. What she needed to do was concentrate on Toby. He was handsome and kind. She could probably learn to like him a lot if she just gave him a chance!

She smiled at him more brightly. "I'm lazy that way too. I work in a bakery, so I like to rest when I can."

"My aunt worked at a bakery in Walnut Creek. She took care to tell me it was much more work than handing out donuts!"

"It is. Absolutely. I've been giving thanks all day for

the fact that I'm not pulling heavy trays in and out of ovens. Some nights when I get home, I have to lie down on the floor to relieve the cramps in my back."

Toby stared at her in concern. Then he said softly, "Those commercial ovens can be dangerous, especially for a slight girl like you."

She'd never thought of herself as slight, but she did like the way he said the word. Like being slight was a good thing. "I'm stronger than I look. Though I have had my share of little accidents while I learned the best way to pull out heavy sheet pans."

"Is this a work injury?"

"Is what a work injury?"

Carefully, as if he feared he was going to bruise her, he looped his thumb and fingers around her wrist and turned her arm.

And sure enough, there was a burn mark on her forearm. Eyeing the dark-red patch that was only about a half inch in length, she said, "I've had that for so long, I'd almost forgotten about it."

His hand remained where it was. Then, ever so slowly, he ran one finger along the mark. She shivered involuntarily.

His brows pulled together. "Does it hurt?"

"*Nee*. Not at all." No, she surely wasn't hurting from his touch. But she was reacting to him in a way that caught her off guard.

With his fingers still on her arm, he murmured, "How did you get it?"

She was becoming flustered.

Nervously, she pulled her arm away, then took another

sip from her water bottle. She tried to think of an interesting way to tell what had happened to her. That would be kind of difficult though, for it was actually a boring story. "I'd love to tell you it was when I was doing something out of the ordinary, but it was just a simple mistake. I was paying more attention to making sure my thumb didn't damage the side of a cake than I was taking care not to touch my arm on the hot rack. Like I said, things like that happen more often than one might expect."

"It happened years ago?"

"*Jah*. Probably five years," she said. Then she winced as she realized how breathless she sounded.

He shifted. She was sure he was going to move away, but he didn't. "That had to hurt."

"It did," she squeaked. "But it served me well. I remembered that experience and minded those racks far better than I had before."

"Put that way, I can see how it might be a blessing."

"*Jah*." At the moment, that was what that burn felt like. A blessing. Looking at him, she said, "I bet you have a scar or two that has served as a learning experience."

"I do." Gripping the bottom of his shirt with both hands, he pulled it off over his head and tossed it to one side. That wide expanse of smooth skin and defined muscle was shocking.

And, if she admitted it, intriguing too. Toby Miller was a handsome man. Fearing she was staring at him a bit too long, she took another fortifying sip of water.

Of course, he misinterpreted her discomfort. Stretching to one side, he kind of twisted his torso to get a better look. "Oh, it ain't that bad, is it?"

His body? No, it was not.

Of course, her discomfort increased tenfold when she realized he was pointing to a thick, jagged scar on his side. It had to be a quarter-inch wide and at least three inches long.

How mortifying that she'd been so intrigued by his chest that she hadn't even noticed what he'd been trying to show her! "Actually, that scar is bad. Really bad. What happened there?"

Straightening again, he looked her way and grinned. "I had a run-in with the corner of some metal siding. It caught me *gut*, and happened in seconds too. It hurt like the dickens, I tell ya. And it was a real mess."

"My word."

"Yeah. Blood everywhere."

She was starting to feel a little queasy. She was also starting to wonder how they'd ever landed on this subject. "I'm sure you needed stitches?"

"I did. Twenty-six."

She gulped, imagining the sight of that. "That's a lot."

"Sure was. That wound was real deep." He grunted. "Then, just when I thought it was healed, I got impatient and did more than I should have." He paused dramatically. "Next thing I knew, I'd torn the stitches and had an infection. Off I went to the hospital again."

Her queasiness was reaching a dangerous level. "Well. Um, I'm glad you're all right now. Real glad."

"Me too. However, my accident had some *gut* consequences. I learned my lesson about taking the time to care for myself, and it's made for a *gut* story."

"Oh, you."

"It's true."

"I'm sorry you have such a bad scar."

"My *mamm* was so mad at me. She said it would have healed far quicker if only I had been a lot more patient. She was tempted to whip my behind for being so pigheaded and stupid."

Sharon giggled. "Maybe you were simply impatient. Ain't so?"

Toby pulled up his knees and wrapped his arms around them. "I used to be impatient. That is true. But now I'm beginning to think I have all the time in the world for some things." He looked into her eyes when he said that.

She smiled weakly as his full meaning hit her hard.

How strange and unexpected life was! Here she'd assumed her biggest romance concern was going to be watching her sister receive Graham's attention while she watched from a distance and pretended not to be affected. Instead, she was entertaining a possible flirtation of her own. To her surprise, it hadn't been uncomfortable, either.

"Toby, I, uh, I think you have a *gut* point. Patience is a virtue. It's definitely a blessing when one is able to appreciate the value of waiting for the perfect time."

He smiled at her, then glanced just beyond her and grinned broadly before lying down on his towel and closing his eyes.

Unable to help herself, she turned to see what he'd seen.

That's when she saw Graham was looking steadily at her. Intently. Not looking too pleased at all about what he'd just witnessed. Just as he had at breakfast that morning.

Figuring that was something to think about, she stretched out on her towel and pulled the hem of her dress up an inch or so above her knees. She closed her eyes then too. Glad to have an excuse to spend some time with her thoughts.

Her mighty mixed-up, jumbled thoughts.

CHAPTER 8

"I t's mighty kind of you to come with me to the Der Dutchman, Graham," Sherry said as they walked along Beneva Road two days later.

"It wasn't out of pure kindness. I wanted to walk with you."

Sherry was so surprised, she almost gaped at him. But then she pulled herself together and told him she'd like a walk. She was looking forward to chatting with him too. She still wasn't sure how Graham felt about her, but she was bound and determined to follow Carla's advice and simply enjoy herself.

After their day at Siesta Key, the heat taking more out of them than they thought it would, the seven of them decided they needed more rest. Graham, Matthew, and Toby had slept in on Tuesday, before ordering pizza for lunch and then proceeding to do nothing more than lounge around the inn's outdoor courtyard for the remainder of the afternoon. The four girls had gone to Yoder's to enjoy a leisurely lunch, followed by wandering in and out of stores. Then the four of them had spent the majority of the evening in the girls' attic room playing cards.

This morning, however, Sherry had wakened ready to explore more of Sarasota. She and Carla borrowed two of the inn's red bikes and rode up and down the streets in Pinecraft. After lunch, Sharon made plans to talk about cookbooks with Beverly.

Since Carla and Vera wanted to sit outside and read, Sherry walked to the front porch where all the guys were. She discovered that, despite all the wonderful baked goods Beverly would provide for tea in just a couple of hours, they'd been trying to convince each other to walk to Der Dutchman and bring back two of their special pies. Sherry volunteered to go, and, surprising her, Graham offered to go along.

Now as they walked down the street together, every so often stepping to the side so mothers with their strollers could get by, Sherry found herself relaxing with him. He'd been teasing her about the way she'd been chatting with every child who crossed their path.

"This is fun, Graham. I'm glad you and the boys were in the mood for pie."

"You came upon us at the right time, for sure and for certain," he said with a smile. "None of us wanted to be seen walking by ourselves with two pies in our hands."

She laughed. "It would be quite a sight, but not necessarily a bad one. And, of course, coconut cream pie is always a *gut* idea."

"To be honest, I didn't really think we needed pie. But Matthew has a terrible sweet tooth. Sometimes it's easier just to give him what he wants."

"I've done things like that with my girlfriends." She smiled at Graham again. Unbidden, hope filled her once more. Maybe she and Graham were meant to be together after all.

As they crossed another intersection, he said, "What do you girls go out to grab? I'm thinking it's probably not pie."

"You're right. It ain't. Sharon is our family's baker, you know. She's always bringing something home from the bakery that didn't sell or experimenting with a new recipe. We never run out of treats," she said as she pushed the crosswalk button at the intersection. "Sometimes we do go out, to run errands or something, but it's rarely for food. I like activity. I, um, don't do well with just sitting around."

"I'm beginning to get that idea." He smiled at her again, remembering how often he saw her get up to wade into the waves at Siesta Key.

Another minute later, when the light turned, they crossed the street, then walked the rest of the way in easy silence.

. . .

As they walked, Graham found himself wondering more about Sherry and even more about his reaction to her. Although he still thought Sharon was special, he'd begun to realize he felt more at ease around Sherry than he did around her sister.

Had he fallen in love with Sherry's letters and simply associated those feelings with a pretty girl, with Sharon? Or had it been the other way around? Had he become so fascinated by his one brief conversation with Sharon that he'd transferred all those feelings to the letter writer?

Surely there was no such thing as love at first sight, was there? Yes, he'd had a strong reaction to Sharon when he met her, but he had become more than interested in Sherry through her letters.

Whatever the case, he was glad his agreement with Toby had prompted him to get to know Sherry better.

When they got to the bakery counter at the restaurant, Sherry pulled out the money she'd collected and asked for the pies. Then they stepped to the side to wait.

Knowing he needed to figure out how he truly felt about Sherry, he thought he better keep their conversation flowing. "Tell me more about your job."

"Well, as you know, I work at a little nursery school as an assistant. I help the teachers with the two- and three-year-olds."

He winced. "That sounds difficult."

"It takes a lot of patience. I'll give you that!"

"But you enjoy it?"

"Very much so."

"Why is that?" he asked after he collected the bag from the hostess and they started their way back home. "Why do you enjoy it? Is it because you like teaching *kinner* or because you want *kinner* of your own one day?"

"Hmm. I never took the time to think about it that way. I guess my best answer would be both," she said with a smile. "I do enjoy *kinner*. I like how free they are. I like how they're unburdened by rules and expectations." She shrugged as they stopped at the light again. "Being with them makes me happy and want to be less worried about such things too." Rather sheepishly, she added, "I hope one day to be blessed with *kinner* like that."

"That's a great answer."

"What? Were you judging me?"

"*Nee.* I just . . . well, you gave me a lot to think about."

Looking up at him, her petite frame so slight but her very being so spunky, something new flickered in her eyes. "Don't take this the wrong way, but I'm starting to think I'm finally seeing the man I've been writing to for the last six months."

"Why would you say that?"

She shrugged again, then admitted, "I don't know how to say this without making either of us look bad. But, uh, looking back at when we first saw each other in the parking lot, I kind of get the feeling you were disappointed when you saw me again."

"I wasn't." This was terrible. He was lying to her.

Looking far more mature than her years, she said, "It's okay if you were. I mean, I know I seem confident, but I also know I'm not much to look at when I'm standing next to my sister."

This was becoming worse and more uncomfortable by the second. "Don't say things like that, Sherry. It's not true. I never thought that, either."

"Maybe not you, but I'm sure a lot of people can't help but compare the two of us. And it's fairly easy to see who'd come out on top."

"I don't think so."

"My sister Sharon is the beauty. She's also cool and reserved."

He hated that she was putting herself down. "Please, stop saying things like that. You're attractive too. And it's pretty obvious you have much to be proud of."

Her expression softened. *"Danke."* When they turned right on Magnolia, she continued. "Graham, please don't misinterpret what I said. I wasn't fishing for compliments. It's just that . . . What I'm trying to say is you shouldn't feel bad if you find me lacking next to Sharon."

"Did your parents do this?" he asked angrily. "Did they make you feel like you weren't as *gut* as your older sister?"

"Nee." With a sigh, she pressed her hands to her cheeks. "I'm just being silly. Please, may we drop this now?"

"We don't have to." Actually, he liked seeing this new, less confident side of Sherry. While he hated for her to have insecurities, her weaknesses made her seem more approachable.

"Well, I'd sure like to." Grimacing, she said, "And while we're at it, maybe we could forget that I brought it up in the first place? That's a fault of mine. I say what's on my mind, then live to regret it."

Just before they turned to walk up the front steps to the inn, Graham stopped. "Sherry, don't apologize anymore for who you are. There's nothing wrong with you and a whole lot that's great. You have qualities Sharon doesn't have. I'm sure she's a little envious of some of your attributes too."

"Maybe so."

"Listen, I'm one of three boys. We all farm together

too. I have a lot of experience trying to keep up with my older brother. My younger brother, Caleb, has said he often tries to keep up with me. It's the way of siblings, I think."

She blinked. "I never thought about it that way." As they started walking up the steps, she looked up at him. "You know what, Graham? I'm starting to think maybe all my experience with preschoolers is going to pay off."

"How so?"

"Over and over again, I try to teach them about the value of patience. But maybe I've learned a bit about patience too." She looked down at her feet. "On the way to Pinecraft, I was sure something good was going to happen right away. But now I realize there's not much value in trying to force anything to happen. Maybe it's best when we have to do a little bit of waiting and praying."

Her words couldn't have been more true. They resonated with him . . . though, unfortunately, they also made him feel more confused than ever. He smiled weakly as he held open the door.

Matthew was lounging on one of the easy chairs in the living room. "Do we finally have our pie?"

Graham laughed. "We do, and *nee* thanks to you. Go round up everyone and tell them to meet us in the dining room."

CHAPTER 9

"Hey, Graham?" Toby asked late that night when they were settled in their beds.

"Hmm?"

"What did you really think was going to happen with Sherry when we booked our bus tickets?"

"You know, I thought I'd see the girl I'd been writing to for months again and fall in love. Instead, I got myself in a real mess."

"Do you still feel like you're in a mess now?"

After his walk with Sherry? He wasn't sure. "*Nee*. One minute I don't want to do anything but relax and have a *gut* time. The next I'm half planning the rest of my life."

"I've been kind of doing the same thing. Do you think it's Pinecraft that's making us so crazy?"

"Maybe." Thinking about Sharon's beauty and Sherry's cuteness and bubbly personality, he said, "Maybe it's the girls. Or maybe I've stopped dwelling on the assumptions I made and started concentrating on the needs of other people. Maybe I'm finally growing up."

"Yeah." Toby punched his pillow and flipped on his

side. "I didn't come here with any expectations other than I wanted to take a break from construction. But now . . ." He blew out a harsh breath. "Now I can't stop thinking about Sharon."

"You and she have hit it off, then."

"I think so. Well, we talked a bit on the beach. And we spent some time together after supper."

"I've seen you together more than that."

"What about you and Sherry?"

Thinking about their conversation on the streets going back and forth from Der Dutchman, Graham said, "I'm starting to see she's more than I thought she was."

"Huh."

The burden was killing him. "Will you keep a secret?"

"Of course."

"Well, these letters? I thought I was writing to Sharon. Not Sherry."

Instead of looking horrified, Toby looked merely amused. "Really? That's kind of hard to believe. They're really different."

"I know that now. I didn't when I was writing."

"The signature at the bottom of the letter didn't clue you in?"

"It would have, if I hadn't confused their names. I remembered meeting Sharon but not her first name. I only remembered her last name was Kramer. So when Sherry wrote and said she just wanted to say hi because she liked letter writing, and I saw the name Kramer, I thought she was the woman I remembered."

"But she wasn't."

"*Nee.*" Wondering why he'd even decided to tell

Toby the truth because now he was feeling stupid, he said, "At first I thought maybe Sharon wrote chatty letters because was a little shy. I thought maybe shy girls liked to express themselves more through the written word or something."

"The amount of information you don't know about the female mind is staggering."

"Like you are any better."

"I have two sisters. I know better." Making a come-closer gesture with his fingers, he said, "So how did you finally figure it out? Did Sherry say something about her red hair or something?"

That would have been great if she had! "*Nee*. I, um . . . well, I didn't actually discover who exactly Sherry was until I got here and we were all standing in the parking lot."

Toby gaped. "*Nee* way."

"It's true."

"What did the girls say when you told them?" He grinned. "I bet you got an earful!"

"They haven't said anything. Because I haven't told them the truth yet."

Toby stilled. "Are you saying Sherry still thinks you knew you were writing to her?"

"*Jah*." He swallowed. "I couldn't figure out what to do. Or how to tell them without hurting anyone's feelings. I mean, either I tell Sherry I liked her letters but had been picturing her sister, or I tell Sharon I didn't remember her name, so she was essentially forgettable."

"Neither option is *gut*."

"I know that." Thinking he might as well confess the

whole story, Graham said, "I almost convinced myself it was okay and that I didn't want to seriously court either of them."

Toby slapped his hands on his face. "But now you do?"

Graham shifted uncomfortably. "*Jah*. I think I do."

"Do I even want to know which one you're interested in now? And before you say anything, I hope you recall that I asked you on the beach who you liked."

"I remember."

"Well? Who?"

"At first I thought it was Sharon, but now I think it might be Sherry."

"You think it might be," he repeated. After a pause, he scowled. "You are seriously playing with people's lives here, Graham."

"It's a mess," Graham agreed. "I feel bad about it too. Anytime either of them mentions the letters, I kind of want to throw up. I hate this secret. But you have to know I'm not playing around. I don't want to hurt anyone's feelings, and I just don't know if I should come clean or not."

He'd known Toby most of his life, but never had Toby looked at him with such disdain. "*Nee*, Graham. That's not what you're doing. You're more concerned with your pride than with being honest. And that's not being grown up at all."

"Hey, now. It ain't—"

"It is. You need to tell those sisters the truth tonight, or I will."

"You can't do that. What about promising to keep my secret?"

"That was before I realized your secret is going to ruin my life," he said before turning away.

After some thinking—and praying—Graham realized two things.

First, Toby was completely right. He hadn't been truly thinking about Sharon or Sherry. He hadn't been thinking about Toby either. He'd been thinking only about his own wants. It was time to change that. He just hoped he wasn't going to be on the receiving end of several cold shoulders for the rest of this vacation. If that happened, this trip was indeed going to go down as one of the worst ideas in his whole life.

Second, he now knew which sister truly made his heart beat just a little faster, and he didn't want a lie to stand between them.

CHAPTER 10

Sherry was doing her best to stifle her yawns on the back patio. But it was late, she was tired, and Graham had been incredibly vague about why he wanted to talk to both her and Sharon at ten thirty at night.

"What do you think Graham wants to talk to us about?" she asked Sharon for about the fifth time.

"Like I said before, I have *nee* idea. Maybe Graham wants our opinion about something."

Sherry was just going to ask what opinion could be so urgently needed when the back door opened and Graham came out. Just behind him was Toby. What was going on?

"Hey," Graham said as he looked at one of them, then the other. "*Danke* for meeting me."

"We didn't know Toby was coming too," Sharon said. "Is this a party or something?"

"I wish it was," Toby muttered.

Graham glared at him. "Toby came for moral support."

Sharon raised her eyebrows. "You need moral support to talk to us?"

"I didn't come for Graham's moral support. I came in case you two needed me," Toby clarified.

Sherry had had enough. "Graham, come sit down and get this over with," she said impatiently. "I'm tired, and I'm done guessing what's on your mind."

Graham pulled out one of the wrought-iron chairs and abruptly sat down. Far more slowly, Toby joined them too.

After exhaling a deep breath, Graham blurted, "I have to tell you both something that's been weighing on my mind ever since you arrived in Pinecraft."

"What is it?" Sharon's expression was full of concern.

Looking as though he was about to have a tooth pulled, he said, "I . . . well, I, um, I had a problem with the letters I wrote to Sherry." Before Sherry could ask what he was talking about, he rushed on. "Sherry, I didn't realize I was writing to you. I thought I was writing to Sharon."

Stunned, Sherry looked at Toby, who seemed irritated, and at Sharon, who was gaping. Then she burst out laughing. "You're being ridiculous, Graham. I signed my letters Sherilyn Kramer."

"I know you did. But I didn't remember meeting you, not until you got here. I only remembered meeting Sharon."

And just like that, all her amusement fled. "You didn't remember meeting me?"

Graham got to his feet and clenched his hands at his sides. "I remembered meeting Sharon, but I only remembered her last name. I couldn't remember her first name. I assumed it was Sherilyn when I got that first letter signed Sherilyn Kramer."

Sherry was starting to feel sick, like she'd eaten a

beetle or something. "So all this time you were writing to me, telling me about your life and how you couldn't wait to see me in Pinecraft, you were really wanting to see my sister."

Graham hesitated. "Kind of."

Sharon tilted her head to one side. "What do you mean by 'kind of?'" Her voice was hard.

"I wanted to see the person who was writing me so many entertaining letters."

"And you thought the author of the letters looked like Sharon, right?" Sherry asked. "What about when I mentioned my red hair and freckles?"

"You never told me that."

"I did in my last letter. I sent it just before I left for our trip."

"I didn't get that letter, remember? I left a couple of days before you did, and it didn't come in time." Sitting back down, he said, "I'm sorry. I don't know what else to say."

"Only that you didn't remember meeting me."

"Don't feel bad, Sherry." Sharon said. "Graham here might have remembered what I looked like, but he didn't even remember my name."

Graham leaned his head back and took another deep breath. When he looked at them again, he said, "I know I sound like a jerk, but I promise it wasn't like that."

"Graham, why didn't you say anything when we arrived?" Sharon asked.

"I didn't know how to tell you," he said after a brief pause. "Then, well, I tried to tell myself it didn't really matter that I got so confused. After all, it was an honest mistake, and it wasn't like I had known either of you well. I thought maybe we could have a *gut* time in Pinecraft and simply be vacation friends."

Sherry knew what he meant, but she wasn't about to let him off the hook. "And by 'vacation friends,' you mean women you weren't serious about. Women with whom you only wanted to have a fling."

Graham's blue eyes widened. "Hold on now. I haven't been flinging with anyone."

"Yet," Sherry said, feeling angrier by the second. Actually, that anger was a good thing. Far better than sinking to the floor in embarrassment.

"See?" Toby interjected. "This is *exactly* why I came along. I knew you girls would need some support."

"For what?" Sharon asked. "Graham just embarrassed both me and my little sister in front of you."

"What he did and said was *nee* reflection on you," Toby said quickly. "You have nothing to be embarrassed about."

"You know what? Let's just stop this conversation before it gets any worse."

"Sharon, I promise that I'm sorry."

Sharon frowned. "Why does that matter right now?"

"Because I want you to believe me. I never meant to hurt anyone."

"Graham, all I need you to do is promise that you'll keep your distance for the rest of this trip."

Graham flinched. "Neither of you will accept my apology?"

Sharon got to her feet. "Why would you expect us to?"

"Because it's the right thing to do."

Sherry hated that he didn't sound more upset with himself. "Graham, I believe you got us confused. I can even understand how that might have happened. But not telling me when I got here? And admitting what you did to Toby before telling either one of us? That was pretty low."

"I didn't mean to upset you both. Toby is right. This is my fault. Not either of yours."

Sharon looked at him with a sad expression. "This might be a shock, but I didn't remember your name either. So I would have understood that you got us mixed up."

"And now?"

"Now? Now I have *nee* idea what to think. I'm angry. I just need a break."

"I'm going up to my room," Sherry said, standing as well. "Do you want to come with me, Sharon?"

"*Nee.* I'm going to the front porch," she said over her shoulder as she started around the house.

Just as she was about to encourage Sharon to come inside after all, Sherry noticed Toby was following her sister, and she went into the house alone. As she closed the back door behind her, she noticed Graham was sitting with his head resting in his hands. He looked despondent and so very alone. Sherry knew she should be glad he was suffering the consequences of his behavior.

So why did she suddenly feel kind of sorry for him?

CHAPTER 11

"Sharon, wait!" Toby called out as she walked along the side of the inn. The narrow flagstone pathway led from the patio to the broad front porch.

Sharon was so mad and confused she didn't want to stop. But she did. After all, it certainly wasn't Toby's fault that his friend had made such a mess of things.

"*Danke*," he said, scanning her face in the dim light. "Are you okay?"

Since it was obvious that she wasn't, she didn't even attempt to hide her sarcasm. "I'm great. *Wunderbaar*."

Frustration flickered through his expression. "Let me rephrase that. Are you really disappointed?"

She realized then that Toby thought she was mourning the loss of a man she didn't really know, the loss of a relationship she'd only had a taste of—not enough to even know how it could be.

That realization was all she needed to know she'd been reacting to the situation, yes, but not feeling pain in her heart.

The difference was notable and significant.

Exhaling deeply, she took a second to gather her thoughts. Then, as they walked to the porch together, she tried her best to convey how she felt in a way that would allow her and Toby both to come to terms with what had happened.

"I'm disappointed Sherry wrote to a man for six months, cast a whole lot of hopes on a grand reunion that might blossom into a relationship, only to get her heart stomped on," she said. "I'm disappointed to learn that while Graham remembered what I looked like, he still found me somehow forgettable, believing Sherry's personality in those letters was mine. But I forgot his name, too, so that makes me disappointed with myself."

She paused, half waiting for Toby to nod and turn around. Or worse, give her a simple platitude that meant nothing to either of them. But instead he simply stared at her in that surprisingly patient way of his. She realized he was waiting for her to tell him everything. Even if it made them both uncomfortable.

When was the last time someone had given her permission to be so open and honest? She knew that answer.

Years. Maybe never.

She sat down on one of the porch's rocking chairs, and then, looking up into his dark-brown eyes with only moonlight to illuminate them, she took another fortifying breath and decided to be even more honest. "I'm embarrassed too."

"Why?" he asked, his tone gentle.

She was completely at a loss. "Why? Because it's, uh, it's been a while since I've taken a chance like this. You see, I found out my former boyfriend had cheated on me, and it hurt."

"I'm sure it did."

"It hurt enough that I didn't want to put myself at

risk again. But Sherry was so excited about all the possibilities with the man who turned out to be Graham, and that made me want to try to trust again."

"There's nothing wrong with that. Although he never admitted it, I could sense Graham's excitement about seeing the author of those letters again, and it made me want to take a chance too."

"Why was it hard? Have you been hurt too?"

"Not like you. I just . . . well, I get uncomfortable around girls. I never know what to say, so I always joke around. Then they don't take me seriously. But Graham's hope for this trip made me a little hopeful too. I didn't expect to fall in love or anything, but I was hoping I could do a little bit better in the relationship department."

"I don't think you have any problems in that area."

"*Nee?* Well, that's *gut* to know."

Sharon found herself smiling at Toby. "I don't know what's going to happen now, but I'm glad we've become friends."

"Me too."

When he sat down in the rocking chair next to hers, she tensed. "Toby, I appreciate you sitting with me and such, but I should warn you I'm not very *gut* company right now."

But instead of backing off, he chuckled. The sound was low and deep in his throat. "Sharon, I neither want nor need you to be *gut* company. I only want you to be yourself."

She ran a hand over her face. "I don't know if what I'm being at the moment is me either. I'm not usually so emotional."

The corners of his lips curved up. "I'm kinda liking this emotional side of you."

Dropping her hand, she stared at him. "Why?"

"Because, until very recently, you kind of intimidated me."

She scanned his face, looking for signs he was teasing her.

But his eyes were clear, his expression earnest.

While she gaped at him, he held out a hand. "Come on. Let's go for a walk."

Not sure where the discussion was leading her or what destination Toby had in mind, Sharon realized she could either refuse or allow herself to be surprised.

Put that way, there was no choice. She linked her fingers with his and let him pull her up. After another moment of awkwardness, she relaxed and picked up her pace to match his long-legged stride. She might not have any idea what was in store for them, but she did know she trusted Toby. That counted for a lot.

Hand in hand, they walked down Bahia Vista, turned the corner on Magnolia, and ended up on the walking path in one of Pinecraft's public parks she'd visited before. It was fairly dark out, though by the light of the streetlamps she could see a few people walking in the distance. But overall, it was quiet and the area was theirs.

"Isn't this something?" Toby asked as they slowed down.

She was confused. "What are you referring to? The park?"

"*Jah*. But I mean something else too." Dropping her

hand, he gestured toward the scene around them. "I mean, look at it around here. Just a couple of hours ago, you couldn't have paid me to return here."

Looking around, Sharon didn't notice anything different—just the small pond, the walking path, the grassy area where groups of teenagers played impromptu kickball games. "Why does it seem different to you now?" she asked.

"Before, it was too crowded, too hot. Too many people, too much noise, too much of, well, everything. But now that it's clearer it seems a whole lot nicer to me."

"Because you don't care for crowds."

Toby laughed. "I don't. You're right. But what I'm trying to say—and not very well—is that maybe I needed to give this place some time, to see it for what it is."

"Is that what you're thinking about our experiences here? And about how Graham has been treating everyone?"

"Maybe. Maybe he wasn't wrong and we weren't right. Maybe he was simply fumbling around, trying to figure out who was a *gut* fit for him . . . and, like me and this park, he changed his mind."

Feeling rather impressed with him, Sharon blinked. "Wow, Toby. And here I thought you were all about having fun."

"I am." Grinning, he reached for her hand again and led her to a bench. "But just like I keep saying there's more to you than most realize, I'm thinking maybe there's more to me than you realize." When she seated herself next to him, he stared at her. "Now, of course, the question is what you want to do about it."

A little buzz went through her as his words settled deep inside her. That was the question now, wasn't it?

What did she want to do? Or rather, what was she willing to do?

CHAPTER 12

I'm blessed to have such *gut* friends," Sherry said to Vera and Carla. "*Danke* for listening to me fret and moan about everything. Sharon seemed to want to be alone, so we haven't even had a chance to talk about this yet."

"Fret away. You have reason."

"You can fret even more if you want to," Carla offered. "I don't mind."

Sherry thought about that, and shook her head. "*Nee* thanks. I'm done feeling sorry for myself."

"*Gut,*" Vera said. "Especially since you and Sharon don't have anything to feel bad about. I think this was all just a mix-up. Graham got confused and then was brave enough to confess it."

"And I let myself get carried away by my dreams. I should have realized people don't fall in love through letters."

"And perhaps that *nee* romance is perfect," Vera said. "My Stefan and I have had our fair share of misunderstandings. No relationship is perfect, especially not at the beginning."

"Point taken." Just as Sherry was about to suggest

they get ready for bed, they heard someone approach their attic door.

"Sherry, can we talk?" Graham called through the door.

She answered from inside. "It's late."

"I know. But I'm not going to be able to sleep unless we talk. Please, will you give me a couple of minutes?"

Heart pounding, she turned to Vera and Carla. "What should I do?"

"Give him a chance, Sherry," Carla coaxed. "He sounds pretty upset."

"I am upset." Graham raised his voice a little. "Sherry, please?"

She couldn't believe it, but she was starting to waver. Was it because she felt sorry for him . . . or because he was the man she really wanted? *Lord, what should I do?* she asked silently. *I want Graham in my life, but I don't want him for the wrong reason.*

"Come on, Sherry. Please?" Graham pleaded.

She looked at her girlfriends, then back at the door. What to do? What to do?

But then she remembered that familiar verse from the book of Luke. *Forgive others, and you will be forgiven.*

What more did she need to know?

"Go talk with him," Vera said. "He sounds miserable."

Feeling much better, she turned and opened the door.

"*Danke,*" he said.

Sherry almost smiled when she saw he looked as miserable as he sounded. His shirt was rumpled and untucked, and his hair was sticking up in all directions.

Obviously, he'd been running his fingers through it. "Oh, Graham."

He blinked, changing some of the desperation she'd spied into relief. "Where can we talk?"

As Vera and Carla giggled, she stepped into the hallway and closed the door firmly behind her. "Not in here. Let's go downstairs. I bet there's no one in the small alcove by the dining room this time of night."

While he led the way down the stairs, she cautioned herself to forgive, yes, but also to stay strong. She was going to listen to him, offer forgiveness, but then politely tell him she'd talk to him tomorrow before finally going to bed.

But when they got to the small room, Graham turned to her and blurted, "Sherry, since I've already made such a mess of things, I'm just going to tell you something straight out."

"I'm listening."

Still staring at her intently, he said, "I really like you. *You*, not your sister. *You*, not the girl I was writing to but didn't really know."

She loved what he was saying. Of course she did! But she was also afraid. "What if you change your mind again?"

"I'm not going to."

Examining his expression, she looked for signs he was keeping his true feelings from her. But everything about him—from the intensity of his gaze to his firm stance—illustrated he was being completely open and honest. "You sound so certain."

"I am, Sherry." He waved one hand in the air. "You

see, this was why I had to tell you and Sharon the truth—and not only because Toby made me realize it was the right thing to do. I realized my feelings for you are real, and I wasn't going to change my mind." He paused. "Distance isn't going to make me forget you," he added, his words practically tumbling over each other. "I like you and it was killing me that I had that secret between us."

His words were sweet. Really sweet. But where did that leave them? "What happens next?"

"That's up to you, of course. But I know what I'm thinking." Before she could utter anything, he reached for her hands. "How about this? I like how you know your mind. I like how you want to stay busy and like to do things and not sit around and wait. I like how you like *kinner*, and I like how you like to organize things too."

As she gaped at him, he added, "I also happen to like your freckles. And since I'm laying it all out there . . ."

"*Jah?*"

"I think you look really nice in that bathing suit."

She felt her cheeks heat again. But this time it wasn't from embarrassment. It was from happiness. She thought of playing it cool. Of pretending she wasn't glad to hear what he said. But that wasn't who she was. She studied their linked hands, how they looked together. Thought about how they felt together.

"That was quite a speech, Graham," she said at last.

"Does that mean you don't want to throw something at me anymore?"

"*Nee.* I mean, not at the moment."

"Well, then. Maybe you'll give me a chance? After

all, we're going to be here for another week. Maybe we could try simply being together? You know, as Graham and Sherry."

As Graham and Sherry. Just the two of them, with no more confusion or misunderstanding twisting everything into knots. "That is quite the opportunity. I'd hate to waste it."

His eyes lit up and he smiled. Rubbing his thumb over her knuckles, he said, "*Danke*, Sherry. You have made me mighty happy."

Funny, making him happy had made her mighty happy too.

CHAPTER 13

The seven of them spent their last evening in Pinecraft Park. Before they left the inn, Beverly helped them pack a picnic basket with sandwiches, salads, chips, and thick chocolate brownies.

After enjoying their leisurely meal, Matthew played a game of basketball with a couple of guys he'd met, and Carla and Vera lay on a quilt and chatted.

Sharon and Toby were near the swings, talking with each other. Each looked more than a little captivated by the other. Sherry was fairly sure her sister was going to be writing a few letters of her own when they got back home. And she smiled whenever she remembered Sharon bravely wearing her swimsuit without her dress the last few times they'd visited the beach.

As for herself? Well, she hadn't wanted to spend a moment away from Graham. When he asked her to take a walk so they could be alone, she'd jumped at the chance. After just a couple of minutes, Graham practically pulled her down one of the residential streets that lined the park.

"This is better," he said.

Sherry laughed. "If you wanted us to be alone, this is the wrong place."

Stepping a little closer, he said, "I guess I didn't want to avoid people as much as I wanted to do everything I possibly could just one more time."

"I've felt the same way. It's going to be so hard to leave here tomorrow."

"It is."

Taking a chance, she added, "It's going to be harder to leave you."

"I've been thinking the same thing about you." After taking a couple more steps, he said, "Sherry, I don't want to lose you again."

She knew what he meant. They'd spent too many days at the beginning of this vacation walking on eggshells around each other, trying to figure out what was real and what they thought the other thought. "You won't. We'll write letters."

"We can do that." Graham paused. "I mean, if that's what you want."

"What choice do we have?" Just then, a dark thought filled her. "You don't want to stop writing to each other, do you?"

He halted abruptly. "After everything we've been through? Absolutely not. Of course not! But I also want to see you every day. I want to court you like my brothers courted their girls, coming to your *haus* every evening and sitting with you on your front porch."

His words made her feel kind of mushy inside. Happy too. Actually, everything he was saying was reassuring. She wasn't alone in this relationship. He wanted the same things she did. "But if we can't do that, then what?"

"What would you think if I visited you in about two weeks and talked with your father?"

Her breath hitched, but she was still afraid to hope. "About . . ."

"About courting you. About one day marrying you, Sherry." Linking his fingers with hers, he said, "Is that clear enough?"

What could she say? After everything they'd been through, all the misunderstandings and all the failed hopes and dreams, they were on the same page in the end.

"*Jah*," she said. "That is clear enough. Even for me."

His blue eyes looked her over, then little by little sparkled in the fading evening light. Then he leaned closer and lightly brushed his lips against hers. It was a sweet kiss. Perfect, because it hinted of a future together. When he shifted and wrapped an arm around her shoulders, she leaned into him.

Everything had been worked out, and nothing more needed to be said.

EPILOGUE

Dear Sherry,

It was so good to see you last weekend. I enjoyed spending time with your family. Has your father spoken with you yet? I asked him for your hand, but before giving me an answer, he wanted to talk with you. Please tell me you won't torture me for too long, Sherry. A man can take only so much.

Graham

Dear Graham,

My father spoke with me not ten minutes after you left. We talked about love and partnerships and the Lord and commitment. I told him all about sparks and laughter and happiness. That's when he said he had better give us his blessing . . . and fast!

So there you are, Graham. We have my parents' blessing so we can be officially engaged.

Set the date, and don't make me wait too long.

Now I am yours,
Sherry

Dear Sherry,

Is one month too long?

I remain yours,
Graham

Dear Sharon,

We're all coming to Adams County on the fifth
of next month for Sherry and Graham's engagement
party. I can't wait to see you! I hope you've already
scheduled lots of time off. If you haven't, do so now.

I think we're going to have a lot to talk about.

Toby

Dear Toby,

I wish you hadn't had to take that early ride home
yesterday! When I was trying not to cry as I told you
good-bye, I felt as though I had just hugged you hello.

Didn't Sherry and Graham look happy? And they
are so excited too! My mother is having quite the time
of it, putting together a wedding in only six months.

I'm looking forward to seeing you in Sugarcreek
next month. I can't wait to stay with your mother and
sisters . . . that is, if they promise to be kind to me.

Sharon

Dear Sharon,

My family all loved you. But you knew they would,
didn't you? You were a perfect houseguest, a perfect

friend, and they all say you're perfect for me. Actually, the girls now think I'm a far sight smarter than they'd ever given me credit for. Your appearance in my life has raised their view of me.

In case you didn't realize it, I'm teasing you. It doesn't matter what they think, as long as we can be together.

I'll see you in a month when I stay at your house for a change. I have a feeling we can expect good things in our future.

Toby

Dear Toby,

I'm still feeling tingly about your proposal. It was the most romantic proposal ever, and right on the heels of Sherry and Graham's wedding too.

My mother looks like she's going to pull all her hair out, but I told her a four-month engagement is going to be just fine. I certainly don't want to wait any longer—especially since we're planning to go back to Pinecraft for our honeymoon. Maybe one of us should write to Beverly and let her know. She might want to prepare herself for that reunion!

Love, Sharon

A NOTE FROM THE AUTHOR

Dear Reader,

Thank you for returning to Pinecraft, Florida, with me! When I heard that this collection was going to be all about summer vacations or experiences, I knew that I had to set my story at the Orange Blossom Inn in Pinecraft. This made-up place was the focal point of four books I wrote two years ago for Avon Inspire. While writing this series, I fell in love with not only the innkeeper Beverly Overholt, but also the city of Sarasota, Florida, and the surrounding areas. I've since returned four times!

I really enjoyed writing about some characters who were on vacation. There is something about vacations that makes me smile. I love the freedom that I feel. I love how anything seems possible. And yes, I even love that feeling of dread that comes with knowing that I eventually have to go back home. Because of that, I try to treasure every minute. Maybe you have felt the same way?

If you're reading this book while on vacation, I sincerely hope you are having a great time! If, instead, you are simply enjoying a nice reading vacation from a busy day, thank you for spending it with me. I love hanging out with friends . . . even through the pages of one of my books.

> Wishing you many blessings and
> lots of sunny days ahead,
> Shelley Shepard Gray

DISCUSSION QUESTIONS

1. I had so much fun writing about reunions and revisiting Sarasota for this novella. What vacation spot are you anxious to visit again? What made it special?

2. Who in your life has been an unexpected "surprise"? Who in your life made a positive first impression?

3. What did you think about Sharon and Sherry's relationship?

4. I thought the following verse from Luke fit this story perfectly. "Do not judge others, and you will not be judged. Do not condemn others, or it will all come back against you. Forgive others, and you will be forgiven." How does this verse apply to a person or a situation in your life?

5. When I found the Amish proverb, "Things turn out the best for those who make the best of the way things turn out," I knew it would work well with this story. Do you find this proverb to be true? Why or why not?

ACKNOWLEDGMENTS

Isn't it funny how God picks the right time for everything? I've wanted to be part of an Amish novella collection for quite a while. When it finally happened, the folks at Harper Collins Christian Fiction placed me with some of the best writers in the genre! Thank you to authors Amy Clipston, Kelly Irvin, and Kathleen Fuller for joining me on this journey. I'm so excited to share a cover with y'all!

Thank you also goes out to the editorial staff at HCCP, most especially Karli Jackson and Jean Bloom. Both made *A Reunion in Pinecraft* something to be proud of.

I also can't help but acknowledge my original editor for the Pinecraft Series, Chelsey Emmelhainz. Because of Chelsey, I was able to write the Amish Brides of Pinecraft series, which this novella is loosely connected to.

Finally, I would never know so many details about Pinecraft without the kindness and patience of my Amish friend. She and her husband took me and my husband all around Pinecraft during our first visit. She's a gem, for sure and for certain.

SUMMER STORMS

AMY CLIPSTON

With love and appreciation for the members of my Bakery Bunch

CHAPTER 1

Happiness bubbled up from inside Ariana Smucker as she leaned back on her palms and gazed up toward the sky. The aroma of sunscreen filled her nostrils, and the hot summer sun kissed her cheeks. Then she smoothed the skirt of her red bathing suit over her thighs before smiling over at her best friend, who was sitting beside her. "This day is absolutely perfect. Don't you agree?"

"*Ya.*" Mariella Ebersol kicked her legs in the water, and the floating dock they were sitting on shifted. She pushed her long, blonde braid behind her shoulder, and her deep-brown eyes sparkled in the bright sunlight. "I can't believe you'll be married in five months." She moved her slim fingers over the skirt on her black bathing suit.

"*Ya*, November is coming quickly." Ariana's heart fluttered and a grin overtook her lips as she looked toward the shoreline. Her fiancé, Jesse Zook, sat on the beach with her brother, close enough that she could see their faces as they talked. They were surrounded by members of their youth group as well as other visitors to Maryland's Cascade Lake.

Resting her hands on the warm wooden dock, Ariana kept her gaze focused on Jesse. He pushed his hand through his thick sandy-blond hair and nodded. With his cobalt-blue eyes and strong jawline, Jesse was the most handsome man she'd ever known, and she couldn't wait for their wedding.

She looked over at her brother, Tobias, and her smile faded as she took in his deep frown and dark expression. Tension gripped Ariana's shoulders and her thoughts spun with anxiety. It was rare that their youth group could take a day off from work at their homes, jobs, and farms to visit a lake. Why would Tobias be troubled on a beautiful day like today?

A group of teenagers swam near the dock, and a girl squealed as a boy splashed her, pulling Ariana from her concern.

"You look worried." Mariella leaned over toward Ariana. "*Was iss letz?*"

Ariana turned toward her. "I was just watching Tobias talking with Jesse. Tobias looks so *bedauerlich*. I was hoping today would cheer him up."

"Cheer him up?" Mariella tilted her head. "What do you mean?"

Ariana blew out a sigh as she recalled the past week. It seemed as if her brother and father had argued nonstop. She'd hoped a day away from their farm would brighten Tobias's mood, but the scowl on his face as he spoke to Jesse indicated he'd brought his trouble with him to the lake.

"Tobias has been arguing with *mei dat* again."

"Oh." Mariella seemed to hesitate, as if awaiting

more details, but Ariana couldn't bring herself to share everything she witnessed daily between her brother and father. "They still aren't getting along?"

"No." Ariana fingered her thick braid as she continued to watch Tobias interact with Jesse. "I'm worried it might be getting worse."

"*Ach*, no." Mariella crossed her arms over her middle. "Do you think you can do anything to help?"

Ariana swallowed a snort. "No. They're both so stubborn. They never seem to listen to each other. I think that's part of their problem."

Mariella gave a little laugh. "That sounds possible."

Jesse and Tobias suddenly stood up from the shoreline and started up the hill that led to the picnic area. They were walking slowly, still talking.

"Is it lunchtime?" Ariana asked.

"It might be. Why?"

Ariana pointed toward the shore. "I think Jesse and Tobias are going to lunch without us." She frowned. Why hadn't Jesse remembered to invite her and Mariella to join them?

Mariella clicked her tongue. "That's awfully thoughtless."

"*Ya*, it is." Ariana turned toward Mariella and raised her eyebrows. "Are you hungry?"

Mariella shrugged. "Sure."

"We'd better go before they eat without us." Ariana stood up on the floating dock, held out her hand, and lifted Mariella to her feet.

She dove into the cool lake water and swam toward the shoreline with Mariella beside her. Ariana relished the feel of the cool water sluicing over her body. When she reached the shallow area, she waded to the beach, where she found her beach towel and pink bandana waiting for her.

She pushed the bandana over her hair and draped the dry towel over her shoulders before trotting up the hill after Jesse and Tobias.

"Jesse!" she called. "Wait for me!"

He stopped and turned, his eyebrows raised. Tobias looked at her, but went on.

"Did you forget I was in the water?" She pointed back toward the lake.

"Whoops." He shook his head as a smile turned up his lips.

She rested her hand on her hip. "I thought I asked you to let me know when you and Tobias were going to have lunch."

"I'm sorry." He ran his hand over his clean-shaven chin. "I forgot."

"You forgot?" She took a deep breath as irritation nipped at her.

"*Ya*, I did. I was caught up in my conversation with Tobias, and I completely forgot you wanted me to call you for lunch." His lips formed a thin line as he walked back down the hill toward her. "I'm sorry."

"It's all right." She shrugged, even though his oversight did send a pang of disappointment through her.

At just under six feet, Jesse stood over her by several inches. She silently admired how the summer sun had already begun to tan his handsome face and naturally highlight his hair to a golden blond. Like the rest of the young men in their youth group, he was clad in swim trunks.

She hugged the towel to her body as her gaze moved to his broad shoulders, and her eyes widened. "Your shoulders are turning pink. You should put on more lotion before you burn."

"I'll be fine." He gestured toward their group of friends as they walked past them toward the picnic area. "We should go before the tables fill up."

He held out his hand and she laced her fingers with his, enjoying the feel of his skin against hers.

As they began the trek up the hill, she glanced around for Mariella. "Where did Mariella go?"

Jesse pointed in front of them. "She's almost up the hill."

Ariana followed his gaze to where Mariella trudged, hugging her blue beach towel around her body. Tobias walked a few feet in front of her.

She looked up at Jesse again. "You and Tobias seemed to be in a deep conversation."

Jesse nodded. "Tobias needed someone to listen."

"Oh?" Holding fast to his hand, she pulled him back, slowing their pace. "What did he need to talk about?"

Jesse blew a breath out through his nose. "I guess he's been arguing with your *dat* a lot lately."

Ariana nodded as worry coursed through her once again. "What did he say?"

"He was venting." Jesse shrugged. "He'll be fine. It's nothing to worry about."

"Okay." She hoped he was right.

"Let's have lunch, and then I'll try to talk to him again later."

"Sounds *gut*." Ariana let Jesse lead her to a picnic table. She sat down on the end beside Mariella as Jesse sat down across from her and beside Tobias. When she closed her eyes in silent prayer, she thanked God not only for their food, but for this beautiful day.

· · ·

In late afternoon, Ariana lifted a bottle of root beer to take a drink. She was sitting on a glider on the far end of Mariella's back porch with members of her youth group surrounding her. They were all enjoying Mariella's father's cold homemade drink and sharing stories. Ariana searched the sea of familiar faces for Jesse and Tobias, but neither was on the porch.

As one of the young men began telling a story about a hunting trip he took last year, Ariana descended the porch steps and walked toward the pasture. She found Jesse leaning against the fence as he spoke to two of his friends, and she gripped her bottle tighter as she walked toward him.

"Jesse?" she called, but he continued talking as if he hadn't heard her. "Jesse?"

"Jesse." Ivan tapped his arm. "Ariana is calling you."

"Oh." Jesse turned toward her. "Sorry. I didn't hear you."

Ariana pressed her lips together as frustration tightened her shoulders. "Could I please speak to you for a moment?"

"*Ya*, of course." Jesse followed her to the far end of the fence. "What do you need?"

"I thought you were going to join me." She gestured toward the porch. "You said you'd have a bottle of root beer with me, and I even saved you a seat on the glider."

"Oh right." Realization dawned in his blue eyes. "I'm sorry. Ivan, Henry, and I haven't seen one another much since they got so busy working in their *dat*'s store. We were getting caught up. I forgot I promised to sit with you."

"I understand." Ariana nodded despite her disappointment.

"I'll come up there now." He took her hand in his and gently tugged her toward the porch. "Let's go. I'll grab you another root beer from the cooler."

"Wait." She stopped him, and they looked at each other. "I wanted to ask you if you've seen Tobias."

Jesse nodded. "I saw him sitting with Mariella on the porch, but then I saw him walk alone toward the barn a while ago. I meant to follow him, but then I ran into Henry and Ivan, and I lost track of time."

A niggling of worry started at the base of Ariana's neck. Tobias had seemed off all day.

"I was hoping today would help him." She looked out over the pasture. The sky was clogged with gray clouds, and thunder rumbled in the distance.

"Would you like me to find him?"

"*Ya*, please."

"All right. We have to get going soon anyway. I think a storm is coming. Also, I promised *mei dat* I'd be home in time to help feed the animals." His expression seemed tentative. "You're still riding with me to get home, right?"

"*Ya*, I'd like to."

"*Gut*." He gave her hand a gentle squeeze. "I'll go find Tobias. You go back to the porch and enjoy the rest of your time with our *freinden*. Okay?"

"Okay." Her earlier worry dissipated as Jesse smiled at her. Before their trek from Cascade Lake back to Gordonville, Pennsylvania, he'd changed into dark trousers and a deep-blue shirt that accentuated his eyes. Ariana admired him as he headed toward the large barn. Her stomach took flight on the wings of a hundred butterflies at the notion of driving home with him this afternoon. Stealing a quick kiss would be the perfect ending to this special day spent with friends.

CHAPTER 2

Dread bogged Jesse's steps as his boots crunched on the rock path leading to Mariella's father's barn. Tobias's glum mood and initial silence, followed by his venting, had bothered Jesse all day. Despite his efforts to cheer up Tobias before lunch, his best friend had never changed. Maybe he could find a way to cheer up Tobias now, before they headed home for the evening.

The scent of rain wafted over Jesse as he glanced over his shoulder. Ariana sat down on the porch glider and then leaned over to talk to one of their friends. The ties from her prayer covering flittered around her shoulders as she nodded.

Before they climbed into the van to head back to Gordonville, she'd changed into a green dress and pulled her hair up under a prayer *kapp*. She was attractive no matter what she wore, but he already longed for another sight of her long, thick braid and the wisps of dark hair falling around her face when she was swimming in the lake. Since he wasn't permitted to take a photo of her, let alone own a camera, he did his best to commit how she'd looked to memory.

Turning, Jesse hurried into the barn. The aroma

of animals mixed with moist earth invaded his nostrils as he walked past the stalls, looking for Tobias. When he reached the back of the barn, he slipped out through the side door and headed around to the back. He stopped short when he found Tobias leaning against the barn wall, holding a translucent glass bottle with a clear liquid sloshing around in it. Was that alcohol? No, it couldn't be. Could it?

Jesse blinked. "What are you doing?"

"Relaxing." Tobias held up the bottle, which was already half empty. "Would you like some?"

"What is that?"

"Vodka." Tobias took a long drink and then cleared his throat as he swiped a hand across his mouth. "It's the *gut* stuff. Have some." He held the bottle out to him.

"No." Jesse approached him, his thoughts spinning with a combination of anger and confusion. "Have you lost your mind?"

"Nope." Tobias took another long draw.

"Give me that before you get sick." Jesse reached for the bottle, but Tobias snatched it away from his grasp. He tucked the bottle behind his back and glared at Jesse. "You said you didn't want any, but don't spoil my fun."

"Spoil your fun?" Jesse gritted his teeth, amazed Tobias had found a way to sneak a bottle out here. "Do you realize how much trouble you'll be in if Mariella's *dat* catches you back here drinking? He's the bishop!"

Tobias snorted. "Please. I'm not hurting anyone. I'm just doing what I have to do to unwind. I don't get much chance to relax, so I need to enjoy it while I can."

Jesse rubbed his temples and flattened his lips

together. In the eighteen years he'd known Tobias, ever since they were six years old, he'd never seen him behave so irresponsibly. The man standing in front of him was someone he didn't recognize. What would Ariana say if she found Tobias drinking alcohol? Worse, how would their father react?

Tobias's expression darkened. "Don't look at me like that."

Jesse took a deep breath in a vain attempt to curb the anger and frustration gripping him. "Is this about your *dat*? I'm trying to understand why you're behaving this way. But I can't—"

"Of course you can't understand me. Your life is perfect."

"Perfect?" Jesse shook his head. "No one's life is perfect."

"*Ya*, I suppose that's true." Tobias studied Jesse, a sardonic smirk spreading across his lips. "It must get tiresome for you to have to hear your *dat* compliment you for your hard work and skill all the time. Honestly, Jesse, how do you put up with all that love and appreciation, day in and day out?"

Jesse balled his hands at his sides and fought to keep calm despite his best friend's biting words. *Be patient. It's the alcohol talking, not Tobias.* "You didn't say today at the lake, but did you have an especially bad argument with your *dat* yesterday or this morning?"

Tobias snorted again and then rested the bottle against his thigh. "Would it make any difference if I had?"

"It would explain why you're acting this way." Jesse

leaned against the barn wall beside him. "I know you're upset with your *dat* right now, but you're doing the best you can. Don't let it get to you. Things will get better."

Tobias narrowed his eyes. "I came out here to be alone. I don't need your platitudes and empty words."

A muscle ticked in Jesse's jaw as his patience wore thin. He had to get the bottle away from Tobias and then get him into his buggy before he was too drunk to walk, let alone guide the horse home. He couldn't possibly tell Ariana that Tobias had been drinking. She'd be furious, and the last thing Jesse wanted to do was ruin this special day. She'd been looking forward to it for nearly a month.

Jesse leveled his eyes at Tobias. "It's time for you to knock it off. You've wallowed in enough self-pity. Get it together."

"I told you. This is how I unwind." Tobias lifted his chin.

"This is how you unwind," Jesse said the words as their meaning clicked into place in his mind. "Are you saying you drink often?"

Tobias averted his eyes, staring at his shoes.

"Give me that." Jesse grabbed the bottle from Tobias's hand and started spilling the contents onto the ground.

"Stop it!" Tobias fought him, pushing Jesse out of the way before reclaiming the bottle.

With a murderous glare, Tobias replaced the top on the bottle. "You act all high and mighty, but you have no idea what it's like to argue with your *dat* every day. When you get home this evening, your *dat* will welcome you with open arms and ask you how your day was. *Mei dat* will tell me I spend too much time with *mei freinden*, I don't work hard enough, I'm not a *gut* example for *mei schweschder*, and the list goes on and on." His face twisted. "You and your *bruders* are everything your parents ever wanted, but I ruin everything I touch."

Jesse held up his hands as sympathy replaced his anger. "I'm sorry your *dat* makes you feel that way, but this isn't how you deal with your problems. I tried to tell you this afternoon at the lake. You need to talk to your *dat* and work things out."

Tobias gave a bark of laughter. "Sure. It's that easy with Marvin Smucker. You've met him, right?"

Jesse sighed and scrubbed a hand down his face. There was no talking to Tobias today. Thunder rumbled in the distance and a light mist of cool rain trickled down Jesse's arms. It was time to change his goal. Instead of convincing Tobias to stop drinking, he needed to focus on getting him home.

"It's getting late. The best thing you can do is get home before you're too drunk to help with chores." He held out his hand. "Give me the bottle."

Tobias hesitated.

Jesse studied Tobias as his frustration returned. "What are you going to tell your *schweschder* when she sees a bottle of vodka in your hand?"

Tobias blew out a sigh and picked up an empty paper bag from the ground. "Let me put it in my buggy, and then we'll hitch up the horses."

"And what if your *dat* finds it?"

Tobias huffed and then handed the bottle to Jesse, who emptied it.

"I'll take care of it." Jesse took the bag and shoved the bottle into it. He'd toss it into the back of his buggy and dispose of it before he got home. Then he turned his glare back to Tobias. "What are you going to do about your breath? It's a myth that vodka produces no smell."

Tobias smirked and pulled a pack of chewing gum from his pocket. "I got it covered."

Jesse gripped the paper bag as he studied his best friend. Lately he'd noticed Tobias chewing gum frequently. Did he have a drinking problem? Thunder clapped above them and the rain became heavier. "We need to get going."

Tobias took a step and then stumbled before righting himself. He turned toward Jesse and held up his hand. "I'm fine."

"Maybe Arie should take you home."

"I'm fine," he repeated with a growl. "Let's go."

Jesse's shoulders tensed as he followed Tobias to their waiting buggies. He tossed the paper bag into the back of his buggy, and Tobias started helping him hitch up their horses. Worry surged through him. He had to get Tobias home safely. Sleep would do him some good. Jesse could tell Ariana and her parents that Tobias wasn't feeling well. Maybe Jesse could blame it on too much sun, and Marvin would be too distracted to notice the truth.

Jesse stole glances at Tobias, who only stumbled once more. Thank goodness he wasn't completely drunk. Now he had to figure out how to get him home.

Ariana joined them just as they finished hitching

the buggies to the horses. With her beach bag slung over her arm, she held a beach towel over her head to shield her prayer covering from the rain. "The rain is a nice break from the heat."

"*Ya*, it is." Jesse tried to smile, but his lips refused to comply.

She tilted her head to the side. "Is everything all right?"

"*Ya*." *No.* He pointed toward Tobias, who was leaning against his buggy. "I was thinking you might want to take Tobias home since he's not feeling well."

"He's not feeling well?" Ariana's eyes widened as she rushed over to her brother. "I was worried about you when you disappeared from the porch. *Was iss letz?*"

Tobias shot Jesse a glare before addressing his sister. "I'm fine. You can ride with Jesse." He hoisted himself into his buggy.

Jesse rubbed the back of his neck as a feeling of foreboding overtook him. He'd wanted to find a way to convince Tobias not to drive his own buggy, but Tobias's stubborn streak had won out again. He forced a pleasant expression when Ariana turned toward him.

"Ready to go?" she asked.

"*Ya*." Jesse turned toward the porch and called to Mariella, who was standing on the porch and still talking to a few friends. He waved and thanked her before climbing into the buggy.

"It was a *gut* day," Ariana said.

He looked into her eyes and some of his worry eased. "*Ya*, it was." He guided the horse down the long driveway toward the road, and Tobias followed.

"I'm so glad our parents agreed to allow us to spend the day with our *freinden*."

"I am too." Out of the corner of his eye, Jesse saw the reflection of Tobias's horse speeding up in his side mirror. "What is he doing?" he mumbled.

"Was iss letz?" Ariana turned, craning her neck to look out the back of the buggy. "Why is Tobias going so fast?"

"I'm not sure." Jesse sat up straighter and looked past Ariana as Tobias's buggy came into view beside his. "What are you doing?" he called. He peered into the mirror, checking for cars. "I thought you were going to follow me."

"Let's race!" Tobias yelled with a wicked grin.

"Are you *narrisch*?" Ariana exclaimed.

As Tobias's horse took off running, Jesse prodded his horse in an attempt to catch up to Tobias. He had to stop him before he got hurt.

"Jesse!" Ariana yelled, squeezing his bicep. "Slow down!"

Slow down? Jesse kept his focus trained on the buggy in front of him. He had to concentrate on what he was doing, not try to explain it. Even if Ariana didn't know her brother had been drinking, wasn't it obvious he couldn't let Tobias race ahead like this?

"Jesse, please!" Her voice broke.

Rain pelted the buggy's windshield as the two horses galloped down the two-lane road, Tobias's seemingly at near breakneck speed. Ariana held on to Jesse's arm, her fingers like a vise digging into his skin.

As they approached a sharp turn, Ariana's voice resembled a sob. "Please slow down. Please!"

Afraid now that he, too, was indeed going far too fast for the road conditions, Jesse slowed down, gripping the reins. Fear coursed through him as he kept his eyes on Tobias's buggy.

He's going to crash if he doesn't slow down!

Tobias's horse took the turn too fast and the buggy wobbled. And then as if in slow motion, the buggy teetered just before the driver's side slammed down onto the road. The horse reared and then struggled to drag the buggy around the corner.

Jesse's blood ran cold as the buggy scraped its way down the road with the rain pounding from the darkened sky.

This has to be a dream. No, it's a nightmare.

Like that stormy night when he and Tobias were only sixteen.

CHAPTER 3

"Tobias!" Ariana shrieked, her voice slamming Jesse back to the present. "Tobias!"

Jesse had no choice. He snapped the reins, signaling for his horse, Rusty, to speed up again. When he caught up with Tobias's horse, he shoved the reins toward Ariana.

"What are you doing?" Her voice pitched even higher.

"Take them!" Glancing at Ariana just long enough to see her eyes widen, Jesse handed the reins to her and then leapt from the buggy, slipping and sliding on the wet pavement as he rushed toward the wreckage.

"Lester," he called to the horse, his voice trembling as adrenaline raced through him. "Whoa, *bu*. Whoa. Calm down, *bu*." He took the halter in his hands to slow him down. Leaning forward, he grabbed the cheek straps and looked Lester in the eyes. The horse was so terrified that Jesse could see the whites of his eyes.

"It's all right, Les," Jesse cooed in a soft, soothing voice. "Just calm down." He breathed in deeply through his nose to calm his surging heartbeat and catch his breath. "You're fine, *bu*."

The horse's eyes returned to normal, and Jesse blew

out a sigh of relief that seemed to bubble up from his toes. He quickly unhitched the straps and led Lester to where Ariana had come to a stop. He tied him to the back of his buggy, then raced to Tobias's buggy.

Ariana climbed out. "Tobias?" she yelled, her voice sounding wobbly. "Tobias! Are you hurt?"

A muffled gasp escaped from inside the battered buggy, and Jesse's heart pounded against his rib cage as he climbed in through the back.

"Tobias!" Jesse hollered. "Are you all right?"

"*Ya.*" Tobias groaned and then snorted. "That didn't turn out the way I planned."

"Give me your hand." Jesse held his out to him. "Let me get you out."

Tobias took his hand and Jesse pulled him out through the back of the buggy.

"*Ach*, no!" Ariana touched her brother's arm as she examined his bloodied face. "You're bleeding." She pulled a tissue from the pocket of her dress and began to mop up the blood on his face.

"It's nothing." Tobias swatted at her hand and chomped his gum. "The windshield busted, but I'm fine." He rubbed his right arm. "Just a little sore. I landed hard on my arm."

Turning, Jesse studied the buggy to survey the damage. The windshield was indeed smashed, the roof had caved in, and the frame was bent. He needed help flipping it back onto its wheels, but it wouldn't ride correctly. How was he going to get this buggy home?

Suddenly aware that his hat was gone, Jesse pushed his hair back from his face as the steady rain soaked through his shirt. He looked at his buggy, wondering if his hat had flown off before or after he'd jumped out of it.

"Are you two *narrisch*?" Ariana's brow furrowed as she turned her glower from Tobias to Jesse. "Why were you racing on a rainy night? Do you realize how dangerous that is?"

Jesse held his hand up to her in defense. "I was only—"

"I can't believe how immature you both are," she snapped, interrupting Jesse as she divided a glare between the two of them once again. "You two were acting like you were sixteen again instead of twenty-four."

Tobias gave a bark of laughter before cupping his hand over his mouth. He swayed slightly on his feet and then righted himself as a smirk overtook his lips.

Jesse's shoulders tensed as resentment crawled up his spine. Had Tobias's drunken haze completely clouded his judgment? He turned to Ariana, but her eyes remained focused on Tobias. Couldn't she tell her brother was drunk? Didn't she realize Jesse was only trying to stop him?

"You think this is funny, Tobias?" Rain trailed down her face and dripped onto her dress. "You could have been badly injured or even killed." Her voice faltered, and she cleared her throat. "This could have been much worse. Lester was obviously spooked, and he could have run in front of a car or a truck."

Her lips trembled, and Jesse's chest constricted. He longed to pull her into his arms and comfort her, to make sure she understood he was only trying to save her brother. As if on cue, a bright bolt of lightning skittered across the sky, followed by a loud crack of thunder that caused Ariana to jump with a start before hugging her arms to her chest. Now was not the time. He had to take charge of the situation and get everyone home safely before the storm worsened.

"Arie," Jesse said, "go sit in my buggy. You're soaked." He reached for her arm, and she took a step back, away from his reach. He gaped at her with surprise. In the three years they'd been dating, she'd never rebuffed him.

Jesse shoved away his concern and nodded toward his buggy. "You should go home so your parents don't worry. Lester is tied to the back of my buggy, so you can guide him. Tobias and I will stay to take care of his buggy."

She glowered at him for a moment before stalking over to his buggy and climbing back into the driver's side.

Jesse checked to make sure Lester's reins were secured and then leaned through Ariana's window as rain continued to soak through the back of his shirt. She was still frowning. Sending her home alone might not be the best idea.

"Are you comfortable riding home alone?"

Her brow creased even more. "I know how to guide a horse."

Jesse winced at her biting words, but pushed on. "Tell your parents Tobias will be home soon. I'll figure out how to get the buggy home as quickly as I can." He tapped the door. "Be safe, all right?" He opened his mouth to remind her he loved her, but before he could speak, she turned, snapped the reins, and started on the trek to her house.

As Jesse watched the buggy's taillights move down the road, cold surged through his veins. But the cold wasn't from the pouring rain soaking his skin. It was from the frosty expression Ariana gave him before she left. She always told him she loved him before they parted ways. But this time she seemed as if she couldn't wait to leave him by the side of the road.

Worry drenched him far more than the rain.

"Don't cry, Jesse," Tobias drawled sardonically as he smacked Jesse's shoulder. "You'll see *mei schweschder* again soon." He swayed and then pointed to the buggy. "So, genius, how are we going to get that home now that you've sent Ariana on her way in the only functioning buggy we have?"

"That's what I'm trying to figure out," Jesse spat back and then eyed him with disgust. "How much did you drink? Did you finish off another bottle before I got there?"

Tobias's eyes narrowed. "Only one, but I don't know how much I drank since you decided to pour out the rest. Do you have any idea how expensive that vodka was?"

Jesse rubbed the back of his head as frustration overtook him once again. Could this night get any worse?

Lightning flashed, followed immediately by a loud rumble of thunder.

Jesse looked toward the road as ideas swirled through his mind. He could jog to his older brother Nathaniel's house and use his phone to call his driver and ask him to come with his pickup truck. But how would they lift the buggy into the bed of the pickup truck without a tractor? Nathaniel's farm was also nearly four miles away, and getting there would mean a grueling run in the pouring rain.

Tobias sank down onto the wet grass and crossed his long legs before pulling his pack of gum from his trouser pocket. After shoving another piece of gum into his mouth, he held the pack up, offering Jesse a piece. Jesse shook his head and gritted his teeth while resisting the urge to smack the pack of gum out of Tobias's hand. Tobias shrugged and slipped the pack into his pocket.

Headlights flashed in Jesse's eyes as a pickup truck motored toward them. It came to a stop beside them, and the driver's window lowered. Jesse held his breath, hoping the people in the vehicle would offer help instead of gawking at the soaked and stranded Amish men with the broken buggy.

"Do you two need help?" a man asked before recognition flashed in his eyes. "Is that you, Jesse Zook?"

"*Ya.*" Jesse approached the truck, recognizing the driver as one of his father's customers. "Hi, Brian." He gestured toward the buggy. "My friend Tobias had an accident. His sister took the horse home, but we need help transporting the buggy. Any chance you know someone with a flatbed tow truck?"

A man sitting beside Brian leaned forward. "I have one. We'll go get it and be right back."

"Oh, thank you. I can pay you," Jesse offered.

"That's not necessary," the other man said. "We'll go

get it right now. I just live up the road. I'm Todd." He reached across Brian, and Jesse shook his hand.

"Thank you so much." Jesse pushed his wet hair back from his forehead. "I appreciate it."

Brian nodded and then hesitated. "You two are soaked to the bone. Do you want to ride back to the house with us?" He pointed toward the bed of his truck. "There's no room in the cab, but you can sit back there."

"No, thanks." Jesse shook his head. "We'll be fine."

"I'll bring you a few towels," Todd offered.

"Sounds good." Jesse thanked them again, backed away from the pickup truck, and swiveled toward Tobias as their rescuers left. "Brian Walker and his friend are coming back with a flatbed."

Tobias chomped his gum. "That's *gut*." He rested his chin on a bent knee as more thunder rumbled above them.

Renewed fury burned through Jesse as Tobias sat quietly waiting for the tow truck. "Why am I the only one worried about getting your buggy home?"

Tobias shrugged. "You've got it under control. Everything will be fine."

Something inside Jesse snapped, and his temper flared. "Have you considered what your *dat* is going to say?" He gestured toward the buggy. "Don't you think your situation at home is going to be worse when he finds you drunk with a smashed buggy?"

"Don't stand there and judge me."

"Who said anything about judging you?" Jesse crossed his arms over the front of his soaked shirt and shivered as the rain continued to drip through his hair and onto his clothes. "I'm still trying to understand you. We have some time to kill, so why don't you explain how you think getting drunk at a youth gathering and then trying to get yourself home was an intelligent plan?"

"Fine." Tobias stood and took a step, swayed slightly, and then righted himself. "Let me try again. You have no idea what it's like to be me. You only know what it's like to be Jesse Zook, the perfect *sohn*."

"I'm not perfect, nor is my home life. I've let *mei dat* down plenty of times, but you don't see me getting drunk and racing buggies as a way of dealing with it. What if Arie had been in that buggy with you?" Jesse's voice rose as his body shuddered with renewed consternation. "How would you have felt if she'd been hurt?"

Tobias glared at him and then slowly shook his head before jamming his finger into Jesse's chest. "Your life is so easy. You have everything you've ever wanted, and you've never had to work for any of it. You've had everything handed to you without any effort."

"That's not true." Jesse slapped Tobias's hand away.

"*Ya*, it's true. You've known for years that you were going to marry *mei schweschder*. You didn't even have to chase after Ariana since she's always been in love with you. She's had a crush on you since she was eight. All you had to do was smile at her and pay attention to her, and you had her loyalty and her heart." He began ticking things off on his fingers. "You have a *haus* of your own, and you're only twenty-four. You have a successful business. Both of them were given to you by your *dat*. You have no idea what it's like to actually work for something."

"I work hard every day." Jesse's body tightened with growing animosity. He took a deep breath in an effort to calm himself. *Tobias doesn't mean it. His emotions are blurred from the alcohol.* "Training horses is hard work."

Tobias sneered. "And you have no idea what it's like to feel like a stranger in your own family's home."

"What are you talking about? Your parents and Arie love you. Your thoughts are hazy because of the alcohol. You have no idea what you're saying."

"Actually, I know exactly what I'm saying." Tobias's expression darkened and his eyes glistened. "All I do is mess up, and *mei dat* criticizes me nonstop."

"Have you told him how you feel?"

"*Ya*, but he doesn't understand me."

"What do you mean?"

"He thinks I should be *froh* to inherit the farm and run it, but that's not what I want." Tobias looked down at the ground and kicked a stone. "I want to work with my hands. I want to build things. Maybe even make furniture like *mei onkel* Titus, but *mei dat* won't listen to me."

"You'd rather be a carpenter?" Jesse was stunned, and then memories filled his mind. He recalled how, when they were children, Tobias used to frequently ask Marvin to take him to visit his uncle Titus's furniture store. He also remembered a time when Marvin yelled at Tobias for spending too much time in the small workshop at the back of their barn where Tobias built birdhouses. His uncle would sell them for Tobias in his store.

It never occurred to Jesse that Tobias longed to become a carpenter. "Have you ever considered suggesting that you sell the farm when your *dat* is ready to retire? Maybe then you can go to work for your *onkel*."

Tobias kicked another stone. "*Ya*, I actually did suggest that once, and he said no. He insisted the farm has to stay in the family, and since I'm the only *sohn*, I have to take it over. He told me to face the fact that I'm a dairy farmer, and I always will be." Glancing up, he gritted his teeth and pointed at his chest. "What about what *I* want? Why can't *I* decide what future I have? What if I want a life like yours, doing a job I love with the opportunity to build a *haus* of my own?"

Suddenly, empathy shoved away Jesse's fury. "You're just upset, Tobias. But everything will be okay. You can have the same things I have. You can have a future. Maybe you'll meet the right *maedel* and get married soon after Arie and I do."

Tobias snorted as a wry smirk overtook his lips. "You think I should get married? And just where would *mei fraa* and I live? In my bedroom?" His expression hardened. "How could I have a family while living under *mei dat*'s thumb?"

"You're a great guy and have a lot to offer. You should try to—"

"Don't patronize me," Tobias snarled. "You know as well as I do that I don't have anything to offer any *maedel* in this community. It's time for you to wake up and see just how easy you have it. Most of us don't have the privilege you're used to."

"Privilege?" Jesse's back stiffened with defiance and

offense. "That's a joke, right? Look, you're very drunk. You should stop talking and shut your mouth before you say something you'll regret."

"Why would I regret the truth?" His voice was barely audible over the rumble of thunder.

Jesse flinched as if Tobias had struck him. Tobias had been his best friend since they were in first grade, and Jesse had thought of him as a brother. Tobias had never shown any signs of considering Jesse privileged and lazy before. Had the alcohol inspired Tobias to speak the truth after their nearly lifelong friendship? The realization sent a pang of confusion and disappointment through him.

Jesse leaned against the buggy as Tobias sat back down on the ground with his back toward him. Jesse tried to ignore the hurt washing over him. Tobias was drunk, and any chance of reconciling their differences would have to wait until he'd sobered up.

The rattle of a diesel engine drew Jesse's attention to the road. He stood up straight and prepared himself for the struggle of loading the damaged buggy onto the flatbed.

In his heart, however, he feared the real struggle had just begun.

. . .

Ariana halted Jesse's buggy in front of the back porch. As his horse came to a stop, a *tink-tink-tink* sounded from somewhere in the back of the buggy. Leaning over the seat, her fingers brushed against a paper bag.

She lifted it, opened it, and found a cool glass bottle. She read the label.

"Vodka?" *Where did this come from?* Her eyes widened. Suddenly, everything came into sharper focus—her brother and Jesse racing in the rain and Jesse blatantly ignoring her pleas to slow down.

Jesse and Tobias had been *drunk.*

Shock cemented her to the bench seat in the buggy. She'd never seen Tobias or Jesse drink alcohol. Sure, when they were teenagers they got into their fair share of scrapes—even a couple of serious ones. But that had been years ago. They were men now, and she thought they'd put that reckless behavior behind them. Jesse worked hard on his father's horse breeding and training farm and kept his promises to her. How could they both be so irresponsible? And worse, how could Jesse, the love of her life, put her in danger by drinking and then driving a buggy to take her home?

Perhaps Jesse Zook wasn't the mature, solid Christian man she'd believed he was. Maybe he was a fraud. He had forgotten about her twice today—at the lake and then again at Mariella's house. Did she really know him as well as she had believed she did? The notion stabbed at her heart.

Her hands trembled as she dropped the bottle into the back of the buggy. She yearned to ask Jesse to explain himself, but obviously she had to wait until he and Tobias brought the damaged buggy home.

For now, she had to push aside her confusion and anger and face her parents. She was already late, and soon her parents would become worried about the delay.

She quickly stowed Lester along with Jesse's horse and buggy in the barn, grateful summer temperatures had been warm enough to keep the horses from getting cold in the rain. Tobias and Jesse would groom them for the night later.

She hurried through the rain toward the back steps of the two-story whitewashed farmhouse she'd lived in her entire life. When she reached the back door, she stopped, sniffed, and swiped her hand over her eyes, hoping to conceal both her raging emotions and the evidence that she'd cried during the ride home.

But she couldn't wipe from her mind the image of Tobias's buggy flipping onto its side. The thought of the smashed buggy sent a shudder through her and stole her breath for a moment. The terror of holding on to Jesse and begging him to slow down overtook her, and her legs wobbled.

Why would Jesse and Tobias risk their lives for alcohol? Why would Jesse risk hers?

Thunder crashed, and Ariana gripped the knob on the closed back door. She peered through the window into the mudroom, and through the open doorway to the kitchen she saw her father sitting in his usual spot at the head of the table. Her mother brought a platter of food over to him. Taking a deep breath, she prayed her eyes weren't puffy. She had to try to act as if everything was okay. If her father knew about the racing, he would be furious. She couldn't bear to witness another argument between *Dat* and Tobias.

Ariana pulled the door open, and as she stepped

into the mudroom, the aroma of baked chicken wafted over her.

She kicked off her soggy shoes and pulled at her dress where it was stuck to her legs. Then she touched her prayer cover, gasping when she felt it was also soaked. She'd been so worried about Tobias that she hadn't thought to take it off before rushing from Jesse's buggy to check on him. She cringed, imagining the lecture her parents would give her for not only getting wet but for not shielding or removing her prayer covering.

"Ariana?" *Mamm* called from the kitchen. "Tobias? Is that you?"

Ariana forced her lips to curl up in a smile and then stepped into the kitchen. "I'm home. Supper smells *appeditlich*."

Mamm's pleasant expression melted into a frown as she studied Ariana. "Are you wet?"

"*Ya.*" Ariana tried to laugh it off, but her laughter warbled. "I got caught in the rain." She started for the stairs. "I'm going to go change. I'll be right down for supper."

"Where's Tobias?" *Mamm* asked as Ariana hurried past her. "Is Jesse staying for supper?"

"They're on their way. They'll be here soon." Ariana reached the stairs and started up, hoping Tobias would walk in before *Mamm* could ask more questions. She couldn't bear the thought of her mother being upset over the accident.

"Wait," *Mamm* said, and Ariana stilled. "I don't understand. Why isn't Tobias with you?"

Ariana swallowed. "They're delayed."

"Delayed?" *Mamm* tilted her head to the side. "What do you mean?"

"They'll be here shortly." Spinning on her foot, she gripped the banister and started up the stairs.

"Ariana Kathryn!" *Dat's* voice boomed, and Ariana froze, gripping the banister with such force that, looking down, she saw her knuckles turn white. "Please answer your *mamm* before you run off."

Ariana slowly turned back toward the kitchen. She cleared her throat, and her mother's deep-brown eyes widened. "Tobias was in an accident, but he's fine."

Mamm blew out a puff of air, rushed over, and grabbed hold of Ariana's arms. "What happened?"

"He's fine," Ariana repeated. "He flipped the buggy, but he's okay. Jesse had me come home in his buggy. I brought Lester home too. Jesse thought he could figure out a way to get Tobias's buggy home."

"Tobias flipped the buggy?" *Dat* pushed the chair back and then stood before crossing the kitchen and coming to a stop in front of Ariana. "How did he flip the buggy?"

"Well, it was raining, and . . . and Tobias was going too fast," Ariana began, her voice small and thin. "I was in Jesse's buggy, and Tobias passed us. Jesse sped up after him, and I kept screaming for him to slow down, but he didn't. I've never been so scared before." The words tumbled out of her mouth as a tear spilled down her cheek.

"And, well, Tobias took a turn and something must have broken on the buggy because the buggy flipped onto its side. Lester kept going, dragging the buggy along until Jesse caught up to him, jumped out of his buggy, and chased him down. It was so horrible and scary. I was so afraid Tobias had been hurt."

"Why were they going too fast?" *Dat*'s voice seemed to echo in the kitchen. "Both Tobias and Jesse know better than to push their horses in the rain."

Ariana opened her mouth and then closed it. While she felt obligated to tell her father about the alcohol, she didn't want to get her brother into more trouble than he would already face when *Dat* saw the condition of the buggy. Her bottom lip trembled and tears stung her eyes.

"What aren't you telling me?" *Dat* demanded. "It's obvious you're holding something back. Tell me what it is. Now."

"Marvin, please." *Mamm*'s voice was quiet but firm. "Calm down. Can't you tell she's upset?" She rubbed Ariana's arm.

Dat's expression softened as he turned to *Mamm*. "I understand she's upset, but I need to know what happened." He focused on Ariana again, but his gaze was warmer. "Please tell me what happened."

"They were racing," Ariana said, her voice wobbling.

"What?" *Dat* exclaimed. "They were racing in the rain? They know from past experience how dangerous that can be."

"I begged Jesse to slow down, but he wouldn't. He just kept chasing after Tobias." Ariana sniffed as tears poured from her eyes. "I've never seen Jesse so reckless and irresponsible. It was as if he was someone else and not the Jesse I know so well." She gaped when she realized what she'd said. "But Tobias is fine, and Lester is fine," she added quickly. "Only Tobias's buggy was damaged in the crash."

Dat gritted his teeth. "When will that *bu* learn? Last week he left the gate open and four of the cows escaped. It's like his mind isn't focused on the present. His head is always in the clouds." He shoved his hands through his thinning hair. "Now he's done this. No matter how much I instruct him to get his life together, he still disobeys me." Grumbling, he stalked over to the table and sank into his chair. "I'll deal with him when he gets home. Let's eat."

Ariana sniffed, and *Mamm* pulled her into a hug. "I was so scared," she murmured into her mother's shoulder.

"It's all right," *Mamm* whispered. "You're home now and you're safe. Go get changed and we'll eat. I'm just thankful Tobias and Lester are okay." She rubbed Ariana's back. "Everything will be just fine."

"*Danki, Mamm.*" Ariana climbed the stairs to the second floor and stepped into her room. After drying off and pulling on a fresh dress, she stood by her window and looked out past the rain, toward the road.

Ariana hoped Jesse and Tobias would be back soon. Anger simmered through her veins as the image of the vodka bottle filled her mind. When she had a moment to talk to Jesse alone, she would demand he explain why he would risk her safety for alcohol. Depending upon his answer, she'd determine if he was the man she believed would build a family with her and take care of her for the rest of her life.

CHAPTER 4

Jesse's heart pounded as he and Tobias stepped into the Smucker family's kitchen.

"Can you possibly explain why you two were racing in a storm?" Marvin demanded. "Didn't you two learn about the dangers of racing when you were sixteen and you both wound up in the emergency room? I would think your broken arm would have taught you a lesson back then, Jesse."

Driving rain pelted the kitchen windows, filling the heavy silence as Marvin speared Jesse and Tobias with harsh and furious eyes. In his early fifties, Marvin Smucker stood just under six feet and had graying dark hair and a matching beard. While his two children had inherited his dark hair, they had received their mother's dark eyes instead of Marvin's bright hazel.

"Well?" Marvin stood just inches from Jesse and Tobias. "I'm still waiting for an answer." His voice was loud as his cheeks flushed pink with anger. "You scared Rosanna and me and also Jesse's parents when you two raced in a storm all those years ago. Were you trying to scare us again? Or did you just forget how to act like adults?"

Jesse looked across the kitchen to where Ariana stood at the sink holding a pot suspended in the air. She glanced at him. She'd changed into a blue dress, and her hair was covered with a matching blue scarf. When their eyes met, her lips pressed together and a frown clouded her pretty face. Her dark eyes moved to Tobias and remained focused on him. Jesse suddenly had the distinct feeling Ariana was avoiding his gaze. Why would she ignore him? Did she really share her father's belief that he had been acting like a sixteen-year-old?

Jesse folded his arms over his chest and shivered as droplets of water dripped down his face and onto his already drenched shirt. Although he'd dried off with a towel Todd had loaned him during the short drive to Marvin's farm, Jesse had gotten soaked once again when they struggled to unload the buggy and stow it in the barn.

Beside him, Tobias leveled a hard gaze at his father, and a muscle in his jaw twitched as he cradled his right arm in his left. Jesse took in the injuries he hadn't noticed as they were working to move the buggy in the rain. Purple-and-blue bruises stained Tobias's right cheek, and a thin cut sliced from his temple to the bridge of his nose.

"Tobias!" Rosanna rushed over to them as she entered the room. She stifled a sob after she touched his cheek. "*Ach!* You're hurt."

"I'm fine," Tobias grumbled, not taking his glare off his father.

"Ariana!" Rosanna called, examining Tobias's arm. "Get the salve and a couple of towels."

Ariana scurried out of the kitchen.

"You still haven't answered my questions," Marvin boomed. "Why were you racing? What were you thinking?" He shook a finger millimeters from Tobias's nose. "What do you have to say for yourself, Tobias John?"

"Nothing," Tobias snapped, then winced as his mother moved his arm.

"Nothing?" Marvin's bushy eyebrows shot up toward his receding hairline. "Why don't you have anything to say for yourself?"

"Because I don't have to say anything," Tobias seethed. "You'll say it for me."

Jesse gaped, staring at Tobias with wonder. Jesse had never dreamt of speaking to his father in such a disrespectful tone. He braced himself, awaiting Marvin's explosion.

Marvin's chubby face flushed bright crimson, and his jaw worked, but no words passed his lips.

Ariana reappeared with two towels and a container of homemade salve. She handed one towel and the salve to her mother. While Tobias dried himself with his left hand, Rosanna began to spread salve over his wounds, causing Tobias to squeeze his eyes shut and hiss in protest.

"Stop squirming," Rosanna said. "This cut looks bad, and we don't want it to get infected. It's awfully close to your eye."

With her eyes focused on the second towel, Ariana stepped over to Jesse and handed it to him.

"*Danki.*" He hugged the towel to his middle. He studied her face, hoping she'd look up at him, but she kept her eyes focused on his hands. "Arie?" he whispered. "Are you all right?"

Ignoring him, she quickly crossed to the sink, and, with her back to him, began washing dishes. Her coldness stung deep into his soul. He stared at her back, waiting for a sign, any sign, that their relationship was still okay, but she kept working at the sink as if she were alone in the kitchen.

"Tobias," Marvin's voice bellowed. "I'm still waiting on an explanation for your behavior. Do you realize how much worse your accident could have been?"

Tobias responded with a sarcastic snicker. "You should see the buggy."

Jesse blinked as he looked at his best friend. *Does he want to start an argument?*

"What do you mean?" Marvin looked over at Ariana and then back at Tobias. "Your *schweschder* said you could get the buggy home."

"*Ya*, on a flatbed." Tobias moved the towel over his soggy trousers. "The windshield is smashed. The roof and frame are twisted too. It's pretty far gone, right, Jesse? It's almost as bad as that accident we had when we were sixteen."

Jesse nodded with a frown. He longed to sneak out and head to his own house, but he couldn't leave without assurance that he and Ariana were okay, that their relationship was still intact.

Marvin shook his head. "I'm so tired of your irresponsible behavior. I'm also tired of your attitude."

"Well, *Dat*, that's one thing we have in common." Tobias lifted his chin. "I'm tired of your attitude toward me. I'm tired of your constant criticism and your lectures. And I'm tired of you trying to force me to be someone I'm not." He handed the towel to his mother and started toward the stairs. "I'm going to take a shower."

"Get back here!" Marvin started after him. "I'm not done with you."

Tobias spun toward his father, his eyes glittering in the low light. "I'm done with you. I have nothing else to say to you." His voice faltered, and he cleared his throat.

Jesse scanned the kitchen, taking in Rosanna's frown and glistening eyes. At the sink, Ariana's shoulders slumped as she sagged against the sink. The tension was palpable, and Jesse's chest tightened. Jesse and his brothers rarely argued with their father or with each other. If only Jesse could help Tobias and his father work out their differences. But how could he help fix this broken relationship when it seemed nearly beyond repair? Besides, this was a private family matter.

"You may be tired of it, but I'm determined to make a *gut* man out of you," Marvin continued. "How do you expect to get married and raise a family if you can't take care of yourself? You need to learn how to take responsibility for your actions. Racing buggies in the rain won't earn my praise. It's time you started acting like a man instead of an overgrown *kind*."

Tobias's expression hardened. "I'm going to live my life the way I want to, and I don't need your permission."

"Is that so?" Marvin folded his arms over his rotund middle. "As long as you live in *mei haus*, you will follow my rules and ask for my permission."

"You've made that abundantly clear. Maybe it's time that changed."

Marvin stood nose to nose with his son, the two men the same height. "I don't see you moving out anytime soon since you don't have any means to live on your own."

"Please stop arguing," Rosanna cut in, her voice sounding thick. "I've heard enough!"

Marvin spun to face her, and Tobias jogged up the stairs.

Jesse finished drying himself, folded the towel, and set it on a kitchen chair. He turned toward Rosanna as she wiped two stray tears from her chin.

"*Danki* for the towel," he told her before looking at Marvin, who was leaning against another kitchen chair. "The buggy is in the barn. You might be able to salvage some of it."

"I'm going to go check on Tobias," Rosanna muttered as she picked up the wet towel and headed up the stairs.

Jesse pulled Todd's business card from his pocket and placed it on the table. "That's the name of the tow truck driver who brought it home. He can take it to the carriage shop if you'd like." He started toward the door and then turned toward the sink, hoping Ariana would look at him.

"Wait." Marvin walked over to him. "I want a word with you too."

Jesse swallowed and cut his eyes back to Ariana. *Look at me, Arie. Give me a sign that you still love me.* When she didn't turn around, he focused on Marvin. "All right."

"I'm shocked you would take such a dangerous risk, racing with *mei dochder* in your buggy." His expression was grim. "I expected more from you. I thought you'd learned your lesson after the dangerous pranks you and Tobias pulled as teenagers."

"Wait." Jesse held his hands up. "I wasn't—"

"It's apparent to me that you haven't learned anything. You're still the same reckless young man who helped Tobias set the back pasture on fire when you decided to have a bonfire in the middle of the summer during a drought."

Jesse took a deep, shuddering breath as fury flowed through his veins. "That was a long time ago."

"*Ya*, it was a long time ago, but your behavior today has shown me you haven't changed. I've lost all trust in you, and I want you to stay away from *mei dochder*. You're not a *gut* influence for her."

Jesse stilled as Marvin's words filtered through his mind, and out of the corner of his eye, he saw Ariana freeze too.

"What . . . what are you saying?" Jesse asked Marvin slowly.

"What I'm saying is that I can't allow Ariana to marry or even date a man who can't be trusted to keep her safe."

"You're breaking my engagement to Ariana?" Jesse's body went cold with a mixture of frustration, shock, and grief.

"*Ya*, that's right."

The floor seemed to fall out beneath Jesse, and the world spun. *I can't lose her.* "But we-we've set the date," he stammered. "We have plans, and I've already built her a *haus*." He turned toward Ariana, hoping she'd defend Jesse and their future plans.

Ariana looked at Jesse, then Marvin, her brown eyes wide. *"Dat?"* Her voice trembled, and her eyes misted over. "You're forbidding me from marrying Jesse?"

Marvin nodded. "That's right. He's not *gut* for you. He's shown his true colors, and I need to keep you away from him. It's for the best. You'll thank me someday."

Tears streamed down Ariana's face. "I don't think that's your decision."

"Ya, it is." Marvin's voice rose, and Ariana cringed. "I'm your *dat,* and it's my job to decide what's best for you." He turned toward Jesse again. "I think it would be best if you left now."

"Please listen to me," Jesse began, holding his hands up again. "I'm sorry for giving you the wrong impression. I was only trying to—"

"You need to leave." Marvin pointed toward the door. "We've had enough stress in this *haus* tonight."

Jesse's body shook and his heart squeezed with anguish as he looked at Ariana. He craved her reassurance. *Tell me you love me.*

Ariana's chest heaved as tears poured down her face. She met his eyes but remained silent.

"Jesse." Marvin's voice began with a hint of warning. "Leave now."

Jesse looked at Ariana one last time and started out.

. . .

Ariana swallowed a sob as Jesse disappeared into the mudroom. When the back door slammed shut, her body trembled and fear gripped her. Her future was crumbling right before her eyes. She couldn't lose him! She was upset with him, but she had to believe there was still a chance they could work things out.

She wasn't ready to give up on him yet. They could work through their problems, if only he would confess he'd been drinking—though she wasn't convinced now that he'd actually been as drunk as Tobias no doubt had been. And if he promised never to drink again and explained why he hadn't slowed down when she pleaded for him to . . .

"Jesse!" Ariana screamed, rushing toward the door.

"Ariana! Get back here," *Dat* snapped, following her.

Ariana hurried through the mudroom and pushed open the back door. Her shoes skidded on the porch floor as she slid toward the railing. A cool mist of rain drifted over her as she leaned on the railing.

"Jesse! Wait!" she screamed as he neared the barn. "Please don't go!"

Jesse spun to face her, his handsome face twisted in a scowl. Her heart squeezed, and tears pricked her eyes.

"Arie, you have to believe I would never do anything to deliberately put you in danger. I was only trying to stop Tobias from racing." He glanced behind her and then took a step back. "I better go. Your *dat* told me to leave."

"Stay!" she begged him. "We'll talk to him and work this out."

"There's nothing to work out," *Dat* growled behind her. "Go back in the *haus* now."

She looked over her shoulder at her father's glare. "But *Dat*, we're engaged, and I—"

"You don't know what's *gut* for you." *Dat* pointed toward the house. "Please go inside now."

Ariana longed to stand up to her father, but she knew better than to go against him. With her shoulders sagging, she turned toward Jesse one last time before rushing into the house with tears spilling down her cheeks. If only she could go back in time and convince Tobias and Jesse not to drink.

Sniffing, she wiped away her tears and returned to the sink. *Mamm* appeared beside her and began drying the dishes in the rack.

"I tried to encourage Tobias to come down and eat something," *Mamm* said. "He refused. If only Tobias and your *dat* could see just how much alike they are. They're both so very stubborn. Their relationship would be so much easier if they could have a civil and calm conversation. They both need to learn to keep their tempers in check."

Ariana nodded while keeping her eyes trained on the frothy water.

Mamm stopped drying the dish in her hand and leaned toward her. *"Was iss letz?"*

Ariana raised her eyes to *Mamm* as a knot of despair swelled in her throat. *"Dat* said I can't see Jesse anymore. The wedding is canceled. He says Jesse isn't *gut* for me because he was reckless today." She cleared her throat. "I'm upset with Jesse, but I didn't want to break things off." More tears spilled down her hot cheeks.

"Ach, mei liewe." *Mamm* pulled her into her arms for a hug. "Everything will be fine. I'll talk to your *dat*." She stepped back and touched Ariana's shoulder. "Don't

worry about anything." She nodded toward the stairs. "I'll finish the dishes. Why don't you try to get Tobias to agree to eat something? He seems to listen to you better than anyone else in this *haus*. I'll talk to your *dat*. Don't give up hope."

Ariana agreed and headed upstairs. She found her brother lying on his bed, staring up at the ceiling. She lingered in the doorway for a moment, waiting for him to acknowledge her. When he didn't, she stepped inside the room and stood at the foot of his bed. "Don't you want something to eat?"

He lowered his eyes to her and blinked. "No, *danki*."

"You should eat something. Lunch was hours ago. I'll bring a plate up to you if you'd like."

"*Danki*, but I've lost my appetite after arguing with *Dat*." Tobias sat up and sighed, resting his elbows on his thighs. "I've had it. I can't take it anymore. I think it's time for me to leave."

"Leave?" Ariana's eyes widened and her stomach twisted. "Where will you go?"

"I haven't figured that out yet." He stood, crossed the room, and took a black duffel bag from his closet. "Nothing is ever going to change around here, so I need to find somewhere else to live." He set the opened bag on his bed and began pulling clothes out of his dresser drawers and tossing them in.

"Things could change if you and *Dat* both compromised," she hedged, hoping Tobias wouldn't get upset with her.

"What do you mean?" He stopped packing and studied her.

"What if you tried just a little harder to please *Dat*?" She fingered the wooden post of his footboard. "He gets frustrated when you don't finish your chores on time or when you wander off into the back pasture when you're supposed to be cleaning the dairy barn. If you just did as *Dat* asked, then he wouldn't get so upset." She held her breath and silently prayed he'd consider her suggestions.

Tobias paused, and then his frown deepened. "It won't work. All *Dat* and I do is fight, so it's better if I leave."

"Don't say that. *Mamm* and *Dat* love you. We're a family and we belong together."

Tobias shook his head as he continued to fill his bag.

An image of the vodka bottle filled Ariana's mind. Jesse and Tobias had been behind Mariella's barn together. She had to know the whole truth before it drove her crazy. She took a deep breath. "You've been drinking."

"What?" His eyes flickered with something that looked like worry, and then his frown returned. "Why would you think that?"

She looked over her shoulder toward the doorway and then leaned in closer to Tobias. "I found an empty bottle of vodka in the back of Jesse's buggy," she whispered.

Avoiding her eyes, he returned to packing. "Look, I'm fine. I'm not drunk. I'm just tired of dealing with *Dat*."

"Please stop packing." Alarm coursed through her. She grabbed his arm, holding it still. "You can't go. You have to stay. You're *mei bruder*. I need you here. *Mamm* and *Dat* need you too." She released his arm and sank down onto the bed.

"It's not that simple for me."

"What do you mean?"

"You're the *dochder*. You're engaged, and your life is planned for you. I'm expected to take over the farm someday when *Mamm* and *Dat* move into a *daadihaus*. I don't want to be a dairy farmer, but *Dat* won't listen. He doesn't understand that this is his dream, not mine. How can I live here the rest of my life with *Dat* always chastising me? It will never work."

"You and *Dat* can work things out if you swallow your pride and talk to him. You're both stubborn and set in your ways, but you can compromise if you really try to talk to him without losing your temper. Swallow your pride and listen to *Dat* without immediately jumping to conclusions." She folded her hands together, pleading with him. "Please think about it. Work things out with him for *Mamm* and me."

"You've had to listen to *Dat* and me argue nearly your whole life, and *Mamm* has had to listen to us too." His eyes misted over. "If I leave, things will be easier on both of you." He turned toward the dresser for the remainder of his belongings.

She sniffed. "I've already lost Jesse. I can't lose you too."

"What do you mean?" He turned toward her.

"*Dat* told Jesse to stay away from me. Our wedding is off." She swiped at her eyes. "He said Jesse was too reckless today, and he can't trust him with me."

Moving the bag, Tobias sank down onto the bed

beside her. "That's my fault. If I hadn't wrecked the buggy this never would have happened." He sighed. "Things will get better for you. *Dat* will forgive Jesse."

"You think so?"

"Definitely. Jesse has his life together. He and his *dat* run a successful business. Just give *Dat* time to calm down, and your wedding will go on as planned."

"I hope you're right."

"You know I am. You and Jesse are meant to be together."

"Just like you're meant to be here. If we do get married, I want you to be here to witness it." Ariana's lip trembled as she looked up at him. "Promise me you won't make any decisions until tomorrow. Just sleep on it tonight and then decide in the morning."

He nodded. "Fine."

"*Danki.*" She stood and crossed the room. Stopping in the doorway, she looked at him again. "I can still get you a plate."

"I'm not hungry, but *danki.*"

As Ariana made her way downstairs, she whispered an urgent prayer asking God to help Tobias and *Dat*—and Jesse too—work out their problems. The three most important men in her life needed help she couldn't give them on her own.

CHAPTER 5

"Tobias!" Ariana hurried up the stairs the following morning, her pulse pounding with every step.

"Tobias!" she called again, knocking on his bedroom door. "You overslept. *Dat* is really upset since this is the second time this week. He's waiting for you in the barn. You'd better get downstairs right now before he starts yelling." She leaned her ear against the door and listened for any movement. "Are you in there?"

She knocked once more and then pushed open the door. The room was empty. Tobias's green window shades were closed, and his bed was neatly made. Maybe he was in the bathroom?

She marched down the hallway to the small bathroom they shared and found it also empty. Her stomach pitched as their conversation the night before echoed through her mind. Surely he hadn't left as he'd threatened. He was only angry, and a good night's sleep should have changed his mind and brought his raging emotions into clear focus.

Ariana entered Tobias's room once again and searched for signs he hadn't left in the middle of the night. But when she checked his dresser, his wallet was gone. Her shoulders tensed with worry. She looked in his closet, and the black duffel bag was also gone. When she opened every dresser drawer and found them empty, threatening tears pricked her eyes.

"No, no," she whispered. "Why didn't you wait another day, Tobias?"

Ariana returned to the kitchen, where *Mamm* stood at the stove making home fries. She took a deep breath as *Mamm* looked at her. "Tobias is gone."

"Gone?" *Mamm* tilted her head. "What do you mean?"

"Last night he told me he was going to leave home. I asked him to sleep on it, but all his clothes are gone. His duffel bag and wallet are gone too."

"Leave? I don't understand."

"He said he was tired of arguing with *Dat*." Ariana explained more as *Mamm* gaped, her dark eyes glistening with tears. "He did it. He left."

"Who left?" *Dat's* voice startled Ariana.

"Tobias did." *Mamm's* voice was thin and reedy. "He told Ariana last night he was going to leave home. That was after you told him he had no way to live on his own."

Dat looked to Ariana as if she held all the answers. "That doesn't make sense. Where would he even go?"

Ariana repeated her conversation with Tobias as *Dat* stared at her. "I tried to convince him to stay, but I guess he snuck out while we were asleep."

Dat's face reddened. "This is all Jesse's fault. He's a bad influence. Maybe he even encouraged Tobias to leave home. And if he hadn't been racing with Tobias this never would've happened. Tobias wouldn't have crashed the buggy, and he'd be out in the barn helping me with the cows. You'd better stay away from Jesse. I mean it, Ariana. He's irresponsible and nothing but trouble."

Ariana blinked as more tears filled her eyes. She recalled what Jesse said before he left last night, that he had only been trying to stop Tobias from going so fast. But why hadn't Jesse done a better job before they left Mariella's house? Jesse could have prevented all this. Not only didn't he keep Tobias from drinking, but most likely he polished off that bottle of vodka she'd found in his buggy himself.

As *Dat* marched outside, Ariana pushed back her shoulders. She had to be strong. She had to find a way to go on without Jesse and Tobias, but it seemed an impossible task.

Then again, maybe *Dat* was right. Maybe she *was* better off without Jesse. But if that was true, why did the thought of losing him rock her to her very core?

. . .

Jesse tied his horse to the fence outside the Smuckers' dairy barn and started up the rock pathway toward the structure's large doors. He'd finished all his chores at home and then rushed over to see Marvin, hoping to convince him to revoke his cancelation of his and Ariana's engagement. He also hoped to explain to Marvin that he wasn't responsible for Tobias's accident.

He reached the barn doors and swallowed a yawn. He'd spent all night thinking of Ariana and trying to come up with a plan to win back Marvin's favor. He couldn't let Ariana go. She was the love of his life, and he couldn't wait to marry her. There had to be a way to make Marvin see he'd do everything in his power to protect Ariana and that he'd never deliberately risk her safety.

When he realized he and Ariana were truly going too fast for the road conditions yesterday, at the risk—and reality—of not being able to stop Tobias from crashing, he'd slowed down. Only when Tobias's buggy turned over had he sped up again, desperate to stop Lester before Tobias could be hurt anymore than he already was.

After taking a deep breath, he stepped into the barn, and the scent of animals drifted over him.

"Marvin?" He scanned the large dairy barn, searching for Marvin. "Are you in here?"

Marvin emerged from the back corner, a glower twisting his face as he approached Jesse. "What are you doing here after I told you to stay away?"

Jesse held up his hands in an attempt to calm the older man. "I just want to talk. You were upset last night and I—"

"And I'm even more upset today." He lifted his hat and pushed his hand through his sweaty, dark hair. "Where's Tobias?"

"What?" Jesse asked, dumbfounded by the question.

"Is he staying with you?"

"No, he's not with me. He's not here?"

"No, he was gone when we got up this morning. All his belongings too. I want to know where he went."

Marvin's voice was harsh. "Rosanna spent the morning calling all the relatives and *freinden* we thought he may have reached out to, but no one has seen him or heard from him. I'm sure you know something."

"I don't know anything at all. I'm just as surprised as you are." Jesse recalled his last conversation with Tobias. "He was upset yesterday. I tried to talk to him, but he was too distraught to listen to me." *And he was also too drunk.*

Jesse opened his mouth to tell Marvin his son had been drinking, but the anger he saw on Marvin's face prevented him from sharing the truth. Learning Tobias was drunk would push Marvin over the edge, and right now Jesse needed him to calm down. He needed Marvin's forgiveness and blessing, not his fury. Besides, telling him about the alcohol now ran the risk of sounding like a lie meant to move the blame from him to Tobias.

"Look, I'm sorry about what happened yesterday." Jesse fought to keep his voice calm despite his galloping pulse. "I know I made some bad decisions when I was younger, but I would never deliberately do anything that would hurt Arie or put her in jeopardy. I came here to ask for your forgiveness for going too fast yesterday, even though—"

"I forgive you, but the wedding is still off. You're not to see my Ariana anymore."

"What?" Marvin's word punched Jesse in the gut. Why was he being so unreasonable? "If you forgive me, then why can't we move past this?"

"I am moving past it. I have work to do. I'm sure you

have chores to do at your farm too. So you should get home." Marvin turned and started walking away.

"Marvin!" Jesse called after him, his voice shaky. "You've known me nearly my whole life, and you know how much Ariana means to me. Why are you treating me like this?"

Marvin spun, lancing him with a hard glare. "If it weren't for you, *mei sohn* would be here, and his buggy wouldn't be in shambles."

Jesse blew out a tremulous rush of air as Marvin disappeared into the back of the large barn. Anguish and despair swamped him. His world was crumbing around him. In less than twenty-four hours, he'd lost his fiancée and his best friend. How had this happened? And, more importantly, how could he fix it?

"Jesse?"

Craning his neck to look over his shoulder, Jesse's body relaxed when he took in the sight of Ariana staring at him. Despite her deep frown, she looked radiant clad in a rose-colored dress with her hair covered by a matching scarf.

"Hi." A weight lifted off his shoulders as he drank in the sight of her gorgeous face. "I didn't hear you walk into the barn."

"What are you doing here?"

When her frown didn't soften, his shoulders stiffened with apprehension. "I came to try to talk to your *dat* and to hopefully see you. I couldn't sleep after the way things were left last night. I worried about you and our relationship all night long."

"You should go." She fingered her black apron and her eyes glistened.

"*Was iss letz?*" He closed the distance between them and reached for her hand, but she backed away before he could touch her.

"Tobias is gone." Her voice was watery. "He left sometime last night, and he didn't leave us a note. We have no idea where he is."

"I know." Jesse sighed. "Your *dat* told me."

"Do you know where he is?"

"No, I don't. Your *dat* asked me the same thing. How could I possibly know where he is?"

"He told me last night he was thinking of leaving, and I begged him to sleep on it. I told him not to make any decisions before morning, but he left anyway." She studied him. "If he was already thinking about leaving before he got home last night, then he could have told you where he was going. You also talked with him for quite a while at the lake yesterday." She lifted her chin, defiance on her face. "You're his best *freind*. Why wouldn't he tell you he was leaving? I would tell Mariella if I were thinking of making a big decision like that. Why didn't you stop him?"

"He didn't say anything to me about leaving. He only talked about how your *dat* treats him." Jesse pinched the bridge of his nose, trying in vain to calm his frayed nerves. "If I had known Tobias was thinking about leaving, I would've tried to talk him out of it."

He studied her eyes. "Where is this hostility coming from? You know me. You know how much I care about you and your family."

She shook her head. "Actually, I don't think I know you at all."

"What does that mean?"

She looked past him as if checking to see if Marvin was there and then lowered her voice. "I found the vodka bottle in the back of your buggy. You were drinking yesterday. The Jesse I knew would never drink. You're not the person I thought you were."

"Wait a minute." He held his hands up. "That wasn't my bottle. I was just disposing of it."

She crossed her arms over her apron. "Do you think I'm that naïve?"

"I'm telling you the truth. It wasn't mine. It was Tobias's." He explained his conversation with Tobias when he found him behind the barn. "I had to wrestle the bottle away from him. I poured the remaining vodka out and then told Tobias I would dispose of the bottle for him. I was going to throw it out before I got home."

"I don't believe you. I don't think you would have risked my safety if you hadn't been drinking."

"Why would I lie to you? I told you. I was only trying to stop Tobias. *Ya*, I was driving fast, and I know you were scared. But as soon as I realized we could be in danger, I slowed down."

"It doesn't matter. *Mei dat* has forbidden me from seeing you." She pointed toward the barn door. "You should go before he catches us talking."

Confusion and hurt flooded him. "Don't you still love me?"

She stared down at the toe of her black shoe.

"We can work this out." He placed his finger under her chin and angled her face so she was forced to look him in the eye. "I won't give up until you believe me and your *dat* allows us to get married."

"I can't see you anymore." Her voice broke.

"It will be okay," he said, his heart breaking as a tear trickled down her chin. "I promise you I'll make this right."

"You can't." She wiped the tear away and then took a step back, away from his touch. "It's over between us."

"Why are you giving up so easily? I know you'll soon realize I'm telling the truth, and I just told you I'll talk to your *dat*."

"If you truly cared about me," she began, tears flowing down her cheeks, "then you never would have been drinking, and you would have stopped *mei bruder* from leaving my family."

Turning, she ran out of the barn. He rushed after her, calling her name, but she kept going until she was inside the house.

Jesse stood beside his buggy and swiped his hand down his face. Somehow he'd managed to make the situation worse. Now he was at a loss as to how to repair his relationship with Ariana and restore their engagement.

As he stared at her house, guilt and regret coiled through him. He should have stopped Tobias from driving last night, but how could he have prevented him from climbing into his buggy? Perhaps if he'd told Ariana her brother was drunk then, she could have convinced Tobias to let her guide the horse home, and none of this would have happened.

But he still didn't understand why Marvin was

so determined to blame him for everything that had happened.

Squinting, he looked up at the blue summer sky. He needed guidance. He needed help getting Ariana back and convincing her father he was worthy of her hand.

As he climbed into his buggy, Jesse sent a silent prayer up to God, begging Him for guidance.

• • •

"You broke up with Jesse and Tobias is gone?" Mariella's eyes widened as she sat on the bench beside Ariana at church.

"*Ya,*" Ariana whispered in response. Despite crying herself to sleep last night, she managed to tell Mariella the entire story without shedding a tear. She left out the part about the empty vodka bottle since she still had a difficult time accepting that Jesse had been drinking and then lied to her.

"*Ach, mei liewe.* Are you all right?"

Ariana shrugged, hoping to give the appearance everything was okay, even though she felt as if her heart had been trampled by a team of horses. "I'll be all right eventually." No, she'd never be all right without Jesse and Tobias in her life.

"Where is Tobias now?"

"We don't know." Ariana moved closer and lowered her voice. "I keep hoping he'll contact us to at least let us know he's okay. *Mei mamm* is distraught. She can't handle not knowing where he is. We've called all our relatives, and no one has heard from him."

"I'm so sorry." Mariella sniffed, and her brown eyes sparkled in the low light of the Fisher family's barn where the church service was being held today. "I hope he contacts your family soon." She looked over toward the unmarried men and her eyes widened. "Jesse is staring at you."

"Don't look at him," Ariana warned through gritted teeth as her cheeks heated. "I've been trying to ignore him."

Mariella raised an eyebrow. "You've loved him your whole life. How can you ignore him?"

"I don't know." Ariana sighed. "You're right. It will take some time for me to mend my broken heart."

Against her better judgment, Ariana sneaked a glance toward the section where Jesse sat, and her eyes locked with his. Her breath paused, and her pulse thrummed as he studied her. His handsome face contorted with a frown, and she longed to rush over and hug him. But she couldn't. Not only would the behavior be inappropriate, but her father had made it clear she was to steer clear of him. Also, she was still angry with him for drinking and then putting her at risk during their trek home on Friday. Tobias was to blame too, but . . .

As much as her heart ached for Jesse, she had to somehow put him out of her mind. She was better off without him. He was too irresponsible.

But how could she forget Jesse when she loved him so much?

· · ·

Jesse leaned his shoulder against the corner of the Fishers' barn. He'd tried in vain not to stare at Ariana during the three-hour service, but his gaze gravitated to her as if pulled by an invisible magnet. She'd looked at him only once and then kept her eyes focused on the hymnal or on her lap, staring at her emerald-green dress. He yearned to talk to her and find out how she could turn off her feelings for him after all their years as friends, then dating.

Last night he'd stayed awake for the second night in a row, racking his mind for an idea of how to get her alone to talk to her. During the service he decided standing outside the barn and watching for her to walk by with a serving tray during the noon meal seemed to be the best solution. Now he just had to patiently wait for her to appear.

When Ariana and Mariella headed from the barn toward the Fishers' house, his stomach clenched. This was his chance.

"Arie!" he called. She stilled for a brief moment before continuing toward the house. "Ariana Kathryn Smucker!"

Ariana stopped and turned toward him. When her eyes focused on him, she hesitated. Mariella gave him a tentative nod. Then she took Ariana's tray from her and whispered something before nudging Ariana forward. Ariana paused and then looked toward the barn before hurrying toward him.

"*Danki*, Mariella," he whispered as his shoulders relaxed slightly.

"What do you want, Jesse?" Ariana hissed as she motioned for him to follow her around to the back of the barn. "I've told you I can't see you. If *mei dat* sees us together, he will explode."

"I know, but I can't stand the silence between us. It's killing me."

Ariana clasped her hands together, and something in her eyes softened. Was he getting through to her? His pulse leapt with hope.

"I shouldn't be talking to you."

"How are you?" he asked, ignoring her warning. He stood so close to her that he could smell the familiar aroma of her favorite vanilla lotion. He bit back the urge to caress her soft cheek.

"It's been horrible. I tiptoed downstairs last night to get a glass of water, and I heard *mei mamm* crying in her bedroom. She misses Tobias so much, and we haven't heard from him. *Mei dat* has been quiet and I can tell he's *bedauerlich*. Tobias told me it would make things better for *Mamm* and me if he left, but he's only made everything worse." She paused and sniffed. "And I miss him too."

"Do you miss me?" Jesse held his breath with anticipation. *Please say yes!*

"I have to go."

Before he could stop her, Ariana rushed back around the side of the barn and hurried toward the Fishers' back door. Jesse kicked a rock and leaned against the side of the barn as disappointment and affliction crawled up his back and stung his eyes.

"Jesse?"

Nathaniel, his older brother, approached him. At twenty-nine, Nathaniel stood slightly taller than Jesse at six feet even. He had light-brown hair, a matching beard, and the same blue eyes Jesse had inherited from their mother.

Nathaniel raised an eyebrow. "Why are you hiding out here?"

"I was trying to talk to Arie."

"Trying to talk to her?" Nathaniel leaned his back against the barn wall and folded his arms over his wide chest. "Are you two arguing?"

"I wish it were that simple. We've broken up. Marvin won't let me see her."

"What?" His brother stood up straight, his eyes wide. "What happened?"

Jesse summarized what had happened between him and Ariana during the past forty-eight hours, leaving out the part about Tobias's drunkenness. Nathaniel listened with interest, his eyes remaining wide.

"I don't know how to get her back," Jesse said after sharing the story. "I can't figure out how to convince Marvin I'm not a bad influence for her either."

Nathaniel shrugged. "That's easy."

"Easy?" Jesse ground out the question. "Now is not the time for jokes."

"I'm not joking." Nathaniel leaned forward, jamming a finger in Jesse's chest. "If you really want to marry her, then you need to find a way to prove to Ariana and Marvin that you will do *anything* to get her back. Show them how much you love her and how committed you are to her."

Jesse blinked as his older brother's words soaked through him.

Nathaniel patted Jesse's shoulder. "Come on. Let's go have a piece of pie."

As Nathaniel started toward the barn door, Jesse looked up at the sky, again asking God for the help he so desperately needed. *Show me, God. Show me how to prove my love for Ariana.*

CHAPTER 6

"How many times do I have to tell you to stay away?" Marvin growled as Jesse entered the stable Monday afternoon.

"I'm not leaving," Jesse countered, standing a little taller as a surge of confidence flowed through him. "I'm here to help with chores."

"I don't need your help."

"*Ya*, you do. Tobias isn't here, so I'll take his place." Jesse pulled on his work gloves, grabbed a pitchfork from the corner of the stable, and started toward the horse stalls.

"Don't you have chores to do at your *dat*'s farm?" Marvin followed him.

"I finished all my chores this morning. Caleb is helping this afternoon," Jesse said, referring to his nineteen-year-old brother. "Caleb said he was *froh* to do a little extra so I could help you." He rolled the sleeves on his short-sleeved tan shirt up to his shoulders. "When I'm done with the stalls, you can tell me what else you need done."

Marvin eyed him as red stained his cheeks. Just like the night he argued with Tobias, his jaw worked, but no words escaped his mouth.

Jesse clamped his own mouth shut to discourage the grin threatening his lips. In all the years he'd known the Smucker family, this was only the second time he'd ever seen Marvin speechless.

"Fine! But only for today," Marvin finally blurted before stalking toward the stable door.

Sweat beaded on Jesse's forehead and trickled between his shoulder blades as he worked. It was another brutally hot June day, but he could take the heat. As he continued to muck the first stall, his thoughts spun. After his strained conversation with Ariana yesterday, Jesse had spent the remainder of the afternoon thinking about the Smucker family and all they were facing after Tobias's departure.

Jesse's chest had squeezed as he recalled the worry and sadness in Ariana's eyes while she talked about how Tobias's disappearance was tearing her parents apart. He loved Ariana, but he also cared deeply for her family. Jesse longed to console both Ariana and her parents. He yearned to find a way to help them.

And then an idea hit him like a bolt of lightning streaking across the night sky. Marvin depended heavily on Tobias since Tobias was his only son, and he needed help with chores now that Tobias was gone. This morning, Jesse briefly explained to his parents that Tobias had left and that he would like to make time to help Marvin. Naturally, his parents were supportive, and Caleb agreed to do extra chores to allow Jesse the time away from the horse farm. He was grateful for his family's understanding and support of the Smucker family.

Tobias's alcohol-induced words had echoed through his mind last night and came to him once again while he worked in the stable.

"Your life is so easy. You have everything you've ever wanted, and you've never had to work for any of it. You've had everything handed to you without any effort . . . You've known for years that you were going to marry mei schweschder. *You didn't even have to chase after Ariana since she's always been in love with you. She's had a crush on you since she was eight. All you had to do was smile at her and pay attention to her and you had her loyalty and her heart."*

Jesse was going to prove Tobias wrong, and he was ready to work hard to show Ariana how much she meant to him. He prayed it would work, because his life was empty without her. He was determined to convince Marvin how much his family meant to him. Jesse wouldn't give up easily on winning back both Marvin's favor and Ariana's heart.

. . .

"Dat!" Ariana called as she stepped into the stable. "I made fresh lemonade. Would you like some?"

Her shoes crunched on the hay as she approached the first stall. *Dat* had been in a bad mood all morning, complaining about all the chores he had to do and grumbling about how thoughtless and irresponsible Tobias had been to leave.

When *Dat* announced he was going to the stable to muck the stalls, Ariana tried to think of a way to brighten his mood. Since he always liked her homemade lemonade, she whipped up a batch and then carried a glass out to the stable with the hope of seeing her father smile. It would be the first time since Tobias left them.

"*Dat?*" She balanced the sweating glass of lemonade and ice in her hand. When she rounded the corner to face the first stall, she blew out a sharp breath. Jesse was there, grinning at her.

"Jesse? Wha-what are you doing here?" she stammered.

His grin widened. "Did you bring that for me?"

Jesse yanked off his work gloves and stuffed them into his pockets before swiping the back of his hand over his glistening brow. Then he lifted his straw hat and raked his fingers through his hair before setting the hat back onto his head. Ariana took in his tall, muscular frame as he leaned the pitchfork against the stall wall, and her words were trapped in her throat. He somehow seemed more handsome than usual. His face was tanned after their day spent at the lake, and his eyes somehow seemed a deeper shade of blue. The sleeves of his shirt were rolled up, revealing his muscular biceps.

When he lifted his eyebrows in question, she realized he was awaiting her response. What had he asked her? *Oh, right. The lemonade.*

"Oh, this?" She cleared her throat as her cheeks flamed. "I was looking for *mei dat*. I thought he might like some lemonade."

"He's not here, but I'll be *froh* to take it off your hands. It's hot in here, and lemonade sounds refreshing."

When she hesitated, the corners of his mouth tipped

up. She held out the glass to him, and when he took it, their fingers brushed, sending sparks of electricity skittering up her arm. She sucked in a breath, and her eyes widened as she looked up at him. *Did Jesse feel that too?*

He seemed unaffected as he took a long draw of lemonade and then wiped the back of his hand over his mouth. "You make the best lemonade."

"*Danki,*" she said as he took another long draw from the glass. "You didn't answer my question. Why are you here?"

"I'm helping with chores."

"Why?"

"Because your *dat* needs the help." He shrugged and took another long drink, polishing off the last of the lemonade.

"Does he know you're here?" She held out her hand, and he returned the empty glass.

Jesse gave her a breathtaking smile, and her knees wobbled at the sight of it. "*Ya,* of course he knows. He was just as shocked as you were to see me, but I convinced him he needed my help since Tobias is gone."

"Oh." She blinked as his words filtered through her mind. Jesse was here to assist *Dat* because her brother was gone. Jesse wanted to help her family. Something warm unfurled in her chest. Despite what had happened, Jesse was still the thoughtful, kind man she'd always adored. Maybe he hadn't lied about the vodka bottle?

But if he hadn't been drinking, then why was the bottle stowed in his buggy? Was it really there so he could get rid of it for Tobias?

She suddenly recalled her father's warning to stay away from Jesse. *Dat*'s mood might darken even more if he found her talking to Jesse. Panic seized her as she peered over her shoulder toward the stable door, in search of her father.

"Arie . . ." Jesse began, his voice sounding thin.

His voice pulled her attention back to him. She stared up at his attractive face, twisted with a deep frown.

"I need to talk to you," he continued. "You've been my best *freind* since we were teenagers. I can't just walk away from you and pretend like I don't feel something for you." The pain in his eyes nearly broke her in two.

She longed to forgive him, but she still had questions. "If you feel something for me, then why did you drink the alcohol?"

"I didn't drink it." His brow furrowed. "Did you see me stumble? Did I slur my words?"

"No."

"Would I have been able to leap from the buggy and stop Lester if I had been drunk?"

She sighed, the fight draining out of her. "No, you wouldn't have."

"I didn't touch a drop of that vodka. I wrestled the bottle from Tobias and poured the rest of it out. It was only in my buggy so I could throw it away. I didn't tell you because I believed I was protecting Tobias, but that was a bad decision. I should have told you the truth, and I'm sorry. I was just so worried about getting you and Tobias home safely."

She let his words marinate in her mind, then asked,

"If you worried about getting us home safely, then why didn't you stop Tobias from driving?"

Jesse leaned back against the stall, bending one knee and resting his boot on the wall. "I didn't know how to stop him."

"Why didn't you try?" She took a step closer to him.

"I did try, but Tobias didn't seem like he was really drunk, and when he got into his buggy, what could I do? Then when he started racing, I yelled at him to stop, and I tried to catch up to him, but he wouldn't slow down."

Her eyes widened as the details of Friday afternoon clicked into place in her mind. "Tobias was acting strangely. I saw him stumble, and everything was funny to him. He was drunk, but you weren't."

"Exactly." He stood up straight. "He was slurring his words, and he was chewing gum."

"What does gum have to do with it?"

"He chewed gum to cover the smell of the alcohol on his breath."

She cupped her hand to her mouth. How could she have been so blind? Hot tears prickled at her eyelids. "And he's been chewing gum frequently lately. Does that mean he's been drinking a lot?"

"It might." Jesse took the glass out of her hand, set it on the ground, and placed his hands on her arms. "Please hear me. I never meant to put you in jeopardy. I would never, ever deliberately do anything that would hurt you. You know that, right?"

"*Ya*," she whispered, her voice trembling as tears escaped her eyes and trickled down her hot cheeks. "I'm sorry for not believing you."

"It's okay. It was a stressful situation. *Ich liebe dich*." His eyes seemed to search hers. "Do you still love me?"

"Of course I do." She choked out the words and then cleared her throat. "But *mei dat* has made it clear he wants me to stay away from you. As much as it hurts me to do that, you know I can't go against his rules." She stepped out of his grasp and picked up the glass. "I need to go before *mei dat* finds us together." She backed away. "*Danki* for helping him."

Before he could respond, she rushed off toward the house, her heart beating wildly.

. . .

"I've told you repeatedly I don't need your help, so why do you keep coming back here every afternoon?"

Jesse set down the hammer he was using to repair the back porch steps. Then he tented his hand over his eyes as he looked up at Marvin, who gazed down at him with his arms crossed over his portly middle.

"You don't need my help, huh?" He wiped his forearm over his sweaty forehead and then stood. "Let's see. On Monday I mucked the stalls and then cleaned the milkers. Tuesday I helped you harvest the hay by running the baler and then helping you store the bales in the loft. Wednesday I cleaned out the dairy barn before mucking the stalls again, and yesterday I repaired the fencing around the chicken coop."

Jesse pointed down at the steps. "Today I'm going to finish repairing the porch and then fix the pasture fence before mucking the stalls again." He rested his hands on his hips. "So, don't you actually *need* my help?"

Marvin shook his head. "You're wasting your time if you think all your hard work is going to change my mind about your relationship with Ariana. You're still not going to marry her."

Marvin's words hit Jesse like a smack across the face, knocking away his smile and replacing it with a frown. Jesse squared his shoulders and lifted his chin. Despite Marvin's cutting words, Jesse wasn't ready to give up. He would paint the house with a toothbrush if that was what it took to prove he would be loyal to the Smucker family and cherish Ariana for the rest of his life.

"I'm going to finish repairing these steps and then move on to the fence," Jesse said, fighting to keep his tone even. "Let me know if you need anything else."

Marvin gave a harrumph and stalked off toward the dairy barn.

Jesse blew out a gust of air he hadn't realized he'd been holding, then squatted down to return to the task of repairing the porch. His mind whirled as he hammered new slats of wood onto the steps.

For five days, he'd rushed through his morning chores at his father's horse farm and then hurried over to Marvin's to work there. Each day, Marvin asked Jesse to go home and then walked off, and then Jesse completed as many chores as possible before suppertime. Every night he fell asleep as soon as his head hit his pillow. He'd never been more tired or sore as he'd been this week.

Tobias's comments about Jesse never having to work for anything in his privileged life haunted him. As much as Jesse loathed Tobias's words, he had also found truth in them. For the first time in his life, Jesse poured his heart and soul into every task he undertook, into all the chores he completed at Marvin's farm. He refused to take anything for granted.

Jesse finished fixing the last step and then looked up at the back door, willing Ariana to walk outside and talk to him. He yearned to hear her voice and see her gorgeous smile. Although he'd had the opportunity to see her from afar while he worked on her farm, he hadn't spoken to her since Monday when they'd talked in the stable. He longed to get their wedding plans back on track, but first he had to concentrate on proving to Marvin he was worthy of Ariana's hand in marriage.

Jesse cleaned up the mess and disposed of the rotten wooden planks, then gathered his supplies to repair the pasture fence. He began replacing the rotten boards at the far end of the fence and worked his way toward the front of the pasture, facing the house.

As Jesse came around a corner, he spotted Ariana in her mother's garden, pulling weeds before dropping them into a bucket. He stilled for a moment, taking in her adorable face as she stuck out her tongue and struggled with one that seemed particularly troublesome. He gripped the hammer in his hand, fighting against the urge to rush over and help her rip up the irksome thing. The emotional distance between them sent a pang through his chest, but he couldn't risk violating Marvin's rules. If Marvin caught Jesse and Ariana together, it might make the situation even worse, and he couldn't chance that happening.

With his teeth clenched in frustration, Jesse turned away from Ariana and continued his work.

. . .

Ariana dropped a long, thick weed into the bucket and then wiped her hands on her black apron. Brushing her hands across her temples, she looked up as the hot sun beat down on her prayer covering and shoulders, warming them both.

She'd been working in her mother's garden for nearly thirty minutes, and soreness radiated down her neck to her back and arms. She stood and rolled her neck and shoulders in an attempt to loosen her stiff muscles.

When she caught movement in the corner of her eye, she turned toward the pasture. Her stomach flip-flopped when she saw Jesse working on the fence. He'd come back for the fifth day in a row to help her father with chores.

She'd seen him working from afar since their talk in the stable on Monday, and he continued to command her thoughts. Yesterday she watched him fix the fencing around the chicken coop while she hung out the laundry. She'd longed to talk to him, but she didn't want to upset her father.

And now as she took in the breadth of his back and arms, watching him hammer a new slat into the pasture fence, she felt an invisible attraction pulling her to him. She couldn't bear to go another day without speaking to him.

Ariana's heart skipped a beat as she looked toward the house and then toward the barn in search of her father. She held her breath, for a moment doubting her decision to approach Jesse. Then, throwing caution to the wind, she ran her sweating palms down her apron before hurrying down the rock path to the fence.

"Jesse." She walked up behind him.

He craned his neck and looked at her before setting the hammer on the ground and facing her. "Hi."

"I saw you working on the porch steps earlier, but you were gone when I finished cleaning the *haus*. I thought you'd gone home." She glanced over her shoulder toward the dairy barn to check for her father once again, and then looked back at Jesse. "Why are you still here?"

He wiped his face with his shirtsleeve. "There's still plenty to do."

"Don't you have chores to do at your *haus*?"

"*Ya*, but I've been doing most of my work there in the morning so I can come here in the afternoons." He rested his arm on the fence post. "Caleb has been picking up the slack for me so I can help your *dat*."

"You must be tired." She took a step toward him while searching his eyes.

"I am, but that's okay. I want to help your *dat*. He can't run this entire farm by himself." He rubbed his chin as he seemed to be carefully considering his next words. "I've also realized I've made a lot of mistakes in our relationship, and I'd like to make it up to you."

Mistakes? Her stomach plummeted. "What do you mean?"

"I've taken you for granted, and I want to make it right."

She shook her head. "You haven't taken me for granted."

"*Ya*, I have," he insisted. "Your *bruder* said some hard things to me last week, but I've realized he made a few valid points. He said I've never had to work for anything, and that everything comes easily to me. He implied I'm spoiled, and he's right. I was able to build a *haus* when I was only twenty-three. You've always had feelings for me, and I never had to work to prove I was worthy of your affection."

He gestured toward the fence. "Now I'm trying to prove how much I care about you and your family." He clenched his jaw. "I'll do anything necessary to show you and your *dat* I intend to take care of you for the rest of my life." He took her hands in his. "I promise I'll always do my best to not take you for granted."

Her chest constricted. "I still don't think it's true that you've taken me for granted."

"*Ya*, I have. Remember when I forgot to tell you it was time to go to lunch at the lake? And then when I didn't join you on the porch at Mariella's, even though I'd promised? I'm so sorry." His voice quavered.

"I told you that was okay." She sniffed.

"No, it wasn't okay." He shook his head. "You're precious to me, and I can't bear the thought of losing you."

Reaching up, she cupped her hand to his cheek. "I promise you won't lose me." Standing on her tiptoes, she brushed her lips across his cheek, and he sighed as his shoulders relaxed.

Ariana cut her gaze toward the barn, where her father stood talking to his driver. She took a step back. "I have to go. We'll talk again soon."

As she rushed back to the garden, she couldn't help but think it wouldn't be much longer before her father realized how genuine and good Jesse truly was.

CHAPTER 7

Discouragement and anxiety settled over Jesse as he moved a paintbrush up and down the slats of Marvin's pasture fence. The early morning July sun beat down on his straw hat, and his shoulders, back, and neck ached after spending the past two afternoons painting the fence.

He'd arrived early this morning to finish the last section so he could concentrate on other chores this afternoon. He'd hoped his hard work during the past three weeks would have gained him at least a pleasant greeting from Marvin, but again this morning he'd growled a half greeting. It seemed no matter how hard Jesse worked, he still hadn't earned an ounce of forgiveness or respect. But he wouldn't capitulate and go home.

As he worked, his mind spun with thoughts of Ariana. They'd stolen glances and a quick conversation here and there, but he longed for more time with her. He'd managed to speak to her alone at the youth gathering Sunday night, but the time had flown by too quickly and their privacy was limited. He hoped to see her again today.

As he moved his brush across the slats, his thoughts

turned to Tobias. No one had heard from him. Ariana shared that she and her mother were consumed with worry about him.

He was painting the last slat in the fence when he heard boots crunch on the ground behind him.

"Did Caleb take over all your chores again today?"

Jesse craned his neck, glancing over his shoulder at Marvin. "*Ya*, he did, and I also worked late last night."

"And then you got up early this morning and came here to work some more," Marvin finished his thought.

"That's right." Jesse set the paintbrush on top of the can and spun toward him. "I think I'm finally done." He made a sweeping gesture toward the wooden fence, the fresh white paint gleaming in the bright sunlight.

Marvin studied the fence and then gave him a stiff nod.

Jesse's shoulders sagged. That was as close to a thank you as he would get, but he would accept it. Any acknowledgment was better than none.

"I don't think that fence has been painted in twenty years." Marvin's words sounded almost wistful as his expression flashed what seemed like melancholy. "I'm going in for lunch."

"Is it lunchtime already?" Jesse wiped his forearm across his sweaty brow.

"*Ya*." Marvin stared at him for a moment, and to Jesse's complete surprise, the old man's scowl softened. "Are you hungry?"

Jesse blinked. Was Marvin inviting him to eat lunch with him? Hope bloomed inside his chest. Perhaps he was making headway with Marvin after all.

"Well, are you?" Marvin asked.

Jesse shook himself from his shock. "*Ya*, I am, actually."

"Come inside. Rosanna and Ariana are making lunch." And with that, Marvin turned and started toward the back porch.

After rinsing out the paintbrush and stowing the paint can in the barn, Jesse went in the back door of the house and stepped into the kitchen. Rosanna was placing a bowl of potato salad and a bowl of macaroni salad on the table. Jesse scanned the kitchen for Ariana, and disappointment filled him when he didn't see her.

"Ariana went to check the mail. She'll be right back," Rosanna said as if reading his thoughts. Her lips tipped up as she nodded toward the sink. "You can wash up."

"*Danki*." Jesse scrubbed his hands and arms before sitting down at the table, which had been set for four. He looked over at Rosanna as she set down a platter of lunch meat beside a basket of rolls. Had it been her idea to invite Jesse in for lunch? Or maybe Ariana's?

The front door clicked shut and Ariana entered the kitchen carrying a stack of mail. She looked beautiful in her light-blue dress. When she met his gaze, her cheeks stained pink and a tentative smile curled her lips. He returned the gesture as his heart squeezed. Oh, how he'd missed her.

"Looks like we received quite a bit of mail today," Rosanna commented as Ariana crossed to the table and set the stack down.

"*Ya*, we did." Ariana held up a white envelope. "This one is addressed to the Smucker family. It doesn't have a return address, but it's postmarked from a town in Florida."

"Open it," Rosanna instructed, coming to stand beside her.

Ariana opened the envelope and unfolded a piece of lined notebook paper with handwriting on it. She inhaled a sharp breath, and then held it out to her mother. "It's from Tobias."

Jesse's stomach clenched as Ariana's parents echoed her gasp.

"Read it." Marvin's voice sounded shaky. "Please."

"*Ya*, please read it," Rosanna said, wiping her eyes. "I don't think I can."

Ariana cleared her throat and began to read.

Dear *Mamm*, *Dat*, and Ariana,

I'm sorry for the way I left. I'm certain you're going crazy with worry, and I want you to know I'm safe.

I'm in Florida. I decided to visit *Mamm*'s bruder Earl. I remember *Mamm* once saying she had a younger *bruder* who left the community. I found his contact information in an old address book in the kitchen and decided to take a chance that he would let me stay with him. I found out *Onkel* Earl and I have a lot in common.

You're probably wondering why I decided to leave the community, and you have a right to know the whole truth. First, I left because I thought it would make life easier for Ariana and *Mamm*. They've had to listen to *Dat* and me argue for years now, and I know it tore them up inside to hear it. I'm sorry for all the heartache I've caused. I didn't mean to be such a burden.

The night before I left, Ariana told me I should try harder and compromise with *Dat*. I've had three weeks to think about Ariana's advice, and I've come to the conclusion that she was right. For years I've been blaming *Dat* for our problems, but I realized it wasn't only *Dat*'s fault. The truth is I've been part of the problem. I haven't been carrying my load as far as chores and responsibilities go. I'm truly sorry. I've been too selfish and self-centered to realize how much pain my behavior has caused all of you. I hope you can find it in your hearts to forgive me.

I also believe Ariana was right when she said that both *Dat* and I are stubborn. While I haven't been carrying my load, *Dat* also hasn't respected my feelings. I understand the farm has been in our family for generations, but it's not my dream to be a farmer. I want to be a carpenter and create things with my hands. I've tried to enjoy being a dairy farmer, but I don't. Instead, I resent it. I'm not sure how we can come to a compromise on this issue when he won't listen and respect my dreams for my future.

Dat, *Ich liebe dich*, but I can't live with you right now. I will come back someday, but right now it's best that I just stay away for a while and work out all my issues.

I've also finally admitted to myself that I need help. I've been drinking alcohol in secret for a few months now. I was using it as a way to deal with my problems, and as Jesse wisely told me the night of the accident, it's not the way to deal with things. I've accepted that I have a problem. *Onkel* Earl told me he had a problem with alcohol, too, and he recommended a facility that can help me. I'm going there soon. In fact, by the time you receive this letter, I will probably be admitted into the center.

Dat, please don't blame Jesse for the accident. It wasn't his fault. I had gotten drunk that night after our trip to the lake, and it was my idea to race. Jesse never meant to put Ariana in danger. Don't punish Ariana and Jesse for my mistakes. Jesse is a great man, and he will take *gut* care of Ariana. He tried to stop me from drinking, and he also tried to stop me from guiding my horse home. I was too stubborn and drunk to listen to him. I'm sorry for wrecking the buggy. I will send you money to repair it when I have a job. Please forgive me for my dangerous and immature actions.

When you see Jesse, please tell him I'm sorry. I was cruel and hateful to him that night. I'm sure he'll recall what I said to him. I said those terrible things because I was envious of the relationship he has with his family. He didn't deserve my wrath. He's been my best *freind* since we were *kinner*, and I hope he finds it in his heart to forgive me too.

I will contact you again soon.

Sincerely,
Tobias

Tears sprinkled down Ariana's face as she sank into the chair across from Jesse. She grabbed a few napkins and mopped up her cheeks. Then she looked at her father, her eyes shimmering in the bright sunlight pouring in through the kitchen windows.

Marvin turned his gaze to Jesse. "Is that true?" His voice quavered. "Was Tobias drunk that night?"

Jesse nodded. "*Ya*, it's true."

"Why didn't you tell me?" Marvin leaned forward in his chair, his eyes seeming more curious than accusatory.

"I tried to tell you the night of the accident, but you wouldn't listen." Jesse shook his head. "After you forbade me from seeing Ariana, I didn't know how to tell you. I was worried you'd think I was lying about Tobias to push the blame for the accident onto him."

Marvin pursed his lips and stared down at the tablecloth. The room fell silent for several moments with only the sound of birds singing outside the windows. Rosanna sniffed and wiped her eyes, and Ariana rubbed her mother's arm.

"I didn't want Tobias to leave," Marvin said. "He kept telling me he wanted to be a carpenter, but I needed him to take over the farm for me. I was wrong not to respect his opinion, but I thought he would eventually agree to help me. This farm has been in our family for three generations, and I didn't want to even think about selling. I just wanted Tobias to take responsibility, for his life and for his inheritance.

"I was wrong. I should have considered his point of view. I never meant to drive him away." Marvin looked at Jesse. "I'm sorry for misjudging you and blaming you for Tobias's actions. I was wrong to take my frustrations out on you. You've never been anything but responsible. I hope you can forgive me."

Jesse nodded. "Of course I forgive you."

"And *danki* for all your help during these past few weeks," Marvin said. "I couldn't have run this farm without you."

"*Gern gschehne*," Jesse said. "I'm *froh* I could help, and I'll keep helping you for as long as you'll allow me to. I'll do anything I can to help your family."

Marvin cleared his throat and quickly swiped his hand across his glistening eyes. Then he motioned toward the food in the center of the table. "Let's eat. We can talk about this more later."

Jesse stole a glance at Ariana, and when she smiled at him, warmth flooded his chest. They were going to be okay, and it seemed as if Tobias was going to be okay too.

. . .

Jesse followed Marvin into the barn after lunch. "I have a question for you."

"*Ya?*" Marvin swiveled toward him, his bushy eyebrows careening toward his hairline.

Jesse cupped his hand to the back of his neck and took a deep breath, gathering all his courage. "You asked for my forgiveness, which you already have. Does that mean I'm permitted to date Ariana again?"

"*Ya.*"

"Does that also mean I can marry her in the fall?" His voice sounded small and foreign to him. Where had his courage gone?

"*Ya*, of course it does." Marvin patted Jesse's shoulder.

"Rosanna and I would be thrilled to have you as a member of our family."

"*Danki.*" Jesse's grin was wide.

Now he just had to ask Ariana if she would still marry him. His chest tightened as ideas filtered through his mind for how he could ask her.

. . .

That evening Ariana laced her fingers in Jesse's as she walked beside him toward the pasture behind the house he'd built for her. "Where are you taking me?"

"You'll see." He shifted the cooler in his hands and bottles rattled inside.

"Do you have homemade root beer in that cooler?"

"Maybe," he said, teasing her with a grin.

Her heart fluttered. "It's a *schee* night."

"*Ya*, it is."

She gazed toward the small pond at the far end of the pasture and gaped when she spotted a bench under a beautiful oak tree. "Did you install a bench?"

"I put it out there earlier today. Do you like it?"

"I love it." She squeezed his hand as they approached the bench and then sat down beside him. He opened the cooler, revealing four bottles of homemade root beer.

He lifted one bottle, opened it, and handed it to her.

"*Danki.*" She took a long drink and then ran her fingers over the cool condensation. "This is perfect." She looked up at him and happiness buzzed through her. Not only had they finally heard from Tobias, but her father had given her permission to see Jesse again. She

thought she might burst from all the excitement cours-
ing through her veins.

Jesse opened a bottle for himself and then closed the
cooler. "What are you thinking?"

"I was just thinking about how *froh* I am." She placed
her bottle on the bench beside her. "*Mei mamm* is relieved to know Tobias is okay, and I am too."

"*Ya*, I feel like a weight has been lifted from my
shoulders." Something unreadable flickered in his eyes
as he set his bottle on the bench too. "I put this bench
out here because I thought you and I could sit out here
together and talk on warm evenings."

His tone and expression were so serious that worry
nipped at her.

"That sounds perfect. I've always loved this pond."

"*Gut*." He looked down at his lap for a moment,
as if gathering his thoughts. "I brought you out here
tonight so we could talk alone. I've been doing a lot
of thinking, and I realized I haven't been a very *gut*
boyfriend, and I wasn't a *gut* fiancé when we were
engaged."

She opened her mouth to protest, but he held up a
hand to stop her.

"Please, let me finish. A *gut* fiancé would put you
first in his life, but I haven't done that. I've been too
busy working for *mei dat* and worrying about my own
life. I've never had to fight for you, but that's going to
change." He tapped the seat of the bench. "This bench
is just a small token to show you how I will always put
you first from now on. I'll always make time for you,
and I'll work on being the best man I can be for you.

If you agree to marry me, I promise our marriage will always be my top priority."

He took her hands in his. "I've already asked your *dat*'s permission and he's said yes, so now I need to ask you." He took a deep breath. "Arie, will you marry me?"

She sniffed as tears filled her eyes. "Of course I will."

"Oh, *danki*." He blew out a deep breath.

"Did you think I'd say no?"

He shrugged and gave her a shy grin. "I was afraid I'd messed up so badly you'd be afraid to trust me again, and that you'd find someone else who would treat you better than I have."

"You're talking *narrisch*." She touched his arm. "I was afraid I was going to lose you when *mei dat* said I couldn't see you. I can't imagine my life without you."

"I feel the same way." He draped his arm on the back of the bench behind her. "I suppose we should start discussing our wedding plans again."

"*Ya*." She rested her head on his shoulder. "I need to start sewing dresses for Mariella and me."

"You do." He rubbed her shoulder. "We should try to convince Tobias to come to the wedding."

Ariana sat up straight. "*Ya*, we should. If we don't hear from him soon, I can write a letter to *mei onkel* Earl and ask him how I can contact Tobias."

"That's a *wunderbaar* idea." He touched her cheek. "I was so worried I wasn't going to be able to marry you. *Ich liebe dich*, and I promise I will always take care of you."

"I love you too. I can't wait to be your *fraa*."

He leaned down and his lips brushed hers, sending

electric pulses singing through her veins. She closed her eyes, savoring the feel of his lips against hers.

Jesse traced her cheek with the tip of his finger. "I will cherish you forever."

Ariana silently thanked God for softening her father's heart toward Jesse, and she prayed that someday Tobias would come back to their family. But as Jesse leaned in for another kiss, all other thoughts retreated as she looked forward to a future with the man she'd love for nearly her entire life.

DISCUSSION QUESTIONS

1. Ariana is devastated when her father forbids her from marrying Jesse. Have you ever found yourself in a similar situation? If so, how did it turn out? Which Bible verses helped you through this difficult time? Share this with the group.

2. Jesse pours himself into working on Marvin's farm as a way to prove to Marvin that he is worthy of marrying Ariana. What do you think caused him to grow as a character throughout the story?

3. Read Hebrews 11:1. What does this verse mean to you? Share this with the group.

4. Which character can you identify with the most? Which character seemed to carry the most emotional stake in the story? Was it Ariana, Jesse, Tobias, or someone else?

5. At the beginning of the story, Marvin blames Jesse for the buggy accident. His feelings toward Jesse change by the end of the story. What do you think causes this transformation?

6. When Tobias leaves home, he finds solace with his uncle Earl. Have you ever helped someone in need?

If so, how did you feel after you helped that person? Share this with the group.

7. What did you know about the Amish before reading this book? What did you learn?

ACKNOWLEDGMENTS

As always, I'm thankful for my loving family.

I'm grateful for my special Amish friend who patiently answers my endless stream of questions. You're a blessing in my life.

To my agent, Natasha Kern—I can't thank you enough for your guidance, advice, and friendship. You are a tremendous blessing in my life.

Thank you to my amazing editor, Becky Monds, for your friendship and guidance. Thank you also to editor Jean Bloom, who always helps polish my stories and connect the dots between my books. I'm grateful to each and every person at HarperCollins Christian Publishing who helped make this book a reality.

Thank you most of all to God—for giving me the inspiration and the words to glorify You. I'm grateful and humbled You've chosen this path for me.

Lakeside Love

Kathleen Fuller

To my husband, James. I love you.

CHAPTER 1

E sther, it's almost time for the next tour."

"Be right there." Esther Coblentz sighed. She loved guiding the groups of Yankees who signed up to tour her family's house and farm, and usually she was the one waiting on them instead of the other way around. But right now she was busy watching Judah King. She had a perfect view of him from the front porch as he helped her father and brother, Reuben, plow the large field her father had purchased last month, adding to their existing farm. Since it was already July, they were working hard to get in some late crops.

"Esther, did you hear me? They're already gathered in the living room."

She barely glanced at her younger sister. "I'll be there in a minute."

"I hope so. I don't want to have to do the tour."

She heard Sarah leave, presumably to go back to the house. Esther knew she couldn't stand here watching for much longer, but she didn't want to leave. Not yet. She wanted one last look at Judah. He really was perfect, with hair the color of black licorice, a sloped nose a little upturned at the end, and a mouth she really shouldn't notice as much as she did.

But it was his dark eyes—soft, kind, and warm—that had caught and kept her attention four years ago when he and his family moved to their district and her father hired him as a farmhand.

Pulling her gaze away, she went inside through the small gift shop. Her father, ever the entrepreneur, had decided five years ago to add on to the house, move the family into the new addition, build the small gift shop, and conduct tours. His business instincts had been spot-on. Not only did the family run a successful farm, but their tourist business also thrived.

Esther smiled at her mother, Fanny. She was ringing up a customer who was purchasing a few of Sarah's homemade jellies and jams. Esther didn't sell anything in the gift shop. She wasn't a gifted seamstress like *Mamm* or a great cook like Sarah. She was . . . average. Average looks, average skills, average everything. Most of the time she was okay with that. Except when she saw Judah. Then she was reminded that average wasn't good enough, not compared to Sarah.

Sarah was the beautiful one. The talented one. The one Judah was in love with.

Esther's smile dimmed. She couldn't think about Judah and Sarah right now. She had a tour to give, and she always made sure to do her best when it came to the Yankee visitors, including speaking only English for them, which her family did with all Yankees.

She entered the living room and smiled at a group of six Yankees standing near the front door. The five women looked to be in their midsixties, and a school-aged boy looked about nine or ten—and very out of place.

"Hello everyone," she said. "My name's Esther. If you're ready, I'll take you on the tour. We'll start with the house, then go out to the barn where you can meet our animals. From there you'll see our fields. All this makes up a real working farm. Please let me know if you have questions anytime during the tour."

The women and boy followed Esther as she moved about the living room. Pointing to the woodstove, she said, "Amish families usually have this going during the other seasons, but it's not needed in the summer, of course." Then she showed the group the gas-powered lamp, explaining how a typical Amish family spends their evenings in each season.

As she observed the group, she realized four of the women were friends and the boy and the fifth woman were together.

"Where's the TV?" the boy asked, searching the room.

"The Amish don't watch TV," the woman nearest to him said.

"So no Xbox?" he said in disbelief. "What about an iPad?"

"Jefferson," the woman with him said. She adjusted her wire-rimmed glasses. "The Amish don't use any electronics at all."

"Actually, that's not true," Esther interjected. "We use some electronics, as long as they're associated with our businesses."

"I see," she said. "I had no idea."

The boy muttered something under his breath, stuck his hands in the pockets of his tan shorts, which seemed a size too big for his slight frame, and shuffled his feet against the spotless wood floor. Esther gave him a small smile. He didn't return it, but she didn't mind. This wasn't exactly the type of tour that would interest a boy his age, and it was clear he'd been dragged along by the woman, who was probably his grandmother.

Esther showed them the rest of the house—three bedrooms in pristine condition, one bathroom, the mudroom—decorated with Amish hats, boots, aprons, and a *kapp* for effect—and finally the kitchen, which was the room that always brought the most questions.

"Can I have one of these?" Jefferson looked at the bowl of peppermint candies in the middle of the table.

"Of course," Esther said, pushing the bowl toward him.

Jefferson reached in and grabbed a handful. Esther waited for the woman with him to say something, but all the adults were busy looking at the "adorable" touches *Daed* had insisted on when *Mamm* decorated the kitchen. "A percolator!" one of them said. "I haven't seen one of these in years."

"And a gas lamp in the corner," another woman said. "Oh, Denise, look at this." She pointed to a cast iron popcorn popper, several gold bracelets jangling on her thin wrist. "Isn't this wonderful? I would love to have one of these."

"I want something to drink." Jefferson plopped down on one of the chairs and shoved a piece of the peppermint candy in his mouth. "It's hot in here."

"I'll get you something in the gift shop." The woman with him looked at Esther apologetically. "His mother didn't sign him up for day camp this week."

"Dad was supposed to do it, Grandma."

Ah, she *was* his grandmother.

"Regardless, there was a snafu. So Jefferson is spending some quality time with me. I thought visiting an Amish home would be very educational."

"More like very boring."

"Don't be rude." She smiled at Esther again, but the smile was strained at the corners of her thin lips. "This is all fascinating. I don't see a refrigerator here. How do you keep your food cold?"

"In the winter we put our food in a wooden pantry my father built. In the summer we use coolers. There's also an ice machine a few houses down."

"You don't worry about the food spoiling?"

She shook her head. "We eat it fast enough, especially my brother and my father." And Judah, who spent a lot of time here, probably more to see Sarah than to help their father. She pushed the thought away. "We also make sure not to buy more than we need."

Another woman nodded her head. Her eyeglasses were on a thin decorative chain that hung around her neck. "That's a wonderful way to live."

Esther thought so too. She'd met a lot of Yankees in her life, especially since she started doing the tours. While some aspects of non-Amish life appealed to her, none of them rivaled her faith, family, and community. Still, that didn't mean she couldn't sympathize with Jefferson. "Let's head out to the barn," she said, looking at the boy. "I think you'll find something to interest you there."

As Esther expected, he perked up when he had the chance to see the animals. As he patted Peanut, their pet miniature pony who loved attention, Esther stood back at the edge of the barn while the women walked through it. None of them were as enthusiastic as Jefferson about the cow, two sheep, one old draft horse, and a pen of cute bunnies. Two of them wrinkled their noses, but Jefferson's grandmother apparently decided to be adventurous. She awkwardly patted the gentle cow on top of its head.

"Small group today?"

At Judah's question, Esther's confidence evaporated. "*Ya*," she replied, but she didn't look at him. She kept her gaze glued on Jefferson, who had turned his attention to the bunnies. Still, she couldn't resist taking a glance at Judah.

He leaned against the barn wall, his handsome face reddened by the heat and farm work. His pants and shirt were dusty, and he smelled like a man who'd spent most of the day in the field. But none of that put her off. Judah King was also a hard worker, which she appreciated. His intention might be to get closer to Sarah, but he was a great help to *Daed* and Reuben.

"Seen Sarah lately?" he asked. He'd straightened, put his hands on his trim waist, and caught her eye. "I looked for her in the gift shop, but she wasn't there. *Yer mamm* said she hadn't seen her either."

"*Nee*. I haven't seen her." She bit her bottom lip.

"Grandma, can I take one of the bunnies home?" Jefferson said, his head popping up over the rabbits' pen.

"No."

"Please?"

"Your parents don't have room for pets. Besides, your

father is allergic to animal dander." Grandma walked over to the pen. "Why don't you say hello to the draft horse?"

"I want to be with the bunnies." Jefferson gripped one under his chin.

"I think an intervention is in order." Judah winked at Esther before moving toward the boy. "Don't hold the bunny so tightly," he said as he climbed into the pen. He picked up another bunny and held it gently in his hands. "Like this, see? You don't want to hurt them."

Jefferson loosened his grip and cradled the bunny like Judah showed him.

All Esther could do was sigh. Or rather swoon. There was something wonderful about seeing a cute, delicate creature in Judah's large hand, safe and secure.

"Now," Judah said, putting the bunny down, "let's go see Maisy. She looks lonely, and she likes company." He led Jefferson out of the pen and over to the draft horse, who didn't look the least bit lonely and only tolerated visitors. Esther smiled.

"Your young man is very good with kids," one of the ladies said to her as she moved to stand beside Esther.

"Oh, he's not—" She clamped her lips. What harm would it be in letting them think she and Judah were together? It wasn't as if they could be confused for siblings. Esther was blond and fair with average blue eyes, a sharp contrast to Judah's dark hair and eyes and tan skin.

"I think we're finished here," Grandma said, wrinkling her nose at Maisy's whinny. "I've seen enough animals, thank you." She smiled, her upturned lips wrinkling deeply at the corners as she turned to Esther. "If I don't get Jefferson out of here, he'll be asking to take home the cow and the horse."

The other women laughed and Esther regained her senses. They'd spent longer in the barn than normal, thanks to her gazing at and daydreaming about Judah. "We'll go outside and I'll show you our garden and fields."

"That sounds boring," Jefferson said, not moving from Maisy's side.

"Remember, I told you I'd get you something to drink in the gift shop when we were finished with the tour," his grandmother reminded him. "And if you're extra good, I might get you a treat."

"Coming!" Jefferson gave the horse one more pat on the nose and jogged to the rest of the group.

Again, Esther wanted a last look at Judah, who was now talking in a low voice to Maisy, gently stroking her nose. Esther had never been jealous of an animal before. *Always a first time.* She watched Judah for another brief moment, then started to follow the group.

"Esther?" Judah called out.

She turned, putting on what she hoped was her prettiest smile. "*Ya,* Judah?"

"If you see Sarah, tell her I'm looking for her."

Her smile dimmed. Of course Sarah was uppermost in his mind. When hadn't she been? "I will," she said, hiding her disappointment. And she would keep her promise. She always did, even though a little bit of her heart shattered every time she was confronted with the reality that Judah was in love with Sarah, not her.

She left to join the tour group, wondering if she would ever get over Judah King.

. . .

Judah gave Maisy one more pat on the nose and the rest of the animals a bit more feed for a special treat, then left the barn and headed for the new field. Enoch and Reuben had taken their break in the family's kitchen, and Judah had used the respite to try to find Sarah. As usual, she wasn't around when he had a break. If he didn't know better, he'd think she planned it that way.

But Sarah wouldn't do something underhanded like that. She was beautiful, sweet, charming . . . perfect. Problem was, he wasn't the only one in their district who thought so. Sarah Coblentz had more men interested in her than should be decent. But again, that wasn't her fault.

How could they not be attracted to her? Judah had fallen head over heels the first day he'd seen her four years ago. And one day he would win her. He was determined to. If persistence meant anything, Judah was ahead of the other guys by miles. It was a bonus that he liked working at Coblentz Farms. Enoch paid well, and he'd rather be farming than working construction, which was what he did in the fall and winter months until it was time for spring planting.

He walked out of the barn into the hot but fresh outdoor air and glanced at the house. Should he check there for Sarah again? He decided not to. Esther would give Sarah his message. Good old dependable Esther. She always kept her word.

He glanced over at Esther as she talked to the group of older ladies and Jefferson. The young boy was kneeling in front of a row of sunflowers and tugging at the stems. Judah was about to intervene when Esther smoothly walked toward the kid, still explaining about the different vegetables and flowers the Coblentzes planted every year, and put her hand on Jefferson's shoulder. Just a light touch, but enough to get the boy's attention. He straightened, and she kept her hand on his shoulder until she had guided him to his grandmother.

Judah was impressed. Esther was not only dependable, but great with children. He'd noticed that after church services. She never hesitated to kick off her shoes and play with the kids, whether it was volleyball, baseball, or horseshoes. Esther definitely liked to have fun.

"Judah!"

His ears perked up at the sound of Sarah's voice. She stopped in front of him, and he was nearly struck dumb by her beauty. Flawless skin, crystal-blue eyes that were so pale they seemed to constantly sparkle, full lips that were perpetually rosy and begging to be kissed.

"Esther said you wanted to see me?" Sarah said.

Danki, Esther.

"I thought after supper today we could go get some ice cream at the Parlor." The Parlor was a small ice cream and sundry shop that catered to both Yankees and the Amish.

"Oh, Judah. That's so nice of you. But I already have plans."

Plans? With whom?

"Maybe we can go some other time. You could invite

Esther, though. She loves the Parlor's ice cream." With that Sarah turned around and left. Although he was disappointed she'd turned him down, he couldn't help but notice that even her walk was perfect.

Hmm. Maybe he should ask Esther to go with him to the Parlor. But what would they talk about? Esther was a quiet and shy woman, emphasis on the quiet. Then again, she might know what Sarah was doing tonight. *Or if she's seeing someone.* It made his head pound to think about it, but if Sarah was seeing someone else, he needed to size up his competition.

Decision made, he went back to the new field. Enoch planned to plant lettuce, beets, spinach, peas, and kale in the freshly plowed ground. They would be harvesting well into October, but Judah didn't mind helping out until then. It meant more time to get closer to Sarah. This wasn't the first time he'd asked her out, and it wasn't the first time she'd said no. But she'd said yes plenty of times too. She was unpredictable. Almost playing hard to get . . . but in the end Judah would get her, and she would be worth it.

. . .

Esther kept her head down as she nibbled on a tiny taste of butter pecan ice cream, one of the Parlor's signature flavors. She glanced up at Judah, who was attacking with gusto a double scoop of Triple Fudge Delight in a waffle cone. They were seated at one of the small, round tables that had room for only two. Around them, customers—both Yankee and Amish—were milling near the counter, trying to decide what frozen treat to order.

She'd been stunned when Judah asked her to go with him to get ice cream tonight. Stunned and confused. He'd never asked her out before, and she wasn't foolish enough to think they were on a date. She could *wish* they were on a date, but she knew better.

Judah licked a spot of chocolate from the corner of his mouth. "*Gut* ice cream, *ya*?"

She looked up and froze. Ice cream was the last thought on her mind right now. "Um . . ." Where were her words? No wonder Judah wasn't interested in her. She was practically mute.

He leaned back in the chair, his mouth lifting in a half grin. "*Nee* need to be shy around me, Esther." He winked and took another bite of his cone.

If only that was more than a friendly wink. Judah was open-hearted and, yes, friendly—two more reasons for her to be attracted to him. But she was . . .

Sigh. She was silent. Nervous. And she didn't stand a chance with Judah.

"So . . ." He pushed back his chair and put his ankle over his knee. "What's Sarah up to tonight?"

Esther shrugged, returning her gaze to her ice cream.

"She didn't tell you about her plans?"

She looked up again and saw the tension underneath his calm exterior. That made her want to ease his mind. "I think she went over to Celia's. She's a Yankee *freind* Sarah has known for years."

"Oh." He seemed to mull that over in his mind.

"Okay." His shoulders relaxed as he polished off his cone.

Esther's ice cream was melting. Forgetting about taking tiny bites, she licked around the top edge of the cone. She started to say something else, but when she looked at Judah, he was staring at her. At her nose in particular.

"You've got . . ." He grabbed a napkin from the holder on the table, then leaned forward and wiped the tip of her nose. "Ice cream," he said, balling up the napkin and putting it on the table.

Her face reddened. She couldn't even lick an ice cream cone without making a mess. "Sorry," she said, tempted to throw away the cone.

He shrugged. "It was kind of . . . cute."

She froze for the second time, barely feeling the cold drips of ice cream over her fingers. Cute? He thought she was cute?

"You going to finish that?" He tilted his head toward her cone. When she shook her head he took the cone from her. "Hate to waste *gut* ice cream."

Normally she did too, but right now she was still trying to wrap her mind around the fact that Judah had not only said she was cute, but he was also eating her ice cream. Maybe there was more to tonight than him quizzing her about Sarah. Maybe he was attracted to her and somehow she'd missed the signals. Missing signals wouldn't surprise her—she wasn't exactly experienced when it came to dating and flirting. Maybe this really was a date—

"Do you know if Sarah's free tomorrow?" He took another lick of her ice cream. "I've got *mei* open buggy all cleaned up and thought she'd like to *geh* for a ride."

Esther's heart sank. She'd love to go for a ride with Judah in his open buggy. "You'll . . . you'll have to ask her."

He grinned. "I will." He polished off the rest of the cone. "You ready to *geh*? I've got stuff to do tonight."

She picked up the napkin and threw it away. She'd eaten approximately three bites of her ice cream. The evening was turning into a big disappointment.

As she climbed into Judah's buggy, her foot slipped. "Hey," he said, catching her elbow. "Watch *yer* step." And although she didn't need his assistance, he held on to her as she got into the buggy.

"*Danki* for *yer* help, Judah," she told him when he got in and took the reins.

"*Nee* problem. Did I ever tell you about the time I slipped and fell facedown in the mud? Almost chipped a tooth on a rock." He smiled and tapped on one of his front teeth. "If I had, I would have deserved it. I was mouthing off at *Mamm* after church."

"I can't imagine you doing that," Esther said, folding her hands in her lap.

"It was before we moved here. I was about ten, and she wouldn't let me *geh* over to a *freind*'s *haus*." He chuckled. "I can't even remember which *freind* that was now. But at the time I thought *Mamm* was the meanest woman in the world."

Esther laughed. "I tried running away when I was about that age."

"I find that hard to believe." He guided the horse onto the street and headed for Esther's house.

"*Ya*, I did. I think I was nine, and I informed *mei* parents I was moving into the barn."

"Wait . . . You ran away to the *barn*?"

"You know how far the barn is from our *haus*. At least five hundred yards."

Judah started laughing. "I thought you were going to tell me you packed *yer* bags and took off down the street."

"Oh, I packed a bag. It was a small paper one that had held apples."

"The ones with the handles?"

She nodded. "It fit exactly one dress, one pair of socks, and *mei* toothbrush." Grinning, she added, "Just the essentials."

"Of course." He tapped the reins lightly as a car sped by. "What was *yer* parents' reaction?"

"*Daed* told me to clean the barn while I was out there."

Another laugh from Judah. "That sounds like him."

"*Mamm* actually packed me a lunch. She was pretty supportive, considering I was running away."

After a pause Judah asked, "What were you upset about?"

"I didn't want to share a room with Sarah anymore." She was tempted to add that Sarah had been almost unbearably messy as a child, but that wouldn't be fair to her sister. She was almost as tidy as Esther was now. And her messiness wasn't the real reason. "I wanted *mei* own space," was all she would admit.

"How long did you live in the barn?"

"Two nights, with some food deliveries from *Mamm*. After that she said I had to *geh* back in the *haus*. I was glad to. It was all right sleeping in the barn for a little while, but I missed *mei* bed. I even missed Sarah." She glanced at Judah. "A little."

She expected him to say something about Sarah now that she'd given him the opening. But he didn't. He stared straight ahead for a few moments. They were nearly to her house when he turned to her. "I always thought you and Sarah were close."

"We are. But we had our fights and scrapes growing up. We're both so . . . different."

"*Ya*," he said, his warm eyes drifting over her face. "You two sure are." He continued to look at her, letting the horse take the lead. Which made her wonder— could he possibly see something in her he liked, even though she was so different from Sarah?

Judah's horse knew the way to her house as if it were his own. Then Judah turned away, taking control of the reins again. When he pulled up in front of her house, she started to get out of the buggy.

"Thanks for going with me," he said.

She glanced over her shoulder and almost smiled. At least he appreciated her company. And she had to admit, it was fun talking about their childhoods. She hadn't felt nervous or anxious at all. It had been nice. Natural. Normal.

"Tell Sarah I'll see her tomorrow."

Friendly. So much for him seeing her as someone other than Sarah's sister. Biting the inside of her cheek,

Esther nodded. As he drove away, she fought the jealousy growing inside her. She loved her sister, and she didn't want to be jealous of her. But when it came to Judah, she couldn't help it.

She also knew she couldn't keep pining after him this way. It was only a matter of time before Sarah decided to settle down, and when she did, Esther knew it would be with Judah. How could she choose anyone else? Not a single man in the district could compare to him. Soon Sarah would realize that, and then what would Esther do? Continually covet? She couldn't live like that either.

Turning, Esther headed toward the house, rubbing her temples. Something had to give, and soon.

CHAPTER 2

The next morning it was blistering hot, even well before noon. Esther carried out a jug of cold water and cups to her *daed*, Reuben, and Judah. She handed Judah his cup and then poured water into it for him. He drained it quickly, pushed his hat back, and smiled at her. "*Danki*, Esther. That hit the spot."

And just like that, she was smitten again, as if he hadn't made it 100 percent clear last night that he was completely enamored with Sarah. Would she ever learn?

"Could I have a little more?" he asked, holding out his cup.

She nodded, mute once again. After she filled his cup, he took off his hat and poured a little of the water over the back of his neck and the rest over his head. All she could do was stare.

Judah handed her his cup, then picked up his hoe and went back to work. Esther walked over to Reuben, who was working farther downfield. She poured a cup of water and handed it to him.

"Had to give water to *yer* boyfriend first?" Reuben said, smirking before downing the water.

"He's not *mei* boyfriend," she hissed.

"You wish he was." He took the jug from Esther and filled the cup again. "Try not being so obvious about it."

She sighed. No sense in arguing with Reuben, since he would continue to tease her until she was fed up. "It's pointless anyway," she muttered.

"You and Judah?" Reuben took another long drink. "I wouldn't be so sure about that."

That made her snap to attention. Did her brother know something she didn't? "What?"

He shrugged. "I hate to admit it, but we men sometimes have blinders on. We don't see that the best thing is right in front of our eyes." He smiled. "Don't lose hope, Essie."

Grimacing, she took his empty cup and walked away. He was the only one who called her that. Most of the time he said it to bug her. Her frown faded as she realized Reuben was trying to encourage her. She glanced over her shoulder at Judah, who seemed to be concentrating on his work. Reuben's words gave her a bit of hope . . . which was suddenly dashed when she heard Sarah call out Judah's name.

"Judah!" Sarah strode toward him, all confidence and beauty and grace.

Not wanting to see the two of them together, Esther walked over to her father. He was crouched on the ground, sifting the plowed dirt through his fingers—his ritual before planting seed every year. When she asked him why he did it, he merely said, "Tradition," then went back to work. "I brought you some water, *Daed*."

He rose from the ground, a little more slowly than

in years past. He was only in his late forties, as was *Mamm*, but both of them had threads of silver in their hair and a few crinkles around their eyes. "You're a blessing, Esther. Hottest *daag* we've had all summer."

She started to hand him a cup, then changed her mind and gave him the jug. He drank almost all of it in one gulp. Wiping the water from his mouth, he said, "We might need some more."

"I'll *geh* back and fill the jug. We don't have any tours set up for today."

Daed frowned. "Maybe we should stop taking reservations and open the place to the public. I've been trying to convince *yer mamm* of that, but she wants to guard our privacy. Can't really blame her for that." He looked over at Judah and Sarah. "Wonder what they're talking about."

Despite herself, she glanced their way. Sarah was talking animatedly, the way she did when she was excited or angry. She didn't seem upset, and from the smile spreading across Judah's face, she must be excited about something. That extinguished the last shred of hope Reuben had instilled. Esther looked away when Sarah touched Judah's shoulder. "I'll get you some more water, *Daed*." She took the empty jug from him, and he was already kneeling back down and touching the dirt again. *Tradition*.

As she walked toward the house, Sarah joined her. "Isn't it exciting?"

"What?" Esther said, not slowing her steps or caring what was so exciting between her and Judah.

"Rhett Davidson will be here sometime tonight."

Esther nodded. She had forgotten about the college student who was staying with them for a month.

Sarah clasped her hands together. "I asked Judah if he would show Rhett around Middlefield. I'd ask Reuben, but you know how he can be."

"Unpredictable." Which was true. As the youngest of the three, he was an excellent and committed farmer, but that didn't extend to any other part of his life. While he still dressed Amish and lived and worked with the family, he had yet to join the church. Esther often wondered if he would. He was twenty, and both she and Sarah had joined by that age.

Mamm and *Daed* didn't seem concerned, but Esther was. She wanted her brother to be a full part of the community, not chasing outside interests. Not that he'd given any indication he was. He just held back from joining the church for some unknown reason.

"I told Judah I'd go with them." Sarah sighed. "I can't wait to meet him. With a name like Rhett, he has to be handsome, right?"

"He's a Yankee, Sarah. Handsome or not, it shouldn't matter to us."

"You're always so serious. There's *nix* wrong with a little appreciation of God's creation."

Esther fought not to roll her eyes. There was plenty wrong with it, and when it came to Judah, it was something she struggled with. But Sarah didn't need to know that. "When does he arrive again?"

"Tonight. *Mamm* said he had to finish up a summer class and then he'd drive right over from Ohio State. Maybe he'll take me for a ride in his car."

"Sarah, are you listening to *yerself*? Why would you want to ride around in a car?"

"Because it's *different*. Don't you get tired of the same thing all the time? Get up. Do chores. Work. Go to bed. Do it all over again."

"That's not all we do. There's visiting with *familye* and *freinden*, church services, weddings, barn raisings, frolics, singings—"

"And that's all fun, but there's a lot of drudgery in between."

Esther stopped, concerned. She faced Sarah. "Are you saying you want to leave the church?" she whispered.

"Good heavens, *nee*." Sarah looked shocked. "All I'm saying is . . ." She tapped her finger against her chin. Even in the sweltering heat, while sweat ran down Esther's back, Sarah's cheeks were a lovely shade of pale pink, and there wasn't a single indication that she was the least bit hot. "I want to experience life to the fullest." She tapped Esther on the nose. "You should try it sometime." Then she practically skipped toward the house.

Esther's shoulders slumped. Didn't Sarah realize Esther wished she could be lighthearted and spontaneous? After all, that's what Judah liked. The one time she'd tried to emulate her sister, it had gone badly. Her cheeks heated at the memory, which made her perspire even more.

She'd approached Judah one day in May. He wouldn't start working with *Daed* and Reuben for the season until the next day, but traditionally the three men got together the evening before to plan how they would divvy up the farm responsibilities. He usually ate supper with them all season before going home to his parents' house, where he still lived with his younger brother and three sisters. She knew he would eat with them this night as well.

She'd practiced walking gracefully for an entire week, imitating Sarah's tinkling laugh and the way she looked at Judah with her chin dipped down and her eyes wide and sparkling. Although Esther thought she looked ridiculous in the mirror, she still worked at it, perfected it, until she thought she was as close to Sarah as she could possibly get.

"Hi, Judah," she'd said when he arrived that night for supper. She'd opened the door and touched her chin to her chest, then batted her eyelids several times.

"Uh, hi, Esther." He frowned. "Something wrong with *yer* eyes?"

"Nee." She stopped batting them, which was good, because it was giving her a headache. She leaned against the doorframe, one hand sliding up the doorjamb and straight into a splinter. "Ow!" she said, jerking her hand away.

"Let me take a look." He backed her up until they were all the way in the living room, then shut the door behind him. He took her hand and ran his rough fingers over the large and obvious splinter. "Do you have some tweezers?" he asked.

A little blood oozed from the place where the splinter was lodged. *"Mamm* does in the top drawer of the little table over there."

He got the tweezers, cradled her hand in his large palm, and paused. "This might sting a bit."

"It's okay—ow!"

Judah yanked out the splinter, then dropped her hand. "You should wash that and put some peroxide on it. Next time, don't slide *yer* hand across wood like that. Even if it's stained it could still end up splintery over time."

She nodded, a little awestruck at his concern and the gentle attention her hand received.

"Is Sarah around?" he'd asked, not skipping a beat. As if she'd heard him talking about her, Sarah appeared, and Esther was immediately forgotten.

Esther shook her head, bringing herself back to the present. Sarah, Sarah, Sarah. For as long as she could remember, and despite being the older sister, Esther had always been in Sarah's shadow, and always would be. Despite that, Esther would never change herself. Trying to be someone else—especially her sister—had been a monumental mistake. She'd never tried to mimic Sarah again.

She went back into the house, pushing Judah out of her mind and thinking about Sarah's reaction to Rhett's coming. Her sister had always had a fleeting attention span, and Esther wasn't all that surprised that Sarah was excited about their impending company. But Sarah seemed a little too excited. And what about Judah? How could she consider showing interest in Rhett while Judah was here? How could Sarah even think about hurting him that way?

Esther paused in the kitchen doorway, wondering if she should talk to Sarah about it. Or maybe mention something to *Mamm*. Then again, maybe she was

overreacting. Besides, Sa— — — —
to gain Rhett's attention. If any— — —
probably have to keep her eye on *him*, not — —
blew out a breath. July was going to be an intere— —
month, to say the least.

Late, after supper was finished and the dishes were done, Esther went outside and sat on the porch steps in front of their addition's front door. The wide porch faced the original house and its front door, too, and the family still used it as long as there wasn't a tourist group scheduled.

Barefoot, she curled her toes over the edge of the top step. It was still hot, stifling so, but a bit cooler out here than in the house. She folded her hands and rested her wrists on her knees, leaning forward, listening to the sounds of the approaching night as she watched the sun move toward the horizon. Her father had built this house in such a way that the sunset was easily seen from the porch, which was what her mother had always wanted.

Over the years, she and her family had spent many evenings here, waiting for the sunset, she and her siblings playing on the porch or in the yard, *Mamm* and *Daed* sitting in the hickory rockers and watching them. When—*if*—she had her own house, she wanted it to face the sunset just like this one. When—if, again— she had a husband and children, she wanted to spend their evenings together, enjoying God's masterpieces in the sky.

But all that was faint hope right now. At the rate she was going, Reuben would get married before she did—and he had stated many times he had no interest in finding a wife anytime soon, if ever.

A car pulled into the driveway as Sarah opened the door behind her. "It's him," she said almost breathlessly. She touched Esther on the shoulder. "Rhett is here."

The small silver car stopped in the middle of the driveway. The engine turned off, the trunk popped open, and Esther found she was almost holding her breath in anticipation, thanks to Sarah's contagious enthusiasm. Telling herself she was acting foolish, she stood and smoothed out her skirt, then went to greet their guest properly.

Only when he got out of the car did she stop short. Sarah, as usual, had been right. Rhett Davidson was a stunningly handsome man. For a Yankee, anyway. He grinned, showing straight white teeth that seemed a little too bright in contrast with his tanned face. He was wearing sunglasses, and when he removed them his hazel, almost gold-colored eyes were revealed. He was broad-shouldered, and as he rounded the car and walked toward her, she could see he was well built, as if he worked on a farm himself—or worked out in a gym. Considering he was a college student, she assumed the latter.

"Hi," he said, extending his hand toward her. "I'm Rhett. Are you . . . Sarah?"

Esther almost laughed out loud at that. She'd never

been taken for her sister before. "No, I'm Esther." She took his hand, and her gym theory was confirmed. He had a firm handshake, but, unlike Judah, his palms and fingers were soft. She pulled out of his grip.

"*I'm* Sarah." Her sister brushed past her and held out her hand. Esther watched as Sarah effortlessly smiled, sparkled, and gleamed so much in front of this man Esther thought he'd have to put his sunglasses back on. "Welcome to Coblentz Farms."

He shook Sarah's hand, but let it go immediately. "I'm glad to be here. Really glad. I'm looking forward to learning about daily life among the Amish."

"You'll learn a lot while you're here, I'm sure. Why don't you come inside? I just made some fresh lemonade."

"That sounds great." He gestured to his car. "Is it okay if I park here?"

"Of course," Sarah said. "My father has a permanent parking spot for you out back, since you said you didn't want to drive at all while you're here. But you can park there later."

"Okay, I'll get my bag and meet you inside."

Esther watched this exchange with slight amusement and a bit of annoyance. Each time she tried not to be envious of Sarah's way with people—especially men—she was drawn back into the green whirlpool. It had happened a couple of times today with Judah already. Tonight she knew exactly what she would add to her nightly prayers.

"I have a better idea." Sarah turned to her. "Why don't *you* get Rhett's bag, Esther?"

Lifting an annoyed eyebrow at her sister, Esther

started for the car. But Rhett moved in front of her. "I can get it." He smiled, and for some reason she felt a little spark in her chest.

Rhett opened the trunk of his car, pulled out a suitcase, then shut the trunk lid and pressed a button on his keychain. The car beeped. "Show me the way," he said, looking at Esther and still grinning as though he was ready for the time of his life.

But Esther remained discombobulated. "You two go ahead," she said, putting her hands over her abdomen. Then when she realized what she'd done, she thrust them behind her back. "I'll be inside in a little bit."

Sarah nodded, giving Esther her secret *thank you* smile. But Sarah didn't need to thank her . . . at least Esther didn't think so. Bother. Esther couldn't remember the last time she was this off-kilter.

After they'd gone inside, she sat down on the bottom porch step, ignoring the sunset in front of her. Surely she wasn't attracted to a Yankee man, one with short hair and soft hands. She liked Judah. She had for so long she didn't know what it was like to be interested in someone else. Which she wasn't. This was just a momentary reaction to a handsome man. Nothing else.

"Esther?" A snapping sound. "Esther, are you in there?"

Blinking, she looked up to see Judah snapping his fingers in front of her, beautiful soft shades of lavender, peach, pink, and coral streaking the sky behind him.

Her hand went to her belly again. No, she didn't feel a spark in her chest or a fleeting feeling of butterflies at the sight of him. She felt a full onslaught, a frisson flowing through her that expelled whatever minute attraction she'd experienced when she saw Rhett. Which relieved her. And irritated. How was she supposed to forget about a future with Judah if her body and heart wouldn't cooperate?

Judah moved to sit next to her. He'd taken a shower upstairs before supper, which he always did after a hot day's work. He was at home here and even kept extra clothes in the bottom drawer of Reuben's dresser. He smelled like soap and sunshine and farmland, and something particular to Judah that made her want to lean her head against his shoulder and breathe deeply. No, this wasn't helping.

"I'm assuming that's Rhett's car?" Judah asked, dipping his head toward the automobile.

"*Ya*. He just got here."

"I'm not so sure about this." He rubbed his chin, which had a sprinkling of five o'clock shadow over it. "I know I don't have a say, being I'm not *familye*—"

"You're like *familye*," she said, interrupting him, something she never did. Great. Now she'd compared him to her brother. Although that might be the trick to putting him out of her mind and putting herself out of her misery.

"Who knows, maybe someday I will be," he said quietly.

His words caused her stomach to flip, and not with attraction. More like indigestion. If only he were talking about their future instead of his and Sarah's. She couldn't respond, so she just stared at the sunset in front of her, willing the colors and shadows and gradients to soothe her.

"I was surprised *yer mamm* agreed to host him for a month," Judah continued. "Enoch I understand. He's a shrewd businessman, and this could drum up some publicity for the farm. Hopefully *gut* publicity."

"Are you worried something will happen?" Esther asked, pulling her gaze from the sunset.

"*Nee.* Well, maybe a little bit. People think they can give up electricity and wear suspenders and they're Amish. They don't know anything about our faith, about why we live the way we do."

"He wants to learn, though."

Judah paused. "Or maybe he just thinks he does. Oh well," he said, shrugging. "It's only for a month." He looked at Esther. "Hold still," he said, then reached over and brushed his finger against the top of her cheek.

She hoped it was because of an eyelash. She'd heard Sarah talk about the time Christopher Mullet had taken her for a ride in his open buggy and reached over to brush an eyelash off her cheek. "It was so romantic," Sarah had gushed. "He made a wish and blew the eyelash off his finger."

Judah wiped his hand on his pants and got up from the porch. "Guess I better get home. Sarah around? Thought I might ask her about that buggy ride."

This time Esther couldn't hide her sigh. "She's inside with Rhett." She pointed to the front door with her thumb, keeping her gaze on the ground.

"Huh."

At that Esther looked up. Judah had his hands on his waist—a pose she would never get tired of—and he was frowning. Something dark flashed in his eyes, an emotion she was familiar with. Jealousy. She rose and moved to him. Without thinking, she put her hand on his arm, wanting to reassure him, knowing how jealousy could eat up a person faster than a child could catch a firefly. "I'm sure they're just talking. And she'll need to show him where he's sleeping tonight."

A muscle jerked in his jaw. "Huh," he said again, the word now sounding like he was shoving it through a cheese grater.

"Why don't we go inside? I'll introduce you to Rhett. You can get to know him a little before you take him on a tour around Middlefield."

But Judah didn't move. "I'll meet him tomorrow." He glanced down at Esther's hand on his arm.

She quickly moved away. "Are you sure?"

"*Ya*. See you tomorrow."

She watched as he went around the house to the barn where his horse and buggy were kept. She waited on the porch until he left, then watched him as he turned out of the driveway and made his way down the road.

. . .

Judah rubbed the back of his neck as he drove home. In his other hand he held the reins loosely, as he always did when he went to and from Coblentz Farms. He and his horse had traversed this distance so many times over the past four years. And he'd always known what to expect when he dealt with the family: hard work, good food, respect from Enoch and—most of the time—from Reuben, a few treasured moments with Sarah, and if he was lucky, a date.

Now all that was changing. He could feel it deep inside. Starting today, things would be different at the Coblentzes. He wasn't sure what to think about that.

His arm itched and he reached to scratch it, then inexplicably thought about Esther's hand. She'd never touched him before. Sarah did it all the time, mostly on the shoulder, sometimes on the forearm. Those little touches always fed the fire of hope within him.

But Esther's touch was . . . confusing. Warm, reassuring, steady. Then again, that was Esther in a nutshell. When he was around her, he could be himself. He didn't have to try to impress her or think about what to say or try to figure out how to gain her attention. He could just . . . be.

Like last night at the ice cream shop. He was used to her being shy, and he usually tried to loosen her up with a little joke to get her relaxed and talking. When she did, he learned new things about her. He'd had no idea she'd run away from home as a child, even if it was to the barn. Esther never broke rules. He liked that about her. There was something to be said for predictability.

He'd felt a churning in his gut when she told him Sarah and Rhett were inside, and he recognized it for what it was—jealousy. For some reason he sensed Esther understood, not only why he was jealous but how it made him feel. But how would she know that? As far as he knew, she wasn't hung up on anyone. If she was, she'd kept it a tight-lipped secret. Not that it was any of his business. In fact, he'd be happy to see Esther settled and happy. She'd make someone a great wife.

Speaking of a wife . . . the churning returned. He was being ridiculous. He shook his head and straightened out his thoughts. Things were fine between him and Sarah, he was concerned about this Rhett person for nothing, and everything would stay the same at the Coblentzes. He was letting his imagination get the better of him, something he often did to his great annoyance. Tomorrow evening he would take Rhett and Sarah around Middlefield, and not only would Rhett see Sarah was off-limits, but Judah would also have done his duty, which would score points in Sarah's eyes.

He really didn't have time to play tour guide. But for Sarah, he would do anything, even spend a few hours with a Yankee who had no business being here.

. . .

Judah was wrong about everything—except for feeling certain their visitor knew nothing about farming.

It was obvious that Rhett had never been on a farm. From the moment the guy stepped on the land, he looked lost. Enoch and Reuben helped him differentiate between the various tools they used, and Judah would give him slight credit for knowing the difference between a shovel and a hoe.

But as far as planting crops, forget it. Judah was finished with his row of beet seed before Rhett was even a third of the way down the next row. He kept stopping and applying sunscreen on his neck and face, which were dripping with sweat before noon. After lunch Enoch gave him an old, battered Amish hat. Judah figured a student of Amish culture would have at least thought to bring a hat.

Things kept going steadily downhill after their planting was done for the day. First, he had to wait on Rhett to finish in the shower, which irked him to no end. Yeah, Rhett was actually living here while Judah had his own home to go to, but still. He always took his showers right after Reuben and Enoch, who spent at the most five minutes each washing off the dirt and sweat of the day. By the time Judah took his shower, the hot water was gone.

But that wasn't the worst of it. When they all sat down for supper, it was clear that Sarah's attention was focused on Rhett. Judah saw the empty chair next to Sarah and tried to sit down beside her. "Rhett's sitting here," she'd said, her voice still filled with its usual sweetness—the same tone he was used to her using with him.

"Huh," he'd said, then went to sit next to Esther, who, as usual, kept her head down and her mouth closed. They bumped elbows once when she passed him potatoes and he was reaching for the jar of bread-and-butter pickles.

"Sorry." Her voice was low, apologetic . . . and for some reason he noticed how pleasant it sounded, which didn't make any sense. He'd heard Esther talk over the years, though never saying much and in a near whisper most of the time. But this was the first time he thought of her voice as *pleasant*.

"No worries." Without thinking, he smiled at her and opened the jar of pickles. "Would you like one?"

She shook her head, and didn't say anything for the rest of the meal. That was fine, because Sarah talked enough for both of them. She peppered Rhett with questions, laughed at his not-so-funny attempts at humor, and batted her eyes at him. The same way she'd batted her eyes at Judah. *Huh.*

"You're still going to take Rhett on a tour of Middlefield after supper, right, Judah?" Sarah said.

Judah was tempted to say no, but he'd already given his word, and he would never go back on a promise. "Yes." He took a bite of carrot and cabbage salad, chewed and swallowed, then looked at Rhett. "We'll probably just drive around Mespo," he said, referring to the small town they lived in near Middlefield, where their community's district was centered.

"We can take him to the gazebo. And the general store. Plus the statue." Sarah looked at Rhett wearing a smile that would instantly melt frozen butter.

"We?" Enoch said with an arch of his brow.

"I thought I'd go with them." Sarah smiled sweetly at her father. "It's a lovely evening for a ride."

"It certainly is," Fanny said. "Esther, why don't you go with them too?"

Esther's head bobbed up. "What?"

"Like your sister said, it's a beautiful evening, not as hot as yesterday. You should join them."

"I'm sure Esther has other things to do," Sarah said, looking at Esther as if she were noticing her for the first time. Which was kind of rude, Judah realized.

"I do have some reading to catch up on," Esther said. It seemed she didn't want to go on the ride any more than Judah did.

"You can do that anytime," Enoch added. He grabbed a slice of bread and slathered butter on it.

"I suppose you want Reuben to come too." Sarah's voice had lost its sweetness, the corners of her pretty mouth downturned into almost a pout.

"I'll pass," Reuben said, digging into the mashed potatoes.

"I don't have to go." Esther picked at the edge of her plate. "I don't want to be in the way."

"You won't be," Rhett said. "The more the merrier, right?"

"Right." Sarah leaned back in her chair. Yep, she was definitely pouting. Which made her extremely unattractive at the moment. Judah wasn't thrilled that he'd agreed out of a moment of weakness to cart around this Yankee, but he'd do it and he'd keep his feelings to himself. Just like Sarah should have.

Like Esther was doing. Judah glanced at her. She scooped up a small amount of potatoes and took a bite. She had a delicate and deliberate way of eating, separating each food from the others and picking up only small bites.

"Mrs. Coblentz, is there a place in town where I can buy some Amish clothes?" Rhett asked. "I'd really like to immerse myself in the full Amish experience."

Judah gripped his fork. Did this guy really think if he put on Amish clothes he would understand the Amish? Judah didn't have anything against Yankees in general, but since he'd been working summers for Enoch, he'd been privy to the conversations of people who took the house and farm tour. Words like *quaint, peaceful, adorable,* and the worst one in his opinion, *simple,* were bandied about with regularity. He didn't like that his faith and way of life were reduced to a few adjectives.

Being Amish was more complicated than that. It took serious commitment to God and to the community. Wearing the clothes and puttering around a farm was not the Amish "experience."

"No need to buy anything, Rhett," Fanny said. "Reuben probably has some clothes that would fit you."

"Or maybe Judah has some." Sarah turned her attention to Judah for the first time. As usual, her eyes sparkled like jewels. Her long, lush eyelashes were moving up and down just enough that they drew his attention, and she bit her bottom lip, drawing his gaze to her mouth. The jolt that went through him when she looked at him this way was still there, but with less intensity—much less intensity since she had looked at Rhett the exact same way.

"I'm taller than he is." Judah shoved his fork into the last bite of his mashed potatoes.

"He can borrow some of mine," Reuben said, not looking up from his plate. "I don't mind."

And with that, Sarah angled her body toward Rhett. Dismissed. Judah wiped his mouth on his napkin and shot up from the chair. "I'll go get the buggy hitched," he said, heading for the door. Then he remembered his manners, stopped himself, and took a breath as he turned around.

"Delicious supper, Fanny. As always." Pleased he'd brought a smile to her face, he went outside, his own, fake smile disappearing. The food was good. It was the company that left much to be desired.

He took his time getting his horse out of the stall, partly because his quick exit had given him even more time to spare while they waited for Sarah and Esther to help their mother clean up the kitchen. And partly because he needed to get his wits about him. If he wanted to show Rhett the real Amish way, he would have to be more accepting and less irritable. Not to mention less jealous.

Before long, Esther entered the barn. Her face was pinched together and she looked like she was being sent to sit on a bed of nails for an hour. She gave him a strained smile, then turned her back to him, her head down as if she was staring at something fascinating on the barn floor. He patted his horse on the nose and went to her. "You okay, Esther?"

She jumped a little. "Sorry," she said, looking at him as she took a step back.

"For what? I startled you." For some reason he felt the need to soften his voice. She was acting like a skittish colt, which she often did when he was around, with the exception of the buggy ride home from the Parlor. Why, he had no idea. But this time it bothered him a little bit. "Have I done something?"

Her eyes widened in surprise. "*Nee*. Not at all."

Judah exhaled with relief. At least he hadn't put Esther off. "*Gut*. It's just that . . ." He rubbed the back of his neck, not sure why he was bringing the subject up.

"It's just what?" she asked when he didn't finish the sentence.

"You always seem to act a little strange around me." At her dismayed face he added, "Not weird or anything like that. Just . . . different."

Then she lifted her chin. "Maybe because I *am* different."

Her response surprised him, because this time she wasn't referring to the differences between her and Sarah. She was speaking solely for herself. He looked at her for a moment. Really looked at her, not just a casual glance, and despite himself he compared her to Sarah. Willowy, graceful Sarah, who had eyes that could melt the ice around a snowman's heart. Esther was shorter, stockier, and, unfortunately, couldn't be called beautiful. Looks weren't everything, but combined with her shy demeanor, the best descriptor he could apply to her was . . . plain. For some reason, that caused a pinch in his heart.

Her chin drooped a little, and he knew he hadn't hidden his thoughts very well, which was one of his drawbacks. Heart on his sleeve, that was Judah King. It had led to more than his fair share of teasing, especially since he started pursuing Sarah. "You're like a moon-eyed puppy dog around her," his brother Stephen had said last year. "The only thing you haven't done is sit up and beg at her feet."

But he didn't want to think about Sarah right now. He moved toward Esther, wanting to apologize. Yet how could he do that and not hurt her feelings? "Esther, I . . ."

She lifted her chin once more. "I should see what's taking Sarah and Rhett so long." Turning around, she left the barn.

Judah clamped his lips together. Oh, he'd hurt her all right. What he didn't understand was why it bothered him as much as it did.

CHAPTER 4

Esther rushed to the back side of the barn, out of Judah's sight and hopefully hidden from Rhett and Sarah, who would be coming any minute. Rhett was upstairs with Reuben trying on some of his clothes, and Sarah had insisted on waiting for him. She'd decided to have a talk with Sarah later. Her flirting with the Yankee man was wrong, and she was doing it in front of Judah. Esther wondered if Sarah even realized her behavior was unseemly, not to mention hurtful.

But Sarah's behavior wasn't making her throat burn. She pressed her thumbs to her eyes, as if she could push her tears back in. It worked somewhat, but a couple escaped. So now she felt ridiculous on top of hurt.

Unlike when she'd referred to her and Sarah being different last night, tonight she'd seen Judah's true feelings when she declared she was indeed different, not like anyone else. At the time she'd been happy with her reply, even a little proud that she'd stood her ground and didn't let on that his comment about her acting weird had hit her square in the heart. Then she risked a look into his eyes, his beautiful eyes with thick black eyelashes that were long, but not too long for a man, and irises that were an unusual combination of dark blues and greens, colors that could only be seen up close.

Judah could never hide his feelings because of those eyes. Everything he thought and felt could be seen. She should know; she'd seen his nearly complete adoration of Sarah every time he looked at her sister.

But he hadn't looked at Esther with adoration. No, when he looked at her just now, his eyes had held pity. When she saw that, she could barely hold it together.

Judah pitied her. Why, she wasn't sure. Because she wasn't gorgeous like Sarah? Because she couldn't keep her own feelings for him locked down tight enough that she could behave like a normal human being around him? That she would always be lacking in looks and personality? Knowing the reason wasn't important.

She lifted her head and gazed out at the farm. The cows softly lowed as they grazed in the pasture. The garden was lush and full of delicious vegetables. Flowers, many of which she'd planted, decorated the landscape with their vibrant colors. She had a part in making this farm a success, and she played a key role in her family's tourist business. She had a good life. An important purpose to fulfill. Yet she spent her time yearning for a man who could feel only pity for her.

Wasn't she better than that? Wasn't she worthy of more?

Despite her pain, she smiled. The invisible cord of hope that she and Judah would be together had finally been cut. It was unexpected, and it hurt, not to mention she would probably have a good cry about it later.

But for now she felt free. She didn't have to live her life wishing Judah would love her or being jealous of her sister. Esther deserved happiness, and she wouldn't find it in Judah, or any other man.

Peace had been within her reach all along. For once she was ready to grab it—to enjoy life and the blessings God had given her and her family.

She walked around to the front of the barn, making one last swipe at her eyes to make sure there wasn't a trace of tears left. She wouldn't cry over Judah King anymore.

Judah hadn't hitched up his horse yet, probably because he was waiting for Sarah to show up. The thought of him and Sarah together didn't bring the thread of jealousy she was used to, and that brought another smile to her face. She glanced up at the sky. It was a beautiful, warm evening. Perfect for a buggy ride.

Rhett and Sarah approached the barn, and Esther's smile widened as her eyes met Rhett's. He actually looked pretty good in Reuben's clothes. He had on a short-sleeved yellow shirt, suspenders, broadfall pants, and a yellow straw hat that didn't do much to hide his Yankee haircut. He was also wearing white sneakers, which looked odd with the pants, since Amish men usually wore work boots.

He stopped in front of her and grinned. He was always smiling, always cheerful. It was contagious, like Sarah's breezy enthusiasm. "What do you think?" he asked Esther, turning around so she could get a full view.

"You look very Amish."

"I'll take that as a compliment. The suspenders will take some getting used to, though."

"You don't have to wear them, unless Reuben's pants are too big."

"They're actually a little snug." Rhett put his thumb in the waistband, which was a bit tight. "But with all the work I'll be doing, I imagine I'll drop a few pounds."

"Don't be so sure. Our mother is an excellent cook. You might even gain some weight while you're here."

He chuckled. "If tonight's supper was any indication, I think you're right." He moved to stand closer to her. "Maybe after the buggy ride you can give me a tour of the old house."

"You can go over there anytime you'd like," Esther said.

"I'd like the tour, though. I imagine as a guide you include details that make it extra special."

Esther couldn't keep from smiling. He wasn't flirting with her. She was sure of that. There wasn't a single butterfly in sight. He was being sincere, and she appreciated it.

"Where's Judah?" Sarah said, sounding a little annoyed. "I thought the buggy would be hitched by now."

"I'm right here." Judah came outside, leading his horse to the buggy. "I'll be ready in a minute."

Esther looked at him, her smile dimming a bit. His voice sounded gruff, which it never did in Sarah's presence. Even Sarah seemed surprised and turned to Esther, mouthing the words, "What's wrong with him?"

Esther shrugged. Judah's moods didn't interest her anymore. The quick glance she was giving him now was only to make sure he was hitching up the buggy, nothing more.

"You need some help?" Rhett asked, walking toward the buggy.

"I've got it."

Rhett stopped in his tracks, obviously because of Judah's clipped tone. He held out his hands. "Okay. Let me know if I can do anything, though."

After the horse was securely hitched, Esther entered the buggy first, sitting in the back and ignoring Judah. When Rhett climbed in after her, Sarah protested.

"You can sit up front with me and Judah," she said.

"Nah, I'm good." He sat down next to Esther and flashed another grin. "I don't mind sitting in the back."

"But you can see more from up front."

"It will be a little crowded with the three of you, don't you think?" Esther asked.

Sarah's expression darkened. "Not if I'm sitting in the middle."

"Esther's right." Rhett settled against the seat, then glanced at Esther again. "Besides, I've got the best tour guide in town right next to me."

She smiled back at Rhett. There was no underlying message to his words, no false sentiment. Best of all, no *pity.* She settled herself in the seat and prepared for a wonderful ride.

. . .

This was the worst ride of Judah's life.

Sarah sat next to him like a statue. There was enough

space between them in the front seat of the buggy for his friend Elvin, who was six four, rotund, and took up more room than anyone he knew. But he barely noticed that because of the incessant chatter in the backseat.

Judah had never heard Esther talk so much. Sure, he'd heard her going through her spiel with the tourists she guided, answering their questions with direct precision. But she and Rhett had chatted nonstop, and not just about the scenery in Mespo. At first Esther pointed out things of interest and answered Rhett's questions. But soon they abandoned the tour. Now they were talking about more personal things—Rhett's studies, his university, and their hobbies.

"You took a quilting class?" Esther said, sounding shocked.

"I did. Actually it was the quilting that led to my interest in the Amish, which led me to changing my major from law to cultural studies."

"What made you decide to learn to quilt?"

Judah, his gaze straight on the road, could almost imagine Rhett shrugging.

"It looked interesting. I'm always game to try something new and unusual. I'm thinking about taking a semester off school this fall and spending the time in the Himalayas."

"That's a mountain range in Asia, right?"

"Yes," Rhett said. "Did you learn about that in school?"

"*Nee*. We didn't learn much world geography. But I do love to read."

"Me too. What's the latest book you've read?"

And that launched them into a literary conversation

Judah wanted to tune out, but couldn't because he also liked to read. He frowned when he learned he and Rhett had the same taste in fiction—thrillers and mysteries. Esther liked mysteries—another fact Judah didn't know—but didn't care for thrillers, and her favorite genre was historical fiction.

Sarah turned back and faced the front of the buggy, her arms crossed. Judah glanced at her. What was wrong with him? He had the perfect scenario here. Sarah was in the buggy with him, and they might as well be alone since Esther and Rhett were doing a fine job keeping each other company.

Judah knew he should say something to break the tension and bring a smile to Sarah's face. But he didn't want to. He didn't like this side of Sarah, one he'd never seen before. She was broody and pouty. Why? Because she wasn't getting any attention from Rhett? He shook his head. "Huh."

"What did you say?" Sarah asked, speaking to him for the first time since supper.

"*Nix*." He glanced at her again. "What's *yer* favorite genre?"

"Genre?"

"Book genre. What books do you like to read?"

"I'm not that much of a reader." She glanced over her shoulder at Rhett and Esther again, then blew out a sigh. "Although I used to love the Little House on the Prairie books when I was a girl."

"What do you like to do now?" He realized he didn't really know. The few dates they'd been on, they hadn't talked very much. Well, Sarah had talked a lot, but mostly about her friends or where she wanted him to take her on their date. Judah frowned. Now that he thought about it, he and Sarah hadn't had a single meaningful conversation. He'd been content to just look at her. Unlike his conversations with Esther. It took time to get Esther to talk to him, but when she did, he enjoyed it.

"I like to cook and sew." Sarah turned around again. "I've made several quilts," she said to Rhett.

"Oh?" He leaned forward. "What kind of patterns?"

As Rhett and Sarah started discussing quilt patterns, Judah contemplated jumping out of the buggy. Goldie was an old, reliable horse who could get the three of them back to Coblentz Farms on her own. Meanwhile Judah would bang his head against a tree or go walk through some thornbushes. Either would be preferable to a quilt discussion.

Finally they reached their destination—a small park in Mespo that split the single road into two separate ones. A general store was on the corner, and the park had a gazebo, small pavilion, trees, and some swings on the grassy area. Yankee houses lined each side, and near the road opposite the gazebo was a huge wooden horse and buggy structure. Judah pulled his buggy to the hitching post.

"I'd like to get some pictures," Rhett said as they all climbed out of the buggy.

"Do you want some with you in them?" Sarah asked, her voice sounding a little high and tight and . . . desperate? Where was the composed woman Judah had fallen for? "If so, I—"

"That's a great idea. Esther, do you mind?" He handed Esther the camera and she hesitated a moment. Judah figured she was trying to decide whether using the camera would be a violation of the *Ordnung*. Being in the pictures definitely would. Then she nodded at Rhett, and they walked together to the wooden statue.

"Good grief." Sarah lifted her hands, her pretty face scrunched into a scowl. "I'm going to get something to drink." She spun away from him, flung her purse over her shoulder, and marched to the general store, her hands clenched at her sides, looking about as willowy as a steel beam.

Normally Judah would have jumped at the chance to follow her. This was another prime opportunity to have some alone time with Sarah. They could get a cold pop and sit in the gazebo. It was a clear evening, with only a few puffy clouds in the sky, and a light breeze that provided a nice respite from the warm temperature. Ideal conditions to convince Sarah they belonged together.

Instead he turned and looked at Esther and Rhett. Rhett was standing close to her—too close, Judah thought—while showing her how to use his tiny camera. Then he went and stood by the statue, leaning to the side a bit, knees bent, and showing two thumbs-up. Judah rolled his eyes. Rhett looked ridiculous. But Esther laughed as she snapped his photo.

Her laugh. Wow, she had a lovely laugh. How had he not noticed that before?

Judah stood guard at the buggy while Rhett and Esther continued to take pictures, with Rhett doing most of the picture taking while Esther observed. When Sarah still wasn't back, Judah was a little worried. He had started walking toward the store when he saw her coming out, talking to an Amish man near his age. Judah squinted and realized it was his friend Samuel Keim.

He waited for the irritation and jealousy to rear their ugly heads like they usually did when he saw Sarah with someone else. This time . . . nothing. Now that he knew she was fine, he turned around and searched for Rhett and Esther. When he saw them sitting on the swings, he groaned.

He couldn't wait for this so-called tour to be over.

CHAPTER 5

As she thought about the evening, Esther sat on the edge of her bed and ran a brush through her waist-length locks. She smiled. Not only had she been set free of Judah, but she had made a new friend.

Rhett was smart—really smart. On the surface he seemed a bit air-headed and more than a little quirky—the quilting class proved that—but as she got to know him she realized he was highly intelligent. He loved reading about philosophy, his third favorite kind of book next to mysteries and thrillers. And as they had walked to the swings and sat down, he told her how much he valued the experience the Coblentzes were giving him.

"I just wish my girlfriend was here," he said. "She would enjoy this."

Esther wasn't surprised to discover Rhett had a girlfriend. "Why didn't she come with you?"

"For one, there's no way the two of us would stay together, even if an Amish family would allow it. We wouldn't want to. But she wouldn't have wanted to stay anywhere alone either. Also, she's in nursing school right now, and she wants to graduate early. So she's taking classes all summer."

"How did you two meet?"

"At church, two years ago." He smiled, but this smile was different from the ones he had given her and her family. "I knew she was special the first time I saw her."

"Is she going with you to the Himalayas?"

He shook his head. "No, unfortunately. Which is giving me second thoughts about the idea of that trip. I haven't booked it yet. It's always been a dream of mine to go, and this opportunity came up with some friends of mine who are missionaries. But I don't know if I can be gone from Shelby for that long. I'm missing her already and I've only been here two days."

"Maybe this is a way to see if you can be apart that long."

"That's what I thought." He looked up at Judah and Sarah, who were standing near the buggy. "Guess they're ready to go." Then he looked at Esther. "What's up with those two? Are they together?"

"Judah would like them to be." She was so pleased she could say that out loud. "But Sarah's not interested in settling down."

"I can tell." He gave her a rueful smile. "Is she always so . . ."

"Flirty?"

"That's one way to put it." He pushed against the ground with his toe and the swing moved forward. "I was thinking overwhelming, though."

"She doesn't mean anything by it," Esther said, feeling the need to defend Sarah. "She's just . . . friendly."

He leaned toward her slightly. "You're friendly, Esther. You're easy to talk to, and you're a good listener. She's . . ." He shook his head. "You two seem very different." He stopped the swing and stood up. "I think that's cool."

Esther smiled again at the memory. She and Rhett hadn't talked that much on the ride home. He'd been focused on the scenery, and probably thinking about Shelby too. Judah and Sarah were also quiet. That surprised her. She'd expected Judah to take advantage of his close proximity to Sarah. Then she reminded herself that she wasn't concerned about Judah anymore, and focused on relaxing.

She set her hairbrush on her nightstand just as Sarah burst into her room, then shut the door behind her. When they moved into the addition, she and Sarah no longer had to share a bedroom. "Are you satisfied with *yerself*?" she snapped.

"What?" she asked, bewildered by her sister's anger.

"Monopolizing Rhett's time like that." Sarah crossed her arms over her chest. "You'll probably get in trouble for using a camera."

"It was *yer* idea to take pictures of him," Esther said, rising from the bed.

"You looked silly."

Esther frowned. "I looked silly taking pictures?"

"You looked silly because he's not interested in you."

Frustrated, Esther said, "I know he's not interested in me. I'm not interested in him."

"You sure acted like it tonight."

"Sarah, we were just talking—"

"We were just talking," Sarah mocked, batting her eyelashes almost grotesquely. "He was talking. You were flirting."

"I was not. I don't even know how to flirt."

"Which is why you looked so pathetic."

Her sister's words hurt to the core. It was one thing to think of herself as pathetic, but to hear her sister say it undid every pleasant and confident feeling she'd experienced for the past few hours. "You better leave now." Esther sat down on the bed. "Before we both say something we regret."

Sarah paused. Esther wasn't looking at her, but she could tell her sister was hesitating to leave. Probably firing up more ammunition to hurl at her. It wasn't enough that she was the sister who had everything— beauty, grace, popularity, men like Judah falling at her feet. She could also be hateful when she was upset.

When Sarah didn't move, Esther turned to her. To her surprise the anger on her sister's face was gone, replaced by remorse. But Esther was too hurt to care. "Leave, Sarah."

Sarah paused, biting her bottom lip as her crystal-blue eyes became glassy. Then she turned, opened the door, and left the room.

. . .

Although it was nearly ninety degrees outside, the chilliness between the Coblentz sisters was palpable. Judah leaned against his rake and watched as Sarah and Esther sat at opposite ends of the bench Enoch had put under a huge oak tree, both of them shelling peas.

He'd never seen them like this before. Even more puzzling, when he'd arrived a few hours ago, he hadn't sought out Sarah like he usually did. But he'd been happy to see Esther right away—until he saw the pain on her face. The same pain was also on Sarah's face. Something had happened between them after he left last night. He had to remind himself it wasn't his business, but that didn't stem his curiosity.

He went back to raking up the grass and stray hay in front of the petting barn. It was Saturday, and Judah normally worked half a day, then went home and spent the rest of the time with his family until Monday. But today he was here longer than usual, mostly because Reuben and Enoch had gone to a farm implement auction, which left Rhett to his own devices. Considering the guy's lack of farm experience, Judah figured he'd stick around and make sure Rhett didn't inadvertently destroy anything. Right now he was cleaning out the stalls in the petting barn, a hot, smelly task Judah was glad to give him and, oddly enough, Rhett seemed happy to take.

Judah paused in his raking and looked at the women again. Sarah got up, took her bowl of shelled peas, and went inside the house. Esther put her bowl next to her, then leaned her head against her hands.

He couldn't stand to see Esther in pain. Although he didn't know what he was going to say to her, he had started for the bench when Rhett came up beside him. Judah smelled the sweat and manure coming off of him, and he hoped that was a result of cleaning out the stalls, not falling into a pile of something he shouldn't have.

"Thought I'd take a little break." Rhett took off his

hat and wiped his forehead with the back of his hand. "If that's all right with you."

There was no sarcasm in the man's voice. Judah looked at him. His smile was faded and a bit work-worn, but still there. He'd eagerly accepted the most menial chore Judah could think of. It was becoming difficult to keep disliking him. "Sure. Get some water too. It's easy to get dehydrated if you're not used to the work."

"Or the heat. I'm a wimp. I'll admit it. I use the gym, but it's air-conditioned. So is my apartment." His face was flushed. "I don't know if I'll ever get used to the heat."

"It takes time. Or so I've heard. I don't know anything different, except when I go into a store or restaurant. Gotta admit, the cold air feels good on a hot summer day."

"That it does." He started walking away. "You want anything from the house?"

"No, but thanks for asking." That was another thing about the guy. He was considerate, and not because he was trying to earn points. Everything about him was genuine. Yes, it was hard to dislike Rhett Davidson.

Despite his complaining about the heat, Rhett moved toward the house with quick steps. He paused at the bench, then sat down next to Esther—too close to Esther, Judah noticed. Without thinking, Judah put aside the rake and went to them.

"You sure you're okay?" Judah heard Rhett ask as he approached.

Esther nodded, giving him a strained smile that didn't reach her eyes. Judah had seen that look in her eyes before, right after he'd hurt her yesterday. Was she still upset with him?

"Do you want a drink of water?" Rhett asked.

"No. I'm fine." She searched his face. "You look like you could use one."

"I'm headed inside now. But if you want to talk, I'm here."

Jealousy stabbed at Judah with intensity. Why would Esther want to talk to Rhett? Had they already become so close that she felt comfortable confiding in him?

"I appreciate the offer." A small smile formed on her lips again. And again, it didn't reach her eyes.

Rhett got up and went inside. Just as the screen door banged shut, Judah slid in next to Esther. "What's wrong?" he demanded.

She looked up at him, her brow lifted. *"Nix."*

"You're lying."

"Judah, I'm not lying—"

"Esther, I've known you a long time, and I can tell when you're lying. You're upset with me, aren't you?"

"I . . . I—"

"I'm sorry, okay?" He took off his hat and ran a hand through his damp hair. "I know I hurt you yesterday. I'm not exactly sure how. I guess I shouldn't have called you weird."

"You didn't call me weird. You said I was acting weird. That's a big difference. Unless you meant to call me weird."

There went the lift of that chin, and Judah had to admit it was cute, even more cute than when she'd had that dot of ice cream on her nose at the Parlor. And when did he start thinking of Esther as cute?

"You're not weird, okay?" He sounded agitated. He

was agitated, and he had no idea why. That awareness didn't stop him from blurting out his next words. "There, does that make you feel better?"

She shot up from the bench, her eyes sparking with anger. "For *yer* information, Judah King, what I'm feeling has *nix* to do with you." She picked up her bowl and went inside the house.

This time Judah flinched as the screen door banged shut. He'd made a mess of that, all right. But if she wasn't upset with him, what was she upset about? More importantly, why did he care so much?

. . .

That Sunday, as Esther sat on a wood bench during their church service held in a barn, she tried to focus on the minister's preaching. Wally Schlabach was hard to listen to, even when Esther's thoughts and feelings weren't in turmoil. He was a fine, kind man, a good minister, but probably the worst preacher on the planet. He stumbled over words, mangled scripture passages, and went off on tangents that even had the bishop scratching his head. Then there was the monotone delivery. But every fourth Sunday, Wally Schlabach delivered the message. Without fail.

This morning Esther desperately wanted something to distract her from what had happened yesterday. Sarah still wasn't speaking to her, and she wasn't all that willing to talk to Sarah. Not until she apologized, at least. Rhett had been his usual kind self, and she appreciated the offer to talk.

But what puzzled her most was Judah's behavior. He'd apologized to her for saying she acted weird, but the apology wasn't necessary. She hadn't even thought about that since it happened. But his apology had not only been sincere, it had been . . . fervent. That was a fancy word, but the only one she could think of to describe what she'd seen in his eyes, heard in his voice. Judah couldn't hide that sincerity, not if he tried. It had reached inside her, pulled out the tiny fragment of that cord of hope that apparently hadn't disappeared completely, and yanked it tight—which had disturbed her even more. The last thing she needed was to have those feelings rekindled.

As Wally droned on, her gaze drifted to the other side of the barn. Sitting next to Reuben, Rhett was easy to spot. He was paying rapt attention to the minister's sermon, as if Wally was the most eloquent speaker he'd ever heard. Reuben, on the other hand, was struggling to stay awake. Although she didn't want to, her gaze strayed to Judah, seated a couple of benches back.

The moment she spotted him he turned and looked at her, as if he'd sensed her watching him. Her cheeks heated and she pulled her gaze away, but not before she saw something she'd never seen in Judah's eyes before, at least not when he'd looked at her.

Interest. He had looked at her with interest.

After the service, Sarah, who had been seated at the end of Esther's bench on the other side of their mother, hurried out of the barn. *Mamm* gave Esther a puzzled look. Esther shrugged. Obviously *Mamm* suspected something was going on with her and Sarah, but Esther didn't want to talk about it. Her feelings still stung from Sarah's verbal assault.

Esther walked outside, pausing for a moment to talk to her friend Julia, who had married last year. She promised to visit Julia during the week, then left the barn and stood in the front yard of Samuel Keim's house. The service was being held at his family's farm, so she was within walking distance of her house, and she didn't want to stay for fellowship this afternoon. She wanted to be alone.

She went to her parents, told them she was walking home, and then started for the road. Rhett stopped her. "You're not staying?"

Shaking her head, she said, "I'm a little tired. I'm going home, and I'll probably take a nap."

"I totally get it. A nap sounds good right now, but I'm staying. Reuben said he'd introduce me to a few of his friends. Everyone's been really nice." He grinned, then said, "Maybe a group of us guys could visit Lake Erie while I'm here. Do you know anything about fishing charters there?"

"*Ya*. Our family reserves one every summer, usually the second week of July. We'll be going this weekend."

"Really?" His eyes grew wide with excitement. "Do you think I could go with you?"

"I'm surprised *Daed* hasn't told you about it. I'm sure he doesn't intend to leave you here by yourself." Esther explained how they always went to Geneva-on-the-Lake. This year they were trying out a new rental area, with nice cottages that had a lovely view of Lake Erie's shoreline. "We're usually there from Friday to

Monday. *Daed* doesn't like to be gone from the farm much longer than that."

Rhett nodded. "Are you sure there's room?"

"Since *Daed* knew you were coming, he probably rented an extra cottage. He hasn't said much about the trip lately, probably because of getting all the extra crops in."

"I'll pay for it," he said quickly. "And whatever it costs for the charter too."

Esther thought for a moment. "I'm sure Reuben will be more than happy to split a cottage rental with you to get that much space to himself. I wouldn't worry about the charter fee—"

"I'm paying my way," Rhett insisted.

"Okay, okay." She chuckled. "You can work it out with *Daed*."

Rhett grinned. "Do you like to fish?"

"I'm not the best at fishing, but I enjoy it. It's peaceful, sitting on a boat or on the shore of a lake or pond."

"I fished a couple of times when I was a kid," he said. "But not on Lake Erie, so I'm looking forward to it." He glanced at Reuben, who was waving him over to a group of his friends. "I'll see you later," he said, then took off.

. . .

At supper the next night, *Daed* said, "I'm glad Rhett brought up our vacation today. We've been so busy with that new field I've been forgetting to mention that all those cottages were already booked for this weekend.

With buying that property and making plans for it, I waited too long to contact them."

Esther frowned. "What about the weekend after?"

"I didn't check." He took a slice of watermelon from the platter in the middle of the table and placed it on his plate. Usually they ate watermelon outside, but it had started raining a couple of hours ago. "We've always gone the second weekend of July. It's tradition."

She knew better than to argue with him. One glance at her mother told her she was right. Her father would forgo vacation before he'd change the date. She pushed at a watermelon seed with her fork, disappointed. She enjoyed their yearly vacations, and she'd been looking forward to this one.

"So we're going camping instead," *Daed* proclaimed.

"Camping?" Sarah said, looking incredulous. "In a tent?"

Daed held up two fingers. "Two tents. Reuben and Rhett can share one."

Reuben was grinning so widely Esther thought his face had to hurt.

Sarah scowled at him. "What are you so happy about?"

"I don't have to share with you two." He pointed his fork at her, then at Esther. "This will be the best vacation ever."

"*Mamm*, are you okay with this?" Sarah asked.

"Of course. *Yer daed* and I used to *geh* camping before you *kinner* were born. I even found our old sleeping bags, and they're in *gut* shape."

"We'll have to get four more." *Daed* took a bite of

his watermelon, then wiped his bearded chin with his napkin. "Plus another tent."

"I called and reserved a fishing charter for Saturday," Rhett added, looking at Esther. "We'll have the boat for the whole day."

"Count me out," Reuben said. He pushed his plate away.

Esther wasn't surprised Reuben wasn't interested in an all-day charter. Her brother could fish for a couple of hours, but he got bored quickly.

"I'll *geh*," Sarah said.

"But you get motion sickness," *Mamm* reminded her.

Reuben nudged Rhett with his elbow. "Last time she was on a boat she barfed over the side. Twice. And that was in a little canoe."

Sarah's lips pressed into a thin line. "That was ten years ago."

"I don't think being on the water all day is a *gut* idea." *Mamm* patted her hand. Her family had been slipping into *Deitsch* with Rhett present from time to time, which Esther noticed he actually seemed to appreciate. "I thought you and I could spend the *daag* at the gift shops instead."

Sarah nodded, her lips still tight.

Esther looked away from her sister and glanced at Judah. He'd been quiet during the conversation, and she expected him to be gazing at Sarah, or at least looking at her with concern since Reuben had just embarrassed her. Instead his attention was on her father. "I've got a tent you can use," he said. "Extra sleeping bags too. Are you camping at the state park?"

"*Ya*," *Daed* said, taking a bite of the watermelon rind as was his habit. A distasteful one, Esther always thought. But he loved watermelon rind. "Already reserved the campsite as soon as I knew we couldn't get cottages. It's probably not one of their best spots, but we're fortunate the park even had one available."

He turned to Rhett. "I won't be able to fish that day with you and Esther either."

"You're going shopping with *Mamm* and Sarah?" Reuben cracked.

"*Nee*." He gave Reuben a pointed look. "I'm meeting with a *freind* from Holmes. Found out a couple of *daags* ago that he'll be in the Geneva area at the same time."

"So it's just me and Esther, then?" Rhett asked.

"And the charter captain," Esther added with a small smile. "Don't forget him."

Sarah pushed away from the table. "The rabbits need feeding."

"I already fed them," Rhett said. But Sarah ignored him and walked out of the kitchen.

Esther half expected Judah to go after her. But he stayed in his seat, his watermelon only partially eaten.

"Sounds like everything is settled," *Daed* said. "The van will be here for us Friday morning bright and early. *Danki* for loaning us the tent and sleeping bags, Judah."

Judah didn't say anything in return. He didn't even nod. His gaze bounced from Esther to Rhett, then back to Esther again. "I'll *geh* fishing with you." His brow lifted, as if he'd surprised himself with the words. "I can meet you on Saturday morning."

"Why don't you just *geh* camping with us?" Reuben

asked. "That would be easier. The van is big enough for all of us."

Esther swallowed as Judah slowly nodded, his eyes never leaving hers. Was he asking for permission to fish? Camp? She was caught so off guard by his sudden decision that she had no idea what he was thinking.

Then he turned to *Daed*. "I'd like to, if it's okay with you, Enoch."

"Sure. The more the merrier." He stood. "You're pretty much *familye* as it is, so why not *geh* on a *familye* vacation with us?"

Esther stared at her watermelon, confused. Judah had never expressed an interest in vacationing with them before. Then again, maybe he realized he could spend more time with Sarah if he went. But that didn't explain him wanting to go fishing with her and Rhett, enough that he was willing to go to the trouble to meet them Saturday morning.

When she looked up, Judah was already standing and *Mamm* was clearing the table. Judah gave Esther a short nod, then left, her father, Reuben, and Rhett not far behind.

Esther saw her mother pause as the men left. "What?" she asked, able to tell there was something on *Mamm*'s mind.

"*Nix.*" She held the platter of watermelon. A few juicy pieces still remained on the large white plate. "It's just . . ." She shook her head, but Esther didn't miss her slight smile. "It's going to be an interesting vacation this year."

Esther glanced at the empty doorway. She was thinking the same thing.

CHAPTER 6

Judah didn't like fish—catching them or eating them. But the thought of Esther being on a boat in the middle of Lake Erie with Rhett had made his thoughts go berserk. Now he found himself helping Rhett and Reuben set up a tent a few feet from where Esther would be sleeping tonight—again.

He'd offered to help set up the large tent where Esther and Sarah and her parents would sleep, but Enoch asked him to help set up the other tent with Reuben and Rhett. They'd done just that, only to have the tent collapse on one side, and for once a mishap wasn't Rhett's fault. Turned out he had a lot of experience tent camping. No, it was Reuben who hadn't secured the tent stakes properly on his side of the tent.

He glanced at Esther as she helped her father, hammering the last of their tent's stakes more firmly into the ground. He hadn't been able to keep his eyes off her since arriving at the Coblentzes before dawn. He'd even tried to sit next to her in the van Enoch hired to take them and all their gear to Geneva State Park, but she climbed into the backseat next to her mother. Sarah made sure to sit next to Rhett, which left Judah to sit next to Reuben on the bench seat closest to the front of the van.

After the tents were set up, Reuben and Rhett insisted Judah go with them for a long and vigorous hike through the park. By the time they came back, Esther had taken off on one of the two bikes the Coblentzes brought from home. She didn't return until suppertime, and then she was busy helping her mother and Sarah—who still looked more than a little put out about the whole camping thing—make a delicious supper of grilled beef hot dogs, packaged coleslaw, homemade pickles, and potato chips.

He sat at the picnic table as he watched Esther. He noticed little things about her, like the efficiency of her movements as she prepared the meal. She didn't have graceful movements like Sarah, but she wasn't clumsy or clunky. He took note of the smallness of her hands, the daintiness of her wrists. The curve of her neck.

The perfect area on her neck to place a kiss.

"Huh," he said out loud.

"What?" Reuben said from the space next to him.

"*Nix.*" He quickly pulled his gaze away from Esther and focused on Sarah, which he should have been doing to begin with. Wasn't this another prime opportunity to spend time with her? To convince her they belonged together? What he shouldn't be doing was thinking about Esther's neck. Or about kissing it. Where had that thought come from, anyway?

As he watched Sarah, he waited for that familiar jolt of attraction he always experienced when she was near. She'd even glanced at him, giving him a tiny smile that should have made his heart do cartwheels. Instead . . . he felt nothing.

"Here you *geh*," Esther said, handing him a full plate.

Jolt. He stared at her, then at the plate blankly, then back at her.

"Judah." She sounded impatient. "Here's *yer* food."

"Right. Sorry." He took the plate from her, said a quick silent prayer, and tried to focus on eating and not on the shot of attraction he'd just felt for Esther. This didn't make any sense. Sarah was the woman for him. The one he was attracted to. The one he loved. Esther was . . . Esther. A friend. Nothing special.

She sat down at the end of the table near Rhett and closed her eyes. Judah couldn't stop watching her. Her lashes rested against her soft cheeks, which were rosy from the summer heat.

Jolt. This one was stronger. Deeper. More confusing than anything he'd felt before. "I'm going to take a walk," he said, standing up and ignoring his full plate.

"We just hiked ten miles," Rhett said.

"You haven't even touched *yer* food," Reuben added around a mouthful of coleslaw.

But Judah disregarded both of them. He needed to get away from Esther, to figure out what was going on. He'd been in love with Sarah for four years. Yet for the past few days he hadn't given her a second thought.

What's going on, Lord? You'll have to tell me, because I have no idea.

. . .

The next morning Esther walked onto the wood dock of the Geneva Marina, carrying her tackle box and fishing pole. She tried to focus on enjoying the upcoming charter and not on Judah, but it was difficult. He was acting strange. Very strange. He hadn't returned from his walk last night by the time she turned in, which was pretty early, even before everyone else had gone to bed. She was tired, not just from bike riding and camping, but also from the strain between her and Sarah all week. They were being civil to each other, which was at least something. But being at odds with Sarah put a damper on everything.

She knew they should talk, but she couldn't bring herself to start the conversation. Sarah had hurt her, not the other way around. It was her sister's job to fix things between them, and so far she hadn't. Between that and Judah's bizarre behavior, Esther was having trouble enjoying herself.

Pulling herself out of those thoughts, she focused on fishing. Rhett said they could purchase worms at the dock, and that's where he and Judah were now. But she wanted to try a few special lures she'd never used. The seagulls soared above them, the waves from the lake lapping against the rocky edges, the sun high and hot in the summer sky. A perfect day for fishing.

As she approached the boat Rhett told her was the one he chartered, she realized Rhett and Judah were right behind her. They carried the cooler Esther packed earlier. After a few minutes, the captain greeted them.

"Another small group was going to come with us, but they canceled at the last minute. So it's just the four of us."

"Sounds great!" Rhett said.

Esther didn't have to look at him to know he was grinning.

They listened as the captain explained the process and procedure.

"Make sure you don't fall over," the leathery-skinned man said with intense seriousness. "And don't take any unnecessary chances."

Feeling like she was back in the schoolhouse, Esther nodded.

They climbed on board, and before long they shoved off. Esther stood close to the edge of the boat, her face feeling the wind that glided across the lake while her body rocked with the boat's movement. Now, this was freedom. She closed her eyes and finally allowed herself to relax.

"Sunscreen?"

She looked at the tube of sunscreen in Rhett's hand. "Thank you," she said. "I'd forgotten about it." She put some in her hand and placed a few dots on her face before rubbing it in. Then she applied the rest to the back of her neck.

"You missed a spot." Rhett reached around and rubbed his fingers on her neck. "There, got it."

She smiled as he took the sunscreen and went to the other side of the boat. Her smile disappeared when she saw Judah looking at her with a mix of confusion, then at Rhett with a look of . . . No, that couldn't be right. Jealousy? Esther blinked as Judah looked away.

She had to have imagined it. Judah would be jealous of Rhett with Sarah, not of Rhett with her. Not that there was anything to be jealous of when it came to either of them. Rhett had shown her a picture of Shelby the other day. She was a stunning dark-haired woman with almond-shaped eyes and a vibrant smile that nearly rivaled Rhett's. He must have told her he didn't plan to use his cell phone, because they'd been sending letters or postcards all week. Esther was pretty sure Rhett wouldn't go on that Himalayan trip after all.

They fished for the rest of the morning, catching mostly perch. They stopped midday and ate their packed lunch beneath the shade of the boat's awning. Rhett, who Esther realized could talk to anyone about anything, was in deep conversation with the captain about the strangest charter trips he'd had.

For some reason Judah had isolated himself and was sitting on the opposite end of the shaded area. He'd been by himself all morning, too, and, she heard him tell Rhett when he asked, had caught only one fish. A small one that had to be thrown back.

Esther finished her apple, put it in a paper bag, and folded down the top. She'd throw all their trash away when they got back to the dock. She set the bag aside, then went to the stern. She peered into the lake water, fascinated by the bubbles and foam floating on the surface. Trying to get a better view, she stood on tiptoe and tried to spy any fish that might be swimming close to the surface.

Realizing she was too short, she looked around for something to stand on and saw the cooler. She tested her weight on it, then stepped up. The bar of the boat rail pressed against her knees as she leaned forward.

Then she saw it—a huge perch. It swam back and forth in front of the boat as if daring her to reach down and try to catch it. She knew it was foolish to try, but she reached out anyway.

"Esther!"

Judah's bellow startled her and she whirled around. The cooler tilted. She grabbed for the boat rail, missed, then tipped right over into the water.

CHAPTER 7

E sther!" Judah yelled as she went overboard. He ran toward the railing and saw her flailing about in the water. Without thinking—or taking off his hat or boots—he dove in after her.

"What in the—"

The captain's angry voice rang in Judah's ears, along with his expletive. He had dived a little bit past Esther, so he turned around and swam back to her, the water seeping into his boots and making him feel as though he had anchors tied around his ankles.

"Judah, what are you doing?" Esther said.

He put his arm around her waist . . . and realized she was fine. She wasn't fighting for breath or stability. She was bobbing in the waves, looking completely comfortable . . . and completely waterlogged. Her *kapp* sagged on her head and water dripped down her cheeks. He tightened his arm around her waist and drew her close, nearly losing himself in the mix of excitement and confusion he saw in her eyes. His gaze dropped to her mouth—

"Are you two okay?" Rhett yelled.

No. He definitely wasn't okay. Right at that moment, holding Esther close—his face only inches from hers—thinking about kissing her breathless . . . he was better than okay. He was fantastic.

She put her hand on his shoulder. "Judah . . ."

Yep. He'd kiss her right now, right in front of the bellowing captain, who was threatening to throw them a rope. Right in front of Rhett, who Judah was sure was grinning from ear to ear since that seemed to be his only expression. He didn't care who was watching.

Then, just like that, Esther wriggled away from him and swam back to the boat, as if he were a poisonous water snake.

He followed her, grabbing his hat along the way. He was a pretty good swimmer, and they weren't that far from the boat, but with his boots dragging him down, it was an effort to reach the ladder. He hauled himself up behind her and sat down on the boat's seat. Unable to bring himself to look at Esther, he focused on yanking off his boots and pouring out the water.

"Here."

Judah couldn't keep from looking up as Rhett put a towel around Esther's shoulders. For once Rhett wasn't smiling. He was sitting next to her, and they were talking in hushed tones. Jealousy twisted inside Judah, not for the first time since they'd boarded this boat. Any clarity he might have gained from his long walk last night disappeared the moment he saw the two of them together this morning at breakfast. Esther and Rhett seemed way too cozy for comfort, especially when he was putting sunscreen on her neck when they got here. Her pretty neck. Which made him want to throw Rhett overboard and finish putting the sunscreen on her himself.

He yanked off a sock and wrung it out over the side of the boat. When he turned around, the captain held out a towel to him, but didn't say anything. He didn't have to. The dark scowl on his face spoke volumes.

"I'm ready to go back to the campsite." Esther's voice sounded small. She even looked small, her shoulders slumped as if the towel around her weighed fifty pounds, her *kapp* pressed against her head, water dripping from the hem of her dress.

Rhett nodded and went to speak to the captain, who immediately started the boat engine. They headed for the marina.

Judah shook off his hat, set it down next to his water-logged boots and damp socks, and stared at his bare feet. Rhett seemed annoyed, the captain was still angry, and worst of all, Esther was upset. With him. He didn't get it. She was the one who fell overboard. All he did was jump in to save her.

She didn't need saving. She didn't need me.

That truth slammed into him. Esther didn't need him. But why did he want her to? Wondering why he cared so much about what Esther did or thought or needed had plagued him the last few days, and he still didn't have any answers.

The ride to the marina seemed interminable. Finally the captain pulled the boat into the dock, begrudgingly offering to let them bring the towels back tomorrow. Rhett conversed with him while Esther made her way off the boat. Judah saw that she'd forgotten her pole and tackle box. He grabbed his boots, socks, and hat, snatched up her things, and leapt over the side of the boat, hoping Rhett would grab the cooler. His bare feet landed on the scorching hot dock, but he barely felt the heat as he went after her. He hadn't realized how fast she was walking, but finally he caught up to her.

"Esther," he said, sounding a little breathless, and he wasn't sure it was from the exercise.

She didn't answer him, keeping her chin down, the towel around her shoulders, and quickening her steps.

"You forgot *yer* pole and tackle box." Judah walked alongside her. When she didn't acknowledge him, he moved to stand in front of her, making her stop. "Esther, talk to me."

"About what?" Her voice sounded strained and high pitched. "The fact that you embarrassed me back there?"

"Embarrassed? How?"

"I know how to swim." She tilted her chin, and he recognized the gesture as defiance and a reach for confidence.

"I know."

"You didn't have to *geh* in after me and . . . and . . ."

His eyebrow lifted. "And what?"

"And manhandle me!"

And then Judah did exactly the wrong thing. He laughed. "Manhandle you? I was helping you."

"You were . . ." She looked upset and confused. "I don't know what you were doing. I didn't need help. I didn't need rescuing." She tried to move past him, but he stepped in front of her again.

"Esther, we need to talk about this. But not here." He looked around. They'd caught the attention of the few people around them, and although he and Esther were arguing in Deitsch, they were making a spectacle.

Why she thought this was less embarrassing than him swimming after her was beyond him. "When we get to the campground, we'll *geh* for a walk—"

"I'm not going anywhere with you."

The snap in her voice cut him, as did the faint quivering of her chin.

She pushed past him and walked away, heading for the bait shop.

The heat from the dock burned through the bottoms of his feet, and he high-stepped it to the grassy area near the parking lot. Although his socks were still damp, he shoved them on, then walked to the bait shop. Judah saw Esther leaving, looking as if she'd quickly tidied up a little in the shop's bathroom. Presumably she was heading back to the campsite. He started after her, only to have Rhett stop him.

"I wouldn't follow her if I were you," Rhett said.

Judah spun around. "Mind your own business."

"I usually do." Rhett set down the cooler and his gear, then pushed back his Amish hat. He hadn't worn a stitch of Yankee clothing since his second day here.

But Judah wasn't in the mood to give him any credit. "You should stay your course, then." Judah started to turn when Rhett interrupted him again.

"You're pretty dense for a smart guy."

Judah walked toward him, stopping when they were inches away from each other. Judah was a couple of inches taller than Rhett, and he took a bit of satisfaction in that since right now he felt as though he was otherwise at a disadvantage. "Don't think I haven't noticed you've had your eye on Esther ever since you arrived at the farm."

"Whoa." Rhett held up his hands and stepped back. "You think I have a thing for Esther?"

"Why is that so hard to believe? Any man would be lucky to have her."

"And you want that man to be you."

Judah froze.

Rhett shook his head, and a bit of his typical smile returned. "First off, I've got a girlfriend. A serious girlfriend. I'll probably ask her to marry me when I get home, I've missed her that much. Second, why are you mad at me? You're the one who's made a mess of things."

"What?" Judah said in a strangled voice.

"You're interested in Esther, right?"

Judah paused. Was he interested in her? He thought about how his feelings for her had changed. How he'd noticed things about her he'd never noticed before. Her sweet kindness. Her pretty smile. The way she took care of everyone, and even how much she was affected by her falling out with Sarah. He still didn't know what all that was about.

Most of all, he recalled the words he'd just said to Rhett. Remembered how he felt holding Esther in the water, the warmth of her hand when it touched his shoulder. How he had wanted to kiss her with a strength and intensity he'd never felt before . . . not even with Sarah.

"See, that's the problem right there," Rhett said, interrupting Judah's confused train of thought. "You can't even answer a simple question when it comes to Esther. Until you get your head on straight, you need to leave her alone . . . before you break her heart."

CHAPTER 8

Aonfter she returned home from vacation on Monday, Esther went through the motions of life. She led the tours, smiled at the tourists at the appropriate times, answered their questions, and helped *Mamm* with meals and chores. She made it through the daytime hours. Nighttime was a different story.

The last two nights at the lake had been bad enough, but for the two nights they'd been back, she'd tossed and turned, tried to pray, tried counting sheep, tried deep breathing. But all she could do was see Judah's face, the way he'd looked at her when he'd held her in the water. If she didn't know any better, she'd think he'd wanted to kiss her. And that's where the anger started. Not at him, but with herself. Not only was she a fool, but she was a love-struck fool for once again believing she stood a chance with Judah.

That feeling wouldn't go away, even though she hadn't seen him since he'd abruptly left the campground after the fishing trip. She'd taken her time walking back from the marina, slowly drying out as she took the long way around the park, not wanting to face Judah. When she finally arrived at the site, Rhett was worried. "I was about to try to find you," he'd said. "But Enoch convinced me you were fine."

"She knows how to take care of herself." *Daed* didn't even look up from the fish he was cleaning.

Esther looked around the campsite, expecting to see Judah close by. But she soon learned he'd used the bait shop phone to call for a driver and had gone back home. "Decided he wasn't cut out for this camping thing." *Daed*'s words were cryptic, and he didn't look at her when he spoke.

Esther should have been relieved, and a part of her was. At least she didn't have to spend the rest of her vacation feeling awkward around him. She had enough of that with Sarah.

But another part of her was disappointed. He hadn't gone after her. Hadn't stayed so they could talk, like he'd insisted they needed to do at the marina. Either whatever she thought she saw in his eyes wasn't real or he'd changed his mind—again.

Judah had not only left the campsite, but also hadn't returned to work on the farm yesterday. And her father hadn't said anything about why he was absent. To top it all off, she and Sarah still weren't on good terms. Even Rhett seemed subdued. Esther felt some guilt about that—he hadn't bargained for all this family drama.

By Wednesday evening, she couldn't take the tension anymore. After a mostly silent supper, she went for a walk. Ohio got its fair share of humid weather in the summer, and the evening air was thick and steamy. Perspiration appeared on her skin by the time she made it to the end of their driveway. She turned onto the road in front of their house as the sun was close to dipping below the horizon. But she didn't stop to admire the colors she loved. She couldn't go on like this, her heart in turmoil, confusion churning in her stomach.

Why was Judah staying away? Was it because of her? He hadn't even been by to see Sarah, not that her sister was concerned. She'd gone out last night with Levi Erb, another one of her admirers. Sarah was living her life, despite being at odds with Esther and Judah being a no-show.

Esther was the exact opposite. She missed Sarah and hated that they couldn't work things out. She'd finally tried to talk to her sister about their fight before they left the lake, only to give up when Sarah barely responded.

Esther's thoughts returned to Judah. More than once recently, she'd felt she was free of him. Yet when she wasn't fretting about Sarah, she was missing him. She glanced up at the sky. *Lord, why am I so confused?* No, she wasn't only confused. She was hurting, and she didn't know how to stop.

She was about to cross the road to turn around and head home when she heard the *clip-clop* of a horse and buggy behind her. She stepped to the side to let the buggy by. When it slowed down beside her, she glanced at the driver and almost tripped over her feet. Judah.

"Hi, Esther," he said.

He wasn't smiling, not exactly. In fact, he looked a little nervous, but also calm. She had no idea how he managed that.

"Do you need a ride home?" he asked.

That was Judah. Polite. Friendly. And acting like

he hadn't disappeared for days without a trace. Which annoyed her, come to think of it. She'd take that over her troubled heart right now. "I'm fine," she said, walking a little faster, planning to turn around toward home as soon as he left.

"It's getting dark."

She hurried her steps, and the horse immediately matched them.

"Esther, I'd really like to give you a ride."

His words stopped her. He pulled on the horse's reins as she turned to him. "Sarah's not home," she said. Although if he wanted to see Sarah, why had he passed their driveway coming here?

He frowned, his black eyebrows flattening in confusion. "Sarah? What does she have to do with me giving you a ride home?"

She sighed. He could be so dense sometimes. Maybe he'd come after her to make some sort of apology or something, but of course he'd want to see Sarah after being away from her for a few days. And now that he knew she wasn't home, she was sure he'd want Esther to give her a message.

"Sarah and I still aren't talking. If you want to get a message to her, you'll have to do it *yerself*." She started walking again, crossing her arms over her chest and feeling sweat trickling between her shoulder blades. How feminine. She grimaced and unfolded her arms.

Before she'd gone more than a few feet, he was right beside her again. "I don't want to talk to Sarah, Esther. I want to talk to you."

"I'm busy." She sounded like a child, but she couldn't

help it. She was tired. Tired of being disappointed, of not being able to let Judah go because she couldn't stop seeing—and wishing for—something that wasn't there. Of knowing that he'd rather chase after Sarah, who didn't care about him, than be with her. She swallowed the sudden lump in her throat.

Esther heard the buggy pull to a stop. She stepped in front of the horse to cross the road—and didn't stop until Judah stood in front of her. She had to halt, or slam into his chest, and she wasn't about to do that. "Judah, please. Just leave me alone."

"I can't."

Shocked at the tender urgency in his voice, she looked up at him.

"I want to talk to you . . . I need to . . ." His brow furrowed ever so slightly, and his eyes darkened in a way that made her toes automatically curl in her sneakers. Her palms grew damp, and not because of the sultry air.

She'd never known Judah to be at a loss for words. She couldn't break her gaze from his or steady her pulse. Or even think clearly. She gasped as he cradled her face in his hands.

"Words later," he whispered, then gently kissed her.

And it was everything she'd ever dreamed of and more. For a moment she melted into the kiss, unable to believe this was actually happening. She regained her senses and pulled away. "Why did you do that?" she asked, then put her fingers to her still-tingling mouth.

"I had to."

"You *had* to?" His words cut through her shock and surprised delight. "You *had* to?" she repeated.

"*Ya.* I mean, *nee.* I mean . . ." He wasn't wearing his hat, and he threaded his fingers through his hair. Then he grabbed her hand, as if he could tell she was about to bolt again. "You're not going anywhere," he said. "Not until we talk."

. . .

Judah was handling this badly. He'd spent the past few days alone and in prayer, seeking God for clarity. Enoch gave him the time off when Judah asked for it before he even left the campsite on Saturday, and Judah had taken advantage of the time. He'd gone on long walks, ridden his brother's horse, sat in the woods, and even tried to go fishing in his neighbor's pond. Fishing had been a mistake, since that reminded him of Esther—of wanting to kiss Esther, to be specific—and he didn't want his thoughts more muddied than they already were.

A little over an hour ago he'd realized what he needed to do. He wasted no time seeking out Esther. Enoch had told him she'd gone for a walk. When he caught up to her, any residual doubts about his feelings disappeared. It was as if everything had fallen into place the moment he saw her.

He'd planned to take her home, letting Goldie lead at the slow, leisurely pace the old mare usually enjoyed. He'd imagined they'd talk, he'd declare his feelings for her, and she might give him a chance to make up for last week. If he was lucky, she'd let him take her to the Parlor again or for an evening ride in his open buggy. She'd get to know him. To find out he was sincere about his feelings for her. And maybe, just maybe, she would start to like him too.

Instead he'd kissed her, which he only regretted because of timing. Kissing her soft lips was more than he could have imagined. But he'd overstepped a line, a huge one. Now he'd have a lot of backtracking to do for her to give him a chance.

She wasn't looking at him now, and her hand laid in his like a limp fish. He did let go of her hand, though ready to grab it again if she tried to disappear.

"Leave me alone, Judah."

"Esther, please listen to me. I know I shouldn't have kissed you."

Her chest heaved as she let out a long-suffering sigh. "Don't worry, I won't bring it up again." She looked at him, her beautiful eyes dull and lifeless. "Sarah will never know."

"I don't care if you tell Sarah."

Her brow lifted, shock in her eyes. Her beautiful blue eyes. "You don't?"

"Sarah's not the one I'm interested in."

She tilted her gaze at him and frowned. "Did you hit *yer* head while you were away?"

He laughed. "*Nee.* I'm perfectly levelheaded."

Esther crossed her arms, her expression dubious. "You just kissed me in the middle of the street. That's not levelheaded."

Behind him he heard Goldie whinny, and he was grateful not only for her patience, but for the fact that the Coblentzes lived on a low-traffic road. "I'm level-headed, except when it comes to you."

She took a step back. "Stop making fun of me."

"I'm not," he said, bewildered she would even think that. "I would never make fun of you."

Her eyes widened, then narrowed as her lower lip trembled. She whispered, "Did Reuben say something?"

"About what?"

"About . . ." She turned away.

He shook his head. "Esther, I promise, *nee* one told me anything." He froze. "Wait . . . Do you have feelings for me?"

She let out a huff and glared at him. "You are the thickest man I've ever met in *mei* life!"

He felt pretty stupid as realization dawned. Rhett must have seen more between him and Esther than he thought. Why else would he have cautioned him about breaking Esther's heart that day at the lake? "I . . . didn't know."

"Because you're in love with Sarah." She wiped her cheek, and he couldn't tell if she was wiping away per-spiration or tears. "It's always been Sarah for you."

He couldn't deny her words. But he could convince her they weren't true anymore. "Until now. I'm in love with you, Esther."

"And I'm supposed to believe that." She crossed her arms again. "I'm *nee* one's second choice. And I won't be used so you can get closer to *mei schweschder*. If you want her, you'll have to get her *yerself*."

Now Esther was freely crying, each tear burning a mark on his heart. The last thing he wanted was to hurt her, and here he was doing exactly that. He started to say something. Words, though, wouldn't be enough.

Despite the heat and the very real possibility that she would reject him, he took her in his arms. "I'm sorry," he whispered fiercely in her ear. "I've been stupid and a *dummkopf* and definitely dense. I didn't know . . . I didn't see."

"Because you could only see Sarah."

She didn't embrace him, but she didn't pull away from him either. He took that as a good sign and held her tighter. "Now I see only you." When he felt her stiffen, he released his hold enough so he could look down into her face. How had he not seen her all this time? How had he missed the beautiful woman who had been right in front of him all these years? Who had been shy and sweet. Always giving him a smile. Always locking her own feelings away to help him gain Sarah's attention.

At that moment it was as if the last cloud lifted, and he was finally seeing—and feeling—everything clearly. "I'm going to prove it to you." He could barely speak past the sudden constriction of his throat. "If it takes every single *daag* of the rest of *mei* life, I'm going to prove how much I love you."

"Love?" She gazed up at him, her eyes wet with tears. "You . . . love me?" She spoke as if he hadn't said he was in love with her only moments ago.

"I do." He'd never been so certain of anything in his life. What he felt for Esther ran deeper than anything he'd ever *thought* he felt for Sarah. With Sarah he'd been able to walk away and not feel like his heart had been torn out. If he walked away from Esther right now . . . His chest squeezed. He couldn't even entertain the possibility. "I know it seems sudden—"

"*Ya*, very sudden. *Unbelievably* sudden."

She wasn't going to make this easy, and she shouldn't. He'd been willing to work for Sarah, and he'd only been infatuated with her. But he loved Esther, and he would *fight* for her. He finally understood what love was, and he wasn't going to let it—or her—go. "Did I mention I was a *dummkopf*?"

She softened a bit in his arms. "You're not a *dummkopf*. You're one of the smartest men I know. It's why I—"

He tilted up her chin with his forefinger. "You what?"

"It's why I love you." Somehow she managed to fold her arms across her chest again in the small space between them. "There, I said it."

"I said it first." He grinned.

The sparkle in her eyes warmed him more deeply than the summer sun ever could. "We're kind of going about this backward, aren't we? Usually people date before falling in love."

"I've never been usual," she said in a straight tone.

A statement of fact, one he'd known all along but had never fully appreciated until now. He was eager to catch up on everything he'd missed about this woman, everything he had left to discover. "I know." He found himself leaning toward her, ready to kiss the tip of her cute nose.

"I need to know something," she said, her voice wavering. "Are you . . ." She averted her gaze, retreating into silence as she'd done so many times around him.

This time, he wasn't going to let her. He brushed his thumb across her cheek. "You can talk to me," he said. "You can ask me anything. I want you to know that."

"*Am* I *yer* second choice? Are you saying all this because you've given up on Sarah?"

He kissed her again, answering her the only way he knew how. When they parted, he said, "Would I kiss you like that if I was still hung up on Sarah?"

"*Nee*," she said, sounding as breathless as he felt.

"Then you believe me?" She nodded, and he pulled back, dropping his arms and putting his hands in his pockets not only for his benefit but for hers. He was more than ready to follow up that kiss with another one. "I do want us to date, you know. I was thinking a trip to the Parlor would be a *gut* place to start."

"Now?" she asked.

"I'm having a sudden craving for ice cream."

She laughed, her smile warming him through. "Funny, so am I."

CHAPTER 9

Inside her living room, Esther shut the front door behind her and leaned against it. She wanted to squeal with delight, but it was late and everyone was asleep.

Judah loved her. He really loved her. At first she couldn't believe it. But over a double scoop of rocky road he'd explained how he'd spent time in prayer, trying to understand his feelings and getting things straight with God.

She admired that. In a way he had stayed away from the farm because of her, but there was a higher purpose involved. That he would seek God's will above his own, that he had to make sure of his heart before talking to her was the final proof he was being genuine. When he'd dropped her off a few minutes ago, he asked her out on a second date, and a third . . . and now they were booked up for the next two months.

The gas lamp hissed to life and she jumped. Sarah appeared in the yellow lamplight, sitting in the rocking chair opposite the couch. Esther pressed her hand to her chest. "Sarah, you startled me."

Sarah didn't say anything, her full lips pressed into a thin line. "Where were you?"

"Out." She wasn't going to let Sarah dampen her evening. "I'm going to bed."

"Not before you tell me where you've been."

"None of *yer* business." Her tone was sharper than she intended, but the sharpness behind the words was real. Taking a deep breath, she started for the staircase.

"I was worried about you."

Esther froze. Then she turned. Sarah's face had softened, and Esther could see the sheen of tears in her eyes. "You were?"

"You've been gone for hours." Sarah sniffed. "I wanted to *geh* looking for you, but *Daed* said you'd be okay."

"Did he tell you I was with Judah?"

Sarah shook her head. "*Nee.* Wait . . . You were with Judah?"

Esther nodded, still keeping up her guard.

"Oh." Sarah tilted her head and looked at her. "You do seem . . . different. *Yer* cheeks are flushed, for one thing."

"It's the middle of summer, Sarah."

Sarah chuckled, although there was a bit of melancholy to it. "He finally figured it out."

"What?"

She lifted her head. "Judah never wanted me. At least not for anything but a trophy."

"I don't understand."

"He's like all the other guys. They think they like me. Or love me." She rolled her eyes. "Then we spend time together and it fizzles. All they can do is stare at me, and I have to force the conversation along."

"Must be awful being so beautiful," Esther said dryly.

"You wouldn't understand."

"Because I'm ugly?"

"For heaven's sake, *nee*. You're not ugly, Esther. You're *schee*. You always have been. I don't get why you would think you weren't."

Because I've spent my entire life comparing myself to you.

"You're so easy to get to know. Everyone likes you. Look at Rhett. He took right to you from the moment he arrived."

"He has a girlfriend."

"I know. I knew that before he got here. *Mamm* showed me the letters he wrote, telling her and *Daed* about himself and why he wanted to stay with us. Right away he mentioned Shelby."

"Then why were you flirting with him?"

"I don't know." She shrugged and slumped in the chair. "I have *nee* idea how to be myself around men. Around anyone, for that matter."

Esther was surprised to hear this. Her sister had always been the confident one, the one who got all the attention. "Why not?"

She didn't say anything for a long moment. Then she said, "They may not like the real me."

Esther sat down on the edge of the couch. "Sarah, that's not true."

"Isn't it? Aren't I just a shell?" Tears flowed down her cheeks. "Something to be looked at?"

"Sarah." She had no idea Sarah struggled with self-esteem. "But you're always so sure of *yerself*."

"I'm *gut* at pretending." She leaned forward in the chair. "I'm so sorry I hurt you. I didn't mean to. But when Rhett ignored me in favor of you . . ."

"You felt rejected."

"I felt hollow. Empty. If I couldn't gain his attention with *mei* looks and flirting, then what else is there?"

"Plenty. Listen to me, Sarah. You are more than a *schee* face. You're fun and a great cook and so wonderful with the animals. Those bunnies adore you."

"They're bunnies, Esther. They adore the snacks I give them."

"And you're the only one who spends extra time with them. You're also amazing with customers. You're *gut* at sewing. Rhett definitely was interested when you brought up quilting patterns."

"True, he was." She laughed. "He's a bit odd, isn't he?"

"But the *gut* kind of odd."

"Definitely." Sarah got up and sat down next to Esther. "*Danki* for understanding."

"I love you, Sarah." She embraced her sister, remembering all the times she'd been envious of her. All the comparisons she'd made. Above everything else there was still sisterly love. And now maybe a friendship was blossoming. But she had to make sure about one thing. She released Sarah. "Are you okay with me and Judah dating?"

"Of course. Like I said, he finally realized you two are perfect for each other."

"But I thought you liked him."

"I do, as a *freind*. Actually more like a *bruder*, so if you two get married, he'll fit right in with the *familye*."

"Then why didn't you tell him how you really felt? Why didn't you tell me?"

"Judah had to figure out his feelings himself. At least when he was after me, he was still around you."

"So you led him on for *mei* sake?"

"*Ya.* You were never going to say anything to him, and it wasn't *mei* place to reveal *yer* feelings. Although you did a terrible job of hiding them. Even *Daed* knows how smitten you are." She smiled. "You're still smitten, right?"

Esther smiled. "Definitely."

Sarah glanced down at her lap. "I have to admit that I liked the attention too. Not just from Judah, but from everyone else." She looked at Esther. "I know it's not right, but I can't help it."

"*Nee.* You can't. Not alone, anyway." She grasped Sarah's hand. "But with God's help, you will."

. . .

The next day Judah arrived at the Coblentzes eager to see Esther, but he needed to talk to Rhett first. When he entered the barn, he found him cleaning out the stables. It was a job best done early in the morning, before the heat of the day made the stench almost unbearable. As usual, Rhett was shoveling the dirty hay and manure with enthusiasm. He looked up as Judah approached. "Hey, dude," he said, holding a pitchfork filled with dung. "You back to work?"

"Yep."

"Good. We could use the extra pair of hands." He

turned and went to the back of the barn, where a large door was open. He tossed the dung into a pile, then faced Judah again. "Everything okay?"

More than okay, but he had to settle one more thing. "You were right," he said to Rhett. "About me needing to get my head on straight."

"And did you?"

"*Ya*. Although it took me a while."

"That happens." He grinned. "Esther looked happy this morning. I'm assuming you had something to do with it?"

Judah was pleased to hear that tidbit of news. "Maybe."

Rhett's grin grew. "Glad to hear it." He gestured to the stall. "I better finish up here. Enoch said the summer lettuce is ready for harvest."

"Have you got another minute?"

"Sure."

"I owe you an apology. Actually more than one. I wasn't nice to you when you first got here. That was wrong of me. I'll also admit to some jealousy."

"About what?"

"You and Esther."

Rhett scoffed. "I explained that. Esther's a great girl. But that's it. She's only had eyes for you, dude."

He believed that now. "Still, I was angry and I took it out on you."

"Hey, don't worry about it." He extended his hand. "We're all about forgiveness, right?"

Judah had misjudged this man. He'd assumed Rhett was here to play at being Amish, but he'd been wrong. Rhett had taken every advantage of the experience.

He'd even picked up some Deitsch. He worked hard every day on the farm and never complained. He'd been attentive during church, and had made friends with other people in the congregation. They realized his sincerity. Rhett was genuine, and in his blindness and resentment, Judah had missed that.

I've missed a lot of things, Lord. But mei *eyes are open now.*

He shook Rhett's hand. Then he got another pitchfork off the wall of the barn.

"You don't have to help," Rhett said. "I know this is grunt work, and I don't mind doing it."

"I know you don't." He entered one of the stalls. "I don't mind doing it either."

CHAPTER 10

ONE YEAR LATER

Esther waved the wedding program in front of her flushed face. It was hot today, even for the end of July. But despite the heat, the bride and groom looked stunning. She glanced at Judah. Sitting next to her, his cheeks were red from the heat too. She waved the program in front of him in an attempt to cool him off. He responded by grabbing her hand—and not letting it go.

"Do you, Rhett Thomas Davidson, take Shelby Marie Monroe to be your wife?"

Esther stifled a swoony sigh. After Rhett had returned home last summer, he'd kept in touch with the family, sending a few extra letters to Judah. They had become good friends before Rhett left. Rhett had decided not to go to the Himalayas, instead finishing his senior year on time. Shelby had graduated from nursing school too.

"I already have my dream," he'd written, right before announcing that Shelby had said yes to his marriage proposal. The couple had visited Middlefield several times and decided to have their wedding outdoors at the Mespo gazebo.

After the ceremony, the guests mingled and congratulated the bride and groom. This was the first time she'd ever been to a Yankee wedding, and while there were differences in traditions, the feeling of love and happiness surrounding the couple was the same. When their turn came, Esther gave Shelby a hug, then to her surprise was drawn into Rhett's big embrace.

"Hey," Judah said. "Stay away from my wife. You've got your own now."

Rhett kissed her on the cheek in front of everybody, which was a very non-Amish thing to do but very much in line with his personality.

As they left the happy couple, Judah pointed toward Sarah and Samuel Keim. They were sitting on the swings even though several long tables were set up, covered with white tablecloths and vases of summer flowers. "I wonder what that's about," he said.

"I don't know." Esther shrugged, despite knowing exactly what Sarah and Samuel were about. Samuel wasn't Sarah's type, or at least Esther hadn't thought so until Sarah admitted her interest in him. He was short and stocky, with wire-rimmed glasses that never seemed to fit straight on the bridge of his nose. But he was so nice, and Sarah adored him.

"He listens to me," she'd told Esther one night after he brought her home from a ride in his open buggy. "Really listens to me. He asks me about *mei* dreams, about what I'm interested in. He sees the real me."

"Huh," Judah said. "They almost look like a couple."

Esther smiled at her husband. They had married in the spring, to no one's surprise, and now lived in the house where Esther used to give tours. With the addition of the new farmland, *Daed* had decided to close down the tourist business. "It's time to have more privacy," he said, which made *Mamm* happy.

Sarah had a job working in a fabric store in Middlefield, and while Reuben was still contemplating joining the church, at least he was talking about it a little more openly.

"Want to go for a walk?" Judah asked.

"But what about the reception?"

"We'll be back in time for the food."

"I wasn't thinking about that."

"You should be, since you're eating for two."

Her hand went to her abdomen. They hadn't told anyone about the pregnancy. It was a special secret to keep between themselves until she started showing.

They walked down the grassy area, then crossed the street. Esther thought they were going to turn around and walk back toward the general store, but Judah took her hand and led her into a small wooded patch near a row of houses.

He put his arms around her waist and drew her close. "There's something about weddings," he said, looking down at her.

"The romance?"

"What, you think I'm a sappy man?"

She leaned forward and whispered, "I know you are. But it's our little secret."

He kissed her, and as with every kiss, he confirmed his love for her. A year ago she'd been hopelessly in love with him. Now she was filled with hope for their future.

"I guess we should go back," he said, pulling away from her but still within kissing distance. "Before someone sees us."

"I wouldn't mind."

"*Yer* parents would."

That worked like a bucket of cold water. They headed back to the reception, where the guests were seating themselves at the tables. Another table was filled with potluck items, similar to an Amish wedding reception.

"They look happy," Esther said, looking at Rhett and Shelby as they sat next to each other on one side of the center table.

"Are you happy?" Judah asked.

She looked up at him, seeing the love in his eyes. "*Ya*," she said, linking her pinky finger with his. "I couldn't be happier. There's one thing I'd like to do, though."

"Name it," he said.

"I'd like to go back to the lake. Just the two of us. Before the *boppli* comes."

He looked down at her, one black brow lifting. "You want to *geh* fishing? In a boat?"

"*Ya.*"

He laughed. "Okay, but you have to promise me one thing."

"What?"

"Don't fall in." Then he leaned over and whispered, "But *I* promise I'll kiss you if you do."

She grinned and whispered back, "I'm holding you to it."

DISCUSSION QUESTIONS

1. Jealousy is one of the themes explored in *Lakeside Love*. How do you deal with jealousy? How has God helped you?

2. If you were Esther's friend, what advice would you give her about her feelings for Judah?

3. Rhett had a great opportunity to immerse himself in Amish culture. Would you do the same if given the chance? What would you hope to learn?

4. *Lakeside Love* is inspired by the story of Leah and Rachel in the Bible. What are the similarities of *Lakeside Love* to that biblical story?

5. Why do you think Judah had a difficult time understanding his feelings for Esther? Has there ever been a time when you didn't see something clearly, only to have God show you what you were missing?

6. Esther struggled with being plain, while Sarah struggled with being beautiful. Discuss a time when God showed you that He sees our hearts and not our outward appearance.

ACKNOWLEDGMENTS

Writing is never a solo endeavor, and as always there are people I want to thank. A big thank-you to my editors Becky Monds and Jean Bloom. We've worked on many books together, and I know this sounds redundant, but I appreciate everything you do, your expertise, and your encouragement. For the friends in my life who get me through my life: Eddie Columbia, Tera Moore, Laura Spangler, and Kelly Long—thank you for walking this journey with me. I love you all.

Special thanks to you, dear reader: I always end my acknowledgments with you. I'm so grateful to every single person who reads my stories. You are all special to me, and I'm honored to call so many of you my friends. Happy reading, many blessings, and thank you for joining me on another visit to Amish country.

ONE SWEET KISS

KELLY IRVIN

To my son Nicholas, who grew up when
I wasn't looking. Love always.

Trust in the LORD *with all your heart, And lean not on your own understanding; In all your ways acknowledge Him, And He shall direct your paths.*

PROVERBS 3:5–6 (NKJV)

Blessed is the man who trusts in the LORD,
And whose hope is the LORD.
For he shall be like a tree planted by the waters,
Which spreads out its roots by the river,
And will not fear when heat comes;
But its leaf will be green,
And will not be anxious in the year of drought,
Nor will cease from yielding fruit.

JEREMIAH 17:7–8 (NKJV)

FEATURED BEE COUNTY AMISH FAMILIES

MORDECAI AND ABIGAIL KING

Caleb

Hazel

Esther

Samuel

Jacob

ABRAM AND THERESA KING

DEBORAH AND PHINEAS KING

Timothy

Melinda

TOBIAS AND REBEKAH BYLER

Matthew

LEILA AND JESSE GLICK

Grace

Emmanuel

LEROY AND NAOMI GLICK

Adam

Jesse

Joseph

Simon

Sally

Mary

Elizabeth

AARON AND JOLENE SHROCK

Ethan

Seth

Amanda

Molly

William

WILL AND ISABELLA (SHROCK) GLICK

Jason

Katherine

LEVI AND SUSAN (KING) BYLER

David

Martha

Milo

Rueben

Micah

Ida

Nyla

Liam

Henry

CHAPTER 1

The last note died away. Smiling to herself, Martha Byler opened her eyes. She always closed them during the German rendition of "How Great Thou Art," enjoying the sound of her friends' voices lifted in praise. Still, her eyelids grew heavy. The temptation to drift off to sleep during the singings mounted as the stifling south Texas heat in Bishop Jeremiah's front room warmed her cheeks. On Sundays, she paid the price for rising early to prepare breakfast for her family before church, helping with the meal after the service, and then spending the afternoon playing volleyball and tag with the little ones. She was worn out by the time the singings started. She wiggled on the hard pine stool. Surely, the ache of her bony behind would keep her awake. Still, she wouldn't miss this special time for anything. The sweet songs of praise filled a spot in her heart like nothing else could.

"Jacob's staring at you." Vesta Hostetler elbowed Martha in the ribs. Her loud whisper carried to the other girls crowded on a bench. They giggled. Vesta leaned closer. "When will you let him off the hook? He's sorry. You know he is."

Martha hazarded a quick glance at Jacob King, lounging between his friends who were busy whispering and horsing around instead of singing. Sure enough, he studied her with that same hurt, puppy-dog look he'd been giving her since that last Saturday night when he'd failed to show up at her farm as promised. With his unruly black hair peeking out from his straw hat, blue-green eyes made more blue than green by the blue of his shirt, dimpled cheeks, and rueful expression, he reminded her of a scholar called to the front of the room after misbehaving in school.

She didn't need to take care of another child. She had six of those at home—six younger brothers and sisters who looked to her every day as an example of what to do next in a home that had lacked a mother for nearly ten years. "He's just sorry I'm mad." She fixed her gaze on the hymnal with its yellowed pages and crumbling spine. "Not that he can't be trusted to do what he says he'll do."

"But he *is* easy on the eyes." Vesta took the pitcher of water from her sister Rachel and helped herself to a drink before passing it to Martha. "And a hard worker. It's not like we have a bunch of choices in this little *Gmay.*"

The sweet, lukewarm water soothed Martha's throat, parched from the heat and from singing for nearly two hours—first the slower German songs and then the old English hymns. She took another sip and passed the pitcher. She wasn't looking for choices. Her family needed her. It was obvious Jacob did not. "I don't have time for courting right now."

"With your *daed* remarried, you don't have to take care of everything yourself anymore." The start of another song didn't keep Vesta from pestering her. Her friend made a habit of reminding Martha of these things. "You're not the *mudder* anymore."

Inhaling the scent of boy sweat mingled with the aroma of baking cookies, Martha pretended to be engrossed in the song. Susan was a sweet woman who made *Daed* happy. The baby made them happy too. She was happy for them. She really was. So why did tears make her throat tight and her eyes burn? She bowed her head and focused on the words of the next song, "Amazing Grace."

It ended far too soon. She took a quick swipe at her face and stood as Rachel carried in a tray loaded with snickerdoodles, gingersnaps, and chocolate chip cookies. The Hostetlers could be counted on for the best after-singing snacks. The boys jostled for the door while the girls milled around in clusters, chattering. The noise level rose in direct proportion to the number of teenage girls in the room.

Martha laid the hymnal in the stack on the spindly end table by Jeremiah's desk and slipped through the crowd. She had a long walk ahead of her. At least the sun had set, taking with it the worst of the June heat. Still, the dank, humid air stuck to her skin as she trudged down the porch steps and headed toward the dirt road that led from the Hostetlers' farm to hers.

"You'll not forgive me then?"

Jacob's deep, sandpaper-rough voice sent a prickle of goose bumps careening up her arms. Why did he have that effect on her when she knew good and well he couldn't be trusted? She halted and turned. "A person is required to forgive."

He clomped down the steps, his work boots heavy on the wood, and kept walking until he stood within arm's length. Too close, in her way of thinking. "Then let me give you a ride home, and I'll convince you of all the reasons you shouldn't hold my transgressions against me."

His white teeth glinted in the light of a full moon that hung heavy overhead. Martha listened to the distant croak of bull frogs and the rustle of a lackadaisical breeze in the leaves of a nearby live oak tree. Tiredness won. Not the way he looked—tall, broad through the shoulders, and tanned from working with his father's beehives. "I would like a ride."

The smile transformed his face. Martha breathed. Looks meant nothing. She wasn't so shallow as to be taken in by a handsome face.

"I'll get the buggy."

"I'm capable of walking with you to get it."

She whirled, stumbled over a rock so rude as to settle in her path, and pitched forward, arms pinwheeling in an effort to catch herself.

Jacob's mammoth hand gripped her arm above the elbow. His fingers were warm and strong. His breath touched her cheek. A soft chuckle floated in the air around her. The danger of face-planting in the dirt passed, yet her balance still wavered with the realization that he was touching her. She looked up at his face, so close she could see a tiny scar on the bridge of his nose. His full lips were a hairsbreadth away from hers. He smelled of clothes soap and peppermint. His smile widened as if he divined her thoughts. "Are you sure? I could carry you, if need be. You don't likely weigh more than a kitten."

"It's not nice to make fun." Her voice didn't quiver, just the right nonchalant tone. "It's rude and I'm not a kitten."

"I'm always nice."

"Not always."

He ducked his head. "Milo and Samuel got the car stuck in the mud. I had to help them move it. We couldn't leave it out where someone would see it."

She tugged free of his grip. "I don't want to know about the car."

The fact that he and some of their friends had pooled their money to buy an old beat-up car and kept it hidden away behind an abandoned barn was none of her business. Two years of *rumspringa* and it was time to grow up. A man who still played at boys' games didn't interest her.

So why did her heart careen into that silly *rat-a-tat-tat* every time Jacob wandered into her line of sight at church? Or *Gmay* picnics? Or singings and volleyball games?

"Do you always do the right thing?" He strode in front of her and then turned so he was walking backward as if he needed to see her face-to-face to talk. His ability to maintain his balance seemed like a slap in the face at the moment. "Name one fun thing you've done during your *rumspringa*."

"I play with the *kinner*. We have fun all the time."

"I'm talking about things you wouldn't normally do." He spun around one short step before backing into his buggy and held out his hand as if to help her up. "This is your chance to be someone else for a little bit."

"I like who I am just fine." She ignored his hand and hoisted herself into the buggy. "I'm starting baptism classes this summer so I can join in the fall."

If she found the answers she sought in those classes. Surely Mordecai King, Jacob's father, would tell her how she could trust *Gott*, even when He let her mother die. Jacob didn't need to know of her uncertainty. No one did. Good Plain girls and boys didn't question matters of faith.

"Me too." He climbed into the buggy and sat. Again, closer than necessary. "That'll be fun."

If committing to memory in German the eighteen articles of the Dordrecht Confession could be described as fun. That Jacob thought so gave Martha hope for him. "Mordecai will make it interesting."

Jacob shrugged. "If we can keep *mei daed* from going off on a wild goose chase with his stories, we might get through all eighteen articles before we're ready for the *dawdy haus*."

The way he said "we" sent a white-hot flare leaping across Martha's face. The *dawdy haus* was for couples who grew old together. Did he see the two of them married, their children grown, grandchildren racing about the yard? It made for a nice picture.

One she couldn't count on. God had taught her not to rely on love when He let her mother die a scant two weeks after little Liam's birth. Hard as he tried, her father could not hide the pain that etched lines around his mouth and eyes in those dark days that followed. He said all the right things—her days were done, we're only passing through this world, God has a plan—yet the pain blossomed every time he thought she wasn't looking.

She studied the stars and tried to think of something—anything—to say that didn't lead to a place she refused to go. They rode along in silence for a piece. The *clip-clop* of hooves and the creak of buggy wheels on the sun-hardened dirt kept time with her thoughts. Jacob turned the buggy onto her farm road. A few more minutes and the ride would end. For reasons she couldn't fathom, Martha didn't want that. Not yet. The memory of Jacob's hand on her arm floated through her mind, sweet and warm. *Stop it!*

"If you've decided to get baptized, you'll need to get rid of that car—"

Her words were drowned in the shrill blast of a horn. Startled, she pivoted. An enormous, shiny tomato-red pickup truck loomed. Dwayne Chapman stuck his head out and waved. "Hey, King! I've been looking all over for you." The words had a strange slur to them. The truck swerved closer to the buggy. He laughed and pulled away again. "I need a backup man for an alligator that has my name on it. You in?"

Jacob slowed the buggy. "Whoa, whoa."

They halted in the middle of the road. Dwayne spun the truck around so it blocked the way to Martha's farm. Dwayne might be nineteen and married with two children, but he still acted like a kid most of the time.

"Have you been drinking again?" Jacob wrapped the reins around his hand, the look on his face one Martha didn't recognize. Humor mixed with concern filled his voice. "Rory will have your hide, if she finds out. Not to mention the highway patrol and the Bee County sheriff."

"I'm fine. I'm fine." Dwayne twisted his Texas Rangers cap around so the bill faced the back of his head. "My posse bailed on me. Bunch of babies who think they have to go to bed early on Sunday night 'cause they got to work on Monday. Me, I can go twenty-four seven. Know what I mean? So I'm looking for another strong back to help me bag me a gator."

"This isn't alligator hunting season." Jacob's gaze met Martha's and skittered away. "It's not something you do in the dark, anyway. You'll fall in and drown—or get eaten."

"I could do it blindfolded, dude. I never caught one during the season. I still have my license and everything. They owe me one."

Dwayne probably thought everyone owed him one. Martha didn't know much about him. Her family had moved to Bee County after Leila Lantz, now Leila Glick, had started working at a day care in town with Dwayne's wife Rory. Leila eventually married Jesse Glick and they both left the *Gmay*. It was a sad story that some blamed on Dwayne and Rory. Martha knew better. People had to take responsibility for their own actions. That included Jacob. If he decided to go with Dwayne, she was done with him.

The thought twisted like a rototiller blade in the vicinity of her heart. Better she should spend her life alone than yoked to a man who couldn't grow up. She'd always have her brothers and sisters—until they grew up and married.

Jacob's snort startled her from her reverie. "I don't think it works that way." He shook his head, his dark curls bouncing under his hat. "Go on home. Sleep it off."

"Don't be a wuss, dude." The words became an almost unintelligible slur. "Thought I could count on my Amish man, man. But be that way, I'll do it myself. Got my raw meat, got my fire power. Got my cane poles in the back."

He held up a Styrofoam package that contained a huge slab of meat that looked like a boneless shoulder roast. The kind Martha passed in the grocery store because it was too expensive for their table. His thumb jabbed toward the back of the truck where a rifle hung from a gun rack.

She knew little to nothing about laws in Texas, but she did know mixing alcohol and guns was a dangerous combination. "You'll fall in the river and drown, or the alligator will eat you." She shouldn't have to explain the obvious. "Or you'll shoot yourself. Then what will your babies do without a daddy?"

"I bagged a gator two years ago. I know what I'm doing."

"Not by yourself, you didn't. Your dad and Nolan and your cousins were in on it." Jacob hunched his shoulders. "I may have to get this."

The last part was directed at Martha.

"You're going alligator hunting?" She knew it. She'd always known it. "With a drunk *Englischer*?"

"That's the thing." Jacob's voice took on a pleading

tone. "I can't let him drive like this. It's not safe. He has *kinner*."

True, but it wasn't safe for a Plain man with no license to drive either. Out of the frying pan, into the fire. "He probably has a phone. Call the sheriff to come get him. A night in jail would straighten him out."

It might be harsh, but her father always said people had to reap the consequences of their actions. They learned the lesson that way. No one could learn it for them.

"Hey, y'all, I'm right here. I can hear you. I'm not going to jail." Dwayne turned the key in the ignition. The truck's engine rumbled. "I thought I could trust y'all. Guess I'll have to have fun on my own."

Jacob held up his hand as if to hush the man. His pleading gaze stayed on Martha. "I'll drop you off and leave the buggy there behind your barn until I can get him home. His father-in-law will bring me back."

He wanted to use her home to hide his *rumspringa* fun? "You really want to hunt alligator right now? You'll never grow up, will you?"

"That's not it. He's a friend." Jacob's voice rose in protest. "You could come with us. You've never been gator hunting. There's a *rumspringa* experience for you. Besides, it's early."

It was late. They'd been doing this two-steps-forward, two-steps-back thing for two years. Every time she thought they might finally make it to that sweet place where she could see the road to a future together, something like this happened. The time he chose to joyride with his friends. The keg party in Mac Moreno's back pasture. Playing pool at the tavern in town. Sure, he invited her, begged her to go. But she couldn't do it. Not knowing the consequences of underage drinking or driving without a license. Her father had suffered enough. The children needed her. She had to think of them, not herself or her desire to have her own children one day. Her desire to have a husband and a life of her own would wait. Had to wait.

She didn't need a special friend. She needed to do the pile of laundry that threatened to take over the laundry room. She needed to sew new pants for Liam. The boy was growing like weeds along a south Texas road. Sunrise would come all too soon, and she needed sleep. "I can't. I have too much to do tomorrow. You go. Do what you need to do. I can get myself home."

"Just wait. Just wait one minute." Jacob hopped from the buggy and strode around to the truck. "Keys."

"What?" Dwayne's head disappeared from the window like a turtle's whipping back into its shell. "I ain't giving up the keys to a guy in suspenders and a straw hat. You ain't got a license, dude."

"And you can't drive drunk." Jacob sounded like Mordecai when he got after the children who decided to chase each other around the yard instead of collect eggs from the chicken coop. "You might run into a car and hurt someone."

"Your concern for me getting hurt really touches my heart. You're sweet on me, aren't 'cha?"

Jacob slipped his long arm into the truck. The engine died. He extracted a silver key chain shaped like a beer bottle with half a dozen keys dangling from it.

"Hey!" Dwayne swiped at the keys to no avail. He opened the door. Jacob took several steps back, keys behind his back. Dwayne growled like a dog defending his supper. "You can't do that."

Fear swept through Martha, making her stomach feel queasy. Would Jacob be all right? Would he get hurt? Anxiety ate at her. "He's right. You can't drive that truck." She tried to keep her voice cool. He didn't need to know how much she cared. He didn't have the same feelings or he wouldn't keep leaving her for others. "Either you'll have an accident or you'll end up in jail for hunting out of season, or worse yet, driving drunk yourself. Mordecai wouldn't like that."

"I don't drink. Not anymore. Besides, I'm more worried about how you'll take it." Jacob made his way back around the buggy and climbed in, closer to her than she would've liked. He tossed the keys up and down in his palm, his gaze on them as if they held the answer to a riddle only he could see. "I'm not worried about driving his truck. It's no different from a car."

He hadn't denied the hunting part. He'd rather hunt than spend time sitting on the front porch with her. It didn't matter. It couldn't be allowed to matter. "You told me you were getting rid of the car."

"I am. I want to, but it belongs to the others too. And we have to find someone who wants it."

"You should give it away, if it's standing between you and baptism—"

"Don't be comparing my ride to that heap of rust you sneak around in." Apparently it took words a while to worm their way into an alcohol-soaked brain. Dwayne sounded truly offended. "Besides this beauty is a standard. You ain't got no idea how to drive a standard."

Martha had no idea what *standard* meant, but Dwayne made it sound complicated. "Is he right? Do you know how to drive this standard thing?"

"You remember Jesse's friend Colton—the one from his youth group? He taught Jesse to drive so Jesse asked him to give me a few lessons." Jacob sounded proud of himself. "Jesse learned to drive a standard, so I figured I could too."

"You've been hanging around with Colton? Have you been to his youth group?" Her heart, already full of holes, stopped beating. The *Gmay* had lost Jesse and Leila to this group nearly three years ago. Leila's mother still mourned the life she would not have as a mother and grandmother to Leila and Jesse's growing brood, as did Jesse's mother and father. They mourned the life their children didn't have with their Plain families. "Are you thinking of joining Jesse's church?"

"Nee. Nee." He shook his head so hard his hat flopped. "I never went to the meetings on Wednesday nights. And we don't party. They're not like that. Colton is married and so is Jesse. We eat at the pancake house together sometimes. Go fishing now and then. But they're busy."

Not too busy to give Jacob driving lessons. He could have pancakes with his family at home. The danger of being sucked into another life was too great. Look at Leila and Jesse. Their families saw the babies once in a blue moon. Jesse almost never came around. It was too hard on his mother and father. They couldn't bear it.

Jacob's expression, the way he stared at her with

those mesmerizing blue-green eyes that reminded her of the Gulf of Mexico on a sunny day, made her want to believe him. Her heart said she could. Her head said don't be an idiot. She couldn't bear the thought of spending time with Jacob, only to have him choose another path. She wasn't like Leila. She would never leave her brothers and sisters to follow him. They'd suffered enough loss already.

It wasn't about her. It was about her brothers and sisters. They all loved their new stepmother, but Susan couldn't take the place of a sister who'd raised them from little bitty.

That was that. It couldn't matter what she needed. They needed her. Jacob didn't. Martha climbed out of the buggy and marched past the pickup truck.

"Don't go away mad, Amish girl!" Dwayne hollered. "Dude, I didn't mean to get you in trouble with the girlfriend."

Martha closed her eyes and reopened them, just in time to see a rut in the road and swerve right. "I'm not his girlfriend."

"Martha! It's not that big of a deal."

"Have fun." She waved her hand in the air without looking back. "Be safe."

He might decide to join an English church. Or he might get eaten by an alligator.

Served him right.

CHAPTER 2

The *clip-clop* of the horse's hooves and creak of the wooden buggy wheels followed Martha, telling her Jacob followed along like a shadow or a faithful puppy she couldn't shake. She didn't look back at the dirt road. *Keep going. Keep going. Keep going.*

"Come on! It's silly for you to walk. Get back in the buggy."

Martha walked faster. Sweat trickled down her cheeks. Mosquitos buzzed around her face. She slapped them away. Her feet and back ached. Finally, the porch was yards away, then right in front of her. The sound of the buggy faded away. He wouldn't come closer. If her father or her brother David were around, they'd want to know why she was walking instead of riding in the buggy. Courting might be private, but some questions begged to be answered.

At the screen door, she dared to look back. Jacob sat in the buggy by the corral fence, watching her, his face forlorn. She loved that face.

How did that thought get in her head? She loved his face like she loved Liam's face. God would strike her dead for lying to herself. *Gott, have mercy. I don't want to love him. I don't even want to like him.*

Sighing, she waved. He raised one hand and waved back, a swift smile bringing out his dimples.

She loved that smile. How could she love that smile, knowing what she knew about him? He couldn't be trusted with her heart. The children could. They needed her.

She slipped inside and shut the door with a gentle nudge, not wanting to wake her family. A light flickered on the wall that led to the kitchen. No one should be up at this hour.

A baby's wail cut the still night air. *Ach.* Someone wasn't happy. Poor Susan. Martha slipped off her shoes and padded barefoot into the kitchen. Susan sat at the pine table, little Henry in her lap. The one-year-old's cheeks were red, his brown curls tousled and wet with sweat. Susan, with her long, brown hair loose down her back and her wrinkled nightgown, didn't look much better.

"Teething?" Martha whispered. "Poor *bopli* looks miserable. So do you."

Susan shook her head, her smile bright. "One day he won't need me anymore. I waited many years for these nights. I don't begrudge him one minute."

Susan always had a positive view on life. Martha loved that about her stepmother. The former schoolteacher had a deep well of wisdom she freely shared. Did it come from growing up with Mordecai King, her brother who was a beekeeper and deacon, or did she give it to him? Women never received the credit for these things. Martha grabbed a peanut butter cookie from the pan on the counter and squeezed into a chair.

"You looked peeved about something." Susan shifted Henry to her other arm. The boy whimpered and snuggled closer. "Didn't you have fun at the singing?"

"It was fine." Martha broke the cookie in half, then began crumbling one side with her thumb and forefinger. "How did you know for sure you wanted to marry *Daed*?"

"Does this have to do with Jacob?"

Martha hopped up and poured a glass of water. She drank half of it before facing Susan again. "I like taking care of the *kinner*. They need me."

"I can take care of the *kinner*. We've had this talk before. It's time to think about starting your own family."

Susan had been a part of their lives for two years. Martha had been the mother for ten years, ever since *Daed* deposited a tiny, restless, two-week-old Liam in her arms and asked her—no, begged her with pain and tears in his eyes—to make him stop crying. "They are my family."

"Wait too long and there won't be anyone around to ask you." Susan rocked. Henry's eyes closed. "I know from experience."

"You didn't marry until later and it turned out fine."

"Because I thought my *bruders* and *schweschder* couldn't do without me." Susan patted her damp, round face with a tattered dish towel. "Sound familiar?"

"There was someone before *Daed*?"

"By the time I realized my *bruders* and *schweschder* were going to go live their lives without me, it was too late." Susan's gaze meandered somewhere in the distance over Martha's shoulder. "Andrew married another. They have half a dozen *kinner* now up in Missouri."

"But it was *Gott*'s plan because you were meant to wait for *Daed*. You were meant to be together."

"I wouldn't dare to assume I know what *Gott*'s plan is." Susan frowned and shook her head. "The young think they know so much. You are a smart girl, but *Gott* knows all. Trust in Him, and He will make your path straight."

Straight to Jacob? The path between them zigged and zagged. There was nothing straight about it.

"I have to go to bed." Martha brushed cookie crumbs from the table and stood. "I hope Henry sleeps through the rest of the night, for both your sakes. We have so much laundry to do tomorrow."

"If he doesn't sleep now, he'll nap tomorrow. It'll make doing laundry easier." Susan tucked the toddler's long nightshirt around his chunky legs. He sighed a sweet, content sound. "Either way, we'll be fine. See you in the morning."

Exhaustion weighing her down, Martha began the trek up the stairs. A shriek broke the silence. Startled, she paused, head cocked, listening. A quieter whimper. Liam. She bolted up the stairs and raced down the hallway to the bedroom the boys shared. Liam sat up in his narrow bunk, hands to his face. Rueben lay on his stomach, arms flung out, not moving in the double bed he shared with Milo, who was likely still roaming the countryside with his buddies. Or maybe he had a special friend by now. She had no idea.

"What's the matter, little one?" she whispered as she crept closer. Rueben had hard work to do. He needed his sleep. David was also missing from the other twin bed shoved against the far wall. Still gallivanting about on his endless *rumspringa*. "What happened?"

"Bad dream." Liam sniffed and leaned into her hug. "The snakes were everywhere."

Bad dream indeed—for Martha. "You like snakes."

"Not huge ones crawling all over the house." His small chin trembled and his voice quivered. "They should stay outside where they belong."

"I agree. Scooch over." She squeezed in and leaned her head against his flat pillow. "Should I tell you a story?"

"The one about the dog who walks all the way from Ohio to Texas to find his little boy after getting left behind when they move." He snuggled against her. "I like that one."

"Me too." She collected her thoughts. Every time she told the story, it came out differently, but Liam never complained. "Once upon a time there was a black-and-white spotted puppy named—"

"Me too."

Rueben's deep voice, husky with sleep, floated from across the room. "Don't leave out any of the good parts this time."

She smiled in the dark and started again.

CHAPTER 3

Doing the right thing should feel better than it did. Jacob lengthened his stride and walked faster. He could see Dwayne's truck still parked half on the road and half off. At least he hadn't decided to take off after spoiling Jacob's plan for this evening. He'd had every intention of making amends with Martha and along came Dwayne Chapman. Father of two, master of nothing. Not to be mean about it. The man had problems. But he couldn't be allowed to race around on the farm-to-market roads in Bee County just because he lacked the good sense and will power to stop partying with his friends.

Rory must be beside herself. The sooner Jacob got her husband home the better. Before Nolan Beale, grandfather to those two little ones, noticed his son-in-law was at it again. Ignoring the urge to whip his hat from his head and slam it into the weeds, Jacob turned his weary bones to the task at hand.

It took ten minutes to walk to the truck—way too much time to contemplate his situation. He'd celebrated his twentieth birthday two weeks earlier, but Martha treated him like one of her little brothers.

He needed to show her he was a man. She needed to learn not to jump to conclusions. She needed to trust in God's plan. No. This wasn't about Martha. She needed to be able to trust him to stick around. He understood that. They'd both lost their mothers far too soon. He had older brothers and sisters to help him through it. She had been the oldest girl in the Byler family. Taking care of newborn Liam had been her job at the ripe old age of ten. That kind of thing left its mark. He understood more than most. He had been at home sick with the flu when the van-semi collision took his mother's life, but the accident left a fat, ugly scar where his heart should be. Not the best thing in the world to have in common, but at least he understood in a way most couldn't.

Gott, *help me do the right thing.* He was tempted to say the words aloud, but Plain folks didn't do that much. Jesus had been mute in the face of His accusers and attackers. Not that anyone attacked Jacob. He simply received the when-are-you-going-to-grow-up looks. Swatting away a horsefly the size of his thumb, he two-stepped around a pile of cow patties and nearly hurled face first into a rut that could swallow a buggy. The road would keep him awake if nothing else.

The truck's headlights were off. No hazards flashing. The passenger door hung open.

No Dwayne.

Lord, give me strength.

"Dwayne? Dwayne!"

The distinct sound of someone puking floated on the dank breeze. Swiping at sweat dripping from his forehead under a hat that seemed too tight after a long day, Jacob tromped through the weeds hoping he wouldn't disturb a rattlesnake out for an evening slither. "Dwayne? Are you okay?"

A half grunt, half whine told him the answer was likely no. It came from his left. He swerved and swept a mass of black-eyed Susans out of his way. Dwayne had propped himself up with one hand against a scraggly mesquite tree that didn't look strong enough to hold his six-foot-plus, one-hundred-eighty-some-pound high school wrestler's frame.

"Are you gonna live?"

Dwayne swiped at gnats and flies that had arrived like uninvited guests to a supper party. He cleared his throat and snorted. "Nothing another brew won't cure. I got a six-pack under the seat." He leaned over and hurled again. This time his swipe removed spit from his chin. "Why don't you go snag it for me? You're welcome to help yourself."

"Give me your phone."

"Uh-uh. You're gonna call Rory and she's gonna yell and throw a hissy fit like she's my mother or something." He staggered away from the tree. His hands went to his knees. Odds were the gnats would get dessert with the main course. He heaved a big breath. "I got chips in there too. Tortilla chips and that bean dip you like. It's a party, dude, come on."

Careful to step around the splash zone, Jacob eyed Dwayne's jeans. One pocket bulged with a wallet, the other had that telltale white ring that spoke of a can of chew. Dwayne had given up smoking in deference to his role as father of two toddlers. Chew wasn't much better in Jacob's estimation, but no one had asked him. He slapped the pocket on Dwayne's blue-and-white striped cotton shirt that bore the logo of the car repair shop where he'd worked since graduating from high school. Rick Santillan, owner of the shop, would be thrilled to know Dwayne had been out drinking in a shirt advertising his business. Sure enough, the phone was in the shirt pocket. Jacob snatched it out.

"Hey, hey, don't be touching me." Dwayne staggered back, both hands in the air, as if doing a little dance. Puke covered one of his pointy cowboy boots. "We're out in the middle of nowhere all alone, but you ain't my type."

"Shut up. Give me your password, then shut up."

"Don't call Rory. She'll just rag on me about how I said I would quit and I didn't. I ain't giving up my hops and barley. I shouldn't have to."

Jacob didn't answer as he contemplated the phone. He preferred not to lie, but he didn't want to argue with a drunk, however harmless. "What's your code to open the phone?"

"Who ya gonna call?" Dwayne guffawed, head thrown back, then slapped his chest with one hand. "Hear what I just said? 'Who you gonna call'? Ghostbusters. It's an old, stupid movie that my parents watch whenever it comes on the rerun movie channel. I guess you ain't seen it."

The man might as well talk gibberish. "What's your code?"

Dwayne swayed and put a hand on the tree. "You can't call her."

"You know she's worried sick about you. Let me tell her you're all right."

"I don't need another mother. Whatever. Six two ninety-seven."

Jacob flicked through Dwayne's favorites and punched Rory's number. After a few rings, it went to voice mail. Jacob knew better. Rory was walking the floor, muttering to herself, talking herself into calling a lawyer and divorcing her high school sweetheart, the love of her life. She was a Dwayne junkie. Jacob couldn't really see what she saw in the guy. But then she'd been sixteen when they'd produced Trevor, followed by Harper two years later. Those babies were worth fighting for.

Biting his lip, he opened the message program and used his one-finger typing skills to tap out a text. "Got Dwayne. Will bring him home. Jacob."

He'd barely hit Send when her response arrived. The phone should've melted in his hand. "Don't u dare. I got 2 babies. Don't need another 1. Take home to m & d."

She didn't mean it.

The cymbals told him another text had arrived, hot on the heels of the first one. "Tell h I sd w'r done. Tell h I'm not j this time. Got lawyer n speed dial."

She couldn't afford a lawyer. Nolan Beale, her father, could. But by morning, she would cool off. She always did.

Jacob studied the star-studded sky for a second. Wispy clouds dressed the moon in lace. The breeze held a hint of coolness, finally. Still, he didn't feel like sitting in a truck all night. He had work to do tomorrow. So did Dwayne. He needed to sleep it off, take a shower, and drink a gallon of coffee. Not at Jacob's house. Dwayne had spent the night in Jacob's barn once before, after crashing his truck into Will Glick's buggy. Mordecai was among the most forgiving of men. He took his role as deacon seriously, but he also had a practical streak. He wouldn't want to expose the children a second time to Dwayne's way of living.

"I'm thirsty." Dwayne started toward the road, giving Jacob a wide berth. He plunged to a stop, then swayed. A couple of cusswords followed, delivered at a decibel Jacob could've done without. "Aw, man, this sucks. Nature calls."

Jacob turned his back on the man and started for the truck. "Hurry up. We're going into town."

"Aw, man, you calling Jesse? Don't call Jesse. He'll rip me a new one." More cusswords. "He's gonna bust a vessel in his brain ragging on me."

Pastor Jesse Glick did have a way with words. And he would not be happy that a member of his small congregation had fallen into his old ways. Dwayne and Rory had joined the Beeville church before Jesse had been ordained, and both their babies had been dedicated there. Jacob scrolled through the contacts and punched Jesse's cell phone number.

Voice mail. Again.

He maneuvered around the truck and opened the driver's side door. It felt good to ease onto the seat. He leaned back and contemplated the wheel. This was a Dodge Ram, four-door with an extended cab. Not new, but Dwayne had spent a lot of time gussying it up. Nice paint job, powerful stereo, new seat covers. If he spent as much time and effort on his marriage as he did the truck, he would make Rory the happiest, most blessed woman around.

"Hey, head to the river." Dwayne climbed into the passenger seat. "There's an alligator with our name on it."

It was a black night out. The Frio River was up by Choke Canyon Lake. A long drive, even in a pickup truck. Besides, even if they caught an alligator, it would take several people to reel it in and then it had to be taken to El Campo for processing. And a man had to show a license to do that. "No hunting tonight."

"You know, you're not as much fun as you used to be. Take me to Shawn's house." Dwayne flopped back against the seat and let out a loud burp that smelled of puke and stale beer. He patted his flat stomach. "Man, that felt good. Shawn'll go with me. He knows how to have a good time."

Jacob held his breath, fighting the urge to stick his head out the window. Instead he punched in the number for Jesse's house. He hated to do it, knowing he would likely wake Leila, mother of two little ones. The phone buzzed and buzzed. Finally, Leila's sleepy voice came over the line. "*Jah*—I mean yes? It's Leila." She cleared her throat. "How can I help you?"

"I'm so sorry. I know you're sleeping, but I didn't know who else to call. Jesse isn't answering his cell so I was hoping to reach him at home. Rory said no way—"

"Jacob? Is this Jacob?" Leila's voice rose. Rustling noise told him she sat up. "Is *Mudder* all right? Has something happened to one of the *kinner*? Deborah? Rebekah? Is Hazel all right? Caleb?"

She ran through the names in a rapid-fire succession that left Jacob with no option but to wait until she ran out. When she stopped, her breathing ragged, Jacob jumped in. "Everyone's fine. Healthy. Sleeping, I reckon. Is Jesse there?"

"*Nee*, he's driving back from the valley. He's been there for the last week working with refugee children. I expect he'll be here in a few hours. He's homesick and the *kinner* miss him something awful, so he decided to drive back tonight. If you tried to call him and he didn't answer, he's driving, that's why." Leila always did talk more than three men put together. Even more than Rebekah, who used to monopolize the supper table conversation until she married Tobias, and now she monopolized all his conversations. Better him than Jacob. Pain throbbed in Jacob's right temple. The start of a headache he could ill afford right now. Sweat burned his eyes. He breathed a gusty sigh punctuated by a trumpet snore from Dwayne. He glanced in his direction. The man was sprawled against the seat, his mouth open with drool forming at the corner. Not a pretty picture, but at least *he'd* stopped talking.

"Dwayne's at it again."

"*Ach*, that man. Rory will take a shotgun to him one of these days if Nolan doesn't get to him first." Crackling came over the line and the next few words were lost. "I'm getting up. I'll call Rory, talk her down from whatever ledge she's on."

Leila talked like that now. Like she read articles in magazines and watched morning talk shows on TV. The English called them stay-at-home moms. The

Plain simply called them mothers. "I need a place to take him."

"Bring him here. I can sleep in Gracie's bed. We upgraded her to a twin a few months ago. She loves it, but she loves sleeping with her mommy too. Manny—"

"I can't bring him there until Jesse gets home. I'll find a convenience store and get some coffee—for him and me."

Dwayne couldn't stay at Leila's without Jesse there. It wouldn't be right.

"Don't be giving him coffee at this time of night. He needs to sleep it off. Bring him here." Her tone turned crisp. "And don't be silly. Jesse brings immigrants here all the time on their way to court hearings and such. His lawyer friends use us as a halfway point to San Antonio. He'll be here in less than two or three hours—"

"Okay, okay. I'll be there in about twenty minutes."

Leila had a way of wearing a man down. She was a sweet, pretty girl. All the Lantz girls were. They just talked too much. Martha wasn't like that. No point in thinking about her now. She probably wouldn't talk to him again anytime soon.

He jammed the key in the ignition and the truck rumbled to life. The stereo followed. Guitars and drums mixed in a high velocity country tune. Something about sitting on the tailgate of a truck drinking from a red cup.

Dwayne snorted and bolted upright. "What, what? Where are we? Are we at the river?"

"Shut up and go to sleep."

"Man, don't be harsh with me." Dwayne wriggled

and shoved his cowboy hat back on his head. The slur had begun to fade from his speech. "I know you think I'm messed up, but walk a mile in my boots, why don't you?"

"I've tried." Jacob swallowed sudden, embarrassing emotion. What had gotten hold of him? A virus, or something worse. "All I see are blessings. A good woman who loves you. Two healthy babies. A father-in-law who gives you shelter. A decent job. What do you have to whine about?"

"You know what my high school friends are doing these days?"

Jacob shrugged. He could only guess. "Going to college?"

"Brent is playing football at A&M. Marshall is in the army, and he's stationed in Germany." Dwayne made it sound like a very special place. "Me, I was born in Beeville and I'll die in Beeville. Rory's the best and I love my kids, but nothing I do is good enough. Ever. Nolan looks down his nose at me every day. Rory's constantly ragging on me to get a better job that pays more. She wants to go to Disney World and Cancun. Meantime, she orders all these expensive baby clothes online. Who knew babies needed so many clothes? And toys and junk. The house is full of it. I'm always stepping on stuff."

He ran down, finally. The man had made his choices, and now he'd like to blame someone else for them. Jacob wanted what Dwayne had, but his path to such riches would be a very different one. Or none at all. "I'm not married, so I don't know much about this stuff, but I do know a man has responsibilities and he doesn't shirk them. Not when he has children depending on him."

"I ain't shirking nothing. Those babies don't want for anything. I work my fingers to the bone to make sure."

"That's good."

Dwayne leaned his head against the window and pulled his hat down over his eyes. "Wake me up when we get there."

Jacob inhaled and blew out the air. He was the last person on earth to give advice about women and marriage. He knew next to nothing about it. If tonight was any indication, he would never get to know more. Ever.

CHAPTER 4

Jacob slammed on the brakes. The truck swerved. The tires squealed, gears screeching, and the engine died in the middle of the road. He'd been doing so well with the gear-shifting stuff. Dwayne snorted and flailed with both arms. "What the—"

"Who is that?" A man sauntered along the farm-to-market road's shoulder, his dark shape outlined by the headlights. He didn't look up. "What is he doing walking around in the dark like that?"

Dwayne muttered and rolled to one side, giving Jacob his back. Whatever. He peered into the dark, restarted the truck, and moved on to the shoulder, well out of the path of any random car that might be traveling the back roads late at night. Cowboy hat or straw? Straw hat. A Plain man.

He wasn't very tall, shaped like a barrel, shoulders hunched. Was he old? What would an elderly Plain man be doing out on the road this time of night? Jacob waited for the man to get closer. Instead he stopped and made as if to turn around.

"Hey, wait." Jacob turned off the engine, shoved open the door, and jumped out. "Wait, do you need a ride?"

The man turned. Not old. Simon Glick. He'd been at the singing earlier. Much earlier. His brother Joseph should have given him a ride home by now.

"What are you doing out here by yourself in the dark?"

Simon peered at him through wire-rimmed glasses that had slid down his nose. He shoved them up with his stubby index finger. "Home. I-I-I can-can find my way home. I'm a man."

Indeed, he and Jacob were the same age, but he always thought of Simon as a little brother. Simon's simple good nature appealed to Jacob. Simon never had a bad word to say about anyone, and he loved to "help out" as he put it. "Where's Joseph?"

"He had to take Vesta home. He said he had to talk to her about something. It's a se-se-se-cret." The stutter and Simon's crestfallen look told Jacob he realized he'd said something he shouldn't have. "Don't tell."

Joseph should have planned ahead better. He should've asked someone else to give Simon a ride. He probably figured no harm could come to a man walking around Bee County alone at night. With a prison down the road, they all knew better. "I won't tell." He wouldn't say anything, except to Joseph himself. "But you should get in. I'll give you a ride."

Simon's forehead wrinkled over his glasses. He looked so much like his father, Bishop Leroy. Leroy hadn't been bishop in a few years, but Jacob still thought of him that way. Simon cocked his head and looked at the truck. "You're driving Dwayne's truck?"

"How do you know it's Dwayne's truck?"

"Seen it around. He drives real fast up and down the dirt roads." Still looking confused, Simon shrugged. "I have to be careful not to get in his way. You drive his truck now?"

Simon hadn't been trusted with his own buggy since he failed to attach the rig properly, which led to a mishap that hurt the horse and destroyed the buggy beyond what the Glicks, well-known for their buggy-making business, could repair. People should be looking out for Simon, not the other way around. "I'm helping him out by driving. He's tired. I have to take him into town, but I can take you home after that."

Simon would likely tell Leroy about Jacob driving the truck, but it couldn't be helped. *Rumspringa* covered a multitude of activities.

"I can help out." Simon's face lit up with a smile reminiscent of his brother Jesse who had the same stocky, barrel-chested body and dark brown eyes. "I like to help."

"I know you do. Why don't you climb in the back seat and we'll get everyone squared away?"

Simon dashed forward as if afraid the offer might be rescinded. Hand on the extended cab's door, he paused, frowning. "Why isn't he going home? Is Ro-Ro-Rory mad?"

He might have the mind of someone closer to Liam Byler's age—about ten—but he still didn't miss much. Jacob opened the driver's door. "*Jah*, she's mad and Dwayne deserves it, but he needs a place to sleep tonight so we're taking him to Jesse and Leila's."

Another big grin. "Jesse is my *bru-bruder*. I like Leila. She has cookies and she shares."

"I know. I like them too."

Once Jacob started driving, he had to concentrate on shifting gears. He didn't try to make conversation, and Simon seemed content to take in the interior of the truck. Likely, he'd never been in one before. The seats had new covers, George Strait seemed to feel blessed that all his exes lived in Texas, and the air smelled like pine trees. A few more shifts of the gears and Jacob managed to stop at the Stop sign and turn onto Highway 59 leading into Beeville. Not bad. He could do this.

"I wan-wan-wanna girl. A girl li-li-like . . . a girl like you got. Li-li-like . . ." Simon's words were so garbled Jacob could barely understand. "I-I-I mean li-li-like Jesse and Leila. Like everyone."

He glanced in the rearview mirror. Simon's face was radish red. His eyes were bright with tears and his lower lip trembled. He wanted a special friend. A girl to take on a buggy ride. Like any man his physical age would. But his mental age? Jacob would never have guessed such a thing.

"I don't really have a girl. Not yet. So I understand."

Simon squirmed. "Can w-w-we both get one?"

The temptation to say he couldn't even get one for himself overwhelmed Jacob. He inhaled the fake pine scent that emanated from the tree air freshener hanging from the mirror. "It's not that easy, but we can try."

"You like Martha."

A statement of fact without the slightest stutter.

"I do."

"My *mudder* says I don't need a special friend."

Naomi most likely wanted to shield her son from the

hurt he would feel when girls chose men who would be the heads of the households they needed. The men who could be *manns* and *daeds* in ways Simon could not. "Do you have someone particular in mind?"

Simon nodded so vigorously his straw hat flopped. He grabbed it. "I like Amanda."

Amanda. Aaron and Jolene Shrock's special girl. Simon had picked exactly the right girl for a man like himself. She was sweet and pretty and she would see him as her equal. Which indeed he was. "Amanda is nice."

"She's pretty."

"She is."

"Jacob will help me." Simon clapped his hands together as if applauding. "This is *gut*. Very *gut*."

Jacob wasn't even able to help himself. How could he help Simon? He kept his gaze on the windshield after that.

They pulled into Jesse's driveway at eleven thirty. Simon had his door open before Jacob turned off the ignition. Leila peeked through the screen door. "There you are. Simon! I didn't know you were coming."

She hugged Simon, a gesture he returned with great enthusiasm. She might have given Jacob one as well if he hadn't taken a step back. Her Plain instincts had definitely eroded. She wore a short robe of shiny material over running shorts and an oversize white T-shirt that didn't hide the fact she and Jesse were adding another *bopli* to their brood. Her feet were bare.

"Let me roust Dwayne out of the truck." Jacob turned away. "Did you get ahold of Rory?"

"She says he can take a long hike and rot at the end

of that trail. Not in those words, but that was the gist of it."

A lot more words, likely. "She's giving up?"

"She'll cool off. Jesse will talk to Dwayne and I'll talk to Rory. Marriage takes work. You don't just give up on it, and Rory knows it. But this kind of behavior . . ." Leila swept her arm toward the truck. "It has to stop. He can't be a good father and husband like this."

"He has a problem."

"No doubt."

Jacob jerked open the door. Dwayne's package of raw meat tumbled to the ground. He scooped it up and handed it to Leila. "This should still be *gut*."

"*Ach*, I could make four meals out of this—five." She took it as if he'd handed her a gift. "*Nee*, I'll give it to Dwayne tomorrow. He can take it home to Rory. They're on a tight budget too."

The Lantz sisters were ones to think of others before themselves. Jacob turned to Dwayne, still passed out on the seat. "Come on, time to go to bed, buddy."

Dwayne didn't budge. His mouth hung open, spittle dribbling from his lower lip. It took both of the men to wrestle him out of the truck. His legs dragged and his head flopped.

"How much did he drink?" Leila laid the package of meat on the steps and stuck her hands on her hips. "Should I put him in the shower or call 9-1-1?"

"*Nee*. He snored all the way here. He's fine."

They dragged him in the house, through a living room littered with dolls, Lincoln Logs, and toddler picture books. The room smelled of baby wipes, dirty diapers, and something sweet recently baked. Ginger-snaps maybe. Jacob heard a crunch under his boot. He'd crushed something.

"Don't worry about it." Leila's tone was airy. "At least you're not barefoot. I do that half a dozen times a day. It's all I can do not to say something I don't want the *kinner* repeating, but there's no point in picking it all up. They just get it right back out."

At the narrow door to the bedroom, Dwayne's head snapped up. His eyes opened. Both arms flailed until he connected with the frame and wouldn't let go. "Where am I? What the—"

"It's me, Leila. You're at Jesse's house."

"What am I doing here?" Dwayne jerked from the men's grasp and hauled himself backward. "I want to talk to my wife. I need to talk to Rory."

"Rory doesn't want to talk to you." Leila shook her finger, eyes narrowed, frowning. "You blew it again and she has every right to be angry. Right now, what you need to do is sleep it off and let her cool down."

"I need to talk to my baby. I need to tell her I'm sorry."

"Tomorrow." Leila relented and patted his shoulder. "She's asleep now. You should be too."

"Where's my truck? Where are my keys?" He stumbled back and smacked his head on the doorframe. "Ouch. You can't keep me here against my will."

"Is it your will to disappoint your wife over and over again? To disappoint God? To take the chance of driv-ing drunk and leaving your children fatherless?" Jacob heaved a breath. Who was he to judge? He had his own sins to confess when it came to a long, drawn-out *rumspringa*. No wonder Martha kept her distance. "Tomorrow is a work day. Get some sleep, go to work so you don't lose your job, then you can go home and make things right with Rory."

Dwayne's gaze swung from Jacob to Leila to Simon, who'd squeezed himself against the wall, his face scrunched up as if expecting a blow. Dwayne's fists unclenched. He sighed. "Okay." His tone had turned meek. He launched himself onto the narrow bunk bed covered with some sort of pink and purple princess blanket. "Take my boots off, will you? My feet are killing me."

His face was covered with sweat and his shirt was damp under the arms. Jacob held his breath as he tugged off the ostrich skin boots and the rank odor of feet floated around him.

"Thanks, dude." Dwayne rolled over, feet hanging off the edge of the bed, and closed his eyes.

The three of them tromped from the room. Leila smiled up at Jacob. "You did good in there. You could be a teen counselor. Jesse needs help."

"Are you trying to recruit me?" An odd, cold feeling whirled round his neck, raising goose bumps. "I'm starting baptism classes soon."

"I would never do that." Leila's cheeks colored. "Don't go home and tell *Mudder* I tried to steal you away from your Plain faith. She doesn't see the babies often enough as it is."

"I wouldn't do that."

She sighed. "I miss everyone so much. All of you."

She and Jesse had made their choice long ago. "A lot of water under that bridge."

"Can I make you some coffee before you go back? Or some iced tea? I have a travel cup I could put it in." She didn't seem the least fazed that he was driving a truck. "I don't want you falling asleep on the road. Precious cargo and all."

Simon's face turned red again. "I like cookies."

"No *kaffi*. Tea would be nice to cool off." Jacob wiped sweat from his forehead with his sleeve. Iced tea would cool him off and not keep him awake like coffee. "*Daed* has me helping with the apiaries in the morning. And I still have to take Simon home and get my buggy back."

"Simon can stay here. I'll take him home in the morning."

And have to explain how he ended up at her house after the singing. And Jacob's role in it. Simon would be in trouble and so would Jacob. "That won't work."

"I like cookies." Simon looked hopeful. "I smell cookies."

Leila laughed. "You have a good nose." She bustled into the kitchen and returned a few minutes later with tea mugs and two sandwich bags filled with gingersnaps. "For the road."

Simon grinned, grabbed his share of the loot, and fairly skipped out the front door.

Moving more slowly, Jacob paused on the top step. He could ask Leila. She and Jesse worked with a church youth group. Jesse did faith counseling, whatever that was. "Do you think it's possible for men like Simon to be in *lieb* and get married?"

Leila crossed her arms, her eyebrows lifted. She

looked so much like her mother Abigail in that moment. "Why, Jacob King, are you considering matchmaking?"

"I don't know." Embarrassment heated his face. He couldn't meet her gaze. "It just makes me feel like he shouldn't be alone because he's different. We say *kinner* like him are special gifts from *Gott*. Don't they deserve the same happiness as the rest of us?"

He couldn't believe he was having this conversation with a woman, who was, for all intents and purposes, English now.

She squeezed his arm. Definitely English. "You are the sweetest thing ever. It would take a special kind of woman to yoke herself to Simon, but he's sweet and kind and hardworking. He looks an awful lot like his brother, and I think Jesse is cute. What more could a woman want?"

Jacob didn't want to think about how cute or not cute Jesse was, but he understood Leila's point. "Like Amanda Shrock. They would sort of fit together."

"The Shrocks came after Jesse and I left." Her skin turned a rosy pink, but she didn't break eye contact. "But if Amanda is half as sweet and nice as Simon, they'd fit together perfectly."

"*Gott* intended for us to be with someone, no matter how smart a person is. I know some really smart people who are dumb."

"You are so much like Mordecai. So wise." Leila rewarded him with another one of those Lantz sister smiles that could knock a man from his boots. "A deep thinker. You'll make some lucky woman a *gut mann*."

He could think of no answer to such a statement. No

one had ever said that about him. Mordecai knew something about everything, and mostly people focused on Phineas because they felt sorry for him and his scarred face. Jacob had been left to make his own way after his mother's death more than ten years ago.

Except for Aunt Susan. Her kisses on his forehead and her soft fingers smoothing back his hair when she thought he was sleeping had gotten him through many lonely nights after Mother died.

He cleared his throat, nodded, and climbed into the truck.

From Leila's lips to Martha's ears.

CHAPTER 5

Set. Spike. *Wham!* Martha whooped and landed hard in the tired-looking weeds that served as a volleyball court in Leroy's yard. Grasshoppers flew in all directions, apparently as surprised as Jacob at the ferocity of the hit. The startled look on his face as he ducked and let the ball sail into the second row gave her a sense of satisfaction. She loved a good game of volleyball. It didn't hurt that Jacob had pushed Rueben aside so he could be directly across the net from her. He'd been doggedly returning her volleys for more than an hour, but this time she got him good.

I'm sorry, Gott. *I'm only human.*

Obviously. Or she wouldn't be questioning His plan for her all the time. How could she consider baptism when she couldn't keep the simplest of rules? Trust *Gott.*

"You've been eating your spinach." Breathing hard, Jacob smiled, straightened, and wiped sweat from his flushed face. "I'll get even, you watch."

"I don't like spinach." Martha hunched forward, poised on the balls of her feet, hands together, ready for the next volley. "How's Dwayne?"

"Dwayne's fine." His smile didn't slip. "Rory took him back. She made him stay at his father's for three days, but she finally gave in."

"Poor babies." She bumped Rueben's serve neatly to Vesta, who grunted and smacked it overhand with more enthusiasm than accuracy. It hit the sagging net and bounced back. "Their daddy prefers alligator hunting to growing up. Like a lot of men I know."

Point for the boys. She tossed the ball over the net to Rueben. The volleys continued back and forth, this time while Deborah, Abigail, and the older folks on the sidelines cheered and clapped. They all loved a good game.

So did Martha, but she liked to win too.

"There was no alligator hunting." Jacob whacked the ball so hard it flew past the second row, hit a mesquite tree, ricocheted, and slammed into the corral fence. "For him or for me."

Game! Martha managed to stop just short of jumping up and down and screaming in victory. It was only a game, after all. Ignoring Vesta's confused looks, she sauntered from the yard to the picnic table where they'd set up plates of cookies, chips, and sandwiches. She poured water in a cup and took a long drink.

"I need your help on something."

She jumped and spilled water on the front of her dress. Jacob took a step back. "Sorry, I didn't mean to scare you."

"I'm not scared of you." Why did she always sound so defensive when she talked to him? He stood close, smelling of soap, sweat, and good cheer. She wiped at her dress, heat spreading across her already warm cheeks. "Help with what?"

He cocked his head toward the cluster of kids clowning around in the yard. Simon chased after Rueben, who had stolen his hat and held it over his head as he ran. Both were hooting and hollering like eight-year-olds. Much like Liam, who tried to keep up on his shorter legs but couldn't. "I want to help Simon ask Amanda to take a walk."

Just when she thought Jacob couldn't surprise her. Grinning despite herself, she swiveled to peek at Aaron and Jolene Shrock's middle daughter, a sweet girl who never stopped smiling but rarely said a word. Amanda sat cross-legged on a gnarly old stump, cuddling a kitten in her lap. She had clapped every time Simon hit the ball during the volleyball game—which wasn't too often, truth be told—and now she giggled at his hat antics. "That's sweet of you."

"You don't have to sound so surprised. I've been known to have a good idea now and then." Jacob grinned that grin that made Martha's breath play hide and seek with her lungs. "Simon told me the other night when . . ." His smooth cheeks turned a deeper red than exertion and sun warranted. "Anyway, he said he'd like to have a special friend too."

She managed a quick breath. Too? As if Jacob had one? Never mind. This wasn't about them. It was about helping two nice people find each other. "What did you have in mind?"

"Ask Amanda to take a walk with you down to the

pond. I'll get Simon to head that direction with me. We'll run into each other, so to speak."

"I can do that."

He nodded. "*Gut.*"

"It's a *gut* idea."

"I'm glad you think so." The smile fading, he shifted his gaze to the chips on the table, then back to her face. "We could take our own walk, once we get them situated."

The trepidation in his voice told her he didn't expect a yes, but he longed for it. So did she. If only she could be sure of him. But nothing could be for sure. Her mother's passing had taught her as much. She studied his face with its blue-green eyes, long nose, and dimples. He knew loss as well. His mother had died in an accident when he was a small boy. Like Rueben. Yet he still sought love. "We could."

"*Jah? Jah!*" He pumped his fist in such an English manner, she took a step back. "*Nee*, don't change your mind. See you down at the pond."

He whirled and strode away as if to stave off the opportunity for her to speak again. Feeling like she had a special mission in life, Martha traipsed over to Amanda's spot, knelt, and petted the tiny, black-and-white kitten. "Your kitty looks comfy."

Amanda smiled. She had a round face, dark-blue almond-shaped eyes, and a smattering of freckles that added to the impression of her as a young child, even though she was the same age as Martha. "She's a sweet baby. She loves me. She doesn't have a *mudder* so I take care of her. *Mudder* lets me."

"You think kitty would like to go for a walk?"

Beaming, Amanda hopped up, her baby clutched close to her chest. "Her name is Patches. She loves to be walked."

"Let's take Patches down by the pond."

Allowing for Amanda's shorter legs, Martha strolled down the dirt path worn by many a couple who decided to sneak away from the frolics held every other Sunday when they didn't have church. The pond came into view. It held so little water it could hardly be called a pond, and it was only the last week of June. They sorely needed rain. A singsong whistle mingled with the croak of frogs and the buzz of flies as big as her pinky. "Jacob?"

"Jacob's here?" Amanda sounded pleased. "He's funny and he always gives me his cookies after church."

Funny and giving. Martha had seen both those qualities in him. So why had she chosen to focus on the negative? For fear. She had never thought of herself as cowardly. She'd been brave when Mother died. Her throat tight, she brushed away a swarm of gnats. "So is Simon."

"I like Simon. He gave me a flower once."

"He did?"

Amanda nodded so hard her *kapp* slid down the back of her head. "*Jah*, a dandelion. We blew on it together."

"That was nice." Martha stopped and fixed the *kapp*, admiring the girl's shiny blond hair. Her own had more frizz than curl. "Simon is sweet."

"He helped me take care of my puppy too. Her name is Star because she has a white spot on her forehead shaped just like a star."

A heart for caring for babies. Was it enough for Amanda to mother puppies and kittens? It seemed sad she might never be a mother. "You have lots to do."

"I'm a *gut mudder* to my *boplin*."

"*Gut* for you."

Jacob stood on the banks with Simon. They tossed rocks in the murky, scum-covered water. "*Gut* job." Jacob slapped Simon on the back. "You have a *gut* arm."

Simon hooted. "I have a *gut* arm."

Jacob turned. "Look who's here."

Simon remained intent on perfecting his rock-throwing technique. Jacob tapped his arm. "We have visitors. Amanda is here."

His face crinkled in a smile, Simon turned. "Amanda is here."

Martha took no offense that he didn't seem to notice her standing next to the object of his affection. She was busy looking at Jacob. He started forward. "I have to tell Martha a secret. You two talk and then you can walk back up to the house together. Simon, you know the way, right?"

Simon nodded his head up and down, but his gaze stayed on Amanda, who held out Patches. "Want to hold my baby?"

"*Jah.*"

They'd already forgotten about Jacob and Martha. She glanced at Jacob. He was watching the couple, his expression delighted. He had a gift for finding joy in life. For someone who'd had a rough row to hoe in his early years, he had no bitterness, no hard edges. His joy wasn't a sign of immaturity, just the opposite. For her to find that same joy would be a blessing. She moved closer. "What's your secret?"

He took her hand in his.

Her first inclination was to faint, but that would be silly. She tightened her grip and prayed her legs would remember how to walk.

. . .

If I die now, Gott, *I would die happy.* Jacob squeezed Martha's hand and led her up the path. The skimpy tree cover consisted of a mix of live oak and mesquite. Not much privacy. Still, he knew of a spot where a fallen tree trunk just off the path could serve as a place to sit for a few minutes. The tall weeds, nopals, and black-eyed Susans would give them cover. There. He pointed to the trunk, suddenly overcome with a timidity he'd never felt before in his life. "Let's sit for a minute."

Martha didn't let go of his hand. She led Jacob to the trunk and sat. He did the same. She didn't say anything. His mind, normally so full of junk he couldn't decide what to think on first, shut down and went out of business. The silence stretched.

"You said—"

"I thought—"

He breathed. "You first."

"You said you wanted to tell me a secret."

"It's not much of a secret." He rubbed a spot of mustard on his pants. "I am in *lieb* with you."

The pause lasted longer than summer in south Texas. "Are you sure?"

Not the answer he'd hoped for. He didn't feel unsure at all. He met her gaze head-on. "A man says he loves you and your first response is to question if he's sure. Are you so unlovable?" To his consternation her eyes filled with tears. "Don't cry."

"I'm not crying. I never cry." She dabbed at her face with her apron. "My *mudder* died when I was ten."

He knew the awfulness of not understanding, of trying to wrap his mind around never seeing *Mudder* again. One morning, she came in and touched his feverish cheek with her cool, soft fingers and told him *Daed* would stay with him while the rest of the family went on a long-planned, much-longed-for trip to the beach in Corpus Christi. He'd been mad at her. He wanted to go, but she said sick little boys needed to rest. There would be other trips to the beach. She'd kissed his forehead and hugged him even though he tried to wiggle from her grasp. Her scent of vanilla and soap lingered long after she left the room.

Aunt Susan had been the one to tell him *Mudder* would never come back. His father spent days with Phineas in the hospital, and Jacob had been sure he, too, would never return. But he had. They both had. "I was eight."

"I know."

"She left and you think everyone who loves you will leave? Everyone will disappoint you? It's not so." The indecision in her face told him he'd careened into the heart of her fear. "You use caring for the *kinner* as an excuse for not taking a chance. Don't do that."

"It's not an excuse. They do need me. But it's true, you can't know."

"No. That's why it's called faith." Never had an argument been more important. "Believing in the unknowable."

"You drive a car. You hunt for alligators."

"For now. Those are things I do for fun. I want to know what life feels like out there. We're only passing through. We don't know how long we have. I want to touch and feel it all. That's part of what *rumspringa* is about." He would settle down, eventually. There was no rush. Life as a Plain man with responsibilities stretched before him. So, for now, he wanted this season of diving into odd, strange, exciting experiences. "It's also about finding that person you want to be yoked to for the rest of your life."

She stood as if to walk away, then sat once again. "I don't know who you are. How can I know how I feel about you?"

"I'm a Plain man who loves a Plain woman and wants to get to know her better. That doesn't mean I'll take her away from her family. They'll always be her family."

She sighed, not looking at all convinced. "That's *gut* to know."

When he most needed words, nothing seemed to come. "Is there any chance you might take a chance on me?"

"When you grow up, it's possible."

Pictures flashed in his mind. The rust-and-green Olds. His friend Milo with a pool stick, his rump in the air as he leaned over the pool table. A red cup full of beer. A season, only a season. "I *am* grown up."

"Not if you're still hanging around boys like Dwayne Chapman."

That again. "Dwayne isn't a bad person. He gets turned sideways sometimes and needs help."

"Is that what you call it when you go to those parties with him in the fields with the beer kegs?"

He hadn't done that in a long time, but the fact that she didn't trust him stung far worse than any bee sting, and he'd had plenty of those over the years. "It's not right to sit in judgment because I chose to help out a friend who doesn't seem to be able to grow up. He needed help getting home. I helped. That's all. You know that. Your self-righteousness is just a cover for your fear."

"I'm not afraid."

"Then why don't you let me get closer? We're stuck. We can't go forward because you're afraid."

"We can't go forward because you won't grow up. I don't need any more *kinner*."

"I don't need taking care of." He drove cars. He helped friends in need. Like Dwayne. Like Simon. He didn't do it to earn her good graces, but surely she could see that he tried hard to be a decent person, a person worthy of her love. "I'm a man, and I'll do what I think is right. A woman who plans to be a good *fraa* would know how to accept that."

"Are you saying I won't be a good *fraa*?"

"I'm saying you have to trust your *mann* to make good decisions and know when to bow to his wishes."

She stared up at him, her blue eyes dark with anger and something else. Hurt. He'd hurt her feelings. "So I wouldn't measure up to your standards for a good *fraa*?"

"I'm sorry."

"I'm not." She sniffed and crossed her arms. "It's better we know these things now, than later. You find me lacking. So be it."

"Not lacking at all. You find me lacking." He'd made her feel bad about herself. This had not gone well at all. His fault. All his fault. He cupped her face in his hands and leaned down, wanting to wipe the hurt from her face.

She stared up at him, her breathing ragged, eyes wide. Her lips parted.

"Mandy? Simon? Mandy!"

A woman's high voice mixed with the lower bass of a man's. Tromping sounds followed. Will and Isabella Glick broke through the high grass and weeds to the tiny clearing. Will halted. His wife nearly ran into him. "You two?"

CHAPTER 6

Disaster averted. A kiss from Jacob would surely lead to disaster. He wanted a woman who knew how to acquiesce to his will. Martha couldn't, not if he wasn't willing to leave behind his teenage ways and English friends. She had to be able to trust him.

Feeling as if she'd been thrown from a runaway buggy, Martha scrambled from the downed tree trunk, hoping her legs would hold her. She moved away from Jacob, but it was too late. From the sly looks on their faces, Will and Isabella knew exactly what was going on. Which was more than Martha could say. He infuriated her, yet she'd wanted that kiss. She still wanted it. "We were talking."

Her voice sounded peculiar. Like she'd just come up for air after swimming underwater.

"*Jah*, about old times." Jacob stood more slowly. He didn't sound at all flustered. "And how important our *mudders* were to us."

"We're looking for my *schweschder*." Isabella fanned her damp, red face with one hand. "She's not supposed to leave the yard, and she's likely to follow a dog or a cat to who knows where. One time she ended up at the Archers on Tynan Road."

"And my *Onkel* Leroy asked me to look for Simon." Will jumped in when his *fraa* ran out of breath. "He wandered off about an hour ago. It's not like him to leave a frolic without saying anything. He's not allowed to take a buggy, so he has to be on foot. You haven't seen him, have you?"

Martha forced herself to make eye contact with Jacob. He raised his eyebrows and offered a rueful smile. Time to own up. It might have been his idea, but she had embraced it with all her heart. "We helped them get together. They're down by the pond."

"Get together?" Isabella's voice rose a full octave. She shook her head. "My little sister with Simon? Why would you do that? You know how special they are. They don't know about . . ."

She floundered.

"These things," Will offered, his expression equally horrified. "Simon and Amanda are like *kinner*. It would be like getting Liam together with one of the little girls."

"Simon asked for my help." Jacob spread out his hands, shoulders hunched. "He says he likes Amanda. Those aren't the words of a boy. Liam would rather eat spiders than touch a girl."

"Mandy says she likes Simon too," Martha added. "She says he helps her take care of her *boplin*."

"Her *boplin* are puppies and kittens." Isabella crossed her arms. "She's not capable of being a *mudder*."

Jacob interceded again. "We're not talking about *mann-fraa* things here. Only simple fun. They have feelings too."

Why couldn't he be as wise about his own life?

Martha swallowed her disappointment in him, a bitter drink. "We weren't thinking that far ahead, only of them having fun together for now. Like others their age. They're included in all the other activities, except this. Do you think they don't notice everyone else pairing off, getting married, having *kinner*?"

"The two of you weren't thinking at all. They are special gifts from *Gott*, given to our care. They think like *kinner* so they don't know what they're missing." Will whirled toward the path. "We need to find them and get them home."

"What are y'all doing here?"

Simon and Amanda traipsed into the now very crowded clearing. They held hands and looked as pleased as two children sneaking a pecan pie from the windowsill after a pie-baking frolic. "We heard people arguing." Simon turned his face to the sun, eyes squinted. "It's too nice a day for arguing."

He didn't stutter. Not once.

"We were talking, not arguing." Will shot Jacob and Martha an accusing look. "See what you've done? Now we have to explain why they can't do this."

"Do what?" Amanda looked puzzled. "Who did what?"

"It's nothing, *schweschder*." Isabella put an arm around her sister and glared at Martha. "Any ideas on how we do that without making them feel bad?"

Martha shook her head. Now everyone would feel bad. What did people say about the path paved with good intentions?

CHAPTER 7

The smell of stink bait in the afternoon could only mean one thing. Fish fry for supper. Jacob grinned at *Daed*, who washed his knife under a nearby spigot in the fish-cleaning area. *Daed* grinned back. It was a good thing they'd staked their camping area with tents a few days before the Fourth of July holiday. A steady stream of campers had inundated Choke Canyon State Park since their arrival. The lake was a popular place all summer long, but the holiday meant a four-day weekend for a lot of folks. It seemed half the Lone Star state had decided to pack up campers and join them.

Jacob rubbed his face on his sleeve, trying to stave off the sweat tickling his cheeks. The haul today included five nice-size channel catfish, three largemouth bass—one a big flopper caught by Caleb who was so excited he fell in the water—and two small crappie courtesy of Liam and Hazel, their youngest fishers. Jacob cut off the head and tail of the last catfish and hurled them in the trash bin.

"Might as well get it off your chest." *Daed* laid a skinned crappie in the ice chest. The snap of the lid sent a long-legged white egret scurrying away. "If it keeps eating at you, you'll be nothing but bone by the time we head home."

Brushing away the flies that buzzed around his ears, Jacob let his gaze travel to the picnic pavilion across an expanse of brown straw that passed as grass in south Texas's withering heat. Martha stood at the Coleman stove, showing Amanda how to control the flames under two dozen greasy hot dogs. The two also sat together at church earlier in the week. Amanda trotted after Martha, helping serve food afterward. She stood next to her when they played volleyball. The two were joined at the hips now. Beyond the pavilion, children played a wild game of tag designed to dry clothes wet from playing in the lake's swimming area. A cluster of women sat at the picnic table husking corn. The aroma of hot dogs floated and mingled with the odor of bait and fish guts. Jacob loved summer. Why spoil all this by talking about his problems?

"Gazing from afar ain't gonna get you much." *Daed* climbed onto a nearby picnic table and propped himself up with both hands behind him. "What's holding you back, *suh*?"

That *Daed* knew of his feelings didn't surprise Jacob. It was a well-known fact in this little *Gmay* that Mordecai King knew everything. His ability to pull facts from seemingly thin air still amazed the children but not Jacob. No one made a big deal about it, least of all Mordecai, and if anyone brought it up, Mordecai would be the first to deny it. His knowledge was dwarfed by his humility. Having a father like that served to make Jacob acutely aware of his own shortcomings. "She thinks I need to grow up. She says she has enough *kinner* to take care of."

"I can see her point." Mordecai leaned forward and put his elbows on his knees, his wrinkled hands clasped in front of him. The silver in his beard threatened to overtake the black, but his blue-green eyes were as sharp as ever. "Gallivanting around the countryside in a noisy, gas-guzzling, fume-belching Olds doesn't beget an image of a grown Plain man."

Mordecai did, indeed, know everything. Shame beat a fiery path from the back of Jacob's neck across his cheeks and down his chin. "We—I plan to get rid of it before baptism classes start." He wouldn't give away his partners in fun—or sin, depending on whom he asked—it wouldn't be right. "Leastways, we've talked about it."

"Not much time left, I reckon." Mordecai jerked his head toward Martha. "Not like the men around here have a plethora of young women from which to choose. Elijah's been talking to her after church."

"A pletho-what?"

Mordecai's vocabulary matched his voracious appetite for reading. Jacob's brother Phineas was the same way. Jacob preferred sports—another way his oldest brother was closer to his father. Not that either Mordecai or Phin ever intentionally made him or the other *kinner* feel left out.

"A lot."

"Right. I know." While Martha had been avoiding him that day after the volleyball game, she'd taken pains to let him see her chatting with Elijah Hostetler as she served potato salad or baked beans after church. "She's mad."

"Should she be?"

"I thought women were supposed to follow the man's lead."

"If the man is wise and fair, *jah*. Even if she doesn't agree. On the other hand, a man who does or says wrong—he should want a *gut* woman to point it out. She will and she should, and then she should bite her tongue and bide her time while he figures it out."

Jacob tried to imagine Martha biting her tongue. She might not be a big talker, but she surely had an opinion about things. She, Vesta, and Amanda laughed as Simon walked by. He stopped and said something. The girls' giggles could be heard all the way across the open field. Simon ambled away, his baggy pants sagging at the waist despite his suspenders. The three put their heads together as if they were whispering. At least he and Martha agreed on that one thing. Amanda and Simon deserved to be happy too. "What do you think about *kinner* who are special gifts? I mean when they grow up and aren't *kinner* anymore. Should they have special friends?"

Mordecai's forehead wrinkled. He smoothed his unruly beard, his lips pulled down in a thoughtful frown. Before he could answer, Dwayne Chapman strode into the fish-cleaning area, a pole slung over one shoulder and an ice chest in the other hand. "Hey, pardner. Long time no see."

"You look better than you did the last time I saw you." Jacob slapped the last bass into the ice chest and closed it. "We're done if you want this spot."

Dwayne cast a glance at Mordecai, who tipped his hat and stood.

"Everyone deserves to have a special friend. *Gott* put someone on this earth for everyone. Read Genesis 2:18–24." Mordecai strode past Dwayne, his words floating behind him. "I'll let you whippersnappers visit. But that doesn't mean you get away with changing the subject. Talk to her."

Leave it to the deacon to know exactly which Scripture applied to a situation. Will was the minister. Maybe Jacob could talk to him again about Simon and Amanda. Or to Leroy. Simon was his son after all. Jacob wanted to talk to Martha too. He eyed the herd of women in the pavilion. The chances of catching her alone didn't seem as good as they had when Mordecai informed the family they would be taking a vacation to the lake.

"What's he talking about?" Dwayne laid the fishing pole on the table and dumped the ice chest on the ground. "Never mind. I wanted to talk to you anyway. You know they have some of the biggest alligators in the state here. They only allowed hunting here like four years ago or something so the gators are like thirty years old. A guy caught an eight-hundred-pound one here a couple years ago. Rory already cooked the pot roast, so I had to buy more meat—"

"Stop with the gator hunting." Jacob tore his gaze from the girls. "They're not in season. This place is packed. Aren't Rory and your babies here? Do you want them to see you breaking the law?"

"Rory, the rug rats, Nolan, Leila, and Jesse—everybody is here. It's a family fling, dude. But it's a big lake. They won't see anything." Dwayne propped open the lid to his ice chest and pulled out a largemouth bass that must've weighed four or five pounds. Its frantic flop caused Dwayne to lose his grip. The fish flipped and landed on the cement, its mouth gaping, eyes wide. He cussed and grabbed the wily fish. "I got fireworks for tonight. Afterward, I'll sneak away and we can do the deed. It'll be cool. Shawn is here somewhere. So is Kyle."

That Leila and Jesse had come with the Beale-Chapman clan didn't surprise Jacob. Leila and Rory had been friends since the early days. Leila and Jesse couldn't be with their real family, so their church family became much more special. It would be good for Abigail to see her daughter and grandkids, even if it was from afar.

Jacob forced himself to focus on Dwayne and his crazy plans.

"Fireworks aren't allowed in state parks. Alligators can't be hunted in July. And I have other plans." An overly optimistic statement, but he would ask Martha to take a walk by the shore once they got the fire going and the children gathered round for s'mores, fry pies, and Mordecai's endless repertoire of funny stories. Amanda loved s'mores and stories. Maybe she'd leave Martha's side when she saw the chocolate and roasted marshmallows. "Plans that don't include you."

"All your folks will be asleep by then."

"Not likely."

Fireworks that made noise might be out of the question—not that it mattered on their skinny budget these days—but the children had their sparklers, worms, and other small treats that wouldn't bother the park's permanent wildlife residents. The older folks would sit in their lawn chairs and enjoy the stars and the evening breeze while the children wore themselves out. Vacation meant staying up later than they normally would. And no chores in the morning. Jacob stuck the knives in a canvas bag he slung over one shoulder. He picked up his ice chest. When he looked up, Martha walked past, arm in arm with Amanda.

The look on her face said it all.

"Hey, we're not here together," he called after her. "He came looking for me. Ask Mordecai."

Martha kept walking.

Jacob kicked at a rock, sending it spinning away.

He turned to Dwayne. "You know anyone who wants to buy a '95 Olds Cutlass Ciera with a hundred-twenty-five-thousand miles on it?"

Dwayne's expression turned shrewd. "That old rust bucket of yours? I just might know someone. Kyle wrecked his truck and his folks won't buy him another one. How much do you want?"

Dwayne didn't know it, but he was about to make up for the trouble he'd caused Jacob.

CHAPTER 8

Sometimes helping others was the best way to shake off a funk. One of *Daed*'s favorite sayings. *Daed* had married Susan in his effort to find happiness. Martha didn't see that option in her future. Jacob had come all the way to Choke Canyon Lake to look for trouble with Dwayne Chapman once again. Tigers couldn't change their stripes, it seemed. She forced herself to smile at Amanda, who sat next to her mother eating a brownie the size of a small cake. She had frosting on her upper lip, a smattering of new freckles, and the start of a sunburn. She looked so content. Jolene, who snapped green beans with an efficiency born of much experience, paused long enough to pat her daughter's knee. "Slow down there, *dochder*, you'll choke."

Amanda grinned, revealing teeth smeared with chocolate. "I like brownie." The words were muffled by a mouthful of food. "It *gut*."

"Don't talk with your mouth full." Jolene went back to her beans, the *pop-pop* like music to Martha's ears. "Take a load off, Martha."

"I should check on the *kinner*. They were getting in the water again."

"Isabella and Will are down there with their two. They won't let them out of their sight."

Relieved, Martha sank into the battered lawn chair. Its frayed, faded nylon seat gave way under even her slight weight. She gazed out at the water, crystal clear in the sun. It might be low, allowing tree branches to stick up along the edges, but it was still beautiful. The pond grass, rushes, and cattails lined it like a green, growing frame that rippled in the breeze. The smell of water, mud, and rotting plants soothed her soul. "It's so peaceful here. I could stay for weeks."

She could camp out, embrace the quiet with no bickering siblings, boisterous boy jokes, or discussions about who should wash and who should dry. She could learn to fish. Fishing made her *daed* content. It might work for her too.

"I know. It's something about the sound of the water and the rustling of the leaves in the trees." Jolene sighed, a contented sound. "A body needs to work hard, but it needs rest too."

Amanda coughed, inhaled, coughed again, harder.

"I told you to slow down." Jolene slapped her daughter's back with two quick whacks. "Go get a drink of water, little piglet. I'll finish your brownie."

"Nee!" Amanda coughed again. "Love brownie."

"Get a drink of water. I'll guard it for you. I won't eat it, I promise."

Amanda bestowed a smile on her mother and trotted away.

"She's so funny." Martha settled back. "She never

has a bad word to say about anyone, and she's always smiling."

"She is a *gut* girl." A pensive expression stole over Jolene's face. Her gaze followed Amanda's meandering progress toward the picnic pavilion. "I know *Gott* has a plan for her, but sometimes I can't help but wonder what the future will bring for my sweet *bopli*."

"You mean when you're gone?" The other Shrock children would care for Amanda. It was expected, but no one would mind anyway. "She's such a sweetheart, they'll argue over who gets her."

"I know. I thank *Gott* for that and for her." Jolene's hands slowed, then rested over the pan of beans. "But that doesn't mean I don't imagine how different her life would be if she could . . . do the things other girls do when they grow up."

The perfect opening. Martha chose her words carefully. "Has she ever mentioned Simon to you?"

"Only every other word." Jolene held out the pan to Martha. "Your turn. I must be getting old. The joints in my fingers hurt. Anyway, Mandy chatters on endlessly about Simon did this and Simon did that."

Martha took the pan and settled it on her lap. "She likes Simon."

"He's a nice boy."

"He's a man and he likes Amanda too."

"You mean likes, *likes*?"

Her cheeks suddenly warm, Martha grabbed a bean, snapped it, and dropped the pieces in the pan. *Snap-snap.* "Special likes."

Jolene held her hand to her forehead and squinted as if she wanted to see the future. "I always think of her as a little girl."

"A little girl's mind in a grown-up body."

"I don't know what to think. I pray for her to be happy." Jolene let her hand drop. "A little bit of happiness isn't too much to ask, is it?"

"Isabella told me I shouldn't encourage her. She was very upset with me."

"She didn't mention it. My oldest *dochder* is very protective of her *schweschder*. And of me too. With Aaron's bad heart and trying to make ends meet, she often tries to carry the load by her lonesome. It's a bad habit."

"So what would you think? Not of them getting married or anything. Just passing the time together."

Amanda traipsed across the grass toward them, arms swinging, face lifted to the sun, and a big splotch of water soaking the front of her apron. Jolene shook her head and smiled. "I think my *dochder* will be happy no matter what, but I don't begrudge her the experience every girl wants."

Martha agreed. Who could look at that shining face and stand in the way? She might spend her life alone, but that didn't mean others should do the same. Something good might still come from her time spent with Jacob King.

Even if he never grew up.

CHAPTER 9

Martha settled the basket of chocolate bars, marshmallows, and graham crackers next to the fire pit and reviewed the contents. Vesta and Amanda had carried over everything needed for the fry pies too. Chocolate. Maybe chocolate would help her forget Jacob for a few minutes. Followed by a hot peach fry pie.

The lawn chairs were strategically placed for conversation and storytelling. Fluffy pink-and-purple clouds huffed and disappeared with the setting sun when the children started their games. Their shrieks of joy as they played olly olly oxen free made her smile despite herself. Life would go on. Chocolate would definitely help. She unwrapped a Hershey's bar and popped a chunk in her mouth. Two little ones squatted side by side, their chubby cheeks dimpled from wide grins, watching as their mother lighted the lumps that turned into writhing "worms" with the heat from a punk stick. She wanted *boplin*. Cute babies who looked like their father.

Back to Jacob.

"Hey."

Martha closed her eyes and opened them. As if her

thoughts were enough to make him appear. That low, sandpaper-rough voice would not affect her. Mind over heart. In other words, *don't be addled.*

Martha inhaled and turned. "Hey, yourself."

Jacob pushed his straw hat back. His face had turned a deep bronze that served to highlight eyes the same color as the lake as the sun set on it. He bit his lower lip and let his gaze wander to the water and back. "I know what you think."

"You do? You read minds now?"

By unspoken agreement they moved toward the water, away from curious gazes. Martha lifted her warm face to a breeze made a few degrees cooler by the lake. The sound of birds chattering and the distant buzz of boat motors soothed her. The water lapped among huisache and mesquite brush along the shores with a peaceful regularity. She tried not to be hopeful. She tried not to think about Jacob's broad shoulders and the way his upper arms bulged against the cotton of his blue shirt. She tried not to inhale his woodsy scent.

Trust. Trust him. Trust Me.

The words sounded so clear, she glanced around to see if someone other than Jacob stood nearby. No one.

Jacob stopped on the path beaten by the many bare feet that had walked, run, strolled, and trudged along the lake, enjoying its beauty. "We sold the car."

She breathed and took a second to let it sink in like her bare feet in the warm soil under them. Trust would be so simple, so restful. Somewhere along the line she'd forgotten how to do it. Jacob's offering fanned the flame of hope. "You sold it for me?"

"We sold it because it was time, and we're not *kinner* anymore, and it's a heap of junk." He shrugged. "I'm a Plain man. Next week I'll start preparing for baptism. That's my plan."

"It's a *gut* plan." She liked it a great deal. "The others were okay with it?"

"All of them. It will be a nice-size baptism class."

"That's wonderful news."

"The other night, I did the right thing." Jacob's tone was firm but somehow respectful. "A man has to do what he thinks is right. Even if it means losing something."

"That's true." Something about his tone was different and no matter how difficult for her, he had a point. A man had to do what was right. She wouldn't respect a man who didn't. Or love him. How could she make him choose? "I understand what you're saying. I just worry that I might have to . . . it's hard to explain."

"Care for me like you do the *kinner*?" He slapped at a swarm of gnats and mosquitoes buzzing around them. "I won't be a burden or a responsibility. I will be a *mann* to my *fraa*. Someone to be counted on. Someone you can trust." He edged closer. "Take a walk with me."

"We tried that and it didn't work out."

"If at first you don't succeed, try, try again."

"I read somewhere that insanity is doing the same thing over and over again and expecting a different result."

"Plain folks aren't allowed to be insane."

Martha couldn't help herself. She laughed. His deep chortle sent goose bumps scurrying up her arms. "I talked to Jolene about Amanda and Simon."

He edged yet closer. "You're changing the subject, but that's okay. I talked to Leroy about Simon and Amanda."

They were on the same page about at least one important thing.

His long fingers brushed hers. She inhaled and tried to think. "Jolene has no problem with them passing the time together."

"Leroy neither. He seemed happy at the thought."

"Jolene too."

"Then we should—"

"*Jah*, we should."

Martha raced to find Amanda while Jacob tracked down Simon. Ten minutes later they met back at the same spot on the water's edge where it ebbed and flowed, sparkling in the last little bit of sun in the dusky beginnings of evening. Amanda clapped her hands, giggled, and covered her mouth when Jacob approached with Simon. "We're all together again." Simon's ears turned red. "We take another walk?"

"*Nee*. It's getting dark and you'll trip over something or get lost. I'll put a blanket down here so you can sit together and talk." Martha shook out a blanket and laid it on the grass close to the narrow shore but far enough away that the water wouldn't reach them. She turned and studied Simon's face to make sure he heard and understood. He seemed entranced by Amanda. "Does that sound good, Simon?"

He nodded but didn't look at her.

After making sure they were settled in, Martha faced the lake. What now? Did Jacob's offer to take a walk still stand? It really was getting too dark.

"We might not be able to take a walk, but we can stand on the pier where it's less crowded." Jacob took her hand. Goose bumps ran up her arm and tickled her neck. "That way Simon and Amanda can have their privacy, and so can we."

"Okay." She couldn't manage much more.

Martha followed Jacob to the short, narrow wooden pier a few yards from where Simon and Amanda sat cross-legged, side by side, looking as if they weren't sure what to do next. She and Jacob were far enough they could talk softly without being heard, but close enough to come back if Amanda or Simon decided they needed some help with conversation. Like every couple in the world, they would figure it out. Another couple, this one English, sat at the end of the pier, dangling their feet over the water, their laughter loud and exuberant over the soft rustle of the cattails in the breeze. Jacob squeezed Martha's hand. "I meant what I said about being able to count on me."

Shyness strangled her for a second. She cleared her throat. "Ever since my *mudder* died, I've felt such a burden—no, that's not the right word . . . such a joy of responsibility for the *kinner*. It's like they're mine. They filled up my life when *Mudder* left it. I don't know what I would've done without them."

"It was different for me because I was the youngest. *Aenti* Susan took over when *Mudder* passed. But I understand." Jacob studied a flock of ducks floating on the lake as if he would find answers to life's secrets in the way they bobbed and floated in the water. "You had a hole that needed to be filled. They filled it. Now Susan is in their lives. She's really good at being an *aenti* and a *mudder*. She's like my *daed*. She knows what to say and when to say it."

"I know. I've seen it over and over again."

"Then you know they're safe with her. You don't have to look for excuses to say no to me."

"They aren't excuses."

"Are you sure? I work hard. I put faith first, then family. I'm an obedient *suh* to my *daed* and to *Gott*. Yet, you push me away. You're scared."

She *was* scared. "I don't ever again want to feel like I felt after *Mudder* died."

"Me neither. I don't know how long *Gott* intends for me to be here, so I can't make any promises on that score, but I can tell you I want to spend those days with you. As many as there are."

"That sounds nice." The future stretched, flower petals opening to the sun. "I will learn to trust."

Jacob leaned closer. "Take all the time you need."

She stood on tiptoes to meet him.

"Jacob, dude, there you are!" Dwayne's holler from the shore had its usual slur. "Dude, come over here. I got Black Cat 'crackers, and a chunk of raw meat."

CHAPTER 10

Timing was everything. Jacob groaned. Martha jerked back and snatched her hand from his. Her fierce frown said it all. Everything rode on how he handled this. He forced himself to look over her shoulder to the shoreline. Dwayne stood in front of Amanda and Simon, a cane pole over one shoulder anchored by a package of meat in one hand, and a bundle of firecrackers with the familiar snarling cat on the red-and-yellow picture in his other hand. He dropped the meat on the ground next to his feet, laid the cane down, and proceeded to pull a lighter from his jeans pocket.

"Don't do that here," Jacob yelled as he strode double-time toward Dwayne. Martha followed, her bare feet slapping on the pier's wood as if punctuating his statement. "Everyone is having a good time. We don't want any part of your so-called fun."

"Chill out, dude. It's gonna be wild. A thousand 'crackers all at once."

Grinning, Dwayne lit the fuse and tossed the bundle to the ground directly in front of where Simon and Amanda sat on their blanket.

Explosion upon explosion ripped the air in a

rat-a-tat-tat like gunfire. The acrid smell of gunpowder burned Jacob's nose. Sparks flew.

Dwayne pumped his fist and held it out for a bump with an imaginary friend. "Yeehaw! Woo-hoo! God bless America!"

Simon leaped from the blanket and planted himself between the exploding firecrackers and Amanda. Her face scrunched up in fear, she ducked her head. Her hands went to her ears.

"Stop-p-p it. S-s-stop it! Amanda doesn't like it."

Jacob sped up to a run. Martha kept pace at his side. "Are you crazy? You threw them right in front of Amanda and Simon. Didn't you see them?"

"Hey, I'm sorry, man." Dwayne threw up both hands as if in surrender just as the noise died away. "I thought they would like their own personal fireworks."

Hissing like a rattlesnake preparing to strike filled the sudden silence.

A mammoth alligator sat in a few inches of water, its long snout raised, only feet from where Dwayne stood on the sandy bank. It flapped its tail in a sharp rap that sounded like a slap. Its eyes shone in the dusk.

Sobbing now, Amanda scrambled to her feet. "I don't like it. I don't like it."

The alligator, at least fourteen feet long, hissed again and bared rows of pointy teeth. Its tail slammed the water again. Waves rippled around him.

"Hush! Hush, Amanda, hush." Jacob careened to a stop less than a yard from her and Simon. He didn't want to rile up the alligator with any sudden movements. The reptile could give chase up to thirty yards or more. He lowered his voice to a yell-whisper. "It's okay. It's okay."

"It's not okay." The pitch of her voice rose. "He'll hurt Simon. He'll hurt you and Martha."

"We'll be fine, I promise." His back to them, Jacob edged between his friends and the alligator, his feet sinking into the sandy, wet soil that led to the water. Dwayne seemed frozen, hands in the air, mouth open, his eyes wide in surprise. "Dwayne, back away. Slowly."

"Dude, this is crazy." Suddenly, Dwayne moved. The guy never did what he was told. He lowered himself in to a squat, his gaze on the gator, his hand patting the ground, searching for something. "I need the meat. This is perfect. Perfect, man."

"*Nee*, it-it-it is not." His face contorted in a fierce frown, Simon shoved between Jacob and Martha. He shook his finger at the alligator. "Don't you-you-you hurt-hurt my Amanda."

"He won't hurt her if you back away slowly." Jacob put his hand on Simon's shoulder and squeezed, tugging him back. He kept his voice soft, gentle. "You're in his playground. He wants this space all to himself. You have to back up."

"Please, Simon, back up like Jacob says." Martha grabbed Simon's hand as if to draw his attention from the alligator. "You too, Dwayne. We don't want to make the alligator mad."

"What if-if-if he comes after Amanda?" Simon's voice trembled. "What if he hurts her-her or you?"

"I'll help Amanda. You do what Jacob says, okay?"

Martha let go of Simon's hand and sidled toward Amanda, one slow step at a time. "We'll be fine."

She put her arm around Amanda. "Can you walk backward?"

"Sure I can." Amanda's tears disappeared. "Like a game?"

"*Jah*, like a game." Martha smiled. "One step, two steps, three steps."

The alligator raised its enormous trap and hissed again.

"We need to move a little faster." Jacob backstepped. "He seems impatient. Come on, Dwayne."

"Nah, I'm fine."

Dwayne knelt in the sandy loom, a big grin replacing his earlier surprise. "The guys won't believe this stuff."

Jacob couldn't worry about a guy acting like an idiot as usual. He and Martha had to get Amanda and Simon away from the danger zone. Then he would deal with cotton-candy-for-brains.

One step. Two steps. Three steps.

Another hiss. Jacob froze. So did Martha. "What now?" she whispered. "Stay or go?"

Sweat ran down Jacob's temples. His shirt was soaked under his arms. "Keep going."

Together, they retreated.

"I don't even have to bait my pole." Dwayne scooped up his package of raw meat and ripped off the wrapper. "I knew that son of a gun was right there. I heard him."

"Be quiet." Contained fury lighted Jacob's words.

Dwayne was about to do something stupid and he would have to stop him. "You need to get out of there."

"We have to keep him here until I get my rifle." Dwayne straightened. "I should've brought it. I don't know what I was thinking—"

The crocodile's tail slapped. His mouth opened.

Now or never. Jacob hurled himself forward, reaching for the meat. Simon moved at the same time. He flopped forward, stretching with both arms.

Jacob snatched the meat from Dwayne's hand and tossed it to the crocodile's left in one headlong motion. He lost his balance and hurtled toward the ground with an *oomph*.

Simon teetered. He fell next to Jacob.

Jacob face-planted in the ground. He rolled and sprang to his feet next to Dwayne, who gaped, empty hands still in the air.

The alligator snapped up the raw meat in its massive jaws and glided away.

With the salty taste of blood in his mouth, Jacob tugged Simon to his feet. They raced away from the water. "Go! Go, everyone, go."

Dwayne followed, cussing up a storm. "Aw, man, why'd you do that? We had a great excuse to snag us a gator! He threatened us."

"Only because you riled him up." Jacob tried to breathe through the ache that had once been his nose. His ribs hurt and a back muscle complained. "Someone could've been hurt bad. You have to stop. Stop drinking. Stop acting like a kid. Stop breaking every rule just because you can. You're not a kid anymore."

"Whoa, chill out, man. I didn't mean for anyone to get hurt."

In the light of the nearby fire-pit flames, Jacob whirled and faced the other man. "That's the thing. You don't mean to hurt other people. But you are. You're hurting your friends and your wife and your little ones. And you can't see it, but you're hurting yourself too."

"Aw, man, you're seriously killing my vibe."

"The alli-alli-alligator could've hurt A-A-Amanda." Simon slapped at dirt on his shirt and pants. "That's not nice. You're not nice."

"He's right." Jacob eyed Simon. Aside from the dirt on his clothes and face, he didn't look any worse for wear. *Praise* Gott. "We're men now with responsibilities. Time to act like it."

"Jacob and Simon are right." Rory Chapman stepped from the shadows beyond the fire. Her baby girl slept on her shoulder, curls hiding her face. Dark circles under her mom's eyes said she, too, was tired. "Am I not enough? Are your babies not enough? You have to drink or chase gators or race trucks on backroads to get your jollies? Do you have to kill someone before you stop?"

"What she said." Jacob planted himself in Dwayne's space. "You have to stop. For your babies' sakes. For your wife's sake." His gaze collided with Martha's. She nodded, her eyes bright. "For your friends' sake."

"I don't mean nothing." Dwayne ducked his head, the words a mumble. "I just like to have fun. Why does everybody have to be so serious all the time?"

"You gotta take responsibility." Jacob took a step

closer. "You have to want help. Seek help. Go talk to Jesse. He helped you before. He will again."

Dwayne raised his head. He let out a gusty sigh. His gaze went to Rory. "I'm sorry, baby."

"I know you are. But sorry isn't enough anymore."

"Okay, okay. I'll do it."

"Say it, baby. You have to say it."

"I'll go see Jesse first thing Monday morning. I'll quit drinking."

Rory trudged across the grass and stopped short of her husband. She smacked his shoulder with her free hand. "Don't do it again. I mean it. No more chances."

"I won't, baby."

Smooching ensued. Followed by giggles from Amanda and Simon. They seemed to be holding hands, fingers entwined, all grown-up with their special friends.

Without a word, Martha turned and walked toward the fire. Jacob followed. Amanda and Simon slipped closer to the fire where Isabella offered them sticks with marshmallows ready for toasting. Jolene assembled the s'mores on the graham crackers and handed them out. The sound of chatter reached a comforting crescendo.

Light-headed with relief, Jacob eased his head back and pinched his nose, trying to staunch the *drip, drip* of blood.

"There's ice in the ice chest. I can get you some." Martha threaded her way between the clusters of folks visiting who were blissfully unaware of the earlier commotion. "It'll smell like fish, but it's clean."

"I reckon I won't be able to smell it anyway."

Martha chuckled. "Such a big honker is bound to bleed a little."

"I don't have a big nose."

"If you say so." She scooped up ice and wrapped it in a white handkerchief. "Take a seat."

Jacob glanced around. No one seemed to notice their exchange. *Gut*. He followed her to a picnic table out of reach of the light of the fire-pit flames. She dabbed at his face with a napkin and then handed him the make-do ice pack. "Looks like you'll live."

"Ouch." He held the pack to his nose. "Do you think Amanda and Simon will recover?"

The words were muffled, but Martha nodded. She eased onto the bench next to him. "Simon was brave. Amanda was scared, but she got to see her friend protect her. It was *gut*. What do you think will happen to them?"

"That depends on *Gott*'s plan for them, I reckon." He laid the ice pack on the table. "We can't see ahead so we have to trust. Amanda and Simon even more so. Their families have to trust He has a plan for them. I don't know if that means marriage or *kinner*. But right now they're enjoying each other's company. That's a special gift to them. And they're special gifts to us. It all works out."

She nodded. "Because we can trust *Gott* to be there, no matter what happens."

"We can. And you can trust me to do everything I can to protect you, just like I did with Amanda and Simon."

"I saw that."

"What do you think of it?"

"I think it's *gut*. I think you've shown me you can be trusted. *Gott* can be trusted." She smoothed her apron. "I like what you said to Dwayne too. You sounded like Mordecai."

"If I were to sound like *mei daed*, I would tell you a man has a plethora of choices, but only one is right." He laughed, but she only looked confused. "A lot of choices, is what I'm saying. I'm joking. I hope to sound like him one day—to be like him."

"Like your *daed*, you did what a real friend does. You called Dwayne out and helped him see the error of his ways." She slid a little closer. "That's what a grown-up man does."

"So you really think I'm grown-up?"

"I do."

She lifted her face. He leaned in. This time no one intervened. The delays only made the kiss all the sweeter. She tasted of chocolate. Her lips were warm and soft. He raised his hands to her face, afraid she might stop. He didn't want to ever stop.

After a few minutes, he opened his eyes. She smiled. "I thought fireworks weren't allowed at a state park."

He laughed and kissed her again.

EPILOGUE

A Sunday afternoon in November at Choke Canyon Lake was a far cry from a July holiday weekend. The camping spots were empty. The pavilions looked lonely. The only sounds were bluebirds scolding each other and a warm, damp wind whistling through thickets of mesquite. The lake had lost its shimmer in the metal-gray clouds that hung overhead. The pond grass and rushes that lined the shores had turned brown. Autumn dressed for the approaching winter.

Martha glanced up at Jacob. She couldn't read his face. He was one stubborn man. He refused to tell her why he'd gone to the trouble and expense of paying the van driver Mr. Martinez to give them a ride to the lake. From the time he'd picked her up at the farm until they arrived at the lake, he'd chatted about everything under the sun except this unusual foray away from home on a Sunday afternoon. Not even a hint. Mr. Martinez seemed happy with the situation. He brought a fishing pole and hiked off on his own the second they hopped from his ancient blue minivan.

"*Now* can you tell me what we're doing here?" She liked the feel of Jacob's hand in hers. He'd been holding her hand a lot in the months since the Fourth of July alligator-infested weekend. They walked and talked on Saturday nights. He took her home after every singing. They stared at each other during baptism classes. They stood in front of their families and friends and declared their faith, joining the church together. But they hadn't traveled before. "What's the big secret?"

He tugged her out onto the wooden fishing pier. "I like it here."

"That can't be why we drove an hour and you coughed up the money for a van and admission to the park."

"*Nee.* I decided I wanted to finish what I started here."

"What you started?"

"I was in a big hurry back in July. I thought we were ready. Maybe you were, but I wasn't. Now I am."

He let go of her hand and planted both of his around her waist. Before she could take a breath, he leaned down and let his mouth cover hers. She curled her fingers around his suspenders and hung on, determined never to let go.

His hands moved up, reaching for her face, cupping it. He leaned back. "I feel a little faint, ma'am."

"I think I'm supposed to say that." Her voice sounded like someone else's. High and quivering. "You brought me all the way out here to kiss me? We did that in July, as I recall."

And many times since.

"I haven't forgotten. This is for starters." And he proceeded to kiss her again. *Please* Gott, *don't let me do something silly like faint. And* danki, danki, danki.

This time, he raised his head and let his hands drop. "I have some questions for you."

Gott, *please don't let me faint. And praise You, praise You, praise You.* "You brought me all the way out here to ask me a question? You could've asked me on the front porch at home."

"With your *daed* watching my every move? Now you're just being contrary." His blue-green eyes mesmerized her. He traced her lips with one long finger. She shivered. He smiled. "Do you trust me?"

"I do."

"Do you trust *Gott*?"

"You saw me profess my faith."

"So I did." He took a deep breath and let it out. His gaze locked with hers. "Will you marry me?"

It would've been humanly impossible to hold back her smile. "I will."

"You will?"

"I said *jah.*"

He whooped like a little boy. He hooted and hollered. All the while looking like the grown man she knew him to be. The blue jays and the sparrows and the mockingbirds took flight.

"I don't know." She pretended to look around him. "Are you sure Dwayne isn't lurking in the weeds over there, waiting to interrupt? Are you sure you're grown up enough to marry me?"

"Dwayne is working at the auto shop and saving to take his family to Disney World." Jacob grabbed her around the waist and lifted her off the ground, twirling her until she was breathless with laughter. "Like me, he is all grown-up now. I want you to know, you'll never have to worry about taking care of me. We'll take care of each other and our *kinner*. Lots of *kinner*."

"I look forward to caring for our *kinner*." She swallowed tears, wishing she could tell her *mudder* about this important day in her life. Someday she would. "I trust you. And I trust *Gott*."

"Then it's settled."

They sealed the promise of a shared future with another kiss.

And another.

Discussion Questions

1. Have you ever had friends who pressured you to participate in "fun" that you knew to be wrong? How did you handle it? How do you think God expects you to handle it?

2. It was hard for Martha to trust after what happened to her mother. What would you tell her about God's love and His plan for her?

3. Dwayne was doing something against the law. Martha thought he should experience the consequences of his actions in order to learn a lesson from them. As a friend, Jacob wanted to help him and keep him from harm. Who do you think is right? Why?

4. Martha and Jacob both experienced the loss of their mothers as children. How did their losses change them? How did they respond differently?

5. Do you believe God has a plan for you even when events occur in your life that are painful or tragic? What does Scripture say about suffering?

ABOUT THE AUTHORS

S helley Shepard Gray is a *New York Times* and *USA TODAY* bestselling author, a finalist for the American Christian Fiction Writers prestigious Carol Award, and a two-time HOLT Medallion winner. She lives in southern Ohio, where she writes full-time, bakes too much, and can often be found walking her dachshunds on her town's bike trail.

Visit her online at ShelleyShepardGray.com
Facebook: ShelleyShepardGray
Twitter: @ShelleySGray

. . .

A my Clipston is the award-winning and bestselling author of the Kauffman Amish Bakery, Hearts of Lancaster Grand Hotel, Amish Heirloom, and Amish Homestead series. She has sold more than one million books. Her novels have hit multiple bestseller lists including CBD, CBA, and ECPA. Amy holds a degree in communication from Virginia Wesleyan University and works full-time for the City of Charlotte, NC. Amy lives in North Carolina with her husband, two sons, and three spoiled rotten cats.

Visit her online at AmyClipston.com
Facebook: AmyClipstonBooks
Twitter: @AmyClipston
Instagram: @amy_clipston

. . .

With over a million copies sold, Kathleen Fuller is the author of several bestselling novels, including the Hearts of Middlefield novels, the Middlefield Family novels, the Amish of Birch Creek series, and the Amish Letters series as well as a middle-grade Amish series, the Mysteries of Middlefield.

Visit her online at KathleenFuller.com
Instagram: kfstoryteller
Facebook: WriterKathleenFuller
Twitter: @TheKatJam

. . .

Kelly Irvin is the bestselling author of the Every Amish Season and Amish of Bee County series. *The Beekeeper's Son* received a starred review from *Publishers Weekly*, who called it a "beautifully woven masterpiece." The two-time Carol Award finalist is a former newspaper reporter and retired public relations professional. Kelly lives in Texas with her husband, photographer Tim Irvin. They have two children, two grandchildren, and two cats. In her spare time, she likes to read books by her favorite authors.

Visit her online at KellyIrvin.com
Instagram: kelly_irvin
Facebook: Kelly.Irvin.Author
Twitter: @Kelly_S_Irvin